THE DOVES OF GALILEE

A STORY OF THE TWELVE APOSTLES

THE DOVES OF GALILEE

A Story of the Twelve Apostles

Vincent Iezzi

Leonine Publishers
Phoenix, Arizona

This is a work of historical fiction based on the Apostles. The stories dramatized herein are based on both fact and legend.

Published by Leonine Publishers LLC
P.O. Box 8099
Phoenix, Arizona 85066

ISBN-13: 978-0-9836740-9-2

Library of Congress Control Number: 2012937168

10 9 8 7 6 5 4 3 2 1

Printed in the United States of America

Visit us online at www.leoninepublishers.com
For more information: info@leoninepublishers.com

To my wife and my love

MARY ANN

who has been unselfish in her support
and understanding

CONTENTS

ACKNOWLEDGMENTS

This is a book of fiction based on fact.

In my research I uncovered many stories about these faithful and unselfish Apostles of Jesus. Some stories were easy to validate in the writings and works of other writers, while other stories of the Twelve were based in legends and traditions. Therefore, they were difficult to verify. In order to capture the spirit of the moment of early Christianity, I chose the most dramatic and more exciting stories. In my journey to write this manuscript, I created some fictitious characters to help support the flow of my story. Some of these people lived and are found in legends, but what they did or what happened to them has been lost in time, so I created their stories from my imagination. If I made any errors, I beg forgiveness from history and excuse myself by saying I remain a writer and a storyteller, and wrote with creativity in mind.

My research was sometimes unorthodox. Besides the normal Biblical searches, the writers of the Early Church, and the many modern day researchers and writers, I gathered information from many other sources including ethnic traditions and legends and dramatic stories in the Apocrypha writings.

No book of this size can be done completely without help. It took ten years of work to complete this manuscript and it took ten years of understanding, support, and care to make this project become a finished product.

My heartfelt thanks to my many relatives, friends and associates, but more so to the following people, who gave more than simple support.

My undying thanks to Caesar (Chay) R. Sabatini who pushed and prodded me along with courage and friendship. I miss you. Rest in peace.

Special thanks goes to Steven Kolter, O.F.S., Phoenixville; Ann Marie Di Cesare, O.F.S., Philadelphia; Tom Stephano, O.F.S., Wildwood; Rev. Father Joseph Kelley, St. Monica's Church, Philadelphia;

Rev. Monsignor George Mazzotta, Philadelphia, and Gerald Du Four, MSPT, Philadelphia, for their help, encouragement, and support. To Laura Rayes and Michael Rayes of Leonine Publishers, a special thanks for their professional concerns and directions.

Other thanks go to Mark, Matthew, Luke, John and Paul and so many other saintly, wise, and talented writers of the Early Church.

Last but not least, a prayer of thanks to my favorite Twelve Men, who for years stood silently by waiting for me to tell of their journeys and their flight from Galilee.

MY PRAYERFUL THANKS TO ALL

PACE E BENE

THE GALILEANS

Silently they each entered the room and embraced each other.

They exchanged quick greetings with smiles and concerns, and then promptly sat on the floor in the center of the room. Others in the room, those waiting for their arrival, stood silently and intently around them hovering, protecting them like the secure walls of Jerusalem. This was a day they all knew had to come. A day they believed was set aside from all time. Some of them were nervous and apprehensive; some excited and anxious, and still others simply resolved to what was to be. One thing they all knew was certain: By the end of these proceedings, all of them would have some regrets. For after this day they would go from each other, from all they had known: the familiar streets and shops, the surrounding hills and valleys, their families, their Jerusalem. They would exchange the familiar for the strange, the old for the new, and find themselves relying completely on the providence of God. They must leave all to do what was apportioned them.

Before them on a long wooden cloth-covered table were a clay cup and a round, flat piece of unleavened bread guarded by two oil-burning lamps, one on each side. Standing behind the table and the covered setting was Peter, their leader. His tall muscular body, with his slightly graying hair and beard, hovered the table like a sentry. His shadow fell away and onto the white wall behind him; it spread wide and huge, almost covering the view of the wall.

Peter called the men sitting upon the floor to prayer. Reverently, the Twelve stood, covered their heads with hoods, and in loud, definitive voices they sang a Psalm for forgiveness, then one of praise and thanksgiving.

Those who stood mutely around the room were moved by the unity of their voices and listened in awe at the new strength and new conviction of the men.

Finally, in a deep, rich voice, Peter chanted the first words of a Psalm for help and strength. Immediately the Others chanted with him. Once again, their strong voices filled the room.

> *May God be gracious to us and bless us:*
> *may He look with favor upon us,*
> *that men may know His way on earth,*
> *His saving power among all the nations.*

After praying, they fell to silence. Their thoughts went back to past days. Each remembered in their own way the Master at different times in different ways. They saw Him walking, eating, sleeping, smiling and perspiring. Some saw His hands raised in blessing or reaching to the sick, needy, and children. Others saw Him in Cana, Capernaum, Nazareth, and Jerusalem, by the Jordan, along the shores of Galilee. No matter where they were with Him, they felt His love, and each was sure of His Spirit working within them. They could feel the urgency of His Spirit wanting to be set free through them.

Peter then called each of them by name. Obediently they came forward to stand silently around the table. The moment deepened the stillness of the room—a stillness so deep it gathered every breath and thought therein, and made it one thought, one exhale, one memory. The memory was of a bygone night at Passover, where they reclined together at a table, and received all of the Master's love. The remembrance of that night long ago filled the inner depth of the Twelve Men standing around the table.

To the many in the room the table was as an altar; to the Twelve it was a table of command that filled them with an inner-depth of holiness. They looked down at the unleavened bread and poor wine. Suddenly, a Presence filled the room; it was familiar to them and small smiles of recognition spread across their lips as they acknowledged this Presence.

The women walked to the Twelve, offering water to wash and towels to dry themselves. After all had finished the purification, the room fell to a solemn hush.

And again Peter, his usual rough and loud voice now soft and low, spoke. "And the Master on that night before He died, while sitting with us took unleavened bread, and raising His eyes to His Father, gave thanks, and breaking the bread said to us…"

Together the Twelve declared, "Take and eat, for This is My Body."

Slowly the Others approached Peter as he gave each a portion of the broken Bread, and each with deep reverence took the Bread and consumed It.

Returning to their places around the table, they gazed at the cup as Peter said, "Then the Master at that same table, while we sat with Him, took the wine, blessed it; gave thanks and said to us…"

Together they declared, "Take and drink, for This is My Blood. Do this often in remembrance of Me."

Each quietly walked to Peter and took the cup from him and gently sipped the Wine.

Deep reverence encircled the room. Everyone felt the warmth and caress of love, for they knew that Jesus was with them, in them.

When they had finished, the women came and gave Peter water. He carefully washed the cup and drank the mixture.

The Others returned to their seats on the floor and fell into silent prayer returning to their own thoughts and remembrances.

Finally, a crude brown bowl was carried by one of the women and placed on the table between the two burning lamps. Slowly, one by one, the Twelve walked to the bowl on the table and each removed a small parchment from the bowl. On each parchment was written the name of a foreign place. *Asia. Greece. Pontus. Cappadocia. Persia. Rome. Crete. Armenia. Arabia. Hispainia. India. Phrygia.* Some had the added note of *North, out of Rome, East, West,* and *South.* Individually they looked at their parchments. With complete understanding and in full obedience, they walked silently from the Upper Room.

The empty Upper Room grew muted as each echoed footstep passed through the door and into the world outside. The Twelve heard the inner sounds of a power greater than any heard before by mankind. To those who remained in the Room, there was a deep understanding to the emptiness, for the Upper Room would never be filled as in the past, nor will the Room hold the courage and faith of that day. The songs of bygone days, the words of bygone nights, will forevermore be voiceless. In their stead was the Spirit of the now different men of Galilee.

High in the sky, far above the Room, the house, the City, close to the sun, a group of twelve pure white doves flew higher and higher in perfect unity.

CHAPTER ONE:

JAMES BAR ZEBEDEE OF BETHSAIDA

PROLOGUE

J ohn sat by the window of the house he shared with his mother, Salome, and the Lord's Mother, Lady Mary. With his hand he shadowed his eyes against the blinding sun that forced its way through the small window. Above, the sky was full of heavy white clouds that towered in the blue heavens.

It was a beautiful day.

A perfect day to go and preach in the Temple, he thought to himself. *First, I must wait for Lady Mary to return from her usual Friday walk with the other ladies. I wonder why they take these walks. Whatever they do does them good, for they return so refreshed. So at peace. Still, I worry. Herod has made it very dangerous for us with his arrests, yet the dampness and the chill of the prison cell have not cooled our zeal or impeded our mission. No matter what punishment Herod burdens us with, the Master's protection further blesses us.*

The recent arrest spared John, but Peter and James the Little were not spared. They were beaten and ordered to preach of Jesus no more, which was nothing new to the Disciples. They had heard it before, and it mattered little.

John rose from his chair and walked slowly to the crude wooden table, which he recently began using as a desk. He slowly moved all the unused scrolls to one side of the table, and the ones he had written on he moved to the other side.

"What an imbalance. There are so many unused scrolls," he thought aloud. "Why Peter, James, the Others, and especially Lady Mary, want me to put in writing what the Master did and said, I will never know. Whatever makes them think I could write? Why does it seem so important to put in writing what Jesus did? Parchments will not make Him any greater. It is what is in one's heart that is important. It is love, faith, and hope in Jesus that are of importance." His mind immediately drew an image of Jesus. He smiled. He forced the image to remain, enjoying the warmth and friendship that only Jesus could give him. He reveled in the moment. Never would he forget the loving, ruddy complexion of the face shadowed by the red hood, or the tall, lean, muscular body covered with the white robe and red cloak. This was one of the many images of Jesus that endured in his memory and which often returned to his mind. His smile widened with the realization that this was the image of Jesus from their first meeting.

∗

He and his brother, James, were busy putting their father's fishing nets in order. He was kneeling on the beach of the Sea of Galilee, busily looking for any recently repaired rips in the net that had not held, while James was tending to the other needs and examining for any new damage. It was a good day. They had a big catch that day, and Joah, their deliveryman, had left many hours earlier with their morning catch for the household of the High Priest Annias. James was talking aimlessly about their mother, Salome, and the long-anticipated wedding of their sister Naomi. The sound of his older brother's voice was always a great comfort to John, for he knew that whatever his brother said was to be trusted. James knew so much about many things; his knowledge was seemingly endless. So as James spoke excitedly, John listened continually, captivated by his brother's thoughts and sounds. Many people observed the two sons of Zebedee with joy, for their mutual love was obvious; they were inseparable and complemented each other. Many observed the deep love that John had for James.

"Mother has plans for a big Sabbath dinner for Justus bar Sabbas and his parents the week before the wedding. Can you imagine, John, our… younger…sis…" His words trailed off, and John immediately missed the sound of his voice; without looking up, John waited patiently for his brother to continue. When James stood up and dropped the net in his hand, John stopped what he was doing and looked up at his brother. He seemed taller, gigantic.

"What's wrong, James?"

James did not answer him. His face had a distant expression—he was living in a faraway place.

John followed his brother's sight and saw that James was looking at a Stranger walking casually toward them. The Stranger was followed closely by Simon and Andrew, the sons of Jonah, a respected master of a fishing boat owned by Zebedee, the father of James and John. Jonah's sons were close friends of James and John. Simon and Andrew were walking in perfect harmony with the Stranger, and John detected a new vibrancy in their steps. He watched the trio's approach with curiosity. He had known Simon and Andrew for all of his sixteen years, and never had he seen Simon so excited or his face so radiant. He usually was plain-faced, serious, a man with no time for nonsense. Andrew, on the other hand, was more adventurous and had been known to sneak off to hear the preaching of that man of the desert, John, whom many called "The Baptizer."

John looked at his brother and was shocked to see on his face the same radiance that was on the faces of Simon and Andrew. For a quick instant, John thought his brother had fallen ill.

"James, what is wrong?" he cautiously asked again.

James did not answer him, and without taking his eyes off the Stranger, he reached down for his cloak, threw it over his shoulder, and walked away.

John's concern for his brother heightened. He never saw James just go off without some sort of explanation or excuse. James was a man of certainties, but without a glance back, he walked away and joined the approaching Stranger. He was greeted with warmth and smiles from the sons of Jonah. As the small group passed John, the shadow of the Stranger fell over him. He felt a strong power wrap around him and he became numb; he slumped and fell back onto the sand, still tightly clutching the fishing nets. He could not see the face of the Stranger because it was silhouetted by the sun, but he could feel the Stranger's eyes pierce his very heart, causing him to grab the side of his chest in defense.

"Come. Follow me," the Stranger said in a soft, loving voice.

John jumped to his feet, dropping the fishing net he had clutched in his hand, and hurriedly walked away with the group. Within seconds, he was walking abreast of the Stranger, who finally turned from the shadows toward him and smiled warmly. It was then that he recognized Him as the one whom The Baptist had called "The Lamb of God," and he knew Him as his mother's nephew.

Many days had passed since that time, but still John relived the warmth of that meeting. It was now a part of his being. Jesus came to his mind with little effort. He appeared in his mind in tableaux, speech, scents, and touch. In times of persecution, that warmth became more intense. John knew this warmth was the kindliness of protection, and the love of family, of father. Suddenly, an image of his father came to his mind, and he smiled warmly with great love. He recalled that tall, thin man with his thick, black-gray beard and his long hair of the same shade. He was a good father and a good provider, in spite of his temper. His father's temper was called to mind affectionately, and never in fear. He recalled his father's anger with the sea when fish were not to be had and his irate name-calling when a sudden storm rose while they were fishing.

Jesus had named James and John "the Sons of Boanerges." Many believed this name was given because of the anger the two brothers displayed during some of the happenings that surrounded Jesus. This was partly true; the other reason behind this name was the anger Zebedee displayed when Jesus took Simon, Andrew, James, and John as his disciples. This left Zebedee without good, experienced fishermen. John smiled pleasantly to himself as he remembered Jesus being reprimanded by his father. Respectfully, Jesus listened to His uncle's thunderous anger, as any good Jewish boy did when being reprimanded by an elder, but Jesus made note, and when the time was right He referred to James and John as the Sons of Boanerges—the Sons of Thunder.

John's reminiscing quickly ended, and he was returned to the surrounding world by the excited voice of someone outside the house calling his name. He recognized the voice as that of his friend, Menachem.

"John! John!" Menachem threw open the door to the house and stood in the sunlight, breathing heavily from his run. His dark shadow spread across the floor of the house and against the wall; it filled the room.

"John, your brother James has returned. This day James' disciples, Hermogenes and Philetus, arrived in Jerusalem. James left Yaffa after they did, and he is to arrive in Jerusalem in two days. From there he will come directly to Bethany."

John stood frozen in disbelief. As Menachem's words settled in his mind, he realized their meaning, and he grabbed his friend's portly body and embraced him.

This was great news!

He had not seen his brother in ten years.

James was coming home!

JAMES BAR ZEBEDEE OF BETHSAIDA

James stood on the side of a hill, looking intently at the city of Jerusalem in the distance. When he and his companion, Stephaton, left the seaport of Yaffa for Jerusalem, he decided not to walk the more-traveled Yaffa Road into the city. Instead, he decided to travel the lesser-used roads in the hope of avoiding the hustle and bustle of eager travelers and of enjoying the long-forgotten countryside. But there was another reason: they needed to avoid detection. He had been warned by friends in "The Way" that Herod Agrippa had initiated a small persecution of the followers to please some Temple authorities. In innocence, James had forgotten that eventually they would have to enter Jerusalem through the Yaffa Gate via the Yaffa Road.

I have been away from you too long, O Jerusalem, he thought to himself. *My familiarity with you has grown stale. You are not familiar to me. You no longer feel like my home.* He took a deep breath and arched the corners of his mouth. *Yahweh's design, no doubt; Yahweh's design.*

As James and Stephaton observed the distant city, other travelers hurriedly passed them. Though it was a warm day and he was tired and thirsty, he had not stopped to rest. The invisible power of the city stopped him. He found himself in awe of Jerusalem. It still had some control over his emotions. Much to his dismay, he found himself remembering more things that happened around the city than things in Jerusalem. His heart beat rapidly as he thought of the unpleasantness he would be forced to remember—and forced to relive. Slowly, he surrendered to his emotions; he rested his tall, muscular body against a nearby boulder and realized that he truly needed to rest. The noonday sun was intense and blinding as it relentlessly beamed down upon the world. Though James welcomed his rest against the boulder, he longed for a place of shade. He could feel the perspiration under his hood wet his deep black hair, and feel the moisture dampen his chest and back. With his open hand he wiped his dampened face, and he drew his hand over his unruly beard. With his rough and callused hands he shaded his dark brown eyes from the sun. He allowed his eyes to look down the hill onto the open plain, then to the small valley that spread out before Jerusalem. Beyond the city, further in the distance and to the right, was the Valley of Hinnom, and his thoughts then went to the unmarked grave of Judas Iscariot.

Judas, you not only betrayed the Master, you betrayed all of us. We had so much trust in you; in fact, you were the most trusted. We gave you our livelihoods, our money, which was the only thing many of us had to give to the Master at that time.

He found distaste in his memory, but grace pulled him away, and his thoughts turned to pity and sadness. He closed his eyes and prayed for forgiveness for his bitter thoughts of Judas. Confident that God had heard his prayer, he opened his eyes and continued his survey of the city and the nearby countryside. His eyes wandered, still marveling, at the high stone walls of the city of Jerusalem, with its array of towers and battlements. At intervals along the thick city wall were the gateways where the hated publicans waited to collect taxes on all goods entering and exiting the city. He suddenly remembered that deep inside the city were two other walls built at different times in Jerusalem's development. He recalled being told that the "Old Wall" with its Hippicus tower, named after one of Herod the Great's generals, was the hardest wall to breach, not because this wall was mightier than the outer wall of the city, but because Jerusalem was built on four mounts and over three valleys, and these landmarks helped to make the "Old Wall" nearly impregnable. His eyes traveled over the wall into the city. He saw the Upper City, where the white marble homes and the palaces with courtyards and gardens were orderly arranged. Their blinding whiteness offended his eyes. Among these homes was the magnificent palace of Herod, which was used by the Roman governor of the province when he visited Jerusalem. He wondered if the Upper Market with its many arcades was still there. He envisioned the countless shops in this market, where expensive items of great social value were bought and sold by the rich. Then, his eyes moved to the Lower City, where narrow, unpaved streets weaved through sun-baked brown and yellow homes. This part of the city sloped downward to the Tyropean Valley. Here lived the poor of the city, struggling to provide for their basic needs. Finally, his eyes fell upon the Temple. Normally, the Temple was the first thing seen, and the first thing every Jew wanted to see when traveling to Jerusalem, but James had purposely bypassed the gold-embroidered Temple because he wanted to remember it in a special way. Most Jews upon seeing it marveled at "the holiest of all holy places," even if they had seen more beautiful structures. The Temple perpetually stood as an exclamation to God. Its square metal rooftop, with the polished vertical spikes that prevented birds from resting on the roof, caught his eye. The bright noonday sunlight reflected blindingly off the metal roof. He was forced to turn his head, for looking into the reflection was like gazing directly into the sun. He had been told that the Holy of Holies was composed of large marble columns and that the walls were all covered with unblemished white marble. He was told, most likely by a Rabbi, that heavy royal purple, crimson red, snow white, and sky blue drapes hung sporadically from the walls and over the Sanctuary. The floors were covered with large unbroken slabs of white-blue tinted marble; when walked upon, they gave the illusion of walking on moving waters. He remembered how the reluctantly setting sun would strike the roof of the Temple and reflect like glistening snow. He wished for a sunset so he could see if this still happened. Years ago, he heard from Jews with greater knowledge of construction say that the Temple—with its many fountains, courts, and ascending levels—drew on the influence of Babylon, but he could perceive only the Greco-Roman, maybe more Roman, influence.

What an unnatural triumvirate: Roman columns and Babylonian walkways and Hebrew footsteps. Again, Yahweh's design, no doubt; Yahweh's design.

His eyes traveled to the northwest corner of the Temple and to the Fortress of Antonia, also called the *Praetorium*, with its palace and Roman barracks. Off in the other direction he saw the palace of Herod Agrippa, and somewhere between these two authorities—hidden yet known and felt—was the house of the new High Priest, Matthias, son of Annias and the brother-in-law of Yosaf Caiaphas. With great emotion, he absorbed everything that he surveyed. Oddly, he did not feel small in its presence, as he did many years ago. In his youth, James believed Jerusalem to be the biggest place in the world, or at least in his world. Everything about the city was huge and overshadowing. The walls, the Temple, the palaces, the many wealthy homes, even the houses in the small, snaky streets that meshed together in many unbroken walls. All were bigger than the houses in Bethsaida. As a child, he visited Jerusalem many times. What he remembered most was being intimidated by its size and frightened by the confusion of so many people hurrying and pushing their way forward. There was one particular trip to Jerusalem that remained with him always. It was the visit during which he became aware of more than merely the size and movement of the city. He was about nine years of age, and his father, Zebedee, decided to take him on one of his many business trips. Naomi, his sister, was younger and his brother John was a baby, so they stayed at home with their mother, Salome. It was the fifteenth day of the month of *Tishri,* the Feast of Tabernacles, also called *Succoth.* For reasons he could not remember, they arrived on the twelfth day of the feast, the day when twelve bullocks were sacrificed to Yahweh. When they arrived, they hurried through the Fish Gate and into the city. His father was very rushed and anxious because he was late. He was expected in the city on the first day of the feast, for he had business with the High Priest, Annias bar Seth, who had just succeeded the High Priest Joazar. The family of Zebedee, which was of the house of Levi, had for years supplied the High Priest, the Temple priests, and the staff with fish for their meals, and the contract was always renewed during *Succoth.* Young James was so excited that it took all of his strength to control his urge to run joyously through the city. His neck ached because he was constantly looking up at the massive structures around him. There was so much to see; he wished for many eyes that day. He and his father rushed through the narrow streets. With one hand, Zebedee held the satchel hanging from his side, which contained his important papers, and with the other hand he held James' hand tightly for fear of losing him, which would be easy to do during any feast in Jerusalem.

Suddenly, they broke out of the narrow streets, and the young boy found himself before the Temple in all its white and blinding glories. He stopped, frozen, unable to move. His father was jerked back.

"Father…"

"Come James, we must hurry." Eager to reach the High Priest, Zebedee pulled his son's hand, but the boy's feet were planted firmly in the ground.

"Father…"

"What is wrong with you?" Zebedee shouted angrily, but he quickly realized what was happening. In similar awe, Zebedee looked at the Temple and reverently bowed. He tucked the boy closely to his side.

"Yes, James. It is the Temple of *El Elyon,* The Most High," the proud father said, pleased to see that his son had felt the presence of Yahweh. He allowed the boy time to become saturated with its glory. As Zebedee watched James' face, he knew that the Lord was touching his son. When he felt that the time was right, he softly ordered his son to bow in reverence, and they continued on their journey, though less hastily.

That was the first time James really saw the Temple in simple faith; for all Jews, the Temple was Jerusalem and Jerusalem was the Temple. Jerusalem was always the City of Yahweh—this is where Yahweh led the Israelites. It was the place where Yahweh rested and stayed among His people. The excitement of seeing the Holy Temple remained with James throughout that day. That night, when he and his father gathered to share a meal with their many relatives who were also in Jerusalem for the feast, James excitedly talked of all that he had seen, but when he spoke of the beauty and splendor of the Temple, his face glowed. The family elders listened patiently with warm and understanding smiles as they beheld the joy on his ruddy face. Among the relatives in the city were some whom he seldom saw, for they lived far from Bethsaida. Among his relatives in Jerusalem for the feast were Joseph bar Jacob from Nazareth, Mary, his wife, who was James' mother's sister, and their young son, Jesus.

It was the year Jesus got lost. James quickly became amused with this thought, and he smiled. *Jesus was never lost—He knew exactly where He was, all the time. We were lost. We had to find Him, just like now, for the sons of Adam are still lost.*

As he looked at Jerusalem for the first time in many years, it appeared less elaborate and smaller than other cities in which he had lived and preached. Cities like Athens in Greece or Carales in Sardinia or Valentia in Hispania seemed larger, busier, and equal in splendor, but none had the Temple, none had the High Altar, the symbol of the enormity of Jerusalem's spirituality. In this comparison, none was greater. Suddenly, his thoughts became heavy with sadness, and he sensed a similar heavy sadness hanging over the city.

Jerusalem. Jerusalem. I see you have not changed since I last saw you. Your betrayals still hang heavily over you, and now even more notoriously. Strangers in foreign lands now know of you and what you have done to your Lord and God. You rest here in your own splendor, but in the hearts of many, you are a city of sadness and shame.

"It still looks the same, does it not, James?"

Startled, James smiled, and turning to Stephaton, he said, "Yes, my friend, it does, only I think a little smaller."

Stephaton gave a small grin and nodded in agreement.

Together, they remained motionless, observing the city, each deep in his own thoughts. Then, without speaking to one another, they began to descend the hill and join the long serpentine procession of people, carts, and beasts of burden on the road to the city; with each step they took, memories continued to flood their minds.

James lowered his head to avoid looking south to the Valley of Kidron and the nearby Garden of Gethsemane, for the thought of that place plunged him into deep shame. He drew his shoulders in a feeble act of defense against the memories of that night long ago, when he and the Others, except for Peter, acted with such cowardice. It was one of the many nights that James could never forget, yet it was a night he seldom wanted to remember. For an instant, his pace faltered and his body shivered. He remained uncomfortable yet wanting, hoping this sad memory of and around the city would fade, but he concluded that this was where Jesus wanted him to be, so he accepted the feelings of shame; in his acceptance, he felt the closeness of his Master.

Certainly, from time to time, the Others have thought of Gethsemane. They too have imagined how alone the Master was because of our weakness. How shameful, cowardly were our actions. That night is our common sin, our common shame and, of course, our common penance. Certainly, I pray that all these years of courage and preaching to the world have erased Jesus' memory of our night of weakness.

Eventually, the shame of this sin passed, as it always did, and again he was free to think of other things. In relief he thought, *It is so much better to remember the good things of Jerusalem.* Quickly he recalled the Holy Day visits his family celebrated and the business visits to the industrious merchants or the Temple officials. He dismissed them and remembered the times that he and the Others spent with Jesus.

He smiled to himself.

Those were happy times. The Master always seemed to make our time with Him special. Times He wanted us to remember as only ours. Those happy memories are the moments that often sustain me in my travels, for those moments were the happiest and easiest to remember. There were nights spent talking and laughing: the talk was for our souls, and the laughter was for our spirits.

Abruptly, James had a picture of Jesus slowly breaking apart a cooked fish because the fish's spine disturbed Him. Then came a picture of Jesus unhurriedly breaking apart a piece of bread, then an image of the way He caringly picked and held a grape. Remembering hot days, like the day on which James was now traveling, he could see the beads of perspiration on Jesus' forehead and the sand and dust covering His face after a dust storm. He recalled the time Jesus slipped and fell, and how with a smile on His face Jesus shook His head in disbelief at Himself; the sound of His delight when He would walk along the shores of Galilee, splashing and kicking at the oncoming small waves; the sigh of satisfaction after a drink of cool water; the deep sound of joy in His voice as He sang the Psalms. These memories were so vivid that James slowed his walk.

How easy it is to forget the happy days with Jesus and remember only the sad and serious ones. Perhaps only a few remember the Master's laughter. What a pity if the world could not hear the deep, tender sound of His joy, or know the humor He had—the joy and delight Jesus was when He was in this world. In our eagerness to make Him known to the world as a Suffering Servant, we have made Him less human. What a pity that we created such a Jesus, for He was happy in His humanity and enjoyed living as a man. To enjoy life was a normal thing for Him; after all, He was living His Father's will, which was part of His Being. He was His Father's greatest gift of pure love.

Suddenly James heard someone behind him laugh, and he turned to the sound.

Andrew bar Jonah?

When he realized the laugh was only similar, he returned his attention again to Jerusalem, but in his mind's eye, he saw the faces and images of the other Eleven. As he remembered some of them, he could recall the sound of their voices, their laughter, and he imagined their smiles.

Why should I not remember them? he thought, slightly reprimanding himself. *I have known these men well, for they are made of the same spiritual mind as I am. We are emotionally, spiritually, and mentally bound to each other.*

After the death of Jesus, the Twelve lived together in the same fears and confusion, and later with the same elation and bewilderment that came when Jesus stood in their midst, early on that first day of the week. They had shared that insurmountable confusion of living with new life after death. How difficult it was, yet how satisfying it was to have Jesus walking and eating with them. It seemed like He never left them, though they realized that Jesus, and knowing Who He was, were not the same.

Certainly the Others, like me, have different feelings and ideas about those days in Jerusalem eleven years ago. It would be interesting to hear their new thoughts on those past times.

James was excited with the prospect of seeing some of his friends. Suddenly, he needed to be with them to be physically replenished by them, as he was so often spiritually replenished. Mostly, he longed for the camaraderie of people who had known Jesus and all the joyful facets of the Master. He needed to have them around him, to be surrounded by the first generation of those who saw and touched Jesus. Above all, he longed to have that family atmosphere again.

The Master knew what He was doing when He threw us together, but I must admit I had doubts. Jesus knew from the start that we would all become one; He knew it from the beginning, though we certainly did not for in those days, we did not know very much of anything.

Again he smiled as he remembered when Jesus chose the Twelve, and immediately he felt an inward shame at his presumption in doubting Jesus and His wisdom.

He remembered it as a clear, warm day with no breeze. Jesus led a huge crowd of followers up the side of a mountain. He stopped to teach them, and when He had finished with the crowd, He left them and continued, alone, up the summit and disappeared into one of the caves. The crowd settled on the side of the mountain, understanding that the Master had gone to be alone in prayer. This was something they understood, because Jesus often would leave them and go off alone to pray. This was His time, and they respected it by simply sitting and waiting for Jesus to come back to them. It never ceased to amaze James how patiently the crowds waited and how willingly they accepted the heat of the day, the lack of provisions, and the discomfort of the land—all to be with Jesus. As always, many began to discuss what Jesus had recently said. All sorts of ideas were voiced, and, as always, nothing was resolved. All their talk confused them more. It was not time for things to be concluded: it was time for things to remain unfinished.

After being in prayer for some time, Jesus returned to the multitude. When the people saw Him coming down the slope of the mount, they all rose to their feet. Whenever Jesus returned, James could feel a great expectation come over the crowd. Everyone wanted to hear more. Some waited with the hope that something Jesus would say would help them to know what He was truly about, others waited for explanations of what He had said, and still others waited for new complications to add to their already confused minds. As Jesus walked toward the crowd, He threw back the hood to His robe and adjusted His yarmulke, which was disturbed by the removal of His hood. His face was tan and had a bright glow of peacefulness. He walked to a large boulder and slowly scaled its round surface. He stood high above them and overlooked the gathering. In a loud, clear voice, He announced that He would be going farther up the mountain, but first He wanted to choose some from the crowd to go with Him. A strange, heavy stillness fell over the crowd, and James felt that everyone was wishing, as he was, to be among the few who would be called. There was no doubt in anyone's mind that to be chosen would be a great honor and that when the time of Jesus' glory came, surely, those chosen would be given the greater places. Jesus looked far into the crowd and then directly at the faces of those closest to Him. His eyes settled on the face of one of the Baptizer's disciples, and He smiled widely and warmly.

In a loud voice He called Simon bar Jonah's name, followed quickly by Simon's younger brother, Andrew. The two brothers walked to Jesus, and He pointed to a place to His right that was above the gathering, yet slightly below Him. Quickly they walked to the indicated spot appearing relaxed, yet James could imagine the pride the two fishermen felt; surely, if he had been called, there would be great pride, and maybe an air of superiority, to his walk. The naming of Simon and Andrew was no surprise, for these two had been with Jesus from the start and were constantly doing things for Him as He traveled about Judea and Galilee. James looked at his two friends. They were of equal height. Both had deep black hair and beards, dark eyes, broad shoulders, and big callused hands. From the back they had often been mistaken for one another, but when one was in their company, it was immediately easy to perceive their differences. Simon was quick tempered and later apologetic, while Andrew was slow and certain. Though older, Simon was more childlike and innocent, while his brother was logical and measured.

With little time passing, Jesus shifted His eyes slightly and looked at James, and with equal clarity to His voice, He called James and then John. This did not surprise James, for he was certain that he and his brother would be called. They, also, had been with Jesus from the beginning and had remained faithful to Him; besides, the Master had always shown interest in the two sons of Zebedee.

Besides, we are related to Him, he thought at that time, *and we gave up so much for Him. We deserve a high place of honor.*

Quickly and with a great deal of pride, James walked to Simon and Andrew's side, and John followed closely behind him. When James reached Simon and Andrew, he embraced the two sons of Jonah, smiled happily, and slapped each of their backs with exuberance. When he turned and looked at the crowd below him, he felt a flow of prestige and great honor come over him. He could sense, most certainly, their envy. He looked at his young brother, beaming with pride. Of the four chosen, John was the most scholarly and the youngest. He still had not grown a beard, though his chin was beginning to show some signs of growth. John's hair was light brown, and perhaps his light brown beard would not be as conspicuous as James' matured jet-black beard was. John was shorter than James and the sons of Jonah, and he was not yet as muscularly developed as the others.

James was happy, pleased in the wisdom Jesus had shown in choosing Simon, Andrew, John, and himself, but he was curious and deeply concerned to see who the others would be. He was anxious to see how much competition he and John would have for the best place in the kingdom that Jesus said was to come. He watched Jesus looking over the crowd; it was obvious he was being careful. Then he heard Jesus call Judas bar Simon from Kerioth. Immediately, Judas flashed a wide smile. James let out a small gasp. He looked quickly at Peter and Andrew and saw the traces of surprise on their faces.

Judas was not one of them. He was not a Galilean, like Jesus and the four of them, but a Judean. Many in the crowd believed he was an adventure-seeker who was political, almost nationalistic, and definitely many saw his worldly side. With the little authority Jesus had given him, such as that of buying provisions, Judas had become very insolent and at times condescending to the crowds that followed the Rabbi. This choice was not a crowd pleaser; James could see the surprise and hear the grumbling voices, and this increased James' disappointment in Jesus' choice.

Judas was a tall man of slight build. He was thin, wiry, and nervous, and he often vanished for hours or days, giving no explanation for his disappearance. He was contrary and could be very argumentative. Many said Judas had a mean streak in his temperament. When someone disagreed with him, he could be very curt and hurtful; James had never seen any of this meanness displayed, though he had to admit that Judas struck him as being very secretive. As Judas rushed happily up the side of the mount, James relaxed when he recalled that Judas was attached to Jesus as messenger and errand boy. He was sure that this was Jesus' reason for making such a choice; perhaps Jesus had chosen wisely. Judas would remain a messenger, nothing more, and certainly he would not be as privileged as the sons of Jonah and Zebedee.

The four of them greeted the new arrival with quick nods and polite smiles.

Jesus ignored what the five men were doing. He seemed too engrossed in His next choice. It was obvious to all that He was looking for someone very special. Finally, in a clear voice, he called Levi bar Alphaeus, who later was called Matthew, and this name caused a greater rumble in the crowd. It surprised many of them, for Levi had been a publican, a tax collector and, therefore, a great sinner; though he had followed Jesus for some time, he still was not a true Jew.

James glared quickly at Jesus, wondering if He had lost His senses.

Does Jesus know what He is doing? he questioned in his mind.

The calling of this tax collector ensured that the Pharisees would be watching Jesus and His group very closely. Merely by association, all of them would be under suspicion.

How did the Master expect us to accept a publican as a companion?

Levi, dressed in a fine robe, new sandals, and a neatly trimmed beard, stood motionless as those near him mumbled and pointed in surprise, and from the look on Levi's face, it was obvious that he was as shocked as everyone else. He looked bewildered and very ill at ease.

James glanced quickly at Simon, Andrew, and John, as if expecting help or some acknowledgment of disapproval; he found none. In his peripheral vision, James could see Judas, and without looking he knew that Judas disapproved. James locked his eyes on Jesus, who smiled broadly as He pointed to a place for Levi.

Levi never took his eyes off Jesus as he hesitantly walked up the mount. Undoubtedly, there was something in Jesus' eyes that was encouraging to Matthew. When Levi walked to them, James moved to the side, not wanting to be associated with this sinner; Matthew stood off slightly, away from the others—alone.

James looked away, pretending to be engrossed in what Jesus was doing; finally, he heard Jesus call Nathaniel bar Tolomai. This man was of some noble birth and was wealthier than most of those who had been called. He had occasionally worked on the Zebedee fishing boats. He was a man who spoke his mind with bluntness. Nathaniel, whom most called Bartholomew, had been a follower of the Master, but he had not associated or become too friendly with anyone. He had two good aspects to his credit: he was liked by Jesus and he had renounced his wealth—though he still wore it—to become one of the followers.

Bartholomew looked with some reluctance at the small group he was about to join. With great apprehension, he walked to the six men and stood near Levi, but a little off to Levi's side. Bartholomew had red hair and a red beard, both of which had been carefully trimmed, and his robe and cloak were of one piece and were of the finest material. His robe had a purple design along the hem that announced not only wealth but pride of station. He was dressed far better than those previously called, and, in fact, better than most of the people present.

James pushed aside his criticism of the choice of Bartholomew with the thought that Jesus was being practical, for this man came from a wealthy family, and his parents had permitted their son the luxury of being a follower of a prophet. The small group would undoubtedly need some financial support, and the family of Tolomai would prove helpful in that respect. Again, James found comfort in Jesus' wisdom, but he made a mental note that Bartholomew would need watching for he could gain more of the Master's affection and thereby become a threat or a problem to John and him.

James examined the crowd before Jesus, and he saw many friendly and familiar faces. There were men he knew who were worthy of being chosen, and there were also many who could be a threat to his position with Jesus. There was his brother-in-law, Justus bar Sabbas, who would be a good choice, for he was a virtuous man and would be another ally for him and John. He uttered a quick mental prayer to Yahweh asking for Jesus to be wiser.

Jesus quickly turned and looked sternly at James, and James could not understand the reason for the look; he had done nothing wrong—he was only silently praying for his brother-in-law to be chosen.

Jesus smiled and returned His attention to the crowd.

James watched as Jesus craned His neck and even elevated Himself by His toes. He was looking far off, further into the back of the crowd for a special person to fill something that was needed. Jesus looked long and hard, and then, smiling, He called Simon of Cana.

More surprised mumblings were heard from the crowd, and the people parted, either to distance themselves from the Zealot or to make way for him to walk up the hill.

In disbelief, James whispered to the Others, "He has picked a Zealot, a Canaanite and a revolutionary."

The Others nodded their heads, or looked away, apparently not as concerned or as surprised as James was. He was disappointed by their carefree attitudes.

How could they not be concerned about this person?

Though Simon had somewhat distanced himself from the Zealots since following the Baptizer and Jesus, he still sympathized with them. Now, the Romans will be suspicious of the small group because of Simon and his half-hearted beliefs. James was appalled at the call of Simon, and he was again disappointed that Jesus had endangered them. He began to question if being chosen was such a great honor; he thought this in spite of his feeling of worthiness for himself and his brother John, and in spite of the apparent prestige that seemed to be attached to being chosen. He could see many problems surfacing among those called, and from his point of view, possibly no relationships at all would be formed. Suddenly, with new insight, James seemed pleased by the decisions, for again he could see little or no impediment to becoming, along with John, the first among them.

Everyone watched the tall, lean man with matted black hair, dark brown eyes, and Galilean face walk slowly up the hillside. Simon's face was wrapped in confusion. Like Levi, his eyes never left Jesus' face. For an instant, James sensed that there was a special bond forming between Jesus and this Simon, and he became envious of what he saw—or thought he saw.

Jesus quickly called another name as if to distract everyone from the naming of Simon. Thomas, the Twin, sometimes known as Didymus, was called. His twin sister had been a follower of John the Baptist, and some said she was the one who brought Thomas to the Baptizer. Short and slightly round with light brown, alert eyes, he made for a handsome appearance. He was not like those previously called; he was by trade a part-time fisherman and part-time carpenter, and he was believed by some to be only a part-time follower. He had made it known that he was deeply unsure about why he was following Jesus. This uncertainty should have disqualified him, but James concluded that Thomas was called as a result of some sentimentality within Jesus, who was the Son of a carpenter and a carpenter Himself.

Thomas came forward timidly. His head lowered. Each step was short and slow. Finally, he reached the hillside and was greeted warmly by the Zealot and by Levi, much to the surprise of James. The choice of Thomas was not memorable. He was unimportant, a nobody, and

James perceived no danger to his position. James concluded that Jesus was being practical: their boats might need repairs, and Thomas would be able to help make them.

Jesus turned to His right then quickly to His left, and His eyes settled on Philip of Bethsaida, a man of many certainties and influences. He was a close companion of Bartholomew. In a low voice, Jesus called Philip's name. Philip was too Greek in his thinking and ways. He had many Gentile friends, and he shamelessly associated with them. James knew Philip from Bethsaida. He was a man of strong independence and had some difficulty with those in authority. He had brown hair and a brown beard with light brown eyes. He was a married man with children from a very close family with many female siblings. James felt again that there was no competition from this man. His brother John and he would still be ranked higher.

Philip walked briskly to the mount with a wide smile and immediately joined Bartholomew; once again they bonded on the common ground of friendship.

Jesus quickly turned to His left, and with his back to a minority of the crowd, He looked at the short, small-featured, frail man standing only inches from Him. He smiled warmly at him and tenderly called his name.

James bar Alphaeus once was a civil servant. He was a cousin of Jesus through Joseph and a brother to Levi, with whom he had made no contact since Levi become a publican. James was very strict in his beliefs and prayed so often that his knees were hardened like the hoofs of a camel. He was regarded as too harsh and too severe, even slightly fanatical. As the two cousins looked at each other, he could clearly see the openly warm and affectionate look on the face of Jesus and the look of total perplexity, confusion, and naked alarm on the face of James.

James bar Alphaeus glanced quickly at the group of men who had so far been called. He was undoubtedly questioning the wisdom of becoming a part of them. His face wrinkled in uncertainty and his head cocked to one side as he stared back at Jesus, searching for some understanding of why he had been chosen. Finding none, he straightened his head and gave Jesus a challenging glare as he walked briskly to the group. Each step he took seemed to be planted firmly. He had been an unenthusiastic follower of Jesus, with Whom he had been at odds because in James' opinion, His cousin, Jesus, was not dutifully tending to Mary, His mother. On several occasions, they were seen speaking secretly. James the Little, as some called him on account of his shortness and the smallness of his features, had for months been trying to persuade Jesus to return to His mother and to a quiet life. It was obvious that this debate would continue between the two cousins. Considering his arguments with Jesus and the chilly relationship between the two sons of Alphaeus, James the Little was no threat to the sons of Zebedee but he was more of a problem for Jesus. Everyone knew that James the Little was friendly with Judas and Simon the Zealot. Many said that he had latent nationalistic beliefs; if this were so, there would be little chance of his assuming any place of importance in the group.

James bar Zebedee felt again that Jesus was putting everyone in jeopardy, as His choices were unsettling and confusing; furthermore, He had inserted a family feud into the group, making conflict practically inevitable. James was confused. What did Jesus hope to accomplish with this band of men?

Now counting eleven men, James leaned over to Andrew and John and whispered, "There are eleven of us. If he calls many more, we will become a mob, and divisions among us will only multiply."

Andrew looked a little annoyed by what James had said, and John looked around quickly, apparently counting the group of chosen men; he shrugged his shoulders uncaringly.

Finally, Jesus called Judas Thaddeus bar Alphaeus, sometimes called Lebbaeus, another brother of James the Little and Levi.

Jude was a young man, as young as John bar Zebedee. He was of simple means and manners and was less controversial than his two brothers and his cousin, Jesus. He listened rather than acted. Not fully matured, his hair was light brown and his face was smooth and devoid of hair. His eyes attracted disquieted looks, for they were light brown, almost beige. In short, he did not look Jewish. He made himself very inconspicuous. His reaction to being called was delightful to observe. His face beamed with happiness, and his eyes seemed to water with tears of joy. This reaction delighted Jesus, Who was smiling vibrantly. The young man walked with a quickened step and lightheartedly climbed up the side of the hill to blend into the group. He was enthusiastically embraced by his brother James and warmly greeted by the others. When his brother James had turned his attention away and was not looking, Jude Thaddeus coyly glanced at his brother Levi and greeted him with a subtle wave. This wave meant much to Levi, for he smiled broadly. Jude glanced quickly at his brother James, and when he saw that he was not being observed, he gave a tender return smile to Levi. It was obvious that his relationship with Levi was warmer and more loving than the relationship between his older brother and Levi.

James counted once again those chosen, and leaning over he whispered softly in his brother's ear, "John, there are twelve of us."

"Yes, I know," John replied without hesitation, and with a wide smile on his young face he added, "like the Twelve Tribes of Israel."

John's response surprised James, for he had not grasped that thought. Suddenly the proceedings on the side of the hill took on a new meaning for James. Perhaps Jesus was not a political leader; perhaps there was a religious meaning to Jesus' mission, and then quickly James lost all care for anything else. His heart beat rapidly, and he felt he was once again a child before the Holy Temple of Jerusalem. The longer he dwelled on the thought of the Twelve Tribes, the more inspired he felt. He sensed a closeness not merely to the Temple's Court of Men but also to the Holy of Holies. As this feeling continued, he immediately resolved that he and his brother John would make themselves more pronounced in the group so that they, like Jacob's sons Dan and Ephraim, would get the better share of this new kingdom. With this thought, James looked more intently at the Others, and with a quick evaluation he felt that he and John were on solid footing. Meanwhile, he again sought the reasoning in Jesus' choices, for he could perceive no unifying thread within the group. If they had been selected for religious reasons, James would have found the Master's choices even more distressing.

He reflected: *How could a publican, a Zealot, a righteous Cousin, two part-time fishermen, two young men, and a group of full-time fishermen lead a spiritual cause? What did Jesus expect to get from these men? As a group, they will become nothing but feeble, and if Jesus expects greatness to flow from them, where is this greatness to be found? We will accomplish nothing!*

Even their different clothing revealed the mixture of their personalities and backgrounds. Some were hooded, some were wearing shepherd-head coverings, and others had nothing to cover their heads but their yarmulkes. Their hair color varied: black, brown, blond, and red. They were short and tall, young and old, thick and thin. Beards of different shapes and trims covered their faces—the younger ones with newly growing beards and the older ones with full beards and gray beginning to travel from their chins. Some were very handsome and strong, others were pallid and scholarly. They seemed so different, so apart and so apathetic to each other.

How could He have chosen some of these? Some are not good Jews. Others did not act as Jews or were born Jews by mistake, and therefore were not meant to be Jews. Some of us are mortal enemies, and others are so close to each other that there will be no room for new friendships. Some are married with obligations, and others are as free as the wind. Finally he concluded:

This motley group of men does not even approach the glory I envisioned. Perhaps Jesus felt sorry for some of them, and that was why He chose them. Then with a raised eyebrow he thought, *Maybe it was all a plan to make it easy for his kinsman to succeed.*

He knew that through their cleverness and careful actions, John, Simon, Andrew, and he would succeed in diverting Jesus from the others, and because he and John were the Master's cousins, they were assured of greater prominence for surely they would receive the greater share in whatever Jesus was to create. Feeling generous, he relinquished a share to the sons of Alphaeus, who also were cousins to Jesus, but the tension between the three brothers was certainly going to diminish their effectiveness.

Jesus turned and looked at the men He had called. Everyone's attention followed.

Quickly, James became uncomfortable as the many eyes from the crowd examined them. He felt on display, and he realized that some of the Others were equally uncomfortable as he observed some of them shift their weight from side to side. He stared back at the crowd and the other followers who should have been called. He was sure that others were also wondering about Jesus' choices.

Truly, they also must see the folly in the choices. Are we the fools? How wise is it to remain with these men? It will definitely become dangerous.

For an instant, James wished he had been overlooked. To be associated with some of these men made him unhappy, but then he saw glares of envy and some looks of disappointment on the faces of those not chosen, and this eased his regrets and disapproval.

Jesus turned his attention to the crowd, and James watched as Jesus carefully tried to dismiss the gathering. After reminding the crowd of the love of *Elohim* God and of the need to seek forgiveness for sins, He raised His hands over the crowd to give a blessing, and everyone knew that all was completed.

James watched the crowd. Their eyes were glued to Jesus.

Jesus has complete control of them.

Adding to his surprise were the mesmerized looks on the faces of the other eleven with whom he was standing. It truly amazed him how Jesus was able to captivate so many.

Well, perhaps my brother and I will have to endure these others, for I truly believe we have found a Man to follow. He pondered with great resolve. *Jesus will lead the Jews to greatness, and John and I will be His perfect right hand.*

It was now late in the day, and the setting sun cast a large shadow of Jesus on the side of the mount. The shadow fell upon and covered the Twelve who had just been called. For the longest time, everyone stood on the side of the mountain in silence, then the stillness of the day was broken by a strong breeze that swirled around the twelve men. It freed them, momentarily, from the heat and the dryness of the day. Soon after, Jesus and the Twelve left the crowd and walked farther up the side of the mount.

Later that night, James sought an opportunity to be alone with Jesus. When the opportunity came, James sat beside Jesus.

"Master, we are curious as to why You picked some of us for Your companions."

Jesus turned His head and looked at James.

Finally, He said to him, "James, I am here for all people, not just those for whom you think I should be here."

He turned His head away from James and looked off into the night sky. "This is your question, James, not the question of the others. I heard your request for Justus."

"But how did you…"

"There are no two people the same in My Father's creation, so I never expected two of you to be the same. Even you and your brother are not the same. I chose these men to show the world that all can walk with Me."

"But, Lord, many of those You have chosen are not worthy to untie Your sandals."

"Yes, I know, but they are Mine, and I will teach them what is needed to be worthy to free Me of My sandals, so that through them I may walk freely."

These words lingered in James' mind for years, and when recalled they seemed as fresh as on the day they were spoken. With each recollection James relived the embarrassment of that past moment.

How wrong I was. God's time cures all ills, James considered as he and Stephaton continued to walk to Jerusalem. *As time passed, our differences became small. Some of us believed Jesus was a prophet and would lead us to find a new way; some believed He was a religious leader with a new idea that would renew Israel and ease the strong hand of the Pharisees; still others believed that Jesus was to lead the Jewish nation to freedom from Rome and all other oppressors. Eventually, we all agreed that He was our Master, our Rabbi, and that He had called us to Him for something important. We knew not what it was, but it nonetheless held us loosely together. We found that we had much in common, such as our history of following the Baptizer.*

We wondered how Jesus knew of this common ground. Many of us had been very careful in not making known our connection to John for fear that Herod would treat us as enemies. As time passed, we came to believe that our time with John was an apprenticeship that prepared us to follow Jesus. We all remembered the words of John when he saw Jesus and called Him "the Lamb of God." We talked for hours about these words, but we never asked Jesus to explain them. Yahweh's design, no doubt, Yahweh's design. In time, it was obvious that our bond was the love we had for Jesus and the even greater love for us that we saw in His eyes. That look made us long for the New Kingdom, but that Kingdom is still a long way off; for now, we are content to be the princes of jails. We still have many "cups to drink." Over the years, we learned the hard truth of a true follower of the Master, and like Jesus, we came to think of persecutors as instruments of blessings. Through our suffering, we are imitators of the Master—we suffered for the love of Jesus as Jesus suffered for the love of many.

As James continued walking along the dirt road, he felt the closeness of the Others. He knew it was only anticipation that made him sense them. After all these years of separation, he wondered what they looked like. For years he had imagined them with gray beards, some possibly bald, some not so strong or agile, some having grown fat or heavy, and assuredly some as thin as he was. These images kept him company over the years, for even when he was far away, they were with him. He missed them as much as he missed his mother, his brother, his sister, and his relatives; in fact, he missed everyone from those early days. Since his departure, he had seen very few of them. Following his departure from Jerusalem and his leaving Matthias in Judea, he met Andrew in Greece. They spent several weeks together in prayer, conversation, and preaching. That same year, he saw Bartholomew and, later, Philip, also in Greece. Philip was the last of the Twelve he saw. In southern Italy, he came upon Nicodemus, who was preaching in a synagogue; then, in southern Narbonensis Gallia, he saw Lazarus and later the aged Joseph of Arimathea, who told James that he was going to Britannia. After these few precious meetings, he saw no one from the beginning. Occasionally, there were letters about the Others from his brother John, and a few from Peter. These letters always pleased him, for they connected him to them. He learned of their work in doing the Will of the Lord and in offering the world a salvation greater then earthly life. Their successes were His successes. He quickened his pace, certain they would be just as curious to hear of his travels through northwestern Italy and southern Gallia to Sardinia, and of his final mission to Iberia, called Hispania by the Romans.

Hispania was composed of three provinces: Tarraconensis, Luistania, and Baetica. The people of this land were colonized by the Phoenicians, Greeks, Carthaginians, and Romans, but it was the Romans who finally subdued the many stubborn tribes of Hispania. The tribes eventually settled into a nation of calm people who allowed themselves to be Romanized. This agricultural province served as the granary for Rome, supplying grains, oranges, grapes, wine, olives, and olive oil. It also, with the help of many slaves, supplied tin, copper, lead, silver, and gold that burnished the glory of the Empire. These riches forced the Roman Senate to safeguard the region by permanently stationing the *Legio VII Gemina* in the province of Tarraconensis. When James arrived in Hispania, its economy was prospering. It was the richest province in the Roman Empire.

Far different from the places my brother Apostles visited, James thought, and he became impatient to tell the Others of his time in Hispania, to recreate for them the great natural beauty of that country. *They will be amazed to hear of this unique land and of its customs. They will be amused by the strange ways of its people, just as I was when I first arrived there.*

The Hispanian Jews were distinct from the Jerusalem Jews. They had developed into a different breed. Perhaps distance accentuated it, or it was, as Stephaton had said, "the different whys and hows of the Jews coming to this place." The Hispanian Jews first traveled as merchants with the Phoenicians during the reign of King Solomon. They settled there and flourished in its rich trade market. They were followed by a group of refugees who escaped the Babylonian captivity. They came to this new land beaten, and they were grateful for a place to live in peace. They settled and became productive farmers, growing grapes, olives, and fruits. Another wave of Jews arrived as purveyors to the Roman legions. They had a degree of superiority that accorded them privileges and prestige. They grew wealthy and remained protected, for they were useful to Rome. The final group of Jews was Herod Agrippa's "Jewish slaves." These were political prisoners captured as a result of the revolt of Yehuda of Gamala. It was said that Herod forced over four thousand of them into exile to Hispania and Sardinia. These Jews lived in constant hatred of Herod. They were a festering wound that could burst open and cause political problems, but even these slaves were grateful to be away from the treacherous mind of that King and the iron hand of Jerusalem. These Jews of different waves of immigration were called *Sephardim*, from the Hebrew word for Hispania, *Serfardi*. Though Jerusalem was still the center of their faith, and the *Sephardim* obediently paid their annual duty of the Temple tax, they lost the rigid thinking and the arrogance of Jerusalem.

They faithfully accepted the Torah and the other Holy Writings with an openness that was both beautiful and childlike. God was God, Who simply was to be believed. His commandments were the rules of life. There was no need for all the dressings. To the *Sephardim*, God was far more personal and reachable than He was to the Jews of Jerusalem. The debates in their synagogues about the Torah were less heated. Their discussions ended with the simple resolution that they were finite and God was infinite and thus they were not supposed to know what He was thinking. They accepted all that was as the will of Yahweh, and they constantly used the adage "Yahweh's design, no doubt, Yahweh's design" to accept the will of Yahweh; this made their lives plain and easy.

James learned to live by this adage. The more he traveled and the more he did for Yahweh, the more he knew that nothing he achieved was of his own doing. He found himself repeating this phrase as often as the *Sephardim* did; it was a great statement of faith and a greater acknowledgment of God. The fact that these people lived this adage helped him to see the *Sephardim* as truly distinct from the Jews of Jerusalem.

After so many years with the *Sephardim*, James concluded that the Hispanian Jews had been specifically called to do something great for Jesus and for the world. He was certain that someday many Hispanian sons and daughters would, with Jesus' guidance, become heroes and heroines.

The general disposition of these people, with their simple childlike faith, made James' teaching of "The Way" easier. When James repeated the words of Jesus indicating that it is necessary to "become like children to enter the Kingdom of Heaven," they immediately related to the Master; when he told them that Jesus had asked them to pick up their daily yoke, they again related to the Master.

The soil of their souls was so fertile from the many years of humility and simplicity that the seeds of Jesus' teaching were easy to sow. The Hispanian Jews accepted the Master's message as a gift from Yahweh.

The Hispanian Jews were a hospitable people. They accepted everyone regardless of color, shape, or origin, and this hospitality inspired many Hispanian Gentiles to accept the ways of the Chosen People. Many Gentiles, by watching the Jews, came to know much about the Judaic religion. This close association between Jew and Gentile made James' mission additionally fruitful. Everyone he met greeted him like a long-awaited relative. They opened their homes and their hearts, and they welcomed him into their community with unbridled excitement. They devoured his words, and when he spoke of Jesus as the Messiah—"He

Who was waited for"—Gentile and Jew alike welcomed their Savior with joy and thanksgiving.

One time, in a synagogue, James preached for fifteen continuous hours, accepting only a small cup of water and even less to eat. Nothing was expected of him except telling them of Jesus. On another occasion, a day after the Sabbath, he preached Jesus to a gathering of thousands of Gentiles for two days without sleep or food, and he spent the third day purifying them in the Iberus River. But not all was easy—that would not be the way of the Lord. Most of the people in Hispania spoke Latin, and James had needed to learn this language more fluently to be able to speak to the people. Stephaton helped by acting in the early days as an interpreter and teacher. Learning Latin was in itself a miracle, the work of the Master, but more miraculous was his simultaneous ability to read and write it.

There was still the restrictive arm of Jerusalem, which often reached out, hoping and trying to re-establish the strict Pharisaic rules. Occasionally, Jerusalem sent emissaries with the intentions of pulling tight the reins and scaring relaxed Jews back into the fold. They would come to dictate orders, but they often left frustrated. On one particular visit, a Jerusalem Pharisee named Josias arrived with the authority to persecute all those who did not fall in line with the wishes of Jerusalem. When he discovered so many converts to the new sect known as "The Way," he became enraged. When he heard that one of the original followers, one of the Twelve, was there among the people, he initiated a vigorous campaign to bring the *Sephardim* back in line. He tried to excite the leaders of the synagogues against James and the believers in Jesus by calling them heretics and ordering that they be killed, but the response that Josias received was very weak. The *Sephardim* Levites, scribes, and priests were not that worried about heresies. If something was wrong, Yahweh would tend to it. Many of the leaders purposely made Josias feel like an outsider, so he approached Liminius Gaius, the Roman Praetor, and accused James and the followers of "The Way" of inciting the "Jewish slaves" to revolt. This lie caught the Praetor's attention, though he normally took little notice of the demands of the minority Jews in his province. He treated them as malcontents and annoyances, and he declared a strong dislike for their barbaric ways. In his view, circumcision was an uncivilized disfigurement of the human body, and the fasts and dietary laws seemed a useless curtailment of human enjoyments. But when he heard that this new group of annoyers was arousing the "slaves," his fears of revolt and trouble overshadowed his contempt for the Jews. He knew he had to keep the peace and ensure that no reports were sent to Rome or

Herod, so the Praetor ordered a number of arrests. The "persecution" was a quick one, and it proved effective. Many were imprisoned or tortured, and some were even killed. The Romans had shown their mighty hand, and the Praetor had proven his authority, but his intent to keep the "persecution" small and short would demonstrate his contempt of the Jews. The last group of arrests included James. Unbeknownst to Josias, one of the quaestors, a financial administrator named Maridius Polis, sympathized with the teachings of Jesus because his wife and entire household were converts. Fearing that his wife would also be arrested, he used his position to influence the Praetor. When James stood before the Praetor and told him that he preached the love of Jesus, forgiveness of sins, and brotherhood, the Praetor laughed. He thought the Apostle harmless and only scourged and released him. Before Josias discovered this, James was quickly whisked away by the followers to a hiding place in the nearby mountains. As soon as Josias and the other emissaries left to return to Jerusalem, the persecutions vanished, but James was sure that many lies and accusations about him were delivered to Jerusalem; nevertheless, James fearlessly continued to do what the Master wanted him to do, for the perils created by men never frightened James. He grew accustomed to the many faces of man's hatred for Truth and of the desire to destroy the teachings of Jesus. He had faced these destroyers as frequently as he had faced the Destroyer of men's souls and the ugly disease of men's sins. Once, at a glance, he looked into a man and saw his sins like open, seeping wounds. After whispering to the man his sins, the man fell to the ground, begging for mercy. The man then denounced his former ways, asked for forgiveness, and pleaded for Baptism. Other times, with the help of the Master, he was able to read the souls of those who challenged him. Often, he had faced Satan in the bodies and souls of persons who came to tempt and test him. He had encountered Satan so closely that he was able to smell the stench of his breath, but with the power of Jesus, he dressed Satan down and made him crawl.

In Hispania, many came to believe and to be baptized into "The Way." Through the power of the Name of Jesus, the Apostle cured many. Many who were washed in the Spirit of the Lord moved on to other cities and, with great love and zeal, began preaching Jesus. Soon, many communities were established. This growth elated James, for he had come to believe that handing off the staff was what he and the Others were expected to do, for the Twelve would not live forever. The Twelve knew that one day Jesus would call them to come to Him and dwell in His shadow, as they once did on the Mount. So while preaching Jesus, James began to assemble an inheritance, so that what was given to him could be passed on to others. Some of those who had gone to uncharted parts of Hispania were reported to have been killed by barbarians, pagans, or fanatics. Others were imprisoned, but like James, imprisonment only reinforced their zeal and love for Jesus.

The world hates us, as it hated Jesus; when they treat us like they treated Him, they make us more like the Master, and our imitation draws us closer to Him.

Apparently there were many who were imitating Jesus, for James had heard of the numerous persecutions throughout the Empire. Though they were regional and few, it saddened him that the young Church was being so viciously treated. He wanted to see the world open its arms to Jesus and His message, but the Church was the representative of Jesus, and she also must suffer as He did. James knew that the world would never accept a message that placed restrictions on its conduct. The world wants to do as it pleases.

In time, God will have His way, for He never blesses the persecutors, only the persecuted.

He reflected on his own thoughts for a moment.

Yahweh's design, no doubt, Yahweh's design. Then in remembering, he thought *Ah, this was all meant to be, for Jesus said it would be so. Did He not ask us to pick up our burdens and follow Him?*

James smiled, and his eyebrows arched as he recalled the day he and John had requested to follow Jesus in hardship and suffering. At that time, they did not understand what Jesus said: no one did, for this was Yahweh's design. Their beloved mother, Salome, with maternal concern and needing assurance from her sister's Son, sought Jesus out one warm late afternoon. She asked Jesus to make certain that her two sons, His cousins, would be ranked highly, one to His right and the other to His left, when He came into His kingdom.

James recalled how his mother's request caused much grumbling among the other Apostles, but their grumbling quickly dissipated when Jesus told them they had to be servants and not masters. The reply Jesus gave to His aunt was not to her liking—she looked disappointed. Jesus, seeing His aunt's face, asked the two sons of Zebedee in a low, grave voice, "Can you drink from the cup I am about to drink from?"

The two brothers, believing that they were being offered a cup of glory, quickly replied, "Yes, Lord!"

Jesus replied sadly, "From the cup that I drink of, you shall drink."

It wasn't until they had been arrested and beaten in Jerusalem, after that glorious Pentecost, that James had perceived the relationship between his cup and Jesus' cup.

I think we all know now what the Master meant. All of us have seen the inside of jails and have been beaten and tortured. We drink from the cup of Jesus; in this suffering, we have succeeded, and we will continue to suffer, for this is Yahweh's design. It is our way to prove our love for Him.

Though he did not realize it, his thoughts had caused him to slow his pace. Noticing that Stephaton had walked too far ahead of him, he quickened his step to catch up with his companion. As he walked, he was filled with great solace. His wandering thoughts stopped for a few moments, and he became removed from his walking and from those around him. So many times, over the years, as he had walked through Palestine, Sardinia, and Hispania, he had walked with a faithful companion; these were prayer-filled walks, for they reminded him of his many walks with Jesus. On those occasions, he had felt the strong companionship and the warm bond between Jesus and himself. Now, with Stephaton, he felt that same companionship and warmth. God had given his companions the insight to know that these walks were a time granted by God to console them. Slowly, his thoughts returned to Hispania, and he found himself amazed at the success of his preaching, yet all that had been accomplished was miniscule next to all that remained to be done. The only satisfaction he received was the knowledge that his labors had made him a tool in the hands of the Master; this gave him great peace and joy, for he had become what Jesus said he must be—a servant. In a low voice, he offered a brief prayer of thanksgiving for the opportunities that had been given him to prove his love for his Master. He felt blessed by all that he had done to spread the Word. Having finished his prayer of thanksgiving, which he usually reserved for the end of his day, he became aware that he had again changed his pattern of prayer. He wondered lately why his prayers were of thankfulness and not of petition. He did not recall his prayers ever being filled with so much thanksgiving. When first he began his mission, his nightly prayers were for strength and eagerness, and energy came to him. He never tired. He knew that no mere human strength could sustain this level of exertion. As years passed, his prayers turned to pleas for understanding and wisdom. When words too wise and too profound came to him, he again knew that he was the vocal tool of the Lord. Then he prayed for stronger faith—when after imprisonment and beatings he emerged stronger in his beliefs, he knew he was living his faith. Now, it seemed that all he needed to do was give thanks.

Perhaps it is time for such a thing, he thought. *Every time I prayed, things came easier to me. My successes are many because of my prayers.*

But as with all human endeavors, not all was successful. Many Jews of Hispania had centuries-old issues that were difficult to overcome. For one thing, they hated King Herod, who they knew was nothing but a puppet in Roman hands. They regarded him with the same intense hatred that they had for Emperor Claudius. Many a native Hispanian did not forget the heavy conquering hand of Rome, the brutality Rome had shown to crush the rebellion, the slaughter of the innocent, or the sale of Jews as slaves. It was the hatred of these two rulers that became James' greatest challenge. Though many Hispanians became true followers, they struggled to achieve love for their enemies. It seemed that no matter what James said, he could not free them from this hatred. He finally left this problem in the loving hands of Yahweh.

"James, do you think Hermogenes and Philetus have already arrived? With two days lead, they should be here by now, do you not think so?"

Stephaton's question disoriented him for a moment. "What did you say, Stephaton?"

"I asked if you thought Hermogenes and Philetus had arrived."

James simply smiled in reply, for he was certain that the two disciples had arrived and were waiting for them. He was equally certain that they were spreading the news of Stephaton's and his arrival. He grew excited with the anticipation of seeing his mother, his brother, and Lady Mary; then, his smile widened as he thought of seeing his two Gentile disciples from Sardinia. These two men were God's greatest miracle of his ministry on that island. With Jesus' help, these two came to him and remained with him throughout the years of his Sardinian mission. They would even join him in his mission to Hispania.

They are as crude and as rough as the jagged Sardinian coastline, he thought to himself. *Their devotion to the Master is as high as the massif that spreads wide and endless throughout the island, and yet they continue to become as gentle, as peaceful, and as simple as the inlets and the fine sands of the beaches.*

Before God's plan allowed them to meet, James had heard of these two men. They were well known throughout the island as sorcerers and, in the eyes of many Sardinians, as very powerful ones. For months, and as long as James preached and converted the Sardinian Jews, these two evil men were not a danger—the sorcerers had no Jews among their followers, so their paths never crossed.

The conversion of the Sardinian Jews became easier for James when Emperor Tiberius exiled four thousand Jews to the island for causing "trouble" in Rome and the surrounding regions. These new Jews added to those exiled by Herod. In this new group were many who believed in Jesus. James began preaching to these new arrivals and found the believers. These new faithful arrivals were revitalized. Soon, he had so many helpers that he could hardly contain their eagerness and fervor. Of course, it was inevitable that the Gentiles would eventually hear of Jesus; soon, they too came to hear James preach, and many were converted.

When Hermogenes, the older and more experienced of the two sorcerers, heard of the miracles that James was performing in Jesus' name, he sent Philetus, his primary student, to challenge James. Well before Philetus arrived, James sensed the approach of evil. Philetus arrived one day when James was preaching. He stood silently in the crowd listening to James with an air of blatant impudence. Many of the people who had gathered that day knew that the sorcerer was present, and they waited with great anticipation for an encounter of the old ways with the new "Way." James chose at first to ignore the young enchanter, but by midday his eyes were drawn to the young man, and he found himself walking through the crowd toward Philetus. As he was walking to the young man, he continued to preach of Jesus. In fact, he was speaking to the crowd about Jesus' miracle of raising the son of the widow of Naim. Many of those gathered were taken by the retelling of this miracle, and they listened intently. James continued to walk through the crowd, relaying the story as he remembered it from that warm spring day many years ago. By story's end, he was standing face to face with the young sorcerer. The young man's Mediterranean face was handsome, but it was decorated with signs and symbols that declared his belief in the Evil One. His young body had many tattoos, and around his neck, arms, and wrists were beads, chains, and ropes with many amulets, bone parts, and animal teeth. His clothing was plain but rich, and his multi-colored robe flowed and played in the soft breeze. In contrast, James was in a single robe that seemed undisturbed by the same breeze. James searched the young man's eyes and saw, hidden behind the arrogance, a dormant gentleness. After detecting this, he smiled with the certainty that Jesus was already working in this young man. His smile widened, and without warning, he interrupted his teaching, placed his hand on the young man's head, and said in a loud voice, "JESUS." That one Name reverberated endlessly through the nearby valleys, echoing and re-echoing. Philetus' body became stiff, and he crashed to the ground like a falling, petrified timber. James let him fall as he proceeded through the crowd, ignoring what had taken place, and he continued explaining his story of the conquest of Jesus over death. He compared the return to life of the boy of Naim to the return to life of all who repent and believe in Jesus.

After he had gone a short distance from the fallen Philetus, he heard someone say in a soft voice, "James!"

He turned to see who had called his name and saw the new Philetus—without evil and without his amulets, bracelets, and chains, which now lay on the ground around him. He was with Christ, for his face was clear of hatred and glowed with anticipation. His body markings had faded into his tan skin.

The crowd gasped at the new man; many moved away, some fell to their knees, and others ran away in complete fear.

The rest of that day and night, James spoke to Philetus of Jesus, and at daybreak the young Philetus was baptized in the Flumendosa River. Shortly thereafter, James sent him back to his former master, Hermogenes, trusting that Philetus' personal conversion would eventually lead to a confrontation with Hermogenes.

Three weeks later, James was awakened by the sounds of someone crying for help. He rose from his sleeping mat and looked around his room. The room was empty. He walked to the door of the house and looked out onto the narrow streets—no one was there. He returned to his sleeping mat, confused and doubting his hearing. Again he heard cries, and the cries did not go away. The cry was from someone in deep, agonizing pain; the sounds were soul wrenching. Not knowing who this soul was, James fell into deep, fervent prayer, begging for some insight, when unexpectedly and quickly, sleep returned to him. A dream came to him. The young Philetus spoke of Hermogenes placing him in a trance that left him paralyzed and unable to speak or fight back. Awakened again, James immediately returned to prayer, and when morning came, he dispatched Stephaton to the poor young man. He gave his assistant his only cloak with the instructions to simply wrap Philetus in it and bring Philetus back to him. Stephaton left and, finding Philetus, did what James instructed him to do. At the very moment that Philetus received James' cloak, the trance was broken. Within a week, the two had returned to James. The next day, the former sorcerer gave witness, praise, and thanksgiving to Jesus before a large crowd. He denounced his former master, Hermogenes, as the Evil One. Word of his conversion spread quickly throughout the countryside, and many came, often out of sheer curiosity, to see the new Philetus. Peace and happiness shone with such intensity from the young man's handsome face that people were drawn to him and desired to hear of his conversion.

Six days after the return of Stephaton and Philetus, Hermogenes arrived. On that day, James was teaching and baptizing in a river northwest of the city of Carales. Everyone in the crowd who came to hear James sensed the anger and vengeance of Hermogenes' presence. One glance at his distorted face was enough for anyone to see that he was armed with all the demons and all the powers of darkness.

When James too felt Hermogenes' presence, he immediately came out of the water; with the Hand of the Master on his shoulder, he walked to the sorcerer. Everyone perceived that an important event was taking place, for they knew that two supernatural powers had come face to face. With silent anticipation and with a stillness of impending awe, the people stood watching. The contrast between the two was obvious and stark. The extremely tall Hermogenes, with his infernal decorations and painted face, was more frightening than the shorter and plain-bearded James. Hermogenes' brightly colored hair was pushed severely back and decorated with teeth, bones, and golden ornaments. His hair was far more striking than the unkempt black hair of James. Black silk and flowing clothes made Hermogenes look spirited in comparison to the earthy Apostle clad in a simple brown cloak and white robe.

They stood a few yards apart. In silence and for the longest time, they looked through unbroken stares into each other's eyes. Hermogenes' face darkened with hatred and evil; James' face gleamed in clear purpose and love.

Unexpectedly, Hermogenes, in a loud, wild, deep voice, began to curse and abuse James with lies and accusations. He cursed his father, Zebedee, as the procreator of an imbecilic son; he cursed his mother as a harlot and his brother as a weakling. He called James a heretic who had been thrown out of his country and exiled from his religion for believing in a crucified criminal of the Empire. He told the crowd that James was betraying them because he wanted to prevent them from enjoying life. He accused him of being a cannibal who ate the Flesh of a dead Man.

James stood with his eyes closed in silent prayer.

The sorcerer's voice grew with anger and cruelty; his curses became more vile and more personal. He accused James of vanity and of preaching Jesus for selfish reasons. He insulted more of his ancestors. He berated him for having many doubts about Jesus and His mission. He reminded James, in perfect detail, of his treachery in Gethsemane and his cowardly absence on Golgotha.

Abruptly, James raised his staff high above his head. Some people gasped, believing that this man of Jesus, this gentle and peaceful man of love, was about to strike the sorcerer, but instead, he forcibly brought his staff down and planted it in the ground directly in front of Hermogenes. Then, turning, he quietly walked away.

The demons within Hermogenes took this as a sign of surrender. With a pleased gleam of sneering triumph, the sorcerer quickly grabbed for the staff and raised it high above James' head in preparation for a fatal blow.

Many in the crowd cried out to warn James, but the staff remained in the air as Hermogenes' muscles strained to deliver the blow. The sorcerer's face twisted in determination, but the staff would not obey him. He tried to release the staff but could not—it had become a burning piece of timber in his hands. His fingers released it and convulsed in the air, but the staff was glued to his palms. Sweat immediately poured from his face as he screamed in pain.

James, who had walked but a few yards from him, slowly turned and saw not Hermogenes but Legion. With a stare that would pierce and permeate the hardest of rocks, James looked at the tormented soul, and while making the sign of the cross in the air, he commanded, "Be gone all that is dark. I command you in the name of Jesus! Be gone!"

As the evil ones flew from him, Hermogenes screamed in excruciating pain; he twisted and crumbled to the ground, the staff still attached to his palms. The dark shadows that were etched on the sorcerer's face slowly vanished. His face went blank, then gray, and finally dead white; slowly, it grew clean of its markings. His body twisted and jerked as raven-black spirits were seen fleeing and flying from him and into dark cracks and caves on the sides of the nearby mountains and cliffs. Finally, the staff rolled free of his hands. It continued to roll over the ground to James, who slowly bent down and picked it up.

Hermogenes laid lifeless in a ball, with his arms and legs tucked tightly beneath his chin. James stood watch over his contorted body.

When holy captivity was completed, James softly said, "Get up, child of God, for you are free. You have been saved by the love and mercy of Jesus."

Hermogenes rose from the ground, fresh and renewed. Quickly and quietly, he began to strip himself of his ornaments, amulets, and robes. Stripped of his clothing, he fell in humility to his knees, pleading for forgiveness. James walked to him and wrapped his cloak over his naked body. Hermogenes rose from his knees and embraced James, then, with equal joy, he embraced Stephaton and Philetus. All that day and into the night, he repeatedly asked Jesus to forgive him. The next day he asked to be baptized, and on the shores of the Flumendosa River, he was reborn into the Christian life.

Following these events, the former men of sorcery from Sardinia had always been ready to serve and to speak of Jesus. They stayed with James and Stephaton, learning more from them and never straying from their sides until the four travelers arrived in Yaffa. In that seaport, the four men separated for the first time in years. They were sent before James and Stephaton with instructions to present themselves to Peter and James bar Alphaeus. James wanted these two men to become familiar with the Elders so that he could present them as part of his report to the Others in Jerusalem and ask that they be sent back to Sardinia as new leaders to guide the growing church in their homeland. After that, he planned to ask that Stephaton be returned to Hispania as the leader of that community because he was so familiar with those people. James, then, was going to ask for another mission, a new mission. The place of his new mission would be left up to the Master, the Will of God, and the Elders.

All is Yahweh's design, no doubt, Yahweh's design, he concluded in his mind.

He would miss all three men, especially Stephaton, for he had been with him so long, but he knew that the former Roman soldier was guided by the Spirit of the Lord. Stephaton knew Jesus from personal experience and from what he had heard, and it was time for him to be sent on his own mission.

James interrupted his thoughts and gave his traveling companion a quick glance. He was so happy to have this man with him, and he was grateful to Peter and James bar Alphaeus for ordering him to accept Stephaton. To lose him now would sadden James, for the ex-soldier had become like a brother to him; in fact, in some things, like height and stature, he resembled James more than his brother John did.

*

Stephaton was tall and muscular, a bit older, but still without graying hair. His days as a Roman mercenary were evident in his neatly trimmed black beard. His dark Hamitic Egyptian skin, further tanned by the Hispanian sun, was an inheritance from his mother. His face, marked with the scars of the many battles he had fought while soldiering for Rome, was a typical Roman face with a strong chin, high cheekbones, and a long hooked nose, all gifts from his Roman father. In bygone days, before his calling, not only his face was scarred but his soul also, for he led a conquering soldier's life of debauchery.

"Are you all right, James?" Stephaton asked automatically, for he felt the Apostle's eyes on him. He asked the question without looking away from the road or from the city in the distance.

James smiled quickly, for he knew that the question was asked not out of concern but from familiarity—he could see by the long unbroken stare in Stephaton's eyes that his traveling companion was also caught in the memories of the past.

Ah, Jerusalem, James sighed to himself with complete understanding of Stephaton's pensiveness, *you still have the power to hold men to yourself. I see you have brought back many thoughts, both good and bad, to our minds.*

The Apostle turned his eyes to the city before him as he walked silently by Stephaton's side; from the expression he saw on the ex-soldier's face, he surmised that Stephaton was lost in thought: he was recalling his days in Jerusalem. James knew especially well the story of Stephaton's conversion, for he had heard it many times—so many times, in fact, that he could retell it as well as Stephaton. Of all the days he spent in Jerusalem, Stephaton recalled only one with frequency and warmth, though for months after that day, he was bewildered by all that had happened to him.

On that day, as a soldier, he had been assigned to assist and witness the crucifixion of three rebels, one of whom was Jesus bar Yosef of Nazareth. Little did he suspect that he would be called that day to discipleship; little did he suspect that God would choose him and touch him with sudden faith.

All during the walk to that hellish place called Golgotha, Stephaton had watched, with more interest than usual, the faces of the people along the way. The Jews did not like this form of punishment, and he knew them to pretend to be stoic and indifferent to the proceedings, but this day he observed a difference. Besides seeing the faces that were etched in torment, or the occasional face of sadness or fear, or the faces of ghoulish observers, that warm sunny day he sensed heaviness, a blanket of hatred over the crowd that seemed woven by something beyond that time and that place. It was a different kind of hate, greater than any human abhorrence; though he did not see this hatred, he knew it was there. He could feel it breathing, seething in anxiety and anticipation. This hatred was different from the hatred he sensed when he walked through the streets of Jerusalem or of any other Jewish city or village—that hatred he was attuned to and could identify readily—nor was this the same hatred that he had felt when stationed in other provinces of Rome. No, what he sensed that day was a much older hatred, one that reached back, way back in time, into ancient days scarcely recorded by men. His Egyptian mother would have called it "evil blood brewed by long loathing." Whatever it was, he sensed it and he had never felt anything quite like it before at any other crucifixion or in any other place. Slightly disturbed by this hatred, he had walked beside the prisoner from Nazareth, and he remembered the young girl who fought to wipe the face of the rebel Jesus. Stephaton had crudely pushed her aside. He remembered the efforts of the old African man who struggled against the soldiers to carry a cup of water to the condemned rebel. He had shoved him into the dirty street.

He had watched this Man, Jesus, stumble and fall.

After each fall, he pulled the Nazarene to His feet, and each time the Man's weight changed—He grew unexplainably heavier. He looked into the Man's face and saw sadness far greater than any he had ever seen; it was a deep, inconsolable sadness. Stephaton found himself believing that this Man was suffering more than the physical pains of carrying a cross; this Man was bearing a tragedy that was not His own.

Stephaton became confused by what he was witnessing. To add to his confusion, he found, for the first time in his life, empathy for someone else. This strange feeling of sympathy for someone else's pain then began to extend to many others, and, more strangely, he felt sorry for himself. During the march, he could not shake this strange feeling from his mind, for it was as strong and as uncomfortable as the heat that pressed against him.

Out of concern for the Criminal, the centurion Cornelius ordered another Roman guard to find someone to help carry the Criminal's cross. An African was pressed into service who reluctantly bore the weight of the Nazarene's cross. Stephaton watched this tall, strong, broad-chested man strain under the rough bark and weight of the tree. But, much later, when he looked more carefully at this African, he saw that the man had an expression of joy on his face, and Stephaton wondered, suspecting that some kind of invisible magic had transpired between the Nazarene and the Cyrenian. He became confused, for he had never been so sensitive and vulnerable to the sufferings of other victims of crucifixion. He concluded, but without much conviction, that duty in Jerusalem was making him soft.

As the march to the hill continued along the narrow, winding streets amidst the mockeries and abuses, the curses and hatred, Stephaton found himself walking in a partial daze. Perplexed and unsettled, he sensed an injustice, a grave wrong, being enacted around him. He felt the need to stop everything, but he did not know how to stop it and he did not have the courage to stop it—nor did he know why he had to stop it.

As they approached Golgotha, his military senses grew keen. It was like combat in the campaign through the forest of Dacia. At that time, he sensed and recognized the eye of an enemy upon him, lurking in the shadows, watching and smiling gleefully in the ability to see him and know his every movement, while he, unprotected, was unable to see the enemy. Sensing this again, he looked around frantically for the face of the foe, but he could not identify him. Then his sight was tunneled toward the family and friends of the Criminal; again, with confusion, he lived His sorrow. His alertness was again heightened when he heard the hatred and ridicule from some of the leaders of the people. Here, he thought, was the real enemy. Without swords, lances, or spears, they were drawing blood and seemed to be the conquerors. These conclusions confused him—they were the opposite of his typical Roman thoughts. This Criminal and these rebels were the enemies of all that was Roman, and whatever they and their families were suffering was deserved, yet he could not understand his softness.

Later, after the nailing, when the Criminal said, "I thirst," Stephaton slowly picked up a hyssop reed, tied a sponge to it, soaked the sponge in myrrh and cheap wine, and lifted it to the Rebel's lips. His only hope was to ease some of the pain of this Man, who, he was beginning to believe, was guilty of no crime.

Several of the nearby soldiers laughed.

"Look, Stephaton is giving the King of the Jews our poor soldier's wine. How insulting for a King to partake of such lowly wine."

He directed the reed to the lips of the Man, tempting Him to take a taste, but the Man refused it. The bitter wine dripped from the sponge onto Stephaton's shoulder and chest; it was so hot that for an instant it burned his flesh. Instead of pulling away in discomfort, he froze and allowed the painful ecstasy and warmth to singe him. He had expected the wine to be warm from the noonday heat, but it was strange that the wine would burn him.

The Man, Jesus, raised His head slightly, not to accept the reed but to show appreciation for Stephaton's kindness. He expected to see a bloody, beaten face consumed in pain, but instead, he saw a smile. Their eyes met, and Stephaton felt something inside himself being ripped away. The sensation was so strong, so real, that it caused him to drop the reed and to put his hand on the side of the cross to steady himself. At that instant he felt as though he was a part of the cross—and a part of this Jesus on the cross—but he did not feel His pains or sufferings. Instead, Stephaton felt a friendship that soon intensified into a feeling of complete belonging, an overpowering feeling of being at home and with family. He felt a fondness from new parents from a different place. Quickly he pulled his hand from the cross and shook his head in an effort to clear his mind of all these strange thoughts and feelings.

When the darkness came, all of the happenings of that day and all of the happenings of his past days were hidden from Stephaton's memory. He felt the wind, which seemed to rise from some unknown, far off place, push and press against him. The flying sand pricked and stung his bare flesh. Lightning pierced the sky, and thunder rumbled and shook the ground beneath his feet as he heard Cornelius, another centurion, declare, "Truly, this was the Son of God." Stephaton fell to his knees, brought there by the trembling world. He looked up at the face of the rebel, Jesus, and saw peace. It was a peace that seeped into Stephaton's soul and soaked the very fibers of his being. It flooded his very spirit. The wine that had dropped to his hand, arm, and chest seared his flesh, his bones, and his soul. He again sensed the enemy nearby; defensively, he quickly scanned the hilltop, determined to find the foe. There grew within him an urgent need to find this enemy. Suddenly, clearly, he found the hidden, lurking foe—his enemy; he recognized the enemy as the underworld in his life and in his flesh. The enemy he sought and found was himself.

Often, after hearing this story recounted, James watched Stephaton's face glow with so great a conviction that James was filled with awe as he gained a new and deeper understanding of what Jesus was to all men. Curiously and yet not surprisingly, James also noticed that after Stephaton spoke of these times, he would become a greater disciple of Jesus; his words, thoughts, and actions would be fired with such passion that James pitied the soul of anyone who had not yet come to believe in Jesus. Stephaton would stalk such an unbeliever as if he were an enemy.

We are all called in different ways with different stories that evoke different feelings and inspire different actions for the Lord. The only thing our calls have in common is the way we respond to them in love and service, James thought.

Certain that both Stephaton and he had relived that day once again, James continued walking on the road leading to the Yaffa Gate.

The travelers and pilgrims on the road were more hurried. From the pushing, the quickened pace, and the sense of excitement in the air, James knew that the other travelers on the road were impatient to arrive, but he and Stephaton were not in a rush. They had learned from the past that if the Lord willed them to be some place soon, they would find themselves at the designated place without delay, but if the Lord did not urgently need them somewhere, they would travel at a normal pace and arrive when they arrived.

We, once again, are part of a design. Yahweh's design, no doubt, Yahweh's design.

The rush around them continued, and James sensed that the hurry and excitement were partly due to the religious fervor of some of the people, who wanted to be in Jerusalem—the City of David, the Place of the Holy of Holies. As James looked at the walls before him, he felt no such excitement, and he sadly accepted that Jerusalem no longer held a place of sacredness in his mind. She had lost her splendor, her holiness, and she did not have the same commitment that she once did. To him, at that moment, it was a city where his family lived and the place where he could find other followers of Jesus.

Without intent, the two veteran travelers suddenly found themselves becoming part of a great crowd, and as they walked, the excitement of the crowd became part of them. Their own anticipation to see friends and family mounted, and their steps quickened.

James, needing to feel the closeness of another person, placed his hand on Stephaton's shoulder, thereby getting his attention. He wanted to share this small moment with him. James wanted to see if Stephaton also was feeling the excitement of coming home.

Just before entering the gate, James stopped. The crowds walking on the road bumped against him or walked around him, some complaining about his stupidity and the inconvenience he was creating, but he stopped because he wanted to capture the emotion of the moment of his return, and because he sensed that there was more for him to see, something more for him to know, find, and experience. His eyes searched ahead of the crowd, over the heads of those walking before him. His eyes scaled the side of the wall, until he saw him, and suddenly he found what he was to know: he knew that the Master was, again, speaking to him. He smiled, for there ahead, above the crowd, standing on one of the parapets of the city wall, was Josias the Pharisee, who once was the ambassador of the High Priest to Hispania. Their eyes locked on to each other. James could see the Pharisee, and he could see the left corner of Josias' mouth arched in a cynical, satisfied grin. Behind Josias and to his right stood another man, whose features forced James to look more closely. He squinted his eyes and shaded them with his hand. He finally recognized the features on the Face—he wanted to call out with great joy the Man's name, but he simply smiled, for a greater understanding overcame him.

In the distance, far off in one of the nearby valleys, there was the sound of roaming thunder.

"How unusual," Stephaton remarked as he looked up at the cloudless sky. "On a clear and sunny day, there is thunder."

James' smile widened, and putting his arms around Stephaton's broad, muscular shoulders, he said with much greater understanding, "Come, my brother, let us go home."

They walked through the Yaffa Gate into Jerusalem and were quickly swallowed up in the maze of narrow, crowded, zigzagged streets. The mass of humanity all around him, along with the many smells and sounds of the city, brought joy to James. He was home. The farther he walked into the city, the more at home he became. He was like that child of so many years ago who was captivated by the size of the city. Soon, he began to recall the many familiar streets, palaces, shops, and houses. They passed Weaver's Street, then Fisher's Street, and finally they came to the juncture of Gardener's Street and Produce Street. At this point, the streets widened, and things, for some obscure reason, seemed calmer. There were less people scurrying and hurrying; there was less noise.

James suddenly remembered that at this time of day all the fresh fruit, food, and flowers would have been purchased, but he was grateful for the calmness, for now there was time and room for them to shop. He grabbed Stephaton's arm and led him to the beginning of Gardener's Street.

"My friend, I think it would be good if we arrived with some provisions for our family and friends. Over there, at the end of that street, should be a merchant who sells fruits and dates. Go down that street and purchase some provisions and meet me back at this spot. While you are doing this, I should like to buy some flowers for my mother and sister, and even for Lady Mary."

"That is a good idea, James, and, forgive me, I often forget the niceties of family life," Stephaton said, smiling, as he turned and walked down to the merchant's shop at the end of the street. It seemed to take Stephaton a long time to arrive at the store, and when he entered, he had to momentarily stand still to give his eyes some time to adjust to the dark interior of the small shop. When his eyes finally adjusted, he walked over to a basket of fruit in the corner of the store. He reached in and gathered two large, fresh oranges in each of his hands. He was certain that these oranges would be a nice gift in addition to some dates, nuts, and figs. Suddenly, an unexpected but familiar chill passed through him. He had experienced this chill before whenever he sensed the lurking of an unseen enemy. He quickly turned and scrutinized every person in the shop. He saw nothing near him that would cause this chill, and he grew anxious. A frightening thought surged through his mind. He dropped the oranges, and with the merchant's angry voice ringing in his ears, he rushed out, pushing and knocking against others in the shop until he reached the entrance to the street. He glanced up toward the end of Gardner's Street and saw James' head above the heads of Temple guards; then he saw Josias, the Pharisee, standing off to the side of the guards.

Stephaton's heart jumped with fear and anxiety. James was in grave danger. He had to go to his aid. He instinctively reached for the small sword by his side, but it wasn't there—he had not worn one there for years. As he dashed up the street, James quickly turned his head and looked over his shoulder at the running ex-soldier; their eyes met, and Stephaton felt the warmth and love from James' eyes. From his look, he sensed a command to remain away and still. Obediently, he stopped and watched as James was led away.

A wind stirred at the end of the street where James had been apprehended, and Stephaton could see it move down the street toward him. It traveled by the outdoor wares of the many merchants and buyers, and as it passed him, he heard in the sound of the wind: JAMES. He became startled at first, but there was a sense that the voice was familiar. He had heard it before. He looked around in confusion for the Speaker of the name. Suddenly, he understood what was happening. He again looked at the small group of guards as they moved away, and he sensed there was a smile on James' face. In sensing this smile, he could easily discern a deep happiness, and he knew that James had accepted willingly what was to happen to him. The guards pushed their way through the crowds. Carefully and from a distance, he began following the small group of guards as they roughly made their way through the crowded, winding streets. He presumed that they were taking James to the Temple, but to his surprise, they continued through the Gennath Gate and passed the Tower of Mariamne. As they continued, Stephaton realized that they were walking to the Upper City, most likely to the Palace of Herod Agrippa I. He grew confused and wondered why Temple guards were taking James to Herod Agrippa I, who was secular and not of the Temple.

If this is all Herod's doings, why is Josias, a Pharisee, involved in the apprehension? he wondered to himself.

As the small group walked through the streets, several other people began to follow. Stephaton was sure they did not know who James was, but a contingent of Temple guards escorting someone was enough of a spectacle to draw a crowd. The farther they walked, the larger the crowd grew. Much to Stephaton's surprise, he heard several people identify James. When they finally arrived at Herod's Palace, the guards took James inside while the crowd, including Stephaton, remained outside in the courtyard. Stephaton pushed and shoved his way as close to the palace entrance as possible, hoping to catch a glimpse of what was happening, but he was unable to see or hear anything. He persisted in trying to get closer until he cautioned himself: *You may be recognized by a soldier, or worse, by one of the Temple guards or Pharisees.*

Suddenly, he saw a few of the arresting guards come out, and he heard them say, "That man was one of the leaders of the heretical group called 'The Way.'"

Many in the crowd began to cheer.

Another guard said, "That man is accused of trying to get the Jews of Hispania to revolt against Rome and thereby embarrass Herod."

I should go and find Hermogenes and Philetus to tell them what has happened, Stephaton thought.

Just then he saw Josias appear on the upper level of the palace steps. He stood looking out onto the courtyard. His eyes were fixed on something. The Pharisee seemed bewildered—from time to time he would glance back into the palace and then back again to the courtyard.

He looks stunned by his own easy success, Stephaton concluded with some bitterness.

Josias stood on the sun-baked steps of the palace, stroking his beard and occasionally wiping his forehead. He paced around, stopped, and again began pacing. At times, he seemed to want to go back into the palace or to seek help. Some members of the Sanhedrin passed, alternately greeting him and congratulating him, but the Pharisee only stared in reply or offered an insignificant smile. None of those who greeted him lingered, for they wanted to see what was happening at James' trial. They quickly left him and entered the palace. Finally, alone, Josias lowered his head. He again began to pace on the top step of the palace. His pacing was a sure sign of his turmoil.

Stephaton witnessed all these things and wondered, *Is this the torment of a soul?*

Without fanfare, James, bound and heavily guarded, appeared on the top steps. He and Josias looked at each other. James was no longer surrounded by Temple guards but instead by soldiers whom Stephaton recognized as Herod's elite guards. James' face had an incongruous satisfaction to it. As James passed Josias, they exchanged words, and James broke free of his captors long enough to embrace Josias. The soldiers quickly regained their hold of James and crudely pulled him away. They roughly directed him to descend the palace steps. Josias stood frozen as if still in James' embrace. His face was lined with bewilderment and twisted with panic. Hiding to the side of the steps, Stephaton watched the Pharisee for several long moments. He could not imagine what James had said to him, but he knew that it had affected him deeply.

Finally, Josias began to descend the steps of the palace.

Stephaton turned away from Josias. He had to follow James. He could not be bothered with Josias and his malady. In the distance, he saw Herod's guards hurriedly lead James away. They were moving toward the Hippseus Tower and the city wall to the Valley of Hinnom. Cautiously, Stephaton followed as closely as possible behind the gathering, which had by now become a large mob.

The mob grew vocal with shouts of hatred.

Stephaton endured all this, and though he cringed with every shouted hostility, he knew he had to follow, if for no other reason than to tell James' family of the happenings.

EPILOGUE

After hearing that James and his companions were arriving, Salome Zebedee, Lady Mary with the other ladies of "The Way," and John quietly left Jerusalem on the short trip to Bethany to await the arrival of the travelers. They had to move quickly, quietly, and separately to Bethany, which was a safer place. It was out of the immediate range of the Temple informers and of Herod Agrippa, who was leading a campaign against "The Way." The house of Lazarus and his sisters Martha and Mary would be perfect. The instant they arrived, Salome, her sister Naomi, and Lady Mary hurried with Martha and the other women to plan a celebratory meal for the joyous homecoming. Word was secretly sent to any of the Twelve who were in Judea or nearby provinces. The first to arrive was Andrew, then Matthew. Later, James the Little and Jude Thaddeus arrived, greatly excited about James's arrival. They told John that earlier, at different times of the day, they had been at the Temple preaching, but they did not draw much attention in order to avoid being followed. Their caution was not so much for themselves, for they were willing to die for Jesus, but for the followers who looked to the Apostles for strength and guidance. Each Apostle was painstakingly guarded, and at the slightest sign of trouble, they were quickly and mysteriously whisked away to safety. John would have joined them, but he had decided instead to escort the ladies to Bethany.

Surely the Master understands our excitement. It has been almost ten years without James, and even the Master longed for family and friends, he rationalized.

He sat for a few moments listening to the excited talk of the women as they busied themselves in the kitchen. When he felt that all was being tended to, he quickly left the ladies and joined James the Little, Andrew, and Jude Thaddeus outside at the back of the house in the shade of the ending day. When he left the house and looked at the sky, the day's sun shone in one last effulgent display. John was in awe of the beauty before him.

"Yahweh is good!" He exclaimed as he took a seat and listened to his fellow Apostles speak excitedly of their day. Jude was surprised that no Temple or Palace guards were near the Temple. Andrew spoke of Saul, whom they had not seen in three years. Andrew heard reports that Saul was planning to leave Tarsus and go to Antioch, and possibly on to Greece or Galatia. Even after all these years and despite all of Saul's accomplishments, the Apostles remained very cautious of him. He advocated quickness and change. He was ambitious, adventurous, and aggressive, and though the Twelve also possessed these attributes, they used them with more discretion and reserve.

John could not become interested in the conversation. He was too excited. He rose from his chair and, looking at James and Andrew, said confidently, "My dear brothers, rest assured that Jesus will take care of all that needs tending. He has been with us until now and He will tend to Saul when Saul needs attending."

Leaving the Others to their discussion, he went into the house and walked to the front room, hoping for seclusion. From the back of the kitchen, he heard the hustle and energy of the women. He was sure that his brother James would be pleased by the meal and all the preparations.

It will be good to see James again. I will spend hours reminiscing with him. I want to hear of his adventures and successes.

John sat on a small chair, and his envy of James and the Others occupied his thoughts. His travels had been limited to Judea, Galilee, and Samaria, with occasional trips to the Decapolis. He longed for other places, those faraway places where his new thirst for adventure could be satisfied. His disappointment ebbed as he reminded himself that his duty was to tend to Lady Mary, under the command that came from Jesus. It fell on him to remain in Judea with James the Little. The pulling of this lot confirmed his responsibility for Mary, whom everyone out of respect now called Lady Mary.

Still, I feel I am not doing as much as my fellow Apostles.

He remembered how James, in his youth, always spoke of traveling. He envied his brother and always wanted to be like him, but he did not have the wanderlust that James had. John enjoyed and needed the comfort. There were times when the two would stand on the shores of the Sea of Galilee, and James would wish that he was standing instead on the shores of the *Mare Nostrum*, that mighty sea of the Roman Empire—on those shores he would set the sails of one of his father's boats and go far and away to distant lands. These thoughts excited John, but he could not see himself leaving his family.

That is why James has traveled so far, and perhaps some of the Others had dreams as big as my brother's dreams. Perhaps that is why they all seemed so excited in going and seeing other places. I never did. Yet now I grow restless, and the desire to be off with them has been gnawing at me.

A picture of his tall brother, with his midnight black hair and full beard, leapt into his mind's eye. He saw his wide shoulders, lean, muscular body, and callused fisherman's hands. He bore an uncanny resemblance to the Master. Many times, people confused the cousins. Their similarities were surprising, for they resembled Lady Mary. The images of Jesus and James brought a warm smile to John's face.

*I wonder if James has changed. He probably has aged and grayed—*he smiled more widely, pleased by the idea—*but surely nothing else has changed; all else will be the same.*

When some Apostles returned to Jerusalem, John noticed that all the poor eating, the lack of sleep, and the imprisonment and tortures had not physically affected them. But time did take its toll, for some showed signs of aging—gray hairs, wrinkles, and even added thickness around the waist.

His thoughts and images were interrupted by raised voices coming from people outside the house. He rushed to the door and opened it wide. A poor, young blind boy was walking and banging against the walls and passersby. Those disturbed by the stumbling boy yelled and swore at him. They roughly pushed him away, causing him to fall several times. John quickly ran to the boy and helped him to his feet.

"Are you all right, brother? Come, let me help you."

"I was looking for the well to quench my thirst. I was certain I was going the right way."

"Fear not, my brother, you were on the right way. It is the others who are going the wrong way. Come into my house and let me help you."

John led the disheveled boy into the coolness of the house. Quickly, he found a cup and filled it with chilled water and gave it to the thirsty child. The blind boy quickly drank the water, spilling some from the corner of his mouth onto his ragged clothing. John found a foot bowl and filled it with cool water; with a clean cloth thrown over his arm, he bent down and began washing the feet of the blind boy.

"Oh kind sir, I am but a blind beggar, not your guest," the child objected, reaching down to stop John, but John remembered the objections and similar protests made by Simon Peter when Jesus insisted on washing his feet.

"That is not true, my brother, you are my guest," he said as he softly moved the protesting hand away and continued to wash the dust and dirt off the boy's feet. As he continued to wash his feet, a strong sense of familiarity came over him. He was surrounded by something he knew very well. He continued to wash the boy's feet, hoping and wanting the sense to become more recognizable. Soon, the water in the basin began to turn from brown to pink, then to red, and suddenly he saw a sore—pierced flesh—on the foot.

"JOHN." Without looking up he recognized the voice. Out of surprise and pleasure and with the desire to greet the voice properly, he bent and kissed his Master's wet, bloody feet.

"John, go to your mother. James, now, is sitting by Me. Know also that Peter has been arrested."

John felt a sudden emptiness in his heart: the place that James had always filled with his strength and guidance was gone. He closed his eyes and let the loss of his brother, who had this day for a short time returned to his world, run through him and into his soul.

This was the way Stephaton and the others found him: kneeling on the floor with a foot basin before him and a cloth over his arm. They told him of James' arrest, trial, and execution by order of Herod Agrippa. They tried to lift him to his feet, but John insisted on staying on his knees, hovering over the foot bowl and wanting to linger in the love and strength of his divine Visitor.

"Up to the very end, your brother was preaching Jesus. Like the Master, he took a soul with him," Stephaton said, holding back his tears as he related what he had been so blessed to see. "The Pharisee Josias, the former emissary to Hispania and he who delivered James to Herod Agrippa, was so moved by James and his defense of Jesus before the court that Josias begged for James' forgiveness, which was readily given. James and Josias walked together to the executioner.

"When they arrived at the place of the execution, James looked out into the crowd. When he found Hermogenes, Philetus, and me, he nodded, lowered his head, and extended his arms, as the Master did on Golgotha. The executioner raised the sword. The smooth blade caught the sun and flashed a blinding light across the crowd. Many covered their eyes, and others turned away."

Stephaton's voice cracked. His face tightened, and he swallowed hard as he fought back his grief.

"John, what I have to say is for you, and for reasons I cannot explain, I feel that you will understand what I am about to say: on a day such as this, with blue heavens and clear skies, as the sword descended, I and I alone heard the distinct rumble of thunder."

Tears flooded John's eyes. He looked at Stephaton, and a wide smile of understanding came to his lips. Now he accepted their help. He stood upright to embrace them all, and he went slowly to his mother to tell her the news.

Moments later, as he sat consoling his mother, John looked at the open window near where they sat, and he saw an immaculately white dove sitting on the windowsill. It was the most beautiful dove he had ever seen. Its small, black eyes pierced him with an unbroken gaze—it seemed to understand what was happening. The dove remained perched on the sill of the window for a time, then it opened wide its wings and hovered over the sill, flapping its wings slowly, softly.

Suddenly, as if called, the dove flew away; John watched it ascend higher and higher into the sky, until it was no more.

CHAPTER TWO:

MATTHIAS OF CANA

PROLOGUE

The man seemed to have surfaced from nowhere, with a gust of anger and a world of hatred.

The first time Paul met the Apostles, John was not with them so he never saw the man and relied only on rumors. He heard that he was a Roman citizen from the tribe of Benjamin who lived in Jerusalem for many years and studied at the feet of the great Rabbi Gamaliel. After his studies, he returned home to the province of Cilicia and grew in the pharisaic tradition. His education was in the strict observance of the Law. He was, so the reports continued, "extremely exact...extremely orthodox." Many said that he had a high opinion of himself and had a problem with authority. It was whispered that the chief priests and others of the Sanhedrin had difficulty with him. Rumors also indicated that the man and a group of other young Pharisees were ordered by the Sanhedrin to investigate "The Way," which was growing in number. These heretics were sometimes called Nazarenes. After receiving this commission, the man from Cilicia and other Pharisees energetically began their investigations. Within days, many people of "The Way" were seized, arrested, and tried. Many were censured and forbidden to speak of Jesus, others were beaten, and those who persisted were stoned. Many Nazarenes fled to neighboring towns and villages, which offered a degree of safety, and some escaped to other provinces of the Empire.

One week after the first arrests, the deacon Stephen—who was deeply loved by Simon Peter, John, Andrew, and many others—was arrested while preaching outside of Jerusalem. His eagerness for debate and his fearlessness in the pursuit of converts put him in grave danger. With cruel efficiency, the young deacon was tried, convicted, and sentenced to death. Many were shocked by the skill of the investigators and by the swiftness with which innocent Stephen was arrested, tried, convicted, and executed. John had been told that Saul held the cloaks of those who stoned Stephen, and so Saul became the name, the face, the image of the persecutors of the Nazarenes. Days later, the Twelve heard that Saul, the Pharisee, went to the High Priest and "asked of him...letters to Damascus, to the synagogues." Saul had learned through the death of Stephen that many followers of the "blasphemer" Jesus had taken refuge in the Jewish quarters of that city. His proposal was to put an end to the large defection of Jews to the new sect in that Syrian city. His request was quickly granted, and he left without delay for Damascus. Word was quickly dispatched to Damascus: the persecutor was coming!

The Nazarenes braced themselves, but Saul never arrived in Damascus with hatred in his heart.

MATTHIAS OF CANA

Matthias was a man of few luxuries and few enjoyments, but he had not always been this austere. Early in life, he was attracted to the Zealots because of their hatred for Rome. He made inquiries and secretly attended several of their clandestine meetings. The illegality of these meetings and the dangers that they posed added a great deal of excitement. He wanted to believe in their cause, but he could not see how hatred would lead to any genuine improvement. He knew that hatred grew deep and could become boundless. Hatred had a way of changing faces; it was ever seeking new victims to satisfy its hunger. For a short period, he was interested in the group, for they catered to his restlessness. He discovered that his nationalistic feelings were not strong enough to make him a Zealot. In essence, the group failed to address the emptiness in his life and to satisfy his need for peace of mind, which was becoming more important to him. He quickly broke off his association and subsequently drifted around for several uneventful years. Unexpectedly, his Jewish friend Zacchaeus, a publican and commissioner of revenue in Jericho, offered Matthias employment as a *scriptor*. Matthias surprised himself by accepting Zacchaeus' offer, though later he admitted that going to extremes was nothing new for him. He seemed to have done that often in his life—changing from anti-Roman to pro-Roman was merely an indicator of his restlessness and his need for meaning in life.

Matthias enjoyed the prestige and the money that this occupation gave him, and a certain peace settled over him; it was shallow, though, and he soon recognized it as false. After several months of employment, Zacchaeus requested that Matthias go to the Jordan River and observe John the Baptist. This request confirmed Matthias' suspicion that Zacchaeus was as unfulfilled as he was. Obediently and filled with curiosity about John, Matthias traveled to the Jordan. From the moment he saw the Baptist, he was captivated by his simplicity and by his call for repentance. Through his words, John compelled Matthias to recall his past sins and his self-indulgent lifestyle. Matthias realized that his sins, though defensively hidden over the years, would not be forgotten without repentance and reparation. Seeing his sins anew, he became sorrowful for them; under the power of John's preaching, he gradually stripped himself of all exterior things, took on the ways of the Baptist, and began to live a life of mortification. The more harshly he treated his body—intense fasting, rough clothing, sleepless nights spent in deep prayer and cries for forgiveness—the happier he became. Soon he felt free of the anxieties of earthly life; he was comfortable in his new way of living and deeply relieved in the knowledge that his sins were being forgiven.

His reports about John to Zacchaeus became less critical and less frequent, and they soon stopped completely. When John pointed to Jesus, Matthias quickly returned to Zacchaeus to report the coming of a new Prophet. Zacchaeus perceived the difference in Matthias, and believing that it was somehow related to the new Prophet, he lost interest in John the Baptist and became interested in Jesus. He requested that Matthias watch Jesus, but Matthias was a changed man. He no longer needed money, so he resigned and began in earnest to follow Jesus. He had to do this—at the very moment he saw Jesus, Jesus looked at him and smiled, and Matthias felt something lifted from him and experienced a sudden, compulsive need to follow Jesus and to learn of this Man's message. It seemed only natural for him to become a follower of Jesus, for it was the course of continuance from John, and within weeks his life began to be filled with hope and love; nevertheless, the Baptist's influence remained with him, and he continued to be severe with himself and to force himself to neglect the joys of the world. He soon found that being with Jesus was different from being with John. Jesus was light and easy, not as intense as John. He heard from Jesus words of charity and joy, even laughter—there was hope. In time, he saw Jesus do things that he could not explain, and these things intrigued him and bound him even more to this "Lamb of God." Assuredly, it was the mystery of the Man and His power over so many people that made Matthias confident that Jesus was the Leader Who would free the Jews from oppression. Unlike so many of Jesus' followers, who were merely intrigued by the Man's actions, he started to pay close attention to the things that Jesus said. Many of Jesus' messages were hidden—only through reflection and careful study would anyone come to know what Jesus was truly saying. Matthias knew that he had to stay with Jesus, not to be part of a new regime, but to help make it all happen. In his confusion, though, Matthias was certain that his limited intellect would be of little help.

As time passed, he was accepted into the inner circle of Jesus' friends. He held many things in common with them, and above all they shared a love for Jesus. As he traveled with the Twelve, he became friendly, but never too friendly. Those who had been with Jesus from the beginning had a certain air of superiority, and at times they were clannish. They were possessive of Jesus, and in spite of Jesus' reprimanding them several times, they did not change their ways.

✳

Matthias felt a hand on his arm, and he was jolted from his reminiscing.

"Let us stop, dear brother," Nescius said breathlessly. "I could use a bit of water to quench my thirst, and a rest to ease my fatigue."

"Are you all right, Nescius?"

"Yes, I am fine, but I would enjoy a rest."

Matthias understood his traveling companion's discomfort. He often forgot that other people did not share his endurance and self-denial.

He is like me when I lived in Cana—back then, at all cost, I tried to ignore discomfort and enjoy the ease of living, he thought as he reflected on Nescius' youth.

He leaned heavily on his staff and watched as Nescius drew water from the water skin. Quickly, a look of relief came over the young man's face. Matthias felt a tinge of pity for his companion, who failed to appreciate the cleansing qualities that moments of denial give to the soul.

A moment of discomfort is what gives weight and value to comfort and what satisfies the need to make reparation, he thought. He looked away with a small amount of disappointment, yet with an equal amount of understanding for his companion.

A cart led by an ox, which was being patiently encouraged by a friendly Judean, passed the two resting travelers. As the man passed them he stared, and Nescius shouted, "Good day, brother."

The man continued to examine them, slowing his beast to a near stop. His head tilted to one side, and his face wrinkled with perplexity.

Again Nescius said, "I hope you are having a good day, brother."

The man did not answer the greeting, but with a look of clarity on his face, he struck the ox and hurried off toward the city, occasionally taking reassuring glances back at them.

Matthias watched this small incident with disinterest, for his thoughts were set on past times, which he seemed compelled to relive. He again allowed himself to begin to remember.

*

Jesus' death left His followers wondering if they had wasted three years following Him. They felt duped and betrayed. They despaired, for Jesus proved to be as mortal and—considering His criminal, infamous death—more human than they were. They moved about like homeless creatures, living in disarray. In time, they gathered. They were drawn to each other, not out of need for support, but out of habit. They did not know what else to do or where else to go. They had been followers for so long that they were unable to lead their own lives. As they gathered, some questioned the reason for their assembling. They saw no comfort in each other. The bond that held them together was gone. Being together only reminded them of their failure to act as men. They looked at each other in quick glances, for long glances were piercing and filled with silent excuses. They ran from Jesus that night—as cowards. Their association enabled them to focus on the weakness in others. It was easier to see the sins of others than to bring to light their own failings. Assuredly, they knew they would not be willing to die for each other; in knowing the fears and weaknesses of each other, they saw themselves. Even in coward-ice, there was strength, false as it was. They accepted the fact that they had the same fears. They understood the confusions that raced through their minds, and this, pathetically perhaps, gave them a common ground.

Then, Jesus showed Himself to them.

They did not know what this meant. It was uncanny, inexplicable.

How could this be?

What did His being among them, again, mean?

Though there was much joy because Jesus was again with them, none sought an explanation from Jesus. They gladly accepted His presence and believed that He had returned just for them. They saw Him. They talked to Him, walked and ate with Him. Though they were happy to hear His voice and capture His scent, and to be led again, they still remained entangled in confusion. Even after seeing Jesus numerous times, they could not comprehend the event of life, death, and life again. It was a contradiction. It was illogical.

The amazing news that the dead Jesus was alive and with the Eleven spread quickly to other followers, and this return to life confounded many. As expected, the news was not confined to their group.

Members of the Sanhedrin knew that they had to stop such rumors before people began to believe that the Nazarene was Who He said He was—the Messiah. In spite of the need to suppress the rumors of a resurrected Jesus, some members of the Sadducees were secretly excited. If this rumor was true, even though it pertained to the criminal Jesus, it would prove the Pharisees' belief in life after death. The Sadducees, on the other hand, needed this rumor crushed, for they understood what Jesus meant when He said, "This Temple will be raised up in three days." They searched Jerusalem for the Eleven, but as they were unable to find them, they sought others seen with the Eleven, and then they sought Jesus' relatives and the relatives of the Eleven; when all these had vanished, the authorities believed that the rumors were false and that the threat was gone.

In reality, the Eleven had left Jerusalem and returned to Galilee and its many remote places.

After Jesus disappeared before their eyes on Mount Olivet, they obediently made the cautious journey to Jerusalem. Witnessing the resurrected Jesus followed by His ascension had left them confused. They entered the city, singularly or in pairs, in the early darkness of the night. They returned to the Upper Room of the house of Mark's parents. It was familiar to them. The warmth and love of the room were still present to them. It was the room where they had the Passover meal with Jesus—their last supper together. Here they found staying together gave them some comfort. Still, they worried about the authorities, they lived in fear—for fear, now, was their way of life.

On the street side of the Upper Room, a steep wooden stairway led to a small landing and to the heavy wooden door. The Room was large, and the interior had plain white walls. Four thin, light-blue pillars supported the wooden beams of the ceiling. The pillars were once decorated with feathers and scrolls, but time had erased these images. There were three windows: one at the back of the room and one on each side. Each window was covered by heavy wooden shutters that kept out the storms and the cold of winter. During the warmer months, they were covered with heavy brown curtains that blocked out the burning sun. The windows on the east and west sides of the room overlooked the rooftops of nearby houses. The window on the back wall of the room overlooked a large courtyard that was cluttered with carts, various empty containers, a few animal stalls, and some other enclosures. Porticos ran along the four sides of the courtyard, and in the center of the courtyard was a well. The Room was normally rented out for large gatherings, but during the ministry of Jesus it had become the gathering place for Him and His followers.

During their first night in the Upper Room, after praying, they sat and remembered. Soon they recognized that Jesus prepared them for His death and for His conquest over death. They wondered how He knew of His death and resurrection. Such things belonged to *Elohim*, the Mighty One. Could He be *Bar Elohim*—the Son of God? Here is where they stopped, for to go further was beyond their thinking, dangerous, and perhaps sacrilegious. Again, their lack of courage caused them to remain stagnant.

Matthias arrived within hours of the last of the Eleven, and he immediately was at their disposal. He and others not so recognizable got provisions from friends who shopped for the Apostles during the daylight. They were also the messengers who delivered and gathered news. When he was not doing things for the Eleven, he joined them in prayer. For the next seven days, they prayed and remained as lost, abandoned sheep. They were like flags in a windless sky with nothing to unfurl their fullness. Strangely, even in their beloved Jerusalem, they felt like strangers. They could not understand this, for Jerusalem was their spiritual home. They could only assume that being hunted was the reason for this uneasiness. Matthias, also, felt this isolation, but he believed it was attributable to being in the city of their disowning—the place where they had remained silent during Jesus' greatest need. Instead of feelings of comfort, Matthias sensed a strong feeling of anticipation in the air. Things were left undone by Jesus, and what was undone would soon be completed. He felt this, though how it was to happen or when it was to happen, he did not know.

On the eighth day of their hiding, Mark arrived at the Upper Room with Joseph of Arimathea and Nicodemus, two Pharisees who had been secret friends of Jesus. They had provided Jesus with a proper burial, which was greatly appreciated by His followers and by the Master's mother. When they arrived in the Room, they immediately went to Simon Peter, and a whispered conversation took place between the three men. Matthias stood far from them. Their facial expressions betrayed the seriousness of their conversation. As the conversation continued, the grief on Simon Peter's face stunned Matthias; he wondered what news could affect Simon Peter in this way. After a few silent moments, Simon Peter embraced the two Pharisees and invited them to sit with the group.

A few holy women rushed to offer cool water and food to the two men. Matthias watched Simon Peter go to a chair and laboriously lower himself into it. He remained silent and in deep thought. After a few moments, he stood up and walked to the long table at the front of the room. He sat on the long wooden bench behind the long table and looked at everyone in the room.

Finally he spoke.

"My Brothers, I have been bothered for a long time about the where-abouts of Judas, who was one of us."

"Today, our good friends Joseph and Nicodemus have confirmed that Judas is dead," he said while acknowledging the two Pharisees with an extended hand. He continued telling everyone how Judas died, and of the purchase of the field on which he died in the Valley of Hinmom. This field had been called, by the inhabitants of Jerusalem, *hagel dema,* the field of blood.

Grumbling voices filled the Room. The very mention of Judas was painful. Many were deeply disturbed by Simon Peter's concern for the traitor.

Simon Peter drew in a deep breath and exhaled in a sigh. He placed his large, callused hands on the top of the table and slowly pushed himself up from his seat. His tall, muscular figure hovered over everyone in the Room.

"Men, brethren, the Scripture needs be fulfilled, which the Holy Spirit spoke before by the mouth of David concerning Judas, who was the leader of them that apprehended Jesus, who was numbered with us, and had obtained part of this ministry."

Matthias gazed at Simon Peter, wondering if the others detected the perplexity on his face. The Big Fisherman of Galilee was totally at a loss—he seemed to be reaching for conviction.

Peter looked at the faces of the remaining Ten, then at the faces of the many other disciples in the Room. He wet his lips and took a deep breath that was heard by all. With new found assurance he continued, "For it is written in the Book of Psalms: 'Let their habitation become desolate, and let there be none to dwell therein. And his bishopric let another take.' Wherefore of these men who have companied with us all the time that the Lord Jesus came in and went out among us. Beginning from the Baptism of John until the day wherein He was taken up from us, one of these must be made a witness with us of His resurrection."

The Room was quickly filled with conversation, and many began looking at each other as they pondered the time period set by Peter. Matthias watched as many faces in the Room registered disappointment—or relief—when people discovered they did not fit the time frame. Slowly, he allowed himself to remember. He was there for the taking up. He was there for the resurrection—and for His death. He was there for the Sermon on the Mount and the teaching of the Lord's Prayer. He was there for the feeding of the multitudes and for Jesus' countless stories and parables. He saw the Master come and go. His mind froze, and he felt his heart beat quickly; his mouth grew dry. He had been with John the Baptizer. He had begun there.

But I was spying on John, not following Him. Zacchaeus hired me to observe the Baptist—that is why I was there. I never became a true follower of the Baptizer, though I admired his ways.

His mind fell to ease. He closed his eyes and uttered a prayer of thanksgiving to *Elohim* for being spared. Completing his prayer, he opened his eyes and was startled by the face of Bartholomew, which was scarcely an inch from his. Bartholomew looked into Matthias' eyes. Matthias returned the gaze. Over Bartholomew's shoulder was Simon the Zealot.

The three had known each other from Cana, and their families were friendly. There were even arranged marriages between the families. Yet they were not true friends.

"You fit the time," Bartholomew declared, with a small smile on his lips.

Matthias returned the smile out of politeness.

"I do not," Matthias replied. The Zealot walked around Bartholomew and stood to the side of Matthias.

"You do. I remember you being with us back to John bar Zachary," Simon said with conviction.

"No," Matthias whispered cautiously, "I was with John to observe him. I had no sincerity. I was there to spy for the publican Zacchaeus. I do not completely comply with Peter's words."

"Matthias." Simon's voice was strong. "Do you not see?"

"See what?"

"You never left," the Zealot replied. "You never returned to your former life. You were captured."

"Enough," Bartholomew declared, and with a flair he turned and briskly walked to Peter.

Matthias felt his legs weaken as Peter looked at him, smiled, and nodded his head.

I stayed! I stayed because I had been captured by the words of John, by the severity of his life, the mortification of his body—he even baptized me in the Jordan. He took a deep breath and slowly let it escape his lips as he again closed his eyes and prayed. *Elohim, judge these moments and do what You will, but truly You know, as I do, that I am unworthy.*

Soberly, the remaining Apostles walked to the long table and sat facing everybody in the room.

Matthias observed them and, for an instant, found warmth with them. He had talked with them about the Master, and they had discussed many things together. They had shared concerns and doubts.

They often tell me I am too severe. They say I punish myself too much. I do not belong with them. I belonged with the Baptizer—I followed Jesus only because John pointed to Him. When John was beheaded, I had no one else to turn to but Jesus.

All this reflection assured Matthias that he was not the likely choice, so he moved to the back wall, separating himself from everyone and the proceedings. He never liked being singled out, and this sudden thrust into the center of things disturbed him. He found himself pressing hard against the wall. From the shuttered window, he felt a light, fresh breeze slip through a crack between the wall and the shutter.

Surprisingly, he welcomed this small luxury.

Peter rose from his chair.

"We have two names that fill the allotted time. Joseph bar Sabas, called Justus by many, and Matthias of Cana."

Voices of approval rose in the Room.

"Justus. Matthias." Peter's voice resounded, and he indicated that they should come forward and stand by the table.

Matthias walked with ease. He was now confident that he would not be chosen, for he knew that Justus was the brother-in-law of the sons of Zebedee—being a relative of the Master, surely Jesus would want Justus. He, on the other hand, had no family ties or any strong friendships among the Eleven. He was so relieved that he almost smiled.

"I beg you all," Peter pleaded, "let us pray for guidance in what we are about to do."

All the men quickly bowed their heads; all fell silent. The women watched. Some closed their eyes, and others covered their eyes with their hands and joined in the silent prayer. The prayer continued for a long time until the Room was suffocating in silence.

Finally, Peter's heavy voice drew everyone back to the task before them. "Master, you know the hearts of all men, show us which of these two you have chosen, to take the place of this ministry and apostleship from which Judas, by betrayal, has fallen, so that this person may go to his own place."

As Matthias opened his eyes and uncovered his head, he caught a glimpse of Lady Mary, the Master's mother. She was smiling warmly. He bowed in respect, yet he was confused by her sudden acknowledgment of him. Despite all their time together, they had spoken but rarely.

They gave Justus and Matthias lots. Each was to mark the lot with a symbol and show the marked lot to someone for verification. Matthias marked his lot with a cross and showed it to the person nearest him, who happened to be Jude Thaddeus, then he dropped the lot in a cup that was on the table in front of Peter.

Justus marked his lot, showed it to young Mark, and placed his lot in the same cup.

Peter covered the cup with his big hand and began to shake it. The rattle and clash of the lots in the cup echoed in Matthias' ears, and his thoughts returned to that day on Golgotha when he watched the gambling off of Jesus' garment. A picture of the Syrian mercenary Abenadar rattling the lots in the cup came to him, and a chill ran through his blood. Peter lifted the cup high above the heads of everyone in the room. He rotated the cup faster and faster. The sound of the lots racing inside the cup continued to press against Matthias' ears. This sound would remain with him, echoing all through the rest of his life. Unexpectedly, both lots flew from the cup into the empty air, and together they fell on the wooden table. One traveled the full length of the table and fell onto the floor. The other rolled over and over until it stopped in front of Matthias. He looked down, and there on the lot was his mark—his cross.

Lady Mary came to him and said softly, "You were always the one."

He wondered how she came to know this and quickly realized the source of wisdom she was.

That day was the day before *Hag ha-Shavuot*, the Feast of Weeks, and provisions had to be gotten. Several men were preparing to go purchase food and drink. When Matthias was preparing to leave to buy provisions, he was stopped by Peter, and soon Matthias felt separated, different.

That night, the Twelve and the other followers gathered in their sanctuary to follow the rules of the feast. *Shavuot* was to be celebrated on the fiftieth day after the Passover Sabbath in the month of *Sivan*. For centuries, Israel used this feast as a thanksgiving festival for the summer harvest. The Diaspora caused the feast, also known as Pentecost, to become known as the Feast of the Giving of the Law. Past rabbis, through careful calculation, concluded that Moses received the Laws of *Elohim* on the Pentecost, and so the feast was celebrated as the Giving of the Law and, therefore, as the birthday of Judaism. The followers celebrated this feast according to the customs set down by the Law. After they secured the doors and windows, they sat and listened to the prescribed reading of *Megillat Ruth,* the Scroll of Ruth. They listened to this story of love, respect, and allegiance—all of which were greater than life and stronger than death. They heard the story of Bethlehem and of the Jewish husband and Gentile wife who became the ancestors of King David. They sang and prayed, they ate and drank, as all good Jews did that night.

Matthias ate little and drank less. His thoughts turned to Pentecost nights with the Master, and these thoughts made him very somber. More sobering were his uncontrollable thoughts of Judas. He formed a mental picture of Judas walking with the Others. The man from Judea had an air of cockiness, a strut of arrogance that intrigued Matthias. He always felt that Judas knew something that the Others did not know. He recollected the quick movements of Judas' eyes when the crowds surrounded Jesus, and the air of pride Judas displayed when he walked close to Jesus. He remembered the times Judas pulled the Master aside to speak to him in private. He remembered some of the Others did not trust Judas and disliked his pomposity, but Matthias liked him; he pitied Judas because he was an outsider, like him.

Apparently, Judas had a better idea for the Master. Like Peter and many of the Others, he did not grasp what Jesus was saying, yet unlike them, Judas decided to force his own ideas on Jesus' mission—he stopped being a servant and became a master.

During the night, while the Others grew more festive, Matthias grew anxious. He, again, felt something pending, something major hanging over them, but he was unsure of what it was. All night, he struggled in vain to discover what was making him uneasy. He grew angry with himself and more obsessed with the unknown. The night passed on, and soon they all grew tired and eased into a restful sleep.

"Matthias? Matthias?"

His thoughts ended abruptly, and he jolted back to the present with the sound of Nescius' voice.

"Yes, is something wrong?"

"No, except you have not spoken to me all this distance, and you seem so far away."

"Oh, my friend, I am reminiscent of bygone days."

"If you are remembering Jesus, please tell me what you are remembering. Were you thinking of one of His stories? Or were you thinking about the day He came to life again?"

"No, my friend, I was thinking of times after His rising. The time after Jesus left forever, the great morning of Pentecost."

"Please tell me of that time," Nescius requested with the simplicity and eagerness of a child.

Matthias looked at him with fond amusement. He loved the childish enthusiasm of this youngster; whenever these childlike things surfaced, he felt grateful that Peter and John had sent him Nescius. He looked around for a rock to rest against, and finding one, he painfully walked to it and sat down. He threw his staff on the ground and, with some difficulty, folded his legs. Becoming somewhat comfortable, he wet his lips and looked off into the distance, willing that day to return to him.

Nescius sat on a small patch of cool grass near the rock and waited.

Slowly and with careful words, Matthias began to tell his story of the first Pentecost.

"Early that day, on the first day of the week, I was jarred from my sleep by the sounds of marching soldiers in the street below the Upper Room. I immediately grew fearful. I was sure that we had been discovered, possibly betrayed, and this thought left me completely empty. Others stirred, and I saw looks of fear and panic on their faces. Simon Zealot jumped to his feet, as did young Jude Thaddeus, Thomas, and Peter, but the others were frozen in their places. The Zealot rushed to the door, checked the heavy latch to make certain it was secure, and placed his ear against the thick wood to detect if any intruders were climbing the steps from the street below the Room. Jude Thaddeus and Thomas climbed over others in the room to get to the closed wooden shutters on the windows. They tried looking out through the small cracks between the shutters. I did likewise at the window near me, but I could see nothing. As I turned from the window, I became aware of the warm, still air in the Room. I was bewildered at how the stifled air had not been apparent to me before that moment. Warm weather never bothered me, but for a strange moment, I had a sudden desire to throw open the wooden shutters and let the morning air into the Room. The marching sounds faded, and a silent relief came over the Room, but the air was heavy with silence and thick with a choking heat. We did not make a sound for fear that the soldiers would return.

"Suddenly there came a thunderous sound that rumbled through the Room, vibrating off the thick white walls. Everyone and everything shook and shivered. The sound became a loud groan that came from the very depth of a Great Being. It vibrated through every fiber, every sense in our being. Just as suddenly, a mighty driving wind came from above us, fell on us, and whipped around the Room. I felt my tunic press against my body. My beard pushed to the side of my face and tugged at my flesh. Sunlight burst into the room, and with it came the sound of a long exhale of breath, a great sigh. I saw nothing but this flash of brightness; I covered my eyes with my arm, and then all was still. Silent. Calm. It was a calm that was never experienced before; a calm that, I was certain, never existed before in all time. It calmed and even soothed my past years. All of the past that tormented me was stilled in calmness. Slowly, I recovered. I looked at the others in the room and, in astonishment, saw that above each head, burning, were parted tongues of fire. They flickered brightly, illuminating each face; their garments looked washed and new. I instantaneously felt a surge of untried ability clear my body. This was followed quickly by an outburst of understanding that raced through my mind—many things that had occurred in the preceding weeks, in past months, and in long ago years became clear to me. The life, death, and resurrection of Jesus were all unmasked, and I understood what Jesus said and did. Words and parables spoken by the Master came back to me along with new and penetrating insight. I had an overpowering surge of eagerness to speak, to sing, and to teach. I felt a flutter of excitement push through my being. It begged—no, it demanded—to explode, to live!

"I saw every face in the room change; I could see the clouds of doubt, which I had witnessed daily, dispersing; the shadow of despair, which darkened our thoughts, being lifted. Each person was upright, confident, and filled with clarity. Their eyes burned with determination. They looked fearless, like fierce warriors armed with invisible—yet invincible—armor.

"'Praise be to Jesus, Son of David, Messiah,' Peter shouted in a proclamation that sought freedom from deep within his being.

"'One in being with the Father from all time,' I heard young John cry out, his voice a declaration that was as revealing as the blinding light.

"From behind me, I heard Matthew shout with great conviction, 'He has fulfilled the prophecies of old.'

"'He has sent His Spirit upon us, and we are His new voices,' said James the Little with fire in his voice, his face and hands raised in fervent prayer.

"We began to shout and cry aloud praises and honor to *Adonai*. The Cenacle was filled with energy and excitement; it was vibrating with the unbridled enthusiasm of a thousand voices, a thousand new songs. Our voices became louder and louder, resounding with great conviction. Some were crying with deep joy; others swayed and weaved from side to side, back and forth, under the influence of a fervor that seemed to recall the first day of creation.

"Simon Zealot, Jude Thaddeus, and Philip threw open the shutters, and the morning sun and air flooded the Room. Peter walked quickly to the door of the Cenacle and flung it wide open. The sun burst from the doorway and struck his face, intensifying its glow. With courage and confidence, he walked out onto the balcony, calling out to the people, the city, and the world. The rest of us, with equal courage and confidence, followed him; out we raced into the free air and the bright morning. Peter stood at the top of the steps with Andrew, James the Big, and John behind him, and the rest of us spilled down the steps. Our cries of praise and glory stopped many on the street, and quickly a large crowd formed.

"I was standing near the bottom of the steps. I noticed the clothing and faces of those listening to Peter. I could tell that many of them were not from Jerusalem or Judea, yet they were listening intently.

"A tall, richly dressed Cappadocian Aryan Jew standing near me said in his native tongue, 'They must all be drunk from the feast.'

"I immediately responded, 'We are not, my friend. We are filled with the Spirit of *Adonai*.'

"'And where did you get this Spirit, my brother Cappadocian?'

"'From Jesus of Nazareth, who was crucified, died, and rose again.'

"'And just how did a Cappadocian come to know this Jesus?'

"'I have followed Him for years.'

"'Are you all Cappadocian?' the man asked as he looked up the stairs to the Others.

"Stunned, I realized that this rich man and I were speaking to each other: I in Aramaic and he in Cappadocian—undoubtedly, he understood me in his own tongue and I understood him in my tongue. I looked quickly at the Others and heard them speaking to Pamphylians, Greeks, Romans, Asians, and Cretans, and I saw expressions of understanding on the faces of these Jews from distant lands.

"I remember thinking, *What great miracle is now taking place? Has the Tower of Babel finally been completed? Have we conquered it with Jesus' help? What form of blessing has fallen upon us?*

"'We are not Cappadocians,' I said with glee, 'we are Galileans, and you are a part of the working of *Elohim* and the promise of the Messiah, Who is called Jesus.'

"The man stepped back. Disbelief streaked across his face and the faces of those with him.

"'They think we are drunk,' I said to Philip with a smile. Philip smiled back and turned to Jude Thaddeus, who then repeated what Philip told him to Thomas, who passed the word up the steps until it was repeated to

Peter. But Peter was beyond all hearing. His face was aglow, and his eyes were fierce—intent on things outside of himself.

"I watched Peter. His loud, booming voice reminded me of the thunderous sound that had raced through the Room only minutes ago. He declared, 'Men of Judea, and all you that dwell in Jerusalem, be this known to you, and with your ears receive my words....'

"I watched the crowd gather. I listened to Peter. I was surprised, for his words were eloquent. He was inspired. Some of the Others were speaking to smaller groups of people near them. I watched in amazement, for truly I knew that a very great miracle was taking place, and all with the help of the Master. I felt a strong urge to laugh aloud. The joy inside me was pushing up into my throat, swelling, choking me, longing to be set free. I felt an overwhelming power come to me, and I willingly surrendered to its prodding and laughed heartily. With joyful tears still in my eyes, I looked at the small group of Cappadocians near me and spoke: 'You have come here to celebrate the giving of the Law, but today a New Law is being given to you from the Hand and Spirit of *Adonai*. This New Law begins with the death and resurrection of Jesus, Who is your Messiah. Today is a day of new birth and of new beginnings, a day of Jesus the Anointed One....'"

Matthias paused and let the rapid beat of his heart slowly ebb. In a low and tender tone, he continued, "A new life was born to me that day. Old yesterdays became new tomorrows. I wondered where this new life had been before the coming of the wind and fire. It did not take me long to understand that it had been a seed within me, resting in fertile soil, and that Jesus and His Spirit watered it with reason, wisdom, and understanding. I understood that Jesus lived through me. I was now His shadow. I cannot explain the joy that raced through me when I came to this conclusion, nor can I express the love I had for Jesus. It was stronger than my need to breathe, and my chest was longing, aching, to be filled. My love was stronger than any army, any storm, any power imaginable.

"We preached all day, and at the ninth hour, Peter and John left us and went to the Temple. We continued to preach and received many. While Peter and John were at the Temple, they were apprehended. We rejoiced for them when we heard this news.

"Can you fathom how strange this was? Those who had been hiding in dark doorways and behind trees and rocks were now laughing at being discovered. How strange that the cowards and deserters were now willing to be arrested and imprisoned—willing to suffer and die for the Man they left to die, alone.

"After Peter and John were released and had rejoined us, we gathered and remained in prayer, thanking the Almighty for our newfound boldness and for the honor of suffering for Him. We sat for hours speaking of the miracle of the many languages, and we eventually spoke of Jesus. His words returned to us like a deluge. We scrutinized every parable, action, and teaching that we could remember. Some of us began writing down the words and actions being recalled. Soon, we comprehended many profound things about Jesus, and from that day on, we lived for Him."

Matthias stopped talking and looked off in the distance. His remembrances had filled him with deep emotions.

Nescius knew not to bother Matthias when he had this faraway look, for when Matthias became this intense, he heard and saw nothing.

After a few silent moments, Matthias whispered, "It was the first time that I knew I was a part of the Master's plan."

Nescius sat looking at Matthias with the wide eyes of a child. He was hungry for more, and when more did not come, he became sad and let out a small sigh of disappointment.

"I envy you and the Others," Nescius said. "When Jesus came to me, it was nothing like this. I would have loved to experience the power of His Spirit."

Matthias felt his companion's frustration, for he knew that the young man came to the Lord through humbler means.

"Elijah found the Almighty in a soft breeze. Not many of us experience light, wind, and fire. *Adonai* comes to us as He wills. He is the Lord of silence and excitement. He comes to ant and elephant, from thunder and breeze, through the Mediterranean Sea and the Black Sea. The Almighty speaks to us in ways that are not ours; our duty is to hear Him."

"But I do not possess the knowledge or diverse tongues that you do. I have understanding of the Torah to show how Jesus fulfilled the prophecies of old, but I do not know how to present this. You and the Others always seem to have the right words. I do not. I have followed your instructions, and I pray always that someday I will be a true disciple of Jesus—that my words will change the hearts and minds of unbelievers."

"Use your frustration as a prayer," Matthias said gently, "and believe me: soon the Lord will come to you, but do not expect a Pentecost. Expect less, and you will receive more. I felt like one of the Twelve on Pentecost, but I did not feel like one of His called ones until He wanted me to feel that way. When I journeyed to Cappadocia and Armenia, then did I truly feel that the Master had chosen me. Believe me, brother, I understand how you do not feel a part of the whole; I understand how inadequate you feel. I know your frustration. Just be certain that you are where the Master wants you to be. It is the Almighty's desire and will that you be this way. The important thing for you to do is to maintain a strong relationship with the Master. Forget your human feelings and shortcomings, and just be as you are—stay with the Master, for He needs you now, as you are. He will make known to you what you are to become. As time passes, you will be called to your own duty. I was chosen to replace Judas when the Master wanted me. It was not Peter or Bartholomew's choice. I came to Jesus, and He found the right time for me. So will it be for you. When the time is right, you will know."

Matthias looked at Nescius, knowing that his friend still had much to learn and that he, the elder, still had much to teach.

"Remember, brother, you came to me when I needed you, and so will the Master come to you when He needs you. But for the moment, you must continue to show Him that you need Him."

Matthias rose carefully from his resting place and bent down to pick up his staff, and grasping it quickly, he stood upright.

"Thank you, Matthias," Nescius said.

"No, thank *Adonai*, my companion, for He has given me an old man's wisdom," Matthias said as he painfully walked away.

Nescius smiled as he jumped to his feet. Hurriedly, he gathered up their few belongings. He knew that to delay would mean lots of catching up, for Matthias, in spite of his limp, had a quick pace. One of the first things he learned about Matthias was how difficult it was to keep abreast of him. When he first came to accompany Matthias, he believed that this fast pace was the Apostle's subtle way of ignoring him, for he believed that Matthias did not like him. Later, though, he came to understand that the Apostle was eager to be everywhere for Jesus.

✳

The two men continued their journey along the road.

Matthias was perplexed as to why they were making such slow progress to Jerusalem, to which he had been summoned for a discussion about the Gentiles. It seemed that this man Paul was pushing for admitting Gentiles as Followers without circumcision. A Gentile being included into the Following was perfectly acceptable to Matthias, for he had preached and baptized Gentiles for some time, and the debate about the necessity of circumcision was of interest to him. He thought that becoming a follower of Jesus should require nothing more than a declaration of belief—and this seemed to be more God's doing than man's. He was certain that what he was doing was acceptable; after all, the important thing was the Gentiles' acknowledgment of Jesus as Lord, Master, and Savior.

I guess we are not urgently needed in Jerusalem, Master, for otherwise You would be moving us far more rapidly. I suppose we must remain plain, simple travelers on this journey, rather than messengers of Your Way.

Matthias, like so many others, found the Roman roads fast and easy to travel, for they were well constructed and well tended. They were Rome's greatest achievement; they connected most of the major cities in the Empire and, more importantly, connected them all to Rome. Most of the roads were straight, but some followed around mountainsides or along riverbanks. The volcanic ash and lime concrete used in the construction of the roads held the stones in place. Using stones and rocks from the local countryside made each road commonplace. The cambered shape of the roads allowed rain and waste to run into the drains that ran parallel to the roads. The wheels of the Roman chariots, supply wagons, and merchant carts had smoothed many of the stones, and in some cases they had etched shallow crevices into them. Many of the roads were constructed and funded by Emperor Augustus, and these roads were called *viae publicae*, public roads. Other roads, known as *viae militares*, military roads, were built at the expense of the military arm of Rome. Rome had learned that it was best to move soldiers on good roads. On these roads, the military had right of way. It was common to see dead animals or people who had failed to make way for Rome's military chariots and cavalry.

As Matthias and Nescius walked along the road, in what many would regard as a rare moment, Matthias began to chuckle to himself. It always amused him how often he had been a part of the many small miracles that Jesus willed to happen. Some people said they were coincidences, but he, and others, knew differently. One of the small miracles was how far the Twelve were able to travel in short periods of time. Upon hearing of this miracle, many people excused it with the statement that their "quick travel was due to the good Roman roads." Though this was partly true, Matthias and the Others did not regard it as completely true. They knew differently, for they saw the hand of Jesus working a small but important miracle. The first time he and the Others experienced this amazing occurrence was when Jesus sent seventy of them out into the countryside. They returned amazed at how they had traveled so far so quickly. At sunset, on the night of their return, when Jesus went off to pray, they gathered at an open wood fire and began to compare journeys and experiences, and soon they all became aware of what had truly taken place. Matthias remembered John, James bar Zebedee, Thomas, and Jude Thaddeus voicing their awareness of the rapidity of their travel. Bewildered by this prodigy, they remarked that it was a marvel and concluded that it was a one-time phenomenon. Years later, when he and

James the Big left Jerusalem and traveled through Judea preaching Jesus in the towns and villages, they came to the town of Arimathea in northern Judea and stayed with Joseph the Pharisee. Out of gratitude and appreciation for all that Joseph had done for the Master and the Twelve, they stayed for several days, preaching and baptizing many from the town and from Joseph's family. After their stay, they decided to move farther north, through Samaria to Galilee. In half a day's travel, they passed through Samaria and arrived in the Galilean border town of Mageddo. When the two Apostles considered the long distance and short time of their travel, they knew that the miracle had reoccurred; thereafter, it happened so frequently that they accepted it as the norm. This was one of the many ways that the Master was present in their lives and in their ministries.

After all, Jesus did tell us that He would be with us at all times even to the end of the world. He makes the roads and the miles go quickly, and He makes time move slowly. If there is no urgency to our travel, the miles and the roads crawl by as slowly as time does. Ah, yes, the Master is with us. I know He is with me when I am cold, tired, beaten, or in prison. I believe He is with me most when I am suffering for Him. He has to be with us, for we are His Living Body. Through us His Spirit breathes, works, and lives. Yes, definitely, the Master is with us, for we could not have endured any of the bad times without His help.

Matthias lifted his head and looked at the long, empty road ahead of him; he thought of James, and an image of his long-ago companion came to his mind. Happily, he remembered the ruddy complexion and the look of resignation on James' face when he recognized the reoccurrence of the miracle of their travels. Matthias recalled the huge grin on James' lips, and he could hear James saying, "Ah, Brother, it seems the Master has hurried us here to do more for Him."

Suddenly Matthias felt James' presence around him. He felt his big, rough hand on his shoulder, and he sensed the peace of his friend's spirit. It was not an unusual moment, for he was often aware of James. He had felt James' presence at every meaningful juncture in his mission. Most especially, he remembered James coming to stand by his side on the day he was chosen to replace Judas. For reasons he never could explain, he was the first of the Eleven to come to him and embrace him. Perhaps James understood more than the Others what it meant to be called—and what it meant to replace Judas. Matthias liked to believe that it was James' way of understanding the pain and suffering that were inescapable aspects of an Apostle's mission. Later, he began to think that James foresaw the difficulties that Matthias would face in fitting into the family of the Twelve. After drawing lots to determine the places of their missions and then deciding to leave two by two, it was James who approached Matthias and asked to accompany him. This invitation shocked not only Matthias but the entire group. It was expected that James would travel with his brother John or with one of his close friends. Though he found James' actions puzzling, Matthias weakly accepted him as his partner. A great bond of respect developed between the two men. They traveled together; after many months in Judea and after making many enemies among the Jews, who called them "heretics," the two Apostles continued into the province of Syria. After being there for a short time, they received word that Stephen the Deacon had been stoned, and soon thereafter came the warning that Saul of Tarsus was on his way to Damascus, so immediately they made plans to move on. Without warning, James announced that he was not going north into Cappadocia but instead to Hispania. This declaration did not surprise Matthias, for he knew that his friend's destiny through the drawing was "to the west."

Their final farewell was etched in Matthias' memory, for he had never seen a person's face glow with such excitement. Matthias knew that James' departure was not only what the Master wanted—it was also what James wanted. So James departed for Hispania, and Matthias continued north into Cappadocia, sometimes called Aethopia by the Romans.

❋

The Roman province of Cappadocia surprised Matthias with its breathtaking landscape. At first glance the land was stark and at times grotesque, yet strangely beautiful. This contradiction made the land interesting. Throughout the countryside, there were volcanic rock formations of tall cones and pillars, each having its own peculiar shape that undoubtedly held an intriguing tale. These formations fascinated Matthias the most, but nothing appealed to him more than the starkness of the land. The mountains were somber and stoic. They seemed to push up to the skies, unaware of their rough might. They erupted from the bowels of the earth like unwanted bits of wasted matter. Their jagged cliffs were like defiant sentries that confronted any invaders who would dare to tamper with the land that they seemed to be defending. The valleys and plains that pushed across the land in scant patches possessed a serene simplicity. They knew nothing of the music that other valleys gave when they were viewed, for they seemed to be unhappy and incidental in their flow. Matthias saw nothing explosive or poetic about the Cappadocian landscape.

The people were very hardy and possessed a strong natural instinct for survival. In their many mountain ranges, in the sides of plateaus, they had built underground cities as retreats because the caves remained cool in the warm months. The caves were also used as protection against invaders, and they were rarely detected by any enemies. Many were living quarters, with places for livestock and food storage. It was surprising to find that Jesus was known by some of those who had been present at the great Pentecost. When Matthias was recognized as one of the Twelve, he was immediately given special treatment and provided with the comforts appropriate for a man of great importance. This made Matthias feel awkward, so after a few weeks of all this attention, he withdrew from the synagogue and silently slipped away into the countryside, much to the relief of the Judaic scholars who could not compete with his brilliant arguments. Amidst the beautiful starkness of the Cappadocian landscape, he preached. Those in the cities who wanted to see the lowly disciple sought him out. Many came and were received in the name of Jesus. Among these successes were many Gentiles, who soon became as numerous as the Jews. He found himself spending more time with the Gentiles and less time with the Jews. With these Gentiles there was a certain freedom, for he did not need to watch what he was saying so carefully or quote the Talmud with such accuracy. He merely spoke of Jesus. Soon, he was preaching with a knowledge that surprised him, and word of the miracles he performed in the name of Jesus spread as quickly as his conversions. But his mission was not all ease and success. He met the blistering attacks of the fire worshippers, who had built a temple on the side of the volcano Argeus—"the abode of the gods"—that continually spewed volcanic fire and smoke into the air. At first, he faced only the resistance of the lowly local priest, but eventually he would face Hoyuk, the much-feared high priest of the fire god, who for months had patiently waited to confront the intruder Matthias.

Matthias made Hoyuk choose the day for their meeting, and the challenge eventually came on a cool, sunny day. With no fears or doubts, Matthias instantaneously took the offensive. Upon seeing the priest in the crowd, Matthias challenged Hoyuk to show his god's strength. Hoyuk and the other priest of the fire god began to chant and dance as Matthias stood, watching in silence.

Finally, Hoyuk's loud, echoing voice called on the volcano to show its divinity. The volcano began to erupt, with fire and lava spewing from its crater. The earth shook and cracked. Rocks and boulders tumbled and rolled all around those who had gathered to see this battle between the two deities. The day suddenly gave way to night. All dark and evil things were felt flying and filling the air.

Terrified people ran. Many stumbled and fell to the quaking earth.

Matthias stood firm, unmoved by the quivering ground beneath him. His head was bowed in silent prayer. After a few moments, Matthias slowly raised his head, then he lifted his right hand high above his head. With a mighty voice that thundered and shook the insides of those nearby, he called out, "Jesus, calmer of seas and storms, powerful over all things in creation, show forth Your might and divinity."

Quickly, the earth stilled. The heavens opened, heavy rains poured down, and the volcano smoldered and died.

When all was calm and people had regained their senses, they found that Hoyuk and the other priest had fled. That day many were baptized in the same water that had settled the volcano. For the several years that he remained with the Cappadocians, his life was in grave danger from Hoyuk and other fervent followers of the fire god, but the many underground cities provided Matthias with a multitude of safe hiding places.

One day, while preaching to an assembly of Nazarenes in one of the cave churches cleverly built by the Cappadocians, two Armenian Gentiles named Tashes and Dikran approached him and asked him to return with them to teach the salvation of Jesus to their countrymen. Armenia was his mission, but Matthias knew that he was not finished in Cappadocia; *Adonai* would make known the right time for him to leave. So he stayed in Cappadocia, but with Armenia nibbling away at his heels and his mind.

The following year, the two Armenians returned and again begged Matthias to go to their country. He took this as a sign that Jesus wanted him to go, and he left for Armenia with the two men. As he crossed the border into Armenia, he immediately found himself captivated by the beautiful topography of the country. Armenia held great beauty in its high, harsh, rugged mountains. The breathtaking magnificence of its lakes and immense plateaus left Matthias in awe of creation and of the Creator. He instantly felt at home among the land, but not so much among its inhabitants. The Armenians were a feisty and difficult people who had artfully kept their country in and out of many empires—their loyalties were to no one but themselves. They were hard to rule because they had an innate and deep-rooted distrust of foreigners and foreign ideas; Matthias and his teachings about Jesus immediately clashed with their isolationism.

There were only a few Jews among the Armenians, and Matthias had easy success with them. He turned to the Gentiles and was soon forced to confront the sun worshippers. The leaders of these worshippers had a strong grip over the people, yet slowly, and very quietly, he began to make converts among them. As time went on, his successes began to bother the leaders of the sun god, and he knew that soon he would find himself face to face with Phias, the feared and powerful high priest of the sun god.

Phias was a man with friends in authority. Most of these friends were the Armenian tribal lords, who protected and supported him. The local Roman magistrate permitted Phias to function, provided he continued to placate the tribal lords and keep the people in fear of their god and at peace with Rome. Phias was known for his clairvoyant powers and his fanatical devotion to the sun god. He had the gift of debate and had humbled everyone who challenged his god. His wisdom was unmatched by anyone in Colchis, which was the main city of the region. Several times Phias sent messages to Matthias telling him to stop "poisoning the people of the sun god with lies and Jewish folklore," but Matthias continued to preach. Many months passed. These two men circled and neared each other but never met for Matthias knew that the time chosen by the Master had not yet arrived.

Finally, after many months, the day came.

It was a hot, sunny morning. Matthias was standing on the side of a mountain describing the storm that almost sank the boat on which Jesus and the Apostles were sailing.

"And the Master rose from His rest, and with the strength and calmness of the Creator, He told the storm to cease and the sea to be calm. Instantly, there was a great calm. Jesus, the Son of God, has power over all that you and I survey. He commands the sky and all its bodies. He breathes, and the air stirs. Jesus smiles, and the small seeds of grain sprout forth. He speaks to the grass, and it grows. He directs the rain and the rivers to fall and flow. He does all these things out of love, a love that never leaves us. His love never diminishes, it is never exhausted—the love of Jesus has no limits. It is eternal. The love Jesus has for us is so great that He died to prove His love and to share it with us. His death was a ransom that sets us free from fear, sin, and yes, even death. His death was not a shame, it was a glory, for it was planned in love. His death is a perpetual memorial of this great love. I assure you, you will never find a love greater than this, or a Lover as giving as Jesus. With this great love comes forgiveness for our sins. This love can be yours. All you have to do is heed His call to become part of this love and know forgiveness."

Unceremoniously, Phias appeared on a cliff high over Matthias and the people. He stood listening to Matthias in silence. When the Armenians saw the high priest, some drew back; others, in anticipation of the confrontation that was about to occur, sat on the ground or climbed trees, hoping to see the war of magic take place. Word of the pending drama was sent to Colchis, to the nearby towns and villages, and to relatives and friends. By late morning, the crowd had doubled in size. Many needed to experience a confrontation such as this to help them overcome doubt and indecision. For months, many had listened to this humble man from far way, who with great strength and conviction spoke of a God Whose love was so intense that He willed His Son to die to show it. The sun god had not done that for them. They lived in fear of the sun god and the power of the high priest. They had never heard of love. But they needed a strong outward sign to convince them further. After months of listening, many compared the miracles of Jesus to the things they saw the high priest do in the name of the sun god. Though they found Jesus more in tune with their daily lives, they saw little reason to leave the sun god.

Fully dressed in his yellow, white, and gold temple robes made of the finest cloth and with his gold sunburst headdress, Phias, along with many richly dressed disciples, stood silently by, listening to Matthias. There was a great stillness, broken only by the flutter of his robes in the wind. For hours, Phias stood listening to Matthias.

Matthias, clad in a tattered, plain robe, and his two converted Armenians stood off to Phias' side. He continued to preach, ignoring the presence of his guest. Suddenly, at high noon, Phias broke his stillness. He raised his hands to the sky. The people gasped in horror, expecting some punishment to descend on them. Because of his position on the cliff, everyone was forced to look up at him. Many had to shade their eyes lest they be blinded by the strong noonday sun that shone behind his tall figure. Standing above Matthias, Phias was massive. He was tall and muscular. His voice was deep and seemed to create thunder inside the very soul of his listeners.

"You are a charlatan, Ma - tie - is, for you preach a weak God. Where is this Jesus of yours? Can He be seen? Can we feel His warmth, as we feel the warmth of our sun god? Can we see any great light from your God, as we see the great light from our god? No! I was told that your God died, killed by His own people with the help of the Romans. This may be the best thing Rome has done for our world."

Many of Phias' disciples laughed aloud.

"He disappeared for days, and it is also said that He has gone into the sky most likely to be consumed by the sun god."

This brought more laughter. Phias, grasping the moment, pranced around the top of the cliff with his chin extended and his arms folded across his chest.

"This Jew speaks to you of a Man called Jesus, Who is a sham. This Jesus was so weak that He died on a Roman cross like a common crimi-nal. So you see, this Jesus he speaks of is nothing but a weakling Who preys on the minds of weak and stupid people, like these two fooled converts who are with Ma - tie - is. They have become slaves of this false teacher. This foreigner is another ploy, an agent of Rome, who was sent to find weakness in our minds and to tighten the Emperor's grip on the noble and proud throat of Armenia. This man preaches weakness, so as to keep us forever in the grip of Rome."

Throughout the day, Phais attacked Jesus while Matthias remained silent beneath the high priest's perch.

When Matthias did respond, he never looked at Phais, but instead continued to look at the crowd, reminding them of Jesus' love for them, of His power over death, and of His eternal presence.

The debate continued into early evening, but the crowds never thinned. Most of them had decided to remain until one of the two men faltered. Phias and his disciples were given food and water, while Matthias and his two Armenian converts ate and drank nothing.

As the night went on, Phias, standing on his high perch, began to grow tired, and he started to waver. He leaned heavily on his staff while Matthias, who had no position to safeguard, stood upright near a group of small rocks, far below the cliff.

Phias' loud, booming voice grew weak, while Matthias continued to speak in his usual tone. In the night, the priest's features became obscure in the darkness while Matthias' face and clothing glowed bright and silvery in the moonlight. Into the dark morning hours, Phias attacked. Matthias preached. The crowd was mesmerized.

When daybreak finally came and the sun began to blaze above the horizon, Phias, in a voice that now sounded like a gasp, yelled, "There is my god!"

For the first time, Matthias looked up at the high priest. His eyes were filled with pity. A rare smile crossed his face. "What a pity, dear Phias. Tell me, where was your god during the night when you grew weak and tired? Does your god go to sleep? Is he only sometimes a god? It seems that your god has no power at night. How sad! My God brings light to the darkness of night. He is the one Who puts your god to sleep and covers him in darkness. My God hides your god with clouds and darkness, as He did on the day of His death, and it is my God Who awakens your god. My God is the One Who refreshes all and Who grants peace to you, your god, and everyone else. My God is your god's God—He is the light of the sun and the glow of the moon. He is light amidst the darkness."

The chief priest stood speechless. He began to shake all over; his disciples declared that he was in communication with the sun god, and they hurried him away.

The rest of the day, Matthias stood in his place and continued to preach Jesus. Many of those who stayed came to believe, and they received the refreshing water of Baptism. Night came, and the crowds were offering prayers of thanksgiving when a mob of men came and arrested Matthias and his two companions. That night, Matthias and his disciples were taken before the Circle of Chieftains on the charges of sorcery and blasphemy. During the night, all three were beaten badly, mocked cruelly, and tortured brutally. Early the next day, the two Armenians, already half-dead from their nightly ordeal, were beheaded, and their heads were impaled just outside the temple of the sun god.

Matthias was spared this fate. Instead, he was stripped naked, tied to four stakes in the ground, and left to bake in the hot sun. His flesh was torn, bruised, and bleeding. His face was swollen and disfigured. He lay in total silence as ants, bugs, and flies began their tiny torments on his exposed flesh. At midday, Matthias cried with a loud voice, "Jesus, Lord of all lights and all living things, let what is now mine become pleasing to You. Let the pains and discomforts of my flesh act in atonement for the sins and ignorance of these people, who hunger for the touch of Your Spirit. Show them, Lord, Your power, so that they can see Your loving greatness."

Suddenly darkness came over the countryside, and those watching scattered in fear. Some ran away, screaming that Matthias' God had killed the sun god; others fell to their knees, begging Matthias to call off his God. Still others denounced the sun god and cried for Jesus to accept them. The screams and pleas continued throughout the long darkness. Abruptly, sunlight came again. With the sunlight came new revelations and many became believers, but when they looked where Matthias had been lying, he was gone.

The people went into the countryside, longing for Jesus and for Matthias' words. When they found him, he was standing tall, unscarred, but when he walked, he walked with a limp. In the years that followed, the limp became worse, and everyone knew that he walked in constant pain. Some days, the limp was so pronounced that he walked like a man under the spell of wine.

Among those who found him that day was a fair, soft-skinned young man who walked up to Matthias and said proudly, "I have been sent by Peter and James bar Alphaeus to accompany you."

That was the day on which Nescius, his new disciple from Jerusalem, joined him.

✳

Peter, James bar Alphaeus, and John were disappointed in Matthias. He was the Apostle who wrote the least and remained the most distant. While the other Apostles corresponded through letters or messengers to keep Peter and others apprised of their missions, no one was sure of what Matthias was doing. Matthias was known for his scarcity of words, but this lack of communication confirmed that he was too secluded. Another disappointment was Matthias' reluctance to ask for companionship. He had been alone since James the Big had left him. The other Apostles, after separating from each other, had asked for companions. As expected, many acquired companions from their mission lands, but these did not fill the same need. The companions given to the Apostles were usually those who had known the Master or had witnessed His message. These companions provided the Apostles with the camaraderie of someone who was both a witness and someone from Judea. There were other reasons why each Apostle received an assistant. Many of those who were sent were known by the Roman and Jewish authorities and were in danger. It was wise to send these followers into safe exile. It was obvious to Peter that Matthias desired and had decided to live his life alone. Their concern heightened when they remembered that he drew the lot for Armenia. Peter voiced his concerns, and everyone agreed that Matthias should not be alone in such an unfamiliar country. So Peter began looking for a companion for Matthias, and John bar Zebedee suggested a young man named Nescius, who had been a follower for ten years and a friend of John for almost as long. The young man was firm in his faith, but he was still searching for a place in "The Way." Nescius had accompanied John on a few missions, and he was found to be impulsive and at times even thoughtless. John knew that Peter would fully understand the implications of such qualities: the young man needed the strong hand of discipline, and Matthias would most certainly provide it. John presented the young man to Peter, and immediately Peter recognized him as one who had been at Cornelius' *villa* on the day of his visit to the centurion's house.

So Peter ordered Nescius to join Matthias with the following warning: "Matthias is a rigid man with few needs, and it appears that he wants no traveling companion because few people could live as he does. I suggest you exercise much patience."

Nescius was dispatched to Cappadocia, Matthias' last known location. Not finding him there, Nescius followed his trail to Armenia, and after five months of travel, he finally found Matthias. From the moment of their meeting, Nescius knew that Matthias was uncomfortable with him, and he recognized that Peter's warning was accurate: a companion was an infringement on his ascetic way of life.

Matthias at first wanted to discharge Nescius, but out of charity he decided to have the young man stay a while so he could rest before sending him back to Jerusalem. Within days, the rationale behind Peter's decision became apparent to Matthias: the young man's conversion came with questions, and Matthias, of quick pace, would give him quick answers. First of all, Matthias had to discipline the young man's energies. Nescius' vision of missionary work was charging into a town on a white steed, banner in hand, shouting the Good News. He had to be taught the many dangers that awaited the Nazarenes. The Apostles immediately pointed out that prudence was always more virtuous than raw fervor. It was evident that Nescius had not yet learned that it was all in God's time, and that it was God Who brought opportunities to the missionary. There was still another problem, and to Matthias this was more disturbing: Nescius had lived a life of luxury. He had lived in royal mansions and the houses of Roman governors. Material deprivation was largely unknown to him. He was versed in Greek, Latin, and Hebrew; he had read many scrolls, and he knew the philosophers. As a result, he was accustomed to being listened to, and he was often the center of attention. The young man was a Jew of mixed parentage. He had no real idea who his parents were, though he was led to believe that he was the son of a Roman officer and a Jewish woman. As an infant, by order of the Procurator Coponius, he was forced on a wealthy, mildly religious Jewish family who for years had been purveyors to the Roman garrison and had consequently been ostracized from the Temple. The family was ordered to raise the orphan as a Hebrew. He was circumcised, trained in Judaic Law, educated in the written Hebrew language, and further educated in Latin and Greek for the benefit of Rome. Eventually, at the age of eighteen, he was pressed into service as a translator. He worked directly under the Procurator Gratus, a predecessor of Pontus Pilate. Having a companion who had been close to Pilate the murderer made Matthias uneasy. Matthias wondered at the plans the Master had in putting them together. As their time together passed, Matthias soon found that Nescius was far from a servant of the Master. The young man had faith, but he could not conform his will to the will of Jesus. He did not understand the subtleties of being a servant, rather than the master, of situations created by God. So Matthias came to understand that he was to finish the work started by the others in Jerusalem—it was for him to form his companion in the ways of Jesus while Nescius labored to purge himself of old Roman habits.

✳

The first time Nescius heard of Jesus was on his return from Caesarea Philippi. He had been in that city on business for Pilate and his wife, Lady Claudia. He was returning to Jerusalem with the centurions Cornelius and Longinus. As they rode their horses casually on the Yaffa Road to Jerusalem, they came upon Jesus and His followers, who were on the side of the road. Nescius looked indifferently at the men and women and quickly decided to ignore them, for they looked like beggars and he hated Jews who begged. They were an embarrassment in the presence of Romans, and it seemed unnatural for the "Chosen People" to allow themselves to be denigrated to such an extent. As they passed by, Cornelius remarked, with a wide smile on his face, that they had just passed Judea's newest Prophet, Jesus of Nazareth. There were reports that this new Prophet was a good magician and a great miracle worker, and there was something in the way Cornelius said this that caught Nescius' fancy. His voice was not sharp and offensive, as usual, but rather soft and understanding. Nescius turned in his saddle to look back. He saw a Man Whom he instantaneously sensed to be the new Prophet; for a second he wanted to stop and go back, but his distaste for beggars was too strong.

Three months passed, and again Nescius crossed paths with Jesus. He was buying some spices for his foster parents. As he walked from the Street of Spices toward the Temple, he saw the Nazarene and His followers, off in the distance. He stopped and watched, not wanting to get too close yet hoping that some magic was in the making. To his surprise, he found all kinds of people—rich and poor, sick and healthy—following this Man. Even more surprising, a contingent of the Sanhedrin was milling in the crowd. He watched as Pharisees approached Jesus and began a conversation with Him, and soon they all seemed to be searching through their robes for something. Finally, someone produced a coin. Nescius was too far from the scene to hear Jesus' words, but it was obvious that whatever He said left the Pharisees speechless. Jesus and His companions slowly walked away. It was then that Nescius noticed that some of those following Jesus were snickering while the questioners were huddled in frantic debate. The discomfort and confusion caused by this Prophet pleased Nescius. Though he respected the power of the Pharisees and the Sadducees, he had little esteem for them. They were too pretentious, too arrogant, and too narrow-minded to be servants of his *Adonai*. In Nescius' eyes, the Holy One was an all-encompassing Deity, never limited.

On account of his Roman background and his employment, the Pharisees had branded Nescius a sinner, and they forbade him from entering the Temple. In spite of the condemnations, he continued to observe the Sabbath, Jewish feasts, and the Law. He was a Jew, and he could be nothing else—he truly believed in *El Shaddai*, the One God, and he was one of the Chosen People.

His foster family, who also were ostracized from the Temple, spared him nothing in his education of the Torah. He studied with *Rebs*—teachers who loved God more than the laws of the Sanhedrin. From his reading and studying of the Torah and the Prophets, he believed firmly in the promise of a Messiah. Like so many other Jews, he believed that the Messiah would come and do great things for the Chosen People. His conviction inspired him to pray often, for he wanted, more than anything, to recognize "the Anointed One."

Though the Sanhedrin did not accept him as a Jew, the Romans did. Pilate granted him freedom from labor on the Sabbath so he could remain a Jew. He was encouraged to live openly as a Jew in the procurator's households. The truth, of course, was that Rome needed him this way, because he could help Rome to understand his troublesome people. But the reasons were irrelevant to him—he was grateful to be a Jew. It excused him from all the confusions and follies of the Roman gods. He could never worship a clay statue whose nature and needs were on the same level as his, nor could he act reverently toward so many gods who tripped and stumbled over each other and acted with pride and vanity. The Romans, like the Greeks, were so unsure of their gods that they created a god for everything, and they lived with many superstitions. At least his *Adonai* was an obvious, present Being, Who above all things was forever mysterious, forever being sought. He was a God with no human deceptions and no human frailties.

His next meeting with Jesus occurred months later while he was leisurely riding his horse on the east road from Bethany. This time, he passed closely by Jesus and saw His Face. The Prophet's upper body was above the crowd because He was seated on a young, gray ass. Nescius stopped and watched, not so much to see this Man, but rather in amazement at what the people were doing. They were climbing and stripping the trees along the road and throwing the palm branches in Jesus' way. Some removed their cloaks and threw them on the path before Him. From the East Gate, known also as the Golden Gate, a group of men, women, and children poured out of Jerusalem, also waving palms. They shouted, "Hosanna! Hosanna to the Son of David. Blessed is He that cometh in the name of the Lord. Hosanna in the highest."

What is wrong with these Jews? Only Romans have triumphant parades. If the Romans see this, they will become enraged. Certainly the Sanhedrin will be infuriated by all this.

Mesmerized by these events, he slowly dismounted his stallion and tied the reins to a nearby bush. He joined the people behind Jesus toward the East Gate of the city. As he walked, he felt a strong, overwhelming power flow over his being. All his life, he had been in the presence of great power— the power of Rome, the power of the Sanhedrin—but this time he felt a far greater power. As the awareness of this power inebriated him, he stopped, paralyzed. The crowd indifferently pushed and bumped him, almost causing him to lose his balance. He watched as the crowd continued to move away. The dust from their steps clouded his sight, and though he could not see the crowd or Jesus, he still heard their shouts. All he knew was that he had been near a power that was greater than any other on the earth.

Out of nowhere, he heard a voice say, "Rejoice greatly, O daughter of Sion...O daughter of Jerusalem, behold thy King cometh to thee, the just and savior...riding upon an ass...." He identified the words of the prophet Zachariah, but not the voice of the speaker. He was bewildered. He did not know what this meant; he had to find answers, but he did not know what question to ask. When he regained his senses, he found himself on the road, virtually alone, and sometime later, somehow, he made his way to the Fortress of Antonia. For the next three days, Nescius' life was unsettled. For the first time in his life, he was thoroughly unhappy. He felt the need for family and the peace he sometimes felt in their solidarity. Passover was approaching, and he was happy that he would be with his family to enjoy the festivities. Certainly, he would regain his senses and stop being so unsettled.

The *Pasch* Passover was the holiday of promise. Nescius vowed to be particularly attentive to his foster parents, aunts, uncles, and cousins. Early that day he overheard the low voices of his parents and relatives as they were speaking of Jesus. They talked of how He fed a large crowd and also of Lazarus of Bethany, whom He raised from the dead. Surprised, Nescius sat listening as they spoke excitedly about Jesus. He wondered why he did not walk away; why, suddenly, did he no longer believe that Jesus was merely a clever magician? He sat with a small cup of wine in his hand and lowered his head, not wanting to appear too interested, but in truth he desperately wanted to hear more about this Man.

"He speaks of another Kingdom," his foster father, Decimus, said with excitement in his voice.

"Yes, a Kingdom that He has come to proclaim," his foster mother, Clarissa, said pensively. Suddenly her mood changed, and she smiled. "He is so tender and compassionate. When He smiles, His face beams with a freshness and joy that make me want to believe Him."

"He makes *Adonai* sound so different from the One described to us by the Pharisees," his Aunt Junia said in a low, brooding voice.

"And how about the stories He tells? They leave you thinking. He speaks often of doing good and helping others. You know, one day after hearing Him speak about the Samaritan helping the Jew, I actually stopped and talked to a Samaritan," his cousin Prescia say with glee in her voice. When no one reacted, she continued, "I heard Him call Himself '*bar* Adam.'"

With shock, Nescius detected an unfamiliar emotion in his family. *This Jesus has filtered into my family. My family has been with Him and heard His words and found meaning in these words. This is what I have missed: I have not heard Him speak, never heard His voice.*

"But we are all 'sons of Adam,'" Nescius blurted, and when he looked up from his cup of wine, he could see his relatives giving each other quick and cautious glances; he knew that by these words he had declared himself a stranger. He was too Roman.

The conversation quickly changed to business, friends, babies, and travel.

Nescius ached to tell them what he had experienced, but he did not know what to ask or what to hope for in their conversation. He had lost the moment; they were too unsure of him to speak freely about Jesus. As the night continued, he tried to bring the conversation back to Jesus, but they ignored all his attempts. He noticed a difference in his family. They were more peaceful, and when the Passover meal began, he recognized a different and deeper feeling in the way his relatives celebrated being "passed over" by death.

The next morning, the sixth day of the week, which was dedicated to Venus on the Roman calendar, Pilate's courier arrived and ordered Nescius to immediately report to Pilate. He left his family's *Pesach* festivities perplexed: he had never been disturbed during a Holy Day or the Sabbath. These days were promised to him, and Pilate never broke his word. He wondered at the reason for this unusual behavior. Nothing urgent came to mind. Before he had left for the *Pesach*, he had completed his Hebrew-to-Latin translations of the Temple Authorities' request to celebrate the upcoming feast of Pentecost, and he had completed the translation of the next portion of Aristophanes' Greek play "The Birds" for Pilate and Lady Claudia. Recalling nothing urgent, he rode his horse angrily into Jerusalem, not noticing the large gatherings before the Hasmonean Palace of King Herod or the heavy and choking silence of the city. He arrived at the Antonia, dismounted, and went directly to the chambers just off to the side of the *Gabbatha*, which was outside the judgment hall of the *Praetorium*. There he was met by his half Roman-half Egyptian mercenary friend, Stephaton.

"Good morning, *Scriptor*," Stephaton said with a small sneer on his lips.

Nescius hated being called "scribe," for it reminded him of the Temple writers. He knew that the garrison often referred to him this way, and when they did, there was a bite in their tone of voice. But hearing the annoyance from Stephaton never angered him, for there was no malice in it.

"Doing nothing, again, *Latro?*" Nescius said with a wide smile, knowing that Stephaton hated being called a mercenary.

In their friendship, they tolerated the playful name-calling. Of course, this bantering was private. It was a chance for them to laugh at each other and deprive the garrison from invading their privacy and friendship. Their relationship was based on a common bond. Both knew they were by-products of illicit relationships, and both knew they were "Roman" only because they were of use to the Roman Senate. They were tolerated, and nothing more. They both acted Roman, but deep inside they were free thinkers.

His soldier friend continued the banter. "Did you get 'passed over' again, Nescius?"

"Of course, I am one of the Chosen People, and this is far greater than being a Gentile."

They gripped each other's forearms in a Roman handshake.

"What is so important to drag me away from my Holy Day?"

"Pilate is having problems today. The Sanhedrin have arrested that Nazarene Prophet for blasphemy."

"Blasphemy is not a crime in Roman Law; besides, the Nazarene is only a magician," Nescius said, forcing himself to be unconcerned.

"Well then, He is a blasphemous magician," Stephaton said, laughing heartily.

Nescius walked away from his friend and went to the heavy draped curtain that hung freely over the entrance to Pilate's sitting room. One part of the curtain fell from the ceiling to the floor, but the other part was draped and held in place by a heavy gold woven cord. Carefully, he glanced around the curtain.

The room was empty.

"Where is Pilate?"

"He is resting. He is not in a good mood. He passed the Prophet off to that slob Herod, but to no avail for Herod is returning the Prophet to him." Stephaton paused and then said, "There is something about this

Man. He has caused much confusion within me, and I cannot figure out why. To be honest, He has confounded me."

"I am confused about Him as well." Nescius was thinking aloud, and quickly he added, "I recently found out that my foster parents are under His influence. I find this somewhat interesting, for they are always cautious in their beliefs."

Suddenly, he realized that Stephaton was no longer behind him, but by his side.

"Did you know this Nazarene, Stephaton?" he asked his friend in a low voice.

"No, but I have heard much of Him, and some believe in Him and in what He does. What I heard I found interesting. There are things about Him that remind me of our soldier god Mithras. I do not know."

"Yes, I feel the same way." Nescius walked back into the side room just as a young Egyptian slave girl came into the room carrying a towel and a water basin. She walked to Nescius, her head low. Without acknowledging her, Nescius sat down and extended his left foot. The girl quickly began to untie his laced sandal.

"Tell me what you have heard, Stephaton."

"Only that the authorities have accused Him of blasphemy. Cornelius, who knows your language better than I do, told me that the Nazarene has been accused of calling Himself *bar Elohim*."

"Really?" Nescius said quickly.

"And just what does that mean?" Stephaton asked, somewhat confused by his friend's deep interest.

"Son of God," Nescius said pensively. He grew more disturbed.

"Ah, finally—after all these killers, robbers, and insurrectionists, we have a god with us," the soldier said, trying to get a smile from his friend. When no smile came, he grew more concerned.

"What is wrong, Nescius?"

"I do not know. I cannot explain it. For some unknown reason, I have become unsettled these past few days. It all is very strange, and what you just said and what I heard in my foster parents' house have disturbed me even more. Strangely, I feel compelled to know more about this Man, Jesus."

The slave girl continued to wash his foot.

Nescius noticed her for the first time. He could see that she was of Stephaton's culture and that she seemed troubled by their conversation. Reaching down, he lifted her face with his index finger. The beauty of her Hamitic face surprised him. She lowered her eyes in respect, but her face was stained with tears.

"Do you know this Jew, Jesus? I give you permission to speak."

"Yes, sire."

"Do you think He is the Son of God?"

"It seems that He is."

"Why do you say this?"

"Because He has performed miracles of feeding many people."

"And of healing?"

"Some say that, sire, but I only saw Him feed the multitude."

"Did you eat of the food He made?" Stephaton asked in curiosity.

"Yes, sire." She slipped back and sat on her feet, looking at Nescius and Stephaton. "He spoke to everyone of loving our enemies, and of caring for the poor and sick. He said that we are to love one another as God, His Father, loves us." She automatically began to wipe Nescius' foot while her eyes, trance-like, remained on Nescius' face.

She continued, "When He speaks, His voice soothes you, and when you think about what He has said, you become warm."

She seemed as if she was about to say more when Cornelius walked into the side room; she lowered her head and, without much thought, returned to washing Nescius' other foot.

Cornelius' entry into the side room was like a storm passing through the portal; he was visibly in distress.

"You Jews are a crazy lot," he said loudly and angrily.

"We, Jews?" Nescius repeated, for he was annoyed by the tone in Cornelius' voice. He had no great admiration for Cornelius, who had persisted in despising the Jews throughout his fifteen years of service in the Province. He knew the language, customs, and religion of the occupied people, but this did little to mitigate his contempt.

"Yes, you Jews," Cornelius retorted with resentment in his voice as he tucked his helmet under his arm and paced the floor. "They have Jesus of Nazareth in custody. The Temple authorities charged Him with blasphemy, and when they took Him before Pilate, they changed the charge to treason."

"What is that to you?" Nescius asked inquisitively.

Cornelius stopped walking and looked at him long and hard.

"Have you not heard this Man speak? He is filled with love and peace. There is no treason in this Man."

What you also? Nescius wondered, and suddenly he was hit with a thought that was so momentous that it almost caused him to lose his breath. *Could it be that Cornelius is a God-fearer? A Gentile? A believer in Adonai?* He instantly saw Cornelius in a new light.

Stephaton cleared his throat, and when Nescius looked at him, Stephaton shook his head in quick, short movements.

"It seems your people cannot decide how to charge this Man. Who ever heard of being convicted of two different crimes? Perhaps if they charged Him with the crime of kindness and mercy I would begin believing in you Jews."

"I have never seen you so bothered. Why are you so passionate about this Nazarene?" Nescius asked.

Again, Stephaton cleared his throat, but Nescius preferred to ignore him.

Before Cornelius could answer, Abenadar, a Syrian mercenary, walked into the chamber. He walked directly to Cornelius and saluted him.

"Pilate wishes to see you, Centurion. The Accused is back from Herod's palace to stand again before Pilate."

Cornelius roughly adjusted his armored uniform, then his helmet. He gave Nescius a quick displeased look, but as he walked from the chamber, his face was clouded with great dread. Nescius sympathized with him.

The power of this Man is truly great. Even Romans become confused, Nescius thought.

Again, the unsettling feeling that had plagued Nescius returned. He looked down at his feet and the girl was gone. He was disappointed, for he wanted to question her further.

"Why did you push him that way?" Stephaton asked, slightly annoyed. "Did you not see how sympathetic he was to the Nazarene?"

"It looked like it was more than sympathy. I think he has been converted by this Man, Jesus, and...." He stopped himself short of announcing his suspicion that Cornelius was a God-fearer. Some Romans who became believers in the One Lord of the Hebrews and began following certain dietary laws were called traitors.

"And what?" Stephaton asked.

"Oh, nothing," Nescius said, unwilling to trust his friend with his suspicions. He rose to his feet and walked to the heavy drape that separated the side room from the *Gabbatha*, with its mosaic, colored floor of small squares, triangles, and circles. This area was called in Greek the *lithostroton*. From behind the curtain, he could see the back of the *bema*, Pilate's judgment chair. Cornelius stood nearby, and Abenadar stood on a lower step. Below the terrace, on the bottom steps, stood several leaders of the Sanhedrin. He strained to hear what was being said, but it was all muffled. It was only when the crowd shouted in unison that he heard it plainly.

"Crucify Him! Crucify Him!" The shouts drew a gasp from Nescius. He became startled at the sound of Lady Claudia's frantic voice.

"Guard, do you know where my husband is?"

Stephaton snapped to attention, and Nescius turned and bowed to her.

She heard the crowd, and she knew the answer.

"Here, make haste to Pontius and give him this small parchment. Now! Quickly!" She stuffed the small parchment scroll in Stephaton's hand.

Leading Stephaton, she pushed him through the curtain and onto the *Gabbatha*. She brought her trembling hand to her forehead and began walking about aimlessly.

"Are you well, my Lady?"

"Yes," she answered, still distracted, and with a wave of her hand she dismissed him.

Nescius was somewhat disheartened by her curt reply. She had always spoken courteously to him. She loved the classics, and with his background in Roman and Greek classics, he was able to inspire her with interesting interpretations of these writings. Their relationship was one of mutual interests and respect, and it had rubbed off on Pilate.

"Pilate, read my note and learn that this Man is innocent," she said aloud, but with no one present.

"Excuse me, Lady Claudia, but do you know this Man?"

"What! Oh, Nescius! I am sorry, I did not know you...what did you say?"

"I asked if you knew this Jesus."

"No... No... I did hear Him speak...but...I just had a sleepless night...filled with dreams of Him...dreams that bordered on nightmares. What is happening here today troubles me deeply." She looked out around the drapes, again.

"I think you should not worry, my Lady, for this Man is believed to be nothing but a magician, though some say that He claims to be the Son of Man and the Son of God. This is a contradiction, my Lady."

He repressed his urge to fake a smile, for he was sure that this statement, though not completely true, would produce a deep, meaningful discussion between them.

Lady Claudia continued to peer around the corner of the drapes, completely distracted and not at all mindful of what he had said.

"Some say He is the Messiah," she said softly, but not speaking to him.

Nescius turned abruptly to look at her.

"Messiah?" he repeated, wanting to make certain that he had heard her correctly. His interest was piqued, and the word "Messiah" echoed and re-echoed in his mind.

Messiah? Could this be He—the One—of Whom the Ancients and the Prophets wrote? he asked himself. His thoughts raced, and he recalled the Scriptures, his knowledge of which surpassed that of most Jews.

Why had not my parents said this of this Man? Why did no one say this word before this moment? His mind continued to search the Scriptures.

There is nothing in Scripture that says that the Messiah must come in great thunderous glory. Could it be that He has come in obscurity, as a prophet? How could He rescue the Jews? What new greatness could this Man give to His Chosen People? Messiah?

The sacred title stilled his thinking.

"Messiah?" he said aloud, though no one was there to hear. *Remember the power you felt, Nescius. Remember it. Could it be that He is truly the One?*

This word, Messiah, aroused a thousand uncertainties in his mind. The more he tried to untangle the mysteries of the Messiah, the more he became bewildered.

I should have stopped and listened to what this Jesus had to say; then, perhaps, I might have detected something in His voice that would have confirmed His claim, or that allowed me to discern His identity.

As he looked out onto the *Gabbatha*, a strange uneasiness overtook his body, and then a great emptiness overcame his being. He had a strange sense that his world was teetering, sitting on the thin edge of a sword, swaying between endless uncertainty and infinite sureness; the fear of falling into uncertainty frightened him.

Have I missed the Messiah? In my contempt for the unwanted of Israel, have I failed to recognize Israel's most longed for?

His attention returned to the proceedings. He strained to hear what was being said. Pilate and the authorities were bickering loudly. He could hear the frustration in Pilate's voice and the insistence of the leaders of the people; he could also hear the weakness in Pilate's convictions and the strength in the demands of the leaders. As he listened, he found himself agreeing with one and then the other. He became impatient with himself, for never in his life had he been so uncertain. He was always able to study, analyze, and conclude, finding solidity and satisfaction in his conclusions. For the first time in his life he felt the sour taste of failure, and it disgusted him—little did he know that the taste was to linger for many days. In his confusion, he felt tears of anger and frustration come to his eyes. Again, he milled over all that he had read about the Messiah, wanting first to discredit Jesus and then realizing that he did not know enough about the Galilean to make any conclusions. His uncertainty drew him deeper into the need to know this Man—again he berated himself for not stopping and listening the few times he had passed near Jesus.

Would He have answered my question if I had asked Him directly if He was the Messiah? He looks so unassuming. He looks so ordinary. But did not Adonai in the past always use the ordinary?

His thoughts were broken when he heard a loud sigh of relief from Lady Claudia.

"Look! Nescius, look how clever Pilate is. He is offering them a choice between that revolutionary Barabbas and your people's Messiah."

Her voice was relaxed, and when she said "Messiah," she displayed a gentle reverence. He did not resent the reference; instead, he found comfort and joy in the sound of the name.

"Give us Barabbas! Give us Barabbas!"

The shouts interrupted his thoughts. He was immediately appalled that the crowd had asked for Barabbas, the criminal, over Jesus.

"Crucify Him! Crucify Him!"

"Do not listen to them, Pilate, please. I have suffered much this night because of this Man."

With shock, Nescius watched Barabbas scurry across the *lithostroton* and into the crowd, which surrounded him and gradually swallowed him up.

"Crucify Him! Crucify Him!"

The crowd grew louder and more demanding.

"He is not listening to me...Pilate did not listen to me."

Nescius looked at Claudia. Her face was pale and stricken with fear. She quickly rushed from the room. He heard her sobs.

Again he heard the shouts: "Crucify Him! Crucify Him! Crucify Him!"

He timidly walked from behind the heavy curtain and onto the *Gabbatha*. This was something he never did without being summoned, but his curiosity compelled him. It was then that he saw the back of Jesus as He was being roughly led away. Jesus, peaceful and docile, walked with the guards. His hands were tied in front of His Body. His hair was matted down with dirt, perspiration, and blood. He turned his head, and Nescius caught a glimpse, but only a glimpse, of the side of His Face. Jesus' eyes met his, and Nescius felt, for an instant, some part of his life—some part of his soul— leave him. He instantaneously felt a bond with this Man, for whatever had parted from him was now part of this

Jesus. Nescius reached the right side of Pilate's chair just as the procurator was washing his hands. It was then that he saw the anger and frustration on Pilate's face.

Pilate flashed a quick look over his shoulder at the *scriptor* and said roughly, "Nescius, prepare a *titulus*. In Latin and Greek…" he stopped, and then as an afterthought, "… and in Hebrew stating that this Man is charged with being Jesus of Nazareth, King of the Jews."

Without responding, Nescius asked Longinus, who was standing nearby, "Where are they taking that Man?"

"To be scourged," Longinus answered with compassion in his voice.

"I gave you an order, Nescius. Do it <u>now</u>!"

The harshness in Pilate's command upset Nescius.

In defiance, he continued to watch Pilate wash his hands in a small bowl, and he heard him say loudly to the crowd, "I am innocent of this Man's blood."

When the people replied, "Let His blood be on us," Nescius flinched and felt a shiver pass through him. He retreated quickly to the anteroom and sat at his desk. He made haste not to do Pilate's bidding, but to distance himself from the words and actions of the people outside. Nescius became afraid, for himself and everyone. Had they not felt the power that radiated from this Man? Had they not stopped to wonder where this power came from? Near his desk were many small planks of wood covered with gypsum. He picked one out of the bunch and began to write what he had been ordered to write, but he could not finish it—his mind was occupied with thoughts of Jesus. Dropping the *stylus*, he rushed from the room in the direction of the dungeons below the fortress; there, he knew, the scourging would take place.

As he began to descend the narrow spiral stairs, he held his breath and concluded that he would have to bathe as soon as he abandoned this insane adventure. He wondered if he would ever be free of the stench and filth of the putrid dungeon. When he neared the bottom of the steps, he could hear the swish of the whip as it sliced through the stagnant, hot air of the dungeon. The scourging had begun.

The dungeon was a round room with four thick pillars. The ceiling arched to a dome and had a round opening about the size of a large table. Through this opening, the sun beamed onto the floor, which was made of roughly chipped stones. This part of the floor rose slightly to form a small mound. The sunlight shining through the opening in the ceiling was the only light in the room.

Nescius felt ill when he saw the brown and red blood stains on the stony mound. He was further sickened by the sight of the most recent blood, which was still rolling and trickling down the slope of the mound into a small gutter. Highlighted by the bright sun were two small pillars that stood about waist high. The criminals were draped over these pillars as the lashes were applied. Hanging from a heavy wooden beam that ran across the opened ceiling was a set of chains from which prisoners were hung while they were being beaten. In the center of the sunlit circle at the top of the small raised floor was a large perpendicular pillar that was taller than most men. This pillar was once a large rock that had been chipped into a rough, jagged post. The post had a small hole not far from its top, and through this hole two heavy chains were threaded. The prisoner's hands were shackled and the chain was pulled through the hole, forcing the prisoner to stretch. He found the naked Jesus chained to this pillar. His arms were pulled high above His head, and He was stretched so severely that He was standing on His toes. The Roman soldiers were seated in the dark shade of the room. They were hidden behind the small dust particles that floated in the sunny air. The particles looked like tiny specks of jewels flowing into the room from the opened roof. The soldiers were nothing more than barely visible gray figures, captured in the shade. They were seated on small wooden stools and were drinking cheap wine. They watched with satisfaction and loudly counted each slash.

"Undecim… duodecim… tredecim…"

"That was a good smack," he heard a Roman soldier shout.

Nescius gazed at the slow stream of blood crawling down Jesus' naked body. The shadowed executioner dropped the whip. Out of the darkness, the whip snapped, cut through the air, and slashed the back of Jesus' legs. New blood appeared. Each cut of the whip made Nescius twitch in vicarious pain. He beheld in wonder the silence of the Man, and soon he was praying to hear the sound of the Man's voice. He was longing, hoping, begging to hear a word from Jesus, but he heard only the sound of Jesus trying to catch His breath. Without warning, without foreknowledge, Nescius was flooded by the awareness of this Man's innocence. A grave injustice was occurring before his eyes, and he wanted to shout *"subsistite!"* stop! But his mouth was clogged with fear of the armor and strength around him.

"Undeviginti… viginti…"

"Hit Him harder!" another Roman soldier shouted.

Finally, he could take no more. He rushed up the narrow steps, out of the stench of the *Hades* of Rome, out of the darkness of the *Shoal* of Judea. Aimlessly, he scurried, and somehow he found his way out of the fortress and into the streets. The sunlight blinded him until he shaded his eyes with his hands. The feeling of the air on his face brought a prayer of thanksgiving to his lips. Suddenly, his stomach wrenched and emptied its contents as tears came to his eyes. He gathered his senses, for he knew he had to write the *titulus*, or be punished. Tired, beaten, and bewildered, he made his way back to his small desk. He hurried to his business, despite the stale taste of vomit that remained in his mouth. As he wrote, he repeated aloud the words Pilate had given him. The words "King of the Jews" echoed and re-echoed in his mind. His mind was taken back to the shouts of the people—"Hosanna! Hosanna, Son of David...King of the Jews!"

They called Him King a few days ago, now they have turned Him into a criminal.

A warm swell overcame him, and he remembered the words of one of the prophets: "Behold, thy King cometh, sitting on an ass colt." At that instant, he understood and believed that this was the truth—Jesus was the King of the Jews. To affirm his belief, and to defy the temple authorities, he posted on the *titulus*, which the official herald would carry and which would be nailed on the cross above the head of the Prisoner, "Jesus of Nazareth, King of the Jews."

He wrote the Hebrew letters of the *titulus* from right to left, in accordance with how the Jews wrote and read. When he wrote the inscription in Greek and Latin, he did likewise—letters from right to left—even though the Greeks and Romans were accustomed to reading and writing from left to right. He did this so that the Jews, and only the Jews, would be able to read what he now believed to be true: that Jesus of Nazareth was King of the Jews.

They deserve Pilate's words, and only they deserve these words, he thought to himself with great vengeance.

As he finished writing, Abenadar entered the anteroom.

"Have you finally finished with the lettering?" the soldier asked with slight irritation in his voice.

Nescius did not particularly like this Legionnaire.

As he picked up the *titulus* and gave it to Abenadar, he knew that he was finalizing the sentence of Jesus.

Abenadar left the room.

He was now alone. He grew troubled, then fearful, and finally morose. Something evil had happened, and he could do nothing about it.

Have we destroyed our final hope of salvation? Where was the power I felt on the road to Jerusalem? Why did not this Man exert all His power to win the people over?

A million thoughts and uncertainties consumed his mind. What bothered him most was that he never had heard the Nazarene's voice, and this tormented him. He would remain in this deep disappointment for days.

When he came to his senses, it was dark.

"I am going to be late for Sabbath at my parents' house!" he said aloud.

He jumped to his feet.

I must go home!

He called for a servant and ordered a chariot to take him home, and then he went to his quarters, picked up his hooded cloak, and wrapped it around himself. As he rushed through the halls and passed the many empty rooms of the fortress, he realized that he was rushing, not to beat the sunset, but to flee from the happenings of the day. The farther he was from the *Praetorium*, the more at ease he would be and the quicker he would forget the Nazarene. Outside, he was greeted by a waiting charioteer. Without responding to the driver's greeting, he jumped on the chariot and braced himself by tightly holding onto the side railing. As soon as he felt he was a good distance from the Fortress of Antonia, he took a deep breath.

"In a big hurry tonight, Nescius," his driver said with familiarity. "It is a good thing. I never saw night come so quickly. Moments ago it was near midday."

Nescius did not hear the driver; instead, his thoughts were drawn to the darkness that seemed to be covering his entire life.

The wind was beginning to pick up. Dust was whirling and picking at his eyes and skin. He wrapped his cloak around himself and threw the hood over his head.

This is the foulest of all nights, he remarked to himself.

They traveled through Tyropoean and went south into the Upper City. As they passed the Hasmonean Palace, Nescius cursed Herod and his part in the day's events. He had to smile, for he knew that Pilate despised this "King," and he saw some humor in how the two rulers tried to pass Jesus off to each other. Another burst of wind caught his breath, and dust swirled around the chariot. He tucked his chin close to his chest and prayed that he might reach home soon. They traveled farther into the Upper City, and they soon passed the house of the High Priests Annias and Caiaphas.

As bad as Pilate and Herod were in today's happenings, he reflected, *they cannot even compare to Caiaphas.*

He became angry with himself for these feelings of condemnation.

It will soon be over, he thought. *I will be home soon, and this day will be forgotten.*

Finally, the chariot stopped. He hurriedly jumped out, purposely ignoring the charioteer's farewell, and he pushed through the garden gate and rushed into his parent's home. Once inside, he dusted himself clean, and the servants greeted him quietly and began attending to him.

"Have my parents started the Sabbath?"

"No, Master Nescius, it is not sunset yet."

"But it is dark as night outside."

"I know, Sir. Some are saying it is because of Jesus that the world has grown dark."

Nescius froze.

Then I did not fall in a trance for a short time—it was for a long time. What has happened to me?

He found his parents distraught. They sat in trances, and fear deeply lined their faces.

"I think they have killed a great prophet, a great messenger," his father said, absorbed in sorrow.

"No, Decius, I think we have killed the Messiah," his mother said with tears flowing from her eyes. "This Man was without sin or fault. We have created trouble for ourselves."

Nescius listened.

He agreed.

He vowed to find out more about this Jesus.

✳

"Nescius!"

An urgent hand pulled him off balance, tearing him from his memories. In his surprise, he dropped his staff and water skin, which crashed on the road and splattered. Its precious liquid washed onto the road just as a small contingent of horsemen, followed by a Roman chariot, rumbled by.

"Nescius, you were nearly killed. Did you not hear me calling you?"

"No Matthias, I did not, my mind was far away."

"My heart is pounding. I truly thought you were leaving this life. What had you so engrossed?"

"That day. The day of the crucifixion. The day of the *titulus* and my fear of missing the Messiah."

"Why do you torment yourself so? Do you not see? You did not miss the Messiah. He is with you and will be with you, now and for all eternity."

"I know, Matthias, but the fear attached to that time is so great that it stays with me. I came so close to ignoring Jesus, and later, on the day of Pentecost, if I had not stopped to listen to Peter's words, I would not have been enlightened by the Spirit. And still later, I almost missed Peter at Cornelius' *villa*. Do you know that I arrived just as Peter entered the *villa?* We had planned to be there hours before Peter's arrival. All the others were there, but Pilate had kept me later than normal. The fact that I just happened upon these things often frightens me."

"But Jesus made you come His way."

"And when Jesus comes again, as He promised, will I be blessed again? Suppose I become as dull and blind as I was that day. Suppose I am not blessed again. What happens then?"

"Your belief in the Master is too great for you to fail to recognize Him. Think of the positive aspects of your relationship with the Master. Think about what has taken place, and not about what might have been. When Jesus comes again, you will know, and you will go to Him."

Matthias watched the young man's face, and for the first time in their journeying together, Matthias envied the youth as he experienced the beauty that sometimes is found in doubt. Matthias had learned that traveling through the detours and bypasses of uncertainties always seemed to unveil deeper truths. Matthias found these roads of doubt and distraction to be places of greater understanding. Upon returning from such a journey, one finds a greater friendship with Jesus. Finding the way to Jesus has made everyone in "The Way" a better believer. He again remembered the doubts that he and the Others had experienced after Jesus had risen from the dead, and he remembered how certain and wise they became after that.

The Apostle smiled understandingly.

"Ah, my brother, it seems this is our day to remember. Perhaps we should ask God why we are being transported back to bygone days."

Still feeling unsettled, Nescius reached for his fallen staff, and he grasped it tightly in his hand.

The two travelers looked at the road, now wet from the wasted water.

Matthias sighed. Looking down the long road at the Judean town in the distance, he said, "It also seems that we are compelled to visit the nearby town for provisions." He placed his hand on his young companion's shoulder, and together they began to walk toward the city.

By early nightfall, they arrived in the town of Phaleaon in the province of Judea, and once in the city they moved quickly through the narrow streets until they came to the house of Abdiel, the tanner, and his wife Devorah, both of whom were Nazarenes. Matthias gently knocked on the heavy wooden door that led to the courtyard of the small house.

From the other side of the door came a timid voice: "Who is it?"

"Abdiel, it is I, Matthias of the Twelve from Cana."

"Do I know you?"

"Yes, I am a friend of *Icthus*," Matthias replied, smiling at the code word used so carefully by the Nazarenes. The door parted, just enough for the occupant of the house to confirm the identity of the visitor, and then it swung wide open. A hand reached for Matthias and roughly pulled him, and then Nescius, inside the small courtyard of the house. Abdiel embraced the two travelers and cautioned them to be quiet. He hurriedly led the men through the courtyard and *atrium* and into the house, and they politely followed him. Devorah rushed to greet the two men and then led them farther into the house.

"When Abdiel heard you were in Judea, he knew you would be coming here," Devorah said loudly as she reached for a bowl of fresh fruit that sat on one of the nearby tables. She held out the bowl, and Nescius quickly reached for an orange.

"You were wise to travel by night," Abdiel said with a small grin on his lips as he directed the two men to nearby seats. Distracted by the offer of the chairs and the need for rest, the two tired men did not catch the full meaning of what Abdiel said.

"You will stay with us tonight. I have made arrangements for you—come sunset tomorrow, you will go to the house of Titos and his wife Portia. They will hide you for tomorrow night."

Both men looked stunned, and Abdiel looked at them with confusion.

"Did you not know that you are being sought?" Abdiel asked, realizing that they were ignorant of the danger surrounding them.

"No," the two travelers said simultaneously.

"Praise God then. It is a blessing you came here first," Devorah uttered in thanksgiving.

"The authorities are looking for you," Abdiel continued. "Matthias, you have many enemies here in Phaleaon and throughout the northern district of Judea."

"What enemies do I have?" the Apostle asked in innocence.

"When you and James bar Zebedee were here last, you received into 'The Way' two young men named Lemuel and Gershom, did you not?"

Matthias smiled; he remembered well the two young men, with their unquenchable zeal to do great things for Jesus.

"Well, those two young men were the sons of the chief Pharisees here in our town. After you departed, those two young men left Judea, along with two other men who also were sons of Pharisees. Last I heard, they were preaching and teaching in the northern part of the Province of Pontus."

"Praise Jesus," Matthias said devoutly.

"Amen," Nescius quickly added.

"The chief Pharisees and the other Pharisees are here. They have received word from an informer who saw you on the road today. The town is crawling with the Pharisees' spies—they are looking for you."

Matthias looked quickly at Nescius. The alarm and concern on his face were unmistakable.

"Then we shall not stay here, for staying here endangers you and Devorah and your daughters," Matthias affirmed. "We will leave under the cover of night and of God's mantle. He will protect us as we travel from here."

"No, you are both exhausted," Devorah insisted. "Stay this night with us and, as Abdiel said, tomorrow night you can travel to the house of Titos. Perhaps things will not be as bad tomorrow as they are tonight."

"No!" Matthias replied with authority in his voice, and Nescius knew they were not staying. "We will not endanger you. We will go and leave you in the safety and blessings of Jesus."

He quickly rose from his seat.

"Come, Nescius. It is the Will of God that we leave our brethren in peace."

Nescius slowly rose. He looked at his two hosts and saw sadness on their faces. He was sure they were hoping for a night of storytelling.

"Here, Brother Matthias, you must take some provisions with you," Devorah declared as she and Abdiel rushed about the house gathering food and drink. She placed them in small cloth bundles and gave them a small wine skin.

Nescius quickly finished eating the orange, silently wishing that he had some sweet bread or a sip of wine to accompany it. He was sure Matthias would be satisfied with having no meal—he was a man of penance. Carrying two small bundles, the men moved to the door. Matthias embraced the couple. He placed his right hand over their heads and called on God to protect and love them. Having completed his blessing, he went through the door and into the darkened street. Nescius had time only to wave to the couple as he realized that they did not know him. He hoped that they did catch his name, which Matthias so casually mentioned. They walked quickly and quietly along the narrow street, staying close to the walls of the houses. They had been rushing through the darkened, shadowed streets for some time when they heard the sounds of marching soldiers. Matthias quickly pushed Nescius into a dark doorway, out of sight, and covered his mouth with his hand.

"Stay. When it is safe, return to Abdiel."

He placed his hand on Nescius' head, as if to bless him, and quickly turned and continued down the street.

Nescius watched Matthias limp away, knowing the pain he was enduring but also recalling his appreciation for discomfort. He watched until Matthias disappeared. Within minutes, Nescius heard loud shouts and heavy quickened steps, then silence, followed by more footsteps that sounded more regimented. As he stole away to the house of Abdiel, he became certain that Matthias had been found and arrested.

The next morning, he was awakened by Abdiel's urgent voice.

"Brother Nescius, we just heard that Matthias has been tried and found guilty of blasphemy and false teaching. He has been condemned to death by stoning."

Nescius sat up quickly. His mind slipped slowly into morning, and when he comprehended what had been said to him, he was jolted into reality. He immediately rose from his mat and began dressing. An empty feeling came over him—the same feeling he had when he heard of his parents' death for the faith.

Oh Divine Master, give me the strength to understand what you are now planning for Your appointed servant, Matthias. Help him to know Your Will...and help me to accept it. He said these words in honesty, but his resolve was weak.

"Matthias will welcome his death in the name of Jesus," he stated to Abdiel. Turning, he looked into his host's face, and as doubt and loneliness slowly permeated his soul, he added, "Now what am I to do?"

"Only let God's Will be done. Continue on to Jerusalem. We have sent word ahead to Titos that you will be coming. Whatever Matthias was to do or say in Jerusalem is now up to you to complete."

"Where is the execution to take place?"

"On the outskirts of the town on the south side...but my Brother, you cannot go there. There is a chance you will be discovered and you will be arrested also. We think it best if you leave now. In the confusion you will be safe—we fear they still seek to harm you."

Nescius smiled.

"The temple jackals cannot harm me. I am a Roman citizen."

Abdiel looked at Nescius with a different understanding of his courage.

"Come. Hurry. I will take you there, but I shall not stay, for if I stay I must cast stones also."

Nescius knew the Jewish laws and customs, so he understood his host's statement.

Together they hurried from the house and rushed through the streets to the town limits, where they found a large crowd standing in a circle and looking down into a pit. In the pit they found Matthias kneeling. The upper part of his tunic was torn. He had red stripes, open wounds, on his back and chest. His hands were clasped in silent prayer. His face was blackened by the many blows he had received, yet it was raised to the heavens nonetheless. In all the blood and scars there was a glow, a snow-white radiance, to his face.

Nescius could feel Matthias' strength and willingness to accept the moment, and he drew peace and solace from this.

Abdiel placed a hand on Nescius' shoulder.

Nescius turned his head slightly to acknowledge the gesture, but Abdiel was gone. Standing nearby was a man whose cloak was tightly wrapped around him; his face was etched in the dark shadows of his hood.

It is daylight, and warm. Why would someone wrap himself so? Nescius asked himself. Suddenly, he felt that he knew this man, for there was something familiar about him.

The man spoke in a deep, raspy voice: "Your friend, Matthias, stands where many of us should be."

Nescius became confused. He moved slightly and strained to look more closely at the man in the hope of identifying him, but he was distracted by the loud, angry voices around him. He heard the call for death mixed with many curses. He watched what he believed was the first rock being thrown. It sailed quickly and forcefully through the air, striking and bouncing off Matthias' head and leaving behind a contusion. He heard Matthias let out a small moan. Another rock hit its mark, then another. Soon, a barrage of stones was soaring through the air, again and again finding their mark, and Nescius felt each stone, each wound. He turned away; he could endure no more. He looked for the stranger, only to discover that he was gone. Confused, he kept his attention away from the stoning. He closed his eyes and silently prayed to Jesus, asking Him to greet his friend. Deep in prayer and with his eyes still closed, he heard a voice cry out, "Father, forgive them, for they know not what they do."

Nescius opened his eyes, certain that the words had been spoken by Matthias, then he saw that the Apostle had fallen to the ground, lifeless. Tears began to come to Nescius' eyes, not out of sorrow, but out of longing to see the greeting that Matthias would receive from the Master.

Stones continued to strike the still body.

He wanted to shout "Stop!" but the word stuck in his throat and choked him.

A man hired by the Pharisees ran down the bank of the pit, and with one strong swing of his drawn sword, he beheaded the dead Matthias. The guard, with a smile on his face, lifted the severed head in the air for all to see. The people cheered.

Suddenly, from his past, Nescius caught the odor of the dungeons of the Fortress of Antonia. As he looked around and saw the faces of glee and excitement, he knew that he was in the presence of evil. This was no place for him; he threw his cloak around himself and walked away, praying and praising Jesus.

EPILOGUE

John walked to the small table and picked a dried date from a small bowl. He would have enjoyed having some honey to dip the date in, but there was none within reach. He was abruptly distracted from his small desire when he heard noise and excitement flowing through the house. For the first time in a long while, the Apostles were coming together. From the other room he heard the voices of Simon Peter, James the Little, Andrew, Bartholomew, and Philip. Their voices were excited and happy as they compared notes and discussed their missions. Their talk of mission frustrated him—he still longed to travel far and wide, but he could not because of his duty to Lady Mary. His travels were diminutive in comparison, yet he was pleased that they were spreading the Word so successfully. Laughter soon broke out among the Apostles, and John smiled. It was good to hear the sound of their laughter.

Lady Mary, his mother Salome, his sister Naomi, Lady Mary's sister-in-law Mary Cleophas, Joann Chusa, and Susanna were busy preparing the evening meal. Other Apostles were expected by nightfall. They expected Matthias shortly, and they heard that Matthew was making his way also. Paul of Tarsus, Joseph bar Nabas, whom many called Barnabas, and others were expected in two days' time. They, like the Apostles, had been summoned to Jerusalem for a meeting of great importance. The question of circumcision of the Gentiles before Baptism had become a major stumbling block for those in "The Way." Much to John's dismay, he found that some of the Apostles were still suspicious of Paul. They seemed reluctant to let go of their distrust. In John's eyes, it was all unfounded. He was looking forward to seeing Paul face to face for the first time.

As John walked through the house to the back courtyard, he passed the table that he was using as a desk. He stopped just long enough to see his latest written words: "And Jesus said, 'Pick up thy yoke….'" He smiled at the words, for he remembered when they were spoken. Suddenly, the sound of Jesus' voice rang in his ears. He paused and reflected. He was always quick to remember Jesus, and lately he was equally satisfied that he could recall more readily some of Jesus' sayings. This inspired him to write more and more. He continued reminiscing contentedly until the voices and clatter of cooking diminished to low rumbles. He felt an unsettling feeling come over him. This feeling seemed to come when he needed to be alone. It meant that something inside needed to be settled, but, at that moment, he could not find anything in need of settling. He walked out of the house and into the small garden cared for by Lady Mary. It was a bright open day with an unblemished sky that wrapped warmly around the world. Off in the distance, he heard the cry of a hawk and looked up. He loved, yet feared, the hawk. He loved it for its ability to glide far and wide over God's world, yet it was a killer that destroyed smaller birds. Just then he saw a white dove—a dove so white that it radiated against the azure sky. It was flying in the direction of the hawk. His heart jumped with fear for the safety of the dove, but for some strange reason this dove was flying at great speed and higher than any bird he had ever seen. It continued to soar and was soon in the blue grip of the smooth sky, and then it was gone.

He then became aware of the sudden silence of the house.

Something is wrong, he thought.

He heard Joann Chusa of the house of Herod talking to someone, then he heard excitement and quick movements. He rose and walked quickly into the house. After his eyes adjusted to the dim interior, he saw his friend Nescius standing in the middle of the room, surrounded by everyone. Cheerfully, they all embraced him and greeted him warmly. John walked to Nescius and embraced him, and he immediately became aware of his lean body.

"Where is Matthias?" James the Little asked freely as he looked behind Nescius.

Nescius' smiling face became serious.

"He will not be coming."

"Busy converting or punishing himself," Bartholomew of Cana said of his old townsman with a wide, playful smile on his face.

"Neither, my Brother." Nescius looked briefly at the faces of the Apostles surrounding him. "Yesterday, Matthias was arrested, tried, and condemned to death." He felt a small lump in his throat. "He is with the Master in glory."

A stillness immediately came over the room as the Apostles became aware of this new loss.

John's thoughts went to Judas, whose portion this should have been, and he closed his eyes, allowing the pain to come over him.

"What happened?" Peter inquired softly, and Nescius related the preceding day's events.

"Where did this take place?" Philip asked somberly.

"Outside of Phaleaon."

"Ah, of course, Judea. The place of Judas," Peter said prophetically. Immediately, Nescius remembered: *Judas, of course, the man by my side. It was he!*

"Let us pray for our Brother Matthias," Peter continued, "and with happiness—he is again in the sight of the Master and is truly blessed. Surely, he is helping to prepare a place for us."

Each of the men looked at Peter, believing his words and foreseeing similar fates. They closed their eyes and prayed. They all remembered Matthias: as a friend, but above all, as a servant of Jesus.

Later that night, long after Nescius had poured out his heart in praise of Matthias' works, miracles, and friendship, and long after he had told the Apostles of the many Gentiles that came to the Master, John pulled him aside.

"You have changed much since last we saw you, Brother. Your faith and love have grown, and from the leanness of your body I see that you have learned self-denial."

Nescius smiled in agreement. "And patience."

This time John smiled.

"Peter is going to ask you to return to Armenia. Are you willing to go back?"

"Yes," Nescius replied.

"He will probably send someone with you."

They became silent.

"You must be tired. I should let you rest, but I feel prompted—forced, even—to ask you a question."

"What is it, John?"

"When Matthias was dying, did he say any last words?"

Nescius thought for a moment, and he soon remembered the words he had heard.

"Yes. I heard, 'Father, forgive them, for they know not what they do.'" The words reverberated in his mind.

"Ah, yes. The words of Jesus on the Cross."

A chill erupted in Nescius' body as he fully grasped how great a servant of the Lord Matthias was. At the same time, the voice he heard at the stoning lingered in his mind. He listened to the tone of the voice, and for one moment, all of time, life, and creation stopped for Nescius.

The voice he heard was not that of Matthias.

Tears of joy flooded his eyes.

Finally.

Now.

He heard the voice of Jesus.

CHAPTER THREE:

JAMES BAR ALPHAEUS OF CAPERNAUM

PROLOGUE

John spent day after day remembering all that Jesus did. After years of gathering his material, he began to connect the thoughts and incidents, and he started writing them on *papyrus*. He still was not sure that he was the one to write an account of Jesus, but many now believed that this was something he had to do. Why they believed this he did not know, though James bar Alphaeus had told him, "You were the youngest, and you watched things differently."

He heard that Mark, who at one time had traveled with Paul but now accompanied Peter, had started a chronicle. It seemed that he was gathering information from Peter and writing with Peter's help.

How unlike shy Mark to do such a thing, he commented to himself.

Equally surprising was the rumor that Matthew had begun a similar undertaking. John heard that Matthew had gathered the notes written by the Apostles and disciples during their many discussions of Jesus. He was certain that Matthew was using these notes for his account.

Now there is someone who should write about Jesus. He was a relative of the Master, and he has the proper schooling. John looked at the *papyrus* on the table before him, and he slumped in discouragement on the small wooden bench on which he was seated. *Could anything be so challenging and yet so compelling as an empty papyrus? What must I do to start this study? O Master, be my guide. Help me to do what You wish.* He looked again at the scrolls. *Things seem to come easy to me once I get started. My trouble is getting started—still, I have no beginning to this account. Where do I begin telling the story of the Son of Man? The Son of God?* He pushed the *papyrus* away from him. *There will be no work today.* He looked to the window and into the skies, marveling at the beauty of creation. *My brother James would have no problem with this task.* He closed his eyes. *James, and you also Matthias, speak to Jesus and ask Him to enlighten me. Even though I feel unworthy of such a duty, there is something deep inside me telling me to do this in order to complete a cycle. Ask the Master to help me find what He wants me to find and to say what He wants me to say—and pray that I do it properly.*

He rose from his desk and walked to the small basin of water on a nearby table. Rolling up his sleeves, he gathered a small amount of water in his cupped hands and splashed his face. He reached for a cloth and wiped his face, paying particular attention to his thick black beard.

Lord, forgive me, for today I am having trouble stepping out with boldness. Perhaps tomorrow I will be able to discover what is hidden so well inside me. Today I seem to be preoccupied.

He surprised himself, for he did not realize that he was preoccupied until that very moment. Now, with this realization, he sighed deeply and said aloud to no one but himself, "For today, we face another grave problem, Paul of Tarsus."

✳

His arrival was seen as a major problem, and some dreaded his visit. Many believed this little man, with his fiery reputation, was too adventurous, aggressive, and ambitious. They felt that he presumed too much, and assumed even more. He had embellished the authority that Peter and the Apostles gave him when first he presented himself to them after his conversion. Some believed strongly that his enthusiasm was excessive; his teaching to the Gentiles was seen as an attack on the leadership in Jerusalem.

Prior to Paul's expected arrival, Peter, James bar Alphaeus, and John bar Zebedee met with several groups and listened to what they had to say. Each group had its own agenda that it wanted to present for consideration. One group was composed of the Pharisees who were of "The Way" and who knew Paul. They believed that Jesus was merely an extension of the Jewish faith and that therefore the Jewish customs and laws were to be followed. They strongly attacked Paul's actions in Syria, where he accepted Gentiles. They were called Judaizers. They sent representatives to Antioch in Syria to stop what they regarded as open sacrilege against the "new" Jewish movement. They believed that only Jews should be included in "The Way," and they condemned the idea of Gentile converts. Paul, they affirmed, baptized Gentiles without authority. Paul had converted these Gentiles without laying on them the duties of Judaism. To become valid, Gentiles had to practice the purifications and penitential rites of Judaism, and to this the Judaizers added, "They must accept the covenant of Abraham with circumcision before they can accept Jesus as the promised Jewish Messiah."

Another group spoke of the biggest problem facing everyone—Paul of Tarsus. They attacked the man as a troublemaker who was insensitive to traditions and to the authority of the Apostles. He was an outsider, not one of the Twelve; his authority was from the Twelve, who in turn received their authority from Jesus the Christ. Another group was still distrustful of Paul, in spite of all of his successes. Fourteen years had not changed their feelings. They constantly reminded the Apostles of the many people who had been dragged from their homes, put in chains, and thrown in jails because of Paul. He would always be the Pharisee—the killer of Stephen and others. Some believed that Paul was a spy for the High Priest and the Sanhedrin. They doubted his "conversion" story, and Paul's verbal attacks on "The Way" confirmed their suspicions. He blatantly challenged the authority and wisdom of the Apostles and the Jerusalem leaders. Others simply believed that he was a man of great ambition on a campaign to strengthen his position in "The Way." They resented the fact that he called himself an "Apostle." He did this without following the criteria of Apostleship set by Peter—those who were at the beginning "with the ministry of John the Baptizer, until the day that the Master was taken up from us, and...a witness with us of His Resurrection." He was not an example of the humility of Jesus. Some who were fearful of change viewed Paul's actions as a major crisis; needing more support in their criticism of Paul, they sent word out to many believers. They told the followers that Paul was undermining the Will of Christ.

So long before Paul's arrival, there was much intrigue and distrust.

For days and weeks, these many views were examined by the "three pillars"—Peter, James Alphaeus, and John. Finally, they stopped listening and decided to address the issue, but after discussing the problem among themselves, they found that they also were in disarray.

James was in many ways fearful of Paul. He saw him as a renovator of the Master's teachings and believed that he had to be brought in line with the ideas of Judaism. After all, the Master was a Jew and He lived the way of the covenant. He reminded Peter and John that Jesus had come "to perfect the Torah, not to destroy it," and he added, "All those who came to 'The Way' had to become Jewish first, for it was written that the whole world would become Jewish." Finally, he reminded his brother Apostles of the time Jesus sent them out two by two. He had told them not to go to the Gentiles or to the Samaritans, but only to the "lost sheep of Israel."

John believed that much of what was being said and done was instigated by jealousy of Paul and his success. He liked Paul; he had never met him, but he liked what he heard of him: his fearlessness, his devotion, and above all his desire to serve the Master.

"True, he is daring and innovative in showing that God is the God of all people. But who are we to say that what Paul does is not from the Master? Perhaps Jesus, seeing that we Twelve are not doing enough, enlightened Paul to lead us in the right direction." John reminded Peter and James of the time he spoke to Jesus about those who were driving out demons in Jesus' name, and of Jesus' reply: "Forbid him not, for he that is not against you, is for you." Then he reminded them that Jesus had commanded them to "Go and baptize all nations...."

Peter simply believed that it was wise to listen to what Paul had to say. "If God wills for us to see things in a different light, then we must do the Will of God, but for the moment we should remain cautious.

"It is imperative that all sides be heard in council. We must listen before coming to conclusions, and above all we need to pray for guidance. Let us not close our hearts before we have the chance to change them. Let us not forget that Jesus cured the centurion's servant, who was a Gentile, and that He helped the Samaritan woman at the well. Consider what that Samaritan did for the Master. She went into her village and told the people, and many were converted."

Then Peter became silent, for in his heart he knew that what Paul was doing was correct. In like manner, he had accepted the Gentile centurion Cornelius and his Gentile friends into "The Way"—he had even been blessed with a vision that guided him in this course of action. He remembered also the deacon Philip preaching in Samaria to the eunuch. He remembered these things, letting them rest silently in his heart. He knew that James and John spoke truly and wisely. They were both right, but he felt strongly that times were changing—that Jesus was showing them a new way. For this reason, he withheld total condemnation of Paul. He wondered if the former Pharisee from Tarsus had been blessed with a vision similar to his, and perhaps this vision inspired Paul to seek converts among the outside world.

Peter then stated with conviction, "I believe that word should go out to our fellow Apostles to call them back to Jerusalem, and we should hear what they have to say. Be not surprised if you find that they also have baptized Gentiles without circumcision. Let me suggest that we wait for

Paul and then evaluate his arguments—if the Holy Spirit has spoken to Paul, as He did to us, we will again be guided by the voice of the Spirit."

Peter knew that a council would receive special guidance from the Spirit, the Enlightener, Who would surely come upon them. Nevertheless, he felt that there was no happy solution. *Some will not be satisfied…a separation is in the making.* Seeing that Peter's suggestion was wise and not confrontational, James and John decided to let Paul have his time in council. They would listen, relying on the Master and His Spirit to guide them, and they would follow His Light. Word was sent to Paul and his companions asking them to return to Jerusalem. Then the Apostles were called back to Jerusalem, and when all had arrived, they assembled and prayed.

Soon, the arrival of Paul and his companions was only days away.

They waited and braced themselves.

✻

Paul arrived with several companions. Among them were Joseph bar Nabas, who was sometimes called Barnabas and who was known to many in Jerusalem, two Gentiles, a young Greek physician named Luke from the city of Antioch, and young Titus, who was of noble birth from the Greek island of Crete.

When James saw Paul enter the room, he was somewhat surprised at how he had changed. He had grown haggard and had lost some of the vitality in his walk.

Quickly James thought, *No doubt the touch of persecution and the trials of preaching have taken their toll on him.*

Peter walked briskly to Paul and embraced him. He held Paul long in this embrace, for Peter was moved by Paul's physical appearance. Peter was shocked and humbled. He could imagine the lack of sleep, the hunger, and the suffering that Paul had endured.

Paul, smothered by the massiveness of Peter and captured by the meaning of their long embrace, slowly fell into a slight repose. He felt an understanding and an appreciation from Peter, and this soothed him to the point of calming some of his anger for the Judaizers.

John was the most surprised of all. He had never seen Paul; he had expected to see a giant of a man with big powerful features, but instead he saw a diminutive man with a light-red, stringy beard. The red hair on his head was thinning—in fact, he was nearly bald. His eyes were tired and red, no doubt from many sleepless nights. His face was small, lined, and haggard. When John embraced Paul, he felt Paul's frailty, and yet he sensed the Spirit of *Adonai* in this man. For this man to do what he was doing with what he had been given was, in John's thinking, true proof that the Master had called him and that he was of Jesus.

Everyone noticed that the greeting between Paul and James was somewhat cool. Paul had come to believe that James and his orthodox ideas were at the root of the problem and that this was the reason for the assembly. Many of the Judaizers were close associates of James, and it was James who had dispatched Jews to Antioch to demand circumcision. All this led Paul to conclude that James was one Apostle that was not on his side.

Paul slowly greeted the other Apostles in a warm and congenial way, then they all sat for prayer and the Breaking of the Bread. Later, they exchanged stories of their missions.

John listened, absorbing all that was being said. When his frustration grew unbearable, he moved away from all the enthusiasm and went off to pray, for he was beginning to feel envy in his heart. He also saw that all this talk was only a way of avoiding the problem that had prompted this gathering.

JAMES BAR ALPHAEUS, OF CAPERNAUM

He was a man of history and heritage. If anyone asked him what was the one thing in life he loved, he would tell them, "Jerusalem," and then as a quick afterthought he would add, "and family." To James, Jerusalem was more than the Jewish faith. It was more than the buildings, whether magnificent or in shambles. It was more than the surrounding arid, rough, beautiful countryside. It was even more than the Holy of Holies.

Jerusalem was the promise of hope for all the world.

Jerusalem was to be the center of power for all mankind.

Jerusalem was to cause the world to change and become better.

He did not know at what age he came to these conclusions, but he knew these ideas had been his for many years. Perhaps he came to these beliefs when, as a young boy, he would recite the *Alenu*, often called the "Prayer of Joshua." This prayer was recited as the last prayer of the Jewish daily liturgy. The words of this prayer, which he believed with all his heart, conveyed his idea of what Jerusalem would be to the world: "...when all the children of flesh invoke Thy Name; when all the wicked of the earth shall be turned unto Thee. And Thou shall be King over them speedily forever and aye...and on that day the Lord shall be One and His

Name be One." As far back as James could remember, he would add to the end of the *Alenu* a petition that this great event, in which all become One with Jerusalem, would occur in his lifetime.

His belief in the importance of the family was as compelling as his belief in Jerusalem, for it had been instilled in him from early childhood by his father, Alphaeus bar Yakob Heli, who desired to keep the family together and to honor their long heritage. He had been carefully taught to place family and family pride above all other secular things. Alphaeus had often repeated to James his firm belief that their family would some-day become famous in the eyes of the Jewish nation.

Alphaeus was the oldest of three sons. After his father, Yakob, died at a young age, Alphaeus took immediate control of the lives of his two younger brothers, Cleophas and Yosef, even though he and his wife Myriam had a growing family. Being much older than his brothers, Alphaeus had the authority to act as their father, and he labored persis-tently to keep his brothers together as a family. He made certain that they would continue to receive education in Jewish family life. They were schooled in the *Tanakh*, the written word, and especially in the *Nevi'im*, the Prophets. To ensure their independence, he had them schooled in their father's trade of carpentry. When they were of age, he began making arrangements for them to marry. Just before Alphaeus completed these arrangements, he suddenly became ill and died, leaving his wife, Myriam, also called Mary, with his children: James, Joses, Simeon, and Levi. Cleophas, Alphaeus' young brother, in order to protect Alphaeus' fam-ily and because Mary Alphaeus was still a young woman, took her as his wife; a year later, they had their daughter, Salome, and after several more years, they had a son whom they named Jude Thaddeus. Continuing the work of his brother, Cleophas held the family close and persisted in the education of his nephews and his children, and he started making arrangements for his younger brother Yosef Joseph bar Yakob to marry Myriam Mary bat Yoachim of Nazareth who also was of the house of David. Soon after this marriage, another nephew, Jesus, was born. At an early age, the two brothers Joseph and Cleophas noticed an instant bond between their sons Jesus and James. Whenever the families were together, James would immediately go to Jesus' side and cling to Him like a bee to an open flower, and it was ordinary to see James showing Jesus how to play or how to conduct himself in the synagogue or in the village. It was a bond that was based on a big brother-little brother relationship; this relationship became especially apparent when Jesus was lost in Jerusalem at the age of twelve.

When Jesus was lost, Mary believed that Jesus was with Joseph's family because of the close relationship Jesus had with Cleophas' children, while Joseph believed that Jesus was with Mary's family because of the strong bond between Mary and her son. When it was discovered that Jesus was with neither parent nor family, Joseph's and Mary's families began a frantic search.

Joseph, Mary, Cleophas, and eighteen-year-old James began to backtrack to Jerusalem, while Mary's family continued on to Nazareth in case someone had found Jesus and had taken Him back to their town.

Cleophas was moved by the concern displayed by his son, James. The boy was constantly suggesting places his cousin could be. As pleased as he was with his son's concern, he could not understand the urgency and distress exhibited by Joseph and Mary. He would have expected a great deal of worry over the loss of a child, but their reaction was surprisingly intense. No one was able to console them. They clung to each other in profound sorrow, and for some unknown reason they found comfort only in the deep, unspoken concern that shone from their eyes. Known to them alone was the knowledge that they had lost the Son of God. The couple remained in this state for three days. Cleophas felt that they were sharing some secret about Jesus. He became extremely curious, and the more he observed, the more he remembered the extra-special care they extended to Jesus. For reasons he could not explain, he found himself comparing them to Adam and Eve on the day they lost Paradise. He resolved to speak to his brother about his observations.

When they arrived in Jerusalem, James insisted they go to the Temple. Cleophas was surprised that James would make such a suggestion, and he was even more surprised at James' insistence. James appeared certain that Jesus would be found there. When they arrived at the Temple, they found Jesus in Solomon's Porch, standing by a long table with scrolls and *papyri* thrown on it. A group of frantic scribes searched for references as another larger group of scribes and teachers sat listening—mesmerized by what Jesus was saying regarding the Messiah and what the Prophets had said about the Messiah. Among those seated at the table were the aged and kind Rabbi Hillel, his son Rabbi Shimon, Hillel's young grandson Gamaliel, and the gruff Rabbi Shammai. James was baffled when he saw all these learned men so captivated by the words of Jesus.

With relief and profound joy radiating from her lovely, weary face, Mary walked to her Son and gently reprimanded Him.

Cleophas and James watched in astonishment at the softness of her reprimand and at the silence of Joseph.

Jesus frowned, as if confused by Mary's reprimand, and with filial devotion He asked, "How is it you sought Me? Did you not know that I must be about My Father's business?"

Mary turned and looked at Joseph. The expression on her face asked a question, and then it turned to sadness; Joseph's eyes filled with tears, and he lowered his head.

Cleophas and James looked on in confusion, deeply troubled by Joseph's reaction.

Hours later, they were on the road home. During this journey, Cleophas overheard James severely admonishing Jesus for His lack of concern.

"How could You be so indifferent to Your parents? You claim to know so much—why did You not have the common sense to tell them and all the family what You were doing?"

"I lost time."

"That is a weak answer, Jesus." James turned and walked away, then he stopped and turned to his cousin. "We were worried sick. We were scared and frightened."

"I know."

"You know we love You and would do anything to help You."

"I know."

"Promise never to do such a thing again."

"The next time I leave, James, you will know less." Jesus smiled.

"Why do You talk so often in riddles?"

"Because it is not time."

James walked to Jesus and embraced him, but James quickly jumped away, as if electrified by some strong surge of energy. Jesus brought James back to Him, and holding him tightly He whispered, "My dear brother James, someday you will know Me and love Me more. Until then, hold fast to being My brother."

From that time on, James watched Jesus more closely and he saw Jesus become more distant and mysterious. Joseph's son Jesus had changed, and Cleophas worried that someday these two brothers would not remain friendly.

Sometime later, Cleophas isolated his brother Joseph and voiced his curiosities. His younger brother simply said, "When the time is right, Jesus will make known what you need to know."

Soon after, Joseph became ill; as he lay dying, he told Cleophas of the dream he had experienced before his marriage to Mary, and he insisted that Cleophas tell no one.

Upon Joseph's death, Cleophas, being the sole surviving son of Yakob, became the patriarch of an extended family that included his brother's son, Jesus.

In the early years after Joseph's death, Cleophas remained close to Jesus and Mary. The two families visited often, and these visits would sometimes last for weeks or even months. At these times, Cleophas would draw his family together and instruct them in the art of woodworking and in being good Hebrews, as his brothers and father did before him. As time passed, he began to notice that the bond between Jesus and James was changing. James constantly challenged Jesus with questions and conjectures that produced long and deep discussions between them. Though Cleophas considered it beautiful that the two men were debating the most profound points of the Holy Book, and he prided himself on knowing that they were his kinsmen, he often had to be the arbitrator in their debates; this disconcerted him, for he seemed to be less knowledgeable than they were.

As the years passed, the visits from Mary and Jesus became less frequent. Soon, Jesus became a stranger, and the world began to change as everyone made their own way through life.

Joses and Simon often worked as part-time fishermen when carpentry work was slow. They had grown devout in their faith. Their beliefs were simple—no complications or controversies—and they did what was expected of them. Levi was a dutiful Jew who did only what he had to do, and nothing more. He did not find carpentry to his liking, so he searched out work as a fisherman, and eventually he became a tax collector, a publican. This caused a great upheaval in the family, and soon Levi was ostracized from the family and the Temple. He later became known as Matthew, and his brother James became Levi's greatest critic.

Jude Thaddeus was the youngest and, therefore, the least controlled. He had more freedom, was a bit of a rebel, and was slightly spoiled. He questioned everything, especially the family's treatment of Levi, and this caused him to be frequently reprimanded by James.

For a time, James worked as a civil servant for the Temple officials, but he did not enjoy the politics and intrigues of the Temple's daily operations. For a short time, he was interested in the Zealots, but their violent ways eventually deterred him. He returned to his family and began to live the life of a traditionalist. Cleophas believed for a time that James would become a priest of the Temple. As James became more conservative in his views, Jesus became more at ease and more comfortable in His ways. The Holy Book came easily to Jesus. He seemed to have a different understanding of the Book; He had a wisdom that came from something deep inside Him. It was a wisdom accented by compassion and flexibility, and because of this He was constantly at odds with the teachers in the synagogue. James considered his cousin's challenges and debates with the synagogue officials to be disrespectful, and this bothered James greatly.

As Jesus grew taller, James remained short, and this physical contrast accentuated their intellectual differences.

Jesus drew people to Him with His calming voice, His frequent smiles. His warmth attracted many people, and especially the needy. James, on the other hand, was rigid and practical, and at times harsh. His attempts to change Jesus' thinking often developed into open rebukes.

James recognized Jesus' fervent belief in the Almighty and marveled at His understanding of the Holy Writings, yet, in private, Jesus would condemn the rulers of the Temple for their obsessive dietary and purification laws and strict observance of the Sabbath. Jesus said that the leaders were becoming too legalistic and were reinterpreting the Laws of the Almighty. This talk made James very uneasy.

In defense of His thinking, Jesus would say with a smile, "*Adonai* is above the law; after all He wrote it."

James became greatly bothered when Jesus would refer to *Adonai* as *Abba,* Daddy. James felt this was a bit too familiar, too casual in respect to the Holy Name of the Almighty.

In reply, Jesus would smile and say softly, "My dear brother, I mean no harm, only the truth. He is *Abba* to all, for He calls us to Him as a loving Father does. Just listen, and you will hear His call."

James was not swayed. Respect for the name of the Almighty was paramount to all Jews. So sacred was the name to the Chosen People that pronouncing it was prohibited. Instead of saying "God," the Jews respectfully referred to Him as "The Name," or more often, "The Only Name," "The Glorious Name." According to the Rabbinical traditions, verbalization of the Name ceased around the time of Alexander the Great. It became a common practice to refer to the Almighty as *Adonai,* which meant Lord, or as *Elohim,* which in its plural form implied plurality of dignity, status, or magnitude. Even when the name of God was to be written, the scribe was obliged to stop and wash before writing the Name. The name "God" was pronounced only on the Day of Atonement in the sanctuary of the Temple, at which time the High Priest would speak the Name; even then, it was spoken in a low, reverent voice.

There were numerous stories and legends of Jews who were threatened with death or promised endless riches in attempts to make them pronounce the Name of God. Few did—they preferred death and poverty to misusing the Name of God. Consequently, it was incomprehensible that someone would refer to God as *Abba*. It was too familiar, too personal—no one had ever referred to the Holy One in such a personal or familiar term. So the disagreements between the two cousins continued over the years. Cleophas looked on with delight, for he knew of no other family who had such debates.

✳

"James, you must come with us the next time we go," his brother Joses said with much excitement.

"Why?"

"Because many believe this man is our new prophet," Joses replied with continued excitement.

"We have not had a prophet in over four hundred years. Why would *Adonai* send one to us now?"

"Because we need one now," Simeon said, amazed that his oldest brother did not realize this.

"This man is filled with great fire and has attacked Herod by calling him an adulterer." As an afterthought and with much caution, Joses whispered, "He has also attacked the Pharisees and Sadducees. He called them 'a brood of vipers.'"

James looked at his two younger brothers with mixed emotions. By condemning the Idumaean King and consequently being disliked by the Herodians, this new prophet had James' admiration, for he had long ago lost respect for the half-Jew King Herod and the semi-religious Herodian Roman sympathizers. However, denouncing the Pharisees and Sadducees was, in James' thinking, profanity and blasphemy.

"This prophet sounds interesting. What is his name?"

"John bar Zachary, or John the Baptist," Joses said, pleased that his oldest brother was interested.

James walked away, and Joses looked at Simeon, who also seemed sure that they had captured their brother's attention.

"John bar Zachary? Do you know if his father Zachary was at one time a priest of the Temple who burnt offerings of incense at the Golden Altar?"

"Yes, I believe so," Joses answered, slightly puzzled by the question.

"Yes, I have heard some say that his father did this once," Simeon added with more certainty.

"Then he is related to our brother Jesus bar Yosef, the son of our father's brother."

James turned and looked at his brothers, whose faces expressed their great surprise.

"You know, I remember father once saying that the birth of Zachary's son was a strange thing. I will have to ask father to explain further." As he realized that his brothers were stunned by this news, he became pleased. Continuing he said, "Being the oldest always has some advantages, one of which is knowing family histories. Tell me what else this John has done that makes you think he is a prophet."

The two younger men began telling James of John's condemnation of Herod's wife, Herodias, and of his call for her repentance—of his call for everyone's repentance. Finally, they told him of the many people who had been helped by John, and how he had guided them in giving up sin and seeking forgiveness.

"There are hundreds who come to see him; they confess their sins as he purifies and baptizes them on the banks of the Jordan River," Joses stated as James showed more signs of interest.

"He insists that he is only a forerunner, a messenger, of One who will follow him and baptize with the Spirit, One who will truly wash away all sins, One who will baptize with more than water," Simeon added.

"Yes, John has said that One greater and mightier than he is to come. This other person will be the Anointed One."

"The Anointed One?"

"Yes, he has said that he is not the Anointed One."

"Where is this John, now?"

"At the lower part of the Jordan," Joses answered happily.

"At Bethany beyond the Jordan," Simeon added with equal joy.

James walked further from his brothers and went to the window of his father's house. Looking out into the dark night, he felt his heart beating against his chest. *Could this be what we have prayed for all these years?*

"When next we go to Judea, we will seek John at Bethany," James announced as he silently repeated again his petition at the end of his *Alenu.*

Weeks later, as the three sons of Alphaeus returned from Jerusalem after the Feast of the Giving of the Law, or Pentecost, they decided they would go down to the Jordan and find John the Baptizer. On the river banks, they found swarms of people listening to John preach about repentance. James was immediately captured by John's thunderous words; they vibrated in James' very soul. He was overcome with the strength of his voice, which tugged at him. He listened to John and eventually discerned that this man was truly from the Almighty. In a rare moment of impetuosity, he joined those going into the Jordan. He needed to be purified. His brothers timidly joined him. The three men stood silently in the heat of a cloud-filled day. Expecting the chill of cool water, James stepped into the river. To his surprise, the water was warm. Finally, he stood before John, and John hesitated. James thought for a moment that John was going to declare him unworthy—too great a sinner to be purified. He felt himself grow weak amidst the shame of rejection.

The two men stood looking at each other for a long time.

Why is he hesitating?

He searched John's eyes for some reason for the delay. He felt that John wanted to say something to him. Perhaps he recognized him. Just as James was about to remind him who he was, the prophet smiled. The smile that came gradually across John's lips—a rare occurrence for the fiery prophet—confounded James further. John closed his eyes, and with the smile still on his lips, he placed his hand on James' head, and with great care he guided him into the warm Jordan. After James emerged and cleared his eyes of water, he looked long at John, who stared back at him. James felt that John was holding a great secret. But James became distracted, for he felt something strong come over him; it weakened him. He staggered to the shore of the river. After his brothers joined him, the three walked further along the shore, and they stood together, drying in the hot breeze. The more they dried, the cleaner and the more different they felt.

James felt Simeon's nudge, but it didn't matter—James saw Jesus bar Yosef at the same time as Simeon did. He had the urge to call out to Jesus, but he froze when he saw the look on Jesus' face.

John the Baptist stopped what he was doing and searched the shores of the Jordan. When he saw Jesus walking into the river, John's face opened wide, and a look of great discovery overcame him.

James detected a hesitation from John, similar to the hesitation he had received. James watched as the two men stood in the river for a long time. After they exchanged words that only a few could hear, John reluctantly and carefully escorted Jesus into the water. Everyone watching these strange happenings seemed to be as confused as James was.

Jesus emerged from the water with his eyes open and skyward. His robe was as white as the snows on the highest mountains around Judea. His face was aglow with some undetectable light. Suddenly, the sun beamed and radiated, and the clouds opened. Jesus stepped from the river, His arms spread wide. His head was lowered, and all the rays of the sun seemed to rest upon Him. James looked to the sky, wondering where the many clouds had gone. The sunlight was so bright that he was nearly blinded.

Then he heard John say, "I saw the Spirit coming down, as a dove from heaven, and He remained upon Him. Behold the Lamb of God. Behold He Who comes to take away the sins of the world."

James felt a stir in those around him and heard their mumblings, but he decided to ignore them—he was too engrossed in Jesus.

Then he heard John sing aloud, "Come, let us praise the Lord with joy; let us joyfully sing to God our Savior. Let us come before His presence with thanksgiving; and make a joyful noise to Him...."

He looked back at John, and to his surprise he found him kneeling in the Jordan with his head and arms raised to the heavens.

When James looked back for Jesus, He was gone. None of them had seen Him go; none had called out to Him.

James left the Jordan perplexed at all that had happened, and he wondered what all these things meant.

✳

Two months later, Cleophas ordered Simeon and Jude to Nazareth with some provisions for Jesus' mother, Mary Yosef. James asked why his father had done such a thing, and he was told that Jesus had disappeared. Days later, James discovered that Jesus had gone into the desert. He could not understand what Jesus had done. To leave His mother in Nazareth and be missing for forty days and nights was unthinkable. Then, when James heard that He had returned to Galilee and begun a life of teaching and preaching, he was dumbfounded.

"How could Jesus leave His mother and go off like that? No son should do such a thing to the woman who bore Him, and who relies on Him for safety and livelihood," James stated to his mother with disappointment and anger in his heart.

"James, ask Mary Yosef," his mother Mary Cleophas said with a smile.

"Has He lost all His senses?"

"James, ask Mary Yosef," his mother said again.

"And you, Mother, why have you not said anything to Him?"

"James, ask Mary Yosef," his mother insisted.

"Why should I ask her?"

"Because perhaps Jesus has spoken to His mother," his brother Simeon answered plainly.

"Or perhaps our mother does not have an answer for you," his brother Jude suggested with a wry smile.

James looked at his two brothers with irritation. Ignoring them, he looked at his mother and asked, "And why has not my father said something?"

"Because Mary Yosef has given your father the reason, and he understands."

"Then I do not understand Mary Yosef's willingness to accept her Son's neglect."

"Well, apparently our sister *does* understand, for she knows her Son far better than anyone else on this earth."

James drew in a deep breath of frustration.

Mary Cleophas looked long at her son. She knew he meant well and that his concerns for his family were sincere, but still she could not understand his strong objection to Jesus' leaving Mary. She shook her head and said to her oldest son, "Sometimes, James, you are too exact. We all have a mission in life. What Jesus is doing is His mission. Try to be more understanding."

"I cannot. Neglect of one's parents is not correct in the eyes of our people or in the eyes of *Adonai*."

Again, Mary Cleophas shook her head in disbelief. She knew that he would never be satisfied with her explanation, so she decided to let him search his own mind for what he needed.

✳

"Father, how could you allow Jesus to go off and begin preaching like a prophet when you know He should be tending to the needs of His mother?" James asked his father several days after speaking to his mother.

"Because it is the will of His mother, and because my brother Joseph once told me that Jesus would someday leave to do what He is doing."

"I cannot understand this. Do you believe that Jesus is a prophet?"

Cleophas looked away from his son and into the distance. He pensively stroked his long, graying beard and softly said, "Who knows?"

"Well I do not believe it!" James retorted.

His father looked at him and smiled.

"My son, you above all others should understand how well Jesus knows the *Torah* and the *Nevi'im*. You have argued with Him many times. You have to admit, He is very knowledgeable."

"This is true, but it has nothing to do with what He is doing. He is making a fool of Himself. He goes about the countryside, teaching things that are not in agreement with the doctrine of the Leaders. Some of the teachers of the Law have questioned me and asked me to explain Him. He is proving to be an embarrassment to our family."

"Have you heard Him teach?"

"No, but I have been told that He teaches in the way of His cousin, John bar Zachary."

"How do you know what the Baptizer has said?" Cleophas tilted his head and looked at his son with a new interest. "Have you heard John speak?"

"Well, yes," James said in a low tone as he walked away from his father, trying to avoid his questioning look. He continued, "Many times have Joses, Simeon, and I been with John."

"Tell me, is John of *Elohim?*"

James turned and looked at his father. With uncertainty in his voice he said, "Perhaps?" Then, with a degree of assurance, he added, "Yes. He has said nothing unorthodox."

"And you got this from listening to John?"

James nodded with some satisfaction.

"Then go and listen to Jesus, and see if you find Him the same."

"But…."

Cleophas got up from his chair and raised his right hand to signal silence. As he walked from the room, he said, "Sometimes, James, we must face things that are hard to understand. We must accept in faith alone what is not understood. Try to be wise, not merely correct. I have heard Jesus speak, and I know from where His teaching stems. I think John and Jesus are of the same understanding—and are the beginning of something that is greater than anything I can speak of at this time."

Left alone in the room, James tried in vain to push aside his cousin's neglect of Mary and to ignore His audacity in thinking Himself a prophet. The more he thought, the more intense was his disappointment in Jesus.

Who does He think He is? He is just like me, we are of the same blood. How dare He think He has something to offer Judea? It is inconceivable that a son of Israel would be that indifferent to his mother and family.

As time passed, more reports of Jesus' strange behavior reached Capernaum, and James and his brothers found their lives increasingly uncomfortable. Many of their friends and neighbors began to ridicule them. Then, one day, they heard that Jesus had come up from Cana to Capernaum. Heeding his father's advice, James decided to find Jesus and hear what He had to say. He asked his brothers to join him; Joses and Simeon were mildly enthusiastic, and young Jude was overjoyed. James assumed that his brothers also wanted to confront and berate Jesus for neglecting His mother, but as the four men walked calmly through the narrow streets of Capernaum to the main synagogue, James soon realized that he was wrong.

"I heard that several fishermen have joined Jesus," Joses said.

I have not heard this; how did Joses hear such a thing? James thought to himself.

"Yes, the sons of Zebedee, who are contracted by the High Priest, and the sons of Jonah, who were in the employment of Zebedee, are among those who are following Him," said Jude with excitement.

James and Simeon looked at Jude with surprise.

Then in a low mumble, Jude added, "I saw Levi with Him."

The brothers stopped walking and looked angrily at Jude.

"You have been forbidden to use that name!"

"I'm just reporting what I saw," Jude said in his defense.

"I also heard that He had been preaching in Judea and Samaria," Joses continued, trying to distract James.

Again, James was surprised by the information that Joses possessed.

"I heard likewise," Jude added, then he shied away, regretting that he had spoken so freely.

James and Simeon looked at Jude again and then at each other. Simeon shrugged, not knowing what to make of his youngest brother's knowledge of Jesus. As they were nearing the synagogue, Joses stated, as if all he said was one continued thought, "And I heard that Jesus changed water into wine at the wedding of Zebedee's daughter, Naomi."

"What!" James shouted. He was shocked. He stopped walking; his three brothers, who had been three or four steps ahead of him, turned and looked at his surprised face.

"Yes. It is true," Jude added. "Many have confirmed it."

"And just how many more things do you know of our cousin's doings, Jude Thaddeus?"

Jude gazed at his older brothers with the look of a young child who has been caught in a wrongdoing. He bit his lower lip and timidly answered, "I have been to see Him."

"And...?"

"Well...He is doing all that Joses said He is doing, and He is good for Judea." Knowing he had overstepped his bounds, he added, hoping to escape their disapproval, "I do not know."

"Well I do," James said roughly and with an edge of mockery in his voice. "If our dear Brother can change water into wine, we will bring Him to the Sea of Galilee and make our fortune."

The brothers laughed loudly and continued on to the synagogue. Soon, the laughter eased, and they continued in silence and doubt.

Jude was anticipating something great, for he believed that Jesus had a supernatural message for everyone and that He was blessed with special powers. Secretly, he was enjoying the notoriety that Jesus was creating, because he was becoming popular. It was not easy to be the youngest brother in a Jewish family—often overlooked and always given the last place. Joses wanted to see if all that was said about Jesus was true, particularly the rumor that Jesus was a messenger of *Adonai*. Simeon was irritated and was determined to make Jesus realize His responsibilities to Mary and the family. Both had suffered from His neglect. James had remained confused; he continued to relive that day on the Jordan with John the Baptist. He had not forgotten John's rare smile or his hesitation with Jesus and himself, and he could not erase from his mind the look on the face of Jesus when He walked from the river.

The synagogue in Capernaum was made of white limestone from a faraway quarry, rather than the black basalt prevalent in Galilee. The building was inspiring; the white limestone created a blinding radiance in the strong daylight sun, and at night it reflected the moonlight, producing a white-blue tint. It was ornately adorned with lintels, cornices, and capitals. When it was constructed, the builders elevated it on an artificial platform, and thus it was the highest and most obvious building in Capernaum. Because of its importance to the town, all the streets led to this place, which was built solely for prayer and the reading of the Torah. There was a courtyard and a garden on the east side of the structure, with an adjacent porch and small room, which served to accommodate the women. The interior walls were painted soft blue, and there was a white ceiling above heavy wooden rafters that supported the roof. On the sides of the main entrance were two *bemata* platforms. These elevated areas were used for the presentation and reading of the Torah. There was an inner assembly prayer hall with benches along the three walls of the room. On the southern wall was an apse with a heavy red velvet cloth covering a semicircular vault that contained the Holy Scrolls. When praying, the congregation would always face the south wall toward the Holy City. The synagogue had a strange history. Capernaum was a frontier town with a Roman garrison stationed just outside its limits. It was the primary duty of this garrison to protect the frontier and collect custom taxes from those entering Galilee. Many years before the birth of James, a sympathetic Roman centurion ordered the building of this synagogue. Various stories indicated that this centurion was a believer and that he did this for political reasons hoping to keep the town of Capernaum forever peaceful and grateful to Rome.

As James and his brothers approached the synagogue, they were amazed to see the large number of people assembled and listening to Jesus; they were especially surprised to see numerous Rabbis and some members of the Sanhedrin there. More shocking was finding Mary Yosef, her sister Salome Zebedee, and their mother Mary Cleophas, along with other women, behind the screened wall.

The brothers had been there for only a few moments when word spread through the assembly that John the Baptizer had been arrested by Herod. James was immediately distraught. He knew that John had attacked Herod and that the Herodians, for Herod's sake, had to silence the Baptist. James found nothing wrong in what John had said; he believed John to be innocent, and this made his arrest all the more troubling. Nevertheless, he was encouraged by the news, for he believed that his visit to Jesus would now be more productive. With the Baptizer arrested, James was sure that Jesus would fall out of John's influence and return to His mother, and perhaps some normalcy would return to the family. He would bide his time, and when Jesus was alone, he would approach and lay the final burden of guilt upon Him. He heard someone speak to Jesus, but he could not hear what was being said. He heard Jesus reply in a loud, clear voice, "Amen, Amen, I say to you, unless a man be born again, he cannot see the kingdom of God."

Suddenly, a man in the assembly, standing not far from James and his brothers, was unexpectedly seized by an evil fit. He growled and cowered in a contorted, deformed posture, and he cried out in a harsh, raspy voice, "What have we to do with Thee, Jesus of Nazareth? Hast Thou come to destroy us? I know who Thou art, the Holy One of God."

The astonished assembly pulled away from the man, and many became numb in sheer terror. All eyes were on the dark, distorted face, with its wild eyes and foaming mouth, but others, like James, continued to watch Jesus; He had lowered His head, and His face was obscured by the shadow of His hood.

Slowly, Jesus raised His head.

James was taken aback. This was not the face of his cousin. This was a different Man, a different Being. Across this face were traces of deep sadness; there was no compassion or tolerance in His eyes, nor was there a smile on His lips. His face quickly tightened, and His eyes narrowed; He stared long and hard at the unrestrained man.

Sternly He ordered, "Hold thy peace!" His voice was more powerful than John the Baptizer's voice had ever been. This voice sent a chill through James' bones.

"Go out of the man," Jesus ordered, His voice even more forceful.

The man continued to convulse, and his face grew darker and more distorted. Shrieks escaped from his mouth. They were painful sounds from a place that seemed beyond all humanity. The tormented screams pierced the ears of all who were unfortunate enough to hear them. Many covered their ears, some began praying, and others scattered in aimless panic. The man on the floor started rolling from side to side. His final screams were caught in his throat; then, as if drawn out by an irresistible force, the screams raced from the room through doors and windows.

Instant silence and stillness fell on the synagogue.

James looked around the room, partly out of relief and partly out of concern for his brothers, who appeared to have escaped. He realized that this was not what had become of them, and his attention again was drawn to Jesus, Whom he glared at with much uncertainty.

What has happened here? What has happened to Jesus?

For the next few moments, all those gathered settled in liberation, then an uproar followed; an onslaught of questions filled the room with uncertainty and accusations.

"What words are these?"

"By what authority does He do these things?"

"By what power does He command unclean spirits to go and they obey?"

James felt a tug at his sleeve. It was his brother Joses. He heard his brother say in a hurried whisper, "Come, let us go. I think Jesus is in danger. It is best that we get away now."

"Come, James," Simeon chimed in as he rushed his brother out of the room and, in passing, grabbed the awestruck Jude.

They hurriedly walked away from the synagogue, occasionally looking back to make sure that they were not being followed. When they were some distance away, they stopped.

"Did you see what happened?" Jude nervously asked.

"What do you think happened?" Joses questioned, breathing heavily, as he leaned against the wall of a nearby house.

"I do not really know, but something evil was there—I felt it," Jude replied with great excitement.

Joses looked at James, than at Simeon.

"I think, young brother, that you should not go to see our kinsman again."

"Why?" Jude retorted. It was apparent that he had decided to return to Jesus.

James raised his hand to command silence. His mind was in enough turmoil. He did not need any bickering.

His brothers looked at him with silent obedience.

"I am inclined to agree with Jude," he said hesitantly. "Something evil was there, I sensed it, but the question to be answered is, Why did Jesus act that way?"

"I personally think that Jesus has lost His senses," Joses stated without much conviction, but he knew he would be appreciated for saying what his older brothers thought.

James, who was still unsettled by the whole ordeal, knew that he would have to see Jesus and be alone with Him, but first he wanted to talk to Cleophas again. When he arrived home, he sought his father out.

"Father, I am troubled."

Immediately, Cleophas dropped his carpentry tools, wiped his hands on his apron, and turned all his attention to his son.

"What bothers you, James?"

"Jesus."

"Oh, James. Not again. I told you we must sometimes allow things to be, and in time we will learn what is to be."

"I have followed your advice. I have gone to listen to Jesus, but I am curious about something that you and mother made reference to, but did not elaborate on. You said that Joseph knew that Jesus was to do certain things, and that Mary approved of it. What could have possessed our relatives to be this tolerant of Jesus' actions?"

Cleophas looked at his son for a long time.

"I am not at liberty to say anything more. I will tell you that Joseph and Mary told me that they knew Jesus was to do these things through special revelations."

James was speechless, and before he could ask further questions, his father raised his right hand and silence was commanded.

"Go and stay with Jesus. Listen to Him."

So that very night, James stole away and sought Jesus; much to his surprise, he found Him with little difficulty. He found Him with several of His friends on the side of a hill, just outside of Capernaum.

When Jesus saw James, He rose from His place and walked to meet him. Jesus greeted him with a warm smile, embraced him, and whispered, "I know what you have in your thoughts, dear brother, and I know your concern for My mother, but please forget about your well-intended mission. Stay with Me. You are filled with great doubts, but time with Me will make you certain."

James was astounded.

How did He know what I came to say? What has happened to Jesus?

He stayed, as Jesus had requested, and from time to time he addressed the issue of Mary Yosef, and each time Jesus told him to be patient.

Several days later, Jesus chose His Twelve, and James was among them.

*

The day after He chose His Twelve, Jesus sat peacefully with them on the side of a mount. They were awkwardly conversing with each other when, suddenly, a great multitude approached them. Jesus stood and looked over the mass of people, and in a loud, understanding voice, He began to speak.

James listened to Jesus and was stunned by the artistry and eloquence of His words. He never suspected Jesus to have such a command of the Aramaic language. His words were peculiarly beautiful and graceful. His words were well balanced—for every blessed deed, a reward was given. All that James heard seemed unique. He felt the weight and the profound meaning of each of the blessings, and he realized that what was being said was deeper than the listeners realized. The profoundness of what Jesus said did not surprise James, for Jesus had always been intense. Jesus' words made James feel comfortable and at home. He was surprised at the tenor of Jesus' voice. His voice moved from tenderness when mentioning the blessing to authority when He mentioned the reward. His voice was clear; it traveled on the wind as each word spread out over the land, going to many places to be heard by many people. James observed Jesus' face and saw a simple, pure love that was greater than any love he had ever witnessed. James knew that He was in a moment of pure ardor. Suddenly, James became aware of a stronger Presence emanating from Jesus, a presence that he could not deny or identify. If this Presence was the *Abba* that Jesus knew, then James wanted to know more. For several penetrating moments, James believed that Jesus was One blessed by *Adonai*.

When Jesus finished speaking, James turned to relay his feelings to his brother Jude. As he was about to speak to Jude, he caught a glimpse of his brother Levi. For a moment, the meeting of their eyes solidified James' feelings about Jesus, for he could see that Levi had understood just as he had. Then James heard Jesus' voice over the crowd, and the words he heard stopped all life.

"Judge not, and ye shall not be judged. Condemn not and ye shall not be condemned. Forgive, and ye shall be forgiven."

He turned and found Jesus' eyes on him, and for the first time in their relationship, he wanted to cower from the presence of his cousin.

Despite all his questions and his irritations with Jesus, he stayed, and over the years he watched all that Jesus did. He continued to struggle in his confusion, but he found some solace in realizing that Jesus knew of his struggles. He listened to each parable that Jesus spoke, and when the Others discussed these stories, there was never any conclusive agreement. In these discussions, James found that he and Levi were close in their thinking, and that they seemed to understand the parables better than any of the Others. Of course, he did not tell Levi how he felt. He still did not acknowledge that brother, but he was sure that Levi had noticed that they were thinking alike.

The miracles performed by Jesus were the hardest things to ignore. They were so utterly overpowering; James watched these events in wonder and confusion. He incessantly wondered how one of his brethren could have such powers, and why *Adonai* would share such powers with a mere human. What kept him close to Jesus were the preaching of love and forgiveness and his occasional understanding of some of the parables.

When members of the Sanhedrin became openly hostile to Jesus, James knew he had to put a stop to what Jesus was doing, for His actions were endangering the entire family. He noticed also that the more Jesus became endangered, the more His mother became impoverished and therefore dependent on her family and Cleophas for help.

He was constantly insisting that Jesus return home, and always Jesus told him to be patient, for in time all would be revealed to him.

After Jesus performed the miracle of the multiplication of the loaves and fishes, James began to believe that Jesus was a prophet—but surely not the salvation of Israel.

In private one night, he approached Jesus and firmly told Him what he believed.

Jesus looked at him and said kindly, "My dear James, the day is soon approaching when you will see Me differently, and then you will believe."

Then came the Feast of the Passover and the arrest of Jesus. James ran the fastest of all the Twelve, and when he finally found a small crevice between two large rocks to hide in, he said aloud, "I knew this would happen, Jesus, I sensed it before You did. This only proves Your folly. Now look at what You have done to our family."

After a few moments of total anger at Jesus and at himself, he thought of his family. Immediately he went to his father's house and found his family still celebrating the Passover, in total ignorance of the arrest of Jesus. Quietly, he pulled his father aside and told him what had happened. His father said, with great resolve, "So this is what was to be."

James did not understand his father's words, and he insisted that they leave Jerusalem before the Sabbath and return home to Capernaum.

"Where are your brothers Jude and Levi?"

"Jude is fleeing, and I know nothing of Levi."

Just then Mary Cleophas entered the room.

"What has happened? I sense a great evil. I have felt it all day."

"Jesus has been arrested."

She rushed to her husband's side, and looking into his aged face, she said softly, "This is not what I thought would take place. We must go to Mary Yosef and help her. She is with Salome Zachary. Come, let us go."

James reached for his father's arm, then his mother's. His face was white with fear and concern, but as he looked at his parents, perplexity overcame him. He could not understand their concern for Mary Yosef. He said, "Father, mother, we must leave Jerusalem. Jesus has put all of us in danger. The authorities who hated Jesus and all He did will come after all who were with Him."

Cleophas pushed his wife from his side. "Go make ready. I will be with you shortly." Looking at James, he said sternly, "And just what is to become of Jude and Levi? If what you say is true, we cannot leave them. We are old; if we are arrested, so be it. But you and your brothers are young. Find them first, and seek us at Zebedee's house; then we will go. Hurry, for the Sabbath will soon be here."

Cleophas turned abruptly, and speaking to himself, he said, "Joseph, I now doubt your words."

James rushed after his father and gently grabbed his elbow. "Father, tell me what you mean by this. In my lifetime, you have alluded to this on several occasions. It is now time for you to tell me."

Cleophas, who suddenly seemed much older, looked at James for a long time. With tears beginning to well up in his eyes, he said, "My brother told me that when Jesus was conceived, he had a dream. In this dream, an angel told Joseph that Jesus had been conceived by the power of *Elohim*. Jesus was to save His people from their sins. Years later, when Jesus was lost in the Temple, Jesus told my brother that he would soon die and that he would not see the reason for Jesus' birth. The next year, Joseph died. With these things in our hearts, your mother, Mary Yosef, and I watched and waited to see Jesus do what He was to do. What has happened today is not what we thought would happen."

Cleophas walked quickly away, leaving his son alone and stunned.

*

James had hidden himself well from the crowd that stood near the Cross. He was far behind the Sanhedrin and the Romans and off to their side, in between two large boulders. He looked around the boulders to see Jesus. He could not believe what had happened to Him, yet this disbelief did not dispel the sadness he was feeling—his best relative, his best friend from early childhood was dying. He saw his mother, the Master's mother, her sister Salome, John bar Zebedee, and the woman from Magdela, all standing by the Cross. He envied the courage of the women, and he wondered why his love was not as great as John's. He heard several Pharisees call out, "He saved others; Himself He cannot save." James twitched.

How cruel are those who claim to be merciful, he thought. *Yet how wrong can they be? Where are all the powers now? Was what was said and believed by my parents all a hoax?*

He heard someone shout, "Come down from Your cross, and we will believe in You."

James was pierced by these words, and without consideration he uttered lowly, "Yes, Jesus, come down from Your cross, and I will believe in You."

Slowly, Jesus lifted His head. He turned His face to the side, in James' direction.

James felt Jesus' eyes on his chest; they burned his flesh. Quickly he fell out of view, behind the boulders. Grabbing his chest and without a glance back, he ran and disappeared into the countryside, never looking back.

Jesus was dead.

There was no doubt of this. Mary Cleophas told James that she saw His side pierced, and she beheld the water and blood that came from the wound. She had helped prepare Jesus for the tomb of the good Joseph of Arimathea, and she watched as the large rock was pushed into place, sealing the tomb forever. These things were confirmed by John bar Zebedee and by Mary Yosef, whom James could not talk to for fear of being disrespectful. He felt that she played a major role in deceiving the family. The family, without shame, gathered to mourn according to the Jewish custom, but out of fear they mourned in hiding. The loss of Jesus was a great blow to all who knew Him, but to the Eleven it was devastation compounded by a feeling of deception.

How could we have been so gullible?

He heard from his brother Simeon that the Others were gathered at the Upper Room of the house belonging to young Mark, so before sunset, he stole away and took up rest in the Room with the Others. When he saw the fear on all their faces, he knew that he had to get his family away from Jerusalem. Nothing would be decided before the Sabbath, and the Sabbath had to be celebrated.

Later that night, they slowly came out of their stupor and began reliving what had happened. Their guilt united them. Eventually, the conversation came to what they were to do, and disputes arose. Peter, out of fear of being arrested, suggested that they stay together. Many believed that Peter's idea was wise for separation could mean betrayal if one of them was captured. Peter reminded them of Jesus' words on the night of the Passover, and he recalled that Jesus had prayed that they be one.

James immediately attacked Peter and those who agreed with this idea. He reminded them of the deception they had just endured, and then he suggested that they leave Jerusalem, separately, and disappear.

"It would be best if we all forgot Jesus," he said with anger and pain in his voice.

Everyone reacted strongly. Most agreed with Peter's idea, but Thomas, Matthew, and Simon the Zealot agreed with James.

Finally, Jude Thaddeus, looking deeply hurt by his brother's hostility, said, "If we have received good things at the hand of God, why should we not receive evil?"

James recognized the quote from Job, and for an instant he wanted to reprimand his brother, but instead he became silent, believing that when all was done, he, James, would be proven the wisest of them all. Seeing the confusion in the room and the weak alliance led him to believe that Peter's proposal would soon be rejected.

Surely, they did not want to admit that they were deceived. Their pride would not allow such a confession, just as I do not want to admit that one of my brethren was the perpetrator of the deception.

So he stayed with the Others, only to draw Jude Thaddeus away from the folly that Jesus had created.

Throughout the second day, they prayed, asking *Adonai* for guidance, but James offered prayers of thanksgiving for their safety from the Jews and Romans. He had lost faith in Jesus and in all He did.

Yet how do I explain all those things Jesus did? How do I explain Jesus' ability to read my mind? He found no answers to these questions.

Early on the morning of the third day, after the death of Jesus, the Eleven were violently awakened by hard, repeated knocks on the heavy wooden door of the Cenacle. Matthew carefully opened the door, which was pushed wide open by the woman from Magdela. Her face was white, and her eyes moved quickly in utter panic. She collapsed onto the nearest stool and began to speak incoherently in short, gasping sentences. Finally, she was able to frantically cry out, "The Master is gone! Someone…someone moved the stone…someone has stolen…the body of the Master."

The room burst into confusion. Questions and doubts poured forth from everyone in the room.

"Please…help…help me find His body."

Peter grabbed his cloak and thoughtlessly raced from the room down the steps and into the city street below. He was followed by John and the breathless woman from Magdela.

Philip went to the door and shut it quickly. He fell against the door and held it closed with his body. His face was white and drained of all life; he looked at the others in the room.

"What do we do? Should we follow Peter and John?" he asked, utterly bewildered.

"I do not know," James bar Alphaeus answered as he became aware of his trembling hand and the cold, clammy perspiration over his body.

"How could this be!" Thomas asked himself, completely baffled as he sought seclusion in the corner of the room.

"It cannot be! My brother John saw Jesus die. Magdela is mistaken," James bar Zebedee declared emphatically, but he looked around the room for further confirmation.

"James, a missing body is a missing body. Did not you hear the woman say she saw that the stone was rolled away?" Matthew interjected with a tinge of irritation in his words.

"Who would have done such a thing?" Jude Thaddeus asked softly, as if questioning himself, for he looked to be in a trance.

"We are listening to the sayings of a woman. Have we forgotten the state of grief she was in days ago? She is confused, and we should not be overly concerned. Let us wait until we have a better report. Let us wait until Peter and John return," Andrew stated convincingly.

"Neither the Jews nor the Sanhedrin would steal a body from a grave," Bartholomew said, and then he concluded, "We have deep respect for the dead."

"It had to be the Romans," Simon the Zealot said harshly.

"But why would they do such a thing?" James bar Alphaeus asked.

His question went unanswered.

Round and round their thoughts were verbalized, and round and round they debated. They grew curt and searched one another's faces looking for assurance, but all they could perceive among themselves were disorientation and bewilderment.

James could feel his heart beating against his chest.

If this is true—it cannot be—if this is true, it is not over. What has happened to Jesus?

The room remained in a state of upheaval, flooded with disbelief.

✳

A short time later, there was another knock on the heavy door, but this was a gentle knock with no urgency to it. Thomas opened the door slightly and peeked out, then he opened the door wide; a forced, uneasy smile raced across his lips out of recognition of those who entered.

James jumped to his feet when he saw his mother, Mary Cleophas; Salome Zebedee, the mother of James and John; and Joanna, the wife of Herod's steward, Chuza. From the moment he saw his mother's face, he knew something was wrong. The three women began to speak almost in unison.

"Jesus has risen!"

"We saw Him, He is alive!"

"Jesus spoke to us! He is alive!"

Everyone, everything in the room froze.

"I went with Salome and Joanna to the sepulcher to complete our rushed anointing of the Master's body. When we arrived, we found the huge stone pushed aside. We hurried to the opening and, before we reached it, there before us stood Jesus. He said to us, "*Shalom.*" We fell to our knees at His feet and began adoring Him. Then he said, "Fear not. Go tell Peter and my brethren that they are to go into Galilee. There they shall see Me."

"We have just left my sister, Mary Yosef. She told us that her Son appeared to her. He was alive again," Salome declared.

James ignored all the excitement around him, but he continued watching his mother as she spoke to Jude Thaddeus and Matthew. He calmly observed her, trying to detect some flaw that would make him believe or disbelieve. He needed something!

Soon the door opened again, and Joseph of Arimathea and Nicodemus stormed in, telling everyone that the Sanhedrin had bribed the guards into saying that the followers of Jesus had stolen His body.

"What has happened to Jesus?" Nicodemus asked.

The women began telling the men of the Resurrection.

In all the excitement, James pulled his mother aside.

"Mother," he said, "are you sure of this?"

"As sure as I am of who you are," Mary Cleophas said, calm and completely certain.

James looked at her for a long time and finally embraced her, only because he did not know what else to do.

What is this? His thoughts screamed. *What has happened to Jesus?*

A thousand questions were asked, and not one was answered. A thousand thoughts were presented, but not one was plausible, and the women's stories were repeated again and again.

In total confusion, tired of wrestling with his mind and his emotions and feeling the need to be logical and to come to grips with what was happening, James silently left the room. He walked down the stairs, around the side of the house, and into the small courtyard behind it. He had always liked this courtyard, but he could not enjoy it at that moment. He walked into the garden and down the garden path to a well that was commonly owned and used by the family of Mark and several neighboring families. His mind was cramped with many questions, many doubts. He knew he had to get things right in his head, but first he had to collect himself. His hands were trembling and his legs were weak. He needed to become logical, rational. He took two deep breaths. He stroked his beard several times, smoothing it. He began to compose himself.

Could Mother be correct? Could all the women be correct? And if they are, what does it mean? How could all this be? No man has died and lived again. Then he remembered Lazarus. *Jesus called him back to life, but who called Jesus back?*

Again, he began to feel his hands tremble and his legs weaken. He covered his face with his hands, as if trying to wash away his internal chaos.

As before, there are always questions, and as before, there are no answers.

He reached the well and leaned over its side, believing he would see his reflection or the reflection of the sky, but he saw nothing; there was nothing but blackness. Finding nothing in the darkness, he raised his head and looked at the endlessness of the clear blue morning sky. For the first time in days, he felt calm.

"Why did not the well reflect the sky and my image?" he asked aloud and in confusion.

A soft, cooling breeze pressed against him. It was so gentle that he almost didn't realize it had passed, and then he felt warmth come over his body.

He felt a hand on his shoulder and a familiar voice say, "James."

The sound of his name was as soft as that refreshing breeze. His heart stopped; he had to catch his breath. He knew he must turn. He had to make certain. He knew if he did that his life would be changed forever, and yet if he did not, his life would not be a life.

He turned.

There, before him in the midst of a blinding brilliance, stood Jesus.

"Jesus," James said, falling to his knees.

"Yes, James, it is I. The Son of Man has risen from among them that sleep. I have come so that you may believe. Believe now. I have gone to *Abba*, our Father. He is pleased with what has happened, and He has opened His arms to the world. And so, I say to you, 'all the children of flesh' will invoke My Name; 'all the wicked of the earth will turn' to Me. And I will 'be King over them,' for this day 'the Lord is Named One.'"

James remembered the words of the *Alenu*, and he lowered himself to the ground, his face now only inches from the dirt.

"Know that if I had changed the Sea of Galilee into wine, as you suggested; if I had come down from My cross, as you wished—you would not have believed."

James buried his face in the dirt, in shame and sorrow.

"Never once did you ask to believe, never once did you pray for belief. Let My Resurrection be your belief. I am here in answer to all your silent prayers, in fulfillment of all your hopes for the world."

"Master…my Master…forgive my disbelief," he said, begging and weeping. A strong, driving wind passed over him.

He rose quickly to his feet, free of darkness, and rushed into the house. The room was in complete turmoil. Peter had seen Jesus. Then, the door to the room flung open, and James' father, Cleophas, breathlessly declared that he and a companion had seen Jesus on the way to Emmaus.

With tears in his eyes, Cleophas declared loudly, "What my brother has said is true!"

✳

The fact that James the Less was given the mission of the Province of Judea was an indication that the Master was instrumental in this choice, for none of the Twelve loved Jerusalem more than James, and none of the Twelve was loved by Jerusalem as much as James. In spite of all that had happened, in spite of all the sad memories that remained in and around the city, James still loved Jerusalem. He still believed that he had to stay in this city, for through His Death and Resurrection, Jesus had made this city holy to His followers. He believed that "The Way" and Judaism would reconcile their differences and work together to announce to the world the greatness of *Adonai* in sending into the world His Son, Jesus the Christ. So in the early years, he tried to regulate things in this direction. When many Palestinian Gentiles, who had heard Jesus teaching, asked to know more and to be baptized, James insisted that they all had to become Jews first. This is the way Jesus left it, to Jews and of Jews, and this is the way James believed it should remain. So before any Gentile was permitted to receive purification, he had to be circumcised.

James was respected in Jerusalem because he was a religious man known for his conservative beliefs. He was just, fair, and righteous. He carefully maintained peace, and he stood, as a mediator, in that wide, empty chasm between "The Way" and the Jewish leaders. Whenever there was an overzealous member of "The Way" who would preach and condemn the Jews for rejecting Jesus, James would take the believer aside and counsel him, then he would suggest to Peter that the zealous preacher be sent off on a mission. This is what he did with Nescius, Pilate's scribe. James sided with John and suggested that Nescius be assigned to Matthias in Cappadocia. And when Lazarus started receiving notoriety, he carefully suggested that he go to southern Gaul to preach. In like manner, Joseph of Arimathea, Nicodemus, and a few others who had fallen out of favor in the Sanhedrin were sent off. Away from Jerusalem, they could not cause trouble for the Sanhedrin or the other Jewish leaders. When the centurion Cornelius became a believer, James suggested that Peter send him to Rome to help those in "The Way" who were being maltreated by the Romans. Likewise, with Peter's approval, arrangements were made for Stephaton, Longinus, and Abendadar, and other soldiers were sent to join one of the Apostles in foreign lands, where they would not embarrass the Roman authorities. When Joanna and her husband Chuza, Herod's steward, and Herod's stepbrother Menahan became followers, James went to Peter, and they also departed so as not to agitate Herod.

On other occasions, when a criminal or runaway slave came to "The Way," James suggested they surrender to the authorities; then, James would seek leniency for the slave, which most often he was able to obtain.

So it was that James was held in great esteem by the religious and secular leaders in Jerusalem. He did, however, have a few clandestine agendas. He cautiously guarded the places that had been made special by Jesus and were therefore holy to the followers of Christ. He used these places as retreats for members of "The Way." If a person came to "The Way" and needed extra time for discernment, James would recommend that they spend time in one of these holy places, and he would leave the rest up to the Master. Soon, these places became assemblies for celebrating the Supper.

The Upper Room, also known to many as the Cenacle—the place of the Last Supper and the room in which the Apostles received the gift of the Spirit and of tongues—was still owned by the family of Mark and remained in the family's care. Here, the followers met often and celebrated the Breaking of the Bread.

The tomb where Jesus was laid to rest was still owned by Joseph of Arimathea and was now tended by Martha, the sister of Lazarus. She, along with Lady Mary and other holy women, visited the grounds and the tomb faithfully.

Malchus, the servant of the High Priest who sought to please Caiaphas and who drew so much attention to himself that he caught Peter's anger, and the edge of Peter's sword, tended the Garden of Gethsemane. On that night, Jesus, Healer of all things, remade the ear that was lost to Peter's anger. This act of kindness left Malchus stunned. Long after all had left the Garden, long after all had been consummated on Golgotha, he was still standing in the Garden. In the days that followed, he sought out the supporters of Jesus. Many of them were not strangers to him, for he had been in their company and knew their families, but his search was fruitless. He sought discharge from the service of the High Priest, and with others who were touched by Jesus in His last hours, he searched for the Twelve. Unable to find them, he and the others talked about Jesus; when God, in His time, felt that all was ready, they found the Apostles and were purified in the Spirit of the Lord.

Unbeknown to many, Malchus returned to the Garden and stayed there. In those early days, he spoke only of the beauty of the Garden. Then one night, one of the Twelve, Bartholomew, came to the Garden. The two talked for hours of Jesus, and from that time on, anyone who came through the Garden found Malchus speaking of Jesus. When the Apostles were beginning to depart for foreign lands, James the Less came to the Garden, first alone, then with many. Soon, the Garden became a meeting place, and the followers came to pray, sing, and hear about Jesus. As time passed, James and Malchus became friends. They often prayed together, and several times they spoke to the multitudes who came for the Breaking of the Bread.

*

James was greatly troubled by the pending meeting with Paul. He knew the gathering was sensitive and, if not handled correctly, could erupt into a major stumbling block. He expected long, exhausting debates to take place, and when Paul and his companions entered the room and made cold recognition of the Judaizers, James became more fearful and his heart sank into deep sadness.

They sat on different sides of the large, rectangular Upper Room. The Judaizers huddled on the left side of the room, and Paul, Barnabas,

Silas, Titus, Luke, and a few supporters sat on the right. Peter, James, John, and the Others sat at a table near the north wall of the room. The position of this table was not to James' liking, for this put the Apostles in the position of judges. James believed that the remaining Ten were to act as deciders. Peter corrected James, saying that the Apostles were there as compromisers. At Peter's insistence, James was asked to preside over the meeting because, in Peter's mind, the meeting was being held in James' mission, but most of the time it was Peter who answered the challenges of the Judaizers.

Throughout the meeting, James listened to both sides. There was long and heated debate, with many quotes from the Jewish writings. What Jesus said was referred to, and His words were quoted with interpretations that in themselves led to disagreements. The debate continued. Each passing hour did not clarify the question; instead, the question festered into other questions.

If bound to Mosaic Law, would "The Way" be lost? Is this what Jesus came to perfect?

How much of Judaism is to be observed by those in "The Way?"

Should the followers be bound to the holidays, customs, and laws of charity and fasting set down by the Sanhedrin?

If agreement is not reached, should "The Way" become independent?

Everyone knew that it was possible for a split to take place. One group would be Jews, separated from Jerusalem because of their belief in Jesus, but still Jews. The other would be Gentiles, who would accept the Jewish writings to prove that Jesus was the Messiah and to build their own traditions.

As the meeting progressed, things looked bleak. The possibility of a break was looming. Peter stood up and spoke. He told the assembly of his dream in the city of Yoppa and of the conversion of the entire household of the centurion Cornelius. Continuing, he told of his joy in these conversions. Finally, he reminded everyone of the many successes that Paul, James bar Zebedee, Matthias, Andrew, and the other Apostles had experienced among the Gentiles.

The room seemed to settle.

After making these points to the assembly, Peter said, "Brethren, you know that in former days God made choice among us, that by my mouth the Gentiles should hear the word of the Gospel and believe. And God Who knows hearts gave testimony, giving unto them the Holy Spirit, as well as to us, and He put no difference between us and them, purifying their hearts by faith. Now, therefore, why do you try to place God on the necks of the disciples, a yoke which neither our fathers nor we have been strong enough to bear? But by the grace of the Lord Jesus the Christ, we believe to be saved, in like manner as they also believe."

All in the room fell to silence.

Paul rose from his seat and skillfully stated his case, and with innuendos he attacked the Judaizers. When he had finished, the Pharisees and the other Jews reaffirmed their stance. They argued well: "Unless you are circumcised according to the custom of Moses," they told the Gentiles, "you cannot be saved."

Everyone in the assembly recognized the limitation this would place on the Gentiles. To comply with circumcision would also mean total obedience to everything Jewish.

Finally, late in the discussion, Paul stood. His face was red with anger and frustration. He closed his eyes, and John bar Zebedee leaned over and said to Peter and James, "I think he is praying." After a few moments, Paul looked around the room. He began to speak carefully and with great patience, but as he continued, his voice rose amidst his heightening emotions.

"Placing the burden of circumcision on the Gentiles would make followers of Jesus nothing more than a sect of Judaism. Those who want this are the same believers who denied that Jesus is the Messiah. If, therefore, all the Gentiles would be circumcised and adhere to all the laws set by Moses, would our Pharisees and the Elders, who seem willing to accept Jesus only as a variation of Judaism, then accept Jesus as the true and one Messiah and change the things that Jesus condemned?" With the sound of his voice, the room froze.

He returned to his seat and sat. He lowered his eyes and waited for an answer.

None came, for the room exploded into complete chaos.

Men rushed to Paul, shouting at him. Those around Paul stood in their way to protect him.

James knew the final question had been asked. The question that everyone was thinking of, but which no one wished to hear, was suspended in the warm air of the room. James jumped to his feet and called for order, and after much insistence on his part, his call was heard.

Peter rose quickly and said that what was needed was a night of thought. The other Apostles immediately voiced their agreement. James ordered a recess.

Immediately after the recess, a group of Judaizers approached James. Their leaders, Abimelech and Eliyakim, two low-level members of the Sanhedrin, pulled James aside.

"We see we have no support from the Others. Peter is blinded by his own mistake and out of pride cannot retract his errors. The other Apostles have been away from Jerusalem, and they have lost their understanding of the Law. But you, James, are a just and righteous man. We believe that you know the Law, as Jesus did, and we believe that you know what Jesus would want to do. Speak on our behalf, and enlighten the darkness of the other Apostles."

In spite of their convincing pleas, and in spite of solid arguments from Paul, James was torn between the two arguments. He sensed that the other Apostles leaned in favor of Paul, especially after Peter told them about his dream and about the conversion of Cornelius and his household.

Left alone for a few moments, James repeated in his mind the arguments of both sides.

Jesus was a Jew, born and raised as such, and all the Apostles were Jews, even Paul. It seemed that a plan was laid: all had to be Jews before becoming followers of Jesus. This strengthens my firm belief that Judaism is to bring the salvation of God to the entire world. The message of Jesus must be carried to the world by Jews and within the confines of Judaism.

He took a deep breath and exhaled heavily.

But look at the reports of Peter, Paul, Matthias, and Andrew, and remarks in letters from the other Apostles, of their many converts among the Gentiles. They went first to the Jews, and then to the Gentiles. The fact that the Gentiles converted in large numbers means that their world is looking for salvation, and they are accepting Jesus as that salvation. This is an answer to my prayers. And there is Paul's question to the Judaizers, which remains unanswered. Unanswered questions…I have lived with too many unanswered questions. There should be no more—Jesus is the answer. If the Judaizers believe that Jesus is the Messiah, they should declare this among the Sanhedrin and then follow His example and go to all people. They should follow His command to baptize all nations.

He stopped thinking and held his head. It was aching.

Still, to break with Judaism…to be without the laws of the undefiled… to lose our entire heritage. I do not know….

Finally, only the Apostles remained in the room, and Peter solemnly suggested that the Apostles pray through the night and the next day deliver their decision to the assembly. As they milled around the room, Peter and the other Apostles seemed to be as troubled as James was.

Peter then whispered, "We will meet at the third hour tomorrow and pray together, and then we will make a decision. James, you will make the announcement of what is decided."

James did not think it was his place to make such a monumental announcement. He did not need this extra burden. His thoughts were thick and heavy with pros and cons. Now, the pain in his head was constant and intense. He needed a retreat, a night of prayer, a night to speak with Jesus. With uneasiness, he left the Cenacle, knowing where he had to go. He walked through the Lower City and the City of David and through the southern gate. He walked slowly through the Kedron Valley, crossed over the brook, and finally walked into the Garden of Gethsemane at the bottom of Mount Olivet. He remembered that this was the place where Jesus prayed and surrendered to the Will of *Abba*, and this was the place where Jesus prepared to accept the fate that His Father had ordained from all eternity.

The Garden was a rectangular enclosure with a rock wall and closely planted hedges that separated it from the rest of the nearby area. Seven olive trees, quite wide at the base and measuring from twenty to twenty-six feet tall, filled the Garden. The rugged, gnarled trees stood watch over the large rocks and over a clearing in the Garden. These trees imparted a sense of permanence and endurance against all perils.

James always found olive trees to be timeless beauties, and as he passed them, he recalled the old Aramaic saying: "An olive tree never dies." As he approached the spot where he and the Others had slept on that long-ago night, he grew sad.

How many times must I remember that night before I am rid of it, he thought. *Truly, I and the Others have suffered much from this memory that seems to never die.*

"Obviously not enough times," he said aloud. "Perhaps we must relive over and over what happened that night so we remain humble and never deny Him again."

He walked further to where Peter, John, and James bar Zebedee had rested, and quickly an image of James Zebedee came to him. He stopped at the small clearing and at the rock where Jesus rested. He stood staring at the large rock. He had seen it many times before, but this night it looked larger and darker. He had never noticed the dangerously jagged sides of the rock; he imagined that if he walked carelessly close to the sides, he could cut himself. The rock looked like it had been a part of another rock. It looked as if it had been sliced in half, and what was left was a relatively smooth, table-like surface. He imagined Jesus kneeling, thrown across the top of the rock. He could never fathom the deep anguish his cousin had endured that night.

"I dare not rest there," he said to himself as he moved to the side of the rock to one of the smaller, insignificant rocks, hoping to find a place to sit and pray.

"James, is that you?" he heard someone ask. The voice startled James. He stopped walking and turned to see who had called him. Coming out from behind the contorted bark of an olive tree was Malchus. His face reflected the moonlight as he offered James a warm, welcoming smile.

"It is you, James. How good to see you. I had hoped you would come to pray, for tonight I am in need of a prayer companion."

"*Shalom*, and yes, I am here to pray. I am troubled much and came to find guidance and enlightenment."

"This sounds serious. Well, my brother, you have come to the right place, for in this Garden, all is made clear, even death—especially death. Come, let us sit."

James sat with Malchus, and together the two fell into a long silence as they placed themselves in the presence of the Lord. Spiritual quietude did not come to James—he was struggling with distraction amidst the echoing sounds of the meeting's dissension. He needed to join Malchus in stillness, but his mind was too troubled.

Then he heard Malchus begin to chant: "The Lord loves His foundation upon the holy mountains: the gates of Sion more than all the other dwellings of Jacob. Glorious things are said of thee, O City of God! I will reckon Rahab and Babel among my worshippers: behold Philistia and Tyre and the people of Ethiopia: these were born there. And it shall be said of Sion: 'One and all, they were born therein and the Most High Himself has established it.' The Lord will record in the book of the nations: 'These were born there' and they shall sing as they dance: 'All my springs are in thee.'"

The Psalm 'for the sons of Core'! Jesus, are You speaking to me? Are You giving me the answer I seek?

Malchus, noticing the silence from his companion, stopped his prayers and said, "I sense you are deeply troubled, James, for you are without words tonight. Am I safe in assuming that you are here because of our visiting brother Paul?"

James looked at the gardener with some surprise.

Jesus, You have sent me my guardian.

"Yes," he said, and without pause he explained his dilemma. When he had finished, Malchus sighed deeply.

"James, you cannot be all things to all people, and that is what you are trying to be. I agree that Jesus came to the Chosen first, but look how 'stiff necked and stubborn' we are—and have been, over the many years.

We should have found it so easy to accept Jesus. After all, we have been tended to for centuries and nourished by the voices of many prophets, yet we remain so stubborn. All the obstacles to the Apostles' missions have been from the Jews, or at least instigated by them. May I be so bold as to say something that you may have overlooked? Look at what happened on the day of our Blessed Lord's death. Look at what Jesus did in His silent and final teaching that day. He brought us Cornelius, Longinus, Stephaton, Abendadar, and many others, all Gentiles. Do you think they would be with us today if Jesus had not willed it? I think not, and just look at the witness these men have given of Jesus' life."

James remained silent as Malchus' thoughts began to take root in his mind. He wanted to be a servant once again to the Master's Will.

"Remember, my dear brother, that the last miracle Jesus performed was on me. I doubt it was performed out of compassion alone. I believe He replaced my ear as a sign to everyone that seeing Him is not enough—we have to listen to His message. I believe He wanted all of us to understand that we need to receive new and different ears in order to hear Him. I believe that we, in order to do His Will, must constantly feel the shift of the wind—not merely see the flash of lightening, but also hear the distant rumble." Malchus paused and looked off beyond the Garden. "After that night, I heard Jesus differently, and I came to believe in Him and seek salvation from Him. We must all listen with new and different ears." He turned to James and, looking deep into his eyes, continued, "Let me tell you, I know these Pharisees. I have been in their employ. They are not as sincere as they appear, but they are serving a purpose designed by the Master. They speak of following the Mosaic Laws because this is what Moses said. If they believed in Moses so thoroughly, they would see that all this debate would be of no importance to the great Moses, who himself promised another Prophet—a Prophet who would be raised up like him but who would be a Lawgiver to all nations. The great Moses tells us to listen to this new Prophet or be 'cast out in utter destruction.' I think Moses was saying that the Law he gave to the Jews could not be applied to all nations, and that the new Prophet would give new direction. All those who came to 'The Way' on the day Jesus died came believing in Jesus, not as a Jew but as that new and great Prophet foretold by Moses, the One who was to be greater than all the Jews. I add myself to this group, and say that we came only as believers, and not as Jews."

James smiled warmly at his friend.

"You are what I needed tonight, my friend, and through you Jesus has set my mind at ease. May you be blessed with Jesus' love."

"And you also, Brother James, but be not so quick to sound my praise. The Master has enlightened me ever since I have been blessed with guarding this place. You see James, I believe that every person who comes in body, mind, or spirit to this Garden must accept, with obedience, death of some sort, just as Jesus did that night so long ago. You came here to die to self, for the only problem you had was your stiff neck. All that has been said to you now you already knew, but you did not listen to it. All you had to do was let go of yourself and let Jesus come through, just as His Father came through Him. This Garden was Jesus' first cross. He had to accept it, carry it, suffer it, and die upon it—here." Malchus shifted on his rocky seat. "See how blessed I am, for He has made me see all these things. What I have said to you I have said to others, like Peter, who was recently here with your same problem."

"Peter was here?" James asked with surprise in his voice.

"Yes, as were Barnabas and Paul."

"What?" James was stunned.

Malchus took a deep breath and smiled. "Yes, as I said, this is a good place to pray. I believe that all people will come to this Garden. Many years or many centuries from now they will come here, for eventually all who believe in Jesus must face a Gethsemane. This is a holy place, a place of surrender, and when anyone comes here to pray, they must be ready to leave much of themselves here and depart with less."

James rose slowly. He was free of all the heaviness that had been crushing him these past hours. When he turned to see where he had been seated, he saw that he had been sitting on the rock upon which Jesus had prayed, and tears came to his eyes.

Malchus sprung from a nearby rock, walked to James, and embraced him. Then he laid his hand on James' head, and with his thumb he outlined the sign of the cross on his right ear.

James smiled and walked slowly through the bushes, rocks, and olive trees to the gate of the Garden, leaving behind a great deal of himself.

The next morning, when James stood to speak and announce to the assembly the Apostles' decision, he saw Malchus standing by the door.

✴

Ten years had passed since that night, since that meeting, since Christianity had experienced its second Pentecost and since the world had swelled with the presence of Jesus. Many things had taken place since that meeting. Many good men and women came to be Christians, and they in turn spread the Word. Peter left Jerusalem for good and, like the

Others, went on to other lands. Even John and Lady Mary left Jerusalem at everyone's insistence because of the dangers in the Holy City.

At Paul's invitation, Lady Mary and John left with Paul and went to Ephesus to live among the many Christians of that city, but John returned often to Jerusalem, more than any of the other Apostles did. His visits were like holidays to James.

Much persecution had befallen the Christians in many Roman provinces. In fact, in Rome itself, Emperor Claudius had expelled all Jews from Rome because of the open debate between the followers of Jesus and the Jewish authorities. This disturbance, it was rumored, was caused by the Christians.

In Palestine, the persecutions were orchestrated primarily by Herod Agrippa, who in his attempts to appease the Temple leaders had jailed Peter and all the Apostles and killed James bar Zebedee. When his son, Julius Marcus Agrippa, who ruled as Herod Agrippa II, came to power, the persecution went on uninterrupted. Meanwhile, abroad, the missions continued with great success. Paul continued with his expansive preaching. His ability to be in so many places proved what the Twelve had come to believe: Jesus made the miles go fast and the days go slow. Paul returned to Jerusalem with a collection, but this did not buy him any friends. Shortly after his arrival, he was accused of taking the non-Jew Trophimus into the Temple, and a riot ensued. Before the Sanhedrin instigators were able to kill him, a Roman tribune, named Claudius Lysias, and a few friendly soldiers rescued him. He was placed in the Caesarea prison. Later, he was presented to the Roman procurator Felix and his Jewish Herodian wife, Drusilla, who according to the Law was living in adultery with Felix. Drusilla's hatred of the Sanhedrin prevented Felix from making a decision about Paul's fate, so Paul stayed in captivity, though with many freedoms, until the new procurator, Porcius Festus, replaced Felix.

Within weeks of his arrival, Festus was faced with "the problem of Paul." He went to Jerusalem to hear the charges against Paul, then he returned to Caesarea to hear Paul's defense of himself. After hearing the two sides in the presence of Herod Agrippa and his sister Bernice, Festus was ready to set Paul free, but Paul shouted, *"Civis Romanus sum!"* I am a Roman citizen. This appeal to Roman citizenry carried with it an automatic appeal to the Emperor and was perhaps the wisest thing for Paul to do, for if he had been released, he would have been killed before he reached Jerusalem. Festus gladly sent him to Rome, and there Paul stayed under house arrest with the Emperor Nero.

During these happenings, James, in the eyes of many, remained the righteous and just man of Jerusalem. He preached Jesus in several towns and cities of Judea, and he was even bold enough to pen a letter to the universal Church on charity and good works. This epistle was widely received and read at many celebrations of the Breaking of the Bread. His life in Jerusalem was filled with balancing the ways of Jesus with the ways of the Pharisees. But discord remained: he found a small group of Judean Christians who remained true to the Mosaic Laws and recognized only circumcised Christians as true believers.

With the spread of the Word among the Gentiles, the Judean Christians in Jerusalem began to see Jerusalem as secondary. When Peter, regarded as the leader of the Apostles, left Jerusalem and settled in Rome, they began to see the authority slipping away from Jerusalem to the Gentile world. They felt more and more neglected, and this became a festering sore on the body of those who wanted Christianity to be nothing more than a sect within the Mosaic Law. At first, the Judaizers blamed Paul of Tarsus for their loss of power, then the blame was placed on Peter; it was inevitable that they would soon blame James bar Alphaeus, for he was an ally of Peter and Paul. James began to be regarded as the traitor as they recalled his words on the final day of the council. The acceptance of dietary and sexual mores was little compensation for the abandonment of the covenant of Abraham. Because they were dissatisfied, some continued to place undue burdens on the Gentiles, and James found himself constantly reprimanding them.

The stubbornness of the Judaizers soon became an everyday problem. In the background, further fueling the dissatisfaction with James, was the High Priest Ananus.

Ananus was the fifth son of Anaias, the father-in-law to Caiaphas, the High Priest who brought charges against Jesus. Ananus had been appointed High Priest by Herod Agrippa II. He was a man who lacked caution. His temper was quick and his decision making was bold and impetuous, leading to numerous conflicts. He was a member of the Sadducees, whose reputation for harshness when judging others was known to all in Judea and to the Roman magistrates. In Ananus' eyes, Peter, Paul, John, and James were all equally dangerous. With Paul arrested and on his way to Nero, and with Peter and John escaping from Jerusalem, he laid a plan to rid Jerusalem of the Christian curse and to remove the final impediment—James bar Alphaeus. He carefully placed spies among the Christians who reported to him all that James said or did. He was very careful, for unlike Jesus of Nazareth, now called the Christ by the Gentiles, James had few enemies. It would take meticulous planning to eliminate this Apostle. He was highly regarded and had many friends among the Romans and in the Sanhedrin. Ananus knew that James bar Alphaeus had become very successful in his conversions. Among these converts were a number of Jews in the ruling class and among the Elders and Pharisees. With rare cunning, Ananus sought known Judaizers among the Christians in the Sanhedrin, and after careful analysis, he found the weak links. So it was that Abimelech and Eliyakim suddenly found themselves invited to dinners at the High Priest's home, and gradually their opinions were sought. They were in discussions about the Christian schism and about James bar Alphaeus, Peter, Paul, and the other "non-Jews." Ananus constantly reminded them of the treachery with which James bar Alphaeus had treated the Christian Jews.

Disillusioned with James and excited by their newfound importance and desiring to ingratiate themselves with Ananus, Abimelech and Eliyakim began plotting with Ananus against James. Almost daily, the two Pharisees presented the High Priest with ideas, but Ananus rejected them all, and each time they failed, Ananus shouted, "I want James dead!"

Finally, their chance came.

Two years after he took over as procurator, Festus died of natural causes. Ananus believed he had been blessed, for now he had a chance to get rid of James. With no Roman authority in Judea, he would create a situation that would need immediate attention and would move to prevent trouble from erupting. So he had James summoned before the Sanhedrin.

James went to the Sanhedrin against the advice of Malchus and of his brother Simon bar Alphaeus, who sensed a plot brewing.

"I am not being arrested. I am being asked to appear. I have been told it is to discuss the situation between us. If this meeting can bring peace, how can I afford to not go?" And so he went.

The Great Sanhedrin was a council of seventy members that at one time had secular as well as religious powers over the Jewish people. The Romans had stripped them of most of their secular powers, though they could still enforce religious punishments such as scourging. Under Roman rule, the sentence of death was not theirs to use, though in former times they had the power to carry out death by stoning, burning, beheading, or strangling. This austere body convened every day, except during Holy Days or on the Sabbath, and always in the daytime. They met in a hall of the temple sometimes called *Gazzith*, the Chamber of Hewn Stone. The Sanhedrin, as it most commonly was called, was composed of three groups of leaders—the Chief Priests, the Scribes or lawyers, and the Elders, sometimes called the Ancients. The High Priest served as the

Nasi, the president of the Council, and was the presiding officer. The *Av bet din*, the father of the court or vice president, also shared the honor of presiding over the Council, but only in the absence of the High Priest. The High Priest and the Chief Priests were the religious nobility of the Council. These posts for centuries were occupied by the descendants of Zadok, a High Priest who lived during the reign of Solomon. Through manipulation and abuse, these two posts were adulterated, and as time passed their authority slipped to other families whose descents were not pure Zadokite, leaving the legitimacy of this priesthood often in doubt. Of the four families—Boethius, Annas, Phiabi, and Kamith—the family of Annas was the most powerful because they controlled the office of High Priest the longest. Annas had served as High Priest for nine years, and each of his five sons (Eleazar, also known as Alexander, Jonathan, Theophilus, Matthias, and Ananus) had also served. Other extended members of his family had also served in the high post, among them one son-in-law, Caiaphas, and one grandson, Matthias son of Theophilus.

The Scribes had the solemn duty of watching over the Law of *Elohim* as set by the interpretation of the High Priest, Chief Priests, and Rabbis. The Elders—composed of prominent, rich merchants and property owners and sometimes influential noble laity or ancient ruling families— served on the Council as the supposed spokesmen of the people.

The majority of those in the Sanhedrin were members of either the Pharisees or the Sadducees. Most of the Pharisees were middle-class and possessed a strong knowledge of the Law. They held great power over the common Jewish people, especially in the large urban areas of Judea. It was the Pharisees who were deeply involved in the education of the Jews, and it was the Pharisees who established the laws that governed services, liturgy, worship, works, and prayers. They believed in the resurrection of the dead and the existence of angels and other spirits, both good and evil. They accepted that human beings had free will, but they also believed in the power of prayer and therefore that *Elohim* could alter the course of events or make known His Will. Furthermore, they believed in a judgment after death by the Almighty One.

Only a small number of the priests in the Temple were Pharisees, but this did not stop the Pharisees from wielding a great deal of power over Temple activities, especially in the area of the form and matter of services.

The Sadducees were mostly rich aristocrats and did not have the common people behind them. They were very Greek in their way of life, favoring Hellenistic games, spectacles, and theater. Most of the members of the Great Sanhedrin were of this party, but few were priests because they were too Hellenistic in their ways. The Sadducees had strong ties to the secular world and, most especially, to the Romans and the Herodians. They did not believe in the resurrection of the dead. The body and the soul died together, with no judgment or reward or punishment after death. They denied the existence of any spirited beings. They believed and preached that *Elohim* was not interested in human beings and would never intervene in their lives. This idea of God's indifference led to a minimal or non-existent belief in a Messiah. The High Priests from the families of Boethius, Annas, and Phiabi were all Sadducees.

James presented himself before the Sanhedrin at their usual daytime session.

Ananus did not attend. His hatred of Jesus, James, and anything else Christian was too severe, but he had his sympathizers strategically placed to push his agenda.

The Sanhedrin sat in a semicircle from east to west. Sixty-nine members of the body formed this semicircle as they sat on pillows or thick cushiony rugs. At the open end of the semicircle, on chairs elevated above the others, sat the *Nasi* and to his right the *Av bet din*. The Sanhedrin Chamber was familiar to James, for he had stood there defiantly with the other Apostles on charges of disobeying the Council's order to "not preach Jesus," and he had been there a few times after that to hear the same charges. Back then, when he stood with the Others, he felt strength, zeal, and conviction emanating from them. They were like twelve lions facing the onslaught of seventy gladiators. Now, years later, as he stood alone, he did not falter, for he still felt their spirit around him. He felt their courage and the same boldness that they had exhibited those many years ago. Also, around him in a palpable reality so strong that James could hardly contain the joy he felt, was the love of Jesus. He felt the truth of Jesus so strongly; it now rested in his throat, almost choking him, waiting to come alive.

Unaware of looking out of place, James stood in the center of the semicircle of the Chamber. He was shorter than most men in the Chamber. He was by far the most meagerly dressed and was more unkempt. Nevertheless, he was aware that he was the most comfortable. He could sense the tension and nervousness of those around him, and he wondered why the tension was there. He slowly looked around the room. As his eyes passed from face to face, he was greeted by some with a smile or a respectful nod, but from most he saw a glare, a bold defiance. His survey made him aware of the Christians among them.

The Pharisees had been more mild in their persecution of the Christians. If Jesus had indeed risen from the dead, it would confirm their belief in life after death. James was aware that there was a closeness between Jesus' doctrine and some of the Pharisees' ideas, despite the conflict that had existed between them.

The Sadducees were the most threatened. Jesus was a contradiction of everything they believed, so they needed to rid the world of His ideas. They had to stop the folly of Jesus and the defections among those in the Sanhedrin to "The Way." It deeply pleased them that there were no known Christian Sadducees in the Sanhedrin.

James knew that the Sadducees were the ones he should fear.

Finally, Abimelech, whom James knew to be a Christian, stood in his place and said, "James bar Alphaeus, we greet you as a man of justice and righteousness."

Many in the Chamber mumbled and nodded in agreement, and James felt humbled, for he was only a servant to the Son of *Adonai*.

Abimelech continued, "We know also that there is no man in all Judea who is so filled with the love of the Law as you are."

The Sanhedrin rumbled in agreement.

"We know that you are comfortable with what the followers of Jesus have been teaching." A voice came from the other side of the Chamber, and James turned to identify the speaker: it was Eliyakim, one of the Elders believed to be Christian.

"But we also know," Abimelech continued, "that you have had many difficulties with a number of the leaders of 'The Way' regarding the observance of the Mosaic Law."

"Again showing your love of the Law," Eliyakim added from his side of the Chamber.

"And because you have so great a knowledge of the Holy Writings, we surmise that you do not truly believe that this Nazarene, one of your own brethren, is the Promised One," Abimelech said with a grin that revealed his fashionable, trimmed beard.

James remained silent and looked straight ahead at the empty seat of Ananus. He refused to have his attention thrown around the room.

"So we are asking you to re-educate the Followers of Jesus and to clarify what you believe," Eliyakim said.

"Convince the Chosen People of Judea to have no misunderstanding about the crucified Jesus." This time it was Abimelech speaking. "They believe in you and will take your word as the truth. Accept our invitation to make known the truth."

"Our Holy Feast of the Pasch is coming, and Jews of every tribe, from many nations, and even some Gentiles, will be here in Jerusalem. Speak to the people then." Again he recognized the voice of Eliyakim.

"And do it from the highest pinnacle of the Temple, so all can see and hear you." This was a strange voice, a stronger voice, and without looking, James knew that Ananus had entered the Chamber.

The words swelled and burned in James' throat, but he held his peace. He closed his eyes and prayed for the grace to remain silent.

Finally, he opened his eyes. "Yes. I believe it is time to settle this matter, before all the people," James said in a loud, clear voice. As he turned to leave the Chamber, he heard the clamor of cheers and agreement. It wasn't until later that night, when he was alone, that he heard also the sounds of shock and remembered the disbelief on the faces of the Christians among the Sanhedrin.

The day before the Passover had arrived, and James presented himself to the Temple authorities. Several excited members of the Sanhedrin accompanied James to the wide walkway above the Temple colonnades. The courts of the Temple were filled with Jews from all over the Empire. Several other members of the Sanhedrin were in the court among the people, and they drew everyone's attention to James, who was now high above them—visible to all. Displaying all the respect that James deserved, many stood silently, waiting for him to speak. In this silence, James looked out over the masses before him, and out over his beloved city. All he felt around him was the touch of a soft cooling breeze, and he welcomed the feel of the earth's breath as it passed over and pressed against his body. His robe spread out and danced in the breeze. He looked spirited, larger than life.

Thirty years ago, when Jesus was lifted up, He must have seen this sight, James thought, and he wondered if sensing this was a sign from his beloved Cousin.

From below, one of the Sadducees shouted out, "O just and righteous one! O great believer in the faith of our ancestors, speak to us, for we are compelled by your holiness to listen to you and do what you say."

From another of the Sadducees he heard, "Our people are becoming lost as they follow the crucified Jesus of Nazareth. Save them from their folly!" Suddenly, the words that days before had choked him and swelled in his throat rushed to his mouth. He shouted in a voice that resounded through the walls and columns of the Temple, "Why…why do you question me about the Son of Man? You know as well as I do that He died and rose again and now sits at the right hand of the Great Power, and He will return one day on the clouds of heaven!"

From the crowd below came a cheer and a roar that stilled all life and sound.

"Hosanna to the Son of David!" the people shouted. Again they shouted, "Hosanna to the Son of David!"

The Sadducees reacted quickly. One of them grabbed James, causing him to lose his balance. He fell from the pinnacle.

James, falling through the emptiness of the air, knew that in life or in death he would be embraced by Jesus. On the pavement below, he was met with more anger, now mingled with hatred and betrayal. Many people began to throw stones at him. Some nearby tried to stop the stone throwers, but they were pushed aside. James felt the clash of the stones against his flesh as their targets were replaced with welts. He began to smile. He tried to stand, but injured by the fall and stunned by the barrage of rocks, he was only able to kneel. He looked into the mob, welcoming, inviting each stone.

Clearly, he saw Him. There, in the midst of the crowd, stood the Master, and Lady Mary behind Him.

He cried, "I beseech you, Lord, forgive them, for they know not what they do."

Some onlookers shouted, "Stop! He is praying for you."

There was nothing that anyone could do. The mob had captured the moment. Suddenly, a man drew close to James' crippled body. He raised high a great hammer, paused for a moment as he beheld a face of inexplicable tranquility, then let the hammer fall upon the Apostle's head.

The last thing James felt was a hand on his shoulder and one soft, warm word—"James."

EPILOGUE

Lady Mary had become ill just before the Apostles' meeting, and she remained unwell during the meeting. Paul suggested to John bar Zebedee that Luke, his dear and devout physician, tend to her. John was reluctant, but when he asked Lady Mary if she would be willing to be examined by Luke, she smiled softly and said, "Of course, I have been expecting him."

John was puzzled by her statement. He held open the door as Luke entered.

Luke stayed with Lady Mary for many hours. Every time someone entered the room, they found the two deep in conversation, with Lady Mary as spry and healthy as she ever was. When finally Luke left, he carried with him several large *papyri*.

*

To leave Jerusalem was suggested by Peter and James bar Alphaeus, but to go to Ephesus in Asia was the suggestion of Paul. Paul said he could guarantee a warm welcome for Lady Mary and the other holy women. So Lady Mary, her widowed sister Salome Zebedee, her newly widowed sister-in-law Mary Cleophas, Joanna Chuza, and John left for Ephesus. They lived in a house that had been given to them by a wealthy Ionian Christian. The *villa* was very spacious and far more elegant than they were accustomed to, but Lady Mary's age and the failing health of the other women made the comfort of the house seem appropriate.

Living in Ephesus was a shock to these new residents, for the city was massive in comparison to Jerusalem. Located on the Aegean Sea at the mouth of the Cayster River, Ephesus was the second largest city in the Empire. It was called *Lumen Asiae*, the Light of Asia, and *Altus ut Roma*, Highway to Rome, because many roads from the eastern parts of the Empire led to Ephesus and to Rome. The city had three major roads. One road from the east went to Laodicea, Armenia, Babylon, and beyond. A northern road led to Smyrna, Bithynia, and the Black Sea. The southern road led to the Meander Valley, Lycia, Cilicia, Syria, and farther south. Ephesus was the capital city of the Province of Asia.

Before the Romans came, the city was very Greek. Then, an earth-quake destroyed it completely, and Rome, under Emperor Tiberius, rebuilt it as a Roman city, complete with Roman architecture and facili-ties. They built a large forum called the *Quadratus Agora* that was con-nected directly to the waterfront. The street connecting the seaport to the square was called *Curetes Vicus*. It was lined with extravagant houses, expensive shops, temples, and monuments, all accented with fountains and works of art. Also in the square was the *Odeon*, the Senate building, which resembled a Roman temple.

Being a great seaport and center of trade, Ephesus was politically strong and commercially successful. As with all the other major seaports, many foreign and exotic imports found their way to Ephesus. Among its inhabitants were many wizards, witches, sorcerers, palmists, and astrolo-gers, all willing to improve the present or warn of the future.

Though John accepted his duty of tending to the Lord's mother, he never lost his desire to evangelize. Occasionally, he would leave Mary in the care of others and go on a mission. He sometimes would return to Judea. When in Bethsaida, his hometown, he would visit the synagogues in nearby Galilean towns. He preached in Samaria and towns and vil-lages near Jerusalem. On several occasions, he had crossed the Jordan and preached in Peraea, Decapolis, and even Gaulanitis and Ituraea, and several times he traveled to Syria. After several months, he would return home, and upon returning he always realized that Ephesus was his greatest challenge. There were believers from hundreds of different religions, and there were numerous places of worship for these religions. Shrines, sanctuaries, and "holy places" could be found throughout the city and the surrounding areas. When John first arrived in Ephesus, he did as all the Apostles did—he went to the synagogues. Because Paul and others had been there before him, he found many Christians, but those who had not been converted were very hostile to the Gospel. He turned his attention to the Gentiles and discovered what Peter, Paul, and the Others had already discovered: the Gentile world was hungry for Christ. It was a life-long dream come true. Most rewarding were the disputes he participated in with proponents of the other religions. He quickly developed responses to all their questions and challenges, and he gained many converts.

Each time he returned to the house, he would spend excited hours telling his mother and Lady Mary of his conversions and victories; they would sit and listen with smiles of joy and approval.

On one occasion, he returned to find Luke at the house and attending to Lady Mary.

"She took to her bed the moment he arrived," Mary Cleophas said with concern on her aging face. "It seems she was waiting for him to arrive."

"We just learned that she wrote to him months ago asking him to come here, for she wanted to finish talking to him," Salome Zebedee said, appearing slightly puzzled.

"Finish talking about what?"

"I do not know, but Luke has been with her for hours," she answered.

"One moment, she was talking to us about Jesus. Then Luke arrived and she smiled and walked to her couch and said, 'I need to rest,'" Joanna Chuza said somewhat mechanically.

Just then, the heavy drape that covered the doorway to Mary's room was pushed aside, and Luke walked out of the room. He saw John and walked directly to him.

"The peace of the Lord be with you," he said.

John answered, "And also with you."

They embraced each other in the custom of all Christians.

"John, I do not know how much time she has, but I would suggest we do what she is requesting."

"What is she requesting?" John asked, bewildered and still stunned by the suddenness of what was happening.

Luke lowered his eyes and bit his lower lip, for he knew the request could not possibly be fulfilled.

"She wants the Twelve here so she can bid you all farewell."

"But that would be impossible. It will take us many months to get them all here," Joanna said quickly.

Salome began to cry, followed soon by Mary Cleophas.

"But not unbelievable," John said as he warmly remembered the ongoing miracle through which the Twelve could travel so rapidly. He walked to the small table that he used as a desk. Picking up a *stylus* and grabbing a *papyrus*, he began to write.

"Joanna, call some deacons. They will act as messengers," he said with urgency in his voice. Turning to his mother and the others in the room, he said "Pray, dear ladies, that my brother Apostles get this message soon."

Looking at the stunned and somewhat confused physician, he requested, "Luke, please help me write to the Others."

Luke walked to the other side of the small table, and together they wrote.

✳

Three days later, Andrew arrived, followed by Philip, Peter, Matthew, and Simon. By the fourth and fifth days, Bartholomew, Jude, and Thomas had arrived. Everyone knew that James bar Alphaeus, who had the shortest distance to travel, would be there shortly. The reunion was too somber for discussion of their missions, and there was no room for comments about how they had aged. They were there for one reason: to see the mother of the Lord embrace her new life. They surrounded Mary's bed and prayed, each sensing and feeling the presence of Jesus.

She looked at each of them slowly, seeing the youth and strength of yesterday among the old and tired. She smiled, giving new brightness to her lovely, aged face.

"Remain always faithful to Jesus. Let your suffering be the greatest testimony of your faith in Him. Do whatever He tells you."

Her breath caught the air.

At three o'clock in the afternoon, she turned her head to the window, and John followed her eyes. There on the window ledge were two pure white doves.

"Ah, James and Matthias, you have come also," she said in a low, weak voice.

John looked back at the Woman.

Then, smiling wide, she continued softly, "and you also, James."

John looked at the window and saw a third dove, as pure white as the others, and he realized that James bar Alphaeus was with the Lord.

The room swelled in light, and the Woman's face became young and beautiful. She smiled. A strong scent of flowers filled the air around them as a soft gasp became the only sound of the room. Lady Mary was new life.

John looked back to the window and saw the three doves hovering, then slowly, one by one, they flew away. He jumped to his feet, the only person in the room to move, and gazed at the doves, longing to be with them and with Mary.

CHAPTER FOUR:

NATHANIEL BAR THOLOMAI, BARTHOLOMEW OF CANA

PROLOGUE

The quickness of Lady Mary's death was a shock to those who loved her, especially the Apostles. They found comfort in knowing that she was always there. Whenever one of them returned to Jerusalem or Ephesus, he would make time to sit with her and talk of Jesus. Often she gave them new insights into the Master's life and doctrine, and this helped them to understand Him better. She had known Him longer than they had, and she knew of His Divinity long before they did. She had been a companion in the Spirit long before their Pentecost. She would sit and listen to the Apostles' stories, and her face would glow with an excitement that matched their enthusiasm. When they told her of their trials and tribulations, motherly compassion would shine from her face and tears would flood her eyes. When they would speak of seeing old friends, Mary would smile gently, and it was possible to see her mind traveling back to bygone days. When an Apostle told of his difficulties, she would comfort him with praise. Her praise was reinforcement. On a number of occasions, she acted as an advisor, but she never volunteered assistance unless asked—she was too humble. When an Apostle would speak of feeling the perpetual presences of Jesus, Mary would simply smile; they knew that above all others, and maybe more often than all others, she experienced the same presence.

At Mary's entombment, John realized that he no longer needed to remain near Mary—he was free to travel far and wide, as the Others did. His discipleship, which made him feel inferior to the Others and like more of a watcher, could finally be transcended. Now, he faced the dilemma of leaving familiar surroundings that provided acceptance and comfort. Unexpectedly, he felt a tinge of apprehension. Certainly the Others had felt this way also, but they had felt it collectively; he had to face it alone, and aloneness was an unfamiliar companion.

Mary's death also made John aware of his own mortality. Even someone as important as the mother of the Master could be called to death, and with great quickness. This made John understand that his desires were not necessarily part of the Will of God, for God had his own ideas and one could be called to His presence when it was time to complete God's plan.

The day after her burial, the remaining Apostles met before continuing their missions. It was to be the last time they would be together. In the gathering were Luke, the physician, and Peter's two trusted companions, Mark and Linus. The talk was first about their fellow Apostles, James bar Zebedee, James bar Alphaeus, and Matthias, and they all remembered these men in special ways.

John watched each of their faces, knowing that they sensed their own mortality. He saw no fear, only resolve and even anticipation, on their faces. Eventually, they talked of the second generation of disciples. They spoke of Stephaton, Philetus and Hermogenes, Nescius, and others.

Soon they began to compare notes and rumors. Peter related the sad news that Joseph of Arimathea had died in Britannia.

Dear Joseph, who gave so much. I wonder if he still had the cup from our last meal with Jesus, John thought.

Mark then gave additional sad news: his uncle Barnabas, Paul's companion, had been called back to the Lord in Cyprus.

"I received word that our dear friend in Jerusalem, Malchus, the gardener of Gethsemane, has been arrested and is set for trial," reported John.

All eyes in the room went to Peter, who had his head lowered. There was news of Cornelius, the centurion, teaching in Italy, and of Lazarus leaving Cyprus and journeying to Narbonensis and Aquitania in southern and central Gaul. They talked about the success in Numidia, Africa, and Cyrenaica experienced by Simon the Cyrenean and other Cyreneans. Some had heard that Nicodemus, after spending time with his close friend Joseph of Arimathea in Massilia in southern Gaul, left for northern Africa. Finally, there was talk of Paul and of all his success. He had been to Galatia, Cilicia, Asia, Greece, and Crete, and rumors indicated that he had even been in Hispania. Now he was under arrest and on his way to Rome to appeal to the Emperor.

"It seems we have more Gentiles being converted than Jews," Peter reflected. "Paul was right—the Gentiles hunger more deeply for salvation."

"But Peter, many of us did not even think about circumcision. I for one was baptizing anyone who professed Jesus. I never thought to ask if they were Jews or not. It did not matter, only their belief in Jesus mattered," Bartholomew stated.

"I did the same," Thomas added with no hesitation. "I believed that if the Spirit of the Lord moved someone, I should not stand in the way. I purified them and never thought of making them Jews first."

"I think we all moved wisely when confronting that situation. Andrew," Peter said as he gestured to his brother, "and Philip told me they were doing likewise, and before our meeting with Paul, we received word through Nescius that Matthias had converted many Armenian and Cappadocian Gentiles. Yes, I think we were following the dictates of the Spirit."

"Luke, tell us, just how successful is Paul?" Simon the Zealot asked.

"He is untiring. It is amazing to watch him and a blessing to hear him. He has written many letters to several communities, giving them further instructions and teachings. I become of use to him when he sends a letter, for I am better with the written word than with the spoken word, but I am in awe of his abilities to do both of these things, and do them well," Luke said with a tone of humility.

"I know that James the Little had written an epistle," John said looking at Matthew and Jude, wondering if they were aware of their brother's writings. He looked at Peter. "As did Peter."

"This conversation brings up a thought we wish to discuss with you," Peter said. "For several years, we have been thinking that it would be wise to put in writing what Jesus did. This narrative must relate the many acts of the Master and the things that proved Him to be the Messiah. Something must be written for those who follow us. So some time ago I asked Mark," he pointed to young Mark, "to put into writing some of the things I remembered about Jesus. He has done this. Mark has with him three copies of his narrative. Others are being scripted as we speak." He stopped talking and looked around the room at the remaining Apostles. "I grow fearful. James the Greater, James the Less, and Matthias are with the Lord, and there are fewer of us who were with John the Baptizer and were there throughout the ministry of Jesus. We have lost the Arimathean, Barnabas, and most of the original seventy-two disciples that Jesus sent out. I think it would be wise to write an account of what we have witnessed, so that others will have no doubts. These narratives would ensure that nothing will be forgotten or left unknown. We must make certain that what we have seen is told correctly."

"Peter is correct. Our ancestors did the same with the teachings of Moses and the Prophets," Bartholomew said.

"I agree. We must do this so that what we have seen remains after us. We must write the truth, with God's help. We do not need to be great Greek dramatists to write the things of the Master," Philip affirmed as he walked and sat by the door.

"But are we not writers? Have we not been writing to one another, giving one another accounts of our works?" Thomas added with a twinkle in his eye.

"Having read your letters, I must say again that we are not drama-tists," Philip added with a grin, and everyone laughed.

"But be aware that what Mark is writing leaves much unsaid. I do not wish to become too important in the narrative, and I have left many things open. I am sure a better narrative will follow." He turned to John. "Long ago, Lady Mary, James, and I asked John to begin a narrative, which I am sorry to say he has not completed."

"I have started, but it is difficult. I am struggling to find a begin-ning," John said in defense of himself.

"You start where we all must start when speaking of the Master: at His Rising. Without that, He was a captivating storyteller with good morals and ideas, but little more." Andrew's voice was very firm.

"Yes, His power over death is what proved Him to be God," Thomas said simply.

John was stunned at the simplicity of his dilemma.

I am sure this is an important point for the Gentiles; they know no founder of a religion who died and rose again. Still, how do I start my account with the end?

"I have begun a journal of what Paul has done. Also, after speaking to so many of you, I have begun an account of your acts after Jesus returned to His Father," Luke interjected.

"Luke, you should only tell what is important. What we have done, even what Paul is doing, is God's work, not ours. Do not spend time on us, for we are only instruments in His hands," Andrew added. "I do not want posterity to think we are so important."

"Agreed."

"Yes, I am of the same opinion."

"I concur."

"Yes, leave us out. Nothing we do is ours, it is from the Spirit within us."

"Yes, we are happy to be mere servants."

"Luke, you should write of Jesus," Peter affirmed. "People have to know Jesus in order to understand what we are doing. If you tell them only about our actions and not about the actions of Jesus, all is empty. You must write a narrative of what Jesus did."

Luke looked at each of them as they continued to ask for anonymity. He was amazed at their desire to remain insignificant. They were more humble than he expected.

"Yes, Luke, you are educated, a physician. Your writing, coming from a doctor, would carry much authority," John chimed in, hoping to be relieved of some pressure.

Luke looked at Peter, then at John. "I believe I will. I have spent many hours with Lady Mary, and she has given me much information about Jesus and His early years. Yes, I probably will write a narrative of the Lord's life, but first I must complete what I have started."

Looking around the table at all those seated, Jude Thaddeus said, "A long time ago, in the earlier days, some of us began keeping notes of what Jesus did. I believe we gave those notes to Lady Mary."

Luke smiled. "Lady Mary gave them to me a long time ago. They are excellent sources, and I will use them."

"I would like a copy of those notes, Luke, for I have started a writing."

Everyone turned and looked at Matthew with surprise, but quickly the surprise gave way to approval. Matthew was educated, and it seemed quite reasonable for him to take on such an important task.

"You, Matthew?" his brother Jude asked.

"Yes. I told Peter about it, and..." he looked at his brother Jude, "I mentioned it to our brother James." Looking at Mark, Matthew continued, "What notes I possessed I have used as references for my writing, along with the account of young Mark, but I do not have all the notes."

John Zebedee smiled broadly with relief. With three accounts of the Life of Jesus left for posterity, there was no need for him to write a fourth.

"I began my story immediately after seeing some of what Mark had put to *papyrus*. I decided to write my account for the Jews." Matthew looked at Mark. "Our brother Mark gave me a good foundation."

Mark smiled and lowered his eyes in embarrassment.

"And could I have one of your copies, Mark?" Luke requested as he looked at Mark, amazed by the young man's humility. Continuing, he whispered, "If our brother Matthew has found you to be so great a resource, I am sure I will also."

Mark, now blushing, said lightly, "You are too kind. Please take a copy, Luke, and use it to do whatever you must do to make the Master known."

Looking at the Others, Matthew continued, "Mark writes for all Christians, whereas I intend to explain things for the Jews in particular. I want to show them that Jesus was the Messiah and that He died for the love of them. We owe this to the Jews, maybe as a last resort, in the hope that they will see the Truth."

"Did you say you were almost done?" Bartholomew asked Matthew.

"Yes, I have seven scribes copying what I have written. They pick up what I have completed almost immediately."

"The same happens to me," Mark added. "My scribes stand waiting for me to finish a scroll, and immediately they start copying. I am sorry that I do not have a finished copy for each of you."

"Please, Matthew, may I have a copy of what you have completed?" Bartholomew asked.

"Bartholomew, are you trying to flatter me, or is your faith so strong that you will be willing to accept what I have written?" Matthew said with a smile.

Bartholomew looked stupefied. "Whatever you write of the Master will be the Truth. I believe that you and Mark have been inspired to take on this responsibility, and I am sure that if Jesus did not want such things to happen, they would not be happening."

John took note of Bartholomew's words and acknowledged that perhaps the Master was not yet ready for him to complete his account.

Everyone looked at Bartholomew and knew that he was right.

NATHANIEL BAR THOLOMAI, BARTHOLOMEW OF CANA

The tree, with its low, irregular branches, spread out over him like a spidery canopy. The large, dark green leaves danced in the persistence of the warm summer breeze. Occasionally, the sun would slip through the leaves and fall on his head and his tan face, highlighting his fashionably trimmed beard and his tightly curled, wavy red hair.

It was too hot a day to be concerned with anything other than comfort. So he came to this fig tree, his favorite place to cool down and relax. Placing his brown seamless cloak on the cool, emerald green grass, he lowered himself onto the soft material of the cloak and sighed with contentment. Carefully, he rested his back onto the rough bark of the tree, shifting and adjusting himself into a comfortable position, and making certain he was not dirtying or damaging his clothes. He looked around. To his right was a road; it was one of those poorly constructed, dusty Galilean roads. To his left were the steep slopes of the many hills of Galilee, and before him was the wide open and beautiful landscape of Galilee. The beauty of his land pleased him. Under the tree, he was certain that the world was right. Nothing could go wrong, and nothing would disturb his peacefulness. Being a man of learning and familiarity with the Law, he naturally quoted from the book of *Devarim,* Deuteronomy.

A land of wheat, and barley, and vineyards, wherein fig trees and pomegranates and olive yards grow: a land of oil and honey.

"The promise to Moses," he said aloud, surprised that these words escaped his mouth. It embarrassed him momentarily, for speaking aloud with no one to hear was definitely not of his station. He quickly looked around to make certain that no one was near enough to hear him. If someone had overheard him, they might have thought that he was out of his senses, and this was something he could never be. After all, he was of the House of Tholomai and was therefore a man of some royalty and position. His family was traceable back to the ancient house of Ptolemy and had a direct line to King David: one of his great-ancestors, Maacah, who was of the House of Tholomai, was one of David's wives. This noble ancestry, though, had done little for his family other than give them pride, some privileges, and enough money to make them a little better off than most Galileans. The pride in his paternal heritage had prompted him to rarely use his given name, Nathaniel. This was the name of his Nazarene maternal grandfather, whom he disliked because of his lack of grace. After Nathaniel matched his daughter to Aaron Tholomai, he shortly thereafter renounced her and her marriage. Some relatives said the problem was all a result of a dispute over a vineyard owned by the Tholomai family and desired by Nathaniel between Cana and Sepphoris. Bartholomew never found out if this was true, and after so many years he did not care to know. So in his disdain for his grandfather Nathaniel, he preferred to be called Bar Tholomai, or Bartholomew.

Taking a deep breath that further inflated his pride, he thought, *Well, it seems Adonai has given me the place to start my thoughts and meditations for this day.*

Immediately he challenged himself to remember the many places in the Holy Writings where the fig tree was mentioned. He thought for a moment, and soon several writings came to mind. He rested his head against the bark of the tree and gave thanks to *Adonai* for the fig tree, his beautiful clothes, his intellect, and his position in life. This fig tree had been his place for years. There seemed to be a direct connection between him and this fig tree that instantaneously produced prayers, consolation, and thoughts of *Adonai*, and when he was in such mental comfort, he hated being bothered. He was not common and did not act like a commoner, even if he worked occasionally as a fisherman. He did have common friends, but they could remain his friends only if they had a degree of self-respect, or if they were interesting conversationalists. He was quick to recognize greatness in other people. He appreciated his life and was thankful for his many other gifts. Perhaps his greatest fault was that he was honest to the point of being hurtful.

Completing his prayers of thanksgiving, he tried to think of a passage of Holy Scripture that he could meditate on, but for some unknown reason, nothing came to mind, and he became impatient with himself. Suddenly, he thought of John the Baptist and remembered John speaking of "one crying in the desert," preparing the way of another. The words of Isaiah, the great prophet, came to him: "Behold, I send my angel before thy face, who shall prepare the way before thee."

Indeed, I would say that John was an angel preparing the way.

With this conclusion came the recurring feeling that something exceptional was to happen to him. This atmosphere of expectation had surrounded him for months. He was certain that whatever this was, it would make him somehow more important.

With his eyes closed, he heard words come to him from nowhere.

"Hear the word of the Lord, you nations, and declare it in the islands that are far off, and say: He who scattered Israel, will gather him, and will guard him as a shepherd does his flock."

Ah, the words of good Jeremiah.

He let himself go, drifting away, and soon he was off in a place of expansive quietude. He sensed he was in the presences of something solemn. He felt he was near *El Shaddai*.

Words came to him again, this time from the *Tehillim* and the Psalmist: "How long, O Lord, wilt Thou utterly forget me? How long wilt Thou hide Thy face from me?"

Certain that he was in the presence of the Most High, he became all still. From nowhere, or perhaps from far in the distance, he heard a heavy sigh, and he was sure that the sigh was the answer to the Psalmist's questions. His face contorted in puzzlement, then he heard the sounds of many people. He became annoyed at their interference, and as the sounds became louder, he grew irritated. Reluctantly, he opened his eyes and saw a crowd walking on a path below his shaded spot. Some people were running ahead of the crowd, and others were walking on the road, encircling a Man. He could not see the Man's face, only His white robe and His red cloak. Amidst this distraction, he saw someone running in his direction. It was his good friend Philip of Bethsaida.

"What is going on?" he asked.

"We have found Him of Whom Moses in the law and the Prophets did write: Jesus bar Yosef of Nazareth," Philip shouted back with great certainty. His face was glowing.

Bartholomew smiled and chuckled slightly. "Can anything of good come from Nazareth?" he said, manifesting again his dislike for Nathaniel the Nazarene.

"Come and see," Philip responded, and he turned away from him to return to the crowd.

Bartholomew stood up and watched the crowd as it passed him. Strangely, he was being drawn to the crowd; something natural, instinctive was pulling him to the Man, yet he did not want to leave his tree, his hillside, his shade, his place. The fear of missing whatever was luring him made him take a few steps, and leisurely he began to descend the hillside. Occasionally, he stopped and looked back to his tree and the shade, but he continued toward the crowd, uncertain and needy. As he approached the side of the road, the crowd stopped. The Man turned to him and the crowd parted, so that the Man and Bartholomew were in full view of each other.

When he was close, the Man declared, "Behold an Israelite indeed, in whom there is no guile."

Bartholomew was immediately flattered. With disbelief and a sneer on his lips, he asked, "How do You know me?"

The Man smiled widely and answered, "Before Philip called thee, when thou wast under the fig tree, I saw thee."

Bartholomew, feeling a sense of being known forever and of finding a perfect resting place, a place of complete and endless comfort, said, in earnest, "Rabbi, Thou art the Son of God, Thou art the King of Israel."

Jesus stopped smiling. He looked into Bartholomew's eyes and saw more than mere humanism. He knew that this man of Israel had the insight and the wisdom to see his God. Placing His hand on Bartholomew's shoulder, He said, "Because I said unto thee, I saw thee under the fig tree, thou believest; greater things than these shall thou see. Amen, amen, I say to you, you shall see the heavens opened and the angels of God ascending and descending upon the Son of Man."

From that day on and without ceasing, Bartholomew believed. When all the others wondered Who this Jesus was, Bartholomew knew.

❊

One week after the Twelve met in the Upper Room and drew lots to determine their missions, Bartholomew and his friend Philip left together for Samaria and then continued on to the northernmost towns and villages of Galilee. After six months, they moved on to the provinces of Cilicia and the cities of Derbe and Lystra, and finally onto Galatia. The two men continued on, knowing that they would have to separate according to the lots they picked, but they stayed together, doing the Master's bidding. They continued into Asia, Lycia, Pisidia, and finally Pamphylia. It was at Pamphylia that the two Apostles parted. Bartholomew continued north into the districts of Lycaonia.

Lycaonia was a harsh land that matched the character of its people. It was a highland country whose inhabitants were poor and backwards. They were plundering, lawless people of simple ways and means. The land was dry and devoid of most vegetation, except in and around the city of Iconium. In the eastern part of the land were volcanic masses, and the rest of the region was made up of hills and plains. For years this land had been known to many conquerors as the perfect place for renegades and bandits to flourish. Many wanted criminals were hiding here, some with altered appearances and some disguised as upright citizens.

When Bartholomew arrived in Iconium, the chief city of the district, Abendadar, a former Syrian mercenary in the Roman Army, was there waiting for him. He had been waiting for his arrival for months, having been sent by Peter. They were to be traveling companions. The two men knew each other from the early days when Abendadar and others who were involved in the crucifixion came to the Apostles to be taught and purified.

❊

Abendadar's father, Sabinianus, immigrated to Damascus from Samaria. Sabinianus was the son of a wealthy cloth merchant. His parents provided him a good education, with Greek and Roman tutors to show him the ways of the world. Soon his parents perceived some degree of economic advantage in being Syrian rather than Samaritan Jew, so they took on Syrian identity but continued to be Jewish in faith. When Sabinianus was nineteen years old, he was betrothed to fifteen-year-old Ligia, the daughter of a Samaritan olive and spice merchant. The youngsters were not strangers; they had known each other from childhood, and it was obvious to all that they were attracted to each other. After a few endearing exchanges of flowers and fruits, Sabinianus told his father to make a contract of marriage with Ligia's father. They soon were engaged, and during the time called the "conduction," which followed all Jewish marriage contracts, the two were expected to get to know each other better. During this period, which normally lasted a year, they lived with their respective parents. Soon, Sabinianus and Ligia found many common grounds for a good relationship, but the most pronounced similarity was their dissatisfaction with the hypocrisy they perceived in the Samaritan and Judean Jews. It was difficult to consider them either as true followers of Moses or Abraham. The dislike these Jews had for each other had broken into open hostilities over the years, and each accused the other of being "second-class Jews." The hatred between the two "chosen people" existed for hundreds of years. King Sargon of Assyria conquered the northern Kingdom of Israel. As part of the Assyrian conquest, Sargon followed the common practice of bringing the ablest back to Assyria.

After Sargon's death, his son Escarhaddon assumed the throne. The new king forced Chaldeans, Cutheans, Syrians, Arabs, and other peoples from eastern Assyria to resettle in Samaria. These inhabitants brought with them their pagan religions. Soon after their arrival, with the hope of blending in and becoming more accepted, they sought the God of the land and became "Jewish." They began eroding Jerusalem's authority, and soon they were intermarrying with the Samaritans. When this period of captivity ended and the Jews were free to return to their "promised land," they refused to associate with this contaminated race. The Judeans referred to Samaria as "the land of the Cuthim," so named on account of the Cutheans. They declared them non-Jews and their clergy invalid. The Samaritans likewise declared that the Judeans were not true descendants of Abraham. The Samaritans refused the supremacy of the Judeans and boldly refused to rebuild the Jerusalem Temple. In retaliation, the Judean Jews proclaimed that no Samaritan could enter the Jerusalem Temple. The Samaritans, in greater defiance, built their own temple on Mount Gerizim. When that was destroyed in 130 BC by the Jewish King John Hyrcanus, they built another temple at Shechem to rival the Temple of Jerusalem. The bitter hostilities festered over the years and turned violent. Around the time of Christ's birth, Samaritans desecrated the Temple in Jerusalem by scattering bones of the dead on the floor of the sanctuary. Samaritans traveling through Judea or Galilee were harassed and often beaten. A Judean never traveled through Samaria for fear of being contaminated or worse. It was common practice for Judeans and Samaritans to create extra space between them when approaching each other, and speaking to one another was unthinkable.

So Sabinianus and Ligia, Abendadar's parents, found a common bond in their dislike for what had become of their faith. They believed that the Jews had traveled too far from their roots and from the ways of *Elohim*. They decided that in their married life, they would slowly separate themselves from Judaism. After their marriage, Sabinianus was sent by his father to Damascus on family business. While there, the young husband got the idea to leave all behind and become Syrian. Ligia joined him, but the journey proved too much for her, and she died while delivering her premature baby boy, who also died soon thereafter. Sabinianus, determined to be free of Judaism, remained in Syria. Angered and saddened by the death of his wife, he abandoned *Elohim* and his Jewish ways and became very Syrian and Roman. He became a Roman citizen, took a Roman name, purchased a *villa*, and quickly found employment as a *stator*, a public servant in the service of Limetanus Titius, the Governor of Syria. He married Kildar, a rich Syrian woman. Judaism was never mentioned again, but it was not forgotten; he still found value in some practices of the Jewish people. Within a year, Kildar gave birth to her only son, Abendadar.

Abendadar grew up with Roman power and life all around him. He knew nothing of Palestine or of his father's past. When he was fifteen, he became a minor *accensus*, an orderly to the Roman officers. By the time he was eighteen, the new governor of Syria recommended him for sixteen years of military service as an *accensus*. It was a perfect opportunity for a young man who loved adventure, but his father's influence with the governor, and the governors who followed, kept Abendadar in Syria. When his father resigned, the governor, Alius Lamius, seeing no need for an *accensus*, transferred Abendadar to the Province of Judea. At the time of his transfer, he had only three remaining years of military duty. Pontius Pilate was the Procurator of the Province, and Abendadar arrived in Jerusalem during the Jewish feast of the Passover. Abendadar came to Jerusalem as a Gentile. As soon as he saw the land of Palestine, he fell under the spell of its bleak contradictions. The land was beautiful but rugged. It was a land of harshness and of softness. The hills were delicate and simple as they flowed across and over the rocky, dry soil like frozen waves. The valleys dipped deep and spread out in many directions, giving the land an appearance of enormity. The rivers, pure and refreshing, snaked their way through the dry and warm land, exhaling coolness. Scattered throughout the countryside were patches of green vegetation, which dressed the land with numerous acacias and jujube trees. Olive, fig, and humble almond trees dotted the rest of the land like small refugees of pleasantness. Vineyards with long, thick-skinned grapes or round, plumb violet grapes sporadically accented the landscape. The weather, like the landscape, was dry and moderate in the day, and it was cool, and often very cold, at night.

On the first day of his arrival, Abendadar sensed he was living on a volcano about to erupt. Daily he felt the faint rumbles under foot, and soon he learned that this feeling was from the restlessness of a stiff-necked populace. The Jews were an extraordinary people. They were very clannish, with little tolerance for any other race or nation. The family was the basic unit of their society. When a person was declared a relative, he was immediately included in their history, blood, property, and struggles— their very spirit. One thing that annoyed Abendadar was the expectation of perfection among the people, especially that perfection insisted on by the religious leaders. It was demanded of the Jews. Those who were ill, lame, blind, or deformed were somewhat shunned and occasionally recognized with a few thoughtless *denarii*. If anyone was suspected of a novel idea that would in some way threaten the status quo of the theocratic system, he was immediately hounded into submission or destroyed. The temple tolerated very few impurities or imperfections, and above all it endured no other religion. Only those who followed the strictest word of the Law were worthy of being called a "Jew." Unscrupulous and impious Jews were never a part of the nation. You could not just be irreligious or religious, you had to be everything Jewish—in living, breathing, acting, and thinking.

After a few months of duty, Abendadar wrote to his father to tell him of the hatred he felt from these people. He wrote, "They hate Romans. They hate non-Jews. They hate Syrians. They hate."

His father's reply plainly read, "I know."

Abendadar became completely indifferent to the people and their ways. Nothing that happened around him held his attention. He just did his duty. He anxiously began counting the months, the weeks, the days that remained with these people, and through it all he was glad he was not a Jew or a Samaritan. He preferred his station at Caesarea Maritima, the capital of the Province of Palestine, to that at Jerusalem. In Caesarea, he felt Roman. The city was opulent and had a metropolitan style, like a Roman city, and it offered many things to keep a restless soldier happy. The streets were lined with Roman temples, public baths, shops, and merchants. Sebastos, the harbor city of Caesarea, was large enough to accommodate three hundred ships. When the Roman fleet was in harbor, the might of Rome permeated the city. Caesarea had a *forum* and a large amphitheater that sat over three thousand people. In the amphitheater, Abendadar enjoyed the Roman and Greek plays, the prose readings, and the acting. Abendadar rarely used the public bath houses; he spent most of his time at the large oval hippodrome, where he enjoyed chariot and horse races and, occasionally, gladiatorial combat. He reveled in the fact that the Jews looked upon this palace and all its forms of entertainment as sinful.

The palace, where he spent most of his time, was a magnificent high-columned Roman structure that projected out into the harbor. It was a peninsula pointing to the promise of distant and different lands, and it provided the best scenery in all Judea. Throughout his time in the military, Abendadar seldom attended physical training because his military job did not demand this training. As was customary, the men exercised without clothing. Cornelius, a centurion with whom Abendadar was somewhat friendly and who also disliked the Jews, asked if he was a Jew. Abendadar quickly snapped a denial, but for the first time he was conscious of his circumcision. With that one simple inquiry, he became an oddity. Only someone in a Judean garrison would have identified his appearance with Judaism. Immediately, Abendadar wrote his father, and finally he learned the truth of his ancestry. He refused to abandon his Roman and Syrian identity. He had no desire to live a life dictated by small-minded people who remained subservient to a God Who had failed them. He had the Roman gods to worship, and they were more like him and more to his liking. For the rest of his tour of duty, he isolated himself from the Jews, and he soon found himself in open contempt of the Jews and their God.

Then, in his final months of duty, when everything grew unimportant, even attending to Pilate, he was asked by his friend Cornelius to assist at a crucifixion. Abendadar found this request a little unusual—he was sure Cornelius knew that he was never involved in such duties. He was going to refuse, but suddenly he saw the look on his friend's face. It was a look of pain and deep aloneness, and he knew Cornelius needed a friend. He never remembered seeing Cornelius so troubled. Abendadar recalled how Cornelius had recently seemed more tolerant of the Jews. Abendadar could not immediately understand the reason for the change, but it was obvious enough for him to notice it. He agreed to help Cornelius out of a mixture of concern, curiosity, and boredom.

As Abendadar listened to the proceedings, his sympathy was with the accused. At first, he thought this was a result of his dislike of the Jews and the authorities, but later he concluded that indeed there were no grounds for an arrest. As the proceedings continued, his pity intensified for the accused Man, Who seemed to be permitting things to happen to Him, not because He was defeated but because He willed it, and this baffled Abendadar. During the trial, he occasionally looked at Cornelius and saw the deep scowl on his face. When the criminal was condemned to death, Cornelius was noticeably tormented, and this made Abendadar even more troubled and confused.

Why would Cornelius be so distressed about what is happening to a Jew? Even if there is an injustice being done, why is Cornelius so concerned? Surely he, like me, has seen Rome's blatant injustice before today.

He cleared his throat, hoping the sound would get Cornelius' attention, but it didn't. He continued staring at Cornelius and felt an unusual feeling come over himself. He felt strange, like there was a need for him to do something, to say something, but he didn't know what he had to do or what he had to say. Slowly, he began to attribute this feeling to the bizarre crucifixion he was a part of, and his unfamiliarity of duty at a crucifixion. For a long time he just stood in the *praetorium*, doing nothing and feeling nothing. He was an ornament.

Sometime later, Cornelius walked to Abendadar and, without looking at his face, ordered Abendadar to go to the *scriptor* scribe, Nescius, to get the *titulus* placard for the crucifixion. Abendadar quickly obeyed, and when he found Nescius, who he knew did not like him, he found the young scribe just as bothered and tormented as Cornelius.

It is becoming a sickness. What does this criminal possess that has captured the minds, moods, and faces of these Romans?

When he returned, he gave the sign to a young, fair-skinned, blond-haired slave named Namenlos, from Germania, who often served as a *praeconor* herald at crucifixions. He then fell into the formation of soldiers escorting the condemned to death.

He occasionally heard Namenlos herald the guilt of the Jew: *Iesus Nazarenus, Rex Iudaeorum.*

As Abendadar walked, he thought, *I will not become part of this death. I will not become like the others, pulled into this confusion and stress. This is only another Jew being taken to a criminal's death.*

As he walked over the cobblestoned, narrow streets, he pushed and shoved the bystanders more roughly than usual, ignoring their aspersions. He was unaware of the crowd, unaware of the entire world, except for one thing—the odor of the streets. For some unknown reason, and from some unknown source, the streets were heavy with an odor so foul that he could not recall ever experiencing such a smell. At first, he ignored the smell as something that would pass, but it did not. It continued to taint the air around him. It grew more offensive as the condemned carried the *patibulum* crossbar closer to Golgotha.

Halfway through the procession, Cornelius walked over to him and, in a soft, concerned voice, said, "This Man grows weak, perhaps too weak. Find me someone to help Him. Someone strong and healthy."

Abendadar looked at the condemned Man. His dirty, bloody, swollen face was beyond any human resemblance. He staggered and swayed with each step under the weight of the crude tree trunk. After giving the order, Cornelius abruptly walked away, leaving Abendadar bewildered as he searched the crowd for an able-bodied man. Then, a man passed before his eyes. The man walked hurriedly away from the procession, completely indifferent to what was happening.

"The perfect person," he said aloud. "You there, *Africanus*."

The tall black man turned and looked at Abendadar. He was shocked.

"Come here, you are being pressed into the service of Rome. Come here quickly."

The tall African hesitated.

"I order you in the name of the Emperor of Rome to come here."

Slowly, the African walked to Abendadar. His reluctance was fueled by resentment and exasperation. Abendadar grabbed his arm and felt the man's muscles tense to his touch. He led him to Cornelius, who ordered the black man to help the condemned.

A fitting duet, Abendadar concluded to himself with complete satisfaction in his choice. He turned his attention to the crowds, and once again his nostrils were offended by the stench around him. He longed for Golgotha and the openness of it, but when he arrived, he became angry with himself, for he quickly realized that Golgotha was the sanctuary of the trash of the city. He then recognized what the stench was—it was the smell of decay and death.

The young herald Namenlos stood with the soldiers. The boy was mesmerized by what he was witnessing, and his face was etched with sadness. Seeing the boy so disturbed made Abendadar become more confused. He knew that the boy had seen too many crucifixions to be so perturbed; he could not understand how this Man had taken possession of this young man also.

Another fool taken up with this Man. I can understand this one, he is but a child, but Cornelius and Nescius are men. What magic does this Man have over others?

He heard Cornelius order him to stand far from the nailing, and he stationed him to control the crowds until the criminal was nailed to the *patibulum* and it was lifted to the *stipes* post for all to see.

Usually, as soon as any condemned was lifted up and his feet were nailed to the *stipes* cross, the soldiers would relax, but much to his disappointment, there was no rest among the soldiers. The bystanders jeered, cursed, and challenged the crucified Man. At times, the people were nearly riotous. So the guards were in a tense situation. Having been in near-riot conditions before, Abendadar kept himself keenly alert of all those around him and of all that was taking place. In this state of acute readiness, he was still bothered by the foul smell around him.

Eventually things settled down, and the guards slowly lost their attentiveness. Abendadar and a few of the other Syrian soldiers sat around and began drinking their soldier's wine, telling jokes and stories. They grew louder in their talk and laughter. Normally, Cornelius would be in the middle of such fun, but this time he was standing solemnly by the cross, looking into the face of the Jew. Strangely, Cornelius' face radiated pity.

What in the name of Jupiter is wrong with Cornelius today?

Abendadar looked at the Jew on the cross, but he could neither see nor feel anything. Turning his attention to Cornelius again, he thought, *I will have to seek out Cornelius later and find out what his malady is.*

Clouds began to build and move across the sky, and the day was beginning to grow grim.

Strange…it was a hot, cloudless day moments ago.

Without warning Stephaton, the legionnaire, appeared out of nowhere, and his sudden arrival diverted and startled Abendadar. He watched as Stephaton walked over to the relaxing guards. He paused there for a moment, then he looked at the crucified Man. Quietly, as if trying to be secretive, Stephaton slowly walked to the skins of wine hanging from a nearby bush; he poured some wine into a drinking bowl, added some myrrh, and then dipped a sponge attached to a hyssop branch into the mixture.

Abendadar watched Stephaton offer the mixture to the dying Jew.

The guards' laughter distracted him from what Stephaton was doing. One of the Syrians had just finished telling an obscene joke, and everyone was laughing loudly. Abendadar, who had not heard the story, laughed as loud as the others in the hopes of getting Cornelius' attention—and as an act of defiance against whatever power this dying Jew had over his friend.

One of the Syrians walked over to Abendadar and the others carrying a red cloak. It belonged to the Jew on the cross. The cloth instantly captured Abendadar's fancy. It was of good material and not fastened by stitches or made of two pieces of cloth.

"Let us do what is expected of all conquerors: divide the spoils of conquest," a guard said with a smirk and a trace of contempt in his raspy voice.

They all laughed, except Abendadar, who was captivated by the fineness of the cloth.

"Should we ask the others to join in dividing the garment?" one of the other Syrians asked.

"I already asked the centurion and Stephaton. They refused. I asked old Calvos, the executioner, and he never answered me. He seems preoccupied with this dying Jesus."

"Is that His name?" Abendadar asked, for suddenly the Jew became a Person.

"Yes. Where have you been, Abendadar? Everyone knows this Man. He is Jesus, King of the Jews."

They laughed. For the first time that day, Abendadar heard the name Jesus, and he remembered Cornelius speaking that name, but he could not remember in what circumstances.

Unexpectedly, a breeze passed by him, and the odor that had accompanied him all day was heavier. It surrounded him, seemingly penetrating his armor and skin.

"Come, let us divide the spoils," one of the soldiers insisted.

"Yes, and the others can go to *Inferi* and play with the gods in the underworld," another Syrian guard added.

"No, let us not!" Abendadar said, surprised at his own objection. He could immediately detect tension from the other soldiers. "Look at the garment. It is all one piece. Few garments in Palestine are like this. Let us cast lots to see who will keep the seamless cloak."

The others examined the cloak and agreed. He was glad they had agreed. The casting of lots would take his mind off the stench that was beginning to settle in his stomach. A soldier produced dice, and they all gathered in a circle around the seamless garment. First, two dice were placed in a small, leathery cup shaken vigorously by each of the soldiers. The six guards cast their lots. The three men who received the highest total of the dice would go on to the next part of the game, in which another die was to be added.

Abendadar got the highest possible total of twelve, another soldier rolled ten, and another got eight. Those with the lower counts were eliminated.

The third die was added to the cup.

Abendadar and the other two soldiers each shook the leathery cup and tossed the dice, and the numbers were tallied.

The first soldier tossed "the dogs"—three ones.

The second soldier tossed a pair of sixes and a one, sometimes called "a family."

Abendadar tossed the dice and received a "Venus"—three sixes. He was the winner.

Just then, the sky grew dark. The wind, carrying a strange chill, blew past them.

"Looks like a bad storm will be upon us soon," one of the Syrians said.

"It is coming quick, and we will have to be here until this Jew dies," another Syrian said.

Oh no, I was hoping for a quick death. The stench is growing unbearable, Abendadar thought to himself.

"He is dead."

Abendadar turned and saw the centurion Longinus standing over them. His face was white and aglow.

"I just lanced His side. He is dead."

Abendadar glanced at Jesus on the cross. The Man's face was obscured by the straggling hair that hung from His head.

Two, three, four cracks of lightning split the dark sky, and distant thunder roared and rumbled toward them—slowly, agonizingly, but with such might that the soldiers swiftly became alarmed.

Abendadar slowly rose from his squatted position and looked around the hill for Cornelius. For some unknown reason, he needed to be with his friend. He found Cornelius standing with Longinus, and he quickly walked to them with his prize, the cloak, thrown over his arm. As he approached Cornelius, he could not tear his eyes away from his friend's face. It was all aglow. He looked as though he were in the midst of a great celestial event. Again, two, three, four cracks of lightning zigzagged and tore across the darkened sky, and thunder rumbled and grumbled all around them. This time the thunder seemed to erupt from the earth, and the rumble was more like a painful groan filled with anger.

Abendadar felt the world tremble beneath his feet.

Suddenly, rain gushed from the sky in heavy sheets of water, and soon everything was wet and washed. The rain was cold, and when it splashed against the hot ground, small clouds of steam and dust rose into the air. When the rain struck Abendadar's bare face, neck, arms, and legs, it sent a chill through his entire body. A forceful wind threw the rain in all directions, soaking every fiber, every particle of life, on that hill.

The world was covered by a midnight sky.

Day was dead.

The earth began to shiver in fright.

Cornelius fell to his knees and cried out, "Truly, this Man is the Son of God!"

The moment Abendadar heard these words, he looked at the dead Jew. He watched as the rain flowed over His body, cleansing it of all the dirt, dust, and blood. As he watched the rain cleanse Jesus, he felt a warmth flow over and through his body. The warmth rose up into his chest and rushed to his head and face. He felt it gather, embrace, and pull all his thoughts, feelings, emotions, taking them to a place within his being that was never before known to him, and he became filled with great comfort. He wanted to shout, to let out a loud, long cry of relief, to welcome a freedom he had never known before, but his throat captured the sound and held it, only allowing it to settle with the rest of him in this place of well-being. He knew, he was certain, that had the shout exited his mouth, it would have echoed Cornelius' cry.

The cloak over his arm suddenly became warm and comforting. Though soaked by the rain, it was not heavy. From it came the scent of incense from the Temple in Jerusalem, and the scent encircled Abendadar's entire person. The foul smell of his bad day had finally lifted.

＊

Abendadar, Longinus, and Cornelius, along with the others who had been on Golgotha, were left in confusion for days. When they heard the rumor that Jesus was alive again, they secretly sought out the guards on tomb duty and questioned them. When they heard the guards' stories, they became more confused. They decided to find the followers of Jesus. They carefully and persistently made inquiries, but Abendadar's approach was a bit unusual for he bribed and spied until finally, many days later, he found them. It was the day before the Jewish feast of Pentecost. He felt like a criminal as he walked, in disguise, to the house. When he found the house, he slowly climbed the many wooden steps to the Upper Room. Occasionally, he stopped to look around and make certain he was not being watched. He tapped softly on the heavy wooden door. Instantly, he heard mumbles and panic on the other side of the door.

To those inside, the knock was loud, demanding.

John bar Zebedee rushed to Lady Mary's side and gently pushed her and the other women into the corner of the room.

Simon the Zealot walked slowly to the door. This made him look the bravest of them all, but his face was white with fear. He opened the door ever so slightly, and everyone heard a low exchange of words between Simon and someone on the other side of the door. Suddenly, Simon threw open the door. In walked Abendadar, and the door was sealed shut behind him.

Abendadar's eyes raced around the room. His small mouth widened to a smile of satisfaction, for he had found what for weeks he had been searching for.

"Simon!" Matthias shouted. "What have you done?" The new Apostle, like some others in the room, recognized the Roman soldier.

"Have no fear," Abendadar said in a loud, commanding voice. "I have been in search of you for weeks. I mean no harm. I want to help you, if you will allow me, and I want to hear more about Jesus."

No one moved or even acknowledged his statement.

"There are many others who would like to know of Jesus—many who were on Golgotha that day." His normally controlled voice turned to a plea. "We need to know, for things happened to each of us that need explaining."

"Look!" Jude Thaddeus shouted as he pointed to the cloak on the man's arm.

"The Master's cloak," Philip declared.

Gasps and mumbles rose from the gathering.

Slowly, as if magnetized, they all began to walk to Abendadar, but he pulled away and tucked the cloak closer to his body.

"No, you cannot have it until you speak to us of Jesus," he insisted.

The crowd separated to form an aisle from the back of the room, and a middle-aged, beautiful woman walked toward him. Tears were welling up in her eyes. She walked directly to him and slowly, tenderly, extended her hand, wanting to touch the cloak, which she stroked very gently.

"That is the cloak I made for my Son over three years ago. I gave it to Him to celebrate His new life. I knew then that it would be the last thing I would give Him. The Almighty had made it known to me that from that day on, I would begin anew. I would give no more, but rather would be receiving from Him."

Abendadar gradually eased his hold of the cloak and extended it to the woman.

"No. No. It no longer is part of me. It is for all to have." Mary turned and looked into the crowd. "Bartholomew, you are the perfect person to bring this man to Jesus. Tell him of the Master."

Bartholomew broke out of the group, walked to the man, and awkwardly embraced him. As they walked away, Bartholomew, smiling, said to Abendadar, "I hope your resourcefulness is a gift from the Almighty and not merely a human ability, for if it is not from the Almighty, we will all soon be in jail."

Abendadar laughed. It was the beginning of a long friendship.

*

Immediately after joining Bartholomew, Abendadar began to see Bartholomew's restlessness. For several months he would be content and would stay in this or that city or town, but then something would trigger an impatience in him. He would begin to become restless, wanting to move on to another place. Abendadar noticed that each move to another place was preceded by a period of withdrawal, with hours and hours of prayer and silence. When Abendadar noticed Bartholomew's withdrawal, he immediately started packing, for he knew the idea of moving on was soon to follow. So after several years of traveling through the many different villages, towns, and cities of Lycaonia, Bartholomew, after a period of drawing away, announced to Abendadar that they were going to continue farther north into Phrygia, which was then part of the Province of Galatia.

The Phrygians were a unique people, highly intelligent and artful. They were greatly respected for their creative wooden and metal art, their farming methods, and their hardy, black, wooly livestock.

They had been conquered by the Greeks after the Trojan War, and the country became a great source for slaves. Like so often before, these resourceful people, though conquered, were able to export more aspects of their lifestyle than they imported. To the Greeks, they gave the legend of King Midas and his golden touch. They disseminated the country's nature-based fertility religion of Cybele, "the great mother of gods," and her male lover Attis. When the Romans came, this fertility goddess caught their fancy, and her cult was added to their polytheistic religion.

Through all this, there remained the Phrygian Jews, who were caught in the grips of many different customs and intolerances and who struggled to remain even more independent than their Gentile neighbors. Though they prospered and were outwardly accepted by the Phrygians, there existed a latent dislike for them. They were disliked not because they were Jews, but because they were foreigners, and the Phrygians were not fond of foreigners. The Phrygians were a closed society, more closed even than that of the Jews.

When Bartholomew and Abendadar arrived, the Phrygian Jews came in large numbers out of curiosity. Some had been in Jerusalem during the Pentecost and upon returning had spoken of Jesus, and Bartholomew reinforced their stories. Those who knew nothing of Jesus began to listen to Bartholomew, and many became followers. When the defections became too numerous, the Jewish leaders sought Roman help and accused Bartholomew of being a revolutionary, but the Romans were not that concerned. This new sect was only a splinter from Jerusalem and was not a great danger. The Jews attacked the Apostle, and soon the enthusiasm in the Apostle's words began to fade, but Bartholomew's words were holy and righteous and unexpectedly found favor among some Phrygian Gentiles. But the Phrygian Gentiles were no easy task. They were deeply entrenched in their ways and did not take to the introduction of new ideas. They were deeply immersed in a polytheistic religion based on nature and the lower needs of humankind. Bartholomew's zeal to save every soul he met was so great that no person could stop him from seeking this goal. When he was in the deepest throes of verbal war with a leader of some polytheistic deity, he did not relent until Jesus had triumphed; because of his persistence, many Phrygians became Christians. Each confrontation Abendadar saw left him believing in miracles—not only because the Phrygians were so difficult, but because regardless of the weather and the conditions of their travels, Bartholomew always was able to appear unsoiled. His clothes, though old and donated, always looked perfect on him; they always looked richer on him. He was able to make any garment look better than it was intended to look and richer than it was worth. This was not done out of vanity or self-indulgence, but rather it just appeared this way because of how he appreciated and cherished all that was given to him.

After many months in Galatia and Phrygia, Bartholomew rose one cold morning and announced to Abendadar, "We must move on. This place will be left for Philip." And with that they began to travel south.

They traveled by boat down the Sarus and Cydnus Rivers, which took them to the Cilician cities of Adana and Tarsus. The city of Adana on the southwestern bank of the Sarus River was built by Pompey the Great and settled by Cilician pirates. It held no great excitement for the two men of "The Way," so they stayed there only three days and preached among the Gentiles. They continued on to the city of Tarsus, and then into Syria and the city of Antioch.

The large city of Antioch was often called "the Queen of the East." It was a worthy rival to the city of Alexandria in Egypt. Antioch, a city of well over a half-million, was a strategic military outpost for the Romans. It was a city of beauty because there were many cultures that came and stayed within its walls. A large contingent of Romans came to this city, adding to its wealth and importance. Every military power that conquered the city contributed to its size and splendor, but it was the Romans who adorned the city the most. During the Roman Civil Wars, Antioch had always picked the winner and consequently was amply rewarded for its loyalty. About six miles outside of the city was the suburb of Daphne, named after the beautiful mountain nymph who was passionately loved by Apollo. Beautiful forests, groves, and brooks surrounded this place of pure white columns and artistic arches. The Romans added temples, fountains, and public baths to make this suburb a place of recreational pleasure. As time passed, the easy life caused Antioch to grow decadent as its inhabitants pursued all kinds of pleasures.

A large colony of Jews flourished in the city. They added to the competitive commercial makeup of the economy, having been settled in the city by the Seleucid rulers and given equal rights with the Greeks. The large colony of Jews never lived within the neat limits of Judaism, so upon the coming of a new Jewish sect, they readily accepted Christianity as an alternative. But as more and more Jews became Christians, the belief in penance and love became deeply rooted.

Bartholomew renewed his friendship with Evodius, who had been made the leader of the community in Antioch by order of Peter. Evodius had been one of the seventy disciples sent out by Jesus, and he had been the first follower to be called a "Christian," which was a soubriquet used by the people of Antioch that soon spread throughout the Roman world. Also living and laboring in Antioch were Lucius of Cyrene and Manaen, who was the foster brother of Herod Antipas. Both these men heard Peter and the other Apostles speak on that first Pentecost, and they were among those received that day. After the death of Stephen, the *diakonos*, they and other Cyrenians fled Jerusalem for Antioch, and while there they were successful in making converts. Soon, they traveled to Damascus, where their successes were greater than they could have imagined. Eventually, they became the objects of Saul's mission to Syria before his conversion.

On the day that Bartholomew and Abendadar arrived, Lucius was readying himself for a return to Cyrene to join Simeon of Cyrene. The Antiochene Christian community made preparations for a small farewell gathering for Lucius, but when word spread that one of the Twelve would be at the gathering, the Christians came out in great numbers, and soon the small gathering turned into a large crowd. Everyone arrived with food and fruit, and as they gathered, Bartholomew sought a quiet place, far off and away from everyone.

My Lord, do You see what has become of Your command to go and preach to all nations? Look at what You have done through us. There are Asians, Syrians, Romans, Pisidians, Cilicians, Jews, and Gentiles, all here because of Your words and Your life. All want to work toward and walk to Your Kingdom. Tears of humility immediately filled his eyes. *Thank You for allowing me to be a part of what You wanted to happen in Your world.*

His solitude vanished as a small crowd found him. They embraced him and drew near to him. Bartholomew knew that they believed that being near him, touching him, they were closer to the Master. Slowly, the people settled into a large semicircle around a table draped with a white cloth that was decorated with flowers and small oil lamps. On the center of the table was a large plate filled with unleavened bread, and to its side were several cups of wine.

Seeing the table, Bartholomew started reminiscing.

He listened to the prayers and Psalms being sung, and like always, he heard only certain words or phrases that jumped out of the Psalm. These words created images of bygone times. He heard, "How lovely is thy dwelling place, O Lord of hosts! My soul yearns; it pines for the courts of the Lord...." The words "...thy dwelling place..." stayed with him, and he relived the comfort that the Twelve had shared with Jesus.

The assembly began a different Psalm, and he heard, "O God Thou art my God: earnestly I see Thee...when I remember Thee on my couch, and meditate on Thee in the night watches...." When he heard, "...I remember Thee on my couch..." this forced him to see, in his mind's eye, the couches around the table of the Upper Room.

They sang another Psalm and he heard, "...I trusted, even when I said: I am greatly afflicted...." When they sang the words "I will take the chalice of salvation and will call on the name of the Lord," his mind traveled to the Passover table and he saw the unassuming cup sitting on the table before Jesus.

The people sang a song composed by one of the Christians, and Bartholomew sat listening but not hearing, for his mind was fixed on the table in the front of the room.

They returned to the Psalms, and he heard them say, "I will thank the Lord with my whole heart, in the circle of the just and in the congregation," and the words, "He has left a memorial of his wonders: merciful and kind is the Lord." In his memory, Bartholomew was there—he was living the moments of that Last Supper so many years ago.

"Bartholomew? Bartholomew!" He heard Evodius say his name loudly. "Bartholomew, everyone is eagerly awaiting your words."

Startled, he looked around and saw everyone standing and looking at him. Their faces were wide with expectation. He was touched. Slowly, he rose and walked to the table. For some unknown reason, he felt very old and tired. The yesterdays he had nostalgically relived seemed to be so many years ago, too many years ago. Standing behind the table, he looked out and onto the faces before him, and he knew what had to be said to them.

"My brethren…." He paused and looked at the table, as if on its pure whiteness he would find written notes of inspiration. He raised his head slowly, and looking at the congregation, he gently smiled. "My mind has been far from this place. It was in a faraway place, many years ago. I was remembering the night the Lord Jesus had Supper with the Twelve. It was His last supper before His death. I remember that night well; in fact, I remember the entire day very well. Before I begin my account, let me tell you that I was blessed by the Almighty with great faith; I seldom doubted. I did not always understand what Jesus said or did, but I believed from the moment Jesus and I met that He was the Son of God. I did not understand how I had come to this conclusion, but I knew it. Do you understand how good God was to me? I was so certain from the very beginning. Through the years, when my fellow Apostles mumbled their doubts and uncertainties, I remained certain. Of course, I did not know in what way Jesus would make Himself known to the world, but I knew, by God's grace and my own convictions, that it would happen. Of course I must say, with great sorrow, that this belief did not stop me from running away when Jesus needed me the most."

He swallowed with some difficulty, choked by the agony of those memories.

Gathering himself, he continued: "The Passover is always prepared days in advance, and I remember how the Master wanted that Passover to be especially solemn. I remember Jesus ordering Simon Peter and John to go into Jerusalem and find a place for "the Meal." They found an Upper Room in the house of our brother Mark, who was a relative of Barnabas and a companion of Paul. As soon as Peter and John found the room, Lady Mary and the other ladies, according to the customs, went to the room and began to clean and decorate. Floors, walls, and beams were cleaned, and flowers, like those here, were placed around the room." He threw open his arms to draw attention to the flowers arranged around him. "Oil lamps were placed around the room, just like here, on the pure white cloth covering the table at which we would sit and sup." He pointed to the small oil lamps on the table before him. "I can recall walking the narrow streets of Jerusalem. The city was submerged in reverent silence. This was not unusual during the Passover, for everyone stayed close to home, and those away hurried home to be with family. The quiet that night was a little different, though. I sensed an air of expectancy. Now, as I recall that night, I cannot tell you what I really expected to happen, I only know that I sensed something serious in the air. If I had told the Others what I was feeling, I am sure they would have thought me mad. I felt that everything in the world that was not human was poised on the edge of anticipation. I wondered what all these feelings meant, but after a few pensive moments, I discharged my thoughts and concentrated on the happenings of the Holy Day.

"The moon was full and bright; the shadows created by the moonlight were dark and foreboding. I do not know if we were uncomfortable with the silence of the night or frightened by the dark places around us, but for some reason we were strangely jovial. We seemed to be forcing happiness into that night, and into ourselves. The Master was solemn and introspective, but He seemed to understand our uneasy lightheartedness. When we entered the Upper Room, everything immediately changed. Jesus became more serious, and sensing His mood, we grew somber. I can tell you that I remember becoming extremely happy in a very different way. My happiness was deep inside me, and my mind told me that Jesus was to reveal Himself to us. I cannot tell you why or how I knew this, but I knew it.

"Then the Master said, 'Long have I desired to eat this Passover with you before I suffer; for I say to you that I will eat of it no more, until it has been fulfilled in the kingdom of God.'

"John, Philip, Andrew, and I looked at each other with deep concern, for Jesus' words were disturbing. They were wondering, as I was, why this meal was to be so different from the other Passover suppers we had shared. Jesus' words reminded me of the question asked by the youngest Jewish male in every family on the night of the Passover: 'Why was this night different from all other nights?'

"The table was shaped like an inverted Greek letter *upsilon*. I am sure you know what that looks like," but to make certain he formed an upside-down "U" in the air. "We reclined on couches, resting on one arm and eating with the opposite hand. The Master reclined at the head of the table, with John bar Zebedee and Peter on his right and Judas Iscariot and James bar Zebedee on his left. I was seated far from Him. Being far from Jesus, away from any place of honor, did not bother me. In the earlier years of following Jesus, I would have given anything to be so honored, but that night, there was no need for pride. Besides, where I was sitting made it possible for me to see all that was taking place, and this was more important to me.

"The ladies who had prepared the room, and in particular Lady Mary, did the cooking. This is the custom: the Jewish mother prepares the meal for the *Pasch*. This custom is extremely important, for the mother is the teacher of the household. She is the teacher of humility and acceptance, and with these virtues, mothers give the Passover an air of modesty and resolve. It is the mother who starts the feast with the lighting of the candles and the chanting of the blessing. Mary did this, and we all sang the *Hallel*."

Bartholomew, with his eyes closed, lifted his voice into the sonorous Psalm. His rich baritone voice filled the room.

"Alleluia! Praise, O ye servants of the Eternal! Praise ye the name of the Eternal! Blessed be the name of the Eternal, from henceforth and forevermore. From the rising of the sun unto the going down thereof, praised be the name of the Eternal...."

In his own world, Bartholomew heard the voices of the other Apostles mingle with his. He smiled with their presence, and his stomach quivered with excitement.

When he had finished, he opened his eyes, now moistened by holy tears, and he again saw the yearning and expectation on the faces of all those in the room, so he continued.

"Lady Mary and the other ladies placed the usual items on the table. There was the roasted, unblemished lamb, which symbolized the sacrificial lamb in Egypt. In baskets around the table was the unleavened bread, in memory of the bread the Jews ate when they were freed from Egypt. Similarly placed around the table were bitter herbs, horseradish or spring radishes, which symbolized the bitterness of slavery. Also on the table was my favorite, *haroses*, which is a paste made of chopped apples, nuts, cinnamon, and wine. Even now, as I think of this delight, my mouth yearns for its taste. This *haroses* mixture was red in color, and it symbolized the mortar our ancestors had to make and use while in slavery. To show gratitude to God for all the goodness of the earth, *karpas* parsley and watercress were placed on the table, to remind the Jews of their earthly gifts. Finally, there was the salt water, which represented the Red Sea. We would dip our greens and bitter herbs in the salted water. Personally, when I ate this mixture, I was reminded of the salty tears of my people.

"After the blessings, everyone ate. Besides the Twelve, there were many disciples, friends, and even relatives of Jesus at the Supper. It was a beautiful night filled with love, care, family, and togetherness.

"There were some Gentile servants from the household who moved around the room, serving the meal as was set down by the Law. We talked, ate, and drank. It was a happy time, so we all drank the customary four cups of wine, which symbolized the joy of being 'passed over.' These four cups of wine also commemorated the four strong verbs that God used when He delivered the Jewish people from Pharaoh: deliver, redeem, take, and bring. Some time passed, and suddenly I became aware that only Jesus, a servant, and the Twelve were in the room. Just as I realized this, Jesus rose from His couch and went to a servant standing nearby.

He took from the servant a towel, a foot basin, and a pitcher filled with water. He removed His tunic, girded Himself, and began washing our feet and wiping them with a towel. I was the first one He washed, and I remember wanting to object. But I knew that whatever He was doing had some profound meaning, and I reminded myself to ask Jesus about the significance of this washing. He continued to Philip, Thomas, Matthew, and Andrew. When he came to Simon Peter, Simon Peter objected, and the Master said, 'If I wash thee not, thou shalt have no part with Me.' I then understood that in order to become part of what Jesus was to do that night, we needed to be cleansed. I had my answer. I looked at the Others, and I realized that they were still a little confused. I wondered what was wrong with Simon Peter—Why did he not understand what Jesus had said? Something important was planned for us, and the Master was preparing us for it by cleansing us. Jesus continued, washing the feet of John, Judas, James the Big, James the Little, the other Simon, and finally Jude Thaddeus. When Jesus finished, He returned to the table and told us that He had just provided an example for us to follow. He made us see that no matter how great we may be in the eyes of others—in your eyes and the eyes of other followers—we are still His servants, and your servants. Jesus said, 'The servant is not greater than his Lord; neither is the Apostle greater than He that sent him.'

"I looked at Jesus. He looked very serious, and I suddenly thought that He had made Himself the servant of all mankind, yet my fellow Apostles did not see it or perhaps at that moment they did not want to see it. I, myself, found the entire idea distasteful. I always believed Jesus to be above everything, especially human authority, and I always believed that He had the power to subject all to Himself, so this idea of being a servant was foreign to me.

"Jesus closed His eyes.

"We watched in silence.

"Softly, with great sorrow and pain in His voice, He said, 'Amen, I say to you, one of you that eateth with Me shall betray Me.'

"I cannot tell you what terror overcame us. We began shouting, 'Is it I, Lord?' 'Lord, is it I?' We were unsure of ourselves. I know many of us were near tears as we begged with sincerity to be declared not the one. I remember thinking that I could not be the one, for I could never permit myself to be a traitor. Nonetheless, I and the rest were the targets of the underworld, constantly threatened by the Evil One and so in this way we were all capable of betrayal. Who could possibly do such a thing? Who among us would find reason to betray Him? And to whom would He be betrayed? The Romans? The Pharisees? The Sadducees?

"In the turmoil, I saw Jesus speak, but I could not hear His words. Suddenly, Judas, who had been sitting to the left of Jesus, walked from the room, off to tend to some charity, as the Master had desired.

"Each of us continued examining ourselves, secretly accusing each other of the possibility of betrayal. We became suspicious of each other. Do you see how easily we humans come to judge others? This is why we often tell you that judgment is in the hands of the Almighty. To judge that night seemed proper, for truly we were all capable of betrayal. I think some of us could have fallen more easily than others. All of a sudden, we grew quiet, and an unexpected calm came over us. This quiet surprised me—we had been joyful and talkative, feasting and celebrating, then there was the swiftness of the silence, as if God had placed His hand over us. It was then that I knew a great marvel was about to take place. Jesus looked at each of us, carefully; truly, I knew He was reading our hearts. When He looked at me, His eyes lingered, and I could see in His eyes an understanding, a confirmation. Slowly, gently, He took into His hands unleavened bread, gave thanks, blessed, and broke it. I watched His hands. They became illuminated—as white as the purest snows on the highest mountain of all creation. They were so radiant that I squinted to protect my eyes. I was so captivated by the seriousness of the moment that I was afraid to breathe, for the mere filling of my lungs would create movement. There was no sound in the room except for the soft, low voice of Jesus, and when I heard His words, they pierced my soul and reverberated throughout my very being.

"He said, 'Take ye. Eat. This is My Body.'

"For a few precious moments, He did not move His hand. The Bread in His hands glimmered, and a light radiated ever so softly from the Bread. It seemed to be reshaping itself before my very eyes into His very hand. He handed the Bread to John on His right and James on His left, who each broke a piece and passed the Bread down the table. I watched the half that was coming to me, and when finally it was in my hand, I heard the sound of a small wind and felt it pass over me. The sound was almost a sigh of relief, and the wind was a breath of repose. The Bread had the fragrance of a newborn child, and as I slowly lifted the particle to my lips, I felt warmth in my fingers. Once in my mouth, there was an embrace so sweet, so refined, so overwhelming that all time, my time, my life, was made present. Nothing else in life, no other moment in life, would be claimed as that moment was claimed.

"Jesus then took a cup of wine in His hands. It was a plain, simple clay cup, but when Jesus lifted it from the table and held it slightly above us, it took on a new and different property. The brown color faded to ruby red, then a light, subtle and yet obvious, blanched the clay cup, making it pure as a white and blessed cloud. It seemed more precious than life itself, more valuable than Caesar's gold. My eyes, and I believe all our eyes, were held by this cup.

"Again the Master spoke, and His words rippled through the room. They resounded and vibrated throughout my being.

"He again gave thanks, and holding the cup out to us, He said softly, 'Take ye. Drink. This is My Blood. It is the Blood of the New Testament, which shall be shed for many unto the remission of sins.'

"He handed the cup to the sons of Zebedee, and the cup was passed to each of us. When the cup came to me, I did not hesitate to taste it. I knew this was the beginning of Jesus' time, but I did not expect the surge created by the cup as it touched my lips, its sacred contents passing down my throat and into my chest. My next breath, my next heartbeat, skipped away from me, lost in infinity. My heart leapt with excitement, and I was filled with something so different from any other feeling. A being within me that Jesus wanted, and which He alone could touch, came to life, and I was emptied of all things—filled only with Jesus. No longer was I the son of Tholomai, of honored family; no longer were my garments the best among the Twelve; no longer was I myself. I was a servant of Jesus! I was part of Him! There was a strange and strong feeling inside me that made me know that I would always be a part of Him, and He always part of me. Even to this very day, I feel this same way whenever I partake of the Lord's Supper.

"As the years passed, I became more and more firm in my belief that this act of communion with Jesus is the totality of His divine giving. He gave wholly; He emptied Himself completely. More and more I find that Jesus' action was not merely a mild gesture, but one without reservation. He did not soften this moment with such words as 'this could be' or 'this should be'—He said 'this IS.' He intended to allow for no misunderstanding: 'This is My Body,' 'This is My Blood.' And so it is!

"When Jesus first said that He was the Bread of Life, the words I heard were 'this is a hard thing.' Jesus' teaching about the Bread of Life, I assure you, was preparing us for this great relationship, and I say to you, and to all the world, that this is from the Son of Man, the Son of God, Who descended from the heavenly realms and took unto Himself our human nature. This giving is from the Son of David, Who poured out His love on those in need, Who transformed souls and renewed lives in the streets, fields, towns, and villages of Galilee. If He could do these things, can He not change bread and wine into His Body and Blood? In all faith, in all reason, we must say that He certainly can. This giving of His Body and Blood under the appearance of bread and wine was His way to expel from our lives the angel of death. This gift spread over us like the blood over the lintels—the sign that we, the new Chosen People, were not to be slain but would be spared for Him to live in us and through us. So our Savior comes to us in the simplest of forms, and yet the most convenient and practical. He remains with us here at the table for us to receive. He left Himself with us so that we would know that He is with us always, until the end of all time. Just as He promised, He has fulfilled. Be glad, for this miracle will always be with us. Come to Him always, humbly and as servants, for if He did all He could for you, you should offer your lives to Him. Approach your God, washed and ready to declare, 'Jesus is Lord and God! Jesus is with me! Jesus is my Redeemer!'"

He looked at the assembly and became confused, for their faces were filled with shock and bewilderment.

Lord Jesus, I pray that what I have said will be of benefit to them. I am at a loss, for as often as I speak of You, the people who hear me look amazed and bewildered.

Bartholomew looked out over the people as he continued. "Then we sang the last part of the *Hallel*."

Closing his eyes, he began to sing, and his voice flowed across the room.

"Give thanks unto the Eternal, for He is gracious; for His mercy endureth forever. Give thanks to the God of Gods, for His mercy endureth forever. Give thanks to the Lord of Lords, for His mercy endureth for ever...."

Abendadar smiled as he looked around the room. He saw the startled expressions on the faces of the people. What they were now witnessing he had seen many times over. Each time Bartholomew taught or spoke of Jesus, the same phenomenon occurred. As he spoke, his robe and cloak became bright and spotless. They looked new. His face looked groomed, and his red hair and beard simmered in fiery brilliance. Unaware of what was happening, Bartholomew continued to sing, and in his mind he saw only the face of Jesus at the Supper table, and he heard only the singing of the other Apostles.

Soon, everyone accepted what was happening as another sign from Jesus, and they too began to sing with the Apostle.

Abendadar stood still, waiting for the other miracle to follow. He closed his eyes in eagerness, and then it happened: he caught the scent. Though he had not had the Lord's cloak in his possession for years, still, each time Bartholomew finished speaking of Jesus, he experienced the heavenly aroma of that sacred garment.

When the Psalm was completed, Bartholomew walked to the table, and facing those gathered, he reached for the unleavened bread on the table. He uttered a prayer of thanksgiving, blessed the bread, broke it, and said, "Take. Eat. This is My Body."

Taking the cup, he blessed it and said, "Take and drink. This is the Blood of the New Testament, given for you and many for the remission of your sins."

Slowly, solemnly, and with a new understanding, those gathered walked up to Bartholomew, and he gave them what he had received years before—he gave them Jesus of Nazareth.

After all had supped and other songs of praise had been sung, everyone departed except for the leaders of Antioch. Bartholomew was given all the latest news about the other Apostles.

John, he was told, left Jerusalem with Lady Mary and travelled to Ephesus. Peter left Syria and went to Italy, and Andrew was last heard of in Scythia, among the barbarians. Philip had gone to North Africa and spent some time with Simon the Zealot. Matthew was last known to be in northern Africa and in Egypt; Jude and Thomas were last heard of in the Province of Osroene.

"The Name of Jesus is all around us, even if it is sometimes spoken in whispers," Bartholomew said, delighting in the news of the other Apostles.

After a few weeks in Antioch, Bartholomew abruptly announced his departure. This time, though, he told Abendadar to stay in Syria and to wait for his return. He was being summoned to Ephesus because Lady Mary, the Master's mother, was near death. That very day, he boarded a ship and set sail.

Abendadar stayed behind, wondering how Bartholomew had come to know this news.

*

One year later, Bartholomew returned, and the moment Abendadar saw him, he knew this was a different man. The change was so stark that Abendadar could not help but blurt out, "What has happened to you?"

"I have been on a trip unlike any other. My trip took me to a far off place, but I never left Ephesus."

Abendadar looked at Bartholomew, fearing that the Apostle was ill or had lost his senses.

Bartholomew smiled then broke into a hardy, robust laugh.

"Relax, my Syrian friend; I have not lost my senses. If anything, I have gained a new one. But tell me, did you miss me?"

"Yes, where have you been? We received word three weeks after you left that Lady Mary had died, and we expected you back immediately."

"I will explain what happened to me, but first, speak to me of this new persecution against the family of Jesus."

"It really has a humble beginning. There was a Pharisee named Chazaya, whose wife and two daughters were converted by Evodius. Soon after they were received, one of the two daughters left for Pontus with her male cousin, Tulumer, who was already a Christian. In retaliation, Chazaya denounced his daughter and nephew, and two days later he went to the synagogue and denounced his wife and other daughter. This caused an uproar throughout the entire city. Soon, every Christian was being sought and accused of bewitching innocent Syrians. Upon hearing of the trouble, the Roman magistrate stepped in to prevent it from growing and sided with the synagogue authorities. We have been hunted ever since, and our comings and goings are cautiously planned."

Bartholomew became distressed. With a deep sigh of resignation, he said quietly, "Similar experiences of persecution and harassment have been reported throughout the Empire. I am afraid we are about to see more troubles."

Raising his head and eyes, he looked at Abendadar. "But Jesus will not let anything happen to us. If need be, we will go to His table more often, for we know He is there."

Abendadar suddenly saw that Bartholomew was far more at peace.

With curiosity he asked lightly, "And what has kept you away?"

"A man. A very strange man. He was not of any province near here; in fact, he was from a strange place called Oxyrhynchus, which is far into Egypt along the Great Nile. This man said the place he is from is also called the Oasis of Al Bahnasa. He was dark skinned and wore unusual clothing. His clothing was long, light, and flowing. His feet were covered in cloth sandals. He had no hair on his face or his head, except for one long strain of black hair that came from the back of his head. The hair was thrown over his left shoulder, down his chest and to his waist. He also wore many rings and necklaces of gold. I never saw such a person, and I was immediately captivated by him. I met him by accident on the road just outside of Ephesus. I was returning to Antioch. It took me one whole year to walk that distance."

"A year?"

"Yes, surprisingly, I did not realize that a year had passed until I arrived here in Antioch." He was sincerely surprised by this fact. "It did not seem that long."

Abendadar looked at his friend with disbelief. Nonetheless, he had been around the people and workings of Jesus long enough to know that nothing is impossible, and that some things are explainable only through faith.

"And where did you two go?"

"We walked and talked. We camped, then we walked and talked more. He had an entire staff with him. He was a man of wealth and position. He told me a strange tale that captured me; I knew that he was sent by Jesus and that I was to do something for this man. He told me that he had been an apprentice to an astrologer who many years ago traveled to Judea on a quest. This Magus had followed a star, an uncommon star. On this quest, he was joined by two other Magi who also were following this same star. Finally, the three astrologers came to Galilee, and the star stopped above the place where a poor carpenter, his wife, and their infant Son was. The Baby was called Jesus. The man's master told him that this Child was the Son of God. The three Magi believed this the moment they saw the Child. After their visit, the three returned to their respective countries and homes. One went to Armenia, another traveled east and beyond Persia, and the other back to Cyrenaica in Africa. Over the years the three Magi remained in contact, and eventually death came to them all. Now himself a Magus, the man went into the service of a new master in Egypt, but he longed to see the "Son of God," so he began a journey to Judea. When he arrived, he was told what had happened to Jesus. He was also informed that Mary, His mother, was living in Ephesus. He was on his way to Ephesus to see the mother of the Son of God, when I came upon him."

Bartholomew looked at his companion and found Abendadar's face beaming with astonishment.

"I told him that Lady Mary had died and that he was too late, and with great sorrow he turned to go back to Africa. I told him I would walk with him, and on the way we talked…."

"…of Jesus?"

"Yes."

Bartholomew looked off to his side and immediately became distant, away from his time with Abendadar. He said, "I could not get away from him. He held me to himself; I was attached to him in spite of my willingness to come back to you and the others. We traveled on and on, and he became more and more enthralled by Jesus. Soon, his entire caravan was listening to me speak of the Master. On and on we went, and with each passing moment I started to notice something very strange. He began to look less and less elaborate. As his appearance changed, I began to notice that his attitude toward his staff was becoming less superior and more friendly. They were becoming like his family. They wanted me to return to Egypt with them, but I knew I had to return here. They professed their belief in Jesus, so as we neared Antioch and approached the Cayster River, I baptized the man and his servants. After that, we celebrated the Breaking of the Bread and went to sleep. When I awoke the next morning, I was alone. They were gone."

Bartholomew's tale was abruptly interrupted as Evodius walked hurriedly into the room where he and Abendadar were talking.

"Brother, you must leave. Word of your arrival has spread, and the Roman magistrate is presently being petitioned for your arrest. We made arrangements for you to hide in a caravan heading north, but you must leave now. Abendadar, you could leave later, for you are protected by Roman law and citizenship, but Bartholomew, please, you must go."

Bartholomew picked up his staff, hugged both men, and walked to the door smiling. Turning to look at the two men, he said, "The Master has something important for me to do. He has given me this strange man who has created a great unrest in me, and now He moves me north. Abendadar, I will wait for you in Commagene. God be with you both."

He went through the door and was gone.

*

Two weeks later, Abendadar arrived in Commagene. To his great surprise, he found that Bartholomew was practically a celebrity. Back in the history of Commagene, a member of the House of Ptolemy had been governor of the small country, and Bartholomew's connection to Ptolemy brought him much notoriety. Soon, people came to believe that their ancestors had sent Bartholomew and that his message had been preordained with the blessing of their forefathers. Of course, Bartholomew casually accepted their conclusion and used it to Jesus' benefit. But soon his celebrity status annoyed the Apostle, so they only stayed in this small agricultural country for six months. Among the numerous converts were many good leaders. Bartholomew laid hands on them and left them to lead the people closer to Jesus.

"We must go on," Bartholomew announced one day. "Begin to pack. I feel the Lord is calling us to go east. I feel a strong call to Osroene and Sophene. I learned long ago that our brother Apostles Thomas and Jude Thaddeus were there, and they have since left and traveled east into Assyria or the Parthian Empire."

A quick chill raced up Abendadar's back with the mention of the Parthian Empire. He had heard of the battles between this barbarian nation and the Roman armies and of the savagery of those people. Truly, God would have to be with them in such an undertaking. So they traveled east to the cities of Edessa, then to Carrhea in the region of Osroene, and into the region of Sophene. They stayed in these regions for many months, and the followers of Jesus grew in number through their untiring labors. They established many communities. Everything was perfect, and they grew comfortable in their successes. Then one day, after many hours of preaching, Bartholomew returned to their humble hut and announced that they must make ready for a move farther north into Armenia.

"This is where the Lord Jesus is leading me, and out of respect for Matthias, Thomas, and Jude Thaddeus—all of whom reported long ago that the souls there are thirsty for the Gospel—I believe this is where we should go. We will leave tomorrow."

Abendadar, who was well accustomed to taking orders, did not ask any questions—he simply packed, and they left for Armenia the next day. But in the back of his mind, he believed Bartholomew was searching for something.

So they arrived in Armenia. For a year they preached, taught, and toiled successfully among those people. They traveled through many cities, towns, and villages and stayed many months around Lake Thospitis. Later, they labored in the city of Artaxata, and finally they arrived in Albanopolis. With the help of several Armenian Christians, they found many eager souls who wanted to know and love Jesus. But still Abendadar perceived a restlessness in Bartholomew, and he knew it would only be a matter of time before they moved again.

Many months after their arrival, when they had settled completely into a daily routine, Abendadar and a few Armenian Christians went into the center of Albanopolis to get some provisions. When Abendadar returned, he found Bartholomew deep in thought. He knew that these moments of reflection were important to Bartholomew, so he left him alone. The next day and the day after that, Bartholomew remained in deep thought, and when he did speak, the usual fire and enthusiasm was missing from his words and ideas.

Finally, Abendadar sat down with him. With deep concern he asked, "Bartholomew, what is wrong? Are you ill?"

"No, my friend, sad, but not ill," he answered, turning to look out the window.

Abendadar followed his eyes. He thought perhaps there was something of interest on the other side of the window, but he saw nothing that could possibly hold Bartholomew's unbroken stare.

"Years ago, in Jerusalem, the Twelve of us pulled lots to determine our missions. Many of the Twelve received specific places, but some of us were confused by the destination we were given. My lot had written on it 'Armenia and beyond,' and that is why we are here. Yet I remain unsettled, so I wait for the Lord to lead me to 'beyond.' I thought perhaps this referred to the Caucasus Mountains and Sarmatia. In the meantime, I seek signs, but none have come, so I labor here in Armenia waiting for a sign. During your absence the other day, a group of men came to me from a place I never thought of as being 'beyond.' They told me they were believers in Jesus, yet they seemed too foreign to know Jesus. So I asked them how they became Christians. They told me that they had been in Jerusalem on the day of the Lord's death and, later, had witnessed the miracle of tongues. They immediately sought to be baptized, and soon after they returned to their country. In their homeland, they converted their families and many friends. Others came asking them questions they could not answer, so they came back to get help.

"I asked them if they were Jews, and they said no, but they knew of Jews in their country. I asked them what they were doing in Jerusalem during that Passover Holiday many years ago if they were not Jews."

Bartholomew turned away from the window and looked at Abendadar with deep sadness on his face.

"One of them told me he had been sent by his owner to find the King of the Jews. It seems his owner had traveled many years before to Judea..." he again looked out the window into the night sky, "...following an unusual star."

Abendadar felt his body go limp, for he remembered Bartholomew's long ago visit with the Egyptian man.

"Then another said to me, 'I know you. I knew you before I met you.'" He looked again at Abendadar and said, though not speaking to him directly, "Such familiar and such fatal words." Bartholomew lowered his head, and after several long moments, he said, "I asked him how he knew me, and he said he had seen me in a dream."

"Where...where are these men from?"

"Beyond Armenia, not north of Armenia—east of Armenia. A place called *India Felix*." Bartholomew took a deep breath, and he exhaled a long sigh of total frustration. "I have failed to see what the Master wanted me to see, so He had to show me—not once or twice, but thrice. Once before, I met a man named Balthazar, who was also a Magus who followed a star. He was in Jerusalem at the time of the Master's crucifixion and resurrection. He stayed with us. He told us of another Magus, but not a third. Perhaps I was to find the third Magus on my own. Today, I met those who knew the third Magus. I am being called to my true mission, Abendadar, the one I should have undertaken before all others. I have failed in my Apostleship, and Jesus has corrected me."

Rising abruptly from his seat with a sudden determination, Bartholomew declared, "Tomorrow I begin my journey to *India Felix*. I will not ask you to join me. The journey will be dangerous and strange. I will write a letter to Peter and have you excused." Abendadar jumped to his feet. He wanted to confront the Apostle and accuse him of being presumptuous and insulting, but he quickly caught himself, realizing that this was not Bartholomew's intention. He was too honest for that. His concern was truly for Abendadar's safety.

"And please tell me, dear Bartholomew, where should I go? I have been everywhere with you. I have endured ice and cold, heat and thirst with you. I have walked with you to the very precipice of death's lips. I have felt the scathe of the whip and the sting of persecution and derision. After all this, do you think I would abandon you now?"

Bartholomew looked at his companion with tears in his eyes. They were tears of joy. He walked to Abendadar, and with a strong embrace, he said, "Then we will go on, the three of us: Jesus, you, and I."

That night they packed for their trip.

The next morning, a group of Armenian men came and offered to travel with them to the borders of *India Felix*. By noon, others had arrived with gold and silver to help pay for the voyage. On their last day in Albanopolis, they gathered with their fellow Christians for the Lord's Meal.

After all the farewells had been said, Bartholomew, Abendadar, and five Armenians finished their packing. As they were just about to wrap the last bundle, Bartholomew came into the room with a red cloth, which was carefully wrapped around something.

"Abendadar, find a safe place for these scrolls."

"Scrolls?"

"Yes," the Apostle smiled proudly, "scrolls. They are copies of our brother Matthew's story of the Master's life, death, and rising. They will be valuable tools to use in our teaching, for they tell of the many things Jesus did for the poor and sick. Matthew gave these to me in Ephesus when we witnessed Mary's journey to her Son."

"You mean you have been carrying these scrolls with you all this time and you never told me of them?"

"I really did not think that they were important—no, I don't mean that, they are important, but I never had need of them. But for some reason, they are now the most necessary thing I have. So please keep them safe."

Abendadar smiled in disbelief and carefully packed the scrolls away, wondering if he would ever stop being amazed by this Apostle of the Lord.

The next day they left for *India Felix*—Lucky India.

*

As they started their journey, the Armenians suggested traveling southwest and down the Tigris River to the seas off the coast of Persia. This was the trade route that had been used for years by the Romans. They insisted that the winds would be favorable for sailing, as this was the time of year when the winds were strong and tended to blow in the direction of India.

"Our guides believe that once we have reached the mouth of the Tigris River and the sea, which they call the Erythraean Sea, we can get a merchant boat to India. It seems they have done this many times," Abendadar explained to Bartholomew, overjoyed because a journey through uncivilized Parthia could be avoided. "They told me that most of their boats travel close to land because the seas outside the Roman Empire are not well charted, and superstitious sailors like to travel with land in sight at all times. This would be good—we could stop, rest, and preach to others on our way to India."

Bartholomew listened and then grew pensive. Finally he said, "I also like the idea of seeing land at all times. Ever since that storm on the Sea of Galilee, which Jesus calmed, I have been a little mistrustful of water. But we will not stop to preach or teach along the way; we are going to India and nowhere else. I have time to make up, for the sake of my Lord and Master—time I have foolishly let slip away."

So the small caravan started out and continued through Armenia, and by the time they reached the city of Amida on the Tigris, three of the five Armenians decided to leave and return to southern Armenia, where they would set up their mission. Bartholomew was pleased to see Armenians tending to Armenians; this was a great accomplishment. At Amida, they boarded a merchant ship that was sailing south along the border with the Parthian Empire, destined for the river ports of Seleucia and Ctesiphon in Mesopotamia. By the time they had reached these river ports, the entire crew of the merchant ship had become Christians. At Seleucia, they boarded another merchant ship that continued down the Tigris to where it met the Euphrates River, and then they sailed on and out of the river basins into the open Erythraean Sea. Three days out to sea, with land to their left, they sailed into a severe storm that almost sank them. Though the ship endured the storm quite well, the two missionaries did not. They both became seasick and spent much of the rest of the voyage below deck, or leaning over the side of the ship's railing. The vessel continued down the coast along the beaches of what once were the ancient kingdoms of Susiana, Persia, Carmania, and Gedrosia.

When they entered the shorelines of Gedrosia, the captain of the ship announced that they had to stop for provisions. They disembarked and found themselves in the midst of merchants from many nations; among these were a large group of Arabians, who immediately caught Bartholomew's attention. He began speaking to them. Soon he was sitting with them in their tents, eating nuts and dates. When he saw the pure white Arab stallions, he thought of his friend Philip, who was a great lover of horses. He walked to the stallions. The Arabians, who knew that their horses did not take well to strangers, cautioned Bartholomew, but he ignored them with a simple smile. The Arabians watched nervously as Bartholomew walked to the horses. These temperamental horses grew complacent as the Apostle spoke to them of Philip. He reminded them of how honored they should be, for they were saddled for royalty and other great people. He told them of God's special blessing on them, for God had made them so beautiful, strong, and fast. He told them that their ancestors had been blessed through the ages. The horses calmly surrounded him. In their midst, he spoke to them of Jesus and His love for all people. As he spoke to the horses, the merchants listened. By the time his ship was ready to leave, Bartholomew had baptized many of the Arabian merchants.

Their voyage continued. From the ship's deck, Bartholomew and Abendadar, when not sick, saw small villages and watched their inhabitants moving around, living their daily lives. The thick, green forest seemed to come to the very edge of the land, somehow defying the salty water; sometimes even the jagged cliffs and mountains brazenly pushed against the sea. Occasionally, small fishing boats from the coastal villages would come alongside the vessel, and they would get sight of the people, with their strange clothing and dark skin and hair.

On several occasions, Abendadar wondered if he had made the right decision in accompanying Bartholomew. He was not a man prone to fear, but radical changes in his surroundings often made him uneasy. The longer they traveled, the calmer the seas became, and soon Bartholomew was holding regular meetings with the crew, eventually baptizing many of them. Finally, on a warm, sunny day, the vessel stopped at a small seaport town, and the captain of the ship told them they had arrived in what everyone called India.

The docking seemed longer than the voyage because they were so eager to feel solid ground beneath their feet and to be free of the confines of the ship. Finally, they walked onto the land, and from the moment his foot touched the earth, Bartholomew knew that his Master had been waiting on these shores for his coming. As Abendadar and the two Armenian Christians began unloading their belongings, Bartholomew ventured a few yards inland and looked beyond the wooden dock into the small seaport town. He was surprised to see straw, mud, and clay huts with thatched roofs. Though neatly arranged, these shelters were nothing like the homes of Galilee. A few of the homes in the town were made of wood. On the sides of the hills that surrounded and overlooked the seaport were several two-story houses made of sunbaked brick. Bartholomew reasoned that these were the homes of public officials or of wealthy families. Everything was chaotic—people bought and sold, children played loudly, and workers yelled orders.

Bartholomew stood watching and smiling, for he heard and understood what was being said; he again thanked God for the miracle of tongues. He knew that if he spoke to these people about Jesus, they would understand his words.

The miracle of Pentecost continues. God is good and is with us always.

He was aware of Abendadar and the others by his side, and together they walked slowly through the crowds on the dock and into the heart of town. The people came rushing out to greet them. As they grew closer, Abendadar broke into a big smile and eventually into laughter when he observed the expression on Bartholomew's face. The village men were half naked. Their torsos were covered with loincloths and their heads were wrapped in twirling cloths, but their chests, backs, and legs were bare. This did not bother Abendadar for he was accustomed to seeing unclothed bodies, but to Bartholomew, a Jew, this was considered unthinkable. Any uncovered flesh was considered improper and even sinful.

The Armenians began to smile at Bartholomew's extreme discomfiture, and Abendadar knew he had to reassure his friend.

"Bartholomew, I am certain that they see us as strange."

"I know," Bartholomew blurted out quickly. After a few moments he added, "But they are naked."

"And so were Adam and Eve."

Bartholomew turned his head and looked at Abendadar, and after a few silent, reflective moments, he smiled.

"I am glad that the Lord chose you as my companion, for sometimes you remind me of the innocence of truth. You are right, they are like the 'first ones,' and we are not here to clothe their bodies, are we? We are here to clothe their souls, and that we will do."

When he turned his attention away from Abendadar and back to the villagers, he saw an entourage of richly dressed people walking through the crowd. The crowd parted, allowing the entourage clear passage to the four foreigners. The approaching group caused Bartholomew to lose his breath. Walking to him in shining silk garments was a man with a turban on his head. Around his neck, wrist, and fingers were necklaces, bracelets, and rings of every size and shape. The man wore an unbuttoned, long-sleeved coat that came down to his knees. Under this coat was a white cotton garment that gently brushed the tops of the cloth sandals on the man's feet. His black beard was trimmed to perfection. To Bartholomew's surprise, the man's lips were red as the skin of a ripe apple, and his face looked painted orange. The man walked with great authority and nodded to the villagers as he passed them. The villagers bowed and pulled away in respect. Beside the man was a woman in a bright yellow silk dress that whirled and draped around her body. It left the upper parts of her shoulders and neck exposed. There were various scrolling designs along the bottom of the dress. The dress's extra material was thrown casually over her left shoulder and over her left arm. Her raven-black hair, with a magnificent sheen, was pulled back rather severely into a bun. Her head was covered with a graceful veil that flowed over her like a delicate blessing. What could be seen of her face was painted just enough to give a blush to her dark skin. Rigid bracelets started at her wrist and continued up her arms. Every finger on her hand wore a ring. Beads of every color and shape circled her neck, and from her ears hung large rings. In spite of all the distracting color, fine material, and jewelry, Bartholomew noted that her beauty was breathtaking.

A tall African slave carried an enormous white umbrella with gold tassels. His muscles straining to hold it properly to provide a pleasant shade for both of these richly costumed people. The slave's face was intent as he concentrated on shielding the couple from any sunlight. Even the slave was richly dressed. He wore a brown coat that opened to show his dark chest. He wore yellow, loosely fitted pantaloons that gathered at his ankles and showed his bare feet. Bartholomew had never seen so large a man as this. He immediately thought of Goliath and imagined how King David must have feared when he faced the giant. Behind the couple protected by the umbrella and the slave was an entourage of color-fully dressed men and women, a veritable walking rainbow. It took all of

Bartholomew's self-restraint to not gasp at the splendor that was before him. He had never seen such opulence in all his life. For one moment his love of fine clothes came rushing back to him, but grace prevailed, and he banished those wicked thoughts.

"Welcome," the man said. He joined his hands before his face and bowed; those around him quickly mimicked his gesture.

"You have blessed our village with your holiness, and we thank our gods and your God for your arrival. My name is Vasu, and this is my wife Nishtha. We are leaders of this district, and several people of your persuasion have told us of your coming. They are waiting for you farther inland. We are not believers in your God, but several of our people are, and some of your own people have come to our land. If you like, arrangements can be made for you to see those from your land and of your God. Meantime, we invite you to have a meal with us."

Bartholomew heard one of the Armenians whisper, "I do not understand what this man is saying."

Abendadar whispered, "Bartholomew does, just be calm."

"My dear Vasu, we are simple people; we need no receptions. A small hut with water and fruit and an opportunity to rest is all we desire. I thank you for your invitation, but it has been a long journey, longer than we would have liked, and we are tired. Please accept our apologies, and be kind enough to understand our need for simplicity and comfort."

"But of course," the woman said softly with a small smile, and turning to a manservant behind her, she ordered, "Gopan, make arrangements for this holy man and his servants to have lodging in a hut."

Vasu softly said, "And perhaps tomorrow after you have rested we can again offer you our hospitality."

Smiling, Bartholomew looked at those around him. Absorbing the words of this "village leader," he knew he had arrived where the Lord had wanted him, for he felt the comfort of home.

* * *

The hut they were given was surprisingly clean and orderly. On the open fire was a large pot, and from it came a savory aroma of boiling fish mixed into a seasoned, watery soup. To the side of the open fire was brown wheat bread, recently cooked. Four large mats for resting and sleeping were neatly positioned around the room on the dirt floor. On the small table, which was just barely off the floor, were large buckets of fresh water, for bathing or drinking, and beside the buckets were several large cloths.

The Armenians dished out the fish and began feasting. From the sounds of their eating, Bartholomew concluded that the fish was tasty. He sat on one of the mats on the floor, gathering his thoughts, while Abendadar washed himself. After Abendadar had washed his face and hands, he went out of the hut to discard the water and soon returned.

"Bartholomew, I think something is wrong," he said with a concerned look on his face.

"What is it?"

"I think this is the hut of a family that was forced out to allow us to stay the night."

"What?" Bartholomew jumped to his feet and the two Armenians stopped eating. "How do you know this?"

"The family is in the jungle behind the house, all huddled together and covered with mats. There is a man, his wife, and two boys and a girl. I asked them to come and join us and they said they were not permitted, then the girl screamed that she wanted me to give her sleeping mat back. I asked her where her mat was, and she said 'in my hut,' pointing to this hut."

"I do not understand," Bartholomew stated.

"This family was ordered by the district leader to relinquish their house, bedding, and food to us," Abendadar replied with compassion in his words.

"Where are these people?" Bartholomew asked, rushing by Abendadar and into the night air.

"Their family name is Ranade," Abendadar called as he followed him into the jungle.

When he found the family, he asked them to return to their house. They were at first very reluctant, so he ordered them back to their hut. Once inside, he realized that most of their food had been consumed, so quietly he reached for what little wheat bread was left. He blessed it, broke it, and placed it into the baskets near the family's sleeping mats. He then extended his hand over the pot of remaining fish stock, and after reciting a silent prayer, he quickly walked out of the hut.

The four men spent the night sleeping in the jungle behind the hut.

*

Abendadar heard mumbling; it awoke him from the recurring dream of holding the Lord's garment. When he opened his eyes, he found many villagers standing around him. The Armenians were startled and alarmed; they thought they were about to be killed.

"Have no fear," Abendadar assured the Armenians. "I do not know exactly what is happening, but I can tell you they are talking about how we returned the hut to that family and made bread for them."

"What bread?" one of the Armenians asked.

The villagers continued to speak all at once. Their excitement was high and rushed. Abendadar had difficulty making sense of what they were saying. Finally, he concentrated on one man and started to understand. He quickly explained to the Armenians what he was hearing.

"It appears that we were expected to take the house from that family because they had been ordered out by the authorities. It is a common practice, and because we gave the house back to the family, we are heroes to these people. The food we ate was all the family had, and Bartholomew made bread for the family after we left. He made seven baskets of bread for them. It also seems that the authorities have arrested the family and have imprisoned them. They accused the family of stealing the bread and of disobeying the order to give up their house. Bartholomew has gone to the house of Vasu, the leader of this district, to defend the family."

The two Armenians started to relax, even though the villagers continued to show signs of agitation.

"They want us to make bread for them," Abendadar stated, and his face registered deep concern.

"What should we do?" one of the Armenians asked.

Abendadar ignored the question and began speaking to the villagers. The villagers soon grew calm and stood in silence as they listened to his ever tranquil voice and reassuring words. He told them that only Bartholomew could make bread, and that he does this with the help of Jesus. Confused and curious, they asked Abendadar to tell them about Jesus.

Without hesitation, Abendadar began to tell them the story of when Jesus multiplied the loaves and fishes. He knew the story well, for he had heard it often, and soon the villagers began to sit on the grass under the shade of the trees.

When Bartholomew returned, Abendadar and the Armenians were teaching the people. They were surprised to see that he had with him the family whose hut they had occupied, along with a contingent of armed soldiers and the manservant Gopan.

"We need to leave," Bartholomew said abruptly.

"But the interest of the villagers is great, and they are beginning to believe."

"I do not doubt that, but if we do not leave, this family will be put to death. Apparently, it is the belief here that to refuse a hut vacated for one's benefit is a grave insult, and it is their custom that the people who have been evicted have no rights. I was able to persuade Vasu of our ignorance, and they forgave me, but they said the family had to be punished for disobeying his orders. I pleaded for their life with the understanding that we would take them with us and leave. In a sense, I have expelled this family to save their lives."

"You must leave immediately," Gopan said sternly.

"We will go farther up the coast where a few Israelite merchants are living. This is the wisest course of action at the moment. Please hurry for the sake of this family."

The two Armenians quickly began packing what little belongings the group had, and the family rushed into the hut and began packing their possessions.

Bartholomew turned to Gopan and said, "Please be patient with us. We will move as quickly as we can."

Gopan, looking around and feeling that he was safe, whispered, "The place you are going to has people who are followers of Jesus. They once traveled to your country and came back with many good and holy ideas. You will be safe there. If you have trouble, continue farther north, and there you will find many followers of Jesus who were taught by another holy man from your country. If you decide to go farther up the coast or if you go south, they will know you are coming."

"How…are you…?" Abendadar asked, yet he knew the answer.

Gopan nodded his head ever so slightly. He reached for Abendadar's hand and traced a cross on his palm.

Abendadar smiled and cupped the manservant's hand, and Bartholomew added his hand to their clasp.

"Were you baptized by this other 'holy man'?"

"Yes. Many months ago, I was on a journey for my master and mistress, and I was baptized by him. He is well known in Kerala and Malabar. He is called Didymus."

"Are you sure of this name?" Bartholomew asked, feeling his heart beat rapidly.

"Well, that is the code name we used, but his real name is Thomas. Do you know him?"

"Know him? He is my brother in Jesus. He and I are of the Twelve. If he is in the south, then we also will go south."

He grew excited with the idea of seeing one of the Twelve.

Fifteen minutes later, the small party was led out of the village. They headed south, and the next day they entered the client state of Kalyana, which was part of Paithan and was under the authority of its rulers of the

Satavahana Dynasty. Here in this place, a completely different and new world was opened to them.

*

Paithan on the Godavari River was once the capital of the Satavahana Dynasty, whose founder Simukha unified city-states and principalities into one kingdom. He started his unification in 230 BC and accomplished his conquest in 212 BC. What Simukha had united stayed strong and prospered. After his death, more principalities were drawn into the kingdom until the reign of Satakarni II, the sixth ruler of the dynasty. During Satakarni's reign, the kingdom had its greatest extension. By 28 BC, the Satavahana Dynasty, through conquest or association with client states, reached from sea to sea across southern and central India and far north, almost to the Ganges River. The able rulers of this dynasty divided the land into *Aharas* provinces. The kingdom was largely decentralized, and each province was administered by an *Amatya* a lord, prince, governor, or appointed minister. Some of these *Amatya* were called "kings." The dynasty could not make all its subjects as prosperous as the kingdom was. The poorest members of this kingdom were the inhabitants of the villages and towns along the coastlines. These people made a living as fishermen or woodcutters, and because this lifestyle provided for their limited needs, they remained satisfied. They were a contented people, for most of the time they were left alone, with no pressure or interference from their rulers. They believed that in servitude they were safe, but their serenity was actually due to the fact that the Satavahana Dynasty ignored these lowly subjects. Bartholomew soon discovered that the coastal people accepted everyone, regardless of color or background. As a result, the region contained a mixture of many people with many religions and cults. The towns and cities of the interior were more organized. These cities benefited from the Satavahana Dynasty's great love of literature and of building cities with temples and bathhouses. The streets were straight and organized, with identical houses on both sides of the street. They were two stories high and made of white bricks. The roofs were flat and were used for relaxing and sleeping on in hot weather. Some had courtyards with wells or fountains. Plants, trees, bushes, and flowers were everywhere. The people were encouraged by the *Amatya* to plant as much as they wanted. The construction and uniformity of these towns and their natural beauty intrigued Bartholomew, for in all his travels he had not seen such uniformity. He was surprised to see that women were permitted to take part in assemblies. This was indeed the strangest thing he encountered, for in all the other societies, women were second-class citizens or worse. His Jewish background made this difficult for Bartholomew to accept, but soon, with the grace of God, he overlooked this society's strangeness. With the help of the locals, they built their own hut and another for the Indian family, who now officially served as their guides and advisors. Bartholomew's first group of listeners was the Ranade children, and following their example, other children soon joined them. They sat around him as he spoke of Jesus and told them of the many good things Jesus did, and especially of how He loved children. The parents began to accompany the children, and soon Bartholomew had to find a more spacious place for his preaching.

The people were astounded to hear that God gave His Son as a Savior to the world and permitted His Son to be sacrificed for sinners, and yet He still loved those who killed His Son. This was not what their gods were like. The gods they knew were aloof, revengeful, and warlike. Hearing about this God of love pleased many of the natives, and soon the Baptisms began.

After six months of quiet and peace, they were visited by a representative of the Governor of Kalyana, who apparently was concerned about the number of people who were becoming believers. From the appearance of the representative, Bartholomew knew that this was no ordinary emissary, for he was richly dressed and weighed down with many amulets, talismans, and ornaments. His garments flowed and played in the wind. His face was dark and smooth-skinned, with dark black eyes that glared unblinkingly. His stare was defiant. It made them uneasy, for he seemed able to read every thought. His dark black hair was meshed with white and gold cords that hung loosely from his head and reached his shoulders. He was encircled by many assistants. Occasionally, one of his assistants would be allowed to whisper to him. Bartholomew surmised that this group was the priesthood of one of the many gods in India. Immediately upon seeing the entourage, the Ranade family became respectful and fearful; Bartholomew could not understand such great fear for another human being.

Visonal, the father of the Ranade family, approached the group. He addressed the representative as the Great Priest Dharmesh. He assured the Great Priest that Bartholomew and his companions were harmless and preached peace and love, and he described how Bartholomew fed the people and cured many of their illnesses. Dharmesh was skeptical about the feeding and the curing, but he conceded that things were peaceful. When Bartholomew stepped forward to speak for himself, the Great Priest ignored him and continued to speak to Visonal.

Flaunting his ornate garments, the Great Priest turned to depart. As he walked, he turned around and told Visonal to warn the Christians to remain conservative in their preaching, for the Governor, known as King Pulumayi, was not a tolerant man and was a strong follower of the fertility goddess. He then reminded everyone that harvest time was near. They would be expected to celebrate the fertility worship, which was to be celebrated in two weeks with the coming of the sixth full moon. The new Christians who heard Dharmesh's reminder became concerned. They did not want to take part in any worship that would be displeasing to Jesus or inconsistent with their new faith. Bartholomew reassured them that all would be made perfect and that he would speak to King Pulumayi on their behalf. Abendadar and the Armenians instantly realized that a confrontation was approaching and once again they would be in grave danger. Abendadar was familiar with the fertility goddess. He knew that the priests of that goddess were very aggressive and more hateful than those of most other religions. This goddess took on many different names in many different societies. She was Ishtar to the Babylonians, Inanna to the Sumarians, Astarte to the Syrians and Egyptians, Aphrodite to the Greeks, and Venus to the Romans. Bartholomew knew her under the title of "Ashtoreth, the goddess of Sidonians and Phoenicians," and he knew that her followers worshipped her in fertility orgies.

The four missionaries continued to preach and teach without concern, and in the following two weeks many of the poor, the sick, and the unwanted came to believe in Jesus. They left Bartholomew feeling rich and needed. When the blind, lame, sick, and dying came to Bartholomew, he would invoke the Name of Jesus, and they would be cured. Several times he multiplied their bread, and on occasion he would help them with their fishing by advising them to cast their nets to the right side of the boat, where a large catch awaited them. Word of his miracles spread rapidly, and soon people from farther inland were coming to see him. Bartholomew reminded them that all these good things were being done through the goodness of Jesus, and many became Christians. When these Christians returned home to their towns or villages, they needed help in teaching others, and so Bartholomew sent the Armenians out to preach Jesus. They became so busy that they stayed at these other towns and villages, while Bartholomew and Abendadar remained on the coast. The Armenians administered many Baptisms, but like Abendadar, they never tried to perform healings, because they never felt worthy. Bartholomew tried to persuade them to invoke the Master's name by reminding them that "all things are possible in His Name." They never tried.

The day of the full moon came, and the fertility ceremony was celebrated by the non-believers in all the towns and villages. The Christians that night celebrated the Meal with Bartholomew and Abendadar.

Bartholomew had decided earlier not to push for a confrontation—at least not yet—but the Armenians, who were inland, did not know this, so they attended the fertility meeting and denounced the sinfulness they witnessed.

The next day, Bartholomew received word that the Armenians had been arrested and were in prison. Before they could go into hiding, he and Abendadar were arrested. They were bound and loaded on the back of an open cart that was pulled by a large, horned bull. They were blindfolded and tied to the sides of the cart; they gathered from the guards' conversation that they were being taken to the palace of "King" Pulumayi, Governor of Kalyana who was known as Polymius to the Romans and the outside world.

As they rode through the streets, they began to hear the sounds of people around the cart. Some began cursing them, and others began throwing stones and garbage at them. Several of the projectiles found their mark, opening seeping wounds on their bodies. Abendadar became angry. He disliked not being able to see his enemies, but Bartholomew remained silent because he could sense that a large number of people were silent and just watching. He could feel their compassion, so he told his companion to pray and turn his mind to other things. The two men began to pray, and the anger around them was made silent. To calm himself, Abendadar began thinking of the cloak. It had been in Lady Mary's possession—perhaps John Zebedee was now in charge of it, but still he longed to have it with him. It reminded him of the physical presence of Jesus. He longed for the feel of the material and the scent of incense. Bartholomew's mind was back to the night of the Supper. His thoughts were with the cup that Joseph of Arimathea had, and in his mind's eye he saw the hands of the Master. He longed to again feel the unleavened bread and the clay cup in his hands.

The cart jerked and swayed, and the two men struggled to remain standing. The farther they traveled, the more difficult standing became, because the roads were in poor condition. From the sounds around them they concluded that they were in the jungle. The deeper into the jungle they went, the more Abendadar was bothered by insects and by the midday heat. He felt his energy being sapped from him; he grew tired as he perspired profusely.

Suddenly, their bumpy ride became smooth. The sounds of the jungle faded away. A short time later the cart stopped, and they were relieved of their blindfolds.

Abendadar looked at Bartholomew and grinned with amazement; the bright sun made Bartholomew's red beard and hair brighter. He was not bothered by the heat or by the cuts and welts on his forehead, face, and neck. Suddenly, Abendadar became unaware of the pain in his own head. He turned his head in the direction of Bartholomew's stare. A small gasp of amazement escaped Abendadar's lips. He was surprised not by the grandeur of the palace, for he had seen Roman palaces and nothing could compare to them. Rather, he was surprised because something so grand existed in such a remote place.

In the distance was the splendor of the palace of Pulumayi. It was a large, square, pink-tinted building with numerous arches adorned by figures of the gods of the region. Each arch told the legend of a different god. These arches were supported by massive, blinding-white columns. The arches and columns stretched across the front of the palace, and under each arch was a beautifully decorated pot containing a large plant with billowing, extravagant leaves. Between each pair of columns stood a meticulously dressed soldier who was as rigid and immovable as the columns. All of the soldiers were of the same height and build, seemingly from the same mold. They stood in perfect discipline, undisturbed by the sun, heat, or insects. Their uniforms were bright blue, and against their dark skins the blue became more pronounced. The uniforms were made of the finest material. Their armor was of silver, highly polished. They were the best-dressed soldiers Abendadar had ever seen; more splendidly dressed than the Persians, Egyptians, or Assyrians and far more beautiful than the dress of the Roman army.

But could they fight as the Romans do? He smiled, knowing that none were equal to the Romans.

The palace walls were set back, away from the columns, creating a large portico that had no decorations except for two tall, muscular guards who were posted at the palace doors. The palace was totally surrounded by tall, thick trees and bushes. They were the tallest, greenest trees Abendadar had ever seen. Every leaf of every tree and every bush seemed to grow into one another, looking like one large green curtain that protected the palace and separated it from the world. Abendadar felt sure that no other part of the world was behind the palace.

The cart jerked forward, and the long-horned animal pulled them over a lustrous, pebbled path that cut through the soft, emerald-green grass that spread out before the palace and ran to the very edge of the jungle from which the cart had just emerged. The path led to three wide steps, onto the portico, to the large door, and into the gaping, black interior. An instantaneous stillness came over the area. No plant, man, or animal moved. The wind was still. Not even the wheels of the cart crushing the pebbles on the path made a sound. The stillness was uncomfortable.

Abendadar took a deep breath. He felt suffocated by the serenity of the grounds and the palace.

The cart stopped. Several guards, dressed differently from the other guards, appeared. They roughly dragged the two from the back of the cart and directed them to walk up the wide steps to the portico of the palace. Once on the portico, they were told to take their sandals off, and the warmth of the sun-baked stone greeted their bare feet. Out of nowhere, six soldiers, dressed like those standing under the arches, appeared and immediately took up places around the two Christians.

From out of the darkness of the interior of the palace, the Great Priest Dharmesh appeared. He was again robed in the finest of clothing and surrounded by a large contingent of priests. With a wave of his hand, the soldiers led the prisoners into the dark interior of the palace. The stone floor of the palace immediately cooled their bare feet.

Abendadar saw massive Roman columns rise to the high ceiling above him. He saw painted images on the columns and rich scroll designs on the top and bottom. Though he could not see any other columns, he sensed that they were there, hidden in the shadows of the room. In the distance, deep inside the palace, oil-burning lamps of all sizes hung from the ceiling, illuminating an area in which a small elderly man sat. He was elevated above the palace floor, forcing everyone to look up at him. An array of pillows of golden silk surrounded him. The prisoners continued walking until they were surprised by the feel of a plush rug that promptly comforted their bare feet. They were ordered to stop.

Dharmesh walked up the six steps, and when he reached the top step, he fell on his knees. The crack of his knees against the stone floor echoed around the room.

"Most High Pulumayi, before your greatness are the offenders of our god."

Dharmesh's words echoed around the room, again and again, yet gradually they faded into silence.

The elderly man sat motionless. He wore a gold turban that twirled and rose to a point. It was bejeweled, with pearls and gems of yellow, red, blue, and black. The man was wearing a black robe trimmed with golden scrolls that opened and revealed his bare chest, which was covered with gray hair. His silk-covered legs were tucked under him, and on his knees rested his hands and his fingers, adorned with rings of every kind.

A long silence and stillness weaved its way around those in the room.

Finally, one of the guards knocked Bartholomew and Abendadar to their knees.

"Kneel before Pulumayi, the Mighty," the guard ordered.

Pulumayi raised his hand to still the guards, who obediently stepped back and away. With a quick motion of his hand, the king instructed the two men to stand, which they did without delay. He leaned forward and Dharmesh moved closer to him. An inaudible conversation was exchanged, and then Dharmesh backed away and stood to the right of the throne of pillows.

"We have been told that you are called Bartholomew and that you are a follower of a Man called Jesus," Pulumayi said. His voice was soft, yet it echoed and danced around the large room.

"I am, Sire," Bartholomew answered in a strong, resonating voice.

"We are also told that you feed the poor through a magical process of addition."

"That is not entirely true, Sire."

Guards rushed to Bartholomew's side as Dharmesh shouted, "Never contradict the Mighty Pulumayi."

"Silence, Dharmesh. We need to satisfy our curiosity. Let this foreign man speak his thoughts," the king said, turning his head slightly to the side, his eyes never looking at the priest.

The king returned his attention to the Apostle.

"Tell us," the king said, his voice still soft yet expansive, "What is wrong in what we have said?"

"I do not feed your poor. Jesus, my Master, does this through me."

Pulumayi looked confused and signaled Dharmesh to his side. Again there was an inaudible conversation between the two of them. Finally, Dharmesh backed away from Pulumayi.

"The mighty Pulumayi wants to know where your Master is," Dharmesh stated.

"Here." Bartholomew gestured toward the great floor of the palace. "There." He pointed to the ceiling. "And there." He pointed to his left, then to his right. "He is everywhere, for He is an all-encompassing God. He is in one place and in all places because He is mightier than all things and all beings."

Dharmesh dashed down the steps and slapped Bartholomew. The slap drew blood, which trickled from his mouth and through his red beard.

"No one is mightier than our god or King Pulumayi," the Great Priest shouted.

Abendadar took a step toward the Great Priest, but he was quickly grabbed by the guards, who roughly held him in place.

Bartholomew slowly raised his hand to Abendadar and to the men around him to signify the end of any possible conflict. Immediately, calm and peace returned to the room.

Out of the darkness of the room came a sound, a cry—a sort of shrill growl. This was followed by the sounds of chains being dragged along the floor. These sounds immediately destroyed the calmness in the air. Bartholomew had sensed others in the room, and he felt their peacefulness, but now he could sense fear. Even from the guards, he sensed a gnawing dread. The room was frozen in fear, and Bartholomew was curious to find out what sort of animal had entered the room and caused such fright.

Pulumayi stood up. His small figure now seemed big and looming.

"We are told, servant of the mighty Man Jesus, that you cure the ill."

"No Sire, my Master does. I am but a servant in His hand."

The sounds of chains dragging across the floor became louder and closer.

Suddenly, out of the shadows of the room a figure pounced. It moved like an animal, crawling, rolling around, and running on hands and knees.

The sudden entry of this figure and its strange condition caused the guards to pull away.

Abendadar could not determine if it was human or animal.

"That is my daughter Esha. She is mad."

Bartholomew turned and looked at the daughter. Her face was dirty, and from the corner of her mouth a thick stream of saliva slipped down her chin and dripped to the floor. Her eyes were dark, empty, and wild. They quickly darted around the room. Her hair was in complete disarray, knotted and tangled. Her fingers were unclean and had patches of missing flesh. Her body was poorly clad, and what flesh was exposed was filthy, smudged, and disfigured. Around her neck was a metal collar, and attached to the collar was a long, heavy chain.

"She is ill," Pulumayi said in a resolved voice. "She is unsafe, part animal from birth, but she is my daughter. We have ordered her to be chained in this way to prevent her from coming too close to the throne of pillows and to people of the court, for she bites and draws blood with her sharp teeth and long nails."

The girl started running around the room, the chain dragging after her, and the sounds of the scraping and clanging of the chain echoed over and over again. From the darkness of the room, Bartholomew heard the sounds of scattering people. Small gasps of fear could be heard. Again, the sounds of the chains being dragged around the cool stone floor echoed and re-echoed through the room. Unexpectedly, she made a dash toward Bartholomew, and everyone scattered. Just as she was about to reach Bartholomew, the chain became taut. She was thrown back and crashed to the stone floor. She let out a painful cry.

As Pulumayi had said, she could not reach anyone.

She clawed the air around her and began barking, growling, and screaming at Bartholomew.

"Esha!" Bartholomew said. The instant the girl heard her name, she stopped growling and clawing. She froze in a crouched position. Her eyes, in a penetrating gaze, fixed on Bartholomew.

Pulumayi took three steps away from his pillow throne. He cautiously stepped down two, then three steps, and in a soft voice he said, "If your Master will cure my daughter, you and your companions can live freely and safely in this kingdom."

"But Most High…." Dharmesh protested.

Pulumayi raised his hand, and Dharmesh withdrew quietly.

Bartholomew walked to the girl, scarcely aware of what had been promised to him. He heard only a cry for help.

"Remove her chains," he said, but no one moved. Too many of them had been bitten or scratched by her. With no one to carry out his command, Bartholomew touched the girl's iron collar, and it fell from her neck onto the ground with a loud clanging sound. Those in the room gasped, and some began to pull away.

Bartholomew stood over her still body, and lifting his head, he began to pray silently. His face glowed with a light that was not of the room, and his garment became bright. After several minutes, he slowly reached down to the girl and rested his hand on her head.

"In the name of Jesus, the Son of God, be free and made whole. Rise, Esha, and give thanks to the God of all." His voice echoed in the room. It was unlike those of the other speakers, unlike any other sound in the room. This echo did not race around the room but rather rose and descended, rose and descended, showering everyone present.

The girl slowly, painstakingly, rose. Her face was dirty but alive in beauty; her hair was tangled, but it shined. Her eyes were bright and alert as she looked around the room at all who were there.

The room burst into frantic confusion as guards left their posts and ran, shouting about the wonder they had seen.

"Most High...." Dharmesh shouted, but again Pulumayi silenced his objections.

Pulumayi descended his pillow throne and drew near to Bartholomew. With tears of joy, he stretched out his arms to welcome his daughter.

"But Most High, this is nothing but magic and trickery, surely you can see it," Dharmesh insisted, but Pulumayi was not listening. For the first time in his life, he held his daughter in his arms.

"Most High, in the name of our god and all her powers of war and love, I demand this foreigner be punished for spreading false beliefs among our people."

Bartholomew looked at Dharmesh and said, "If your god was of love, then why did she not cure this child, who lacked only love? And if this was an act of trickery and magic, why did not you and your magicians do what Jesus has done?"

Dharmesh rushed to Bartholomew with his hand raised to strike him.

"Enough!" Pulumayi shouted, and the Great Priest's hand froze in the air.

Dharmesh timidly backed away.

"This man has done us a service, and it has always been our custom to reward people for services rendered. There will be no more talk of punishment. We have given our word that he shall have freedom in our district, and so it shall be done."

With a flash of his robes and with amulets jingling, Dharmesh turned and rushed from the room, followed by a group of priests.

Pulumayi clapped his hands, and a group of frightened women, who had been in the dark shadows of the room and who had witnessed the miracle, slowly walked to him. He ordered them to take his daughter to be washed, bathed, and dressed anew.

The girl looked at the women and smiled. With great grace and dignity, she walked from the room, but not without a glance behind her and a wide smile for Bartholomew.

She disappeared.

Pulumayi turned. With tears in his eyes, with deepest sincerity, he said pleadingly, "Come, Bartholomew of Jesus. Come and sit with us and tell us of your Master."

By day's end, Pulumayi and his daughter Esha were cleansed in water, filled with the Spirit, and made followers of Jesus. Over the next few days, many members of Pulumayi's family and court became Christians.

The next day, the Armenians, Abendadar, and Bartholomew had supper together in the palace. They talked of their successes and the greatness of Jesus, Who was ever present in their lives. They were all calm and at peace with the knowledge that they were under the protection of Pulumayi. Later that day, Bartholomew asked Abendadar to return to the village to get the scrolls with the writings of Matthew.

"I think that we know the language of these people well enough to tell the stories of Jesus in their language."

Abendadar agreed that this was a good idea, and he left immediately for the village.

Three days later he returned, and when he entered the palace grounds he was immediately seized by guards and taken to another part of the palace, where he was met by a frantic Pulumayi.

"Oh dear friend, much has happened since you left. Dharmesh, after leaving us, went to my brother, King Aristakarman, whom some call Astriagis. He told my brother about my friendly treatment of Bartholomew and you. When the king heard of my conversion, he immediately set out to confront me. Bartholomew was with Esha at my wife's palace. Upon arriving here, Aristakarman immediately arrested your Armenian friends and had them put to death by fire. Later that night, they found Bartholomew and arrested him. He was placed in jail, and we have been told that he has been tortured and has suffered many beatings—but still he refuses to deny the Master Jesus. They searched for you, also, but we mentioned that you are a Roman citizen and a former soldier, and the king, who is afraid of Rome, said he would only exile you. That is why we intercepted you. You must return quickly to your former village and make plans to return to Roman rule."

"And you, most kind king, what will happen to you?"

"Nothing. My brother is actually a reasonable man, and he will only take Dharmesh's advice for so long. He tolerates the Great Priest only because he knows he can control him. My family and I will be safe with Aristakarman, but Dharmesh has ways of bringing you harm. You must make plans to leave immediately."

"I cannot do that, Sire, I must stay and finish what the Apostle has started."

"But your safety cannot be guaranteed."

"I must stay, for this is my call. This is my service to Jesus, Who has called me to Himself. To leave now would be a betrayal of that call."

A young boy came into the room. He was about twelve years of age. He had brightness in his eyes, and his demeanor was that of a mature man. He had an air of importance to his features. It was readily apparent that he was accustomed to being in a position of authority.

"This is my son, Irfan. He has been my source of information. Bartholomew has touched his soul in a special way."

Abendadar bent from the waist slightly out of respect for the young boy. "I am grateful for your help, kind sir."

The boy returned the gesture and turned quickly to his father.

"Father, I have bad news. Dharmesh has not relented...the situation is deteriorating rapidly." The young boy was struggling with his words from shortness of breath, and from the tears that had begun to well up in his eyes.

"After Bartholomew was beaten, they put the knives to him, and I have just learned from one of Uncle Aristakarman's guards that they have pinned him to a tree at the edge of the jungle, overlooking the village."

"Do you know the place?" Abendadar asked urgently.

"Yes, sir, but...."

"Take me there. Immediately."

"No, you must not go. What they have done to Bartholomew is... most disturbing."

"Kind sir, have you forgotten that I was a Roman soldier? I am well accustomed to gruesome sights."

"But if you go, you will be immediately arrested, and then what will we do without a leader?" Pulumayi said.

Abendadar took a deep breath. Pulumayi's wisdom tempered his anxiety. Softly and with deep concern, the former soldier said, "But I must see him. I must let him see that he is not alone—that I am here to continue in Jesus' name. He must see this."

Pulumayi considered Abendadar's reply, knowing that he could not change his mind. He reached for and tightly grabbed Abendadar's muscular arm.

"Come," Pulumayi commanded, and the three quickly left the room and entered the great privacy of the palace.

Abendadar was left alone in a room, and soon many servants entered. They quickly went to work on Abendadar. His dark skin was darkened with some brown skin dye. They bound his head in a turban and gave him a *dhoti* a long loincloth to wear.

He was carefully instructed on how to wrap the *dhoti* around his waist, run it between his legs, and tuck it into the wrapping around his waist. He was naked except for the *dhoti*.

Pulumayi ordered his son and two of his servants to take the disguised Abendadar to where Bartholomew was. The two men and Abendadar ran from the palace, and swiftly they fell into the cover of the nearby jungle. Without looking back or hesitating, they continued to run until they came to the edge of the jungle and to the village. Swiftly they made their way through the streets, and finally they reached the hill.

Abendadar slowly walked up the hill, not because he was tired from his hasty journey, but rather because he could hardly believe what was before him. The closer he got to the scene, the more he understood what the young boy meant by "they put the knives to him." They had skinned, cut, and ripped the flesh on Bartholomew's body. Pieces of flesh, sliced and torn, hung from his chest, stomach, legs, and arms, like strips of red and purple ribbons and rags. In some places, bones were made bare. His face was cut, swollen, bruised, and beaten. Blood flowed from all the wounds, and hundreds of insects were feasting on the sweetness of the blood. His red beard and hair had been torn from his chin and head. These people were not Romans, so they had no crude crosses on which to crucify people. Their cross was a live tree with a wide trunk and two large branches.

Bartholomew was held in place by a heavy rope around his arms and the nails in his wrists. His legs were spread apart and fixed to the side of the tree by large nails driven through his ankles.

Abendadar approached the cross.

These barbarians!

Anger began to penetrate deep into his soul, and he faltered as hateful, malicious thoughts slithered into his mind.

Lord, why did You let them do this?

His eyes burned with tears, and he uttered a profound request for forgiveness. He closed his eyes and felt warm tears stream down his cheeks.

A weak voice descended from the tree: "How good You have been to me, Lord Jesus, for You have permitted me to be robed in garments of royal purple and kingly red. I praise You, for You have not forgotten Your servant. I come to You dressed in this honor."

These words of joy and happiness helped Abendadar to accept what he was witnessing. He opened his eyes and saw a smile across the Apostle's swollen lips. In the small slits of Bartholomew's swollen eyes, the disciple sensed a command: "Continue." Realizing that his companion understood his thoughts, Bartholomew broke eye contact and raised his head. Off in the distance, far from his perch, Bartholomew saw a small hill, and on this hill he saw a fig tree. The shade from the tree, though far out of his reach, gave him comfort. Soon, he saw a Man slowly ascending the side of the hill. The Man was dressed in a white robe and a seamless red cloak. The Apostle pulled against the nails as he tried to leave his cross and go to the hill, and to the Man, but he was held by the pain, though this pain was nothing in comparison to the pain of longing he felt in his chest.

With a smile on his swollen, bruised lips, he shouted, "Lord!" With great excitement, Bartholomew cried, "Abendadar, look over there, under the fig tree. See what good has come from Nazareth!"

Abendadar looked in the direction of the small hill and then heard Bartholomew sigh the name: "Jesus."

Abendadar did not need to look. He knew Bartholomew was dead.

He searched the small hill, and saw no fig tree.

EPILOGUE

John rolled up the scroll, rose from his stool, and walked to the window opposite the table that he used as a desk. His eyes searched the landscape. For a few quick moments, he was captivated by the wind playing through the leaves of the tall trees. After this delightful respite, he glanced back at the scrolls on his desk, and he sighed with frustration. For years this had been his daily exercise. He would sit at his desk and remember an event in Jesus' life, and slowly words would flow from his memory into his *stylus*. Often, he became so immersed in the life of the Master that he would reach a state of ecstasy. Later, he would return and edit what had been written, and then it would end. Nothing more would happen, and he would be dry and empty. He would become unhappy with his progress and begin to doubt if he truly was to be the transcriber for Jesus. He knew that many were eager to see his finished account, but he never seemed to finish. He felt as though he would never finish, for he could find no beginning. Every attempt he made to write a beginning ended in dissatisfaction and disappointment, but still he tried and tried, every day.

He returned to his desk with renewed frustration and disappointment. He had to be free and comfortable of all thoughts before he could put a beginning on parchment. He knew he would find and write the beginning Jesus wanted him to find. Assuredly, the words to his *epistulae* letters were truly guided by God. He would again be guided. Besides, he could not afford to damage any scrolls; they were too rare and too expensive.

In the past year, he became certain that deep inside him was the perfect beginning for his account, but this certainty had not trickled down to his hand and onto the parchment. He was convinced that the beginning he was to write, when he realized it, would somehow burst forth onto the parchment. He just had to find the right words for the beginning.

Where do I begin? Should I begin with one of the stories Lady Mary told me? No, those early years are so unimportant in comparison to what Jesus did later. Should I begin with the day I saw Jesus? No, that would be self-centered. I could start when John bar Zachary called Him "the Lamb of God." That truly was the beginning, but I am not comfortable with that. Perhaps a genealogy of His family? No, I know only Mary's side of His family. Joseph's side of the family is better known by the Sons of Alphaeus. Slowly, he began to rearrange his desk. *Where do I begin? At what beginning? When did it all begin?*

He took a deep breath and released it in an exaggerated sigh, hoping that somehow this expulsion would rid him of his frustration. Still perturbed, he walked away from the desk, leaving his rearranging undone.

With resolution, he thought, *All I can do is wait for the beginning to come. I have no control over it. It will come when God wants it to come.*

He walked again to the window and found himself gazing into the last warm breaths of daylight. Lady Day was ending, and she was giving way to Sister Night. He felt the last heat of day depart, and the first cool of night skipped lightly across his face. This was always a strange time of day, when nature did not know what it was, when it was caught between two doors that were both partially opened. As he pondered this dilemma, he grew sad at seeing an ending, yet eager to have the beginning. This time of day always made him nostalgic. It was during these hours, in bygone days, when the Twelve would gather to discuss what they had seen, heard, and witnessed during the day with Jesus. John always enjoyed this time, for it allowed him to learn what the Others were thinking. It gave him a chance to match their observations with his. Often, what the Others saw would confuse him. Many of them elaborated on what they had seen, or they would tint it according to political or social ideas. He never did this. To him, the actions of Jesus were simply sacred and marvelous. Only he and Bartholomew had believed from the very beginning that Jesus was a special and spiritual Person, directed and inspired by God. From the first moment of his calling, Bartholomew would often repeat, "Jesus is the Son of God." None of the others saw this clearly, at least not at the very beginning. At one time, some thought Jesus was an angel, but He spoke of *Elohim* as "*Abba*," and no angel would do that. Then, some began believing He was a prophet, and many of them maintained this idea because He acted like a prophet, condemning the sins and excesses of those around Him. Toward the end, some even began believing He was the Messiah, but no one was totally faithful to this conclusion, and above all things, not one of them knew where Jesus was leading them. Jesus made no call to arms or to revolt; He spoke rather of love, compassion, and sacrifice. He never attacked the Romans. He never disobeyed the laws of Rome. So what was He about? They did not know. They only speculated and guessed. John could not understand how the Others could not see that Jesus was truly good and that His miracles were from a Higher Power. Could they not see and feel the goodness that Jesus radiated?

Surely they must have seen that everything He did was of a spiritual nature. He was leading them to a kingdom not of this world. Why did they miss this? He chuckled to himself. *Ah, how could I figure out the ways of my brothers when they unknowingly were under the shadow of Adonai? Certainly, all this was in Jesus' plan. Most likely, He wanted us to be receivers of a miracle. It was something we had never been. We had seen miracles, but it was the Master's final wish that a miracle be performed on us and just for us. The Master wanted to make us the cure for the confusion that was in the world, and to do that we had to be a miracle. On Pentecost day, when the confusion had become staggering, we became physicians for the Lord and healed many wounded souls.* John smiled to himself as that day passed quickly through his mind. *What a mixture of joy and wonder that day was. None of us realized that a miracle had taken place—or that we were the miracle. We became filled with the same courage that Jesus had, and like Jesus, we defied governments and laws.*

As these thoughts slowly faded, the image of all the Others came to him, and he grew lonely. He missed their friendship, and when finally the image of his brother James came to him, he grew melancholy. It was twenty years since James had been killed by Herod, and still John missed his brother. But in his sadness he was able to find joy, for he knew that his brother was with the Master. He recalled how the Others moved farther away to spread the Word because James' death proved that Jerusalem was unsafe. Jerusalem was no longer to be the center of "The Way." Many of them never returned from their distant journeys, except when they gathered for Mary's death.

His thoughts were interrupted by something that passed the window. Quickly he looked to investigate the distraction, and he saw a dove hovering. He pulled away from the window, knowing that the dove was a messenger, for he remembered the news that followed the appearance of the other doves. He felt his heart beat rapidly. With no control over his thoughts, he quickly began whispering the names of the Others: Peter, Andrew, Thomas, Matthew, Jude, Philip, Bartholomew, Simon.

The dove landed on the windowsill. Its wingspan was longer than that of most doves. It cooed, as though wanting to be understood and recognized.

John drew close to the window, no longer afraid or apprehensive.

He sensed the dove's joy and peace. The dove was pure blinding white, but near the center of its chest was a small blemish; it was a spot of royal purple. This mark was scarcely noticeable, but John knew that he was meant to see it. He heard a light knock on the door, but he could not remove his eyes from the dove. He heard his mother walking to the door and then the sounds of low voices. He did not move or turn, but instead he stood watching the dove as it lifted from the windowsill. It lingered a moment, hovered, and then pulled away and flew with great exuberance into the early night sky.

He heard someone call, "John."

The voice was familiar, but he did not want to turn to acknowledge it or to see who the speaker was. He associated the voice with a disciple. When he thought of that disciple, he knew what time in Jesus' life he would write about tomorrow.

Tears welled up in his eyes.

Taking a deep breath, he turned and saw Abendadar, and the meaning of the royal purple mark on the dove became Bartholomew.

CHAPTER FIVE:

SIMON PETER BAR JONAH OF BETHSAIDA

PROLOGUE

John's many trips on the Sea of Galilee had its rough and stormy moments. Never had he experienced sailing as rough as the seven weeks he traveled on the *Mare Inernum* the Mediterranean Sea. Before this journey, he traveled over land, across lakes, navigated up or down rivers but never a long, confined voyage. He began to understand that it wasn't the distance but the enormity of the sea that was taking a toll on him. When he first boarded the Greek merchant ship *Thalassa Aetos* the Sea Eagle in Ephesus, he was excited and anxiously waited to depart. However, as the ship pulled away from the dock and slipped into the Aegean Sea, he surprisingly grew remorseful. He quickly missed the security of being on solid terrain.

On his first night, he stood on the deck of the ship, and watched the heavens and the sea mesh together in darkness and fell under the splendor of the vastness of God's creation. Caught between nature and his own finiteness, he was humbled and in awe of God. He listened to the soft hiss of the parting waters as the ship met and cut into the dark, oncoming, infantile waves. The sound brought back memories of the many trips across the Sea of Galilee from Capernaum to Gamala or Gergesa and to the mouth of the Jordan River. With the silver moonlight coloring his face and hands, he started to remember his many nights on the Sea of Galilee before and after the arrival of Jesus. He heard his father's rough orders to Simon, Andrew, and his brother James. He heard the chatter and hearty laughter of these fishermen. He heard them sing their songs of adventure and of fishing, songs which were always filled with stories of inflated catches. He remembered the many nights, when he and the Others listened to the Sea of Galilee as it became black in night's hand, and of the soft gentle exhale the Sea made under this dark blanket. He felt a strong longing for the Others, and his thoughts returned to a place of comfort. He heard the Twelve laughing and joking with each other, and could even hear their words of bickering and teasing. He heard their quiet whispers and questions of what Jesus said and did. He heard them asking what they were doing following a Man whom they did not know or whom they did not completely understand. He heard Jesus speak in a low restive voice that seemed to put an end to all worldly problems. He heard the popping of the flames that warmed them and saw the twelve amber faces sitting in a circle.

He felt Jesus and the Others near.

He caught the aroma of Jesus.

The comfort of companionship brought a long missed stillness to him. Whenever this stillness came, he knew that his Master was preparing him for a new direction; it was the way God spoke to him. Throughout the night, he grew certain that something was to be found, and so he waited that first night for something to be revealed, but by night's end he was filled with a heavy melancholy and went to sleep sad filled with an intense desire.

The next day the ship caught a strong wind and the sails bellowed with billowy pride. The ship cut and slipped across the open sea, and John was sure Jesus was hurrying him to Rome. The wind stayed with them all day and into the night, but by dawn the seas were stilled. The ship was dead in the middle of the giant Roman Lake. The sails hung uselessly from the mast like discarded laundry. The small waves, which playfully slapped against the ship's sides and beneath her, lifted and lowered her in a soft easy rhythm. This gentle treatment by the sea reminded John of a baby cradle that was slowing down to a sleepy rock. The crew took to the oars, but the Sea Eagle went nowhere.

The ship stayed this way for two days and nights.

The captain and sailors talked about the oddity of the dead wind and blamed it on the fact of their sacrifice to Neptune but not Mercury.

John smiled and knew that this was all the work of Jesus, so on that night, he again stood on the deck of the ship and with the calm around him, said aloud, "Speak to me, Master, so I may come to know what You wish of me."

On the third day, the rains came and then the winds, which were so violent and so powerful that even the most experienced seaman was filled with fear. The ship became helpless in the hands of the sea, as the waves roughly toyed with it. The storm intensified. Many aboard began to believe that they were going to die. The captain, crew, and the few passengers began invoking Neptune and other gods for protection.

John smiled at their ignorance. He had learned long before that he and the Others would always be protected from the anger of the sea, and that none of them would die by drowning. Confidently, John stood on deck in defiance challenging the wide-raging sea. Wet and salted, jolted yet un-swayed, he held his post, and as he stood there, he remembered a similar storm and the fear of death that was in the minds of those aboard the boat. It was early in their journey and they became confused by many of the things that Jesus did.

One day, Jesus told a twisted lowly leper to go show himself to the priest. The Disciples were confused by this order, for the man still had the stench of leprosy. As the leper passed them, however, he had a clear face and pure skin. Later that day, Jesus was beseeched by a Roman centurion named Cornelius to cure his manservant. Jesus became filled with compassion and immediately started out much to the dismay of the Twelve. As they neared the *villa* of Cornelius, the Roman sent a messenger to meet Jesus, saying that his house was "not worthy to receive Him." Jesus marveled at these words, and said He had "not found so great a faith in all Israel." These words disturbed and hurt the Disciples.

"How could He say such things of a Gentile, and a Roman at that, while we have given up so much to follow Him?" Judas asked.

"I agree. Have we not shown faith by following Him, though He says so little of what He is about?" Simon the Canaanite stated with an edge to his words, for he found the idea of a Roman being helped by Jesus repulsive.

"Let us wait and watch more closely before we judge so harshly. Truly, Jesus saw something in this Roman that He did not see in us. Let us wait," Bartholomew added softly.

So they waited for things to be made clear to them.

Whenever John remembered incidents like this, he became angry, for he never seemed to react to any of the events. He wished he could have been as passionate as Bartholomew or Peter. All he did was sit and listen.

I was never to be a leader, to say what was on my mind, he thought. *I had to traverse a different way, and at journey's end come to know differently.* He smiled and allowed past and bygone days to return to his mind.

Later, after the servant of Cornelius had been healed, they dined at Simon Peter's house, while many remained outside waiting for Jesus. The crowds had become bigger and more demanding of Jesus, and the Twelve could see that Jesus was weary. After eating and clever planning, they pulled Jesus away undetected and sailed to sea. When they were in the middle of the sea, and land was but a shadow in the distance, Jesus rolled His cloak in a ball and using it as a pillow rested His head on it, and "in the stern" slept. The sea was serene, and it was a cloudless night deep in dark blue with soft blinking stars, as a slither of the moon illuminated the night.

Suddenly, a strong wind arose and captured the waters around them. The listless sea and peaceful night swiftly turned into a storm of great anger, and it seemed that all nature had grown vicious. Peter's boat was captured by the confusion of the sea, and the Twelve grew concerned for their safety. Immediately, the experienced fishermen took to the mast and dropped it before the valuable cloths were ripped or destroyed, and then they ordered everyone to brace themselves. Some of the fishermen among them said, "This is one of the Sea of Galilee's sudden storms that usually pass as quickly as they start."

The statement gave some comfort.

The storm lingered seemingly centered on Peter's boat. The sea began to pour into the craft, and larger waves lifted and heaved the craft to and fro. They slipped and fell against each other despite holding on to the mast or the side of the boat with tight white-knuckled grips.

John never remembered a storm like this. It was as if all the anger in the world was in this storm trying to hurt and destroy them. He was struck with fear, though he tried not to show it, but he could see the fear, alarm, and panic on the faces of the Others.

Later, some told him that they were so fearful that they cried, though it was impossible to differentiate their salty tears from all the salty water on their faces.

"We are surely going to die," Bartholomew shouted above the sound of the wind.

"We could never swim to shore for the sea is too violent," James the Less said, as he held closely onto the mast of the boat.

"Wake Jesus," Jude said with the unfamiliar sound of an order.

John heard James, his brother's voice, above the confusion, "How could Jesus sleep so peacefully? Does He not know we are in peril?"

"Simon, the boat is filling with water faster then we can bail it," Andrew said as he filled a cup of water and threw its contents into the sea. "Wake up the Master; He will know what to do," Andrew added with urgency.

Rehearing all the voices of the Disciples, John thought to himself: *How afraid we were even with the Lord with us. No wonder after His death we were more fearful. What lost and confused children we were, and yet Jesus daily tried to make us understand who He was and what His mission was about.*

Finally, Thomas began nudging Jesus roughly.

"Lord, save us, we perish," Thomas shouted. His voice was lost in the sounds of the tumultuous wind and the splashing sea.

The Master quickly sat up. He looked at the fear on their faces. His expression was one of disappointment, and John remembered that everyone was soaked and drenched by the rain and sea, while Jesus' clothing was dry.

"Why are ye fearful? O ye of little faith," He said in a low, saddened voice, yet all Twelve heard Him.

He stood up undisturbed by the rocking boat. With His head lowered, He slowly raised His arms, and after a moment raised His face to the sky. His face was bright and radiant.

"Be still," He said, and the sound of His command pierced the anger of the wind and the strength of the sea like a sharp dagger. All went still and a great calm followed.

Jesus returned to His seat, and rested His head again on His cloak.

Embarrassed, the Twelve looked at each other. They had witnessed each other's fear. They were exposed to each other. Without speaking, they hurriedly hoisted the mast wanting to act normal, needing to forget what they had discovered about each other.

Perplexed, Matthew questioned, "What manner of Man is this that the waters and the winds obey Him?" His question remained unanswered, but it confounded the Others.

"One thing is for certain," Bartholomew said more to himself than to the Others, "We do not have the faith of the centurion Cornelius."

They said nothing more as they made for the shore and "the country of Gerasens."

They were not even aware of their dry robes.

*

John never forgot the look of disappointment on Jesus' face. It was a look that was forever present to John, and present also was his remembrance of the silent pledge he made that night. Long after the sea had calmed, he remembered looking at Jesus and promising that never again would he, John bar Zebedee, be afraid of the sea.

The sea's spray stung John's face and the salty water slipped into his eyes burning them. He slowly lowered his head in small protest to the pain. In the turmoil of the raging storm, John felt a warmth pass over him; he was dry. A wide smile opened across his mouth and when he opened his eyes, the sea and the storm were calm.

Have I the faith of Cornelius, Lord?

From the quarters below, the sailors and the few passengers slowly came onto the deck and when they saw the calm sea, they began to speak of the greatness of their gods. Then they saw John standing with open arms and outstretched hands. They saw that his face and hands were wet from the storm but his clothing dry. They watched in silence and confusion until John lowered his arms and turning to them, said softly and with a smile, "Let me tell you of another storm and of a Man named Jesus of Nazareth."

SIMON PETER BAR JONAH OF BETHSAIDA

At one time, the house had been the home of the *villicus* guardian to the Camolius vineyards and groves. It was a small house with a garden and small fountain in the back. Simon Peter used the garden nightly for his prayers and meditations. The small garden was a far cry from the rooftop of a Galilean home, but it served him well. He had learned many years ago to accept what God gave him. His heavy body leaned back in his wooden chair while his broad shoulders overlapped the back of the chair. The once brown hair was now streaked with clean white hair; a contrast to his closely trimmed and totally white beard. The many furrows on his tanned face were the result of his many years of squinting to protect his sensitive brown eyes from the sunlight of Galilee and other places. At sixty-nine, he still looked powerful, but appearances mattered little, for he knew that age had sagged his muscles and abuse had eaten his strength. Slowly, he brought his big calloused hand to his face and leaned his head into his open palm. His hands still showed the strength and the power of a fisherman. He inhaled deeply to capture the clean open air. A tinge of pleasure passed over his face as he looked out the back of the house and on to the distant landscape. It was a peaceful sight, and one he knew he would remember long after he left this *villa*. The tall pine trees, with their long thin trunks and bushy leaves, swayed softly from the push of a late afternoon breeze. In the far distance, to the left of the house, were white barked trees, a few majestic redwoods, and a few willow trees that marked the end of the *villa* of the patrician Larius Camolius. The enormity of this *villa* amazed Peter; this was the largest parcel of land he ever saw owned by one family. He could remember nothing like this existing in Judea and he had seen nothing as vast or prosperous in any of the other Roman provinces.

His admiration fell away from his mind as he looked with great satisfaction at the trees which began to throw a welcome shadow over the neat rows of grape vines and olive trees.

Soon the shadow will slip over the small house and all would be cool, he thought, knowing he would welcome the cool and damp of the night, conditions he preferred, for the heat of the day made it impossible for him to stay in the house or to deal with his boredom. In desperation to escape the heat and the monotony, he walked through the *villa* and in recent days joined the workers in tending to the grapes and olives. He found great happiness in being a novice among the seasoned harvesters of the fields, and was proud that he had conquered his ignorance so quickly and received approval from the harvesters. He laughed, for being a harvester was foreign to him. He was a fisherman not a farmer, but again he saw the artful workings of his Master because he found many fertile ears and willing souls in the groves.

For a few precious moments, he closed his eyes, burning as they were from use, and rested his head against the back of his chair.

Perhaps tonight will be cooler and I will find sleep, he thought, pondering the many warm sleepless nights he had endured these past weeks. His nights had been filled with uneasiness and a strong feeling of expectation.

Truly the Lord is trying to speak to me. There must be a reason for these sleepless nights. An inventory of the things that could make him uneasy raced through his mind. *Perhaps it is the Emperor's hatred? Perhaps my fears for the infant Ecclesia Church? Or is it my sorrow in sending Mark away which I had to do for his own protection and because I knew the Master had other things for him? No, it is none of these. These things were God's Will.* He nodded his head in agreement. *Possibly, I am not comfortable being in the house of a Roman patrician, or of enjoying the comforts of a person of high birth.* His thoughts stopped and for a moment he felt he might have found the source of his sleepless nights.

It was a year since he met Larius Camolius through the centurion Cornelius. The two Romans were childhood friends and had been centurions in the Roman Army, but Larius had retired earlier than Cornelius because of a wound he received from an Armenian terrorist. His wound left him partially crippled cutting short his military career. He returned to Rome and his prosperous family, and began a life in Roman politics like his father, Crispus Camolius. Being a wounded veteran had its benefits, for he was given hero status and his popularity soared. After his father's death, he inherited the lands and farms that his father had neglected. Soon Larius turned these lands into a lucrative business and grew even wealthier. He then married Livilla Natilius, who was not of a patrician family, but a merchant family with equal wealth. They immediately started having children—a girl named Liva and twin sons named Agrillius and Adessius. At the age of eight, Agrillius died of seizures. Several years later, the remaining son, Adessius, began suffering the same illness as his twin brother. One day, after the teenager had suffered a bad seizure and remained unconscious, Cornelius told Larius of Peter who could heal in the Name of Jesus. Later that day, on a cold windy night, a clandestine meeting took place in the *domus* main house, where Peter in the Name of Jesus cured young Adessius. Livilla, her son, and many servants and household slaves, immediately came to Jesus, but much to Peter's dismay, Larius did not.

When the Emperor began ordering the arrest of known Christians, Larius, in the dark of night with the help of Cornelius, whisked Peter away just moments before he was to be arrested and housed him in the *villa*. Everyone was told that Peter was the new *villicus* and that his name was Bar-Jonah.

Livilla and her household were delighted with Peter's presence, for nightly he was invited to the *domus* house to speak of Jesus. On several occasions, he led the Supper, but each time he went to the house, Larius was away on business which bothered Peter greatly.

It is frustrating that Larius has not been open to the Lord. He is, I am sure, more concerned about his position in Roman society than in being redeemed. Could my failure to win him over be the cause of my uneasiness? The cause of my feeling incomplete? Most definitely my being here is the Will of God. This family must be special to the Master for He placed me in their way two times. Assuredly, the Lord has a need for Larius, and that is why I must bring Larius to the Lord. I must finish what I have started with this family. He grew contented with these thoughts, but after weighing them further he still found no relief from his uneasiness. Then he dismissed his conclusion with a vigorous shake of his head. *No, Larius is not the problem; well perhaps he is a bit of it, but not all. Certainly, in recent days, my presence on his estate has made him fearful. In my enthusiasm to teach Jesus to the field slaves, I destroyed my disguise and revealed that I was a Christian. I am now a great risk to Larius, his family, and household. As long as I quietly worked in the vineyards my disguise was good, but when I began preaching, things became dangerous.* Putting the Camolius family in danger did not sit well with Peter, and for this reason he would leave and find another place to live.

He jolted into an upright position and felt a cold icy chill run through his body which made him shudder. It was back again. The thing he prayed constantly to be protected from; the moment he never permitted himself to relive. He quickly rose from his chair and began to swiftly pace the floor in total panic. Suddenly, he fell to his knees. Sleep would not be his companion, for now he was afraid to sleep; sleep would conjure up dark thoughts. He glanced out the back of the *villa*. The entire world became a black outline against the dark blue sky. In the distance, he saw the hills of Rome and returned to the hills of Judea and that night on the Mount. He allowed the remembrances of that night become his companion believing that this was the lesser of two evils. Tightly clasping his hands and closing his eyes, he began to pray; and with prayer came tears in his eyes.

On that long ago night, Jesus bade nine of the Twelve to remain at the foot of the mountain while He allowed James, John, and Simon Peter to go up the side of the "high mountain." Once the Apostles reached the place appointed, Jesus went off to pray while the three Apostles reclined on the ground and slept. After some time, without any known cause, the three awoke and together they saw Jesus "transfigured before them." His face held the radiance of the sun, and His entire being was in an aura of blinding light. His clothes appeared dazzlingly "white like snow." Confusedly, there appeared two men, one on each side of Jesus, whom the Apostles understood to be "Moses and Elias conversing with Him." Jesus became brighter while the two Servants of *Elyon* Most High grew dimmer and withdrawn. With exultation and equal confusion, Simon Peter said, "Lord, it is good for us to be here: if Thou wilt, let us make here three tabernacles; one for Thee, one for Moses, and one for Elias." While he spoke these words, a brilliant cloud descended over their heads and from this cloud thundered a voice that announced: "This is My beloved Son, in Whom I am well pleased: hear ye Him."

The three terrified Apostles threw themselves onto the ground, burying their faces further into the dirt. Simon Peter dared not raise his head to see any more, for he understood that something was happening that was too significant to comprehend. He knew and believed, without any doubt, that he did not belong in the company of such magnificence. Apparently, he was the first to feel the stillness of the night, and when he looked up, he saw Jesus standing on the Mount alone.

Jesus said to them: "Arise, and fear not."

The excitement that night and moment still sent a flutter throughout Peter's body, and though he now understood what had happened, at that time, he felt bewildered for he did not know what it all meant.

How confused and baffled I was; I had no idea what happened. On the way down the mountain, Jesus told us not to say anything of what we saw. Dare we? How could we explain what we saw? We could not understand it ourselves. For the first time in my relationship with Jesus, I was afraid of Him and of what He was. At that moment in time, I could not judge what or who He was. I walked well behind Him as we descended the mountain. I had to; I felt foolish for what I had said. Why, why did I always have to be the one who spoke? And why did I always say the dumbest things? Lord, what did You see in me that I did not know was there? What did You sense from my senselessness? Why did you not pick James bar Alphaeus? Or James bar Zebedee? Or John, Your most beloved? They were wiser, even of Your Blood, and more prayerful. They were more worthy. Why did You allow me to speak first and be the loudest? As You gave others tongues to speak, why did You not help me loosen my tongue?

Exhausted, he fell to the floor and stretched out on the cool tiles which gave him comfort. Away from him, he heard the soft trickling sound of the fountain in the small garden behind the house. The gentleness of the sound slowly mesmerized him. Drifting, he soon fell into a state of inertia. Peace came to him and drew him deep within its dwelling. With his mind blank, free, and still, he took rest.

He saw a figure walking to him. It was a known figure; it looked like James bar Zebedee, and then he acknowledged it as Jesus. He was walking to him and smiling.

In this dream he heard, "Be of good heart; it is I, fear ye not."

The ground that Jesus walked on, then, became water.

He shouted, "…bid me come to Thee over the water."

Jesus called back, "Come!"

He lifted his foot over something and felt a cool silky feeling under his foot. Quickly, and with great confidence, he brought his other foot beside his first foot. Looking directly into his Master's face, he began to walk: one step then another, one foot before the other. Every step he took was miraculous, and soon things of greater wonder surrounded him. He was enveloped with things he did not know. He was aware of their existence, but he did not need them, because all the joys of his life were in the Face of his Lord. Unexpectedly, the sensation of water beneath his feet began to tickle; He was walking on water! He looked down, and the water rose swiftly to meet his face.

In panic, he looked at Jesus and cried: "Lord, spare me."

Jesus said, "O ye of little faith."

In a different voice he heard: "Why do you doubt even now, Peter? Know this. You had to speak first and be first because you were the one who heard My Father before you heard Me."

A hand rested on his shoulder.

"Peter! Peter!"

He shot up from his stupor.

"Peter, are you well?" He heard a familiar, soft voice ask: "You were crying and you are wet from perspiration. Are you well?"

"Yes. Yes."

"Why were you sleeping on the floor?" The young man asked in innocence and confusion.

His mind still hazy from sleep, Peter looked at the diminutive man before him. Slowly, he recognized Linus, and the message of the dream jumped into his conscious mind.

"Deo Gratias!" Thank God!

"Yes, *Deo Gratias* for another day to serve Him," Linus said as he helped Peter to his feet.

Linus felt Peter's wet robe. "Are you sure you are all right?" the young man asked again.

"Yes. Yes. I am fine. Just a dream, but a real one." Peter sighed. "It was a message from the Master. I forgot to keep Him and only Him before me. He came to remind me to stop doubting. It was something I failed to do. Jesus must be tired of me constantly questioning Him and myself. I fear when I meet Him again, He will have a great deal to say about my doubts."

Linus laughed and said, "I am sure what our Good Lord will say will be all good, for you have been a faithful servant."

"No." Peter quickly interrupted, "I have been many things but I have not always been a faithful servant."

Linus looked at him with some misgiving and then with understanding. He knew the story of the denials and the torments that remained. He heard the story many times and especially when Mark was recording Peter's thoughts.

"Peter, I have something from your wife," young Linus said, hoping that thoughts of his wife would change the moment. He walked to the cloth bag that he first disregarded when he came in the house.

"She sends you some clean linens and her love."

"How is my wife? And daughter?"

"They are well, and being tended to very kindly by Cornelius and his family. Speaking of Cornelius, he will be here later. He apparently has some news."

He looked at Peter, and saw the older man was distant; maybe he was not fully awake, or perhaps he was still thinking of his dream.

Linus abruptly left the room, as Peter unsteadily walked to his wooden chair and sat in it.

Peter heard the small seeping sounds from the fountain in the corner of the garden. Listening to the small dribble immediately comforted him.

"Living water," he uttered aloud as the sound of the trickling water overcame him. Water was always a companion to him and an important part of his life.

I must keep the Master and only the Master before me and let all my doubts fall away. I am accountable only to Him.

"Water?"

"What?"

"Here is some water to bathe yourself. Your clean garments are over there," Linus repeated as he again turned to leave the room.

Clearing his throat and throwing his shoulders back, Peter murmured, "*Deo gratias,*" then loudly, "and thank you, Linus."

The young man smiled and continued to the door.

"Did you say that Cornelius was coming?"

"Yes, Peter. He should be here shortly."

"Good, I have a favor to ask of him," Peter said, knowing Cornelius would provide a new place for him.

Linus walked out of the room closing the curtain over the door entrance allowing Peter some privacy. He walked to the front of the house and opened the door. He looked out over the estate, and in the field he could see the vineyard workers. Then he glanced up the small stone road that led away from the small house to the *domus.* The main house was quiet which was odd. Looking beyond the house, his eyes followed the nicely constructed road that led away from the *villa* towards Rome. He slowly walked back into the house and closed the wooden door wishing Cornelius would arrive soon.

The small house was silent, and Linus assumed the silence meant that Peter had dressed, had returned to his chair and was thinking of the past or in morning prayers. He smiled knowing that prayer and remembering were the same thing to the Apostle.

These two things become one, for it is impossible to pray and not remember bygone days. How could Peter or Cornelius, or any of those who saw Jesus, pray without remembering something, or some moment with Him? They were on familiar ground with Jesus and so were blessed, while many like me did not know Jesus when He was alive.

He stopped thinking and listened intently for a sound from the other room. Hearing none, he concluded that Peter was visiting the Lord. Again he smiled to himself, for he believed that Jesus visited Peter and the Apostles. After all, they were friends, and friends visited each other. He looked around the small house for something to do. Normally, when Peter was in morning prayers, he and Mark would review Peter's previous day's dictations. They would copy what they had written and eventually discuss some of the writings. This copying was an education for Linus, and he often received new insight into the nature of Jesus. In contrast, Mark, who wrote in a restrained manner, was lively in his discourses on Jesus. He described so many details that Linus often had to remind himself that he did not know Jesus. At times, Peter and Mark described Jesus so well that Linus could picture Him in his mind. They spoke of the tone of His voice, His frequent wide, warm smile, and His deep laughter. Their description of Jesus' laughter was so vivid that Linus believed that he heard it once.

After updating their work, the two young men would have a breakfast of dates, nuts, and some bread while waiting for Peter to join them for prayer. Now Mark was no longer here. Linus missed him and the copying which was finished long before Mark left for Northern Italy. Linus would not have to worry about breakfast, for Cornelius would be arriving with the meal. With nothing to do, Linus began his morning prayers.

On the other side of the curtain door, Peter had bathed, and as he dressed he thought how good it would be to see Cornelius. It had been some time since he visited, and he wondered where he had been. He knew Cornelius was not preaching. He couldn't be, because that would reveal his identity as a Christian. Cornelius' silence was very important to the *Ecclesia* since this helped him conceal people and make arrangements for quick and clandestine departures.

Cornelius was full of surprises. He even surprised the Lord with his request, for his servant and message of not being worthy. He surprised me when Abendadar came to invite us to his villa in Judea. Oh! How well I remember that day. I remember the overwhelming feeling I received when I entered his villa. I sensed Cornelius was a believer in Elyon, the One God, as quickly as I was aware that his household was of the same mind. It was a house alive with the Holy Spirit. Again, he surprised me with the request to be baptized, and when I agreed, he showed me his family and guest. His guest included those whom I should have feared. However, I knew Jesus had touched them. There was the young Namenlos, the herald of the Master's crime; Calvos and Dorimius, the executioner; Longinus the lancer; Nescius the titular; the Legionaries Abendadar and Stephaton, and even Malchus of Gethsemane. It did not matter, because on that day they were just children longing to come home.

The clean smell of his clothing distracted him, and he grew thankful for this small gift from his wife whom he thought of with great affection.

He remembered Linus who, he assumed, was in prayer and waiting for Cornelius.

Linus is a good and a loyal servant of the Lord, and I know that he misses Mark as much as I do, but I had to send Mark away. Things were not safe here. He has much more to do for the Master such as making copies and distributing the manuscript.

Having dressed, Peter walked and sat in his chair. He quickly gathered his thoughts, closed his eyes and began to pray. He began by thanking Jesus for coming into his life and for his family and loved ones; their faces passing through his mind in an unending procession. Cornelius came into view, and Peter remembered the rumors he heard of how disturbed Cornelius was when he had been assigned the duty of leading the crucifixion of Jesus. He remembered John bar Zebedee telling how Cornelius helped carry the Body of Jesus to the tomb. The procession of images continued, and the faces became vibrant. He thanked Jesus for Linus. He was thankful for his protector Larius and his family who, at great risk, harbored him.

My young Linus, who like Mark, is like a son. I will dismiss him from my service when I leave this estate. He will be safer away from me. Perhaps I will send him back to his hometown.

His prayers continued but not without distractions. Occasionally, he heard the soft steps of the young man on the other side of the curtain, and each time he heard a distracting sound, Linus came to mind.

✳

Linus was an Italian Gentile born in Volterra, Tuscany. His grandfather was one of the first Praetorian Guards created by Augustus to protect his throne. After serving the mandatory twelve years, he returned to Tuscany and his farm. When he died, the land and farm went to his son, Herculeanus. Shortly after his father's death, Herculeanus married Clorisa, a woman he had loved all his life and who was the sister of Cornelius, the centurion. Soon after the marriage, Linus was born.

The day after his eighteenth birthday, Linus and his mother, Clorisa, were in the *platea* main street in Volterra where they heard Paul preaching. The mother and son were immediately taken by Paul's powerful message of Jesus. Immediately, they were both filled with great comfort and love, and on that day they were baptized. Linus and Clorisa quietly joined the small Christian community in Volterra. When Cornelius returned from Judea, they learned that he was a Christian and had seen Jesus and partook in a miracle, and had even been near Jesus on the day of His Crucifixion, they were elated. Linus stayed close to his *avunculus* uncle picking at his memory and hungrily demanding more about Jesus. Later Cornelius learned that Peter was in Rome, and so he prepared to leave for the capital city to offer his services to the Apostle who had baptized him and his household.

Linus begged his mother and father to let him go with his uncle. His father, who had not accepted Jesus, was very reluctant to grant Linus permission, but after days of debate, he was persuaded by Clorisa and Cornelius to let the boy go. So Linus came into Peter's service and would never leave his side.

∗

"*Vale*"Farewell. Cornelius shouted, as he watched his friend Belginius, a Roman and an informer for the Christians, disappear into the crowded *Forum* of Rome. He stood motionless as passing Romans bumped and pushed against him. He could not move because he was staggering under the information he had received and the information angered him.

Why are all these things happening? Do Your chosen ones deserve such torments? Have they been so sinful as to deserve this?

His own words sent a shock wave through his mind. He asked similar questions of God years ago. Unable to control himself, he found his mind being transported to that day on Golgotha. He tried to control his thoughts, for he never sought to return to that time, but he was unsuccessful. Immediately, the faces in the Forum were lost. His thoughts were captured, and he returned to Judea. In the pit of his being, he felt the same disgust that he experienced that day. He felt the hot, dry, Judean sun bearing down on him. The heaviness of his helmet crushed against his head, and he now felt the same ache in his head that he had that day. The discomfort was so real that he needed to throw off his helmet. Also real was the weight of his armor as it contained the heat. He relived his contempt for the Jews whom he never liked, and as a Roman occupier, he humiliated them as often as he could. He relived the desire to escape everything, everyone, and worse, the need to strip himself of his uniform and become free of being Roman.

In all the years he was in the province of Judea, the only thing Jewish that appealed to him was their firm, undying belief in One God. He esteemed the uncomplicated idea of One God, so in secret, he studied this Jewish principle. Soon he experienced an unusual interior peace that he did not understand, so he continued his pursuit. Discreetly, he began questioning Jews with whom his household did business. Later, he hired a Jew to answer all his questions about *Elyon*. As his interest grew, the Roman and Greek gods became unappealing. Equally unappealing to him were the many things that seemed to complicate the idea of One God. In the end, he believed in One God but not through Judaic practices. Circumcision, purifications, dietary laws, and other pharisaic principles were too difficult to accept. He also rejected the idea of a Messiah to liberate the Jewish people, yet deep down he believed that *Elyon* would come and clear the affairs of mankind.

When Cornelius first heard people speak of Jesus, he believed Him to be a prophet, but when he heard Jesus speak of love, his idea of Him being a simple prophet faded. In place of this thought came a frightening thought: that Jesus was a messenger of *Elyon* with a purpose to save. Where this idea came from he did not know. What was so surprising was why he felt such conviction in this idea. Dressed as a Judean, he went into the crowds to listen to Jesus' words of love and compassion. He found Jesus' stories profound, and eventually believed in the goodness of this Man and felt a softening in his heart towards Him.

Jesus' voice echoed in his mind days after hearing it. It was haunting yet soothing, and he began to change his feelings towards the Jews. Though Cornelius felt a kinship he never knew, he could not completely agree that goodness could conquer evil. It was naïve to believe that wrong was corrected by the "turning of a cheek" or forgiveness should be "seven times seventy." He knew better. He was a soldier and he knew that force and only force could turn the other cheek; that forgiveness was received only after the fear of pain or death, but still, he wanted the words of Jesus to be true.

When Cornelius' Etruscan manservant, Pavilius, his companion from childhood, became ill, Cornelius was sure that Jesus would be able to help. He invited Jesus to his *villa* to heal Pavilius. After sending the request, he began to feel unworthy. He was a Roman, a non-Jew, and not a full believer in the Jewish ways. He had been a man of the world who had done many evil things: he had killed and brutalized and even knew harlots. He did not surrender his way of life completely to the Jewish God though he believed in Him. He could not expect this holy Man of that God to come into his unworthy abode. So he sent a second messenger asking Jesus to merely say the words of healing. When Pavilius was cured, Cornelius received a humbling revelation: apparently, he was worthy of this holy Man, because Jesus had shown that the love He preached so often was also for him. He suddenly felt all his transgressions being forgiven, and that Jesus made him worthy of *Elyon's* love.

When Pilate ordered him to lead the crucifixion procession, Cornelius reacted instinctively and hurriedly made preparations, but soon lost the awareness of being a soldier and felt disloyal. In kindness, Jesus healed his manservant Pavilius, and Cornelius never thanked Jesus for this benevolence.

How could I now lead Jesus to death?

He had the unheard of desire to ask Pilate to relieve him of this duty, but stopped short for he knew Pilate was having a terrible day and he respected Pilate's command. It was a day that produced a slither of weakness in the Procurator who had lost control of the situation. As he left Pilate's side, Cornelius wondered if Pilate knew from one of his informers that he and Jesus had a loose relationship and that Jesus cured Pavilius.

During the long journey through Jerusalem, Cornelius leered at the crowd wondering how they could kill a Man, who fed, cured, and taught them goodness and love. His feeling of superiority over these people returned. While riding Nimbus, his horse, he looked down at them and thought that they were less civilized and far more barbaric. They had allowed a great injustice to take place with their pettiness, jealousy, and their fear and blindness. He grew angry and hateful.

He wanted to break all codes and stop the carnage as he had earlier stopped the scourging, but he knew he could not stop this procession of death for to do so would lead to his own death. He was a Roman centurion and was one longer than he had known Jesus. Furthermore, helping the Nazarene would mean disobeying the Procurator. In his many years of service, he did soften occasionally by inflicting limited punishments, but he had never blatantly disobeyed an order. Still, he felt that what was transpiring contradicted all that was good; this Man had done no wrong. He grew sad, for he knew that he did not have the same love that Jesus so strongly preached.

How could God allow such an injustice? Why are these things happening to Him? Does He deserve such torments? What did He do that was so wrong? He questioned himself knowing the answers would be given by others. He felt sick and ached to yell at the world. Then he thought: *Perhaps by performing my duty, by being here, I will find a way to help Jesus.*

He fell under the weight of his duty and did what was expected of him and continued in a daze.

Remembering that day in Jerusalem caused Cornelius to increase his pace through the *Forum* and the streets of Rome. He foolishly raced through the streets hoping to outrun his remembering, but his mind would not remain in the moment. He came to the *Vicus Pontum* the Street of Bridges and stopped. His breath was short; the perspiration rolled down his face, chest and back.

He longed for water as he did that day long ago.

The procession came to the crest of the Mount where Jesus had been attached to the Cross. Cornelius was amazed to see the impression Jesus had on the men in his unit. In some subtle way, they all seemed influenced by this Man. The routine surrounding crucifixions were changed.

Calvos, the thick-skinned executioner, the torturer of the Nazarene, stood under the Cross mesmerized by the dying Jesus. His face froze under a mask of sadness. In shock, Namenlos, the herald and deliverer of the *titulus* placard, who normally raced back to the barracks to get away from such events, stood staring at Jesus like a frightened deer. The legionnaires, Stephaton, Abendadar, and Longinus, were subdued and solemn. The usual, loud camaraderie among the soldiers was missing. Everyone in the unit seemed to be holding their voices, jokes, and laughs to a respectful murmur. He could not understand why this was happening. They never showed any interest in Jesus when He was free, and surely none heard Him preach, so why this?

Curiously, Cornelius observed his men, but his inspection was interrupted by the words Jesus spoke. He heard Jesus ask "forgiveness" for all, and he heard the promised "Paradise" to the rebel Dismas. When Jesus gave His life to His Father, Cornelius knew he stood in the presence of something far greater than Tiberius and Rome. Instantly, nothing became more urgent than Cornelius finding out what Jesus wanted to say to him.

"I believed You were a Good Man. Please give me a sign that you are God." He challenged Jesus in a low voice, "Call me to be Your disciple."

It was then that the storm came!

The storm was so great that it demanded all creation to tremble. The rocks and mountains shivered; mighty trees bent and snapped. Dust, dirt, and sand flew, attacking and blinding everyone so that all covered their eyes and faces from the debris.

It was a rage so great that it threw a mourning shroud across the sky and gave a new meaning to darkness. Neither did the world experience darkness such as this, nor had the world ever known such anger, because this anger came from a deep wound that had been opened in the very heart of existence. It was anger so violent and strong that it wanted to destroy but could not. It wanted to punish but it would not, yet it wanted all to know that something was wrong.

Cornelius knew this was no ordinary storm. This was a mighty storm from an Almighty Being.

He heard the screams of all those around him.

"Almighty One, save us!"

"*Elyon,* have mercy!"

"*Adonai,* help us!"

People ran aimlessly stumbling and falling. The mules that carried their supplies up the Mount whined and panicked in fear. The horses of the legionnaires reared and snorted in terror.

Suddenly, all the confusion and cries were stilled and silenced, and Cornelius now knew what he had failed to understand. All that he had heard and seen before were made clear to him, and from deep inside him emerged a new understanding and a new freedom. He shouted affirmatively, "*Verum, est Filius Dei!*" Truly, this is the Son of God!

The skies opened and the flooding rains came.

At that moment, the darkness, rain, and quaking stopped for Cornelius.

✳

As Cornelius' horse galloped quickly down the empty road towards the Camolius *villa,* he felt heavy trepidation in the news he carried. After receiving Belginius' report, he verified parts of the news and sent a messenger to the *villa* for Linus to meet him. He wanted both of them to speak to Peter. It would make things easier for him, but not make his duty any lighter. Besides, after breaking the news to Peter, there would be no time to comfort the Apostle since he had to hurry to Ostia to meet John and the ship, the *Thalassa Aetos.* He would have to leave Peter to Linus and the young man's abilities.

Finally, he arrived. He dismounted his horse and walked toward the house. Standing at the door of the house to greet him was Linus, whose face was glowing with a smile.

"Linus, where is Peter?" Cornelius asked grimly.

The smile on the young man's face quickly vanished when he heard the seriousness in the centurion's voice. When he saw the look on his fellow Roman's face, his excitement died, and he quickly matched the seriousness of his guest.

"What is wrong?" Linus whispered.

"Where is Peter?" Cornelius demanded.

Linus pointed in the house, and suspecting something was grievously wrong, covered Cornelius' mouth with his hand.

"He prays," Linus said in a whisper. He slowly and carefully grabbed Cornelius' arm and led him away from the house and into the small courtyard in the front of the house.

"I have grave news," Cornelius said.

"What is it?"

Cornelius hesitated for a moment, then swallowing hard, he blurred out, "Peter's wife and daughter have been arrested. They were taken early this morning, and I don't know where they are. I have several of my guard friends, fellow Christians, including Belginius, looking for them."

Linus leaned against a nearby tree to steady himself. The news took him by surprise. Peter's wife's arrest must have happened soon after he left her to begin his trip to the Camolius *praedium* estate.

Cornelius took a few steps away from Linus and looked off into the distance. After a few moments of reflection, he said, "I do not know if finding their whereabouts would be good, for I know that when Peter learns of their arrest, he will try to find them and risk being arrested. He is too important to us for that to happen. He must leave Rome as we had said he should."

"I agree. But we know there will be no stopping him. We will have to leave this all in the hands of the Lord."

"Yes, you are correct. It is in the hands of the Lord, but there is more."

Cornelius looked at Linus, who quickly stood erect to brace himself for more.

"Paul has been arrested. He was arrested while he was in Greece and arrived here late yesterday and is again under house arrest. He is scheduled to appear before Gaius Ophonius Tigellinus, the Prefect Praetorian, tomorrow or the next day. Tigellinus' judgments lacked fairness. Tigellinus is the Emperor Nero's puppet, and he will do anything to gain favor with the Emperor. To convict and sentence a man of Paul's position would be a great achievement for Tigellinus. Though he has not been arrested yet, Luke of Antioch, the physician, is with Paul and Mark."

"Mark!" Linus shouted in shock, and Cornelius rushed to cover the young man's mouth and pulled him further from the house. When they were a safer distance, Cornelius took his hand from Linus' mouth.

"What is Mark doing in Rome?" Linus whispered hurriedly and in distress. "He was supposed to be in the north."

"When I heard Mark had returned, I immediately went to see Paul. His guards, who are fellow Christians, made my visit possible. Later Luke and Mark arrived. I asked Mark about his reason for being in Rome, which was in disobedience to Peter's command. He told me that when he heard of Paul's arrest he came back to make peace with his former mentor or have no peace with the Lord."

"This is serious news," Linus said, as he slowly started walking down the dirt road and further from the house.

"Luke and Mark are not in immediate danger. They are carefully and secretly being escorted to Paul's cell by Christian guards, but still there is danger. I know Paul is aware of this, and I am sure he will send them away as he did his other disciples."

Cornelius followed Linus down the dirt road.

"And there is additional news."

Linus stopped and looked at Cornelius. His face was expressionless.

Cornelius stopped. His eyes met Linus' expectant stare, as he said calmly, "Last night, I received a letter by courier from Sylvanius, a fellow centurion from the South, saying that John is on his way and will be arriving today at Ostia."

"John?"

"John bar Zebedee is one of the Twelve, is the brother of James the Big and a good friend of Peter. I do not think you have ever met him."

"No, I have not, but why is he coming to Rome?"

"I have no idea, but I am certain that he does not know what has happened in Rome or of the danger here. What is worse is the thought that Peter, Paul, and John are here together and that the Emperor could have all three in one clean swoop of his hand."

"What are we to do?"

"Immediately we will have to get John, then I do not know. What do you think?"

Linus could not think because his mind was heavy with concern and worry. Fumbling with his words, for he knew Cornelius was waiting for an opinion, he said slowly, "Yes. I agree that you have to get John. I will stay with Peter and..."

"And what?"

"We must tell Peter all these things. He must know."

"Yes, I know. Giving him the news is not what is bothering me. It is what he will do that bothers me."

"I agree, but with John here, Peter may become still and not seek his wife and daughter. Perhaps John will be able to control Peter and show him the wisdom in leaving Rome."

"True. Come, let us tell Peter this news. I must leave to get John and return here."

"No, Peter will not stay here. He feels that he is endangering the lives of the Camolius family; besides, for reasons I cannot explain, I feel uneasy being here."

"Then take him to my *villa*."

"Agreed," said Linus as he turned abruptly and started back to the house.

Cornelius followed and quickened the pace, for he had to hurry to meet John in Ostia.

"Oh, I forgot. I do have a bit of good news. Simon Magus is dead."

"When? How?"

"Early today. He had persuaded the Emperor and others in the Imperial Court that he had stolen the Apostles' power and could fly. So the Emperor built him a tower, and Simon climbed the tower with great conviction and flew to his death."

"May he be found worthy."

"Of what? The man was an impostor and all that was evil…"

"And a baptized Christian," Linus interrupted, "He must have had some worth."

Cornelius shook his head.

"Sometimes I find it very difficult being a Christian," Cornelius lamented.

"And so I, for being a Christian is an uncommon thing. Trying to live as a Christian is what we are called to be."

Cornelius slapped the young man on the back.

"Linus, sometimes you are wiser than some of the ancients."

Linus looked at him quickly, not believing what he said, but smiled in politeness.

Quietly and slowly, they walked up the road and into Peter's house.

✳

The instant John's foot touched land he thought the earth beneath him moved, and he froze to gauge and adjust himself. It was a joy to stand with no need of the ships railings, the sides of the mast, or the safety ropes strung across the deck of the ship.

The soft hissing sound of the sea was replaced by the loud voices and clatter of people around him. Standing in the middle of all this confusion made him feel like an obstacle in everyone's way. Everyone was hurrying about moving things, taking things, and carrying things. He quickly deduced that he was unsettled because the entire seaport of Ostia was in perpetual motion. Looking around, he saw merchant ships of different sizes and shapes. The features of some were familiar but others were unrecognizable. For a few brief moments, he wondered what their history and place of origin was. A sea of slaves was unloading the many ships docked, and he watched as jars, jugs, baskets, and containers of all sizes and shapes passed him in long rows. In other places, he saw cargo being passed from one slave to another.

The *curator* overseer barked orders at the slaves who unloaded the cargo and carried it from the newly-arrived ships to nearby barges that were waiting to be loaded for the trip up the Tiber river and to the city of Rome. Other slaves were loading small amounts of cargo on waiting carts for the road trip to Rome.

His thoughts went to the slaves and their exhausting toil.

Lord Jesus, give them strength, and free them from their bondages, and give their owners kindness, compassion and Your peace.

Suddenly, he felt the presence of Rome. Even though he could not see it, as it was some twelve miles away, the sense, enormity, and the liveliness of Rome was with him. He sensed it waiting, pulsating, and ready to devour all that came into its gates. From this distance, he could hear, or imagined hearing, the city's heartbeat. Unexpectedly, he became frightened, and wondered what this unknown fear was. He continued observing all that was going on around him. Ephesus was not as busy, or as urgent as this, and nothing in Palestine could compare to it. He had never been in such a din before in his life and had never been in a place like this.

Ah, you have never been to Rome before, you silly Jewish fisherman.

He smiled to himself and feeling totally acclimated, he walked confidently, swinging his arms and enjoying his independence, which gave him a welcome joy to return to this plain and fanciless self.

"John?"

He turned quickly when he heard his name. It was said softly and almost in a whisper. The face he saw was familiar, but he could not immediately identify who the man was. Years had put grayness in the beard and hair, and the weight of years had rounded the shoulders.

Who is this familiar yet strange person?

"John? John bar Zebedee?"

"Yes." Then he remembered. "Cornelius!"

The two men embraced, and the former centurion quickly grabbed John by the arm and moved him through the crowd.

"Come we must hurry. The barge that is to take us upriver will soon depart."

"But my things…"

"They will be attended to. It is not safe for you to be here. Hurry."

In their urgency to get to their destination, they bumped and shoved through the maze of people and supplies. John grew annoyed. He did not make any excuses for his rudeness, nor did he have time to enjoy and appreciate the new adventure exploding around him. He never saw such a variety of foodstuffs or goods. He never saw in one place so many different manners of dress or shades of faces. He wanted to enjoy and watch everything. He found it amusing, and he wanted to remember this moment.

Occasionally, he saw some rich merchants standing on a platform overseeing what was being done. Their richness was ostentatious and their refinement obvious. Out of annoyance and anger, he slowed, but Cornelius' strong grip left no room for leisure.

"Why are you hurrying so?" John asked with irritation, but he was ignored.

Before long, he was led up another boarding plank and onto a barge that was being loaded with goods of every imaginable item. Cornelius led him directly to a bench behind some cargo at the end of the barge.

"John, stay behind this cargo and remain unseen. If anyone asks who is accompanying you, tell him you are waiting for me and make certain to tell them that I am a centurion."

"But Cornelius, you have not been in the service of Rome for many years."

"I understand, but they do not know this, so you must say precisely what I have said to you."

"Why must I pretend so?"

"Because your life is in danger."

John drew back in surprise, and Cornelius was confused by the astonished look on his face.

"Not all those men on your ship were willing to listen to you. When they arrived in Ostia, they immediately went to the authorities and reported you as a Christian."

Cornelius calmed himself and remembered that John had been at sea a long time and was unaware of the danger approaching him.

"While you were at sea, a large fire broke out in Rome in the market-place near the *Porta Capena* and the *Circus Maximus*. Ten of the fourteen regions of Rome were burned and many lives were lost. When it was over, the Christians were blamed for the fire. Nero quickly started arresting our brothers and sisters. No Christian was safe. We learned, from some friendly sources, of your arrival today, but before we could meet you, we heard that you were reported. Some of the new Christians who were aboard your ship were arrested, but thankfully many were able to escape. However, it is only a matter of time before they will be sought, captured, and arrested. We thought you were also taken until I saw you milling aimlessly around the dock. Thank the goodness of Jesus that I did find you. Now that you know all these things, please remain here."

John sat stunned. Persecution of the young Church was nothing new, but what surprised him was the idea that Rome, the all-powerful Rome, and her Emperor, now laid siege to the Body of Christ. He could only see much suffering and many deaths and he grew mournful.

"Simon Peter? Is he…"

"No, he is safe and awaiting your arrival. Now stay here. I must attend to some business. Pray for my safe return. I should be back before this barge leaves for Rome, and if for some reason I do not return and the barge leaves, stay hidden in Rome until a fellow Christian will meet you and take you to Peter. The Lord be with you."

"And with your Spirit…," his words trailed off as Cornelius sped around the tall containers and from his sight. He sat on the deck of the barge alone and listened to the river lazily slap against the side of the barge. He listened to the monotonous beat and again yearned for the feel of secure land. From the other side of the tall cargo, he heard the sound of rough, commanding voices and the soft grunts of the slaves; then nothing. Silence…

He felt the late day sun beaming on his head. He ran his hand through his wet, pitch-black hair. This suddenly made him aware of his perspiring. He felt the perspiration slip down his back and chest. He was certain that this *Tallit Katan*, a garment worn to honor the Commandments, was wet. He thought he should stop wearing the *tallit*, but he could not get himself to abandon the comfort he felt when wearing it. Though he had no proof, he was certain that the Others had stopped wearing this garment. Wearing it now did not hold the same meaning it did years ago, and now he wore it as a memorial to Jesus who never stopped wearing His. Even on Golgotha, John remembered that the *tallit* being among Jesus' discarded clothing. The sun continued to cause discomfort, so he covered his head with his hood. In the shade of the hood, he found safety and comfortable repose from the sun. From under his hood, he looked over the side of the barge and into the Tiber. The river was not as blue as the Jordan; it had a brown-reddish tint mixed with the blueness of the water. He saw twigs, leaves, a sandal, fruit skins, and other trash floating past the barge.

Nothing like the Jordan. Then in disgust and with a touch of revenge, he thought, *the waste of Rome, the pigsty of the world.*

Curling up in a fetal position, he closed his eyes and longed for Galilee. Soon his thoughts returned to Cornelius, and remembering his request, he uttered a quick prayer to Jesus for the former centurion's safety. Then he thought: *It has been years; I cannot begin to remember when last I saw him.*

Disciplining himself, he forced himself to focus on a place in time, and when he found that time, he smiled slightly with satisfaction. It was when Cornelius was transferred from Palestine and returned to Rome. He compelled himself to focus on a place in time and when he came to a conclusion, he smiled slightly with satisfaction.

Ah yes, it was years ago, when we left for our mission. A small feeling of satisfaction crossed his mind, for now he could use the plural; now he was in the missions. *The last time I saw Cornelius, he left Jerusalem to return to Rome. He was held with great affection by those in Jerusalem. Many of us knew him before he came to be a Christian and many suspected he was a "God-fearer" before becoming a Christian. I saw him on Golgotha. Of course, I had no idea what was happening to him or what Jesus was doing to his soul, but by nightfall, when all had gone and we removed Jesus from the Cross, he remained. He helped us carry and bury Jesus. After Jesus rose, we heard that he and other Romans were inquiring about us. I still can remember the fear unleashed in us. We were sure that they were all out to harm us. Soon, Simon Peter reminded us that Jesus had cured Pavilius, his manservant, and that his manservant was a disciple of Jesus and of what Jesus had said about the centurion's faith, but still there was fear. We did not have the courage to accept him until the wind and fire came to us and we grew bold.* He smiled with amusement. *Afterwards, Simon Peter went to Caesarea, and upon his return, told me the entire story.*

Having grown very comfortable, he shut his mind off to these memories. Again he heard the monotonous river beating against the side of the barge. The tempo matched the sway of the wooden vessel. Contented, he slowly dozed off and rapidly saw the image of his brother and then all of the Others. They were still young like in the early days, only they showed zeal and dedication on their faces, and there was boldness, love, and bravery in their eyes. He once again felt their friendship. Finally, he saw the Face of Jesus and his soul lurched, leapt, and he longed to rest his head on His Master's Shoulder.

*

He felt like he was gliding, and then realized that the craft was moving. He heard the whishing of the passing water, and for an instant he refused to open his eyes; he just wanted to be still. During the past weeks, being still had become an important thing for him, but he felt the nearness of another person and this alarmed him. He quickly opened his eyes and was startled by the image of another person seating opposite him.

The figure was wrapped in a cloak and the face was hidden in the dark shadows of the hood. John slowly pressed against the side of the barge wanting to put a distance between him and his unknown guest.

"I did not want to disturb you. You looked so peaceful, and you were smiling so often that I believed you were having pleasant dreams."

He was relieved to recognize Cornelius' voice.

"Ah, Cornelius, I was visiting my fellow Disciples. It was good seeing them again, but more importantly, I was remembering Jesus. There will be a time, I believe, when I shall dream these dreams and shall not awake. I wait earnestly for the call of my name."

"Oh my dear Brother, I too have such dreams. Do you realize how blessed we have been to have seen and known the Master? To have walked with Him or felt the pull towards Him? To have the tone of His voice resonate within our beings?"

"Well put, Cornelius."

"But John, you and I have much more to do, and sometimes the need to labor is greater than the desire to die. We have much more to say and even more to write."

"Ah, so Simon Peter has told you of my writings."

"Your letters? Yes. What other writings are you undertaking?"

"Nothing," John quickly said, pleased that Simon Peter had not said anything of his writing an account of the life of Jesus, for this project was moving slowly. He understood even if no one else did, that this slowness was willed by God.

"How long have you been sitting here? It is night."

"Not too long. I arrived once we began up the Tiber."

"Have you finished your business?"

Cornelius' face darted from the shadow of his hood and smiling, said, "Yes, and all is well," as he retracted his hood.

"Good." John looked away and into the dark night. He moved his head to his left, and in the not too far distance, he saw the torches and lamps of Ostia. Even though he could not see the port, he still sensed the disorder and chaos.

"Is Ostia always that chaotic?"

"Yes, and it is good that it is, for many of us are able to arrive and depart with little detection."

"Are things that bad?"

"Yes, Nero has moved on us with great vengeance and the *populus* people gleefully accepted his measure with added brutality. We are new toys for the children of Rome. We have become a new game for their amusement. They call us *maleficus* harmful and *periculosus* dangerous.

I have heard names like *infidus* disloyal, *proditor* traitor, and *haereticum* heretic used when they speak of us. Words like these are poison in Roman society. We hide. We have gone underground for our meetings. We hide always. We meet in secret. Men, women, and children are arrested and thrown in prison. Many are tortured and beaten. I know the ways of the Romans, and I can assure you that kindness and mercy do not exist within the walls of Roman prisons."

"You say that Simon Peter is safe?"

"Yes, for the time being, but he is in grave danger."

"I have heard that Paul of Tarsus was released and was later arrested again in Greece. Has he returned to Rome?

"Yes, at the moment he is safe. He is under house arrest again, but we have accepted that his fate is sealed. Within the grips of Rome, even if it is a loose grip, one can be quickly choked. We are in contact with him through his guards who are Christians."

"He is an amazing man. He has become a good disciple of the Master. I read his letters to the Ephesians and they were well done and I heard that he has written more. With all that you say has happened, I was wondering if he was still with us. He has a sharp tongue which has gotten him into many troublesome moments."

"Yes, I know, but he has also gained many converts."

"Praise God for His wisdom."

"And His protection of you. You have no idea of the anxiety your unexpected trip to Rome has caused. We were so afraid that you would be discovered before we found you. Can you imagine what a prize you would be to Nero? Even that madman would realize the value of one of the Apostles."

"I am the least of the Twelve. I have not endured half of what the Others have endured."

"It matters not; you are one of them. Now tell me, for I am curious, why did you decide to come to Rome?"

John looked long at Cornelius. The question was never asked of him before and John was without an answer.

"It seemed the thing to do. I had no reason to come here. In the first days of my voyage, I thought I would go to Hispania and perhaps continue my brother James' work, but during the voyage, as the days passed, I felt a sudden need to see Simon Peter. Now in rethinking this, it was not a need but a calling. Something had to be found and maybe resolved, and then I thought of Mark and realized that I had to see him to talk about his writings."

"I presume that you were called here to talk to Peter and tell him to leave. As for Mark, he also has returned to Rome after being ordered by Peter to go north. We all thought he was there, but he returned to Rome when he heard Paul had been arrested. This is very dangerous. He is well known as Peter's companion and also as a fellow traveler of Paul. He also would be a big prize for Nero."

"When do you think I can see Mark?"

Cornelius did not answer him. He weighed the heaviness of his answer to this question and finally, after some thought, blurted out, "I hope never. You must realize the fear created with all of you in Rome at the same time. Suppose all of you were arrested, what would happen?"

John smiled. "Nothing, for Jesus said He would be with us always. He is the one who is here, and as such, is the one who is important, not Peter, Paul, Mark, or me and you."

"We understand that, but wonder if we have played into the hands of the Evil One. Allow us our fears and our selfish needs. We still are not that strong to be without shepherds. There is a great comfort in knowing that there are some who saw and knew the Christ. Your living witness is the greatest proof we have to offer the world."

"Cornelius, I have heard what you said many times, but you cannot expect to lock us up like invaluable treasures. We have the command of Jesus to go out and baptize. We all knew its meaning. We knew that we could not be safe or saved indefinitely. We cannot live forever. The true test of Jesus' mission will be when we are gone and other disciples are left in charge of communities who have not seen the Master."

"No one, and least of all me, mean disrespect to the Master's command to you or your understanding of His command, but still, we need the parenting. We learn through visible things and Christ knew that, and that is why He gave us the Supper to celebrate in His memory; it is His 'Visible Presence' among us. All we are trying to do is keep Peter, Paul, and you safe among us as long as the Lord wills."

John did not answer him for he could hear the fear in his friend's voice, but he had to answer him, so he softly said, "God will provide."

"I pray so, but we will try and help by being careful," Cornelius immediately stated. "Besides, John, there are no capable disciples in Rome. Things are uncertain here because there is no one to leave in charge. We did have Simon Peter who came, stayed, and led, unlike Paul, who came, stayed and left. Until we have someone to fill Peter's sandals, we would like to protect what we have, and besides, what good are dead Apostles to the cause of Jesus?"

John looked off into the distance and decided to leave Cornelius in his foolish insecurity. His mind filled with regret for he had hoped to see Mark. He read Mark's account of Jesus and felt Mark left much unsaid; that his work was incomplete. He did not want to criticize what was written but wanted to find the motive behind the short account.

Cornelius got to his knees and looked around.

"We should be arriving shortly." Giving John a bundle, he continued, "Before we arrive, it would be wise if you changed your clothes."

"Why?"

"Some whom you converted on your ship have been arrested, and some have spoken to the authorities and gave a description of what you look like and what you were wearing. A change of clothes would help disguise you and make your discovery more difficult."

John watched Cornelius' moonlight face and saw a grave and worrisome expression. Suddenly, he had a different feeling about Rome and a deep fear came over him.

Could this be the reason for my coming to Rome—to die? But Master, I have not even begun to work for You!

"This new policy of the Emperor is not like the persecutions we have seen in the provinces, is it, Cornelius?"

"No." Cornelius responded without hesitation. "This has spread throughout Italy and will spread throughout the Empire until being a Christian will be the worst thing that one could be." He paused to take a deep breath, emphasizing the despair he felt. "No, my dear brother, what we have here will be worldwide. This will be our Golgotha."

"'Blessed are they who suffer persecution for justice' sake, for theirs is the kingdom of heaven,'" John thought aloud.

"'Blessed also are you when men reproach you, and persecute you and, speaking falsely, say all evil against you for my sake,'" Cornelius continued.

"'Rejoice and be glad for your reward is great in Heaven; for so did they persecute the Prophets who were before you.'"

The two men stared at each other for a long time as they both remembered, so long ago, Jesus and the teaching on the Mount.

Finally, Cornelius stood erect.

"Come, you must hurry and change your clothing and above all remove your *tallit*," he said as he walked around to the other side of the cargo where containers were protecting them.

John wondered how Cornelius knew of his *tallit*. Forgetting his curiosity, John immediately stood up and began to undress. The open air cooled him. He looked out onto the calm water and had the sudden urge to jump in and be rid of all the perspiration and the heat. This urge soon passed as his mind wandered and he remembered such a memorable night.

As he dressed, he heard Cornelius say in an adamant tone, "You are to keep your face covered and under your hood. There are few in Rome who will recognize you but still I want to make sure you arrive safely to see Peter. We expect you to convince him to leave Rome and out of harm's way. If we are stopped you are to remain silent. Your Latin has a Galilean tint to it and is detectable. I will say you are a mute and my manservant and I will do all the talking."

John agreed though he was slightly amused by the charade and the seemingly clandestine act. Although he was fully aware of the dangers, especially after learning of the arrest of Peter's wife and daughter, he found all this very exhilarating and enjoyed all the adventure that was coming his way.

The barge, moved by muscular slave rowers, continued up the Tiber River. Slowly, the barge navigated the first of the three bends in the river Tiber, and Cornelius remarked, "We are in the southern part of the city." He pointed to a small hill and continued, "That over there is *Aventinus*, one of the Seven Hills of Rome." John looked at the Hill with the curiosity of a visitor, but his interest was distracted as the docks, wharves, and warehouses along the riverbank came into view. They were brightly visible from all the torches held by workers who planted them in the ground or by the torch holders attached to nearby buildings. He could see many people unloading barges and loading open-backed carts with jars, jugs, and baskets for the voyage into the heart of the city.

With a sudden jerk, the barge moved eastward and neared the riverbank.

John became confused for a moment. *We are going too fast to stop; why the change in directions?* Suddenly, he smelled burned wood and when he looked he could see thousands of specks of light from many torches and lamps spread out over the city and up a small hill.

"This is where the *Circus Maximus* is. It was badly damaged by the fire, but only the wooden portion of it was damaged. That tall object you see in the distance is the *obelisk* that Augustus took to Rome from Heliopolis. It stands in the *medius* center of the Circus. You would have enjoyed the Circus," Cornelius continued as he leaned forward to see into John's face. "There were many good horse races there, and at times they even raced dogs, ostriches, and camels."

John detected the Roman pride in Cornelius' voice.

"Nero and the Senate did not waste time. They have imported more slaves to rebuild Rome, and those lights are where the slaves have begun working. It is good that we travel by night, for you would become sick at what is happening to great Rome."

John detected the sadness in Cornelius' voice and he strained his eyes, wanting, even praying, to see the damage, for he did not have the same devotion to Rome that the former centurion had.

The barge slowed slightly and turned another bend. John looked ahead and could see they were approaching a bridge.

"We will soon be passing the *Insula Tiberina* Tiber Island. On the island you can see the temple to the Roman god of medicine, Aesculapius. The bridge we will pass under was built by Tiberius which leads directly into what is left of the Forum."

The sounds from the rowers stopped as the barge slipped slowly between the island and the rest of the city of Rome. As soon as it passed under the bridge, the rowers were heard again, and John uttered a silent prayer for them.

"You cannot see it but we are passing that part of the city called *Subura*. At one time, Julius Caesar lived there in a modest house; of course it was before he became *pontifex maximus*. Many Jews lived in this section, and at one time it had the only synagogue in Rome. It is the poor section of the city and many believe the fire started there."

Cornelius' voice dropped as he drew closer to John, and whispered, "Many of those killed in the fire were Christians."

John became less interested and somberly began to pray.

"Nearby is the *Campus Martis*. Many in the Roman Army train and live there. It is filled with barracks, temples and baths. I trained there many years ago."

The barge continued and the two Christians grew silent.

Cornelius was too despondent to continue, for his beloved Rome sat in ruins. It was his country and was not his enemy yet. John was silent because he was so taken by the death of all those innocent people. He was not sad for the Christians who had died, because they were now with the Master and His peace was over them; his sadness was for those who died not knowing Jesus. For those souls, he prayed, beseeching God's mercy and forgiveness since he and the Others had failed to reach them.

Minutes later, the barge turned the final bend in the river and Cornelius said simply, "To our left is *Mons Vaticanus*. It is not one of the hills of Rome because it is on the opposite side of the river. It was built on the Etruscan city of Vaticum."

John did not hear him because he was deep in thought and sad that he had not come to Rome sooner. He was sure that he could have brought those ignorant dead to Jesus.

Moments later, they slipped beside a dock. They immediately disembarked from the barge and were quickly and silently escorted by a number of hooded men to a horse-drawn cart with baskets, jars, and jugs in the back of it. Cornelius quickly jumped onto the driver's seat, signaled for John to climb up beside him, while an unknown teenage boy sat quietly on the back of the cart. Without a word to anyone, they pulled away and slowly moved north and away from Rome.

Along the way, Cornelius greeted his fellow Romans in Latin.

"*Ave amices* Hail Friends."

"*Ave.*"

Everyone seemed so friendly, which further made John feel they were being cautious without reason.

Occasionally, Cornelius would yell back to the boy in the cart, "Adessius, are you still with us and safe?"

The boy, Adessius, would laugh and yell back, "Yes, centurion, I am well."

Once safely out of Rome's view, Cornelius quickened his pace over the mostly desolate road. With gentle but persistent coaxing, Cornelius encouraged the horse to pull the cart, with its cargo and riders, to the estates of Camolius.

John sat watching Cornelius, and frequently through the night, thanked Jesus for this convert from Golgotha.

✲

The room was dimly lit. The moonlight relentlessly poured into the room from the portal that led to the garden behind the small house. Light from under the cloth-covered door slipped into the room reminding Peter of the outside world. The world did not matter, for he was tired and had no desire for anything but rest. In fact, he knew he could think of nothing for any extensive period that night. His thoughts were scattered and rambled to and from.

When he heard of his wife's arrest, he remembered their life together and the love they had for each other. The image of her long, soft, black hair, of her dark, olive complexion and big, wide, black eyes stayed in his mind for a long time. Thoughts and images of their engagement and wedding day flooded his mind. He remembered her daringness and coquettish glance when they first passed each other as she, her mother, and sister, returned from the early morning chore of getting well water. It was their first sight of each other, and he shamefully remembered the flutter that passed through him. Men were not to be so taken by a woman, but she was different, and he sincerely believed that *Adonai* had made him understand that she was to be his companion.

Warm thoughts of yesterdays came to mind but their warmth could not extinguish his sadness.

He recalled, with a wide-open smile, the day Jesus honored him and his family by walking into his house in Capernaum. Peter and Andrew had expected a meal to be ready for them, but there was none, for his mother-in-law had unexpectedly become ill. Peter's wife, who was tending to her mother, did not have time to prepare a meal. Embarrassed by the lack of hospitality, Peter began to apologize to Jesus, but Jesus set the apologies aside and without a request went into the room where the sick woman was.

The old woman was lying on a bed mat on the floor. Her head was slightly elevated by a cloak under it, and she was perspiring profusely. Jesus walked to her and she struggled to rise from her floor mat out of respect of Jesus, and began making excuses for not having prepared a meal for them and asked for forgiveness. Smiling, Jesus told her to relax, that He did not need any food, but was there to heal and to feed her.

The old woman's eyes moved quickly around the room in a panic. "But, Sir, You cannot cook," she mentioned innocently and Jesus broke into hardy laughter.

"You are correct, dear mother, but I can feed you with hope and love."

With a sigh of relief, the old woman eased back onto her mat. She was too sick to care.

"You have a fever?" Jesus asked.

"I do, and I feel pain everywhere," she replied tiredly.

Jesus extended His hand to her forehead. The woman's body gave up a shiver and her body and clothing became dry. She looked at Jesus wide-eyed. As He withdrew His hand from her head, she captured it and kissed it respectfully. Then with great exuberance, she sprung to her feet.

"Simon, do not stand there like a stone idol, get a fire started and tell my daughter to fill the bowls with water and to get some wheat for bread. Well, do not stand there Simon, move!"

Recalling that day made Peter smile, for he remembered thinking how sorry he was that Jesus had cured the old woman, because after that she put him to much work.

My wife was so much like her mother. After that day, my wife, like her mother, had total belief in Jesus and they followed Him and us as often as they could. At every turn, they encouraged me to remain with Jesus.

Easily, he recalled his wife saying to him: "He is a Man who will do great things for us, because He is filled with love and kindness. He will fill the empty things in our world. He is a true Jew sent by the Almighty to teach us. Stay close to Him, Simon. Do not be foolish."

He heard her voice, and truly she was one of the reasons why in the beginning he stayed with Jesus.

She knew, before many of us, the great value of Jesus. For this faithfulness, I am sure, the Master will take good care of her and my daughter.

Now the image of his daughter, a smaller version of her mother and grandmother, sprung into his mind's eye, and he warmly remembered the softness of her skin when he held her as an infant. He remembered the constant joy her voice carried when she first started to put words together and make her thoughts known.

Still, he felt her skin.

Still, he heard her voice.

One of the joys of parenting is the ability to remember such memories long after a child matures. She too knew Jesus was a special being, but her knowledge came through the simplicity and plain innocence of a child.

He remembered one time when his wife and daughter came to Bethsaida to be with him after he had been away for several weeks. When they arrived, they went and stayed at the house of Jonas, his father. It was the time following their preaching two by two, and proclaiming of all of *Adonai's* forgiveness and love. He and Andrew were together, and they even healed a woman who could not hear and a man who could not speak without a stutter. When they finally returned to Jesus, they were ecstatic at what they had accomplished.

How foolish we were. We thought we did it all, but it was Jesus who had done it. He gave us this experience so we could understand the power He could bestow on us and what we could achieve in His name. We were so arrogant with our own importance. Jesus just listened to us as we rambled on telling Him what we had done. How silly we must have sounded. How ignorant we must have appeared to Him and how little we had learned. The next day, He performed His great miracle of feeding the many. My wife, her mother, and my daughter were among those present that day. I still can see the look of wonder and awe on their faces when they realized what had taken place. I, of course, tried to act much at ease as if the miracle was a daily occurrence for Jesus. How weak and egotistical I was.

His remembering continued. To avoid being noticed, Jesus and his Apostles left Bethsaida and traveled up the Jordan to Lake Huleh, also known as the Waters of Merom, famous from the days of Joshua. Next they traveled by land to the city of Caesarea Philippi in the land of Ituraea. During this trip, the Apostles were confounded and discussed what had happened. They could not comprehend how Jesus was able to feed so many. Again they questioned Andrew about the number of fishes and loaves in the boy's basket. They questioned Bartholomew, Jude, James the Little, and Judas asking if they had correctly counted the remaining fish and loaves. When the questioning started to border on insults, they talked among themselves and came to the conclusion that Jesus had the power to provide provisions. Some of them thought that Jesus had finally revealed what He was going to bring to the Jews; He would lead them into economic freedom and Judea would no longer have to depend on other nations for necessities. He would be the new provider of *manna*. They were satisfied with this conclusion, and, of course, never disclosed it to Jesus.

The next day, Jesus said to them: "Who do men say that I am?"

Jude Thaddeus quickly answered with a wide smile of innocence on his lips, "Some say you are John the Baptist."

Several of the Apostles laughed at Jude's innocent answer.

"Others say you are 'Elias.'" Andrew said quietly.

Thomas frowned in open mockery of Andrew's statement.

Young John took a step forward and said, "Others say you are Jeremiah."

Several of the Apostles snickered.

With a coy look in his eyes, Matthew straightforwardly said, "One of the Prophets."

James the Less cleared his throat as a sign of his irritation at Matthew.

"But who do you say I am?" Jesus asked them.

They were stunned and stupefied by the question. They thought the answers that they gave Him were sufficient. They were speechless. No one had ever asked them such a question. They only thought of Him as a remarkable man and a prophet.

Jesus slowly moved His eyes over their blank faces. Each passing face made Him grow sad, and then from His right side He heard a deep voice say, "Thou art the Anointed One, the Son of the Living God."

All the Others moved aside, for this announcement by Simon was grave; it challenged their Jewish mind and stood on the brink of heresy.

Jesus turned to face Simon. Slowly, He walked to Simon and stood before him. In an unbroken look, Jesus intently examined the eyes and face of the tall fisherman. Simon felt the penetration of Jesus' eyes. They were piercing and Simon grew uneasy. He thought he would be reprimanded again, and he wished he could retract his words but the world had heard them. For some unknown reason, Peter believed the words he uttered, and he believed they were expected by many. Consciously, he heard a sigh that seemed to come from all the things around him, from the things and people who stood in this place years, many years before.

Jesus smiled and His face brightened with delight.

"Blessed art thou, Simon bar Jonah, for flesh and blood hast not revealed this to thee, but my Father in heaven."

Walking closer to him, with the smile on His face gone, Jesus continued somberly, "And I say to thee, thou art Peter, and upon Peter I will build my Church, and the gates of hell shall not prevail against it."

Now their faces were inches away from each other and with their eyes locked in unbroken stares, Jesus said in a deep, commanding voice, "And I will give to thee the Keys of the Kingdom of heaven; and whatsoever thou shalt bind on earth shall be bound in heaven and whatsoever thou shalt loose on earth shall be loosed in heaven."

Finishing these words, Jesus slowly backed away, step by step, leaving Simon Peter standing alone. The other Apostles looked at Simon Peter and for an unexplainable moment, for an instant, he looked taller, stronger, better, but more alone. As the years passed, Peter would return to that day over and over again, and each time he did, a chill ran through him. Afterwards, he would question those mysterious words every time he recalled them.

I did not know where I found those words, or where they come from. They came from nowhere!, he thought. *Not from me; I never knew them. They came like an arrow shot from some Unknown Archer and pierced my head. I thought of no other thing, not even my next breath which was caught in my throat. I was compelled to say them. They flew out on their own. Jesus said they came from His Father, but I did not understand what Jesus meant.* He shook his head showing disbelief and doubt, then became still, for the entire memory baffled him. *I had no idea what Jesus meant with these words. Nor did I understand what He meant by giving me the Keys to the Kingdom. How many times after that day did I ask the Others if they understood what He meant. What Keys? What Kingdom?* Again he smiled and his right eyebrow arched slightly. *Ah, it was Andrew who then came to me months later and reminded me of the story of King David choosing one head, a primary minister, above all the other ministers to carry the 'keys of the kingdom' with more authority than the others. I became frightened with Andrew's words. I did not want such a responsibility.* The thought sent a chill up his back, and he shook his head again.

His thoughts were broken by the sounds of excited voices in the next room, but he had no desire to listen to what was being said or what was happening. He was too absorbed in thought to care for the outside. He was at peace with his own thoughts and his reminiscing took complete control over him and he was compelled to stay with his remembering. Contemplating Jesus' strange words, he began to feel that the Others thought of him as being different. They seemed to believe that he was set apart from them, and soon they respected him silently. Henceforth, they gave way to him, expecting him to speak first for them.

I did not feel greater. The only thing I felt was the weight of their silence. I was like them; ignorant and a sinner. As time went on, Jesus changed my thinking. Whenever He prayed, He called me first to go with Him and that perplexed me.

Later, Andrew told Peter that John and the two James' were envious or at least disappointed that he was given some prominence. He laughed at his brother's remark, until Salome Zebedee, the mother of James and John, asked Jesus for her sons to be treated better than the rest. Then he knew that Andrew was right and for days he believed they resented him.

I always thought that either James or John would have been the better choice. They were related to Him. James the Greater even resembled Him. I could not understand why I was the one to speak. Jesus said the Father had revealed it to me. If so, why had the Father nudged me and not James, John or James? I was the least worthy and...I proved that...later....Look how faithful John and James, his brother, remained. Look at Andrew, who was the first to be called to the Lord; that should have meant something. The Father should have prodded one of the Zebedee brothers. It should have been one of them. I could understand why James bar Alphaeus was not chosen as he was not yet a complete believer in Jesus. Yet he was given the mission of Jerusalem and surely that was the Father's doing. Even now, with the fire of the Holy Spirit deep inside me, I still do not understand the ways of Adonai. So why me?

He got up from his chair, and in the silvery moonlight found a jar of water on a nearby table. He poured a small amount of water in a cup and quickly drank it. With the empty cup still in his hand, he froze as he remembered the news that John was on his way to Rome. John's visit made Peter believe that an important message was coming to him.

Earlier that day, a well-thought-out plan was set. Peter was going to leave the Camolius estate and he was going to send Linus and Cornelius away while he stayed in Rome. If things became too difficult, he would leave at a later date for the east to find his brother Andrew who was some-where north of Greece. Also he would try to locate Mark or his brother or one of the Others. Later, he planned to go west to Southern Gaul, but these plans had changed due to the happenings around him. Paul was arrested, as was Peter's wife and daughter, and with John coming to Rome, Peter concluded that the Lord was moving him in a new direction. Perhaps he was called to come home and John was to take his place.

Lord, I hope this is what You are showing me? Or have I again misunderstood You? Whatever it is, I am at a lost and I need a nudge from You, Master, to tell me if I am correct.

He sincerely believed that a response would be forthcoming but when no response came Peter sat numb. After a few fleeting moments, a big sigh escaped his mouth which reflected his disappointment and helplessness. He rose from his chair and walked slowly to the portico in the back of the house. The world around the house was shadowed with only the gray and blue moonlight visible. It seemed surreal. Watching this sight only made him grow sadder, so he turned away and returned to his chair. His large body fell onto the chair, and he quickly threw back his head and looked at the ceiling above him. The heavy wood supporting the roof of the house ran across the ceiling from right to left and his eyes followed as if reading a scroll. The wizardry of imagination took his mind to his letters and to those he received from others. Finally, his thought returned to Mark.

Mark gives me great concern. I never believed he would disobey me, but if he felt he had to make peace with Paul then I have nothing to do with this. It is between Paul and Mark and of course the Master.

He reflected on his thoughts momentarily and wondered if he also should make peace with Paul for they had not been on the best of terms since Antioch.

I too should make peace with him, he thought, and wondered how this could be done. He was told and even read that Paul had belittled him on a number of occasions for what had happened in the city of Antioch.

Paul was right. I behaved poorly; no, shamefully. Like Paul and Barnabas, I was living as a Gentile and had celebrated the Meal with the Gentiles. I stopped dining with the Gentiles before the Judaizers arrived in hopes of talking to them before they saw me with the Gentiles. I was afraid they would start trouble again. I wanted to find time to explain myself. What I failed to see was that my actions were insensitive to the Antiochene Gentiles. When Paul saw this, he grew furious.

In his mind, he could see Paul's fiery eyes and his tense, red face.

"Is God only the God of the circumcised?" Paul demanded. "No!" He continued and drew closer to Simon Peter's face. "He is the God of all, for Jew and Gentile can believe the same thing. There is no limit to anyone's belief."

Paul publicly reprimanded Simon Peter, disturbing many, but Simon Peter defended Paul's actions. He committed the error in example and he told them that Paul was justified. When he was alone, he remembered that Paul compromised himself when he circumcised his companion, Timothy. In that moment, Simon Peter wanted to remind Paul that he too was guilty of the sin of appeasement. Thereafter, Paul's reprimand angered him. He regretted not being bold enough to defend himself. For days his thoughts festered into revenge, and when he realized these thoughts were becoming sinful, he fell on his knees and asked forgiveness. However, the turmoil in his mind remained, and he did not find complete release of his feelings until he spoke to his brother Andrew. He confessed his anger and desire for revenge. Andrew simply reminded him that Paul and he were only weak human beings. "You both fell into the hands of earthly power and forgot the power of the Master," Andrew said, "and Jesus used Paul to make His displeasure known to you, so forget it, and pray for Paul and yourself."

So this is what Peter did.

But Paul is a difficult man. He drove Mark and Barnabas from his side because of his fire and passion, but he was not always this way. Immediately after he came to the Lord, he was unsure of himself. I do not think he fully understood what had taken place within him. I remember he wanted to see and talk to us, and I recall how we reacted with great distrust. Regardless of his conversion and no matter what others said happened to him, we still felt uncomfortable. We all thought it was a ploy set in our midst. After all, he was a Pharisee and the image of Stephen the deacon's death was fresh in our minds. Repeatedly, Paul asked to see us. Filled with uncertainty, we had to debate meeting with Paul.

"I think he wants us to give him our blessings." Peter remembered his brother Andrew saying with a great deal of conviction in his voice.

Philip looked quickly at Andrew and slowly said, "No, I think he is in need of some human confirmation of his conversion."

"He needs legitimacy, a legalistic thing that appeases his pharisaic mentality. Seeing us will give him the legal status he needs," James bar Alphaeus had remarked aloud.

Everyone became silent. Then from the far end of the room came the soft voice of Jude Thaddeus. "I see it differently. I think he is coming to us for direction."

"And I believe he needs to come to us for forgiveness," Peter remembered saying. "He needs to make a confession of the sin he committed against Stephen. There is a need for reparation. Meeting with us will be that reparation."

Peter reached for a cup of water.

Paul's coming to the Lord was different from ours. We were with Jesus and were called by Him not only to work in His name but also to be living witnesses. We heard His voice and were captivated by His wisdom. We lived with His hurt, His thirst, and hunger. We saw and felt His disappointment. We saw His miracles and were astonished by them. We walked and traveled with Him. We saw Him confront the non-believers, and how He condemned and forgave the sin. We saw His death and His resurrection. To die is human but to rise again, that truly is being God!! In a way, we died as He did and we rose to new life. Paul knew none of these things; he seemed to know only the glorified and not the human Man. Paul lacked the sights, sounds, and memories of those things that are in our daily thoughts and memories. He paused, for he felt himself becoming upset. *With the help of the Holy Spirit, Paul came to believe in what we personally saw and it was that same Spirit who was our common ground. The same Spirit, who came to us so that we might understand and be convinced, came to Paul to convert and correct. Many see a difference in our callings, but we recalled Jesus saying that we believed because we saw, but blessed were those who did not see yet believed. We began to understand that those who did not see the Lord, although set apart, were equal to us.*

Again he paused and the image of Paul coming into the Room to meet the Twelve for the first time slipped into his mind. Simon Peter watched Paul. Each step he took was unassuming, almost fragile. He was more uncertain of the Twelve than they were of him, but one thing was apparent to Peter and some Others—Paul had met the Lord, for his enthusiasm showed this.

I know he sensed our distrust and I know we surprised him due to our lack of fear. I am sure he knew that he could do nothing to harm us for in torture or in death we were victorious. I think we saw that this frail and insecure man sympathized. We saw a man who felt great comfort in the grips of hatred who was now a novice in a palm of love.

Peter walked to the smaller man with red hair and embraced him. They stood for a long moment looking into each other's eyes, and Peter read the threefold confession: forgive me for my unbelief, forgive me for wounding you, and forgive me for helping in the death of Stephen.

As Paul told the story of his conversion and of what followed, the Twelve and others in the room listened silently. He talked about his successes, and as Peter watched him something strange began to happen. Paul became bold, and with each spoken word, with each completed sentence, an air of condescension rose in Paul's mannerism. With equal boldness, Peter realized that with or without the Twelve, Paul was going to preach Jesus any way he saw fit. We all knew that we were not going to match Paul's feelings of superiority.

Paul must have seen our lack of commitment. He knew that he was more educated than we were and more knowledgeable of the Holy Scriptures. Whatever the reasons, he began talking to us, and soon several of the Others began shifting in their seats as they also became aware of what Peter had observed. He departed without asking for any permission or for a mission. Even though he did not have to, still, it would have been respectful had he asked. It also would have shown his humility and that he learned how to walk humbly with the Lord. He loudly cleared his throat, needing to break his thinking, for the swell of resentment grew in his soul. One thing was certain, his energy seemed unmatched, and what Paul had, was given to him by the Lord. He rested his head on the back of his chair and closed his eyes. *Lord, help me. I have so much to learn. I have to understand Your ways. I have to be more of You and less of me.* He opened his eyes and stared into the dark ceiling above him. *I think Mark has shown me that I also should seek Paul's forgiveness or maybe Paul and I should seek each other's forgiveness. Master, please allow me this moment of reparation.*

He reached over the side of his chair and placed his empty cup on the floor. Again he heard the sounds of low voices in the next room and for an instant hoped they would not disturb him for he still sought solitude. The idea of having people around him made him tense. His thoughts returned to his wife and daughter, and he closed his eyes as his concern for them surged. In his sadness, he felt he was receiving a gift, for this was his opportunity to return these loved ones to God. *We are only leased to one another, so I place them, Master, in Your warm and loving hands. Your will be done. Only, I beg You, allow them little pain and little fear for they have been true followers of Your commandments. If need be, let their lot fall and rest on me.*

He thought of Lady Mary and remembered the pain, yet also resignation in her eyes the day Jesus was crucified.

Now there was strength but a strength I did not understand at that time. In fact, Andrew and I were sure she was just in a state of shock and that this was the cause of her tolerance. However, I now understand that she was the example of acceptance with faith.

A familiar image of Mary sitting off in a corner came to his mind. When she was with them, she always seemed to be distant. Seeing her this way made him want to sit next to her to talk. In his mind, he walked to her and decided to speak to her.

Lady Mary, help me to bear this loss as you did yours. A swell of humanity grew inside of him and he thought, *If only I could hold my child as you held yours.*

He rested and allowed his prayer to drift from him. He instantly felt Jesus near. With peace and tranquility, a pleased and satisfied smile spread across his lips. He welcomed and enjoyed the few small moments of calm in his turbulent world.

Suddenly, he felt a chill. The chill threw his thoughts back to the many cold prisons he experienced. Though this was unpleasant, there were no regrets and no complaints. *Those were times offered for Jesus,* he quickly thought, and this thought filled him with joy. Again the chill passed over him, but this time the chill held the dampness of the earth. Into his memory crept the feeling of the damp, hard earth of that night in Gethsemane. He felt the roughness of his cloak as he wrapped it around himself. He curled and shifted his body closer to James and John.

During his sleep, he heard Jesus ask him to join Him in prayer.

John also heard the request, for he remembered hearing John mumbling some feeble excuse and Jesus walking away.

Sometime later, this same request was made.

Later, he heard the clamor of the oncoming soldiers and guards which stirred him from his sleep, but he could not comprehend what was happening. Then came the touch of a rough hand on his arm, and then another, and he was jolted from his warmth and forcibly dragged to his feet. He was startled and irritated, still suffering from the stupor of the Passover wine. He saw Judas approach and kiss Jesus on the cheek. They spoke softly to each other, making it impossible for him to hear what was said. His uncertain eyes watched as Jesus walked directly to the guards and soldiers.

Peter's heart began to beat rapidly and he heard Jesus say: 'Whom seek ye?'

"Jesus of Nazareth," they answered.

"I am He."

They fell back in shock at His authority.

Ignoring their confusion, again Jesus said, "I have told you that I am He. If therefore you seek Me, let these others go their way."

Jesus freed us from death, for we had to continue His mission. I did not know or grasp the meaning of this, for I thought only of defending Jesus. How foolish I was since He already told us—me—that this was necessary but it was not what I wanted to believe.

He remembered the rage bellowing deep inside his chest as he awoke. He wanted to reach out to Judas and harm him. In his memory, he could feel the leather handle of his dagger, and again he could feel his need to injure and kill if need be. He saw the flash of his blade in the moonlight and the feel and sound of flesh being sliced.

Ah, poor Malchus. How stunned he was by my assault. I am sure he did not expect that from me or from any of us, for he saw us many times cower before the authorities and the many times that Jesus defended us. Even more shocking was the Master's compassion and mending of his ear. He smiled as he remembered the astonished look on the face of the High Priest's hireling. *Weeks later, when Malchus and I met again, his facial expression was one of joy, and he thanked me for being so aggressive and enthusiastic because my actions had given him a new insight of Jesus. He became a good servant of the Lord and a great help to all of us, especially James bar Alphaeus.* Remembering these things made Peter uncomfortable. *But what I did was not pleasing to the Master. I may have been the one privileged, as the Others thought, but I was the one most reprimanded. Truly, the Master wanted me to remain humble.* He sighed loudly. *I do not remember what happened after that. I remember Andrew and Thomas tugging at my sleeve and pulling me away. I ran. All of us did! I remember Philip and Matthew, followed by the Zealot, and James bar Alphaeus scurrying over the low gray stone wall and disappearing into the Valley of Cedron. I can remember Jude and Nathaniel darting away and quickly fading in the dark shadows of the Garden to hide among the olive trees. I ran like the rest, only to stop and hide behind a large rock. I watched as they led Jesus away and I saw Judas looking on. Suddenly, I felt a body near me. It was John, and he whispered, "Simon Peter, we must follow them and see what happens."*

He opened his eyes, needing to break free from those moments of fear.

He laid his face in the palm of his hands. His memories of that night always created anger. His emotions were still as mixed as they had been that night. He recalled the deep feelings of disbelief at Judas' betrayal. He recalled wishing he hurt Judas and not Malchus. It amazed him, after all these years, that he was still saddened when he remembered Judas. He knew his sadness also had a lot to do with pity. For some unknown reason, at the very first moment Judas and he met, he felt a pity for Judas and always made excuses for him and gave him the benefit of the doubt. Peter believed that Judas had miscalculated the High Priest's intentions. He did not perceive that the authorities wanted to have Jesus put to death. *He knew, as we all knew, that there could be no trial because Rabbinical Law forbade night trials. He knew that witnesses for the accused had to be pre-*

sented, and certainly, many would come forward, especially us, His Apostles, for we knew more about Jesus than the rest of the world. Judas realized that the timing of the arrest was in the Master's favor, for even if the Sanhedrin decided on a guilty verdict, they could not execute Jesus because again the Law forbade execution the day after a trial. Moreover, the next day was the Sabbath and all work ceased on the Sabbath. Furthermore, Roman law forbade the leaders the right to execute. With all these things, Judas believed that Jesus was safe. Eventually, people would be alerted and a large protest would follow and the hand of Jesus would be forced and His kingdom would follow. This is what was on Judas' mind; he wanted Jesus to perform miracles and assert His authority. I remember him saying so often that Jesus was teaching and talking too much instead of acting. If only he had stayed closer to the words of Jesus and less to his own ideas.

His remembering made him grow tired and weary. He yawned and tears came to his eyes and then he wiped his eyes and cheeks with his rough hands.

Life is a thousand 'if onlys' that are easily solved in tomorrows than when they happened.

He mentally saw the image of Jesus and smiled warmly.

How blessed are we to be able to close our eyes, sometimes opening them, and see the Face of the Master.

Once more, his mind drifted to the Garden. He saw the guards roughly grab, shove, and move Jesus out of the Garden. Once inside the city, they quickly traveled through the dark and barren streets of Jerusalem. John and Peter followed the mob but at a distance. They were constantly darting behind the dark shadows of trees and rocks, in doorways, behind pillars and empty carts, always trying to stay hidden. From the direction of their travel, John and Peter knew that they were heading toward the house of Ananias, the former High Priest, who had been deposed fifteen years earlier but whose advice was still sought by his son-in-law, Caiphas.

"Simon Peter, do you see? The High Priest only wants to speak to Jesus. There is nothing to fear." He heard John say. "There are no grounds for an arrest; Jesus is guilty of no crime," John continued.

I believe John said these things more for his benefit than mine, but he, like me, remembered the incident in the porticos of the Temple with the money changers. Jesus had infuriated the authorities by condemning their business in the Temple grounds.

Peter yawned again while his body grew heavy. He took a deep breath and slowly exhaled. It was a breath of exhaustion and he passed from alertness to partial stupor, until he slowly slipped into blankness and deep sleep.

And then that night, so long ago, vanished into a dream.

They easily entered the courtyard of the house of the old High Priest, because many in the household knew John bar Zebedee through the family fishing business. The two Apostles stood by a large fire with many of the household servants. He felt the night's chill down his back, feet, and hands. The only part of his body that seemed warm was his face, which was warmed by the big fire before him. He stood by the fire and looked pensively into the flames, mesmerized by the comfort the fire gave off and the danger within it. As the two warmed themselves, John constantly looked over at the house, shifting his body while trying to get a better view of the interior. It was clear to Peter that John wanted to get into the house to see what was happening. Peter was hoping that he would not do this for he did not want to be left alone.

Suddenly…

That woman! Where did she come from? Who was she?

"Are you not one of His Disciples?" the woman asked in a loud voice while everyone around the fire looked at the two of them. She questioned both of them, but John simply walked away from the fire leaving Peter behind.

His heart beat hard and fear sprang into his chest.

Defensively and with a hint of indignation, he replied, "I am not."

It is only a tiny lie.

It left distaste in his mouth. Next to him, he heard someone say in Greek and in a low hoarse voice: *"Prodotis!"* Betrayer!

He looked in the direction of Ananias' house and saw John edging his way inside and became angry that John had left him.

Around him, people were talking about Jesus. They were saying how dangerous He had become, and that He was trying to undermine the religious leaders and cause a division between the people and their leaders. Peter wanted to correct them and tell them how loving and gentle Jesus was but he held his tongue for fear of betraying himself.

The heat from the flames made his face feel feverish.

Again…

A man who knew Malchus saw Peter and said, "Are you one of them?"

Fear tightened his chest and he heard the loud thump of his heart in his ears. His hands grew clammy.

He replied slowly and with great control. He knew that if he displayed any anger, the man would remember his flare-up in the Garden and would recognize him.

"I am not."

The man walked away with a glance over his shoulder as he left. The man still had doubts, but Peter felt relief and welcomed the servant's retreat.

It is only a small lie.

Suddenly a bitter taste came to his mouth. Off in the distance, he heard someone say in Latin and in a coarse voice: *"Fugitivus!"* Deserter!

He slowly extended his hands to the flames trying to act normal and undisturbed by the questioning, but he noticed his hands trembling, so he quickly drew them to his side. He swallowed hard, needing to repress his fear.

Soon those around him returned to their talking and condemnation of Jesus, so he slowly moved away from them to another fire closer to the house.

This group of servants talked about Jesus as well, and speaking of how dangerous he was.

"He is a revolutionary."

"He associated with sinners and zealots."

Peter's eyes shifted to the face of each speaker.

"A blasphemer and a charlatan," another said.

"He and His followers could bring Rome down on us with a vengeance," still another said.

He wanted to correct them but his mouth grew dry and his body was shivering.

Then another servant looking closely at Peter said, "This man was with Jesus for he is a Galilean."

"Do not be a donkey keeper and a damned fool," Peter exploded. "I swear on all that is holy that I do not know this Man. If I were a follower, do you think I would be a jackass and be here?"

Now nothing existed but this answer.

His words had stilled the air around him.

All eyes were on him.

At that moment came the sound of a cock's crow, and Simon Peter turned quickly and looking up saw Jesus being led from Ananias' house by the guards.

Their eyes met.

Jesus' eyes did not accuse; They were filled with sadness.

Again, the cock crowed.

Off to his side, he heard someone say in Hebrew in a low raspy voice, *"Oyev!"* Enemy!

He heard his Master's voice echoing: "before the cock crows you will deny me three times."

A hot burning tear scourged his cheek, then another equally burning, slipped down his cheek, and then another until his face was moist with tears. He felt them seep through his beard and slide down his neck. Staggering, he took a step back, then another, and another until he was running. He threw his hood over his head and gathering his cloak, covered himself as he ran hiding from the darkness of the night. In blindness, he stumbled and fell. Wet with tears, his face hit the ground and the dust of the earth stuck to his face. His cry turned to wails, then to screams of pain, as he felt the searing flames of his denial of Love. Somewhere in his dream, he heard his own cries. They separated him from his thoughts and he jumped back to the present, with tears real and burning on his face.

He heard someone, something, moving in the room, causing him to look into the darkness. His stare was hard. He strained his eyes as he peered into the void. He heard the sound of deep, heavy breathing and he quickly looked into the corner where he found a round figure. He did not have to look for a face; he knew he would find none. A demon was there, perhaps it was his own demon, but he knew it was a demon, for he felt uneasy and a foul scent that displaced all the air of the room. The voices he heard in his dream—the voices that had invaded his mind—were the voices of the Evil One. He knew "Legion" would never leave him alone, since he was an easy target for many years. The Evil One is a persistent being and never lets someone forget his sins or his unworthiness.

"You do not need to remind me that I am a sinner or that I should not 'cast the first stone,'" he said aloud and then with great confidence continued: "I know what I am, but I also know when I cry, 'Lord, save me for I am drowning' He is there to lift me, and there to save me."

He heard the shuffle and the moan of discomfort.

Then with a voice of great authority and courage he said, "Be gone, thing of the night, thing of my past, in the Name that is above all names; Be gone in Jesus' name!"

From the corner of the room came a loud painful moan that blended with a growl, and a foul, stomach-turning odor passed quickly through the room, causing Peter to cough.

Then the room returned to night.

With his big, rough hand, he wiped the cool tears from his face and quickly thanked Jesus; He had been saved again and protected from the storm and his own stupidity. Once again, Jesus had been in his boat to protect him. He threw his head back, hitting the back of his chair and for an instant his head pained.

A sigh of exhaustion escaped his mouth.

He had to rest for he was very tired and this weariness was no surprise to him, for each encounter with the Evil One left him fatigued. This encounter with "Legion" even left Jesus drained, but it did not seem to bother Jesus as much as it bothered Peter. He closed his eyes and prayed a short prayer for Jesus to remain with him his entire life.

"Peter?"

"Yes!" He replied instinctively being startled by the sound of his name and another voice.

He turned his head, and at the doorway with candles to brighten the room was Linus, Cornelius, and behind them, John bar Zebedee. He jumped to his feet and rushed to embrace his friend. They held each other long and John realized, for the first time, that Peter was older than he was. He also could feel Peter's tiredness seep through his clothing; this was not due to age but from years of travel, torture, abuse and worry.

The two men sat, quickly exchanged greetings, and then settled down to those simple conversations that take place between two old friends.

Linus and Cornelius busied themselves bringing in dates, nuts, fruits, and some wine and water for their enjoyment. Occasionally, they sat to listen to the conversation. John welcomed Linus and Cornelius in the conversations because it gave him time to look intensely at Simon Peter. Soon, after some examination, he recognized a familiar strain on Simon Peter's face, which he wanted to address immediately, but decided to wait until they were alone.

Meanwhile, the two Apostles continued to exchange information about the Others.

"I received letters from Philip and Andrew recently. They are both in Greece. I have not heard from Thomas, Matthew, Jude Thaddeus or Simon, and that is expected for they are in remote lands," John said as his face was lit with joy.

"I have heard from none of them. I would not know what they were doing if you did not tell me." Peter stated, not out of envy, but through conviction.

"I hear from the Others because I am more stationary, but it matters little, as long as one of us hears of them."

"I did hear that Lazarus was in Gaul with Martha and Magdalene. They are doing well and have made many converts, as is Barnabas, who is now in Cyprus."

"We have all been blessed and have done well for the Master in spite of all that the Evil One has placed in our way," John stated as he tilted his head to get a better perspective of his friend's face. "And how are you doing?" John finally asked.

"We are well."

"But disturbed," John observed.

"The news of my wife and daughter's arrest is disturbing but they are in Jesus' Hands and there is no better place for them," Peter replied plainly and with sincerity.

"I hear Mark has returned and is with Paul."

"Yes." Peter's forehead scowled. "Mark has returned to do what he has to do. I am certain, as soon as he has resolved his problems, he will continue on his journey away from here. He knows how important he is and how much the Master relies on him."

"And Paul?"

"Ah, dear John, you know as I, that Paul will always be Paul. He will face this crisis as he has faced all crises with the determination and the stubbornness given to him by the Lord." Peter paused and looked away for a moment, then turning; he looked directly into John's eyes. "There is no need for concern here, brother. It is the will of the Lord and we will come and go as He wills."

John studied Simon Peter's face for a moment and could see his sincere attachment to the will of God. Taking a sip of wine, he slowly lowered it, never allowing his eyes to leave Simon Peter's face. He, again, read something familiar on Simon Peter's face and knew he would have to mention it; what he read on Peter's face he knew Peter would not address.

"And Simon Magus?" John asked, breaking his evaluation.

A small smile spread across Peter's lips.

"Hmm. Would you believe with all the other news of this day that I never even thought of poor Simon? May God forgive my negligence."

"Well, dear brother, rest on your own words, Simon Magus, like all the others in today's news, is in the hands of the Lord."

The two men looked at each other for a long time as they remembered the Simon Magus of bygone years. Breaking their long stares, Peter said, "Perhaps we should pray for his soul."

And together the four men prayed for Simon Magus and for all the happenings of that day.

*

John reached for some nuts and dates and, after his first bite, realized his hunger.

Peter watched as John wolfed the food down.

"Linus, I think we have neglected John's appetite for he eats as if he were starving," Peter said with a wide smile. "Do we have any food to give him?"

Linus quickly jumped to his feet.

"Oh John, I apologize; I truly forgot my hospitality."

Linus was moving around gathering plates, dates, nuts, olives and grapes.

"I will warm some bread and fish for you. Please forgive us...me... I was so engrossed with the joy of being in the presence of two Apostles that I forgot myself."

"Easy, Linus," Cornelius said with a chuckle, "you are so flustered that you might hurt yourself. I am certain John understands, and besides, he has been unfed before, is this not true, John?"

"More times than I care to remember. Simon Peter, do you remember the time we were walking down the road to Bethsaida and we came across those orange groves..."

Cornelius and Linus left the room—leaving the two men to talk and reminisce—and Linus immediately went about preparing a better meal for John. Cornelius stood by the curtain, and for a brief moment listened to the two men recollect. He heard them laughing and their laughter made the Roman feel comfortable. Turning to Linus, he said, "Linus, take your time. Peter and John have much to talk about; there is much on both of their minds, and we should allow them time to be alone."

"But I was eager to hear them talk of the Lord."

"Later, after they finished speaking to each other," Cornelius said as he walked to fill a pitcher of water. As he drank, he again looked at the curtain that divided the two rooms and silently prayed for Jesus to be with his two favorite Apostles.

"Simon Peter, you are troubled again," John remarked.

"It has been a day filled with anxiety and unexpectedness."

"I do not mean today or today's news, though I would admit, it is a day filled with repentance."

John leaned forward and looked directly into Peter's face. He examined the wrinkles, the general condition of Peter's face, and then he looked into his eyes. Now sure that his eyes were not deceived, he leaned back in his chair.

"No, Simon Peter, I am speaking of your troubles with the past. I can always tell when you have relived that night; your shoulders slump and your face becomes haggard. Your eyes reflect confusion and your face shows a look of fear. Your insecurity seeps from your body like the scent from a flower. Why do you do this to yourself? Do you not realize that Jesus forgave you?"

Immediately, Peter reacted by sitting erect. His head jerked and twitched in shock.

"Do you know me that well, John?"

John chuckled. "Come now, my good friend. Was I not the one who found you the next day mired in self-hatred and self-condemnation? Was I not the one on whose shoulder you wept? And how many times since that night have I surmised and told you correctly that you were reliving that night? Yes, Simon Peter, I know you that well."

"It is a sin that has a thousand lives."

"Oh, Simon Peter, have you not learned of the Master's forgiveness?"

"I know more than any one of His forgiveness. The Others wrote telling me of their torment of Gethsemane, and I write telling them that they were forgiven and I am sure they were relieved. I, on the other hand, have received my three-fold forgiveness on the shores of the Sea of Tiberius." Peter stopped and looked at John. Slowly, he leaned forward putting his elbows on his knees and continued, "John, you never had these feelings. You stood with Lady Mary and the Holy Women. You proved your love. I never proved my love for Jesus in an open theatre, as you did." He pointed to his chest. "My love is here and it is unseen. I never manifested it." He sat upright and said in a low voice: "All that I do now, I do in reparation to prove my love. Is it enough?" He swallowed hard. "Do you remember that night on the shores of the Sea of Tiberius? Do you remember? After I girded myself and went to the Master; you had said you knew who it was on the beach and then I came upon Him standing. He had started a fire, and when you and the Others came onto the shore I returned to my boat. Do you know why I returned to my boat? Because of the fire. I could not find myself standing near it; it reminded me of that night of my denials, but worse, Jesus was by the fire reminding me of my accusers. I knew He remembered, and I could not bear the light of the fire on my face and Jesus seeing it."

John rose and walked around his chair saying, "Do you not see, Simon Peter, each time you relive that time you doubt."

"Yes, I have doubts. Doubts in and of my worth. You and the Others always put pressure on me to be the one to speak up—to be the first among you—when I was not."

"That is not true! Jesus chose you. Have you forgotten that day when He called you Peter?"

"No, in fact, this very day I recalled it and wondered why it was me."

"Because His Father appointed you." John walked around his chair and returned to his seat. "Do you want to know what we thought of that day? Well, I will tell you. Most of us believed that Jesus knew one of us was to be the leader, but He did not know the manner in which this was to be revealed. He knew someone must lead, had to lead, because the continuance of His mission was to be through that person, that leader. Jesus came for the future and the future needed a leader who knew who He was. So the Master was forced to ask us directly '…who do you say I am?' No one knew who He was. If the Father spoke to any of the Others, none came forward. They did not have the boldness, but when the Father, through the Spirit, moved your will, the lot fell on you. Not because you wanted it, we all knew you did not; not because you deserved it, we all knew you did not, but because it was revealed to you who Jesus was. It came from the Father and all Jesus had to do was confirm His Father's wishes. It had nothing to do with who was better or who was right for leadership; it had to do with who was certain and bold enough to speak out. That was you, Simon Peter, it was always you. After you spoke your words, I wondered if you knew what you said but when I saw your face, I knew, as Jesus knew, that there was no doubt in your words. You knew who Jesus was. You answered His question with the greatest of truth."

"But have you forgotten the time he called me Satan and told me to get behind Him? I rebelled because I did not want Him to suffer. I wanted to help Him."

"He had to rebuke you; you were working against His mission."

"But, John, I was the one who spoke the words; I was the one who received His disfavor."

"Because the rest of us did not have the courage to say the words. Do you not think we also wanted to protect Him? Do you not think we wanted to stop Him from washing our feet? Do you not think we wanted to walk to Him over the water? Of course we did, but we never acted; we never said the words; we never took the step, because we had not been chosen. All those words, actions, and steps were for you to accomplish; you were our voice. You were meant to be the leader."

Peter grew silent and John was not sure if what he said helped his friend.

"Simon Peter, you have a short memory. Do you forget that at the Passover Meal, Jesus told you that He had prayed for you? I do not recall Him ever singling one of us to tell us that; and do you remember His other words after that? He said 'you must strengthen your brothers,' and this is what you did.

"And how have I done this?"

"Simon Peter, listen to yourself. Think! Who called for the replacement of Judas? Who was the one who opened the door on Pentecost and led us out onto the porch to the awaiting world? Who lead us in courage when we were thrown in prison that day? Who called for the naming of the seven deacons? Who reminded us that the reason Jesus washed our feet was to show us that we had to wash the Judean dust off our feet and go elsewhere? Who lead us in the pulling of lots for our missions? It was you, Simon Peter; it was you."

Peter sighed and began to speak. "And lately...no, even further back...I believed it should have been your brother, James, or you and even James bar Alphaeus."

"James? Me? James Alphaeus? Why? Because we were related to the Master? Oh Simon Peter, we were the least worthy. I cannot speak for James bar Alphaeus, but for James and myself. At first we thought of Jesus as a man who would lead our families to prosperity and power. We saw ourselves as heirs apparent to His kingdom, and I think James Alphaeus saw Jesus as a rebel and a wayward member of his family. We did not understand that Jesus was working for a heavenly kingdom. Jesus could not pick us, for He had to show that it was not a family affair. He had to show that He came for the world and not merely for His family. But you, you came out with the words that stopped our thoughts; it was perhaps the first time we understood a little about who Jesus was. Remember what Jesus said to you when you spoke your proclamation. He said the words were given to you from His Father. Even if Jesus wanted to make the sons of Zebedee or Alphaeus the leader of the Twelve, He could not, for His Father had made the anointment."

"But you, your brother, and the other James, always made me feel that you resented the Master's choice."

"Maybe, at first, because of our worldly mentality but later we never did. If you felt that, it was from your own doubts; not from anything we did. If we exercised any authority over you, it was because your doubts forced us. Remember the meeting with Paul and Barnabas where you told James Alphaeus to take the lead? I am sure he would not have done this without your consent. We always moved on your examples and orders, Simon Peter."

"And your mission here? Have you not arrived here on a mission to take over my lead? I remembered the prophesy that Jesus gave that I would be taken away and you would remain."

John was stunned and then he allowed himself time to ponder Peter's statement.

Was that the reason the Lord sent me here? He thought and reeled in the question.

John remembered what Cornelius and Linus mentioned before he came into the room. They pleaded with John to convince Peter to leave Rome, not to seek out his wife and daughter, or Paul, or Mark, but to leave before it was too late.

"I do not believe I was sent here for that reason, Simon Peter," John said. "I am here to tell you to think of saving yourself. I am here to tell you that you are too valuable to the Church and that you should leave to fight another day."

"But, John…my wife, my daughter…"

"They are, as you said, in the hands of the Lord. Rejoice and be glad for they are in a better position than we are."

The younger Apostle could see that Peter was perplexed. There was no doubt that Peter believed his wife and daughter were protected by the Lord, but his heart was still anguished. It was understandable that he would feel this way for his family. His love for them was long-standing and instinctive. But his trouble went beyond these things; it was his human passion—that element that all had witnessed time and time again—and the thing that always got him in trouble with the Master.

John closed his eyes. He needed guidance to control his thoughts but none came. As he was preparing to ask for the Lord's help, a thought surfaced and opening his eyes, he looked at Peter and said, "On the shore that night, the Master asked you three questions."

"Yes, I know these questions for I have answered them many times over."

"Let me ask you these same questions as I write them in Greek."

"You are writing your account in Greek?"

"Yes, because Greek is more widely spoken. As you know, even the Romans send their instructions to the provinces with a Greek translation attached; but alas, I shall write in the common Greek the *koine* for I want the common people to understand it."

"John, I am so happy to hear you are giving an account of the life of the Master."

"Well, it is far from finished, so be at ease. Nevertheless, do not distract me; let me tell you what I know of your conversation with the Lord on that evening. He asked you: 'Simon, son of Jonah, lovest thou Me more than these?' and you said…"

"Yes, Lord, You know that I love You."

"And He said to you, '*Boske* feed My Lambs.'"

The two men looked at each other, both seeing in their minds the flickering flames of the fire, the dark night in the background, and Jesus sitting by the fire, poking it with a long stick held in His Pierced Hand.

"Again He said to you, 'Simon, son of Jonah, lovest thou Me?' and you said…"

"Yes, Lord, You know that I love You."

"And He said, '*Poimane* tend My Lambs.'"

They both remembered Jesus dropping the stick into the fire. Jesus turned to Simon Peter on His right and looked into His Apostle's eyes.

"He then asked a third time, 'Simon Peter, son of Jonah, lovest thou Me?'"

Peter remained silent and John waited.

"I was so deeply hurt when He asked a third time."

"He had to ask you again, Simon Peter, because He had to erase the three denials, and because each question was more intense than the one before. You were answering Him with a human love and that is not what Jesus wanted. When He looked at you the third time, He wanted a love that involved your mind, soul and eternal life."

"And my answer was filled with those things, John; I felt His healing power. I felt His love, but more importantly, I felt my love for Him. It was so intense at that moment that I lost the feeling of life."

Peter looked at John, through eyes swimming in tears that distorted his vision but not the sight of his heart or his inner sight.

"Lord, You know all things; You know that I love You."

"And He said, *Boske* feed, pasture My sheep. Simon Peter, you are to feed and pasture His Lambs with His love and your love. You are to *Poimane* tend and shepherd His lambs. You are to guide and guard His Church. You, a fisherman, are now to shepherd in His name and for Him. Your life is never to be yours again. Your life, all our lives, belong to the Master. There are still many yet to hear of God's love and of His Son's redemption. You must leave Rome, and go, be safe for more sheep are to be found and fed, and more lambs are to found and shepherded in Jesus' name."

Long and heavy moments passed.

Peter finally broke the quiet when he cleared his throat.

"Now I know why you have come, John. If I go, you are the one who will take my place."

"No!" John's voice was a gasp. "No. No, never…" John was being distracted. "No…it cannot be one of us." At that moment he understood why he had come to Rome. "Now I see why I am here…Peter, I was sent here to ease your doubts and to be a witness and messenger of the Lord. Peter, it is time to let go. We must pass the Word to the next Disciples…"

Peter slowly rose from his chair.

"Do you realize this is the first time you called me Peter? Throughout the night you called me Simon Peter."

"For now you are *Petros*. You are the rock—*Cephas*—the leader of His Church. You are the chosen one of God."

"Linus, Cornelius." Peter called out loudly.

The two men charged into the room only to find the Big Fisherman and John the Beloved facing and staring into each other's eyes.

"Linus, I will leave Rome, immediately," Peter said without breaking his stare. "It is time."

Cornelius looked at John, smiled an unspoken thank you, as Linus then poked Cornelius in the back to signify his pleasure at this announcement.

Peter turned and looking at the two men who had gotten a few steps of the doorway, said: "Cornelius, please send a message to my brother, Andrew, telling him I shall join him in Epirus. Then you will accompany John back to Ephesus; his work here is done. Linus, make ready my trip and wake Adessius and make sure he is ready to leave Rome with me."

In a soft but authoritative voice, Peter had spoken as head of the Twelve.

John fell to his chair. He closed his eyes and folded his hands in prayer with a smile on his lips, for the Lord never ceased to amaze him. He was thankful that Jesus never stopped whispering to him.

"Going with Adessius is very wise. No one would look suspiciously at a young boy and a grandfather walking the Roman roads," Cornelius spoke with assurance.

"I agree. I will make preparations. Adessius and I will be ready to leave when you are," Linus said with relief in his voice.

"No, Linus. No. You shall stay. You will take my place to continue on. Come here my son, and kneel"

"But Peter, who will care for you?"

"The Master."

"And what am I to do here in Rome? I am not a leader."

"You will receive the Spirit of the Lord; as I did, as John did and as the Others did. He will be your guide. None of us can call ourselves leaders for we are chosen to serve and do the Will of God."

Peter pointed to the space in front of him.

"Come, Linus, child of God and Herculeanus of Volterra. Come."

Linus glanced affectionately at John, who ignored his look but who quickly rose from his chair, walked, and stood slightly behind Peter. Slowly, Linus walked to Peter and knelt before him, and then Peter laid hands on his successor.

*

That night, Peter, Linus, and Adessius traveled into the city of Rome and found shelter with one of the many Roman Christians. In the dark early hours of the morning, Peter and the young boy, Adessius, slowly made their way down a street called *Vicus Cyclopis*, then to *Vicus Drusianus,* and finally through some winding Roman streets where they left Rome through the *Porta Capena.*

Peter decided to take the south *Via Appia* and eventually splinter off to a minor road and reach one of the seaports on the *Mare Hadriaticum* Adriatic Sea.

The *Via Appia* was an easy road to travel, for it was straight and superbly surfaced with massive blocks of volcanic stones. The road was called *regina viarum* queen of roads and was named after Appius Claudius Caecus, a Roman Senator who organized its construction. It was built to connect Rome, the *caput orbis* Head of the World to its provinces in the south. As the boy and Peter walked, the road grew busy with the early morning transportation of products for the city's population, thus creating a degree of anonymity. Adessius walked quietly by Peter's side holding his hand; not for guidance or help, but to protect this man whom he believed was a messenger of Jesus. The boy knew all about Jesus and of the love and goodness of God from this tall robust man. For hours, days, and years, he sat at Peter's feet and listened to the many stories, lessons and explanations this fisher of men relayed. He felt a strong and special relationship with this Galilean which was sealed eternally by God. Years before, his mother, Livilla, told him how Peter cured her son's illness.

As they walked along the Road, the boy occasionally glanced at Peter. Even in the dark, he could see Peter's face, and from the glow and distant look tried to imagine what story or time Peter was remembering about Jesus. Whenever a charging chariot or a fast wagon passed them, the boy would tighten his grip on Peter's big calloused hand, and Peter would look down at him and smile. The smile was to assure Adessius that everything was all right and that the boy did not need to fear. As they walked further from Rome, Peter began to feel uneasy. Something was missing. In all his travels through Judea, Samaria, Asia, Pontus, Bithynia, Cappadocia, Galatia and Rome, there was a feeling of companionship. He was never alone. He felt and knew that Jesus was with him—ever walking with him—but in this journey, he did not have this feeling and he worried. Peter found himself waiting to feel Jesus' presence.

The two travelers continued walking, and occasionally Adessius would ask Peter if he was well or if he wanted to stop, to which Peter would shake his head and continue along the road with his long heavy walking staff clicking loudly on the stone road. Other times, Peter would ask Adessius if he was well, and the boy would gleefully nod his head and smile; He was very happy to be with the Apostle, and at times, the sound of his small staff also could be heard clicking on the road.

After several hour's journey, noon came upon them. They both covered their heads with their hoods to provide some shade to their eyes.

Suddenly, Peter realized the cause of his uneasiness. It was going too slow. They should have been several miles away from Rome but they were not. This did not fit in with the other trips Peter had taken. He decided to stop to pray, in the belief that in conversing with Jesus he would find the reason for his slowness and of his feeling of loneliness.

As they sat on the side of the road, many travelers, vendors, merchants and military chariots passed. It was beginning to look like a normal day on the roads to Rome.

When Peter had finished his prayers, Adessius brought some oranges and some grapes and the two ate and talked.

"How are your parents, Adessius, and have you seen them lately?"

"They are well, Peter, but I have not seen them. My mother has left Rome for her sister's house. My father is in Rome. A few servants are at the *domus;* some with father but most are with mother.

"I thought the house was quiet earlier."

"Peter, do you think my father will ever come to be a believer?"

"My boy, you have no idea of the hours I have spent in prayer for that to happen, but it will happen in the Lord's good time. When the time and place for your father to come to Jesus is right; it will happen."

"I too have prayed and I am sure it will happen."

Peter smiled at the boy's admiration and love for his father.

Suddenly, in the distance, the two heard the sounds of loud singing.

Peter and Adessius jumped to their feet and looked up the road. People on the road scattered and hurried out of the way of an oncoming contingent of Roman soldiers running in tight formation around an open cart, which was drawn by two black stallions. In the back of the cart was a group of men, women and children huddled and singing together aloud. They were singing a psalm and Peter immediately recognized the Psalm.

"The Lord is my light and my salvation;
whom should I fear?
The Lord is my life's refuge;
of whom shall I be afraid?
When evildoers come at me
to devour my flesh,
My foes and my enemies
themselves stumble and fall.
Though an army encamp against me,
my heart will not fear...."

Peter immediately walked to the edge of the road. He planted his staff firmly in the ground, threw back his hood, and raising his right hand shouted, "Have faith in the Lord Jesus; He is with you."

Adessius was sure that with all the noise of marching feet, clanging armor, rumbling wheels on the stone road, and the singing prayer from the cart that no one could hear Peter, but still he looked up at Peter's face in esteem at his courage. Suddenly, he saw Peter's face change to surprise, and Peter looked down at the boy and drew him closely to him, hiding his face in his brown cloak and from the face of his mother on the cart.

After the cart had passed, Peter said hurriedly to the boy, "Come, we must move faster, Adessius, for we have more to travel."

He grabbed the boy's hand and quickly walked away.

"I must get you to safety," Peter said with great urgency.

At a faster pace, with his head lowered and his mind deep in thought, Peter wondered to whom he should deliver the boy. Many good Christian people came to his mind; among them were Clorisa and Rufus Pudens, who had befriended both Peter and Paul in days passed. He grew less anxious and sure he found someone to care for the youngster.

No wonder the large domus of the villa was so quiet today.

Walking along, Peter saw his sandaled feet jump out before him and from under his robe. He became totally engrossed in the act of walking; how it seemed to be of his will yet not of him, and then he became aware of his wooden staff and the road. Suddenly, he felt a very familiar presence and he smiled; Jesus was walking with him. He felt at peace for now he was certain he was doing the right thing by leaving Rome and Linus. He raised his head. He saw a Man in the distance walking to him going to Rome. He stopped walking when he saw the Man because he recognized this Person instantly. His face exploded with joy, and then in a moment his expression registered confusion.

The youngster walking by Peter looked up at him with concern.

"What is it Peter?" the boy asked and then following Peter's sight saw a Stranger walking towards them. He never saw the Stranger before, but for some strange reason he felt he knew Him for he immediately became comfortable. His concern for Peter faded as he watched the Stranger. He was awestruck by the expression of the love on His Face, and because of the color of His robe, Adessius recognized the Stranger as a Galilean.

Peter spoke with an apprehensive voice.

"*Domine, quo vadis?*" Lord where goest Thou? Peter asked in Latin.

Adessius was surprised that Peter would speak to a fellow Galilean in Latin.

"*Venio iterum crucifigi.*" I go to be crucified again, the Man answered in Latin.

Peter felt rebuked again and then his face glowed and his mind raced to the conclusion: *Lord, I will not abandon or deny You again.*

"Then I shall go with You to be crucified," Peter said quickly as he firmly planted his staff in the roadside. Leaving it there, he turned and started walking back to Rome.

Stunned, Adessius quickly raced after the two men and fell in step with them.

They walked in silence for a long distance and when Adessius looked over to the Stranger, He was gone. He looked quickly at Peter wanting to question him about the Stranger but was momentarily taken back with the look of joy and happiness that beamed from Peter's face.

"Peter, where is the Man?"

"Adessius, He is with us and we are with Him. I know that what will happen is His wish, and I will not desert Him or try to change His mind. Our God is good, for He always gives us other chances to amend our lives."

The young boy pretended to know what Peter was saying, but it was unimportant in comparison to his confusion over the disappearance of the Stranger. He was sure that he would eventually understand; until then, out of politeness, he returned to silence and continued to walk by Peter's side, glancing back occasionally in search of the Stranger.

They walked some distance when suddenly out of nowhere, Larius Camolius appeared by the side of the road. It seemed he was waiting for them and was expecting their arrival. On seeing his father, Adessius quickly started to run to him, but Peter, out of concern for the boy's ignorance, firmly grabbed him and held him to his side. With excitement and simple glee, the boy looked longingly after his father and it was then that he knew something was wrong. His father was not properly dressed.

He was clothed in plain, coarse material that did not flow over his body but simply hung on him. His sash was a cord and he had no cloak over his shoulders or sandals on his feet. The dirt and cuts from the road had blacked the skin on his feet. He looked like a slave, not a rich merchant. Equally disturbing to the boy was the missing tenderness in his father's eyes that the boy always got when he and his father met. Instead, he saw a tight, controlled face with sad eyes. Finally, Peter and Larius stood looking into each other's eyes.

Adessius immediately broke loose from Peter's grip and walked quickly to his father and embraced him.

"Peter, you know?"

"Yes, I saw as the cart passed us. What happened?"

"Her sister. She found out and reported them to the *Cohortes Urbanae* Roman City Police."

"Them?"

"She and our servants."

"Oh, Larius," Peter was filled with regret, but immediately he spoke with the authority of an Apostle, "My friend, they are with the Lord; there they will find fulfillment, and believe me, that is where they wanted to be."

"I know…and…I want to be assured of my place with them."

"Larius, do you believe?"

"Livilla and Cornelius were right; they told me that you did not know. My wife was recalling all the things you told her and the household. I always believed, Peter, but I had to continue on with my life to do good things for you and others. This was the reason for my absence at the *domus* when you came; I was making sure all was well while you stayed there."

Peter looked deeply into his eyes and could see the truth in what he was saying.

"They have burned our house and your quarters also. Linus could not recover any of your documents. They burned all your correspondence from the Others and everything of yours is lost. I am sorry." He fell to his knees before the tall fisherman. "I come to you looking like a slave, empty. Now I will accept Jesus openly and be like those in my household."

Peter smiled widely. Looking down he saw the expression on the face of Adessius. It was filled with greater joy than Peter could have imagined.

"Livilla has worked her first miracle. Come, Larius, let us find some running water and let me give you to Christ, your Redeemer."

"No, we cannot waste time, Peter. The authorities know you are on this road. Some people informed the contingent of soldiers escorting the cart that they heard you call to the prisoner; they know you are our leader."

"So we have little time left. Come, let us hurry and look earnestly."

The three hastily walked away and soon came upon a small rushing stream. Standing in the stream with Larius and Adessius standing nearby, Peter baptized his newest convert. As soon as the action was done, Peter instructed him to leave with Adessius.

"I am going back to Rome with my Lord. Peace be with you."

He promptly walked up the bank of the stream with great vigor. Larius watched Peter hurriedly walk back to Rome looking as if he had to catch up with someone.

A short distance from where he left Larius and Adessius, a group of well organized Roman soldiers were marching to him where they quickly surrounded him.

They girded him, and lead him away.

✳

Nero had his prizes, but the arrest of Peter was kept quiet for many days. When Linus heard of the arrest, he assembled many and prayed for Peter and Paul that God spare them much suffering. It was also rumored that Peter was being held in the dreaded *Tullianum* prison, later known as *Mamertine* Prison, and that Paul was soon to join him.

Tullianum was regarded as the worst prison to be incarcerated. Prisoners were known to die in this jail before trial, dying from disease or going raven mad. It was a jail located near the *Capitoline* Hill in the northwest corner of the Forum. It consisted of two rooms, one on top of the other. *Carcer,* the upper room, which was shaped like a *trapezium,* was used to hold prisoners awaiting trial or execution. The room was composed of blocks of tuff-stone, and before its use as a jail it had been used as a stone quarry. The lower room, which was a conical vault, was called the *Tullianum.* It was named after Tullus Hostillius, the creator of the jail, and was used for the maliciously condemned prisoner. It was a horrible dungeon that was dark, damp, cold and slimy. The odor it released was stomach wrenching, for it was never cleaned. It was the most isolated place in the world. Jugurtha, King of Numidia, and the Gallic leader, Vercingetorix, two great enemies of Rome, had been held and died in this prison and when facing death they both rushed to it with pleasure.

At his arrest, Peter was chained to a column in an upright position in the *tullianum* lower room. He was unable to sit or lie down. The darkness of the cell devoured him, and he was greeted by vermin and large, hungry rats. Without fear, he accepted his fate as a blessing, and at this moment he thanked Jesus for this gift; he was untouched by anything in the cell.

Softly, he began to sing: "Have mercy on me, O God, have mercy on me:

For my soul trusteth in Thee.
And in the shadow of Thy wings will I hope,
until iniquity pass away.
I will cry to God the most High:
to God who hath done good to me.
He hath sent from heaven and delivered me;
He hath made them a reproach that trod upon me.
God hath sent His mercy and His truth, and He hath
delivered my soul from the midst of the young lions..."

The guards on watch, who were used to cries and screams of near insanity, listened in complete shock, for this prisoner's voice was filled with softness and warmth. Processus, a jailer, stood and watched the trapped door to the cell and was astonished to see light radiating from the small cracks in the wooden floor. He was immediately unnerved. Many moments passed and finally, when the light failed to go away, and believing that what he was seeing was an evil sign, he prodded his companion Martinianus.

"Please see what I see?" Processus asked with a trembling voice.

"By Jupiter! How in Pluto could that be?" His amazed companion shouted.

"It's a sign from the netherworld. I heard that Christians do such things."

"Nonsense," Martinianus said. "Open the trap and see what it is."

"Not I!"

"A great Roman soldier you are." Martinianus said as he walked roughly to the trap door. Covering his nose and mouth, he threw open the door and quickly jumped back and fell to the floor. Processus was quickly forced to cover his face with his cloak, not from the stench, but from the blinding light from the cell.

Soon they regained their composure and with a bravery they never knew they had, slowly approached the trap and looked into the circular chamber. To their astonishment the prisoner, Peter of Galilee, stood between two illuminated images. The two images cast a light so bright that the two jailers could not make out their facial features.

"Come down, Processus and Martinianus. Join us. Let us tell you of Jesus."

The two men cautiously descended the steps to the dungeon and into the light.

For seven shifts, these two jailors listened to Peter. They remained very secretive about these conversations with the Apostle, and as time passed, they discovered that other jailors were talking to Peter as well. After three weeks, forty-eight jailors had been guests of Peter and none of them remembered the darkness or the stench of the dungeon.

One day, Processus and Martinianus descended the steps of the dungeon and told Peter that they felt the breath of Jesus and asked to be received into the new faith. The moment they made their wishes known, a small stream of water miraculously sprung from the side of the dungeon wall, and Peter baptized them. Before Peter left the dungeon, he would baptize forty-eight of his guards and all from the same stream of water.

Three weeks later, a Roman centurion of the *Augustan Cohort* and a member of the *Region VIII Forum Romanum*, named Julius Marcus Solarius, arrived at *Tullianum*. His arrival prompted Processus and Martinianus to once again become Roman guards. The centurion walked around the *Carcer* inspecting the condition of the prison when he finally came to the two jailors. He looked at them for a long, penetrating moment. Finally, he smiled.

"Relax, guards. I have heard that you have jailed Peter of Galilee, is this true?"

The two jailors looked at each other obviously not wanting to answer the centurion.

"Guards, I have asked you a question."

Still they remained silent.

"Has the prisoner been speaking to you?"

The jailors lowered their eyes, but their eyes bolted up when Julius Solarius drew his sword from his scabbard. They believed they were doomed.

Slowly, Julius lowered his sword and with the point of the sword drew a poor replica of a fish. When he finished, he spoke lowly and in Greek, the word, *Ichthus*.

Immediately, the tension on the faces of the jailors turned to joy as they recognized the Christian sign.

"So he has spoken to you." He smiled. "Have no fear; I know the power these men of Christ have. I escorted Paul from Caesarea and was subjected to his power."

He replaced his sword and took a step closer to the two guards.

"Paul has been sentenced to death by the Prefect Praetorian, Gaius Ophonius Tigellinus. He will be taken here today. You are to inform Peter. You are also to tell him that we have news of John and Cornelius' safe departure out of Rome. We have nothing more on their whereabouts but they are safe. Assure Peter that I shall try to make his and Paul's stay here as pleasant as possible."

He turned to walk, then stopped, and looking over his shoulder said warmly, "Do not be foolish. Your bravery and your loyalty to Peter is commendable, but let me repeat to you what I was told by Paul. 'Let the Lord's will be done. Do nothing to stop it, for it is His Will. I have done my part; after I leave, you must do yours. Live on to fulfill your calling; to prove your own work; to glory in Christ alone.' My brothers in Christ, we have many hours, days, and years to make recompense for our lives. Live to make that recompense by remaining alive in the example of these two men."

He turned and walked out of the jail.

The two guards immediately went to Peter.

Three hours later, Paul of Tarsus arrived with the centurion Julius Solarius and two troopers of the *Praefectus Urbi* Urban Cohorts, who were from the Office of the City Prefect; the Roman Police.

Processus and Martinianus examined the small man and then looked at each other in silent disbelief. Without speaking, they knew what each was thinking: How could this diminutive red-haired man be the fiery lion of Christ?

Once the door of the jail was closed, Julius and his two accompanying troopers hastily removed Paul's restrains.

"Thank you," Paul said in a soft voice to the guards. Peter's two guards felt a strength in this man's voice. With equal softness, but with authority, he asked, "Where is Peter?"

Quickly, Processus moved to the floor door and opened it and descended the steps to the dungeon, and with equal speed brought Peter up to the carcer.

The two disheveled men stood silently looking at each other. From their appearance and clothing they looked like two long forgotten beggars.

Martinianus and Processus removed the chains on Peter's hands and the two men embraced.

Peter's height and girth enveloped and smothered the short and thin man, but somehow they appeared as equals, and when they parted they both had smiles on their faces. They continued to hold each other at arm's length.

"Well, Paul, we have finally arrived. It seems the Lord is calling us to Him. My soul and heart beat with boyish anticipation."

"No more or no less than mine, for finally I will once again see the glory of His Being."

"Your companions, Luke and Mark?"

"Gone. All are gone but Tychicus whom I just released, and yours?"

"Cornelius has left with a guest," Peter replied with caution, but he was sure Paul knew the guest was John bar Zebedee, "and I have appointed Linus to take my place."

"So, the baton is passed to a new generation. We have run the race," Paul said with a smile on his small face.

"We have little time. I ask your forgiveness. I once harbored ill thoughts toward you in the beginning," Peter said as tears began to build in his eyes.

"Peter, there is no need for any apology, but I forgive you. I have a certain roughness to my personality that I know is abrasive to people. This is my thorn. I thought you and the Others were not suitable for the ministry and I thought I knew better than you. However, James, Matthias, James, Bartholomew and the Others have given as much as I have and perhaps more. You must, in the name of the Others, forgive me for being so condescending and disrespectful. You were first to the Lord; I sometimes forgot that."

The guards watched in reverence as the two forgave one another.

"Then we are done here?" Paul asked with a small smile on his face.

"Yes," Peter replied with great certainty.

"I am a little afraid. Not of pain and death, but afraid if we have done all that we were called to do."

"What we had to do is now accomplished. The rest is for others to do. As you said, we have run the race that was ours to run."

Paul smiled.

Julius walked to a small table off to the side and unwrapped a red cloak he was carrying. He prepared the unleavened bread and wine. The two guards that arrived with Paul immediately walked to the heavy wooden door of the jail and stood against it.

"Come Paul, let us for the last time celebrate the Meal together."

Silently, they walked to the small table.

Processus took one of the oil lamps, which hung from the wall, and placed it on the table. The two Apostles repeated the words and the actions of the Last Supper. When they finished, Peter was chained and returned to the dungeon. Paul was chained to the wall and all night the two prayed for each other, for their murderers, and for forgiveness from anything they had failed to do for Jesus.

During the night, two unknown Praetorian Guards, and fifteen guards of the *Praefectus Urbi*, arrived and relieved the Centurion Julius Solarius of his charge. Paul was quickly and quietly escorted outside the walls of the city of Rome past the pyramid of Cestius and on to the *Via Ostia*. There, just at dawn, he was beheaded in accordance with the privileges of a Roman citizen, on the charges of propagating a forbidden religion, which was regarded as treason against the Emperor.

Moments after Paul was taken, a small cohort of the *Praefectus Urbi* arrived and relieved Julius Marcus Solarius, Processus, and Martinianius of their duty and bound Peter tightly. He looked at Julius Marcus and said in a whisper, "Seek out John and tell him what has happened, and tell him that I am waiting for him."

One of the guards heard part of the conversation and quickly stuffed a dirty cloth in his mouth.

"This will be a precaution," the guard said, "for I have been told that his words could change the minds of men."

Quickly, they rushed Peter out of the jail with Julius Marcus Solarius, Processus and Martinianus following.

Blinded by the early sunlight, unkempt and tired, Peter walked upright to the cart that was to transport him through the city. During his ride, his face beamed with joy, for this day he was promised a meeting with Jesus. This was the day he was born into eternity. They drove him past the Temple of Juno and into *Campus Martius*. The faint smell of the burned *insula* apartments of *Subura* was still in the air. Soon, they were joined by a unit of Roman executioners, the Lectors with their rods and axes, the Titular who heralded the crime of Peter, and other who would pin him to the cross from the *Region VIII Forum Romanum Capitoline Mons*. The procession crossed over the Tiber and onto the foot of *Vaticanus Mons*, which was also called the Mount of Prophesy. In this marshy district of ill repute, on a low-lying part of Rome, the soldiers bound two tree trunks together to form a cross. Someone had axed the bottom of the tree so that it would penetrate the soil of Rome while the rest of the tree was left crude.

Just like the Cross of Jesus, Peter thought in retrospect. Delighted that he was to be crucified, he shouted loudly in Latin, "*Ecce Crucem Domini*" Behold the Cross of the Lord.

Two of the executioners grabbed Peter and threw him to the ground and with crude and harshly fibered rope tied his body to the tree. They nailed his arms to the *patibulum* crossbar and then began nailing him to the *stipes* upright. As they began to raise the cross to plant it in the hole in the ground they had prepared, Peter shouted, "NO!" He looked in the crowd at familiar faces and seeing Julius, Processus and Martinianus said in a tearful voice, "Tribune, I am not worthy to be crucified as my Lord was."

The executioners stopped and looked at the captain of the *Praefectus Urbi* for directions and without hesitation, he quickly shouted, "Give the traitor his wish; it will only cause him more pain."

So they crucified Peter upside down to make him worthy.

Julius Marcus Solarius watched the look on the captain's face and he knew that the two guards, Processus and Martinianus, had been discovered. Their faces, full of grief, did not help distract the captain's suspicions. Julius Marcus Solarius quietly slipped away and soon was far from the scene. He had one more thing to do for Peter: he had to send word to John that Peter and Paul were with the Lord.

From his cross, Peter saw the world upside down, but he still could recognize the Phrygian, the sanctuary of Cybele, and Attis in the near distance. Overjoyed with the knowledge that his time was near, he began to sing Psalms of thanksgiving and praise to God. Those around him mocked him and some threw stones at him but still, he remained joyful and accepted all this for the love of Jesus. He began preaching to those near him and shouted to boats and barges passing on the Tiber; and his voice was heard by the multitude.

Later he was heard, saying softly, "Lord, this time I have not denied Thee. Lord, with Thee I have gone to prison and death, and now I lay down my life for Thee. Let my sufferings be offered for my sins, and let my blood become the root for your Church on earth."

A crowd formed. Some were Christians who courageously stood watch over his dying moments with silent prayers. Many just passed by wanting to appear as observers. Regardless of who came, the many Roman soldiers observed all who were there, for they had been ordered to give a report of anyone who was suspected of being a Christian.

After several hours, Peter's chest began to grow warm. He knew within a short time that his chest would begin to burn and thirst would come to his mouth. He could feel the blood warm his face, scalp, and his eyes, and he was sure his eyes were red with blood. With no regard for his pain, he continued to preach to all those around him. He began giving instructions to those who understood the Christian way. Finally, he called on God to bless his executioners and tormenters and show them mercy.

It began to rain and the raindrops chilled him. As the raindrops raced down his naked body, they washed some of the filth from his body and some of his blood streamed away like small veins over the dark brown earth. Some of the drops eased his thirst; some rushed up his nose burning the passages.

An hour passed, then another, and as he approached his third hour, he grew silent.

A Praetorian guard walked over to Peter carrying a thick heavy club, and with a great swing of the club broke both his legs. No one knew why this was done, though some concluded that it was only to torture Peter and give joy to the Romans. Peter did not react; his thoughts were elsewhere.

Looking across the Tiber, he saw four young men walking towards him. The rain did not bother them and in each of their hands were thick staffs which did not serve any practical purpose. He knew who they were and the sight of them excited him. They stopped in the distance watching as if they were waiting for him. He tried to shout their names, but his mouth was too dry and parched. Then he saw another Man coming from the other direction. He walked briskly up the mount and joined the Others. His hair was playfully tossed by the wind. The wind pushed the snow-white robe against His body outlining His chest and legs. His face wore a wide smile; it was Jesus. The five of them stood watching and waiting, when suddenly the Man in white began walking down to the banks of the Tiber River and stood by the shore.

The day slowly faded into night.

With all the strength he could muster, Peter moistened his parched lips with his tongue, and taking a painfully heavy breath shouted, "Lord, I know it is Thee, bid me come to Thee."

Jesus turned, opened his arms and Peter heard the thunderous, "Come."

Peter felt free and he could see and feel himself walk slowly over the refreshing waters of the Tiber and as he walked he heard His Master say, "Come Peter, Fisher of men, Shepherd of My Flock, Rock of my Church; I know Thou truly loves Me."

Peter smiled and his eyes were fixed on the face of Jesus as he continued to walk on the waters.

Epilogue

Cornelius and John boarded a barge by the Tiber dock and traveled down the river away from Rome to Ostia. In Ostia they walked briskly down *Decumanus Maximus*, the main street, and were swallowed in the confusion and commotion of the street. John could not control his curiosity. His eyes moved in all directions, touring his surroundings; trying to capture everything. He glanced with fascination at the many living quarters stacked on another called the *insula*. He wondered why people would willingly live in these tall wooden structures on top of each other. On the right side of the street, he saw the Baths of Neptune and with disdain looked away. This was a place where naked men bathed together. The shamelessness of viewing naked bodies was an affront to his Christian ideas and Judean heritage. Walking further, they approached the *horrea* corn warehouses and the shouts and bartering of the merchants drowned out all the noise of the city. They hurried along with the intent of boarding a ship that was destined for Ephesus. Arriving there, they found the docks well-guarded. The Roman soldiers were stopping all passengers, and Cornelius could see several informers standing with the soldiers identifying Christians. Somehow, the Roman heard of Peter and John's escape. Knowing that they would be identified and arrested, Cornelius quickly directed John away from the ship. They rushed through the city and down the *Cardo Maximus* to the southern *Porta* gate that leads out of Ostia. Once outside the city walls, they took an infrequently traveled dirt road that cut into the thick pine and cypress trees of the nearby forest. After several hours, they left the forest and traveled south on the coastline of *Latium,* which for the most part was sparsely populated. As they passed the *Albanus Mons* Alban Hills with its two crater lakes and the extinct volcano Mount Cavo, Cornelius explained that many of the *villas* on this mount were owned by Roman Senators.

"They were built so that the Senators could escape the oppressive heat of Rome. The Consuls often celebrated the *Feriae Latinae* Holiday of the Latins on the summit, at the sanctuary of *Jupiter Latiaris* Temple. The volcano has been dormant for many years but someday God will have His way."

They moved along the dirt road, cautiously avoiding contact with anyone, and if they did cross paths, Cornelius' greetings were quick and uncaring.

"We have to get to Antium before dark. Though these roads are guarded by mercenary soldiers at scattered way stations, it is not good to travel by night. It is a dangerous and a foolish thing to do; there are too many robbers, revolutionaries, and other unsavory citizens that prey on travelers," Cornelius said, then as an afterthought he added, "and much to my regret, some unscrupulous Roman soldiers."

John felt very secure with Cornelius and trusted the decisions he made. Nevertheless, he could not help but see a shade of uneasiness on Cornelius' face.

"What is wrong?"

"John, remember, you are not to talk."

"But no one is here."

"All the more reason for you to practice silence." Smiling, he looked ahead and continued, "Antium is a favorite sea resort for Nero. In fact, it is where he and Emperor Claudius were born."

His face wrinkled as he spoke, "I do not think the Emperor will be there. Still, the very idea of being that close to anything of Nero is frightening, but we have no choice. Staying at a roadside inn is almost as dangerous as the roads at night, besides, I am sure all the inns leading from Rome will be guarded, so we must travel to Antium, for it is beginning to get dark."

They quickened their pace.

"When we arrive at our destination, I will not reveal your identity to anyone. It is best that few people know you. Tomorrow we will leave early so as to travel safer and longer. Eventually, we will join the *Via Appia* and go deeper into Campania."

They arrived in the small town of Antium where a Christian by the name of Maximus Bolarius, the son of a companion of Cornelius, made them stay in his *villa* which was built on the side of a cliff. They were greeted with old news that Peter had made it out of Rome and was on his way to Southern *Italia*. They were overjoyed to hear this; certain that they too would be soon out of Rome's reach. They were immediately given water and a change of clothing that was a grade below their own clothing which made them look like ordinary travelers. The servants gloated, and during the night after resting, the family gathered for the Meal, which Cornelius conducted which John silently and happily partook.

In the early morning, Maximus Bolarius supplied them with a horse, a cart and some provisions. With a cart filled with hay, a horse, the livestock fed, and their well hidden provisions, they continued south along the coastline and before night they arrived at the town of Tarracina on the Tyrrhenian Sea. Once again, Cornelius found lodging in the *villa* of a very wealthy Christian named Octius Doracius who was a friend of Cornelius. Octius had been stationed with Cornelius in Judea and was baptized by Peter. They were assigned a room that was immediately tended by a servant who told the travelers that he was a Christian. After they bathed and rested, they were taken down the long central hallway into a large common room where they ate and enjoyed many fruits, dates, and nuts dipped in honey. Later fish stock soup was served and after all had calmed, Cornelius spoke to their host of Jesus. Throughout his talk, John yearned to speak but didn't and when the Meal was celebrated with Cornelius presiding, John longed for his voice to be heard.

Early next morning with a fresh horse and jugs of water, the two refugees traveled in silence over a narrow picturesque road with giant crags and pointed rocks. They continued for some time and eventually left the road and began traveling northeast to the city of Fondi, which was on the *Via Appia*. During this trip, Cornelius reminded John that he was to continue acting as a mute and to keep himself well-covered.

"Your Latin is poor and it will give you away. Your Galilean face will cause suspicion but being a slave of a former centurion is common and being a mute will kill all suspicion; so remain silent," Cornelius cautioned.

As they traveled, they came upon a group of slaves repairing the road. Encompassing the slaves were soldiers and guards. Some of the sentinels and senior Roman soldiers were lounging on the grassy roadside. The sight immediately disturbed John and Cornelius. Cornelius was disturbed by the presence of the Roman guards, but John was distressed by the condition of the slaves who were being physically abused. One of the slaves, an elderly man, slipped and fell. A guard ran to the slave and whipped him while he held the man in place by standing on his ankles. The slave was screaming in agony but the soldier continued to beat him.

John immediately jumped from the cart and getting a jug of water, ran to the slave. His hood flew off his head and beamed on his Galilean face. He knelt by the man and using his palm as a cup offered the slave some water. The guard's whip came down, and John offered his back in protection of the slave.

"B'shelya! Silence!" Cornelius shouted in Aramaic to John as he raced to the sentry who was about to strike again.

"Fellow Roman," Cornelius said as he gripped the sentry's arm. "Excuse my slave; he is a mute and does not understand that slaves are not treated as kindly as he is."

The sentry immediately eased the tension in his arm and looked long and hard at Cornelius.

"I am centurion Cornelius Sabatinius of the *Cohors II Italiac Civium Romanorum,* and this is my servant."

"Sorry, centurion."

"It is fine. Forgive my servant." He reached down and lifted John by the arm and pulled him away.

The sentry grabbed the old slave and pulled him to his feet and the slave, knowing he was spared, limped away.

Cornelius led John to the cart. They climbed aboard and nonchalantly drove away. As they moved away, Cornelius called back to the sentries, "Rome is proud of your work," but from his tone, John knew that Cornelius was controlling his temper. When they were some distance from the work crew, Cornelius, in a controlled voice, said to John, "Son of Zebedee, if you ever do anything like that again, you will not have to worry about the Romans killing you."

"I was not worried about Rome or your wrath, Cornelius; I was worried about the wrath of God for our indifference."

Cornelius turned and looked at John. "You are right. Forgive me, but you did not come to Rome to die. Jesus has other reasons for you being here, and we are trying to get you out of Nero's reach, so that you will have a long life to do the Master's Will."

Cornelius stopped the cart and started tending to John's wounds, and John felt the gentleness of this Christian brother.

That night, they arrived at Fondi and were taken in by Lucius Dartinius, a retired Tribune whom Cornelius knew from childhood. The Tribune was an old friend of Larius Camolius.

John could not determine if the Tribune was a Christian. He listened as the two Romans exchanged niceties and bits of news from Rome, when suddenly, the Tribune stopped talking to Cornelius and looked at John and said, "And you John, the Apostle, how is Cornelius treating you?"

John looked at Cornelius for instructions.

"You may speak, John, Dartinius is a convert of Peter. He visited Lacius' *villa* often and was there the night you arrived; though you did not know it. He is the one who has made all the arrangements for our departure, which we have so easily abandoned. He is now making new arrangements for us."

"John, I apologize, the living quarters are a bit primitive, but they are the best we can do. Everyone is in danger these days and is being careful."

John let out a gasp of relief and spoke, and did most of the talking the rest of the night. After he celebrated the Meal, they retired.

Before dawn, they rose. With a fresh horse and a mule attached to the cart with fresh water jugs and a wine skin on his back, plus more hidden provisions in the hay and feed, they left. Sitting on the back of the cart were two Christian servants from Lucius' household. Lucius Dartinius escorted them on horseback for several miles until he was certain of their safety. He was able to get them through some heavily guarded road checks. After some distance from their last road check, they stopped.

"You see how things have changed since you left Rome. From here the road checks will be less frequent. Cornelius, I am certain you can get by them." His mouth widened to a big broad smile. "If, Cornelius, your name does not carry any authority; you can invoke my name." Dartinius dismounted and knelt for John's blessing. He mounted his horse and left them calling back, "The Lord be with you. Cornelius, tell Priscus Capuanius that I send my regards."

They continued down the *Via Appia* all that day making good progress. That night, they hid deep in the bush and forest far from the road, purposely avoiding the city of Mintrunae because Cornelius knew of no Christians in the city. Early the next morning, they continued their journey, again making great progress. Late that night, arriving just outside of the city of Sinuessa, they took refuge in the barn of a Christian named Vincus Tarminius who was a blacksmith. Very early the next day, the two Christian servants of Dartinius went on ahead of John and Cornelius to the city of Capua, because Cornelius knew the two slaves would be able to get into the city cunningly and avoid the sentry post. After the two departed, fresh provisions were loaded on the cart and they continued on their journey. John noticed Cornelius was deliberately driving the horses at a slow pace. As they moved along, they passed a small group of travelers traveling north from Capua. After they had passed, and they were alone on the road, Cornelius said lightly, "John, we are alone now, you can speak."

John looked at him and stubbornly made several silent moments pass before he spoke.

"You are worried."

"Yes," Cornelius said, "Capua is at the end of the *Via Appia*; from here, many small roads lead further south and to the seaports. There are many soldiers and sentries in this city. They know many Christians are trying to escape."

"If you are so worried, why did we come here?"

"Because we have connections here, and they alone can take us out of *Italia*. You heard Dartinius asked to be remembered by Priscus Capuanius; he is our contact. Peter converted him and made him leader of the Christians here."

"Why are you telling me all this?"

"To appraise you of our situation and in case we are separated."

Cornelius turned and looked at John.

"I'm afraid the Romans know of me being a Christian more than they know who you are. This worries me, for I may be putting you in danger. I am not afraid of Rome or of dying, but I am afraid of you being captured."

John was surprised, for he did not realize that Cornelius was a burden to him, because John thought that he was a burden to the centurion.

They returned to silence.

"Capua gives me unpleasant memories," John said, desperately wanting to ease the moment, and because he was unable to remember why the name of this city created a shadow in his mind.

"Ah, John, you know your history. This is the city in which the slave Spartacus was trained and revolted against Rome," Cornelius said, pleased to discover John was somewhat versed in Roman history.

Cornelius returned his attention to driving the cart. Looking over the head of the horse and seeing the road was becoming crowded again, he said, "John, remember you are a mute."

"Again," John said in a low whisper.

Cornelius smiled.

They had traveled for half an hour when, Cornelius suddenly sat erect. John followed his sight, and saw Dartinius' servants and another man riding on a cart and approaching them on the opposite side of the Appian Way. The on-coming cart stopped and both slaves jumped from the cart and one of them called out, "Sir, please, we seem to be having trouble with one of the wheels on our cart; could you help us?"

Cornelius passed them and pulled over to the side of the road at some distance. He quickly jumped from his cart and rushed to the other.

"Stay here," He ordered.

John looked back and saw the servants and Cornelius pretending to make some repairs to the cart and surmised that they were conversing. He looked at the man who stood away from the cart. The man smiled at John, and John sensed this was Priscus Capuanius. John was extremely surprised with his youth and the glow of sanctity that radiated from him. The man whom John believed was Priscus slowly walked back and forth watching the road. Priscus quickly went and stood by Cornelius who was pretending to repair the damaged cart. John could not see what was happening, but he was sure there was much discussion.

Finally, Cornelius stood up and backed away from the cart, inspecting what repairs were supposedly made. He loudly said, "That should make things right. I hope you have a safe trip."

"Oh, thank you good Roman," Priscus said.

Cornelius swiftly walked back to his cart and when he reached it, he climbed into the seat and quickly gave the horse charge to move.

John immediately knew something was wrong, for Cornelius' face was pale and his lips were quivering and he wore a grave and somber look.

Priscus and the servants remained by their cart.

"We are not going to Capua. It is too dangerous. It seems they know we are headed this way. Everyone who has helped us has been arrested. Arrangements have been made for us at Neapolis, but we must hurry and be cautious. Cover your head and remember; you are a slave and a mute," Cornelius said as he pulled his hood over his head, and John did likewise. Cornelius proceeded to turn the cart around and away from Capua.

As they passed the two slaves and Priscus once again, the young man slightly nodded his head and John accepted this as a sign of Priscus' respect. They rode away and soon Priscus and his companions were far from their sights. Then they made a quick turn and were off the Appian Way and on a small road swallowed up by the forest. They traveled in total silence for a long time, bouncing and rocking on the poor road with its many holes. Each passing mile and the heaviness of their silence made John become aware of the weight of concern the centurion carried. Quickly, he uttered a prayer for Jesus to protect Cornelius and to ease his concern, and then having nothing more to do, he further prayed in thanksgiving for those who had helped them and finally, in thanks for Peter's safety. Unexpectedly, a stabbing thought crossed his mind. *Paul!* In their excitement to leave for safety he had forgotten that Paul had been under arrest, and immediately he uttered a prayer for God's mercy and protection. As soon as he completed his prayer, a strange awareness came over him; he was certain that Paul was dead; that he was killed by the Romans, and that he was with Jesus. Instantly, he accepted this revelation as truth and turned quickly to say something to Cornelius, and it was then that he became aware of the Roman soldiers coming quickly towards them.

✳

Since his arrest, his hands were tied behind his back and attached to a metal bracket in the floor of the cart. The rope was so tight that his hands were numb. The rope burned on his flesh and he was certain that his wrists were raw and stripped of skin from his twisting and pulling. Cornelius and he were separated immediately when suddenly Cornelius was quickly whisked away and hurriedly sped off in a chariot. The fact that John was a slave made him secondary and of less importance. There was no doubt in his mind that Cornelius was the target of the arrest.

The two guards assigned to transport John mostly ignored him, except to occasionally harass or mock him. For hours they traveled along small bumpy side roads. John was hungry, thirsty, and tired. He was impatient that he had to remain a mute. At first, he enjoyed the part, but he was growing tired and was beginning to think that he should suddenly pretend to be cured. The thought of creating a cure amused him momentarily, as he imagined the chaos such a cure would create. He knew he would enjoy watching the expression on his captor's faces, but he quickly rejected this idea; it would trivialize the Lord's miracles.

Like Cornelius said, they do not know who I am, and being unknown helps me remain safe. Like Peter, I have more years to live. I am sure the Master has other things for me to do before He calls me to His Side.

His sore and bonded wrist became less of a concern as he worried what had become of Cornelius. His guard's conversation caught his attention.

"They are killing them off by the hundreds. Many of them are being crucified like that criminal they follow. Others are being burned alive, and still others are simply being given to the wild animals. I never realized there were so many of them. They are all over the Empire," the young guard said.

"I also heard that there was a lot of loot to be had. The homes and properties of the Christians are like an open market after they have been put to death; that's the best way to treat a heretic," the older guard added.

John closed his eyes and wished he could close his ears as well; so he quickly prayed. *Master, I know there is a reason for this persecution and I accept Your will, but please, I ask You to help those in pain and suffering for Your Name's sake; may they come to You with little suffering.*

"I agree, but it seems the more they kill the more there are. I was surprised to hear that Cornelius was one of them, and now I am told that there are many others in our ranks," the young guard said.

"May the gods urinate on them and vomit them into Hades," the older guard said with anger in his voice.

They became silent.

"We must be nearing the city," John heard one say.

"Yes, I can see that the roads are getting busy."

The cart moved onto a better road and continued slowly. John saw more people and more passing carts.

In the late hours of the night they arrived at their destination where John was roughly whisked away and placed in a barn chained between his two guards. The next morning, the guards chained him to a post and disappeared. John spent his morning in prayer, thinking of the many people who might be suffering for the love of the Master. Finally, he gave thanks for all the joys the martyrs would experience in being with Jesus. After completing his prayers, he grew peaceful and was sure that his life was not endangered and that nothing other than a beating was awaiting him, yet the idea of suffering for Jesus enflamed him with anticipation; he became jubilant.

His guards returned and with them was a very young centurion. John surmised that the centurion must have been recently promoted to this rank for his breastplate, scabbard, and other parts of his uniform, were new and polished. One of the guards pulled John to his feet.

"My name is Gaius Taminius." The young centurion said. "I am a centurion for the magistrate of Herculaneum who sent me to interrogate you about your master Cornelius."

"Centurion, we were told when we arrested him that he could not speak," the older guard said.

"But he can hear!" Gaius Taminius shouted roughly wanting to appear firm and in command. "Did you not interrogate him?"

"No, sir, that was not our orders."

The centurion shook his head in disbelief and in frustration said, "Leave us. Go stand guard outside. I'll question him."

The two guards saluted and swiftly left the barn.

Alone, the centurion looked intensely at John, then with a small smile he said, "Cornelius has been charged with being a Christian and..." The centurion removed his sword from its scabbard and with its point, drew a crude fish on the barn's dirt floor. "...he stands before the Magistrate of Herculaneum while we speak. He will most likely be put to the sword."

John looked at the centurion's drawing and recognized the crude image of a fish - *ICHTHUS* - and he knew what it meant, but he did not dare speak. Cornelius had made him suspicious of everyone and had told him of the tricks and deceptions Rome was capable of doing.

"There were enough witnesses against Cornelius to have him executed three times over. As soon as you are comfortable and presentable, I will take you to the city."

The centurion looked over his shoulder and from the wide spaces between the wooden slats of the barn wall could see that the guards were still posted where he had commanded them. He moved closer to John, and in a low voice said, "They do not know who you are, and if things remain this way we should be able to get you out of Herculaneum and on your way."

Again, John showed no reaction.

"Guards," Gaius Taminius shouted loudly and the unexpected loudness and sharpness of his voice startled John.

The two guards came running into the barn.

"You are correct, this man is useless and as stupid as a barbarian. Get the prisoner some water to bathe. He smells like a barn animal; see if you can get someone to give him new clothes; do it immediately."

The two guards rushed out of the barn and disappeared.

"We do not have much time," Gaius Taminius said in a low controlled voice. "Just remain silent and dumb and we will have you out of harm's way by nightfall. The magistrate, Malius Fulatus, is an elderly man who already is tired of this day's work. Being Cornelius' traveling companion was not made known to Fulatus, because the orders to stop Cornelius came from Rome. If he knew who you were, he would have ordered you to die."

John closed his eyes and prayed to Jesus.

Soon the two guards returned with water, clothing and food. Leaving everything on two wooden stools near John, they quickly left the barn, followed by Gaius Taminius. John washed and changed clothes, which surprisingly fit him perfectly; Gaius Taminius entered the barn and ordered his old clothes to be burned.

Now clean, he was given some stale bread and olives, and after eating, his hands were again tied behind his back, but not as severely. A unit of four Roman soldiers appeared, and Gaius Taminius discharged John's former guards ordering them back to Capua. He advised them that he and his small unit would escort the prisoner into Herculaneum.

The two guards happily saluted and quickly took the cart heading back to Capua.

Another cart came to the barn door. John was placed in the back, and with a jerk began his journey to the town. After traveling a short distance, Gaius Taminius ordered the cart to halt and one of the Roman guards went to John to free his hands. Then they continued on and twenty minutes later they arrived in the town of Herculaneum.

Herculaneum was a small town founded by the Greeks and named after Hercules. It was a pleasant town that had many oddities to it, among which were its neatly organized streets with simple, close, rectangular houses and shops. It was a town without a *Forum*, a trademark of the Romans; every Roman city had one. Nonetheless, Herculaneum had an arena and a gymnasium where athletes wrestled, raced, and boxed. The main street, the *Via Maximus*, had homes with extended roofs and second story porches supported by large beams, shading the walkways where venders sold their wares out of baskets and jars. Pedestrians ruled the *Via Maximus*, because it was against the law for chariots or carts to use this street. The street was dotted with three fountains: one surrounded a statue of Hercules, another washed over the statue of the goddess Venus, and the other at a tribute to the Emperor Augustus Caesar.

The moment John entered the town a deep sorrow came over him. He grew uneasy and could not understand what was wrong. Suddenly, a breeze passed carrying a strong and definite odor. He instantly grew nauseous. He covered his mouth and held his breath. Only once before had he experienced this odor, it was the day Jesus called Lazarus from his grave. It was the stench of death. He knew he was being shown something, something in the future, but he did not know what it was. The cart continued on its way, and they drove onto one of the secondary streets, and from these roads, John saw *Mons Vesuvius* in the distance.

True to his promise, Gaius Taminius boarded John on a ship heading south and away from Rome, but before boarding the ship, Gaius Taminius went aboard and John watched as he spoke secretly to a man whom John concluded was the captain. When Gaius returned, they boarded the ship and were greeted by a short plump man with a long, graying beard, and a warm, smiling face. His name was Mihay; John instantly knew that he was a Roman Jew. The three walked away from the boarding plank as the ship continued to be loaded with goods to be carried down the coast of *Italia*.

"I shall travel a small ways with you and then you will be with Mihay, who is a Christian," Gaius Taminius said while Mihay bowed to John. "He will escort you to Epirus near Macedonia. Once you embark there, he will give you over to another one of our contacts and that person will escort you to Ephesus. Once again, you must continue to remain silent, and please, for our sake, refrain from preaching. If you must speak, please wait until you have traveled far down the coast and away from Rome. Please understand that this is for your safety and for our benefit; we cannot lose you." The centurion sat on the deck and patted it with his hand for John to sit beside him. John obeyed. In a whisper, Gaius Taminius continued, "All those whom you knew, met or saw in your time here have been arrested or killed for the love of the Lord."

John looked sadly at the young centurion; he had guessed this.

"Well maybe not all, Linus is the exception; he is in hiding." The young centurion looked around quickly and moving closer to John continued, "What is happening here will spread throughout the Empire, it would be good for you to return to Ephesus and remain quiet for the time being. Timothy, Paul's disciple, is waiting for you."

John struggled to his feet and walked a short distance from Gaius Taminius. It bothered John to be told to remain silent when he ardently desired to preach Jesus. It all seemed so improper for him, one of the Twelve, to be hushed.

When is it my mission?

He leaned against the boat's railings and felt himself grow in sadness. *My time will come by the will of my God, and not by the wishes of men.*

He let out a deep sigh, for suddenly there were no questions to be answered; no more help to be offered or places to hide or people to hide from. All of a sudden the quick changes in Rome and his abrupt travels seemed like an experience that had happened so long ago. Now he had to face travel by ship and he was not looking forward to another long voyage. He took a deep breath as an act of resolve and surrender to the will of God. He stood silently as the ship was freed from the docks and moved out into the open seas.

He stayed by the railing of the ship until it was night.

Looking up into the dark blue sky, he felt the moon on his face and marveled at the many flickering stars in the sky—they blinked at him like a thousand eyes. He grew in awe of the magnificence of God's creation.

"Here, Yochanan, it would be good for you to wear this," he heard a new voice say to him. It was Mihay and besides him Gaius Taminius. Being called by his Hebrew name surprised John. He looked down and saw a *tallit katan* in Mihay's hand. John touched the cloth reverently and slowly folded Mihay's fingers around it. He smiled kindly at the captain and walked away. The final tie had been broken and with a small tug of sadness in his heart, he uttered a short prayer.

Lord, I feel a revelation—a sad revelation coming to me. Please give me the strength to endure it according to Your will, and to have the wisdom to understand what I must do with it.

"I have never seen anything like that before. Look! A dove flying by night." Mihay exclaimed.

John turned quickly and saw the dove gliding in the moonlight. In this light it did not look white but as shining silver. He felt his heart beat rapidly, and he closed his eyes not wanting to see the dove, hoping to get rid of it and its revelation. He dropped his chin onto his chest, remaining still, forcing himself to be silent. He tortured his body with small short breaths, yet a quick flash of a face came to him. In silent acceptance, he nodded his head acknowledging what he already knew. He glanced at the dove as it continued to glide. Slowly, it flew onto the sea and for a quick moment it touched and then walked on the shimmering waters. Then it dipped its wing and climbed higher and higher into the stars.

John let out a silent cry, a cry of longing, and his eyes, filled with tears, blinded him.

"Why did you not tell me that Peter had died?" he asked breaking his silence of many days.

Mihay and Gaius Taminius looked at each other, for they did not understand what he was saying.

CHAPTER SIX:

Andrew Bar Jonah of Bethsaida

Prologue

The Greek merchant ship *Anassa* slipped from the shore and into the Tyrrhenian Sea. It moved so slowly, so carefully, that it made no sound. It seemed to just slide away from the coast and instantaneously blend into the dark night, like the shadow of a thief creeping through a darkened house. When the lights from the torches on shore became mere flickering dots, a strong wind caught the sails, and the ship cut through the sea with the smoothness of a sharp dagger. Even the captain of the ship, a big strapping Greek man named Mixalis, was amazed at their quickened speed.

So through the night, cloaked in swiftness, the ship continued.

Early morning found John bar Zebedee on the deck of the ship. He had been at this post all night, so deep in prayer that he forgot to sleep. Far off, John saw what was left of *Italia*—a slither of land that was barely visible under the cover of a morning haze. The haze made the memory of Rome a long-ago dream; that was what his voyage to Rome had been. He had moved in, over, across, and from this land so quickly that he could not intelligently think of his visit as anything else. As he continued to observe this mystical view, the sliver of land hued in pink and gray and black, he acknowledged that the colors he saw were taking on meaning for him: blood, ashes, death. From deep within his being, he heard the cries of his fellow Christians. His eyes filled with tears, and he welcomed them and the painful sorrow they represented. He felt the warm salty tears slip down his cheek, onto his lips, and into his black beard. He remembered what Mihay, his Roman Jewish companion, had told him about what was happening in Rome—the many killings, tortures, rapes, and beatings, and the few denials. He closed his burning eyes and thought, *Master, You have a reason for allowing all this to take place, for surely we are completing Your prediction that we would suffer persecution "for the sake of righteousness."* He let out a heavy, deep sigh. *Thy Will be done.* With this resolution, a solace came over him, and he was at peace with himself and with Rome. He opened his eyes and with his right sleeve wiped his face of tears. He strained to see Rome. *All I did in Rome was move,* he thought, and he remembered the barges and carts that took him from one place to another. He mentally revisited the *villae* and countrysides where he spent his days and nights, and they all blended together. The only thing he knew for certain was that he had seen Peter and for selfish reasons he, like the others, had tried to push Peter out of Rome.

But we were thinking for ourselves and trying to move the hand of the Master according to our desires. We were so sure that it was right for him to leave, but right for whom? For us, who were afraid to be left alone.

He shook his head in disbelief of everyone's actions, but he stopped as a new and more revealing thought came to him.

We were...stumbling blocks to the Will of God...We acted as Peter once did. Suddenly he had a new understanding of Peter.

John's shoulders immediately slumped when he heard the sound of Jesus' voice saying, "Get behind Me, Satan. Thou art a stumbling block unto Me, because thou savorest not the things that are of God, but the things that are of men."

Lord, forgive us. Forgive me.

This last thought made him feel alone. He longed for the companionship of a fellow disciple.

It was the plan of the Lord that Rome would be the place for Peter to rest his head. We must learn that the Master sets our course, and never are we to worry about His Church, for He is there to tend to it and to us, His servants. For an instant he believed that he had not done anything pleasing to Jesus in this journey, but quickly, in self-defense and with the desire to ease his own disbelief, he thought, *But my journey was not wasted, for I truly feel I was to be there to help Peter do the right thing—to pass the Keys to someone else. That was my mission and nothing more; Jesus made this obvious by having me come and go unharmed.* He envisioned young Linus. *Lord, protect young Linus. Praise God!*

The remembrance of Peter's death pierced his being. It was so great a realization that he staggered under its weight and was forced to grip the railing of the ship. Peter's death rolled over him. The pain and the emptiness of the loss intertwined in his soul. His entire being was mournful, and deep inside his being he cried out. He allowed this emotion to take hold of him until he could mourn no more, then he regained his control. He uttered a small prayer to Jesus, and quickly a smile crossed his lips, for in his mind he had a picture of Jesus greeting Peter and of the two greeting Cornelius.

I will mourn them, as Jesus said I must, but I will not mourn them in my soul, for there they will be alive. I wish I knew where Andrew is—I need to go to him. I know the sorrow one has with the loss of a brother. The death of James left me half alive and half complete.

The swollen ocean was around him. Suddenly a chill passed over him and he reacted by throwing his cloak over himself. *Early morning coolness,* he thought, but the chill stayed and began to settle in his bones. By the time Mihay arrived, John was shivering and his teeth were chattering.

For weeks, John laid ill in his small compartment below deck, shivering and then sweating and then shivering again as his fever raged. To Mihay, his companion, and to Mixalis, the ship's captain, who served as physician to the crew, one thing was clear: John was dying.

In his delirium, John saw many things pass before him. He relived moments with Jesus and heard the Master's voice. He saw himself lay his head on the Master's chest. He heard the soft, steady heartbeat and felt the strength from the muscles of His chest. He saw James, Matthias, James bar Alphaeus, and Bartholomew. He saw an older, almost scholarly Philip, a thinner Andrew, a grayer Simon, a younger Thomas, and an older Jude Thaddeus. He saw a tired Matthew laboring over a *papyrus*. He saw Peter standing alone as Jesus bestowed on him the Keys of the Kingdom. He saw Paul in chains and Mark preaching in Alexandria, and finally he saw Luke talking to Mary. He heard the laughter, the excitement, the debates, and the idle conversations as they walked the roads of Palestine. He crossed the Sea of Galilee and relaxed by the Salt Sea as the Twelve grew to appreciate each other. He felt the cold of the Judean nights when they would sleep out in the countryside. He saw the multitude of people following and studying Jesus. He saw the Sadducees and Pharisees peering and questioning, and he felt their condemning eyes. He felt the waters of the stormy sea and saw Jesus walking, coming closer and closer to him.

Amidst this strangely providential illness, he committed all these things to memory, for he had to continue his account of Jesus. As he noted these things, he knew he had much to write. There were many things that would never be told. There were things that happened daily that could not be reported.

How could I write of the private lessons Jesus gave us? Can I write of the times He sought each of us out because He perceived something lacking in our relationship with Him? How could I tell others of the daily miracles Jesus performed by simply tapping our hands or placing His hand on our shoulders when He detected something troublesome in our lives? Who would want to know about the respect Jesus had for Lady Mary or for the other holy women?

In his feverish confusion, he heard a heavy door slam shut. It startled him and he jumped, and then the cold night air passed over him and he was chilled almost to death. He found himself sitting at a table with the Others in the Upper Room. Those around him thanked Simon Peter and him for having found such a nice, comfortable place for the Passover. He wanted to tell them of the unusual occurrence that happened that day, when Peter and he, following Jesus' orders, had gone into Jerusalem in search of a man carrying a water jug. The idea of a man carrying a jug of water, the duty of a woman, at midday made Peter and John doubtful. Upon entering the city, they saw a manservant carrying a water jug, and quickly they walked to him. They followed the manservant to a house, and there they asked to see the Goodman. Upon seeing the master of the house, they said, "Our Master says to thee, 'My time is near at hand, with thee I make the Pasch with my disciples.'" The master of the house showed them a large upper room, and they requested that the room be made ready. Again, he heard the sound of a heavy door being slammed shut; again, startled, he jumped, then the chill of the cold night air passed over him, and again he was chilled almost to death.

In his delirium, John saw parents and relatives in the Room. Several followers and other disciples of the Master were also there. He heard greetings and joy—it was a holiday! He heard young Mark ask the Passover question, "Why is this night different from any other night?"

John gazed into this vision of the past. His attention is drawn to the towel that Jesus is using to dry their feet. Though it is used to wipe their soiled feet, the towel remains white and clean.

Then John hears the words, "…then you are clean, but not all."

Jesus moves from one to the other, and finally he is before John. Ignoring John's mild objection, He takes John's feet and John feels his feet in Jesus' hand. The water is chilly and John almost pulls his feet back, but remembering what was said to Simon Peter, he shivers and makes the chill rest within him. Jesus moves to Judas, who quickly lifts his feet to Jesus, and Jesus washes his feet. John watches as the water is poured onto Judas' tanned feet, and he sees the dirt and dust fall from the disciple's skin, but when Jesus wipes Judas' feet with the towel, John sees that the towel is soiled. John looks at Judas in surprise and almost comments on what he is seeing, but he lets his observation pass as Jesus continues around the table to the Others. Finally, Jesus returns to His place, and John sees that the towel is clean again.

All of their eyes are on Jesus as He dresses and sits again.

"Know you what I have done to you?" He says, looking around the table. No one answers Him, for Jesus' display of humility has only embarrassed and confused them.

"You call Me Master and Lord, and you say well, for I am so. If then I, being your Lord and Master, have washed your feet, you also ought to wash one another's feet. For I have given you an example, that as I have done to you, so you do also. Amen, amen, I say to you, the servant is not greater than his lord; neither is the apostle greater than He that sent him."

Jesus continues to speak, but John cannot hear what He is saying.

Then Jesus becomes silent, and soon the Twelve see that He is growing troubled.

"Amen, amen, I say to you, one of you will betray me."

The room is thrown into tumult, and they look at each other and begin speculating as to who it could be. Suddenly they all doubt each other and themselves.

Simon Peter pulls John's shoulder roughly and says to him, "Ask who is it of whom He speaketh."

John quickly asks the question, but before he can hear the answer, they all begin shouting, "Lord, is it I?"

We asked this question because we all believed He knew the future.

Jesus says something, but John cannot hear what He is saying. No one hears the Master's words. John watches Jesus pass a morsel of bread to Judas. He watches Judas walk from the table, across the room and to the door.

The door opens.

And it was night.

He heard the sound of a heavy door being slammed shut, and again, startled, he jumped. Then the chill of the cold night air passed over him; again, he shivered.

His eyes remained on the heavy, closed door, and he heard words, the Lord's words, fill his mind.

"Now is the Son of Man glorified, and God is glorified in Him."

"Whither I go you cannot come."

"A new commandment I give unto thee; that thou love one another, as I have loved thee."

"By this shall all men know that you are My disciples, if you have love one for another."

"Take, eat, this is My Body...this is My Blood...."

John turns his head to ask Jesus where Judas has gone, and he feels the love from his Master's eyes. He feels warmed. Slowly, he opens his eyes and sees Mihay and Mixalis staring at him.

He ignored the two men's happiness and relief as he thought, *The Master washed our feet to prepare us for the Meal and to tell us that we had to wash the dust of Jerusalem from our feet, to travel far for Him so the world would come to know His love and redemption. What a pity so many things happened that we did not understand.*

The boat stopped moving.

They arrived in Epirus, and John was happy, for he had learned much in his sleep.

✳

John was carried off on an enclosed litter because he was too weak to walk. They placed him in a covered cart that had been supplied by a Christian merchant from the city of Ambracia, which was located near the mouth of the Arachtus River. Then, John and Mihay boarded a small boat and continued up the Arachtus to the estate of Anker, who had a successful fishing business. After a short boat ride, they arrived at Anker's home. John was quickly taken inside and examined by a number of physicians, some of whom knew Paul and Luke. He was ordered to bed and given certain herbs to cure him and others to sedate him.

The next morning, he awoke. Gaius Magnius Longinus was standing nearby. Longinus had been a Roman Legionnaire on Golgotha the day Jesus died.

John had to look hard at the man, for he was not the tall, strapping soldier of long ago. He was now heavy and gray and slightly bald, but the handsome features were unmistakably those of Longinus.

"John, relax. The physicians have given you some strong medicine to cure your malady. Mixalis, the captain of the *Anassa*, did a commendable job in containing your illness, and Mihay, by the grace of our God, helped greatly with some of his old-fashioned Jewish remedies."

"If the remedies are Jewish, they will work," John remarked with a weak smile on his face.

"They were Christian and Jewish, and no illness can beat that combination," Longinus replied, smiling as he reached for a cup of wine mixed with cool water.

"Here, take this liquid, it will help you regain your strength." Longinus lifted John's head slightly to make drinking the mixture easier.

John felt the strength of Longinus' arms and thought, *Old but still strong, what a good gift Jesus gave us from Golgotha.* As the wine passed over John's lips and into his parched mouth, he gave thanks to God for this soothing relief.

Longinus gently lowered John's head onto the folded blanket being used as a pillow.

"Where is…."

"You should not be talking. The physicians suggested that you relax and be peaceful so that you can regain your strength."

"My dear Longinus…when a disciple of the Lord does not speak… all will be lost." He watched as Longinus again smiled, only this time not out of politeness but out of sheer delight.

"I was supposed to meet Timothy here. Where is he?"

"He has gone to Corinth to again try to help that troubled church, and then he will go to Ephesus to make things ready for you."

"Good. I will see him there. Now, my good friend, tell me, where is Andrew? I must see him."

"He is not here. When last I saw him, he was crossing the border between Thrace and Macedonia. We were together until that time, but he had a dream that you were ill and were coming to Epirus. After telling me of this dream, he ordered me here to await your arrival and told me to take you back to Ephesus. He instructed me to tell you that he knows of your thoughts and thanks you for thinking of him in his grief, but he is happy that Peter is with the Lord. Also, he begged me to tell you that you and he are blessed for having known Peter."

"Andrew was the strong-minded one. He was a friend and made my fears disappear with his optimism. He had the idea of a universal Church long before most. Did you know he was Paul's strongest ally? Well, he was. When I am well, you must make arrangements for my return to Ephesus, and on the way to Ephesus, you can tell me all about Andrew and his many travels."

Having said these things, John slipped into sleep, and in his dreams he learned that his traveling days were over—his mission was to finish his account of the life of Jesus.

ANDREW BAR JONAH OF BETHSAIDA

James bar Zebedee said to Andrew, with the Others present and able to hear, "You were the one who led many of us to the Master, and still you lead more to Him."

His brother Simon once said to him, "You were the first chosen by the Master, and I feel you are the greatest of us all."

"Andrew, we respect your brother, Simon, but we come to you because you are the boldest among us and the one who has the ear of Jesus," Matthew once said to him.

Of course, Andrew did not agree with what was said by the Others, for he did not consider himself any different from his fellow Apostles. They were all chosen, and none was better than any other. They were all equal in being sinful, weak human beings. What made him different was that he never wanted to be first or be considered first, and he spent much of his time standing in the shadow of the Others.

When the moments of clarity came, as when Jesus challenged them and asked them who people said He was, it was not Andrew, for then he was without a firm thought, but his brother Simon who spoke. It was with Simon's proclamation that the Others stopped thinking of Andrew as being the first. Andrew was always grateful to the Almighty for not giving him the words to answer Jesus' question.

After the death of Jesus and the coming of the Holy Spirit, his understanding changed slightly, for he then began to believe that being called first meant that he was to be the loudest in speaking the words of Jesus to the world. Because of this belief, he was the first to leave Jerusalem and begin his mission.

*

Many months after the death of the deacon Stephen, Jerusalem became a dangerous place for the Twelve. The Pharisees, with the help of Saul of Tarsus, had jailed and beaten many of the believers of "The Way." Many escaped Jerusalem and scattered into towns and villages in the nearby regions, and some traveled far from Judea. To protect and minister to these believers, Peter sent some of the Twelve out to those in exile.

They were to minister to all in the remote areas of Galilee, the Decapolis, and Samaria. The Twelve left Jerusalem firm and strong in the belief that God would protect them from harm. All readily accepted imprisonment and beatings, which some had endured only to find glory and blessings in their sufferings. Nonetheless, they believed that they were more valuable when they were free and able to do what Jesus wanted them to do. They could not "go and preach to all nations" if they were in jails, in chains, or crippled by beatings.

As the Others scattered, Peter, James bar Alphaeus, and John bar Zebedee remained in Judea, in hiding or in constant movement. When they preached, they soon disappeared—whisked away and hidden by members of "The Way." They were safe in the small towns and villages, but in Jerusalem they were in constant danger of arrest and imprisonment. Occasionally they would make clandestine visits to their families in Galilee.

From time to time, the Others would return to Jerusalem. They all returned except Andrew, yet everyone knew of his travels from his letters, which came from Cappadocia, Galatia, Phoenicia, Lycaonia, and Asia. Several Apostles had traveled into Syria and Cilicia, some to Cyprus, and some even to Arabia Petraea, but none seemed to have traveled as far as Andrew.

In those early days, it was becoming more dangerous for Peter to be present in and around Judea. Many tried to get Peter to leave and travel with them, but he always refused, until Andrew unexpectedly returned to Jerusalem. At that time, James Alphaeus and John bar Zebedee encouraged Andrew to take Peter into the wilderness of southern Judea. Andrew was not too pleased with this proposal because he had returned to Judea to say goodbye to Peter and the Others, for he had decided to go to Greece and beyond, as the Lord was leading him. After watching Peter in action, he agreed that Peter was becoming too bold and impetuous. Peter was far too valuable; they could not allow him to be arrested, jailed, or killed, so Andrew agreed to rein in his own zeal. He made the suggestion to Peter to travel south; Peter's quick reply astonished Andrew.

"You look surprised, Andrew, or are you disappointed because I seem so eager to run away from Jerusalem?" Peter asked in a soft voice, which had become his normal tone, but it was still strange to Andrew, who was accustomed to his coarse, harsh tone.

Peter continued, "I am not afraid of the Sanhedrin, or of Herod, or of Rome. I only wish to be with you, my brother, for I see in the future that we will be separated for a long time. I know you have nothing to hold you back. Our father Jonah has been dead for some years, and our dear mother Joann died soon after the Feast of Pentecost, so you have no obligations, nothing to confine you or impede you. You are free to go and fulfill the Master's command to 'baptize all nations,' and I am sure you will do just that by traveling far and wide."

Andrew remained silent. He examined his brother's face. There was a certain wisdom that was fixed in Peter's large features. It was a wisdom that Andrew had not noticed before this moment. He was pleased with this revelation, for Peter was no longer in need of Andrew's opinion. Immediately a weight was lifted from Andrew, for his eventual departure for Greece was made easier. He now knew that his return was to be according to God's will and that his travel with Peter was meant to be. Filled with peace, he bowed to the Will of God. But as he realized these things, a great sadness came over him, for he knew that bidding his brother farewell would be painful, for he loved him greatly. They had been more than brothers—they were friends and confidants, with many similarities and only a few easily settled differences. There was, however, one exception: Andrew had always been more of a Hellenized Jew than Peter, even to the extent that he refused to be called Amir, his Hebrew name, which meant "strong and mighty." Instead, he found great pride in his Greek name, Andrew, which meant "manly and valorous." Though they had often debated this issue, Andrew's position could not be altered.

"It is selfish of me to want this time," Peter continued, "but after much prayer, I believe that the Master saw fit to grant me this time with you. I have great fear on account of your boldness, and I believe that you will challenge everyone who doubts your words about Jesus. You will argue strongly against dissension, and you will wear your opponents into the ground with your firmness. You are destined to make many strong enemies, and as a result you are destined for much persecution and suffering; truly, you could be the first among the Twelve to go to the Master."

With sincere joy, Andrew smiled at his brother's prediction. He had thought that being the first to be called on earth would perhaps make him worthy to be the first called to heaven. It pleased him to see the understanding Peter was displaying.

The brothers departed Judea with the silent understanding between them that their time together would not last, and that this would be their last time together. They traveled south and southwest to the holy city of Hebron.

Hebron, the ancient royal city of the Canaanites, was home to King David, who ruled his Hebrew subjects from this city for seven years. The Jews believed that Abraham and his wife Sarah, as well as Isaac and

Jacob and their wives, were buried in caves near the city. For this reason, it was regarded as the second most holy city in Judaism. It was no surprise, then, that the two brothers were met with hostilities and were constantly at odds with the religious leaders. Many times they were challenged, and they were frequently ordered before the Council of Elders to explain themselves and their "heresy." The two were spending more time before the council and less time with the people, so they decided to leave Hebron, for they could not make any converts. They shook the dust from their sandals and traveled to the town of Engaddi, known for its growth of beautiful palm trees, which contrasted with the town's location on the shores of the Salt Sea, sometimes called the Dead Sea. They were received warmly and decided to stay and preach Jesus. They visited the small villages around Engaddi preaching of their risen Lord and many came to believe. Soon, Jerusalem and Hebron heard of their successes in Engaddi, and emissaries were dispatched. The two, forewarned by other followers, decided to move farther away and out of the reach of the Council of Elders. It seemed that the farther away from Jerusalem they traveled, the less they were met with distrust and anger. They crossed the Salt Sea and came to the land called Perea, which was sometimes called "the land beyond the Jordan" and which was known as the homeland of the prophet Elijah. This land, far from the authorities, was a safer place for the two of them to preach and enjoy each other's companionship.

Perea was the homeland of the Moabites and Ammonites, the archenemies of Israel. It was located on the east side of the Jordan River, spreading from Decapolis in the north to Idumea and Arabia in the south. It was conquered by King David and remained part of his kingdom until the death of Solomon. Israel then lost control of it, and it became known as Gilead. Many years later, it was reconquered by King Johanan Hyrcanus, who forced Judaism on the inhabitants.

The Apostles traveled northward along the shore of the Salt Sea to the mouth of the Jordan River. Andrew became sentimental, for in the nearby town of Bethany beyond the Jordan, John the Baptizer had made Jesus known to him, and it was near here that he and Peter had been called by Jesus. These memories gave him a closeness to Jesus and the Baptizer, and he felt that he was the most blessed of all the Twelve. Perhaps the Lord had made this trip possible more for his benefit than for Peter's. Together the brothers preached in many villages and towns of Perea, and they were surprised at the kindness with which they were received. After many months, a messenger from James bar Alphaeus found them. They were asked to return to Jerusalem because Saul the Pharisee was seeking an audience with the Twelve. Apparently, James and John were uncertain of what to do. The two, who had become attached to Perea, reluctantly began their journey to Jerusalem, promising that someday they would return. They never did.

They both felt distrust for Saul, though Peter's distrust was stronger. Andrew reminded Peter of Saul's successes in preaching and teaching Jesus to many in Syria. What Saul was doing was not opposed to their understanding of Jesus or to the betterment of "The Way." Though he did not tell his brother, Andrew had a strong feeling that Saul would take the lead in bringing the doctrine of Jesus to "the other world." Andrew believed that Jesus wanted the Twelve to go beyond the Chosen People and into the Gentile world. He would not admit it to anyone, but during his travels, when potential converts approached him, he never asked if they were Jewish, so he was certain that he had already crossed that threshold and had accepted Gentiles into the fold.

They arrived in Jerusalem with their minds set on seeing this man from Tarsus, but the Others proved to be more apprehensive than they were. Just as it seemed that they were going to deny Saul an audience, Yosef bar Nabas, called Barnabas, a follower of Jesus and cousin to young Mark, sought to speak to the Twelve. He relayed the story of Saul's conversion on the road to Damascus and described Saul's bold preaching in Syria. After hearing Barnabas speak on Saul's behalf, the Apostles felt more trusting, and they allowed Saul to speak to them. It did not take them long to get the feeling that in Saul was a great voice for the Truth, for his zeal and his wisdom were forceful. They then sat with him and talked to him of Jesus and of the things they remembered. After several days of camaraderie, they all decided to go and preach Jesus. Saul demonstrated such zeal that his life was soon in danger, so the Twelve rushed him off to Caesarea and Tarsus. From then on Saul was called Paul.

The Twelve then assembled, and Peter told them to turn to prayer, for they were to rely on God to direct them in their missions. In nine days, they would assemble again and draw lots to find out what the Lord had chosen for their missions. Amidst their prayers, they drafted twelve fundamental beliefs about the life, death, and resurrection of Jesus. It was a creed. The day after they had completed this work, they drew lots. Now knowing their missionary destinations, they left Jerusalem two by two with the promise that soon each of them would be sent assistants from the great number of fearless and faithful followers. Before any of them left, Andrew bid them all goodbye and left by himself, needing to return to Perea across the Jordan. The call and pull to Perea was so strong that Andrew felt he would die of unhappiness if he did not return. Besides, he had to fulfill his promise to return. For this journey to Perea, he crossed the Salt Sea and traveled directly to the fortress of Machaerus.

Machaerus, which was called "the Black Fortress," was about ten miles east of the Dead Sea and north of the Arnon River. King Herod the Great built this fortress to safeguard Perea's border towns from the nomadic Arab tribes, who often raided the villages and towns of Perea. Now, the Romans were using the fortress for the same reason.

The moment Andrew arrived at this outpost, he knew he had been drawn back for a reason. He remembered that at this fortress John the Baptizer had been imprisoned and beheaded by Herod Antipas at the request of Salome, the daughter of Herod's wife. Seeing the fortress made Andrew think more deeply about the effect John had on his life. He did not want to enter the fortress; in fact, he refused to enter it. He was satisfied merely to look at it. So he sat on the slopes of a nearby hill, praying and listening.

For two days Andrew sat watching the structure, knowing he had to find the reason for his presence there. As the hours passed, he felt the strength of the Baptizer come over him. He heard John's words echoing in his ears, and he recognized how much he missed his old friend.

His first encounter with John was nothing more than a sighting. Simon, James bar Zebedee, and he were in Peter's fishing boat traveling down the Jordan when he heard John's voice coming across the water. It was so loud and clear; it seemed that the speaker was standing beside him, but he could see no one. He was pulling in the nets with a great catch when he became paralyzed by the voice.

"That is John bar Zachary. His father is one of the Temple priests," James said nonchalantly. "His mother is a distant cousin of my mother. I hear he is calling for people to repent, and he has openly attacked Herod for adultery and the Herodians for their hypocrisy."

"A dangerous thing to do," Andrew replied with little thought.

"But it is the truth, and the truth should be spoken," Simon said with conviction as he pulled their early morning catch out of the river and onto his boat.

James and Simon were not affected by John's voice as much as Andrew was. The next day, when he was in another boat with his small crew of fishermen, he brought the boat closer to the shore and disembarked, telling his crew to continue up river and on returning he would join them. He waded ashore, not knowing why he had to be there or what he would find, but the closer he came to John's voice, the more certain he was that he was meant to be by John's side. He felt that an important thing was about to take place. Within hours, Andrew was so impressed by this great prophet of the desert that he knew he wanted to become his disciple, but his practicality forced him to return to his crew and his fishing. Each time he learned of John's whereabouts along the Jordan, he would make a point of fishing in nearby waters, or he would find a reason to repair his nets near where John was speaking.

When Zebedee moved his fishing boats to the Sea of Galilee, Andrew and his crew remained in the vicinity of the Jordan. Andrew continued to leave his boat and wade onto the shore to listen to John, whose followers now included young John, son of Zebedee. Andrew's distraction continued until the crew complained to Zebedee's son James and to Andrew's brother Simon. Andrew's neglect of his duties was putting a strain on them all.

James and Simon pulled Andrew aside to talk to him about the complaints, and he told them of the powerful message of John the Baptizer. Andrew was so enthusiastic and filled with such fire that they decided to investigate for themselves. Their commitment to Zebedee was somewhat stronger than Andrew's, so their stays with John were brief and their visits were sporadic.

As the months passed, Andrew began noticing several other fishermen among John's followers. Several times, he saw Philip of Bethsaida and his wealthy friend Bartholomew. He became acquainted with two other fishermen from Cana, Simon and Matthias, and with three part-time fishermen from Capernaum named Thomas, James bar Alphaeus, and Jude Thaddeus. Among the followers of John were many men he knew, and on some occasions he even saw Levi, the publican. They all seemed to come and go, and none was as faithful to John as Andrew was, for Andrew thought that John the Baptizer was the *Mashiach* the Messiah. How he arrived at this idea he could not remember. The Baptizer was the first truly spiritual person Andrew encountered—and he seemed to be the transcendent reformer that Andrew wanted the *Mashiach* to be. Years later, he would feel a small degree of shame in having had such thoughts.

When the time seemed right to Andrew, he walked into the Jordan to be cleansed. As he entered the waters, John looked at him with an unbroken stare. After several long moments that seemed an eternity, John said to him, "Andrew bar Jonah, you will travel far from this river and you will stand in mightier rivers than this, and many others will come to and from you."

Andrew did not bother to question John about his words because he was mesmerized by the man's eyes; they pierced him and seemed able to read his every living moment. He grew weak in his knees and felt like the water of the Jordan. He began to slip under, and then John caught him and slowly guided his head into the water.

Later that day, the Baptizer identified Jesus as "the Lamb of God." Andrew instantly left John and followed Jesus, and after spending a day with Him and hearing Him teach, he ran to his brother, Simon, with only one thought in his mind. Finding his brother he gasped, "Come, for I have found the Messiah."

The remembrance of those bygone times caused Andrew to grow calm. Deep in thought and overlooking the fortress of Machaerus, a warmth passed over him. It was the same warmth that he had experienced years ago with the Baptizer. Suddenly, he thought he and John were very much alike. He instinctively rejected this idea because it was so pretentious, but the more he tried to rid himself of this thought, the longer it lingered, until finally it settled comfortably in the corners of his mind. His thoughts were pushed aside, for he assumed that he needed to learn something in this moment. He settled and let the Will of the Lord come upon him.

Finally he thought, *It all began with John because Jesus ordained it this way.*

Later the Baptizer, to appease his doubting disciples, sent them to get assurances. Andrew, in a similar moment of weakened faith, doubted Jesus, and like Thomas, he had to touch the feet of Jesus to be satisfied of His return from the dead. It was then that he, like the disciples of the Baptizer who diminished in the presence of Jesus, had to diminish and become lowly and "poor in spirit" to understand the totality of Jesus.

With this new realization, Andrew began to weep, and standing with his arms open to the heavens he cried, "Oh Lord, You have brought me here where John stopped to make my new life begin. It is from this place that You wished that I should begin my voyage through the world in Your name, and with John as my companion." Falling to the ground, he lay prostrate, crying tears of thanksgiving.

When morning came, he briskly started south toward the town of Dibon-gad, and he arrived there in two weeks. He rested for several weeks and then preached in the small synagogue in the town, welcoming many into "The Way." Leaving Dibon-gad, he crossed the Arnon River into Arabia and continued on to the town of Rabbath Moab. This town was a mixture of many beliefs and had a small population of Jews, who welcomed Andrew and his teachings. Surprisingly, several of them had been in Jerusalem on that glorious Pentecost day and had experienced the Twelve's first burst of boldness. They returned home, telling others of the miracle of tongues and of the death and resurrection of Jesus, but they soon found that they needed help in persuading others. Andrew was that help, for many came to "The Way" during his visit. He even accepted Arabs and other non-Jews into the fold. While in Rabbath Moab, several Arabs came to him from the nearby town of Kir of Moab, asking that he go with them to their town, for they wanted him to speak of Jesus. The nomadic nature of these people was a bit unsettling to Andrew, who believed in a strong central family life, but after living with them a few months, he began to relate to their way of life.

A man named Saleb, who owned a caravan of pack animals and who had traveled farther into Arabia after being away from Andrew for several months, returned to Kir and walked up to Andrew and said, "So after Jesus fed the people with loaves and fishes, what happened?" Andrew continued telling Saleb the story of the multiplication as if they had never been apart and had never stopped talking. This was the way these people lived. Life was events that were interrupted but continued; eventually, they would be returned to.

So Andrew continued preaching and received many into "The Way," and again he found Arabs and other non-Jews willing to accept Jesus as their Lord and God. Several times when in the desert, with no rivers or brooks available, he simply poured water from their water skins and cleansed them. On one occasion, when he had an entire tribe to baptize, he put his hand into the barren ground and water came forth, and long after he left this place, it continued to provide drink for the nomads. Caught up with the energy of success and his speed of travel, Andrew left Arabia Petraea and turned north back to Perea. He traveled along the coast of the Salt Sea to the mouth of the Jordan. He continued north on the Jordan and finally arrived at Bethany-on-the-Jordan. Here, he felt the presence of holiness, for it was at this very place that John had baptized him. He paused and remembered. For nine days he fasted and prayed, asking for wisdom to match that of his brother Peter and for stronger determination to do what the Lord wished him to do. He had pulled the lot for Greece and "to the north." He had no fears of Greece, for he had a strong understanding of these people, though he did not think himself able to match their intellect. "To the north" was a great uncertainty. He feared he would not be strong enough to challenge the cultural elements that were "to the north." After nine days, he broke his fast with some wild fruits that were nearby. He left Bethany armed with the knowledge that Jesus would always be with him and, as He did for Moses, would fill his mouth with the words of the Spirit. He knew he would never again feel alone. For the next few years, Andrew preached in the Syrian country-side and in such cities as Tyre, Sidon, Damascus, Palmyra, Emesa, and

Apamea. He traveled to nearby Cilicia, Pamphylia, and Lycia and farther north into Galatia and Pontus. In Bithynia, he unintentionally found Peter, who had been preaching in the province, and together they went to the seaport city of Sinope. This city had a large Jewish population, most of whom made their living from fishing. The brothers were in their element, and they reveled in the idea of returning to their boats and fish. After many months of working in their trade and preaching, the two brothers parted. Peter headed to Pontus, and Andrew remained behind. One day while fishing with some Bithynians, Andrew was unexpectedly mocked by a group of soldiers who stood on the shores of the Black Sea. Andrew requested that the boat turn and head back to the shore. Once on shore, he was confronted by a young Roman soldier named Varianus. This young Roman attacked Andrew with much verbal abuse, to which Andrew made no reply. Finally, Andrew walked directly to Varianus. The soldier's eyes widened in terror, and he shrank back like a caught animal facing death.

From this soldier came a foreign, throaty voice that bellowed, "O brave Varianus, what have I done to you that you should send me this God-fearing man?"

Andrew placed his hand on the soldier's shoulder and Varianus collapsed to the sandy beach. He thrashed and rolled about, screaming in pain and foaming at the mouth. Some soldiers grabbed Andrew while others lifted Varianus to his feet. Andrew, in a voice that covered the land like a mighty wind, ordered the demon within the soldier to leave. Liberated and restored, Varianus removed his uniform and threw it at the feet of the Apostle. His fellow soldiers reminded him that the penalty for desertion was death, but the soldier declared, "I am now a soldier of Jesus of Nazareth, and I wear the uniform of the Eternal King." He then boarded Andrew's boat, and they went out into the Black Sea. After two days, Varianus was baptized by Andrew. Some Christians learned that the Roman Magistrate of Sinope had ordered Varianus' arrest and death, so he was whisked away and put on a ship destined for Amisus in Pontus. Andrew immediately sent a letter to Peter asking him to protect Varianus among the Christians. Later, Andrew was warned in dreams to leave Sinope. He obeyed the dreams and continued north into Armenia and onto the very border of the Caucasus. At every river, he stopped and preached and baptized. He led many to "The Way" in the lands he visited.

After many months in Armenia, he continued south away from Armenia and passed through Osroene and into Syria. He was heading for Antioch in Syria when he was met by Gaius Magnius Longinus.

Longinus, after his conversion on Golgotha and Baptism by Peter at Cornelius' house, went into the desert. During his retreat, Longinus was called by Peter to leave his hermitage. Peter sent him to Andrew requesting Andrew's return to Jerusalem for a council meeting regarding the problem of circumcision for the Gentiles. Andrew and Longinus returned to Jerusalem, and with the other Apostles Andrew attended the council.

The feeling of companionship, of seeing and being with the Others, was uplifting. When they all spoke of their travels and adventures, Andrew became eager to return to his mission. During the meeting, Andrew and Peter supported Paul, telling everyone of Paul's preaching and conversions among the Gentiles. Andrew had always preached to Gentiles and had never required them to be circumcised. He believed that Jesus had come for all people.

When Andrew spoke during the debate, he quoted Zephaniah regarding the Messiah: "Then I will restore to the people a chosen lip, that all may call upon the name of the Lord, and may serve him with one shoulder." When he had finished, he looked at James bar Alphaeus, who had a startled look on his face, and in that look Andrew felt that he had said something of importance to James and that God was speaking through him, so he continued: "Truly, the Prophet was showing that the Messiah came for all nations and that all nations would come to obey Him. This seems to have been intended from all time—there is no mention of how they should come to Him. Therefore, I do not believe that the Law of Moses or the ritual of circumcision has any bearing on the Gentiles."

Later he approached James bar Alphaeus and said, "Why did you look so surprised at what I said, James?"

"Only because I knew you were speaking to me. I had forgotten that once I thought as you do. You reminded me of my old convictions, and I feel at ease with the way I voted. Once again, you are leading people to the Master."

Andrew quickly walked away, not wanting to hear more.

After the meeting, the Apostles sat and enjoyed one another's company. They reminisced about their time together with the Master. They enlightened one another's thoughts with stories of their preaching and teaching. Later, they sat and spoke of James and Matthias and glorified God, for these two Apostles were now living among the blessed in the presence of God. Throughout the night, one thing remained obvious: they all were eager to get back to their missions. So they retired early and prepared to leave the next day. Once again they dispersed, going north, east, south, and west, but before any of them departed, Andrew and Longinus were gone and well on their way to Tyre and Greece. Andrew traveled peacefully, thinking he was going the correct way.

✳

On the first night of their voyage back to Ephesus, John and Longinus sat under the open night sky. It was a pleasantly cool night. They ignored their tiredness and the slight chill, and they prayed deep into the night. The cloudless sky and the open sea became their holy places. When they had finished, they sat in silence, allowing the Lord time to respond to them; this was their most important time, for in these wordless moments they were refreshed and enlightened.

It grew late and Longinus, concerned for John's health, suggested that they retire, but John insisted on hearing about Andrew's mission.

Reluctantly, Longinus, who had been Andrew's companion for many years, began his tales of Andrew's missions. These stories lasted for three days, and not once did John grow weary of Longinus' monotone voice. The only time Longinus was not telling his tales was when he was sleeping. But even then, rest was not rest, for his mind was remembering times he would tell John the next day.

Longinus began telling his stories in poor Hebrew, but he would eventually resort to speaking *Koine,* the commonly used Greek, or Vulgar Latin, the language of the plebeians.

John knew that Longinus was a learned man, a man who loved history. He remembered from long ago that when Longinus spoke, he was very descriptive, almost poetic, so John was sure he was about to be enlightened as well as informed. Each night he edged closer to Longinus, like a child anticipating a legend of a great hero.

Longinus began night one of his story.

"In Tyre we boarded the *Agenor*, a Greek ship named after the mythical King of Tyre and father of Europa. The ship was filled with cargo and was headed for the island of Cyprus, and from Cyprus on to Greece. During our trip, we decided to read a copy of Paul's letter to the Thessalonians, with the hope of understanding the problems that would face us when we returned to Greece.

"When we arrived in Salamis, the chief seaport of Cyprus, an exchange of cargo took place, and several new passengers boarded the *Agenor.* Among those boarding was a rich Cypriot Jew named Cenon, who was going to Byzantium and then would return to Adrianopole in Thrace. He was a short, pudgy man with dark eyes and dark hair. He was a friendly person, and his happiness was contagious. He was well dressed, not too lavishly, but he still looked to be more affluent than we were. It did not take Andrew long to recognize that the man's inner peace was brought about by spirituality, and when the man mentioned that he had been in Jerusalem when Pontius Pilate was procurator, Andrew suspected that the man was a 'Nazarene,' so he found a piece of charcoal nearby and drew a cross on the deck of the ship. Immediately, the little man raced to Andrew and embraced him as a fellow Christian. With little forethought, he began talking about Jesus, then he spoke of Paul, and when he seemed to have run out of things to say, he apologized and asked our names. When he found out who Andrew was, he knelt before the Apostle and asked for a blessing. After, Cenone remained in silent respect and this made Andrew very uncomfortable.

"In an attempt to change the subject, Andrew asked him, 'Tell me, Cenon, why are you going to Thrace?'

"The man's face lost its glow of awe and beamed brightly. 'Because I have business there, and because I am to take you there.'

"I chuckled slightly and said, 'But brother, we are going to Greece.'

"Cenon's face broke into a wide smile. 'No, I think the Lord wants you to go to Thrace. We are without help. The Thracian Nazarenes have no elders or leaders. I and about seven others have been teaching and preaching, with what little we know, to so many of our countrymen. Paul came close to Thrace, but he never crossed the border. What Paul told the Philippians trickled into Thrace, but still we thirst for the Living Water. What we have received thus far has been secondhand, but now we could have one of the Twelve—one who walked and spoke and ate with the Master, one who witnessed the life and death of Jesus. We need you, Andrew. You can always go to Greece, it is just south of Thrace.'

"'Thrace is to the north of Greece,' Andrew said in a low voice that was really only for him to hear.

"'What did you say, Andrew?' Cenon asked.

"'I think he said no,' I interjected, but with uncertainty, for I did not hear clearly what Andrew had said.

"Andrew placed his hand on my arm to quiet me. Turning to Cenon, he continued, 'My brother, you are right, we must go north.' Returning to me, Andrew stated, 'I think this man is a messenger from the Master. We will go north.'"

"And that is how Andrew and you got to Thrace?" John asked with a smile. "I often wondered. Of course you know, Longinus, that Andrew always insisted on going north to preach the Lord. Tell me of Thrace, for I know little about it."

"It seems a vast land and is a recent Roman conquest, so Romanization of the land has not yet occurred. In fact, I do not expect that Romanization will ever occur, for the Thracians are a stubborn people, though most people in Thrace would agree they have benefited from Roman rule. Thracians are considered barbarians by the Greeks because they did not absorb the Hellenistic culture but rather remained as a loosely organized collection of warlike tribes with no central government. Once they were united under a chieftain named Sitalces, but his reign did not take hold for lack of succession. Years later, Philip of Macedon drew them into his kingdom, but even a man as strong as Philip, or an Emperor like Claudius, could not change these people. They have an aversion to urban life—the closest they have come to urbanization is living in small, open villages. As a result of this lack of centralization, the region is open to attacks from many countries. I found these people to be quite cultured. The Greeks' tendency to denigrate these people is not correct in my view. They have developed beautiful forms of poetry and music, and their polytheistic religion is similar to that of the Greeks. They are a race of superb horse-men and were recruited by the Greek, Macedonian, and Roman cavalries for military purposes. I fought several battles with these horsemen, and I can assure you, John, that they are almost without equal. They also have supplied a number of gladiators, among them the rebel Spartacus. They created the Thracian sword, a slightly bent blade that is in use in amphitheater combat. All the conquerors of Thrace exploited it for its gold and silver mines. It also supplies the Romans with wheat, olive oil, and fruits." Longinus stopped speaking and shook his head. "I am sorry. I am digressing. Let me continue. When we arrived at Byzantium, we taught everyone whom Cenon brought to us. Among these was a young, strapping man named Stachys. Stachys was a childhood friend of Cenon and also was a Cypriot Jew, but because of business with Rome and the Greeks, he was living in Byzantium. Stachys housed us and provided us with much needed support. He was invaluable to us, and his simple faith was so fervent that I for one stood in awe of him."

"Was not Stachys a friend of Paul?"

"Yes, you surprise me, John."

"I know of him as one who befriended Paul and Barnabas when they were in Cyprus."

"Yes, that is true. Stachys was a *quaestor* under Proconsul Sergius Paulus."

"A stronger tie than I would have suspected, but please excuse me and go on."

"Within a short time, many in the Jewish community came to believe in Jesus, and news of our presence spread across the Bosporus into Bithynia, the ancient city of Calchedon, the nearby cities of Nicomedia and Nicaea, and farther south to Prusa. Jews from these cities began journeying to Thrace to hear an eyewitness speak about the life of Jesus. Some came because they were of "The Way," and others came out of curiosity. Some Christians from these cities spent much time with us. After learning more, they returned to lead their communities.

"News of Andrew's presence in Thrace also reached inland to the interior Thracian cities of Adrianopole, Philippopolis, and faraway Serdica. Soon these cities sent delegates asking Andrew to visit them. Their desire to know more about Jesus was so overpowering that we found ourselves preaching at several different places in one day, and the overwhelming response and enthusiasm we witnessed brought us much satisfaction. Soon Andrew truly believed that this was where he was meant to be. Daily he praised and thanked Jesus for showing him this place, and daily he gave thanks for the Lord's messenger, Cenon. With little rest, Andrew preached to everyone. We stayed a year in Byzantium then moved inland with Cenon, who had sold all his belongings to join us. We left Stachys as *episkopos* of Byzantium."

"A wise choice, for I have heard that Stachys is doing a good job," John said with conviction. "I have heard also that his life is in danger because of his condemnation of the Roman Army's immorality, with which he is very familiar."

"I pray he remains safe, for I know, as you do, that he is a very holy and righteous man."

"Again, my apologies, Longinus. Please continue. But do tell me, is it true that Thrace is a beautiful land?"

"Magnificent! The interior of Thrace has two large plains that are divided by a vast mountain range. The wide-open, windswept plains are breathtakingly beautiful. The grass and wild vegetation sways in unbroken motion as the steady wind weaves its way through those wild lands. The gently varying shades were so beautiful that it often moved Andrew to poetry, and much to my surprise, I soon found myself admiring the glories of Creation. The terrain was mountainous, but not overpowering. The land flowed like a soft sigh, like the melodious sound of a fine harp. It looked delicate, almost fragile."

John sighed at Longinus' description. He wished to tell Longinus that his descriptions were picturesque, but he did not want to interrupt his companion's tale.

"The interior cities are actually just ancient settlements that are gradually expanding through the establishment of Roman garrisons. The army attracts many camp followers, farmers, and traders. Many of these people stay and build homes, but they are not totally Romanized. Most of the merchants that settled in the cities of Adrianopole and Serdica represent a blend of many cultures. Our missionary work was exceedingly difficult in these cities. The worst city was Philippopolis, which is far more backward than the others. The city was renamed and rebuilt by Philip of Macedonia. Philippopolis became an outpost and a barbarian town, and matters only became worse when Philip imported criminals, exiled enemies, and other social outcasts. When the Roman garrison arrived, the town was opened to further depravity, and it became filled with all manner of immoral, irreligious, and wicked people. The people live day by day and worry little about tomorrow. They live a life of instant gratification, and anything that opposes their revelry is ridiculed and attacked. The citizens obey few laws, and they have no respect for anything Roman. When off duty, the Roman soldiers only contributed to the depravity of this forsaken city.

"A few people, along with a small Jewish community, welcomed us, but the majority of the people were openly hostile. After months of frustration, Andrew gave Philippopolis up for lost, and we went on to Serdica and Adrianopole. From time to time, he was drawn back to the city of his failure, and with new fervor, but it was never enough to capture the hearts of these hardened people.

"On his last trip to this city, he met his next messenger from the Lord. As he was preaching in the northern section of the city, he noticed a young man whose face seemed to express a plea. Amazingly, the face had an uncanny resemblance to that of Mark, the companion of his brother Peter. The resemblance was so great that for an instant Andrew lost track of his thoughts. I soon realized that something was wrong, so I followed Andrew's sight and saw the young man and his resemblance to Mark. I abruptly left Andrew's side and began walking and pushing through the crowd, but before I could reach him he sidled his way out of the crowd. Finally, the young man and I cleared the crowds, and I reached out and caught him by the arm. When he turned, I was stunned to see that he bore no resemblance to Mark. My shock and disappointment must have been very obvious, for the young man asked me what was wrong. I quickly gathered my senses and apologized. We talked for a long time. I heard the young man's story about a people that longed to know more about Jesus. I pleaded with the man to stay with us, but he told me that he had many miles yet to travel. He urged me to heed his pleas and tell Andrew what he had told me. That night we were guests at a house of one of the local farmers, and as the three of us sat by the open fire, we talked about the young man.

"'Longinus, believe me, I was about to call out to the young man,' Andrew said.

"'He looked just like Mark. I thought perhaps he had come from Peter with a message, but now you tell me that he looked nothing like young Mark. That is so hard to understand,' Andrew remarked with a great deal of confusion in his voice.

"'I tell you, as I followed him and got closer to him, I became more certain that it was Mark, but when he turned around, nothing—not even the smallest resemblance to Mark,' I declared with equal confusion.

"'Could our eyes deceive us?'

"'Apparently so.'

"'Did he say where he was from?'

"'Yes, from the city of Tomis.'

"'Ah, Tomis, the capital of the province of Moesia,' Cenon added as he moved around the room. 'It is the city to which the poet Ovid was banished and in which he died; he hated the Moesians, called them barbarians. Tomis is a nice place, better than this forsaken city, but it is heavy with Thracian habits.'

"'The young man told me that the citizens in Tomis and the rest of the province have heard about Jesus from returning travelers,' I continued. 'Some people are claiming to be followers of the Lord, but their knowledge of Jesus is incomplete and unreliable. He told me that the people are eager to learn more about Jesus.'

"'Did he give you his name?'

"I could not answer him. I was dumbfounded by Andrew's question, and I answered him slowly, 'I…never…asked him.'

"Andrew smiled.

"'Where is Tomis?' Andrew asked.

"'In Moesia. North of here,' Cenon quickly responded.

"Andrew's smile widened, and his face glimmered with wisdom.

"'North?'

"Cenon and I nodded.

"'Tomorrow,' Andrew said as he threw his cloak over himself, 'we will leave for Moesia.'"

"Ah, there you see it, Longinus, Andrew's obsession with the north," John interrupted proudly, but he was not telling the Roman something he did not know. "Now please go on. I am very interested, for I am not at all familiar with Moesia," John stated with urgency.

"I know, John, so let me give you some information about it. Moesia is a buffer province for the Romans—it separates Macedonia, Thrace, and Greece from the undesirable Sarmatians and other barbaric tribes. The Roman general Marcus Licinius Crassus conquered this land during the reign of Caesar Augustus. In spite of the fact that the Moesians have competitions, gladiatorial events, and other games in honor of the Caesars, and though most of them speak Latin, they have not become completely Roman. The Greek influence prevails among these people. Moesia is west of the *Pontus Euxinus* Black Sea and important for the trade routes to Bithynia, Pontus, and Armenia as well as the Caucasus and Sarmatians often called Scythians. The great *Ister Flumen* Danube River with its tributaries separates Moesia from Dacia. This river connects Moesia to the interior provinces of the Empire, and consequently it is common to see trading ships from Pannonia and other land-locked provinces pass through Moesia on their way east to the Black Sea. Moesia has rich farmlands and pastures and supplies Rome with wheat and other grains. It also supplies Rome with livestock and the gold that allows the Romans to continue to live in luxury. Many of the men have served Rome as soldiers and warriors. Titus Plautius Silvanus Aelianus, a governor of the province and a friend of my grandfather, arrived in Moesia several months before Andrew and I did. He took command of the *Legio V Macedonia* with orders to produce more wheat and, above all, to keep peace in the province. Within a short time, Titus Pautius improved the standard of living by developing urban areas and encouraging people to live in cities and towns. Because of the close relationship between the Moesians and the Greeks, he permitted and encouraged certain Greek cultural ideas that ran parallel to the customs of Rome. The polytheistic Greco-Roman mythological religion was one of the things he gave the people.

"We arrived in the Moesian port city of Odessos, which because of its importance to Roman trade on the Black Sea is regarded as a city of privilege in the Empire. The city is primarily Roman with a large garrison and many camp followers. A number of Jewish *quaestors* accompanies the garrison. There is a fairly large population of Moesians living in and around Odessos, but most of them are poor, serving as laborers, if not outright slaves for the Roman military.

"As the young man had told us, there were people eagerly awaiting our arrival, and we were greeted by many commoners who were searching for hope. They had heard of Jesus but understood little of the Messianic message of forgiveness and everlasting life. Surprisingly, we found the people practicing the ritual of the Supper, which came to them from converted Macedonian travelers and merchants of Thessalonica and Philippi. Day and night, we preached. We strengthened and reinforced the beliefs of many lukewarm followers. Soon, we had converts, but not in large numbers.

"I went to the garrison and preached to the soldiers; being of Roman blood and a former military man, I had full access to these people. Unfortunately, they were not at all willing to listen to me condemn their lives of sin and debauchery. The military commander, Quintius Vibius, the son of a friend, forbade me from speaking to the soldiers and secretly warned me to leave Odessos. I know the feeling of the breath of Rome on my neck, so I wasted no time. I relayed the warning to Andrew and reminded him that the young man was from Tomis, and perhaps that was where we were truly meant to go. I pointed out that our lack of success in Odessos was further indication that we should move on, but Andrew did not accept defeat so readily. We stayed a while longer, but each day it became more dangerous. Little by little we moved away from Odessos into the surrounding area, and eventually we headed in earnest to the city of Tomis.

"Now Tomis is the capital of the province of Moesia; the governor and all his entourage are treated like royalty. The city is far more advanced than Odessos, but still not as advanced as many other cities within the Empire. It has a large commercial complex with a spacious bathhouse and numerous warehouses that store olive oil, wheat, and other agricultural products for export to Rome. In the center of the city, in what could be called the *forum*, was a statue of the Greek god *Pontus*, the "god of the deep sea," who represents the Black Sea. Farther up and to the left, just outside the temple dedicated to *Serapis*, stood a statue of *Glycon*, the snake god, whom the Moesians worshipped before the Greek and Roman occupations. The followers of *Pontus* and *Glycon* became the objects of our first efforts because the cult of these gods was very shallow and was no match for the zeal and truth that we could offer them. Many people threw aside these dead gods and readily accepted Jesus. Our successes were among the poor and despised, who found great comfort in the Master rather than in snakes or deep waters. As our successes multiplied, I saw a deep contentedness come over Andrew, for again he believed that he had arrived where the Master wanted him to be. But the real challenge was still waiting for us, and when finally we came face to face with it, we found ourselves in perilous waters. The challenge we had to meet was the god *Serapis*."

"Is that not an Egyptian god? What are its followers doing in Moesia?" John asked.

Again Longinus was surprised by John's knowledge but neglected to acknowledge it, for he was now tired and wanted to finish his story. "John, you are partly right. *Serapis* is a blend of Egyptian and Greek gods. It is mainly a combination of *Osiris* and the bull *Apis*, hence the composite name of *Osirapis*, which is the Egyptian name for this god, but through the ages and after years of gradual change, the god became known as *Serapis*. The occult followers of this god existed in the Delos, one of the holy cities of Greece, and I am told there are believers even in the province of Britannia. I know of a large fanatical following among the Egyptians of Alexandria, and for some reason this god has a great following with the governor, magistrates, legates, and centurions of Moesia. Most surprising is the fact that there are similarities between *Serapis* and the Hebrew God, so much so that when Emperor Tiberius expelled the Jews from Rome some years ago, he ordered the followers of this cult expelled also, because he thought they were Jews.

"These people believed that *Serapis* was the supreme god and was the embodiment of the soul of *Osiris,* the god of the underworld. *Serapis* was, so to speak, the incarnation of *Osiris* on earth. Another name for *Serapis* was *Chrestus,* which of course sounds quite similar to *Christus* from the Greek *Christos* Messiah. When word spread that two foreigners had arrived and were preaching about the Messiah, the people began to arrive in multitudes. They told us that they knew all about *Chrestus,* the messiah, and that they had a temple dedicated to him. At first, Andrew and I thought that some of Paul's teaching had found its way into Moesia, but after questioning the people we soon discovered the confusion. We immediately started correcting the error, but there was stiff resistance. Each day, when we preached Jesus and spoke of His sacrifice and resurrection, long, heated debates followed. Little was accomplished because there were so many voices against Andrew, Cenon, and me. Oddly, our nights were filled with visitors who covertly approached us and asked questions about Jesus and His promise of salvation through forgiveness and love. These nighttime visitors became engrossed in our teaching, but they did not accept Baptism. We rarely saw these night visitors in daylight, and when we did, they would stand idly by as the followers of *Serapis* continued their attacks.

"I began to suspect that those disrupting our teaching were troublemakers from the Roman garrison, and soon I observed that they not only were disturbing our teachings but also intimidating those who were interested. I sensed a great danger developing, one which I was familiar with, for when I first came to the Lord, I was intimidated by the garrisons, most especially the Antonia garrison in Jerusalem. Those days seemed so long ago, but I remembered them, as I do today with equal clarity."

"Though I want to hear more, Longinus," John said, "I think you are weary. It would be wise for you to end your story for tonight, and we will get some rest. Tomorrow, we will continue. Go below and rest; we have many days and nights for you to continue."

"Thank you, John. What I have to tell next is lengthy, and my eyes are heavy."

"Good night, Longinus."

"*Dominus vobiscum.*"

"And with your Spirit."

John watched as Longinus walked away. His body was still upright and his steps fell solidly on the boards of the ship—a true Roman soldier.

That poor man looked exhausted, John thought.

John gazed at the sky around him and surveyed its vastness. The open sky in its enormity reminded him of the Sea of Galilee, and a twinge of homesickness came upon him. Quickly he forced it away, but he knew it would not stay away for long. He turned his head and looked down the deck of the ship where Longinus had walked, and his thoughts of home and of Rome returned.

He remembered Longinus and the others who came to "The Way" in the early times. He remembered them telling the Twelve how they hated their assignments in Judea; Longinus called his assignment a curse because he disliked being away from his beloved Rome—"When I am deprived of Rome, I am only half-alive."

He joined the military at the age of seventeen against the wishes of his family, most especially his father Rematius. His father, a Cappadocian of Roman citizenship, had trained Longinus in the family business of making and repairing armor. Young Longinus, however, was far more inclined to the wearing of armor than to the making of it. Whenever Rematius was summoned to Mazaca Caesarea to make repairs to Roman armor, or whenever the *loricatus muneris* armor officer arrived at his father's place of business, young Longinus would sit and listen to the soldiers talk about all the strange lands and barbaric people they had lived among. He was captivated by their stories of adventure and by the respect and fear they received from the people. Above all, he was enticed by the arrogance of the Roman soldiers. They were the conquerors of the world, and as soldiers they represented the Emperor. The soldiers encouraged Longinus to pursue a career in the military, and they assured him that his extensive experience with armor would make him extremely valuable.

He joined the Roman Legions and trained in Cappadocia, and because of his trade he was quickly made helper to the *quaestor*. In addition to making and repairing helmets, shields, javelins, daggers, and swords, he was responsible for ordering provisions for the garrison. He was assigned to the province of Asia in the same capacity and stayed there for several years. His wanderlust induced him to ask for a transfer, and he was moved to Narbonensis in southern Gaul. Here he got his first taste of battle against the rebellious Gallic tribes. His Gallic tour lasted a number of years, and finally he was transferred to *Italia*. The prospect of being in Rome was extremely exciting for Longinus. He would be at the center of the world—the city to which all the world looked. His tour of duty took him up and down the Italian peninsula; this lasted for ten years, and it was ten years of the easy life. Soon he was made a centurion. Being a centurion in the *quaestors* gave him a degree of non-military living. There were many privileges attached to this position. He did not have to deal with crowded, uncomfortable quarters. He had few military duties—some guard duty and a little combat training. He was free to come and go with little regulation. He was more of an administrator than a commander. Some under him were freemen, but most were slaves who had blacksmith or weaponry backgrounds. He hoped he would continue to enjoy these privileges throughout his time in the army, but during a short tour in eastern *Italia* he began having trouble with his eyes, which started to burn and became sensitive to the sun and bright fires. His eyes were continually irritated, and as a result they frequently became teary. His eyes twitched uncontrollably. In an attempt to see better, he constantly squinted. He was ridiculed and mimicked by his military companions. The army doctors blamed the forge fires for his damaged eyes, and soon he understood that this malady would impede his advancement in the service. He was soon assigned to Judea to finish out his remaining military obligation. He and Pontius Pilate, two bitter Romans, arrived in Jerusalem around the same time. Because of his rank of centurion and his disability, he was assigned the duty of being a ceremonial centurion to Pilate. He was constantly at Pilate's side; the mundane duties associated with this position added little excitement to his life. His unhappiness soon sank into depression. He found fault in everything around him, and eventually his generalized anger turned into a hatred of the Jewish people. He saw them as an inferior race and found amusement in their strange customs. They had barbaric ways of mutilating their bodies and practiced pointless dietary restrictions. They had men who believed in the value of virginity, which was unnatural to any Roman. They had the odd concept of a single God and somehow convinced themselves that this God had made them His Chosen People. They were a conquered people, yet their arrogance amazed him. He believed that their religion was wishful thinking, for if ever there was a "chosen people," it was the Romans. By their very actions, the Jews proved that they did not truly believe they were the chosen ones, for instead of bursting out with confidence in their God, they drew inward and became clannish. He concluded that if they truly were the Chosen People and their God was ever with them exerting all His power, then they would not be subject to Rome and other nations. If they believed their God so superior, they should be confident enough to let the rest of the world know about Him and proselytize to all non-believers, as the Romans did. If their beliefs were right, they would be the rulers of the world, but instead they build great walls around themselves and keep the rest of the world away. The only thing their narrow-mindedness did was invite hostility and ridicule from the rest of the world.

Unbeknown to Longinus, God was beginning to work within him, for the angrier he grew with the Jews, the more he found himself drawn to them. In this perplexity, he had the gnawing feeling that the belief in one unseen, all-powerful God was far more acceptable than the belief in the many handmade gods of Rome, who were more human than divine.

The very mystery and mystique of this God *Elohim* held his interest. Here was a God Who played no games with His people, as the god Jupiter did. *Elohim* gave moral codes that guided His people to Him—laws that showed them how to live, act, and think. More importantly, He appeared to truly care for His people, in spite of their failings. Armed with these thoughts, Longinus sought out Jews, including young Nescius and a few renegade Jewish employees of the Roman Army, to make inquiries into this religion of the One God. Soon, he came to understand *Elohim* more, but knowing *Elohim* did not help him to understand His Chosen People.

Several months after arriving, he heard of a man named John who lived in the desert and ate locusts and wild honey and who preached repentance to all. Many of the Jews went to hear this man, and many became his followers. Some people called this John a *navi* prophet. Longinus was curious, so he disguised himself and went to hear this man; after hearing him, he found himself needing to learn more. It was on one of his trips that he saw the centurion Cornelius in the crowd. After seeing Cornelius on several other occasions, Longinus approached him with confidence, and the two talked about John and became friends. Much to his surprise, Cornelius, who was well known as a "Jew hater" among the garrison, was deeply captivated by the words of John. Furthermore, he learned that the centurion, who read and spoke Hebrew fluently, had been secretly studying some of the Jewish writings after purchasing some scrolls, at great expense, with the help of his beloved servant Pavilius. Longinus, in turn, listened to all that Cornelius discovered, and though he did not embrace the Judaic religion, he remained interested.

Longinus noticed changes within himself, and the changes made him accept, to some degree, the world he was a part of. He even began enjoying his life in Pilate's service, and he appreciated the company of his fellow soldiers and even the people of Judea. It made him happy when he saw the Jews listen to John, and when some changed their lives, he grew less severe in his perception and treatment of the Jews.

One day, the half-Jew Herod, with the blessing and help of a sympathetic sect called the Herodians, had John the Baptizer killed. This angered Longinus. He began slipping back into his old hatred, in spite of sound advice from Cornelius, who explained that John was not killed by the Jews but by Herod, who had a great fear of the prophet. Though this somewhat appeased Longinus, he was not completely satisfied. He watched as Cornelius grew interested in a new prophet named Jesus, Who was preaching about the kingdom of God. For some reason, Longinus could not commit himself to Jesus, though he feigned interest because Cornelius was so excited about this Man. Cornelius told him that this new prophet was performing magic, but still this did not inspire any interest. Longinus learned that Cornelius began disguising himself so he could go to hear Jesus. Their friendship started to decline as Longinus remained indifferent to Jesus.

Many months later, he heard that Cornelius' manservant Pavilius was ill. Longinus liked this manservant a great deal and knew how much Cornelius loved him—even respected him as a sort of father figure. Out of concern, Longinus decided to go to Cornelius, hoping to be of some comfort. On the way to Cornelius' house, he heard that the servant was not sick, so Longinus returned to the Antonia Fortress, believing that a renewed friendship was not meant to be. Days later, Cornelius pulled him aside and told him that Jesus had cured his manservant.

"My friend, I sincerely believe that this Man is blessed by the Jewish God. I am equally certain that He is a holy and righteous Man Who has come to set a new way for the world," Cornelius said with conviction. "He, more than John, has changed my ways. Come with me and see for yourself."

But Longinus never went. His time for release from the army was very close, and he did not want to be concerned with anything but the thought of returning to Rome and marrying.

✳

He rested on the mat, enjoying the small bath house in the garrison. He was bathing with three other centurions. It had been a busy day for the entire garrison. All were compelled to attend drills. The garrison was on full alert. Tension was in the air, for the Jewish holy feast of Passover was about to begin. In the past, there had been trouble with the Jews during this holiday. Pilate ordered Longinus to be at his side and on duty the next day.

Relieved of duty, Longinus enjoyed his time off because he believed that he deserved this pampering. A hair-plucker removed the hair on his back and chest, and now he was relaxed under the services of a slave who was rubbing him down with oil in preparation for a hot bath. His mind was at rest, and he was almost slipping into semi-consciousness when the others in the room began to mock the Jews and their great feast.

"I hear that they do not sit during their meal," one said, laughing loudly.

"They do that so they can get a fast start in case they have to run," another one said and laughed aloud.

"They eat lamb, weeds, and drink salt water," the first one said.

"That is why they are so miserable. They eat bad things," the second one said, and they both laughed.

"Well, for certain, the alert will continue into tomorrow," another man said.

I wish the Jews to Hades, Longinus thought as he slipped into nothingness.

The next day, as expected, the garrison was on alert, and when Longinus saw Cornelius, he was shocked at the anger he saw on the centurion's face.

"You were right, my friend, these Jews are not worth anything. Last night, they arrested Jesus and charged Him with blasphemy. I hear He was found guilty and is now to go before Pilate. This is going to be a long, long day."

So the long, long day began.

Longinus stood by Pilate, observing the proceedings, and he was overwhelmed with confusion. He could not understand how blasphemy, a Jewish concern before the Jewish people, could turn to treason, which was a Roman concern. The more he heard, the more sympathetic he became to the man Jesus. The longer he stood by Pilate, the more his eyes burned. Soon he developed a headache so severe that he wanted to rip off his helmet. His eyes twitched uncontrollably, and he was forced to close them to stop the burning and the pain. He became oblivious to all around him and was consumed by his own misery, which was more important than anything else.

Finally, he heard Pilate say aloud, "*Ibis ad crucem,*" Thou shall go to the cross. Following the Roman custom, when the death sentence was announced, Pilate broke a long stick in two and tossed it at the feet of Jesus. The loud condemnation and the snap of the wood jolted Longinus back to reality. He was relieved that Pilate had made a decision, for his standing and suffering would soon be over. His pains had made him lightheaded.

Suddenly out of his pain came a thought of Jesus, and he felt pity for the accused. A great injustice had been dealt. He looked at the accused as He was being led away, and then, with painful and burning eyes, he saw Cornelius, whose face was an open wound.

In ten minutes, the crowds were gone and their shouts had died to occasional bursts of crude laughter. The death march to Golgotha had begun, and Pilate returned to his chamber. Longinus slowly and carefully walked to a shadowed area off to the side of the *praetorium* and hurriedly removed his helmet; he laid his sweaty head against the side of the fortress. He pressed his head against the wall, desperate to relieve his pain. He stayed in this position for several minutes, satisfied with the small relief he was receiving.

From nearby he heard someone say, "Look at my fingers and hands. They are all torn up from those cursed thorns that I weaved into a crown for that criminal."

There was silence.

"Ah, but it was worth it. It hurt Him, and it made Him look ridiculous."

"I think not. I think we are hurt more, and we look ridiculous. I have an uneasy feeling that Judea, Rome—the world—will not be the same for what has happened today."

Longinus recognized the voice of the regretful legionnaire Marcellius.

Again Longinus felt the uneasiness he experienced earlier.

Hours later, as he sat drinking a cup of wine, Marcellius came to him and told him that Pilate wanted to see him immediately. He rose from his table, quickly finished his wine, and slowly put his helmet on his head.

As he neared Pilate's office, his eyes began to burn and twitch uncontrollably. He entered the room to find the governor pacing back and forth across the floor of his chamber. As he walked, he was wringing his hands over and over again as if trying to wash them.

"These damnable Jews!" Pilate shouted. "They are never satisfied!" He noticed Longinus standing at attention near the door. "Centurion, get a horse and hurry to Golgotha and break the legs of the three who were crucified today to hasten their demise. When this has been completed, report back to me." He stopped pacing. "The leaders have beseeched me to make certain that the crucified die quickly. They say the bodies must be removed before sunset. The Great Sabbath begins at sunset, and the bodies of these men must not remain on their crosses. I can never seem to satisfy these people. Now go!"

Longinus rushed to the stables and mounted a horse. Ignoring his burning eyes, he galloped to Golgotha. When he arrived, he quickly dismounted and was surprised at the number of people on the hill. The Pharisees and other leaders of the Temple were mocking the man Jesus. Some family and other friends of the crucified were there, and he saw Abendadar and other soldiers casting lots for the dying men's garments. He watched as Stephaton offered wine and myrrh to the man called Jesus. He saw a few other soldiers of the garrison standing and milling around in unusual seriousness. He looked for Cornelius and saw him off in the distance. He was mesmerized by Jesus, and Cornelius' stare caused Longinus also to look at Jesus. For an instant, his eyes met Jesus' eyes, and for the first time in his life, he felt aware of being in the presence of holiness. This privilege weighed heavily on him, so that he could not move from where he stood nor take his eyes off the Man's face.

In a low, weak voice, Jesus said something in Aramaic. Longinus did not understand.

"What did He say?" he asked, impelled by some strange sense of urgency.

"He said, 'It is consummated.'" It was the voice of Cornelius. Though he was surprised that Cornelius was near him, he could not take his eyes off of Jesus' face.

"Why are you here, Longinus?"

"To make sure these men are dead. Pilate wants their legs broken to hasten their death."

"It will soon be over. Jesus is dying quickly," Cornelius said. "If this is what you have been ordered to do, I will get Dorimius, the executioner, for you."

Moments later he realized that Dorimius, a member of the Auxiliary Legions, was standing by him.

"Pilate has ordered us to break the legs of these men. Do so," he ordered, still not able to take his eyes off the face of Jesus.

Dorimius remained unmoved.

Longinus, still looking at Jesus' face, continued, "Leave the man called Jesus for last."

Dorimius slowly walked away.

Jesus lowered His head, breaking the stare between them. Longinus believed that Jesus did this to pray; then, remembering that all Jews lowered their heads for blessings, he wondered if perhaps Jesus was seeking a blessing.

Startled, Longinus jumped as he heard loud cracking sounds and a loud scream, followed by an abusive curse coming from one of the other crucified men.

The wind began to blow, and the clouds in the sky grew heavy.

Unexpectedly, Jesus raised His bowed head, and looked to the sky above Him. In a strong voice, Longinus heard Him say: "*Pater! in manus Tuas commendo Spiritum Meum.*"

Longinus was surprised to hear Jesus speak in Latin, but it was even more surprising to hear a dying man speak in such a loud voice.

There was another great cracking sound, followed by a cry of pain.

The wind began to rage against the mount, carrying sand around and around, like a whirlpool picking up whatever was on Golgotha and taking it into the sky. The wind shifted the sands, which were thrown against the unprotected skin of all there. The skies turned from gray to black, and day turned into the dark of night, into the midnight hour.

Longinus took his eyes off of Jesus and saw Dorimius slowly walking to His cross.

"Dorimius!" Longinus shouted above the din of the wind. "No, wait!"

Dorimius looked at the centurion and almost smiled in relief, for he did not want to harm Jesus. Without any thought, he quickly walked away and took up his previous post.

Longinus walked slowly to the right side of the cross, and gripping his lance tightly in his hand, he raised it and plunged it into the side of Jesus. Instantly he felt the flesh split and heard the sound of the wound. This was something he had never experienced before, and he cringed and recoiled in the experience. Longinus withdrew his lance, and immediately there gushed forth warm blood mixed with water, which burst forth from Jesus' side and splashed Longinus' face. At first it burned his skin and eyes, and then it soothed them. His eyes stopped burning, his twitching ceased, and his headache faded. When he looked up, he knew Jesus was dead.

In a great rage, lightning and thunder ripped and roared around the mount and across the skies. The earth shivered and then quaked, bellowing a cry back to the sky. Rains fell from the darkness with such strength and vengeance that each drop felt like the prick of a sharp blade. In the darkness, amidst the angry rage of nature, came a cry—a declaration—from Cornelius, now kneeling in adoration: "*Vere Filius Dei erat Iste,*" truly, this Man was the Son of God.

Longinus looked up into Jesus' face with new eyes and saw Jesus in a new way, and in that moment he began his new journey.

✳

John slept late the next day. After the conversation with Longinus, John wrote notes about the reasons for the piercing of the side. He grew grateful for God's goodness, for he remembered a great deal of that day on Golgotha. To show his thankfulness, he fasted that day until supper. When the coolness of the night came upon them, he grabbed Longinus, and they left the crew and passengers to return to the deck. There, under the night sky with its thousands of stars, John insisted that Longinus continue with his story of Andrew.

Longinus began night two of his story.

"I had a sleepless night, John, as I relived all that happened to Andrew and myself while we were in Tomis, and soon the fears of that time came and stayed with me all night long."

"I am sorry, my friend, I did not want to revive any bad memories," John said with annoyance at his selfishness.

Longinus permitted a few moments of silence to pass between them as he gathered his thoughts of the past.

"John, what I am about to tell you will truly sound unbelievable, and I know that only a fellow Christian could understand it."

John's curiosity heightened, and he grew ever more eager for the Roman to begin.

"The difficulty we encountered in Tomis was totally diabolical. Word spread that we were in Tomis to replace *Serapis* with another Messiah, and the Grand Eminent Priest of the temple of *Serapis* was not about to let this happen. One day, while we were preaching, a storm of stones came flying at us. One jagged rock hit Andrew in the jaw and cut him badly, and for days he had a wide, open wound with black, bruised skin. Cenon was hit in the eye and for days was not able to see; from then on he was partially blind in that eye. I received several hits on the head and back because I had protected Andrew with my body. There seemed to be no end to the bombardment, but out of nowhere came a wind so intense that it quickly put an end to all the rock throwing. The people were blinded by the flying sands and scattered. That night, we slept in a nearby forest and tended to our numerous wounds. The next day, a large crowd came seeking us. They were not at all friendly, and they began taunting us with sharpened sticks. They cursed us as enemies of their god. I did not believe they were there to kill us, but I knew they were there to harass us in the hope that we would leave. I remember wishing that I had a lance or a sword, and the moment I thought this, I received a pain in my eyes. I must tell you, John, that every time I stray, the Master speaks to me and draws me back to Him by making my eyes ache.

"But let me return to my story. Where was I? Oh yes, in the midst of all this jabbing and cursing, Andrew stood firmly and courageously in one place with his eyes to heaven. He eventually raised his arms, and then quickly all was stilled and silenced.

"Andrew spoke: 'People of Tomis, slaves of *Serapis*, I know that you act not under your own will but according to the will of your pagan god. You persecute my companions and me out of fear of the truth, not out of fear of what we will do to your god. Our God is the One Who created all things, including the rocks from which you have carved your god, and I assure you that if I called on my God, He would destroy not only your god but his temple. I warn you, do not tempt my God, for He is all powerful.'

"Many of those around backed away, but some remained and continued to taunt us. Andrew closed his eyes and said in a loud, clear voice, 'Jesus, let it be Your Will that these hearts be turned to You.' Those taunting us continued, but not so aggressively. Cenon and I joined Andrew in prayer. Suddenly, the sticks held by the people crumbled in their hands. Some gasped in awe, and others ran in fear, screaming that Andrew was a sorcerer and a demon. Andrew looked around and invited those who wanted to stay to come to him so he could tell them more about the 'Messiah of Love.' Many stayed. By night, we had baptized many, and after we attended to our stab wounds, we again slept in the forest. As I slept, a quick and rough hand covered my mouth. It was Soberex, one of the Docian soldiers I knew from the garrison. He had been baptized in secret and had come to know the gentleness of the Master.

"'Longinus,' he whispered in my ear, 'do yourself and your companions a favor. Go! Tomorrow they will come to arrest and kill you all. Tonight, all who were known followers of Jesus were arrested, and most have been put to death. This night has turned into a bloody night. Our lives are nothing in comparison to yours. Please, go with the Lord and go quickly.'

"He released me and was gone. I immediately sat up and looked over at Andrew, and to my surprise, I found him sitting up; the firelight flickered across his face. Apparently he had been awakened by someone who told him of the danger we faced.

"'I know what you have heard,' Andrew said to me. 'Let us move fast, for there is something new awaiting us.'

"I called Cenon and we swiftly gathered our belongings and walked through the forest in the direction of the sea. When we reached the shore, morning was upon us, and there by the shore was a ship with three men sitting in it. Their faces were shadowed by their hoods.

"'Look, Andrew, a ship to take us far from this place,' Cenon said with great excitement.

"Andrew glanced at Cenon as if he were mad. 'What good is that boat to us? Look at the size of it. It is too small. It can barely hold the three men already aboard.' Yet oddly, he did not stop walking to the small boat. When finally he arrived at the boat, he turned to the hooded helmsman of the ship and shouted, 'Tell me, Sir, where are you going with this small ship?'

"'To the city of Mermedonia,' the helmsman replied in a soft voice.

"My heart jumped and fear took hold of me.

"Andrew turned to us and asked in a low voice, 'Where is the city of Mermedonia?'

"'In Scythia and Sarmatia,' I replied with great trepidation; I longed to say more but was unable.

"'Farther north,' Cenon said, looking at me in the hope that I would say something to stop Andrew, but I could not. My heart skipped a beat, and I was deep in prayer, pleading that Jesus would find a way to stop Andrew from making a commitment to go to Mermedonia."

"Ah, north again," John interjected with much wisdom.

"Yes. North again. Andrew looked at the helmsman and with a smile on his lips said, 'Sir, take us with you on your ship and sail north to this city.'

"The hooded helmsman replied, 'Are you sure of this request? All men flee this city; why do you wish to go there?'

"Andrew walked closer to the small boat. 'During the night I had a dream that a friend, Varianus by name, was imprisoned there and in grave danger. I have a task to perform there. It is a solemn task that I must complete for my Master.'

"'Well then, pay your way and I will get you to that feared city,' the helmsman said.

"The three of us looked at each other. Jesus had answered my prayers, for we had no money and the trip would be impossible. You see, John, I knew of this city and of the people in that region, and there was nothing good there.

"Andrew smiled, 'But sir, we are disciples of the Lord Jesus Christ. He gave us orders to go and preach His Good News to all people and to take not bread or water or money or clothing. So we have nothing to give you. If you cannot take us, then please tell us how to get there, and we will be on our way.'

"'If your Master has indeed told you this, then out of admiration for your obedience, I will take you there. Come aboard, if you are ready.'

"My heart skipped another beat, but I decided immediately that we were in the hands of the Lord. Andrew got in the boat, but Cenon and I were reluctant. The helmsman looked at me and then at Cenon, undoubtedly noticing my lack of enthusiasm.

"'Good traveler, your two companions are not as happy about this journey as you are. May I suggest that you give them the opportunity to wait for you here, until you return.'

"Andrew looked at us. Seeing our apprehension, he asked us, 'Brothers, do you wish to stay and await my return?'

"Cenon immediately said, 'No, for it is unsafe here.'

"I looked at Cenon and then at the helmsman, and for an instant I thought that I knew who the helmsman was. I quickly turned away and looked at Andrew and said, 'Holy Andrew, where would I go? How could I be away from all the good things that you have been empowered by God to do? I do not want to go to this place, but I will follow you wherever you feel the Master is directing you.'

"I climbed aboard.

"Andrew turned and smiled at the helmsman.

"'There, Sir, you have your answer.'

"The helmsman smiled and the ship pushed away from the shore and headed north.

"Soon Cenon was fast asleep, and I sat comfortably between him and Andrew. Andrew was strangely intrigued by the helmsman, whom he could not stop looking at. For some reason, I felt that I was not meant to be there. I looked at the other two members of the crew who just sat there, saying and doing nothing. I remember thinking they were there as guards, but as guards, they were too calm and serene—almost angelic. I remember concluding that they must have been men of peace, for they certainly were not men of war.

"'Tell me a story about this Man, Jesus, your Master,' the helmsman said. Andrew began telling him about the night Jesus calmed the stormy sea, and it was then that I fell asleep. Andrew told me later that as he was telling the story, the face of the helmsman began to change into a face he knew very well. When he stopped speaking, the helmsman insisted he continue. When he came to the part of the story in which Jesus calms the sea and the Apostles find peace, the helmsman said, 'Andrew.'

"'My Lord!'

"'I say again to you, Andrew, be not afraid, because the Lord God will not forsake you.'

"When Andrew heard these words, he laid his head upon my leg and slept.

"At morning we were on the shore. The soft strikes of oncoming waves against the boat woke us, and quickly we were surrounded by the barbarian Scythians in the land known as 'the land of the *anthropophagi* man-eaters.'"

Longinus shivered, and John was taken aback.

"Why are you so uneasy, my friend?"

"Because what happened to us was so horrifying. These people are flesh eaters and worshipers of the evil one."

John felt his inner being lurch, then he felt himself fall into a place of revulsion. He closed his eyes and instantly remembered the last time he felt this lurching feeling. It was when he and the other Apostles discovered that Jesus spoke to Samaritans; this disgusted them. John opened his eyes, prepared for what he would be told. The look on Longinus' face alerted him to the fact that the experience was too fresh in the Roman's mind to be seen as a blessing. John waited for Longinus to continue.

Slowly, Longinus started: "I really cannot tell you too much about the country, because we did not see much of it; for what I saw, it was a flat and barren place with no sunlight or joy of nature. It was a world without thought of another day. The barbarians quickly bound us and raced us through the countryside with our hands tied before us, and running behind us was a horseman whose face was painted a hideous brown and black. Soon, we arrived at what these nomadic people called a village. We were placed in a compound that was supposed to be a jail, but it was poorly constructed in comparison to Roman standards. In the center of this construction was a large tree trunk. It had been cleared of all its branches and life. They tied us to this tree and left us.

"When our eyes adjusted to the darkness of the hut, we realized that other people were present, and soon Andrew began calling out, 'Varianus.' No one answered, for they were all drugged with some herbal mixture that made them unable to think or speak. A person stumbled over to us. We did not know who it was until he spoke, and then we recognized Varianus. He had been blinded by the barbarians, but they did not give him the herbal drink that drugged the others. He told us that an angel came to him and told him that he would not be affected by the drink.

"'How did you get here?' Cenon asked him.

"'The ship taking me to Amisus was attacked by renegades, who took us here. All the members of the crew have been killed, and my days are numbered.' When he said these words, he picked up a tag that was tied around his neck. 'When you come here, they number you, and before the next full moon, you are killed and eaten. Somehow they had forgotten to number me, and I sat for days, speaking to everyone about Jesus. Many left this life believing in our Master, but my preaching caused me to be discovered. I was beaten and then given grass to eat. They have fattened me up to their liking, and now I believe that my time is approaching.'

"'No, my friend, the Lord has sent me to set you free in His name,' Andrew said in a low voice.

"'No, Andrew, you were sent here to prepare me for my voyage to the Master. Your presence makes me sure that all I have done has been pleasing to God, and I am confident that I will be welcomed into His arms.'

"At that moment the door of the prison opened. Seven guards entered the cell and began checking the tags around the necks of the prisoners. As each was picked, Varianus shouted, 'My brothers, be brave, for soon you will be with the Lord Jesus Christ, Who loves you.'

"One guard kicked Varianus and then dragged him out of the cell.

"'Andrew, thank you for giving me new armor. Praise God!'

"Andrew raised his hand and made the sign of the cross.

"Another guard came to Cenon. 'Ah, we have a fat one. We will not let you waste away. We will give you to our rulers.' Laughing, he walked to the prison door and slammed it shut, and moments later we heard loud screams and then silence. Moments later, the door opened; they came for Cenon and dragged him out of the prison. The last thing I heard that night was Cenon screaming. The next morning, we were awakened by the guards, who were laughing as they carried in food and drink. The other prisoners quickly scrambled to the buckets to eat and drink.

"Andrew told me not to fear, for the Lord had told him that we would not be harmed. As I turned to tell Andrew that I was willing to die for Jesus, then we saw Cenon sitting on the other side of the prison.

"We rushed to him and could see that he was without eyes. They had blinded him, and he was still in great pain. We immediately tried to comfort him, but he needed no comfort...he was smiling.

"'Andrew, the last thing I saw before they blinded me was the helmsman who took us to this place. Tell me, was that Jesus?'

"'Yes,' Andrew replied simply.

"'Good! Thank you. Praise my Lord. Finally, I have seen the Lord, and I have no fears. I pray that I will be a good dinner for our captives.'

"'You will not give more to these sinners, for the Lord has promised that we will not be killed,' Andrew declared as he struggled to stand. He raised his hands, arms, and face to the heavens and began to pray. Just then, a large cloud came over us. It covered us for some time, and during this time we all felt the love and presence of Jesus. When the cloud vanished, we were free from our bondage. The door to the prison was wide open, and the guards were all asleep. We walked out of the prison and traveled through the city unseen. When we reached the village limits, Andrew took us to a huge tree whose leaves and branches draped to the ground. We walked through the branches and found food and drink waiting for us.

"'You are to stay here and wait for me,' Andrew ordered. 'As long as you stay here under the protection of this tree, you will not be found out. I will return shortly. Wait for me. The Lord be with you.'

"Before I could object, he was gone. I knew he would be protected, so I immediately began to attend to Cenon, who was still in pain and was losing much blood.

"During the night, Cenon's condition worsened and he was gasping for air.

"'Longinus, do nothing more for me. I hear my name being called for a new mission. This is the Will of the Master. Tell Andrew that Varianus did not deny Jesus, though they tore at him. I was spared for this sleep and will awake to be with Varianus.'

"With these words, he took his last breath. After saying prayers over his body, I buried him under a pile of rocks. The night passed, and seven nights later Andrew returned. It was then that he told me this next story.

"He had returned to the village and boldly sat under a brazen pillar with a statue of the half man and half goat god on top of it. He sat, invisible to all, and secretly disrupted all that the Scythians were doing. He impeded their executions and cannibalism by turning the swords of the soldiers into stone. All these strange occurrences made the rulers of the people confused and panicky. One of them said that there must be a wizard in the village, and he insisted that they begin a search. Just then, an old man who was barely able to walk came into sight. He slowly walked up to the seats of the rulers and shouted, 'Woe be to you, for you all will starve. Search for a stranger from the south named Andrew; he is the cause of all your troubles.'

"Andrew knew that the old man was the devil, so he shouted, '*Belial!* My God will throw you back into the abyss.'

"Others, after hearing his voice, began looking around the area, bewildered and in terror.

"The devil answered, 'I hear you, but I cannot see you. Show yourself to me, Andrew, brother of Peter, the denier of his Master.'

"A bitter wrath welled up in Andrew's heart, and he shouted, 'You are still blind, you stupid and unclean pig!'

"The Lord removed his invisibility, and he was seen.

"The people fell back in fear upon seeing a man appear from nowhere.

"'There is the cursed one who tried to starve you. Take hold of him! Do what you need to do,' the Devil shouted with glee in his voice.

"The soldiers ran to Andrew, bound him, and began to beat him. They dragged him through the streets, where everyone threw stones at him. Torn and bloody, he was taken to the leaders, and with swords and spears they began to stab him.

"'He seems ripe, perhaps we should have him now,' one of the rulers shouted.

"'No!' shouted the Devil. 'Gag his mouth first, then tie him to the pillar beneath the image of your god. Let him see the face of the god who will take his life.'

"They did what was suggested, for they were under the Evil One's influence.

"During the night, the Lord came to Andrew and spoke to him. 'Andrew, you allowed anger and evil to come into you, and that is why you ceased being invisible. Why do you need to have anger and revenge in your heart? Do you not know that I could dispatch the entire heavenly host on Satan and have him silenced?'

"'Forgive me, Master, for I am but a sinner.'

"'Arise,' Jesus said, offering His hand.

"Andrew continued to pray for forgiveness.

"At midnight, Andrew stood up before the image and made the sign of the cross in the air seven times, and from the image water poured forth in a great flood. It swept through the village and extinguished all the fires, which were used for cooking. By morning, the village was flooded and the people began to flee, but they could not, for a wall of fire had surrounded the village. All of them were trapped within. When the waters came to their necks, they began crying for help and mercy. Andrew, seeing that their evil was crushed, picked up a rock and smashed it against the pillar; the image fell, the water ceased to run, and the land was instantly dried. All of the people ran to Andrew. He blessed them and asked for the remains of Varianus. Andrew prayed over the remains and called the Roman back to life.

"'Tell us of your God,' they demanded, and Andrew told them of Jesus. The next day, he baptized them and gave them the Lord's instructions and prepared to leave, establishing Varianus as the *episcopus*. The people begged Andrew to stay, but he told them he had to go to his disciples and on to other missions. As Andrew prepared to leave, he was approached by a young boy who reproved him, saying, 'You must stay for seven days. You have yet to leave your mark on these people. Finish what you have begun, cleanse these people further, and give them all of the Lord.' Andrew knew that the Master was speaking through this boy, so he stayed with them for seven more days, after which he returned to the tree where I was waiting.

"Upon his arrival to the tree, he asked for some rest, but first he told me his story.

"'Andrew, Cenon was taken to the Lord,' I told him.

"'I think not, Longinus, for he is working with Varianus.'

"These were his last words as he entered sleep. I was surprised by his statement but did not have the heart to continue a conversation, for I could see that he was exhausted. I suspected that he was confused, but his reply remained in my mind. Cenon's last words echoed in my memory. In doubt, I went to the pile of rocks that was Cenon's grave and began removing the rocks.

"There was no body. Cenon was indeed with Varianus.

"I wept, for I had doubted the Lord and Andrew. I prayed through the night, asking Jesus to forgive me and to help me to always believe in His power.

"The next day, I woke and found Andrew awake and eager to move on to our next mission. We gathered what little belongings we had, and soon we were on our way.

"'When we arrive at the shoreline, there will be a boat waiting for us,' Andrew said to me. 'You are to go to Epirus and meet John bar Zebedee. He seeks me and thinks I am in need of consoling. Peter, my brother, has been crucified. Tell John he is to return to Ephesus; you will escort him home and then join me in Greece at Achaia. Our time going north has ended. We are being told to go south, and there we will go.'

"We continued to walk and came to the shore, and there a boat awaited us. I tell you, the more we walked and sailed, the more joyous Andrew became, for Peter was with the Master, and Andrew felt that we had accomplished great things in that forsaken land. There was one final marvel on the day we left Scythia: the land around us changed, and the fields were gold with grain that swayed and moved to the will of the wind, and the breath of God."

"You are right, my dear Roman friend," John said. "Only a believer in the power of God could understand and believe such a story. I thank you for your account. You have been a good servant of the Lord, and of Andrew. The Twelve are blessed to have so many of you with us as we travel and do the Will of God. Many of you continue our labors after we leave a place. As I told Peter, it is time to hand over the reins to others who will follow us."

"My coming to Jesus was easy in comparison to that of many others, though I must admit that being an early follower of Jesus was not easy. After Peter baptized me at Cornelius' house, I went into the desert to find myself. While I was there, I suffered greatly. I was a follower of Jesus the Christ, yet I felt that I was failing Rome. In coming to Christ, I deserted all that I knew as a Roman and as a soldier, and this made me feel strange and out of the world. To conclude that Rome was not the most important thing in my life made me feel empty and alone. I met my demons in the desert, and when I was near collapse, I received word that Peter wanted me. He sent me to Andrew, and I found my new life."

John stared into his companion's face. It was silvery gray from the moonlight, and his well-trimmed gray beard was white and glistening. He wished that he had been on the journey with them. This is what he missed: the joys and the sufferings in traveling and preaching the salvation of the Lord.

"Tomorrow," Longinus said plainly, "we will arrive in Pylos on the Peloponnesian Peninsula. If you wish, we could disembark and visit some of our Christian friends."

"I will consider it. I intend to pray this evening, perhaps late into the night. I may not be up early. You should get some rest. Now that you have told me all about Andrew, you should have no need to stay awake and think of what to tell me. Go to your rest, Longinus."

"Thank you, John. Good night, and the peace of the Lord be with you."

"And also with you."

✳

After Longinus and he parted, Andrew traveled to the city of Philippi. In Philippi, he was greeted warmly by Christians, and within hours he was preaching and baptizing. Unfortunately, the persecution of Nero arrived in the city while he was there, and many went into hiding. Andrew's bold and open Baptisms caused him to be an immediate target, and he was quickly arrested. After a vicious beating, he and several other Christians were taken outside the city and thrown in a pit with three large hungry lions, but the animals did not touch them, and during the night they were rescued by some militant Christians. He was rushed off to Pella in Macedonia, where he was greeted again by Christians who had known Paul. They pleaded with Andrew to stay, which he did, but his stay was cut short by the persecution that followed him. He departed quickly, not only because he was being hunted but also because he was drawn to the cities of Thebes, Athens, and Sparta. These were the historical jewels in the crown of Greek history. Paul had passed through these cities but had not left that great of a mark. Andrew traveled to these cities and preached with great zeal, and many became Christians.

✳

Andrew believed the Greeks to be superior people. He learned of their culture through Jews who had visited and worked in Greece, from the Greek Jews who had come to Jerusalem, and from the Greek fishers who came to Galilee seeking fishermen. His friends Milippos and Leonides of Thebes were such recruiters. They had been raised in Greece and were as proud of being Greek as of being Jewish. Their stories of Greece made Andrew's adventurous blood boil and perked his interest in the Greek world. The two were employed by Alexion of Athens, who sometimes accompanied them on their trips to Galilee.

Alexion was a Gentile. Andrew knew this but never told anyone, for association with a Gentile was considered a grave wrong among the Jews. Alexion made Andrew see that Greeks were not like other Gentiles. He learned that the Jews had borrowed names, architecture, medicine, nautical knowledge, and much else from the Greeks, and this proved that *Elohim* had blessed and elevated the Greeks above other Gentiles. Alexion was knowledgeable, and through him Andrew heard of the great philosophers, Socrates, Plato, and Aristotle. Alexion told him about the minds and souls of these great teachers with such depth that the Apostle was in awe of Greek wisdom. He was amazed to hear that men sat and did nothing with their lives but think, and he was equally amazed at what they said was good and reasonable. He longed to hear more and frequently sought out these Greeks when they were in Galilee. He was eager to learn of other worlds, and the proud Greeks were always ready to tell of their greatness. On occasion, there were debates that did nothing more than solidify their respect for each other. None of the arguments solved anything or converted anyone. These talks elevated the Greeks to a special place in Andrew's mind. At one time, he even thought of joining the Greek fishing fleet, but he knew that his father and brother would not permit it. He thought of telling his brother but then remembered that Simon had no time for Gentiles, so he kept his learning to himself.

One day, Alexion told him that Socrates believed in one God.

"We Greeks think him an atheist," Alexion said, and the bright light of Greece dimmed at that moment.

How could the Greeks deny the wisdom of Socrates? Had he not told them so many wise things about life, the soul, and the world? How could they think that he was wrong? Great minds are given to man so God can be found through them. Andrew thought these things knowing that the great minds of the Talmud, the Torah, and the Holy Writings had heard the whisper of the Almighty.

To Andrew, the mind of Socrates had a special connection to God; God had used it to reveal Himself to the Greeks, and they had ignored this revelation. Surely, if God has revealed Himself to other people, other nations, but without acceptance, God remains a far away idea.

When finally the Twelve were assembled by Jesus and had started to bond, he spoke to Philip and John about the Greeks, telling them what he had learned. They appeared enthused by what he said. He recalled especially how Philip found some comfort in Greek thinking, and he was sure that he had piqued Philip's curiosity.

✳

After months of travel and preaching, Andrew arrived on the outskirts of Olympia. He sat on a rocky hillside and surveyed the land. The peacefulness of the landscape matched the serenity of his mood. He had not felt this stillness for years. It was a reward. He had accomplished much for the Lord, and he was now with the people he knew as well as his own. This is where he was meant to be, and though others had passed through Greece and left their marks, Greece, he believed, was meant for him.

In the distance sat *Oros Olympos,* the mythical home of the Greek gods. The mountain soared into the sky in a way that seemed to verify the belief that it rose from the center of the earth.

Andrew swallowed hard at the sight of the mountain. He could easily understand why the Greeks chose this colossal, majestic mount for the home of their gods, but he could not understand why the Greeks believed that their gods were there. The traditions of the Greek gods seemed contradictory to the Greek mind. They were a people devoted to searching, to asking and answering questions. They gave great minds to the world and explained many things about the soul, life, love, and purpose. How could they believe in gods with the same humanity as theirs? Their gods were humans playing at being gods, yet the Greeks could readily destroy such stupidity with their own logic.

Andrew stretched out his legs and fell back onto the grassy earth. He closed his eyes, but still in his mind he saw Mount Olympus.

Ah, Andrew, the Greeks need gods like all people. They innately knew that everything around them came from a Greater Power. No mere accident or human effort could have created all these things. So they looked for a Great Power, and with the simple minds of children, they created gods like themselves, believing in the godliness of humanity. Like them in many things and above them in other things. Yes, the Greeks, like the Babylonians, the Scythians, and the Armenians, felt a need for a god, but not the God that I have seen. I, like many others, saw both God and Man—like me in all things but sin, and above me in all things as God.

He sat up, and as he looked again at Mount Olympus, he forgave the Greeks, not because they needed forgiveness, but because he understood them better. Standing up, he looked down into the plains below him and said aloud, "My Greek friends, I have come like Peter and Paul to tell you of the God Who died on Golgotha. I will show you a God Who will fulfill all the dreams of your philosophers and playwrights. I will offer you life everlasting with forgiveness and love, not thunder, lightening, or human drama."

Again feeling the need to travel, he lumbered down the side of the mount and walked east into Arcadia and further to Megara, where he would meet Longinus. Suddenly and with much understanding, he realized that he missed his traveling companion.

✳

The city of Thebes was the city of his two Greek friends Milippos and Leonides. Many years before, the two informed him, with great pride, that their city had been founded by the Phoenicians and became a city-state like other Greek cities. Like all Greek cities, it was built on high ground known as an *acropolis*. As with all city-states of Greece, with the exception of Sparta, it was protected by high walls. He knew that Thebes was the home of the ancient lyric poet Pindar, who believed in the immortality of the soul and in judgment after death. He remembered thinking that Pindar was a sort of Greek Pharisee, for he saw similarities in their beliefs. Thebes was also the home city of the mythical figure Heracles, who was half man and half god. Andrew was amused by the trials and tribulations of this strong man of Greece, with his exaggerated feats of strength.

"But all religions have strong men who were champions of their god," Milippos once remarked. "Even we Jews have Samson."

As Andrew walked through the High Gate of Thebes, he wondered who would be the strong men of the Christians—surely none of the Twelve, for they were too human.

His stay in Thebes was crowned with his meeting with Milippos and Leonides. To his great joy, Andrew found that they had been baptized by Paul and Barnabas. They had been waiting for him, for they knew he would come to them. In fact, they had prayed for his arrival. With pride and joy, the two Greeks assembled as many Christians as they could, and that night Andrew held the *agape*, which was the Greek word for the celebration of the Meal.

The next morning, Andrew and his two Greek friends went to the *agorai* marketplace, and he began preaching. During his preaching, he mentioned that Jesus was both God and Man.

"Ah, He is like our Heracles," a Gentile shouted.

"No, *Christos* was both God and Man, not half god and half man like your Heracles."

The people began to shout and curse Andrew and some tried to grab him, but Milippos, Leonides, and some other Christians came between the mob and Andrew. They whisked him off and hid him until nightfall, when they took him out of the city. The three of them headed for Athens, where the Greek Gentile Alexion lived. Having insulted the pride of Thebes, he was never welcomed there again.

✳

Even before one sees Athens, the idea of Athens lives in the mind. It is a city of long history, great minds, prodigious power, and vast wealth; it commands respect from anyone who enters its gates. It is a white city of pure beauty. At the center of all that is breathtaking is the *Acropolis*, which demands immediate admiration and attention. To the north and west of the *Acropolis* stood the Council building of the *Aeropagus*. The *Acropolis* is often called the "sacred rock" of Athens, for on it were built the three important temples: the Parthenon, the Erechtheion, and the Nike in honor of Athena, the goddess of Athens. These temples commanded respect. The power of Athens had waned, but these buildings hearkened back to its former greatness.

Andrew entered through the main gate of the city, called the *Diplyon*, with childlike enthusiasm. Immediately he felt the soul of the Athenian legacy. As he and his escorts walked down the *Panthenaic*, the main street that led to the *Acropolis*, Milippos and Leonides rattled off names of dramatists, sculptors, and painters who lived during the glory of Athens. Andrew heard nothing of what they said, for he could not remove his eyes from the *Acropolis* and its temples. He came to the marble gateway called the *Propylaea*, which led up and into the *Acropolis*. He stopped. His Jewish sense and Christian spirit would not permit him to go any further, but still he felt a deep appreciation for the human minds that had created the magnificence around him.

Leonides told Andrew that the temples had marble and clay statues of Athena and bronze figures and mosaics that depicted parts of the mythology of Athena. Around the temples were sacrificial altars and sections for group prayer. The services of the temple were open to everyone, believers as well as non-believers, but in deference to the goddess's solitude, no services were ever held directly inside the temple.

"Look, there is Alexion," Leonides said with joy in his voice.

Andrew turned to look behind himself, but he did not see his old friend.

"He is coming from the temple," Milippos added in a low voice.

Andrew turned back to the *Acropolis*, then looked at his two companions. "Is he not a...."

"No, Andrew, he is not a Christian, and he does not know that we are. When Paul and Barnabas were here, he was away. He has remained staunchly and fanatically faithful to the Olympians."

"Welcome to Athens, my friend," Andrew heard Alexion say, and Andrew turned quickly. Walking toward him was Alexion, and Andrew almost gasped with surprise at the man he saw. He had aged greatly and looked frail. They embraced, and Andrew felt nothing but his small frame and bones.

"Come, let us leave here and go to my house where we can relax and enjoy conversation," Alexion said as he pulled Andrew quickly away from the *Propylaea*. He led them north through several narrow streets to a well-constructed road that rounded the *Acropolis* known as the *Peripatos*. After a short distance, they were met by a cart, and on the cart they began the scenic and leisurely ride to Alexion's home.

Andrew listened to all that was being pointed out to him, but he was more interested in Alexion, whose physical appearance bothered him greatly.

Soon they came to the open countryside.

"What ails you, Alexion?" Andrew finally asked, unable to control his curiosity.

Alexion explained that he was very ill, and nothing that the sons of Hippocrates did had helped him. Even the prayers of the High Priestess of the Temple of Athena had not helped him, so that day he had decided to go and make an offering to Athena on his own. The same malady had also stricken his wife Zosima, who was more ill than he was, and equally as ill as his grown son Glaucus, his daughter Dictynna, and several of their slaves.

The moment Andrew walked into the *aule* courtyard, he felt uncomfortable. The first thing that bothered him was the opulence of the *spiti* house, and clearly Alexion was proud of this opulence. He was also disturbed by the many pedestalled idols of Greek gods scattered all around the atrium.

The courtyard was a perfect rectangle with shrubs, small trees, and many flower beds planted along the four sides of the yard, with eight small stone paths leading to eight doorways, which were the entrances to eight rooms. In the center of the courtyard was a small pool with a statue of Athena rising from the center of the still water.

The four men were greeted obsequiously by six male slaves, who immediately asked to take their *himation* cloaks. They then hurried away only to return just as quickly with urns, basins, and foot cloths. Their feet were washed, and again the slaves quickly disappeared.

"Come, my friends," Alexion said. "Let us go into the *andron* dining room where we can relax and talk. We will have some food together."

He led them quickly across the courtyard, to the right and through a doorway. Immediately the coolness of the room greeted them, and Milippos and Leonides swiftly reclined on the couches nearby. Andrew timidly walked into the room and sat on the edge of a couch, remaining uncomfortable in spite of the pleasantness of the room. The floors had mosaic images of satyrs, nymphs, and other pagan remembrances. The walls were plastered and painted a bright red that almost hurt his eyes. The ceiling, with its heavy wooden beams, was white. From the beams hung lamps burning olive oil; their fumes and fires soiled the white ceiling with black marks. Along the three closed sides of the room were twelve couches, four on each wall, and in front of each couch was a small table on which food was served.

"Gamelion, go call your mistress and tell her we have guests," Alexion ordered, and one of the slaves quickly exited the room as two female slaves entered carrying bowls filled with figs, grapes, nuts, honey, and bread. They were followed by two other female slaves carrying jars of wine, which was quickly poured into clay bowls. The Greek Jews immediately began to eat and drink, but Andrew sat observing all the moving and ordering. Finally, Andrew resigned himself to Alexion's wealth and power, and he silently rejected it.

"I will have the servants prepare a feast for this evening, and you will stay here as long as you wish. It is good seeing you all; I truly missed you," Alexion said with a wide smile on his face, but upon looking at Andrew his smile faded. "Andrew, you are not hungry?"

"No."

Alexion tilted his head to the right to examine Andrew further. "You look uneasy."

"I am not accustomed to being served by slaves."

Milippos and Leonides stopped eating and quickly sat up; they sensed the tension growing in the room.

"Slaves? Oh, you mean my servants."

"You own them?" Andrew questioned softly.

"They have been in service to my wife's family for years. Their grand-parents worked in the Lavrion silver mines, which my wife's family had interest in. When the mines began to fail, they came into service to her family and eventually to me. They are of my *oikos* household. They are dealt with justly."

"You own them?" Andrew questioned in a raised, agitated voice.

"Yes!" Alexion said quickly, then he smiled, hoping to change the atmosphere in the room. "I am sorry, my Jewish friend. I feel I have offended you, but I am Greek, and I, like Plato, cannot imagine society without slaves."

"You give them a life of mere obedience, but man is not contented with such a life. They have souls with ambitions and desires and intel-lects," Andrew replied.

"My fellow Greeks," Alexion said looking at Milippos and Leonides with a forced smile on his face, but the smile did not hide his annoyance, "we have a Galilean philosopher with us." His sarcasm was obvious.

Returning his attention to Andrew, he said, "I have no desire to argue with you, Andrew, on the morality of slavery. I know you are a good Jew and that the Jews think they are better than other races, but believe me, we Greeks have found slavery to be necessary to sustain harmony in our society."

He paused and tilted his head to one side and frowned as he recalled something. With careful, slow words, he continued: "If I recall, you Jews also had slaves, and even your father Jacob was indentured to his father-in-law."

"That was all in the plan of God," Andrew answered.

"Well, these servants are in the plan of Athena."

"Oh Alexion, do you not get exhausted at being an Athenian?"

Alexion quickly jumped to his feet.

"My old friends, here is my wife, Zosima."

The men turned their attention to the doorway, where they saw a feeble woman. Her rich clothing hung on her like meaningless rags. She was thin and looked old. Walking by her side and holding her arm was Gamelion, the slave. She slowly walked into the room and sat on the edge of the first couch she could reach.

After helping Zosima to the couch, Gamelion walked to Alexion and whispered something to him.

"My friends, I have a visitor. Business. Please excuse me. Zosima, be gracious to our guests. I will be back shortly." With these words he left the room.

"It is good seeing you again, Milippos and Leonides. I trust your families are well. And you, good sir, I do not know you."

"I am Andrew, son of Jacob of Bethsaida in Galilee."

"A Jew?"

"Yes."

"I trust your family is no longer in that land. I am certain that the Romans will crush the revolt with much brutality."

"What has happened in my homeland is not a surprise to me," Andrew replied as he remembered the prophesy of Jesus. "Still, I have my people in my mind, and they are ever in my prayers."

"You must be thought of very highly, Andrew, for Alexion does not take kindly to *metoikoi* non-Greeks. He is exceedingly proud of everything Greek."

"I am sorry to see you are not well, Lady Zosima. I trust you are not in pain."

"No. No pain, I am just slowly fading away. My husband believes the gods will help us. He reminds me often that our gods have made us great, and they have helped us when we were suffering under the heel of others." She leaned forward slightly and whispered, "I do not have Alexion's faith, and maybe that is why we continue to be ill; I have angered the Olympians."

Gamelion presented her with a cup of water. His concern for her was apparent from the look on his face and from the way he hovered nearby. She carefully took the cup and sipped from it.

"Thank you, Gamelion," she said with a smile. "My faithful Gamelion has suggested that I pray to the 'Unknown God.'"

"The Unknown God, *Eromenee* madam?"

"Yes. You see, we Greeks build altars to every god there could be, and to make certain that we offend no god, we build an altar to one that we may have forgotten—the Unknown God. See how practical we Greeks are."

She returned her cup to Gamelion.

"Gamelion has great faith in this Unknown God, whom he calls *Prosopikos Theos*, his Personal God. He tells me that his God has strong friends who walk the earth. I remember years ago a man who came to Athens and did much good; he spoke beautiful things and even healed sick people. He said he came to tell us about the Unknown God. Some listened to him, but Athenians are hard-headed people. I am told that his followers are still in Athens. I wanted Alexion to seek them for their help in curing our family, but he has refused. If this God can heal my family, as the Olympians have failed to do, then I will believe in Him forevermore." She paused and took a deep breath, which seemed to cramp her stomach, for she grabbed it quickly.

"Are you unwell, Lady Zosima?" Andrew asked with deep concern.

"No. It is nothing." Swallowing hard, she whispered again, "I prayed to this Unknown God, asking that this man return to Athens. If he does, I will forsake my husband and the Greek gods and seek him out."

"This man who came to Athens, where was he from?" Andrew asked.

"He was Jewish," Zosima said, "from Judea."

"No, my Lady, he was from Tarsus in Cilicia," Gamelion corrected her softly as he stared directly into Andrew's face. The two Greeks seated behind Andrew looked at Gamelion in surprise.

"Andrew...." Milippos said quickly, and Andrew raised his hand to silence his friend.

"What was the man's name?" she asked her servant.

"Paulos," Gamelion answered.

"Do you know him?" Zosima addressed Andrew. "He is a Jew."

"Yes, somewhat. I am sorry to say he is dead. Killed at the hand of the Emperor."

Zosima began to cry and soon looked like a child whose dreams had been crushed. This transformation made Andrew compassionate.

"Now I know that my children are doomed to *Kerameikes* a nearby cemetery. He was my last hope. Oh, Gamelion, what am I to do now?"

Gamelion rushed to his mistress's side and touched her shoulder.

"My Lady, do not lose faith," Gamelion said. "The death of this man does not hurt the goodness of my God."

"For He is full of compassion and mercy," Andrew said in a low, reverent voice.

"Yes sir, He is, and I know He will not fail me, for I believe in Him." The servant turned and looked at his sobbing mistress. "Sir, please help her. She is a good woman. Kind and gentle. I have prayed for mercy ever since I heard Paul speak of the *Christos.*" He turned to Andrew. "I know who you are, you are one of His fishers. *Iesous Christos Theou Uiou Soter,* Jesus Christ God's son, Savior. You see, Paul and Barnabas taught me well."

"Does your master know that you are a Christian?" inquired Milippos.

"No!" Gamelion glanced quickly around the room and walked to the open doorway, looking out into the courtyard. Returning, he continued, "Master thinks that Christians desire to change the face of Greece by introducing a new religion that stems from the Jews. He thinks the movement is a Jewish plot to convert the world to their religion. He hates Christians for denouncing all the gods, including the Emperor. No, if he knew that I was Christian, he would have me scourged, reported to the Romans, or worse, he might sell me."

Andrew walked to the woman and knelt by her side. He whispered, "Lady Zosima, do you wish to be cured and saved by the Unknown God, Whose name is *Iesous Christos*?"

The woman's eyes moved across Andrew's face, and in an instant her countenance shone with hope.

"I am one like Paul, and believe what I say to you: *Iesous* is the God of love, mercy, and faithfulness."

"Yes. I will believe in such a great God. And my children? Will this God love them also?"

"His love knows no limits."

Andrew came to his feet and suddenly towered over everyone in the room. Immediately, Milippos and Leonides were on their feet, and they walked to Andrew's side and fell on their knees. Gamelion followed their example.

Zosima raised her eyes to Andrew. Her face was wet with tears, yet glimmering in hope.

"Help my family, oh God of love, so that we can be witnesses of Your mercy and declare Your goodness throughout all of Greece," she whispered.

Andrew raised his hands above Zosima and began to chant in a language that was strange to all present, then he said in a loud voice, "God of all love, cleanse this body and soul of all sickness, and give her Your peace. Give her the life of Your Spirit. I ask this blessing in the name of Him Whom You have sent to us with Your love. Amen."

Zosima collapsed onto the couch, and the three men made her comfortable as Andrew continued to pray in an unknown tongue. When he finished, he laid his hands on her head and blew his breath on her face.

"Let her rest," he commanded, then he asked Gamelion to take him to the children.

The two Greeks stood watch over Zosima, and eventually Leonides removed his cloak, rolled it up, and placed it under her head. Then he sat and silently prayed. They were so deep in prayer that they did not see or hear Alexion and the Roman soldiers coming across the courtyard.

"What is wrong with Zosima?" Alexion shouted in alarm.

"She is resting," Milippos said.

"Where is Gamelion?" he asked, looking around the room. "And where is Andrew?"

"Gamelion and Andrew are…"

"…gone," Leonides quickly said, completing Milippos' sentence.

"Why did you not tell me that Andrew was a Christian and a follower of that poisonous sect?" When Alexion uttered the word "Christian," his voice rang out with contempt. Milippos and Leonides grew uneasy.

"We thought you knew," Milippos simply stated.

"If I had known, he would not have been welcomed here."

One of the Roman soldiers stepped in front of Alexion and looked directly at the two Greeks.

"Do you know where this man Andrew has gone?"

"No, he just left because he felt unwelcome," Leonides said, glancing over the Roman's shoulder at Alexion.

"Well thank the gods he did. I have no time for men who try to change the ways of Greece…or of Rome," Alexion said. After walking to his wife and taking her hand, he stated, "She feels feverish."

"She is well," Milippos said.

The Roman turned and clamped his hands, and the soldiers in the detachment surrounded the two Greeks.

"Now tell me: Are you two Christians?"

The two men stared at the Roman soldier.

"No, they are not," Alexion said, still by his wife.

Leonides looked at Milippos, and together they smiled.

Milippos took a deep breath and threw back his shoulder, expanding his chest in pride.

"Yes, we are Christians."

"What? What are you saying?" Alexion jumped to his feet in shock.

"As I suspected," the Roman soldier said. "Take them; tie them in the cart and take them off to prison for Magistrate Cyriacus Gallius. Tomorrow we will see if they have the strength to remain Christians."

The soldiers roughly grabbed the two men and pulled them away.

"Milippos and Leonides, you have betrayed my friendship, but I am glad to see you have been found out and will die because of your folly," Alexion said.

"The Lord be with you and forgive you your sins, Alexion," Leonides said to him.

"When I am with the Lord, I will pray for you," Milippos said sincerely.

"To hell with you and your Jewish Messiah!" Alexion shouted.

The Roman captain turned to Alexion and said, "Thank you, Alexion, you are a true Greek and a true Roman. It is people like you that allow these cursed ones to be captured. We have not found this Andrew of Galilee, but at least we have some of his followers, and that will make the magistrate happy. He will remember you for this."

"I trust you will find my slave Gamelion and arrest him. Undoubtedly, that quiet snake also is one of them."

"We will hunt him down. May the gods be pleased with you." With a Roman salute the captain turned and followed his men out of the house.

The room was silent, and Alexion returned to his wife. Wiping her face with one hand and holding her hand in the other, he whispered her name.

"Mera! Mera!" Alexion shouted with urgency.

A small, young, female servant came running into the room.

"You called, Master?" She ran to Zosima. "Is Mistress ill?"

"I do not know. Where are all the servants? I need one of them to go for the physician." He jumped to his feet and walked quickly from the room. "Where are the servants? Mera, stay with your Mistress."

Mera went to a nearby table for some water and a towel. When she returned, Zosima was sitting up.

"Mera, hurry! Go to the children's room and tell the man Andrew to leave quickly. Tell him that his life is in danger and that his friends have been taken away for being Christians. Tell Gamelion to leave with Andrew, for he also is in danger."

"Madam, you are well!"

"Never mind me, do as I say, child."

Mera began to cry.

"No time for tears, Mera, go and do as I say, and hurry."

The young servant ran from the room and did as she was told.

*

After Andrew left Athens, many Christians were rounded up and imprisoned or killed. Half of Alexion's household, including Lady Zosima and her son Glaucus, were arrested. Alexion fell into disgrace with the Roman Magistrate, and his daughter Dictynna somehow was not discovered and remained free to do the Will of God.

Andrew had been taken away from Athens by his new companion Gamelion. They traveled through a clandestine network of Christians in Athens and other cities until they arrived at Achaia. The quickness of their travel was certainly a miracle from the Lord. He was sure that he was where God wanted him to be.

Life in a cave greatly pleased Andrew. During the day, he welcomed its natural coolness. At night, the cave with its dark chill was unpleasant, but this discomfort became his reparation.

The cave was outside the Greek city of Patras, and he was covertly kept alive with food supplies provided by the local Christians. Non-Christians secretively came to Andrew; he preached about Jesus to them, and many were baptized. After a month of hiding in Patras, Andrew remembered that Longinus was still in Megara.

"Gamelion, you must go to Megara and find Longinus and return with him. I was supposed to meet him weeks ago, and I am certain he is worried as to why I have not arrived. You know all the quick, underground ways to come and go, so I am sure you will be safe on this journey. Besides, you will be protected by God, for you are doing His Will. Now go and hurry back, for I miss Longinus greatly, and when you leave I will miss you greatly."

Gamelion left quickly, heading south to fetch Longinus.

Two days after his departure, the governor of Achaia, Aegeates, made a proclamation denouncing the Christians as enemies of Rome and of the Greek people, and all citizens were encouraged to inform the Romans of anyone whom they suspected of being a Christian. Within one week, hundreds were arrested, and many were martyred because they refused to worship the Roman Emperor or the Roman or Greek gods.

The Lord made Andrew understand that it was just a matter of time before he would be found and arrested. On the first day of the week, Andrew knelt in his cool cave, praying and meditating on the love of God. His mind went back to Jesus telling the Twelve that He would be with them always, then he thought of the night of the *Pasch* with Jesus.

He thought of how Jesus was keeping His promise by being always present to them in the *agape* which was their thanksgiving of the love God poured out to them through the life, death, and resurrection of Jesus. His mind wandered to the cold, chilling night in the Garden of Gethsemane. The night became so real in his mind that he felt the chill, and he could see the silver moon shining amidst the darkness of the night; he felt the heaviness of his eyes and heard the whispers of Jesus off in the distance. He heard the clang of armor and the sounds of rushed footsteps against the solid earth.

Then he heard a familiar Voice say: "Whom do you seek?"

Then he heard a strange voice say: "Andrew of Galilee."

And Andrew said aloud: "I am he."

So they took hold of him, arresting him in the name of their god, the Emperor Nero, and dragged him to jail.

The damp chill of the cell pleased him greatly. He had forgotten the ache of prison, and he was pleased to be reminded of it again. He welcomed the stench and the troublesome varmints, the fleas and the buzz of insects. He went into himself and prayed as he never prayed before, knowing that what was to be was the Will of God. He thought of his brother, of days gone by. A strong longing to be with Jesus and Peter came over him. He remembered James bar Zebedee, and the often forgotten Matthias, James bar Alphaeus, and Bartholomew, and he longed to see them again. He thought of John bar Zebedee and felt the warm care and friendship between them. He was confident that young John would be ever cared for by the Master. He prayed for the safety of Thomas, Matthew, Jude, Simon, and of course Philip. It was of great comfort to know that they were in the places appointed them and were doing the Will of the Master. With regret, he remembered Alexion and prayed for forgiveness if he had harmed his Greek friend, then he hoped that the Spirit of the Lord had come upon Alexion.

Late in the second night of his imprisonment, Andrew was awakened by the rats nibbling at his toes. He sat up and began talking to them, telling them they should be more considerate, but they continued to scurry about the cell. He began telling them about Jesus and how Jesus showed respect for animals during His time on earth. The rats stopped attacking each other and started to listen. Suddenly, the door of the cell swung open. The light from a torch burst into the room and attacked Andrew's eyes. He quickly shaded his eyes with his hands to avoid further discomfort. He was violently dragged from the cell. Once outside, he was ordered to strip, and as he stood naked, protected only by his hands, he was drenched with cold water and given a clean robe to wear. His hands were bound and he was led away. As he was pulled up the steps of the dungeon, he was approached by one of his guards who had been kind to him and whom he suspected of being a Christian. The soldier's name was Ifidamius.

"Be calm, Brother," Ifidamius said in a low tone. "I have been asked to take you to see a very important woman who is very ill and who is in need of your help. I know that taking you to her is dangerous, but she asked for you. She has heard of the *Christos* and of the many good things that have been done in our Lord's name. She knows me as a Christian and has asked me to carry out her request. The good and the bad of this is that she is the governor's wife, Maximilla."

"If God is with her, we must go," Andrew said simply.

They rushed out of the prison into the dark night, and Andrew felt comfortable, for in his cell, it was always night. Ifidamius ordered him onto an open-back cart. He was bound to the side of the cart. Ifidamius climbed on the cart, took the reins and roughly ordered the horses to gallop away. When they had traveled a safe distance, Andrew was freed of his bindings and was asked to sit next to Ifidamius.

"My Lady is so sick that her husband, the governor, has placed a dagger for himself next to her bed, for with her death he wishes to die also. He is extremely devoted to her and loves her more than anything in life. I am certain that if you heal Maximilla you will be set free."

"I will heal her only if she accepts the *Christos* as her God and repents of her sinful ways."

"She will do this, for she is no stranger to Jesus. She knows of Him, for many in her household are Christians. She has learned much from me—she trusts me completely. She knows who you are and was going to seek your release, but then she became ill with fever and pain."

"You see the hand of the Lord in this, my brother?"

"Yes, that is why I am certain you will be set free to continue doing the Will of the Lord. If you are set free, I will seek to be released from the army so I can accompany you, for I want to do more for the Lord."

Andrew smiled, for he knew that feeling well.

"We have moved Maximilla to a small *villa* owned by her husband's brother, Stratocles," Ifidamius said, urging the horses on to a quicker pace. "Stratocles is not at all pleased with what we do, but my Lady pleaded so fervently that he acquiesced to her wish. I do not know if he can be trusted, and I leave him and us in the hands of the Lord."

They arrived at the *villa*, and Andrew was hastily led through the gate, into the courtyard, and through the portal into a large, airy room where many olive oil lamps brightly burned. He saw nothing but the woman reclining on the couch surrounded by many female servants, all of whom were in prayer. He readily perceived that the woman was in great pain, for her moans were loud. Several of the servants came to Andrew and, reaching for his hand, kissed it. He became unnerved by their displays of respect and ignored their actions. He walked to Lady Maximilla and felt the side of her face with the back of his hand. He first observed her fever, but then he felt something radiating from her, something he had only observed once before—the time the woman from Magdala came to Jesus. He felt a living spirit in Mary of Magdala then, and he felt the same spirit in Maximilla, and without hesitation he called for water. While the water was being brought to him, he knelt in prayer. When the water arrived, he slowly poured the water over the woman's head, and she grew still and her skin lost its moisture. Everyone in the room was awestruck by her stillness and the peacefulness in the room. Andrew stood and placed his hand upon her head, and in a commanding voice he shouted, "Woman of faith, awake from your sleep, for you are now full of the life of Christ, the risen Lord and God of all."

With these words, Maximilla elegantly lifted herself into a sitting position and cried, "Jesus, You are my God!" All the servants began to shout praises and to give thanks to God, and in the midst of all the jubilation Andrew stepped back, allowing them their moment. Suddenly he was grabbed and pulled away behind a large column, and a Roman dagger was soon at his throat.

"Are you a sorcerer?" the man holding the dagger asked.

"No, I am an instrument of my God."

"How were you able to cure Maximilla when all the physicians and charmers could not?"

"I did not do it; my Lord and God did it."

The man holding the dagger eased his grip on Andrew.

"What name do they know you by?"

"I am Andrew of Galilee."

"The renegade?"

"A renegade only from the Evil One, but from no one else."

The man with the dagger laughed.

"I must ask you to do something for me, renegade from the Evil One. My servant Alkman is sick with the same maladies as Maximilla. Heal him, also, so I can come to believe."

"Take me to him."

The man with the dagger grabbed Andrew's arm tightly and hurriedly led him from the large room, through a maze of corridors and halls, into a much smaller and more austere room. Upon entering the room, the man called Alkman opened his eyes and struggled to sit up on his pallet. He struggled to speak, but he was too weak to say a word.

"Alkman, be at peace. This man has the power to heal people. He is going to help you," the man with the dagger said.

The servant continued to struggle to speak, and finally the man with the dagger leaned over and listened to the sick man's whispers. After hearing his words, he stood up and said to Andrew, "He said that he saw you in a dream and has been expecting you."

Andrew smiled and said to the man, "Then you know who I am, good man, and you know who sent me?"

The sick servant nodded his head.

"Then in the name of Him Who sent me, I say to you, arise, and find new life in the name of Jesus Christ your Savior."

Alkman closed his eyes, and after a few quick moments he rose from his pallet and embraced Andrew, saying, "Sir, tell me of Jesus, for I want to be completely His." Turning to his master, he said, "Thank you, Master, for you have saved my life here and in the hereafter."

Andrew then learned that the man with the dagger was Stratocles, brother of Aegeates, governor of Achaia. In the house of Stratocles that night, Andrew spoke of Jesus and told the household of the love and sacrifice of their Savior. They heard of the miracles and of the wonders that Jesus performed, and by morning they were pleading to become Christians.

In the morning, as they all sat listening to Andrew speak of Jesus, the house became filled with Roman soldiers. When the entire household was assembled in the large room, Aegeates arrived, and one could easily see the fiery anger on his face. He walked directly to Andrew and ordered him to be bound and led back to Alkman's room to be guarded. Immediately, Aegeates questioned everyone in the household, and those who admitted to being Christians were quickly herded away. Among those bound and led away were Alkman and Ifidamius.

Maximilla and Stratocles tried in vain to stop the arrest by explaining what had happened, but the governor would not hear anything they had to say.

Alone with his wife and brother, Aegeates became enraged and called them "betrayers of Rome."

"The Jews are in revolt against the goodness of Rome. Roman Legions are marching on Jerusalem to crush the revolt, and you both have sided with the enemy of Rome by becoming Christians. You have betrayed Rome and endangered my position as governor of this province."

He ordered them to be confined to the *villa* and to their rooms.

Andrew was called in to see him.

"Jew! Christian! You have two charges against you. You are of the Jews, who are at war with the Empire of Rome, and you are of the Christians, that subversive group of Jews who wish to undermine Roman gods. Show me that you are a subject of Rome by denouncing that rebel and criminal Jesus, and I will set you free."

Andrew and Aegeates looked at each other for a long time.

Finally Andrew said, "How can you set me free, Aegeates, when I am already free, and by my death I will be free for all eternity."

"You insolent Jewish pig!" With the back of his hand, Aegeates slapped Andrew, and the ring on his finger opened a gash above the Apostle's eye. He moved closer to Andrew, so close that Andrew could feel his breath on his face and smell the wine and onions on his breath.

"By your bewitching charisma and enchantments, you have taken my brother from me, and it would have been better if you had left my wife to her death, for you have killed not only her but also my love for her." He spat in Andrew's face and yelled, "I damn you to Hades, Christian!" Stepping back, he commanded in a loud voice, "Guards! Take this Christian pig and crucify him. Do not nail him to the cross, but tie him tightly to a *chi* X so that his death will be slow."

They led Andrew away. As he walked from the *villa*, he felt his heart pounding from the excitement and joy.

EPILOGUE

A young, exhausted Greek courier arrived at John's home in Ephesus. John directly saw to the young Greek's comfort before he sat to read the scroll that had been delivered. As he loosened the leather tie around the scroll, he grew anxious, for he was sure it was from one of the other Apostles, or possibly was about one of them. He did not recognize the script, so he presumed that someone wrote the letter for one of the Apostles. He became disappointed when he saw that the *epistula* letter was from Longinus.

To John bar Zebedee of Jesus Christ

From Gaius Magnius Longinus, son of Rematius

May the peace of our Lord Jesus Christ be with you,
Brother.

I am writing to tell you of my meeting with Andrew
in Greece after leaving you in Ephesus. I arrived in
Megara as planned, and in ample time, but Andrew was
not there. This did not surprise me, for I expected him to
be late. He always found distractions in his voyages.
After being in Megara for several weeks, an elderly
man named Gamelion found me and said that Andrew
had experienced trouble in Athens with his old friend,
Alexion. Perhaps you remember this man from his visits
to Galilee years ago. He was truly a Greek. It seems that
Andrew irritated Alexion and was forced to leave Athens
with Gamelion. They traveled far from Athens and
arrived at Patras in Achaia. In hiding, Andrew began
preaching to the people. Gamelion was ordered to Megara
to fetch me. Together we returned to Patras.

I must tell you that things have gotten bad in Greece.
Our brothers and sisters are being pursued relentlessly.
Many have been imprisoned, and many, firm in their
faith, have died. It is dangerous to be a Christian.

When finally I arrived in Patras, I found the city
in heightened alert. The governor, Aegeates, had ordered
the arrest of all known Christians. This persecution had
been going on for days. Roman soldiers were everywhere,
and each time we saw a unit of them, we hid or fled.
Gamelion knew all the hiding places, but it was obvious
that we were running out of options. Finally, by the
grace of God, we found a home just outside of the city.
It was then that I learned that Andrew had been arrested
and condemned to death by crucifixion.

John lowered the parchment and covered his mouth with his hand. A sudden and familiar chill raced through his body. He closed his eyes, hoping to hold time, but flashing across his mind was the image of Andrew walking in the midst of the Twelve. Andrew, the *Protokletos*, the first called! After many long moments, he returned to the letter, ready to accept the Will of God, yet he felt his hands become wet with perspiration and his heart was beating loudly in his head.

I insisted on going to where Andrew was and, reluctantly, Gamelion escorted me. We walked along a dirty road that went around the city. We came to a small stream, and there on the side of the stream was Andrew. I was ready to declare the report a hoax, because the man on the chi looked nothing like Andrew. His face was unrecognizable; it was cut, bruised, swollen. He had been hit and beaten by the Roman and Greek passersby. The blood from his wounds was caked dry and brown. His chest was scarred, cut, and ripped. There were more wounds than I could count. He was weak, and his lips were sore and brittle. He had been on the cross for three days and nights with no food or water. He needed water, but no one could give him any, for the Roman guards were everywhere—anyone who assisted Andrew would have been revealed as a Christian. This did not stop Gamelion or me. Gamelion found a cup of water and rushed it to Andrew, but before he reached him, he was stopped and taken into custody. I removed my cloak and rushed to cover Andrew. A Roman stopped me, but I declared my Roman citizenship and military rank and was left alone.

Andrew slowly raised his head; he recognized me, and his head fell back. I stood watch over him for a long time. Several soldiers came to me and told me that Aegeates had ordered Andrew to be crucified this way so that the wild animals would devour him, but none came near. They told me that when Andrew saw his cross, he welcomed it with open arms. He called it his "beloved cross" and spoke to it as his friend. As they spoke, Andrew moved. He looked up, and with his parched lips he cried aloud, "My time has finally arrived. There, over there, is John bar Zachary showing me the way, and there is Jesus waiting for me. O Master, I see You! Call me once again by name, and receive me with the same love. Call me to Your eternal peace, that I may enter the mansion You have prepared for me." Lowering his voice, he said, "For this day I was born, for this day I came into the world."

And he died.

Later, a woman named Maximilla came and had him buried.

May my news be not of sadness, dear friend, but of joy, for now Andrew is with our Lord. He has the better part. May you be protected by our Lord and Master. I go now to Italia.

Peace of the Lord be with you. Longinus.

The letter fell to John's lap. He wanted to cry, not for the loss of Andrew but out of longing to be where Andrew was. Suddenly he remembered something, and he looked to the window. Not finding what he expected, he rushed to the opening and looked around the sky. There was no dove. He was confused.

Behind him he heard a flutter. He quickly turned around, and there perched on his desk was a white dove. John walked slowly to the dove and it jumped away, flew about the room, and returned to his desk. It walked back and forth on the desk with what seemed a great deal of impatience.

John stood intently watching the dove and becoming a bit amused by its actions.

"Friend, are you trying to tell me something?" John asked.

The dove cooed.

"I believe that you cannot leave until I figure it out." John thought for a moment, watching the dove march back and forth across the desk.

A thought came to him.

"Is the Master growing displeased because I have not finished my account?"

The dove flew to John and perched itself on his shoulder, and for an instant it stayed happily there. With a flutter of excitement it flew around the room. John followed the flight of the dove, which was fluttering around and around, until finally it stopped on the window sill. John wanted to cry out a plea for it to stay, but he could not deprive his brother of the joy of Jesus.

The dove fluttered and lifted off the sill.

John rushed to the window and watched it fly in the direction of the sea. Once over the sea, the dove swooped down and then ascended into the blinding sun, and there it disappeared.

Another void filled John's life.

CHAPTER SEVEN

JUDAH THOMAS, THE DIDYMUS OF CAPERNAUM

PROLOGUE

Returning from Rome, John settled into a daily routine at Ephesus. Early each day, at the first sign of daybreak, he rose from his sleeping mat and prayed. Sitting on a mat that had been woven by his mother, Salome, and his sister, Naomi, he began to pray Psalms of praise and thanksgiving to God. Soon he felt himself in the presence of a Greatness so acute that he fell on his face and continued:

> *"To Thee, O God is due a song of praise in Sion,*
> *let a vow be paid to Thee who hearest prayers.*
> *To Thee every mortal comes…"*

He soon lost himself in the memorized words of the Psalm, then suddenly felt himself being drawn towards the presence of Jesus. Immediately he was surrounded by a Power so immense and overwhelming that he could scarcely breathe. He heard himself say:

> *"…Happy the man whom Thou dost choose*
> *and take to dwell in Thy courts.*
> *May I be filled with the good things of Thy house,*
> *and with the holiness of Thy temple…."*

John saw Jesus moving to him seated on a cloud. His heart beat rapidly with anticipation. Soon shapeless images floated slowly and reverently around Jesus. John saw those who had been called by Jesus coming into view. He raised his voice in a song of praise and those whom Jesus called also entered in the praise. Soon a thousand more voices joined them saying:

"...By wondrous signs Thou dost answer us with justice,
O God, our Savior, Thou, the hope of all the world
and of distant seas..."

From memory he prayed one Psalm after another. The words of praise in each Psalm gave him happiness for he knew that they were being heard.

When the vision passed, he opened his eyes and rising slowly came to a seated position on his mat. His hands trembled slightly and his clothes were wet from perspiration. This did not bother him, for he expected such things to happen; after all, he had been before the Almighty. He gathered his senses and laboriously pushed himself to his feet. He was unsteady but soon regained his balance. He walked across the room to a table on which rested a clay pitcher and cup. He slowly poured a cool cup of water. He walked to a nearby table and reached for the unleavened bread on the plate and broke off a small piece then reached for a small bowl of warmed milk. He ate the breakfast his sister Naomi had prepared for him. No longer hungry, he returned to his mat to continue praying. His prayers this time were petitions for others and for guidance, courage, and love of enemy. He gave these requests to Jesus in a soft tone. After completing his long list of cares, his prayers turned to the war in Judea. News of the war had disturbed him, but all wars disturbed him for the suffering and lack of reason and love that lived in wars. Every war seems to be the darkest of times, the time of the midnight hour, the devil's hour.

News was that Jerusalem had fallen, burned and leveled. Many hundreds of thousands had died and tens of thousands had been carried off into slavery. He felt a chill run up his back and he offered those suffering into the arms of God's mercy. He wondered how many he knew were killed or now were suffering. His eyes teared for no matter where he was in his new life with Christ, he was still a Jew. Unexpectedly, his compassion shifted to the Romans. Now all men were children of God, all were His Chosen People and war was bad for all participants. Finishing his long litany of petitions, he tucked his legs close to him and sat motionless, allowing Jesus time to inspire him. It was during these moments that John was enlightened and filled with the past. He allowed Jesus to tell him what he had to write that day. His mind was emptied becoming a blank scroll. Slowly the world around him faded and all he heard was his own breathing.

Time passed.

Around him were the sounds of shuffling steps along a dirt road. It was a long road just outside of Jerusalem. They were walking to a small garden called Gethsemane at the foot of Mount Olivet. They were familiar with this place, for they had gone there often. This was where Jesus prayed. They had just finished the Passover meal with Jesus and there were just Eleven of them, for Judas had gone into the night to complete a task for the Master. He heard plainly the voice of Jesus which he remembered word for word.

"If the world hates you, know ye, that it hath hated Me before you. If you had been of the world, the world would love its own; but because you are not of the world, but I have chosen you out of the world, therefore the world hateth you…if they have persecuted Me, they will persecute you also."

John felt the night air against his face and the mumbling and confusion of the Others, but he quickly pushed these voices aside longing only to remember what Jesus was saying. With this persistence, he, with ease, recalled the expression on His Face as Jesus spoke these words. He relived the moment as the passing breeze moved the locks and shining black hairs on Jesus' Head while the gentle wind pushed against His beard. John experienced the gravity of the moment and of the soberness of the Others in spite of the many cups of wine he drank at the Table.

"…all this is done so that the Word may be fulfilled which is written in their Law: 'they hated me without cause.' But when the Paraclete cometh, whom I will send you from the Father, the Spirit of Truth, who proceedeth from the Father, He shall give testimony of Me: And you shall give testimony, because you are with Me from the beginning."

As soon as the moment began; it ended. John quickly returned to the present, rushed to his "desk" and began to put on parchment what had been revealed to him. The words came rapidly, more quickly than his hand could write; it was difficult to keep up with his thoughts, but somehow he was able to get them scribbled. Finished, he fell back in his chair and felt relieved that he had accomplished something. The ache in his hand and shoulder from all his writing rushed him back to reality. It was then that he realized much time had passed and he accepted his pain with joy.

Later, Ignotus, a former Roman *scriptor* writer and companion of Nescius, would come and rewrite what he had scribbled. Ignotus had been injured in one of the Zealot attacks near Jerusalem and was left walking with a limp until he came to Jesus. At his Baptism he was cured and made whole. Ignotus will ask questions and John will delight in telling him more about Jesus which will transport him to the past. Only this time he will be aware of all those who were around Jesus and the past would be flooded with the vibrancy of people. He will experience again the time of day and the weather. He will feel the company of his father and mother and again see the pride on their faces as James and he stood by Jesus. He will feel the spirit of Lady Mary and become sad for he missed the role she once filled by counseling him with soft guidance. She always told him he would be remembered as one of the great Disciples in spite of his limited missionary work. He could hear her say in a soft voice, "Your undertaking is to tell a different side of Jesus." To humor her he would remain silent for he never could see himself in this light. These memories of the Disciples, of Jesus and those who were with him seemed to come alive as he almost could hear their voices and laughs stir the air. He even heard their nervous coughs, sneezes and even an appreciative belch after a good meal cooked by the Good Ladies. He found great solace in these recollections and grew thankful for these moments.

He decided to rest before going to eat his mid-day meal prepared for him by Naomi. She had taken on the responsibility of tending to him soon after their mother, Salome, died. Naomi's care was nothing but a continuation of his mother's, especially since her husband, Joses, also known as Justus, had left for the missions. Joses, like John, had been held in place by the family and had preached and taught Jesus in a limited way. Two days after Salome's death and because they no longer followed the Jewish format of seven days of mourning, Joses asked John's permission to leave with Sopater, Secundos and Caius of Derbe, three former companions of Paul, for the provinces of Dalmatia and Illyrium. Their journey to these provinces was instigated by Luke who was preaching, teaching and writing there. Since his departure, Joses had written of their success and this validated John's belief that the mission was something approved by the Lord. He rose from his chair and walked into the cooking area of the house and found his sister Naomi busily moving around the room cleaning and washing things.

"John, your meal has been waiting for you. When I came to call you, you were busy writing so I let you be. I have prepared something simple: bread, olives and some beans and lentils that were given to us by Trophimus. He arrived earlier this morning and said he would be back later in the day. He has an important message for you."

John barely listened to his sister for it was normal for her to talk for long periods trying to push everything in the time allotted to her. She always updated him of all that had to be known. After this she remained silent the rest of the day. As she continued to report things to him, he walked to a stool by the table and near his sister. Sitting down, he lowered his head in thanksgiving and began to eat his midday meal. He broke a piece of bread, took some olives, and by-passed the beans and lentils. In his mind jumped the short nervous image of Trophimus, who was a man in constant motion. He would pace back and forth while speaking and never sat in a chair long enough for the seat to get warm. He was born in Ephesus and was a companion of Paul in the Province of Asia and Greece, and stayed with Paul during his first captivity. While passing through Asia, he became ill and was left in Miletus by Paul. He was a constant companion to Tychicus who also was a traveler of Paul. Tychicus was often the letter carrier for Paul especially in regard to Paul's letters to Titus. He was a man with no time for nonsense. When he preached, he did so with great vigor and conviction that it left little or no doubt of his faith and sincerity. He was a short man with small features but a big heart. He was known to give his last *denarii* to anyone who cried alms, and at each meal would divide his meals in half giving half to the poor. Like Trophimus, he was sent to Ephesus to help Timotheus, also known as Timothy, of Lystra and Southern Galatia. In Ephesus, Trophimus and Tychicus helped with preaching and converting of the Gentiles and did many acts of charity for the poor and sick. The three of them had established themselves as a strong presence in the city and were deeply loved and respected by the Christian Community. Their presence diverted any attention to John who lived quietly in his home writing his account of Jesus and who uncomfortably was sought out for advice.

John read some of Luke's account that Joses sent and found Luke's account far more superior in structure to Mark but it did not quench John's need and hunger to say more of Jesus.

The knock on the door startled John and he became aware that his sister had stopped talking. She rushed to the wooden door of the small house. When she opened the door, Tychicus was standing there and he immediately walked into the house and to John.

"Good day to you Brother. Peace be with you," They embraced each other in the familiar Christian way.

"Good day to you, Tychicus, and the peace of the Lord be with you. I trust you are well."

"Yes I am. Timotheus sends his best wishes and the Lord's blessings to you." He stopped and looked at Naomi who followed him from the door and was passing him.

"And the peace of the Lord be with you, Naomi."

"And also with you, Tychicus. I am surprised to see you; earlier Trophimus said he was to return with some news for John."

"Trophimus is with Timotheus on some important business, but I am here to deliver what Trophimus was to deliver."

He removed a large size satchel that hung heavily from his shoulder and quickly gave it to the Apostle. John reached for the satchel and the weight caused his arm to collapse. He recaptured his strength and caught the satchel with both hands.

Tychicus smiled slightly. "I forgot to tell you they are weighty," he said as he immediately sat in a nearby chair seemingly exhausted from his journey.

"A cup of cool water, Tychicus?" Naomi asked.

"Thank you, Lady Naomi, that would be perfect," he answered while fixated on the confused look on John's face.

"What are these?" John asked.

"I believe they are letters from Thomas, the Apostle. I was instructed by Trophimus to advise you to read them in the order they are written."

"These may take days to read," John said in amazement.

"No doubt," Tychicus said casually as he reached for the cup of cool water offered him by Naomi.

"What would possess Thomas to write all these letters?"

"The young and strange man who delivered these to Timotheus said that some of them were very old letters and were written many years ago."

JUDAH THOMAS, THE DIDYMUS OF CAPERNAUM

To John, son of Zebedee, my brother Apostle, may the peace of Our Lord be with you and those with you. I pray that this finds you well and safe. The dangers you and our fellow Apostles face are far more serious than mine for I seem to be safer than you. These letters were long promised to you, and I hope you will forgive me for not keeping my promise. It seemed every time I attempted to send you a letter something delayed me and I never followed through with my commitment. I continually wrote to you but never seemed to find the time to send you what I had written. As you read these scrolls, you will see they cover many years. You may be familiar with much

of what is written but I decided that I would keep my promise
and send you letters telling you all that I am doing in my mission in the Name of Jesus, Our Lord and Savior. Time and
the duties to labor for Our Master were more pressing. I have
moved quickly and never expected to be where I am. The fact
that things move so swiftly hopefully will account for my not
writing you. When last I wrote you, it was in response to the
death of Peter and my letter was filled with sorrow and joy.
It is amazing how these two emotions can come to us at the
same time. Your responding letter arrived many months later
and I was pleased to hear that Peter had picked a successor.
Because I do not know Linus, and know that you do, I will ask
you to forward these parchments to him in Rome. When for-
warding these letters please attach a letter of introduction so
that I may not be a total stranger to our dear brother. When
last we met you asked me to write of my voyages, and you constantly repeated this request over the years. For some reason
you found the news of my activities of interest, and I hope my
letters will not disappoint you. I promise I shall write often to
tell you more of my missions. When we pulled lots many years
ago I was given "outside of Rome," which made me happy for
I did not want to be near that City because of its sinfulness.
Even the mention of that City caused me to feel the heavy
heel of Rome on my back. So I was pleased to learn that the
Lord in His infinite wisdom had given me the best of choices.
Some of the Others got specific missions but my mission was
open and I was happy with this. As you know, I left with Jude
Thaddeus and we traveled north finally arriving in Syria,
where we met both fervent believers and hateful leaders. We
stayed there until we heard the warning that Saul was coming
and then we hurried into Commagene and parted. I stayed
in this small province finding some safety among the many
friendly Jews. My stay in this comfortable place may sound
cowardly but the truth is I was trying to get direction, after all,

I had the entire Roman Empire to evangelize and I was having a difficult time trying to see which of the Provinces captured my imagination. Finally, I felt a call to move on and went into Osroene and the city of Edessa, where many Jews had lived. It was in this City that an unusual thing happened which I wish to relay to you....

✳

Thomas was carefully escorted into the palace. He knew from his treatment that he was not in any danger. He was preaching in Edessa three weeks and his successes, though great, had not caused any trouble. His converts were Jews who surprisingly seemed very receptive to him. One day, while preaching in the synagogue, he was shocked to find himself surrounded by royal guards where he was then asked by the captain of the unit to follow him. When Thomas was some distance from the crowds, he was placed in a chariot and whisked away to the palace.

The palace room was a long narrow room with barren walls and two large heavy black doors—the one he just arrived through and the other at the end of the room. In the middle of the room was a long narrow table that was almost as long as the room and on this table, neatly arranged, were clothes, rugs, jewelry, silver and gold plates and cups, bejeweled knives, and shields. Thomas stood, momentarily looking at those articles before him, and began walking the length of the table. As he walked he looked at the articles on the table with awe for he had never seen such an array of wealth. The sudden sound of a heavy latch opening startled Thomas and he looked at the door at the end of the room. Slowly the door opened and coming through the door was a tall man dressed in long flowing white robes with black swirls that trimmed the sleeves and the hem of the robe. A black, leather band was tied around his head. The black band ran through his thick black hair and across his forehead. He was the tallest man Thomas had ever seen.

Bowing to Thomas the man said softly, "Sir, I need you to follow me." The man spoke in perfect Syriac, which was a dialect of Aramaic.

"Thank you," Thomas replied in Aramaic and the man glanced up and smiled impishly. Then standing upright, he led Thomas through the large wooden doors and into a larger and wider room. The walls of the room were decorated with swirls and curls that reminded Thomas of the curls of the ocean waves before they hit the shoreline. The swirls on the walls were the same swirls that trimmed the clothing of his escort, the guards and the servants standing in the room. Four huge pillars painted light pink stood powerfully holding the blue, star-studded ceiling. Suspended from the ceiling were two large fans made of palms that swayed lazily and peacefully to and fro. They moved in perpetual motion by two strong men pulling thick, heavy rope. The cool room rewarded their labors. He walked on a huge rug of white, black, grey and gold swirls. At the far end of the room, elevated slightly above the floor, was a white, ivory throne beautifully carved in gold and silver swirls. Behind the throne was a massive, royal, purple drape that flowed and fell from the ceiling and crumbled into layer and layers on the floor.

"Please wait, Sir." The tall escort said timidly.

Thomas stood in the center of the room and soon became conscious that he was the center of attention for everyone had stopped moving and all were looking at him. The only things moving and making small, hissing sounds were the two huge fans swaying back and forth above him.

The sudden long blast of a trumpet shattered the room's tranquility. A cymbal clashed and its echo rushed around the large room vibrating off the walls. The sound caused a quiver to race through Thomas' body.

The tall escort shouted in a loud, booming voice, *"Abgar V Ukkama bar Ma'nu"* and everyone in the room lowered their bodies to a deep bow while some even prostrated themselves.

From out of nowhere, an elderly man appeared. His head covered with a gold turban and a gold robe trimmed with white swirls.

In a louder voice the tall escort bellowed, *"Jaay-baa-raa,"* and in equal tone but with greater enthusiasm everyone in the room repeated over and over, *"Jaay-baa-raa."*

Thomas recognized the words, "noble" and "mighty" and deduced that this elderly man was their King. Undeterred by the grandeur of the moment, Thomas looked at the King with simplicity.

The King's face, though wrinkled and lined, still had a glow of youth to it. His eyes sparkled with an inner delight and there was an aura of solitude about him.

"Teomaa," the King said.

Thomas was taken back for he had not been called by his Aramaic name since Jesus called him to be one of the Twelve.

"Yes, I am Thomas," he replied politely.

"I am told that you are a follower of the Man they call *Eesho*, Jesus."

"Yes, I am a Christian. I am one of the Twelve."

"Forgive me for not greeting you properly, *Shlama Alookh*, Peace be with you.

"*Shlama Alookh*," Thomas replied quickly. Suddenly the Book of Ruth came to his mind and being prompted he added further in Latin: "*Dominus vobiscum.*"

The King sat upright with these words and smiled with great joy.

"*Deo Gratias,*" he replied.

Thomas knew immediately that what was implied was understood only by the King and himself, and he knew he was standing before a friend.

"Please come closer. My eyes are weak and I want to get a good look at you."

Thomas walked closer and as he did a scent of flowers filled his nostrils. He wondered where this scent had originated.

The King looked at him for a long time then said softly, "Ah yes, you look like a Hebrew. You say you knew Jesus the Christ? Did you walk with Him? Did you hear Him teach?"

"Yes I did all these things."

"Then you, *Teomaa*, are a blessed man. A holy man."

"I am indeed a blessed man, Sire, but not a holy man. I work to be a holy man."

"You minimize your value, *Yaa loo-Pa*."

From that moment on Thomas became known as *Yaa loo-Pa* the student.

"I need to be alone with this man."

The tall escort clapped his hands loudly and repeatedly emptying everyone but the King and Thomas. The tall man surveyed the room and seeing none bowed to the King and began to back away.

"No Parlan, you can stay."

A smile of appreciation spread across Parlan's face.

"Tell me, *Yaa loo-Pa*, did you see Him work all His miracles."

"Yes, Sire, I did."

"I do not mean to correct you, *Yaa loo-Pa* but I do not think you saw them all. I know of one you did not see. You did not see the miracle your *Ru-bee* Teacher performed in Edessa."

Thomas muffled a laugh and then smiling said, "But Jesus never was in Edessa."

"You are correct in your thinking, but His Spirit was. Come sit by me and let me tell you the story of the miracle of Edessa and after my tale you will tell me all I need to know about Jesus."

Thomas sat on a large, plush pillow to the right of the King.

Parlan clapped his hands and servants came scurrying in carrying trays of fruit, raisins, dates, olives, and bread. Others rushed in with white jugs and pitchers and poured water and wine in the cups that were now before the King and Thomas. As quickly as they came they were gone and once again the room was still.

"Many years ago, when I was young and filled with much life, I came to the throne of Edessa. Things were good, for my father King Ma'nu III Saphul had ruled wisely until his death. We had no wars with our neighbors and our people lived well. The first six years of rule my reign were filled with prosperity and benevolence. I even married. As I entered my seventh year, a new illness broke out in my kingdom and within a year many died. Soon I myself became ill and my many physicians and herbalists worked feverishly to try and cure me. I escaped death several times, but I grew weaker after each episode. Finally, I knew I could rule no longer and abdicated in favor of my brother Ma'nu who ruled as Ma'nu IV bar Ma'nu. Away from the duties of state, I found myself in search of a cure for my illness. For six years I suffered with this illness and then one day was advised that my brother Ma'nu had contracted the illness and was near death. I believed he would survive just as I did many times, but my brother died and I reclaimed the throne. For eighteen more years I suffered, sometimes in so much pain that I asked the gods to end my life. One day, Parlan, my manservant, came to me with a tale of a Galilean who was reported to be like a God for it was reported that He had cured people of blindness, leprosy, and muteness. Parlan told me this Man gave peace to those who were troubled; that He even had power over the underworld and that He raised the dead. I asked Parlan to verify these things, and the next day he brought before me a man named Hannan who was a Judean merchant. Hannan claimed he heard the same as Parlan, but added that many in Judea despised this *Ru-bee* and were planning to kill Him. He told me this miracle worker's name was Yeshua bar Yosef of Natsraya. With great need, and with the greatest belief in His Power, I dictated a letter to Jesus. In this letter I told Jesus that I heard of all the things He did and that I knew He was a holy Man and that I truly believed He had come from a Great God and was the Son of that Great God. Finally, I offered Him refuge in my small peaceful country. I gave the letter to Hannan to deliver to Jesus. Three months later, Hannan returned with an oral message from Jesus thanking me for my faith in Him. He also thanked me for offering Him my kingdom as a shelter but said He had a mission to complete and it had to be with the Jews. He concluded His message by saying that He would soon complete His work on earth and would return to His Father and after His return He would send someone to me who would heal me because of my faith."

Thomas sat waiting for more to be said. He had no idea of Jesus cor-
responding with anyone outside of Judea. Thomas never believed he knew
Jesus but now he realized he knew very little of his Master. This entire
episode left the Twelve more ignorant of Jesus. Furthermore, Thomas saw
that the teachings of Jesus were not narrowed to the Jews. The fact that
Jesus did such a thing made Thomas sure that he and all the Others were
to open the world of love, sacrifice, and salvation to all people.

The king slowly stood up and Thomas jumped to his feet in order to
remain in respect of the King.

"Jesus kept his promise. He sent a man named Addai. This young
man sought out Hannan, the Jewish merchant, and together they came
to me. The first thing I noticed was the change in Hannan. His mercenary qualities and his ability to barter were tamed and he walked with
peaceful steps. The young man surprised me. He was so fragile and innocent. I thought to myself that he could do nothing for me. He told me of
the death of Jesus, which saddened me especially because of the manner
of His death. Then he told me the unbelievable tale that Jesus rose from
the dead. I looked at this young man in total disbelief, and I thought him
mad. I then discharged him. The young man had no sooner gone when
Hannan and Parlan came to my help. Knowing that Addai was not able
to hear, I told them I wanted Addai taken to the border and sent on his
way. The two of them thought I was mad. Parlan reminded me that Jesus
raised others from the dead and if Jesus was able to do this for others
what would stop Him from doing the same to Himself. Hannan asserted
I had to believe that Jesus rose from the dead on His own power to be
cured. I knew that these two men said these things because they loved me
in a way that was far different than my wife and children, or my people.
They loved me with a new love that I wanted to possess. I had Addai
brought before me again and asked him to tell me about Jesus. For three
days I listened to his stories of what Jesus said and did and for three days
I suffered greatly. Finally, on the third day, I said to Addai, 'Son, you must
know that I believed Jesus is the Son of God. I do not know what God,
but I knew of a God. In my mind I see He was a Man of simple ways, yet
He has command of the world and nothing is beyond His reach.'

"Addai stood over me and poured water over my head and demanded
the demons in my body to leave in the Name of Jesus. I tell you, *Yaa loo-
Pa*, I felt the pain rise up from my feet to legs, to chest to head, and I felt
new life cover in its place. I am sure that I was experiencing what Jesus
felt when He rose from the grips of the demon of death. I suddenly lost
feeling and collapsed into Parlan's arms. When I awoke, which seemed
like mere moments, but was in fact days, I was freed of my past life and

began a new one. Addai sat with me and for another three days talked to me of Jesus."

The King reached for Thomas' right hand and cupped it in his two big hands. Thomas felt the heat from them and was comforted by their warmth. When he looked down he was surprised to see how old the hands of the King were.

"What I have told you seems like a long time ago, *Yaa loo-Pa*, but it is not. Jesus kept His promise to me and I pledge to you, as I did to Addai, that I shall give my kingdom to Jesus for we have been blessed with the promise of Jesus and of two of his Twelve."

Thomas looked at the King for a long time wondering what he meant by "two of the Twelve."

"Sire, I am confused, what do you mean 'two of the Twelve?'"

"Addai is here."

Out of nowhere, Thomas heard his name shouted in a surprised and thrilled tone. He knew the voice but was too stunned to quickly identify it. He looked away and there, rushing across the large rug before the throne of King Abgar with great familiarity, was Jude Thaddeus bar Alphaeus.

✳

Can you imagine the delight it was to see Jude and finding he was Addai. He looked far more mature than I remembered him and yet he still was young Jude. When we embraced I was surprised to learn that he had filled out, and from the look in his eyes and the smile of confidence on his face, it was apparent he had matured. I was pleased to see him. With the King nearby, we talked about Jesus for hours and days and soon began to instruct the household of King Abgar. During the following weeks, we received many and we were very happy with all the good works we were doing. With the King's backing we were not disturbed except by a few zealous Jews in the capital. Dorimius arrived with word that called us all back to Jerusalem for a Council due to the controversy about the Gentiles and circumcision. Jude Thaddeus, ever obedient, left immediately. I stayed back a little longer. I had nothing to hold me, nothing pressing me; I just had a great many doubts about Saul and did not want to face him again without clearing my mind of any ill thoughts that would affect my judgment. Our previous meeting with Saul left me very uneasy. More importantly, I resented his arrogance and Pharisaic airs. Meeting him again would only make me more displeasing to Our Lord, so I avoided the possibility of sinning by staying away. I also lingered back knowing that I did not have to make such a decision for I knew that Jude Thaddeus could speak for us both. What I was not immediately aware of was the effect I was having on Abgar and his household. They knew of the message and they observed Jude Thaddeus' immediate departure, but not mine, and soon they began looking at me as a contradiction to obedience. I began to experience glares from everyone in the household, and soon less and less began coming to the Meal. Of course, I attributed this to the fact that Thaddeus, whom they loved, had left and they were not that used to me. Several days later, something unusual happened. I left the palace of King Abgar and decided to walk to the bazaar, which is a large open area like our Galilean market place. On the way there I saw a man running from tree to tree. He was sneaking about obviously hiding from some fearful thing. When he arrived at the tree of his destination, he would press his back hard against the tree trunk and then look around with quick, sudden, jerking motions. I was confused by his actions and yet intrigued. I stood watching him for some time then decided to find out what he was doing and walked to him. "Sir, may I ask what you are doing?" I inquired. "I am hiding from the sun," he quickly replied. I laughed. "That, kind sir, is impossible unless the sun helps you with clouds." "So others say, but still I try," he replied and raced to the next tree to hide. I pursued him and again I said, "Sir, I am curious; why are you trying to hide from the sun?" "Because it is a powerful thing that watches me always; I am blinded by it and cannot see my own way." He continued to his next tree leaving me laughing, then he said without looking back, "Do you not prefer seeing the things you want and not be blinded into seeing only what the sun wants you to see?" I stood watching as the man continued to hide behind the trees and from his back I could see that he resembled me. I tried to dismiss the encounter but I finally surrendered knowing that what I saw was also an important lesson. I quickly returned to the palace and prayed for understanding. Why did I have to see this man and his strange doings? After many hours of asking the Master to forgive me — again — I announced to all that I was leaving for Jerusalem. I arrived at Jerusalem just before the Council met and I am certain you remember what happened...

✳

John slowly lowered the parchment. He had to rest. Thomas' Greek was not the best and often he would sprinkle Aramaic and even Latin words in his writing, just enough to make it tedious. He leisurely reached for the large, smooth stone he had taken from the shores of Italia. It was a memento of his trip. He laid the stone on the scroll to hold his place. He leaned back in his chair and thought of Jerusalem so many years back. His remembering immediately focused on Thomas, who arrived later than all the Others for that important meeting. Thomas was welcomed by the Others and he blended quickly into the camaraderie. It was like old times with the Disciples together laughing, joking, teasing and speaking of Jesus. These moments were needed for they had missed each other. Their togetherness returned them to being with Jesus. Once again they felt the air and space around them being stirred by Jesus. Soon the feelings between them grew serious and the problem of Paul and Barnabas came into the discussion and their concerns lingered into the next day.

The day of the meeting, John recalled the conviction that Thomas displayed when the Twelve met privately. He firmly believed that the Gentiles had to be preached to and had to be liberated from the Jewish dietary laws and the laws of circumcision. Of all the Twelve, he was the first to side with Paul and Barnabas. John thought Thomas' position very peculiar especially given that Thomas did not trust Paul or like Barnabas. He would have to speak to Thomas privately, but before John could inquire about Thomas' irregular behavior, Thomas rose from his seat at the assembly.

"Let me remind you that things happen according to the mind of The Almighty and that everyone is subject to His Will. Without advice or consent, many of us have been accepting Gentiles into the Way. Was this ever disputed by any of the Twelve? No, because we unconsciously knew that by 'all nations' Jesus meant everyone in His Father's domain. Let me also remind you that most Jews have not accepted us so easily; in fact they are, in all places, our chief adversaries. Further, let us not forget that Jesus, when multiplying the loaves and fishes, or speaking His Blessings or saying anything, did not hesitate to see if Gentiles were there; He spoke and acted. We soon learned that the Gentiles were in our midst. Confidently, they heard His words and were blessed by them. How then can we stand in the way of Paul who speaks Jesus' words and does His Will? How can we say that this is not of the Almighty? How can we dare feel we have the right to impose Jewish Laws on non-Jews, when the Master Himself did not say to do so?"

That entire speech was so unlike Thomas. He had always been a man of few words. He always liked complete security and safety. Truly he was inspired by the Spirit of the Lord. Suddenly John stopped his thinking. His forehead wrinkled and his lips puckered as he reheard his own thoughts. Quickly he acknowledged that his thinking was incorrect. *Thomas was not always so careful in his thinking. There were times he was almost as quick and rash as Peter. Like the time Lazarus was very ill. We were in Perea at the time when we received the sad and discouraging news from Martha. Many of us were shocked at Jesus' tranquility on hearing the news. Many were happy, for Bethany was only fifteen furlongs from Jerusalem, and that was too dangerous for Jesus at that time. When Jesus announced "Lazarus is dead" and that Lazarus' death was for our benefit, we became sad and perplexed at how this possibly could be for our benefit. Of course, "his death for our benefit" was added to the long list of things we did not understand. Jesus began walking away from us, alone, down the road. We all searched after him and then Thomas said, "Come, let us go that we may die with Him." How certain and brave Thomas was. I wondered then if he was truly brave, fool-hearted, or enlightened by the power of Adonai. I watched as he began following Jesus. Jude Thaddeus, Simon Peter and I joined him, and slowly the Others followed. We believed that nothing could harm Jesus. No matter how dangerous it was, if Jesus could calm the seas, He would calm the Leaders and the People.*

John looked around the room making a mental note that he should write this remembering in his story of Jesus. He was shocked in realizing it was twilight.

Where had the time gone? he wondered, and then he felt guilty and bothered that he had neglected Tychicus. He looked quickly around the room for Tychicus to apologize but Tychicus was nowhere to be found. He heard mumbling coming from the next room. He rose from his chair, walked to the portal and peering through the folds of the curtain found his sister kneeling by a stool in mumbled prayer. He decided not to bother her, and as he returned to his chair, he berated himself for being so selfish and in not being a good host to poor Tychicus. He sat in his chair and looked at the scroll held in place by the smooth, Italian rock. He touched the rock and smiled warmly as images of Peter, Cornelius, and Longinus flashed into his mind. He dwelled on the two Roman soldiers and wondered how well they were. He looked at the scroll and knew he would have to finish reading it now that Thomas had captured his imagination, but he was tired and decided to rest a bit. Soon Naomi would finish her prayers and come into the room and burn a candle for him. He would then continue reading but for now he needed to rest his burning eyes. He closed his eyes and rested.

When Naomi came into the room, he returned to his reading and found nothing of great interest. Thomas told of his return to Edessa, and of living comfortably and of the death of King Abgar. He then wrote that he was expecting to leave Edessa and anticipated a journey to Armenia to meet Jude Thaddeus.

The scroll ended there.

Several days later, after John had completed more of his account of Jesus' stay on earth, and after a short rest, he returned to the scrolls Thomas wrote. He reached for a new scroll which was not of parchment but of *papyrus*. *Papyrus* was a far more expensive material to write on then what Thomas used. He immediately concluded that this scroll was part of King Abgar's legacy. As he looked at the scroll he saw clearly that it was marked with the Roman number II. He picked it up and slowly, almost reverently, unrolled the scroll. As he read, he became confused as to where he was in his friend's life and mission, reading further he concluded that this *epistula* had been written many months, maybe even a year later after the previous letter. He immediately felt cheated, for he selfishly wanted to know what had happened during those missing months.

In Armenia south of Lake Thospitis I found Jude Thaddeus. I was happy to see him again. It always made me feel good to see one of the Twelve; there is great joy and solidarity that

exist between us. To my surprise Dorimius was with him. This
surprised me for Dorimius was far too serious, mature and
old for Jude and yet they were so at ease with each other.
The three of us briefly stayed together because Jude was
intensely restless. He told me he was being led south, and
he said he finally understood where he was heading. So he
and Dorimius left me. There were few Jews in this province
so I began preaching to the Gentiles, who were somewhat
receptive, because their gods were ruthless and without the
love, mercy, and forgiveness of our Lord. I received several
letters from those in Jerusalem telling me of the persecutions
and I longed to return and give support or my back to be
beaten, but something held me in Armenia. After laboring for
months and winning many for Jesus, I received word that I was
needed back in Osroene because of a falsehood about Jesus
that was being taught. It was the longest journey of my life.
It took me twelve weeks to arrive at the Armenian Osroene
border. I should have realized something was wrong then but
I did not. I attributed my loss of time to the poor Armenian
roads. Once I crossed into Osroene, a great storm rose up
and it made travel impossible. I took refuge in a small farm
just inside the border in what was once called Sophene. The
farmer who worked the fields had been a Roman merchant. His
name was Zelet, but the Romans called him Pharnaces. He
allowed me to stay in his small hut with him. We spoke long into
the night about Jesus and he was surprisingly familiar with
"The Way." We prayed together then retired for the night.
During the night I had a strange dream. In this dream, I was
walking down a long, endless road and as I was slowly walking,
the trees, bushes, farmlands and other landmarks were passing
by quickly, as if being pulled by time or pushed by a strong
wind. I remember thinking that this was what happens when we
do the will of the Lord and are on a mission in His Name. I
am certain you know of what I speak. Suddenly, in the dream,

Pharnaces is walking with me. He is speaking in Aramaic but
still I cannot understand. I asked him where he was going.
He did not answer me but then said in Aramaic, "Just follow
me. I know the way." We continue to walk. As we walk, the
landscape around us begins to change from rocky mountains
to plush valleys and then to deep ravines. There are no plants
or trees, just large boulders and rocks that run up and down
roughly along the land. I felt the passing wind as it pushed
through the channels of the rough terrain. I asked, "How
can I follow you if I do not know where you are going?" He
answered softly almost with surprise, "Out of Rome as you
were to do, but if you do not know where to go I will go before
you and prepare the place for you." I stopped walking for his
words became like an invisible wall before me that I could not
pass. Strangely, his words echo in my mind and I know these
words were said to me before but I am unable to remember
where I heard them or when they had been said to me. I do not
or could not dwell long on these words for I became distracted
by the landscape around me. The path that I was walking was
now surrounded by an open desert with shifting and moving
sands. The sand of one hill slowly shifted away to be made
into another sand hill and the process continued constantly
changing the landscape. I said to Pharnaces, "I do not like
where you are going. I think I shall go back and stay where I
was." He replied, "then you will never know me." Just then a
strong breeze passed us and pressed my cloak and robe to
my skin and a scent of sea water came to me. I looked around
and the long, endless path was passing between two large
bodies of waters. I heard Pharnaces say, "I am going to the
place you were going but refused to go." I turned to him but
he was gone, yet I sensed that he was still with me. Waking,
I looked around the small hut but no one was there but me. I
slowly rose from my sleeping mat and reexamined the hut and
walked to the door. The hut, which I believed was on farm land

was not on it at all, but in the middle of a town that I did not recognize. I immediately thought to myself - I am lost! I looked to my left and up a long lane of small, white huts similar to the one I had used to sleep. There were many people walking and working around their huts. Looking to my right, I saw huts leading to the gates of the town. At the gate, I saw a man wearing a red, silk cloak, a yellow robe and yellow turban. His grey beard was trimmed meticulously; his fingers bejeweled. His dark skin and dark eyes were sober yet friendly. In his presence, I felt an immediate warmth toward him and curiously enough I felt that I somehow knew him. I saw him standing by the gate of the town talking to another man. It was certain that the man with the turban had just arrived. The man he was speaking to seemed to be giving him directions, but I could not see the other man for he had his back to me. It was obvious that this well-dressed man was a man of some means, but still I concluded with satisfaction that he was not a man of royalty. I decided that he was a merchant from some distant place. The two men were carrying on a long conversation and though I could not hear what they said I could not stop looking at them. All of a sudden, I knew the man with his back to me, and at that moment, he turned and my heart instantly began pounding in my chest nearly at the point of breaking free. IT IS THE MASTER! IT IS JESUS! I wanted to run to Him and kneel but I could not move. I plainly saw Jesus point, directing the merchant to me. With great joy I smiled at Jesus. The merchant handed Jesus a small cloth bag which I somehow knew contained coins. The merchant began walking to me, but my eyes never left Jesus and my longing to be with Him was tormenting me but I could not move. Finally the merchant reached me and stood blocking my view of Jesus. I could see and feel the merchant's eyes searching my face. Finally he asked, "You are Thomas also known as Didymus?" I looked at him and said, "Yes, I am he."

"I am told you are a carpenter," his tone of voice exuded confidence. "Of sorts," I replied slightly perplexed by his tone and inquiries. "Is that your Master over there by the main gate?" "Yes, He is my master and I am His servant." "Good, for He has just sold you to me and you are to follow me."

"What?" I heard myself shout.

"Your Master has sold you for thirty pieces of silver. He said that you would understand and that you should come with me without delay. He further said that He would lead the way and that you would find truth in your voyage."

Thirty pieces of silver, John thought as he interrupted his reading. *The price of betrayal? NO! It was the price of confirmation of what Jesus now needed Thomas to understand.*

John returned to his letter.

I looked to the town gate wanting to question Jesus why He would do such a thing, but He disappeared. "Did He tell you why I was being sold?" "Yes, among my duties here was to find a carpenter for my master. Your Master said you were familiar with that occupation."

"I am familiar with that trade, Sir," I said with no hesitation believing that Jesus had just set a new direction for me and that I had no choice but to go where He wanted me to go. "You may call me Abban," the merchant said to me. "I am an envoy of King Gondophares who sent me to seek out your Master. A long time ago, your Master promised to send one of His servants to the land of my master to fulfill a promise to one of our ancient Magus named Melchior. I believe, Didymus, you fulfill that promise and that you are that servant." "I am my Master's servant," I answered with great pride. "But tell me kind Abban, of what Roman province is King Gondophares the king?"

"He is out of Roman rule. He is in India." The word "India" rang loudly inside my head and my thoughts lunged back to

the time when we pulled for our missions. I remembered when
I received my mission those many years ago. I read the parchment that said "Out of Rome" and the name India came to me.
I remember quickly rejecting this outlandish idea. The thought
of going to such a place with so many mysteries and being
so far removed from all the things I knew and understood
frightened me. Now here I was faced with this same foreign
land — "Outside of Rome" — with a firm commitment made to
this strange man, Abban, who had purchased me through the
wishes of Jesus. Once more faced with this same destiny, I
grew frightened even more for now I knew that this was the will
of Jesus from the start and that I had failed Him. Soon I grew
comforted in knowing that Jesus sold me to this strange land
and that He was going before me to prepare the way. How
blessed I was, for now I no longer have any more doubts. It
seems that the Master always had to clear me of doubts and
yet I believed that I was not a doubter but simply stubborn.
Yet I wondered how many more times did Jesus need to prove
Himself to me. That very day Abban began preparing for our
trip and I relived the day Jesus told us He was the Way, the
Truth and the Life. Like so many of the Twelve, I heard but
did not listen.

John watched as the scroll rolled into itself. His mind wandered back
in time, needing desperately to capture the moment Thomas was speaking of for he could not recall it. Like passing hours in a day, the many
events in the life of Jesus passed in his mind. Several moments swiftly
came; others lingered for brief moments. Places, faces and words scurried
on and on and then like a bolt of lighting the scene was in his mind and
he saw Jesus and the Twelve seated around a table. The moment was just
after Jesus had washed their feet. Jesus then gave them the command
to love. But He said this in a tone that was not as a command but as a
gift. "A new commandment I give unto you that you love one another
as I have loved you…" For a frightening moment his mind went blank;
he grew anxious, tormented that he had lost the moment. In complete
despair and near tears he said aloud:

"What happened next? Please, Lord, help me remember…Ah yes. Simon…Peter…Jesus predicted that Peter would deny Him. Yes and then Peter slumped back on his couch and I looked after him. He was so rejected. That was why I do not remember so readily what Thomas was speaking. I was concerned with Peter who was hurt that Jesus could even think that he could deny Him. I remember hearing Jesus speaking of mansions and going before us to prepare places for us."

I do not know what he said next because I was away from Him and He was absent from my thoughts. How lonely a moment that was for me as I needed to hear all of it but needed to see how Simon Peter was doing.

Stillness came over John as he experienced the loneliness of being near Jesus yet apart from Him.

Unexpectedly, he heard Thomas' voice, speaking anew as if near him, and in that moment said, "Lord, we know not where Thou goest. How can we know the way?"

It was after Philip spoke that I returned to listening to Jesus as He spoke at great lengths of His Father. I can still see the looks of bewilderment on all the faces around Jesus. Their silence seemed to both answer and ask questions.

Quickly, John began looking for a *stilus* and parchment, and being relieved in finding one, he quickly began to write what he had relived. The words reverberated through his mind and onto his hand as he wondered at how hurriedly he wrote. The revelation continued until late into the night when mentally exhausted and muscles aching, he slumped onto his desk and instantly fell asleep. He did not even hear or feel the loud thump of his head hitting the wooden table.

In his sleep he relived that moment and heard himself say to Peter, "Look how Thomas and Philip question the Master so freely. They expressed their doubts and concerns effortlessly. Why am I not like them?"

And Peter said to John: "Be blessed, for sometimes boldness brings you to the front which can leave you lonely and without certainty."

Through the night he dreamed, and when he woke the next morning he found the *stilus* still upright in his hands. He blinked rapidly to adjust to the morning sun and then looked at the blackened, soiled fingers that held the *stilus*. His eyes fell on his written words: "Amen, Amen I say to you, he that believeth in Me, the works that I do, he also shall do; and greater than these shall he do…"

John smiled. Sitting upright he prayed by giving thanks to God for having used him.

I did not write these words Lord…they are Yours and You gave them to me to record. Help me Lord, for I forgot many things You did. When You spoke them, they were difficult to understand. I was not born in Your Light. Enlighten me so that I can remember well what You want me to say. Let me finish the task You gave me so that all may come to know You better. Above all things, help me to overcome my forgetfulness and remember all that You did or all that You said.

He put his hands flatly on his desk and pushed himself up. Now standing, he looked down at all that he wrote and deep inside felt the gnawing feeling that he still had more to write.

Master, help me to not only hear Your words but help me to listen to them, anew with understanding.

He walked to a large, clay bowl on a small wooden table in the corner of his house and cupping his hand, gathered water. He rubbed the chilled liquid and rough hands onto his face. His skin was stimulated and his face felt alive.

Thomas was right; we heard but did not listen.

The picture of Thomas, whom he had always regarded as his friend even before their calling by Jesus, froze in his mind and he smiled for he remembered how Thomas resented the shortness of his own legs, and disliked being the shortest of all the Disciples, even shorter than James the Little. His remembering caused a smile. *But being short did not make him look younger than Jude or I. He always looked and acted like a short, old man.*

He reached for a cloth nearby and softly patted his face lingering and patting a little longer at his deep, black beard. The contrast between his rough hands and the soft cloth was stark, and he enjoyed the difference. Quickly, he turned and looked at the scrolls from Thomas. They had fallen on the floor by his desk, and he thought himself very careless for having treated the scrolls so badly.

Quickly he said aloud to himself, "But John, they only tell of what Thomas did. How important are they to you? In truth, they are unimportant. Everything we do is unimportant. Everything we write is unimportant. It is not about us—it never is about us—it is always about Jesus."

He nodded his head several times in agreement to his own words and thoughts, *We always believed this. What we said, did or wrote was nothing.* He turned and ran his eyes around the room until he came to several, large, clay jugs sitting in the corner of the room. Flowing out of these jars resembling bound unadorned flowers, were many parchments and letters to him from the Disciples and others.

They are unimportant. But they are important only if they tell of the Master. What they did in their voyages and their trials tell us human things. We should only keep records of what the Master did when He was teaching us.

He took a small step in the direction of the corner, stopped and thought: *I shall have to ask Tychius to burn them.*

He returned his attention to Thomas' scrolls on the floor and slowly walked to them, carefully gathering and then placing them on his "desk." As he did this, he wondered how old the remaining scrolls were and if they filled in the missing years. Long ago, he heard Thomas was in India. With quick calculation, he concluded that it was nearly twenty years ago. In those twenty years he heard from some passing Arab merchants who were Christians and even some Persian and Babylonian Christians that Thomas had brought many to Jesus and that he was beloved by the people of that far away land.

✳

Abban had other trade duties to complete before returning to his master so they avoided the rough and fast moving Tigris River and traveled the Euphrates with its low banks and slower flow. To get to the Euphrates they traveled south overland through Sophene into Osroene. Thomas was given a mule and though he was experienced at riding such a creature, he found this trip difficult. There were poor, dirt roads with small and large pits or gullies. His mule, which he sarcastically called *Haa-saa-naay* and which in Aramaic meant "easy," was a joke to everyone in the group, for the mule was far from being easy. He was stubborn and unfriendly having kicked and bitten several members of Abban's traders. Above all else, he was overly obstinate and as a result most of the time Thomas walked beside the mule talking and reprimanding him for being so obstinate.

The thought of passing through Osroene excited Thomas, and he asked Abban to stop at Edessa. He wanted to see his old friend King Abgar and the manservant, Parlan. Abban quickly agreed, but as soon as they crossed into Northern Osroene they learned that King Abgar had died and that his son, Ma'nu V bar Abgar was King, and did not inherit any of his father's belief in Jesus. Thomas wanted to see the new King, for he remembered him as a young man and hoped to correct the young King's ways, but the elders in Edessa told him that it was dangerous. Thus far, the King had only voiced a personal dislike for Christians and still did not try to stop the Royal household or his subjects from practicing their beliefs. The Elders made Thomas understand that to make himself known and to confront the King may instigate Ma'nu into acting against the Christians. Further, they insisted that Thomas not make himself known for fear that he would be arrested. Many in Edessa remained faithful to their conversion, but the new King had many spies among the *populous*. Jude Thaddeus, who returned before Thomas arrived, was secretly rushed out of the Osroene and headed east into Assyria. Abban hearing the reports of the King's displeasure with Christians held Thomas close to him, and quickly settled his business and whisked Thomas out of Edessa under disguise. They hurriedly headed for the port city of Nicepherium on the Euphrates River. The city was founded many years before by Alexander the Great. In Nicepherium, Abban hired the first boat that was sailing south and down the Euphrates. The boat they used was a spoon-like reed boat made of thick grass and common to this part of Osroene and for travel up and down the Tigris and Euphrates. The boat was called *Dilhun* and from the time they boarded the boat, Abban openly spoke of his dread and distrust of reed boats. However, he had to forget his fears, for he knew he had to get Thomas out of Osroene and away from King Ma'nu.

The quickness of their passage through Edessa and Osroene did not rest well with Thomas. He felt he abandoned an opportunity to preach Jesus and this made him forlorn. His first day on the boat was spent sulking. As night came, he positioned himself away from the others and deeply prayed for Jesus to save the people of Edessa and to gently touch the confused heart of the new King. He was in prayer for many hours and was so deep in conversation with Jesus that he was unaware of anyone abroad the boat.

"How can you stand up in this boat?" He heard Abban ask him which quickly shook him out of his meditation. "Standing up in a reed boat is a dangerous thing to do."

Thomas almost laughed aloud, but instead, he simply smiled, "My friend, that is merely your fear of reed boats speaking."

"Call it what you wish, Thomas, but it is still a very unwise thing to do. You may fall over the side."

"I am not afraid of falling over the side, because I am praying."

"Do you always pray standing, open-handed and with closed eyes?"

"Yes. This is how all Jews pray."

"If I were you I would find a new way of praying."

Thomas politely ignored Abban and returned to his conversation with Jesus.

Moments passed and again Abban interrupted him saying, "To whom do you pray?"

"To my Master."

"Your Master! The Man at the gate?"

"Yes."

"Why pray to a mortal man?"

"He is not a Mortal Man. He is the Son of God."

Abban instantly grew pensive.

"If you believe that your Master is truly the Son of God then I would suspect you would be on your knees as you would a king and act a bit more humble."

Thomas looked at Abban with some surprise.

"And you, when you pray to your god do you not also stand?"

"I used to, but since meeting your Master, I have been kneeling."

Thomas was stunned by this answer and felt ashamed, for he neglected to become conscious of his companion's encounter with Jesus. He should have known that the entire incident at the gate was more amazing to Abban than it was to him.

Abban looked away from Thomas and gazed off into the distance. "I find your Master bewitching. Since I have met Him I have been very uneasy…very anxious…very needy." His face tightened and his forehead wrinkled in bewilderment. "I cannot forget His eyes for they singed my flesh. Nor could I forget His voice for it echoed like a chant in a large temple."

Thomas smiled widely and put his hand on Abban's shoulder.

"My poor Abban," Thomas said sympathetically, and Abban quickly looked at Thomas for he was not used to pity or such concern; he was only a servant. "Please do not feel you are being singled out, for Christ often creates unrest within people but He never does this to harm anyone; it is only to make them accept Him. He did this to me and to others. At first, I thought I felt my unease and need for Him because I could not understand His hold on me. I was attracted to Him like a tree to water. I have seen many leave Jesus because they could not live with the need He created in them. This need is like a desert thirst that Jesus alone can quench and this discomfort always caused people to race away from Him. To stay with Jesus also means the need to find and be found.

"Eventually, the search would lead to the discovery that this need for Jesus is love. If I speak to you of Jesus' love, Abban, believe me it is a love so great and so strong that pushes its way into life. I felt it grow daily within me until it was life itself. I lived on and for His love, and soon realized that Jesus welcomed the moments to receive love. As you learned, I am one who fully needs to understand everything that comes into my life, yet unconditionally I loved, even when I didn't know who He was or what He was about, I was compelled to continue to love Him.

"Once, when I thought I had lost His love, the void was so immense that I forgot the next moments of life. I remember the day this happened well. It was our last Passover meal. Jesus told us He was leaving and that we knew the way to the place He was going, but we could not follow Him. His departure, coupled with my inability to follow Him, was more than I could bear. I did not want Him to leave without understanding why He came and what I was to do with my love. So I questioned Him and He answered by saying: 'I am the Way, the Truth and the Life.' I quickly fell silent for I did not comprehend what these words meant. I knew that if I continued dwelling on His words I would be confused even more, so I let it go—I often did that—just let things go, and many times it seemed the wisest thing to do. I am glad I did, for that night turned into a 'magical' night due to the continuous love felt at the dinner. The Others sensed the same thing and we remarked to each other that now was the time for Jesus to remove any doubts we may have had on who He was. How blind we were after all those years of showing us He was one with the Father. His actions alone should have made us understand Who He was. We saw Him do things that we knew only a messenger of the Almighty could do.

"We saw Him cure the sick and we became confused. 'How could this be?' we asked.

"We saw Him feed the multitudes and we became uncertain. 'How could He do this?' we asked.

"We saw Him raise the dead and we became uneasy. 'How can a mere man do such a thing?' we asked.

"We saw these things with our own eyes and we knew they happened. There was no choice but to believe that He had great powers which most of us believed came from the Almighty."

"And did you get the power to work in His Name?" Abban asked with impatience.

"Only after Jesus died and I was left searching in much turmoil."

Suddenly a strong wind passed over them and the night sky was filled with heavy clouds.

"A storm comes," Thomas said looking into the sky, and when he turned to look at Abban he saw a look of terror. He walked to the man and stood directly before him just as the boat hit a swell. Abban quickly reached for the side of the boat.

"You should have no fears Abban, for I am sure we shall not capsize. Long ago my Master calmed the sea and since that day none of the Twelve fear the seas. No, if we are to die it will be on land and by the hand of men."

Abban grabbed Thomas' hand and pleaded, "Help me to be as sure as you."

"Stand up."

"What?" The terrified man shouted as he recoiled and gripped the side of the boat, "Are you mad?"

"Stand up and show you have faith in Jesus."

Abban could not move.

"Stand up!" Thomas extended a hand to the fearful man.

Thomas reached down for his hand and gently took it into his own hands. Abban gripped Thomas' hand so tightly that Thomas instantly felt the pain. Abban searched the Apostle's face and was immediately assured and briefly felt enough courage to want to stand. Suddenly Abban felt a kindling warmth pass from Thomas' hands into his. He grew comforted and slowly rose to his feet. His jaws clutched tightly; his eyes shut and his breathing was short and gasping. He no longer felt the boat beneath him, or the wind and water around him. When he opened his eyes, the river around him was churning and a strong wind tossed his beard, cloak and hair about wildly, but the boat remained stationary and it thus seemed to be the safest place in the world.

"Believe in Jesus. Believe in the Man at the Gate and He will make the waters still," Thomas said in a loud commanding voice that bellowed above the forceful wind.

Abban closed his eyes and saw anew the Face of Jesus; he heard His Voice echoing softly in his ears and his body became warm. When he opened his eyes the night was calm and bright in the moonlight while Thomas was seated on the deck of the reed boat and he, Abban, was standing alone. Mystified, Abban said in a shaken voice, "Please tell me more about your Master."

"I shall," Thomas said as he was smiling for he knew that Jesus had called another to Himself.

Early the next day they arrived at the port of Circesium in Osroene, took on provisions, and continued down the Euphrates and by noon arrived at the Mesopotamian river port of Dura. There Abban traded for some *papyrus* and some silks and they departed again. Surprisingly that night and all the next day, the sails of the boat ballooned with strong winds that came from nowhere and surprised everyone for they had never experienced such winds. With these forceful airflows, the boat sped quickly down the river making the crew extremely happy. At this speed, it would be difficult for someone to attack from the shores. There were many tales about vessels being attacked and crews murdered by marauding, nomadic tribes who cunningly hid along the shoreline. These tribes lived in the barren wasteland and nearby jagged mountains and used all possible diversions to capture cargo, people and wealth. These tribes had no law and nothing seemed to be able to curtail them making such travel extremely dangerous.

Seeing Thomas so often in prayer, the crew concluded that this holy man was the cause of their good fortune.

Thomas remained unfazed by these not-so-natural events. He knew Jesus was rushing his trip, for He was needed in India. Meanwhile, several crew members came to Thomas and they became believers, and though Abban was receptive to the stories and teachings he still remained uncommitted. Thomas remained patient knowing that he would come to Jesus when Jesus wished it.

For the next two days, the sails ballooned but on the morning of the third day, as suddenly and as mysteriously as the winds began, they died, and the boat slipped slowly down the river. The sails dangled from the masts like old, sagging flesh and it seemed that the entire world had stopped and was fixed in time. Surrounding the boat, on each side of the river, came a view of a desolate and destroyed city. The void of wind matched the stillness and the barrenness of what all aboard the *Dilhun* recognized as a once great city. Thomas felt the hurried beat of his heart against his chest. He felt the loneliness and bareness of all that he saw and for one quickened moment he felt he had to know this place. This place had personal meaning to his life. In complete silence the small crew stood like clay statues looking at the ruins. The silence of that moment was broken by Thomas' soft question, "What is this place?" and from behind him came Abban's voice: "The great City of Babylon."

Babylon! The place of the great captivity. The prison that held the Jews away from their beloved Jerusalem. Slowly he felt his life draining from him. He felt empty and deserted by all that he knew. He felt no love but only rejection. From the pit of his dark memories, he thought of another time and quickly remembered having experienced this feeling before; he felt these emotions before—*When?* Then gripped by a black, uncaring hand from his past, he felt a tug at his being and it caused him to physically jerk and to almost convulse.

Seeing Thomas in distress, Abban quickly grabbed his arm, and Thomas turned to look into his traveling companion's face when all went black.

Waking, he saw the darkening sky above him and the white sails of the ship bellowing obediently in the cool night air.

"Ah, my friend, I trust you had a good rest. Thank all that is good that you have returned to us."

Thomas tried to raise himself but he was gently pushed back onto the blanket on the floor of the reed boat.

"No, you must rest. I think your collapse was due to your need for a good rest, and besides, the scenery was very depressing. All dead civilizations are depressing."

"That was Babylon." Thomas said the words with much pity.

"Yes, what was left of it. Every time I see it I try to imagine the hate others must have for that empire. They hated it so they destroyed it completely leaving only rubble and silent cries, but thank all that is good that we have passed it," Abban remarked as he looked away and then snapping his head back he looked intently at Thomas who was breathing more easily with a look of relief. "I was sorry to see that affect you so much."

"I relived a terrible time," Thomas said as he wrinkled his forehead as if in pain.

"The slavery of your people by the Babylonians? That happened so long ago. One has to forget the pains of the past. It is unnatural to dwell on yesterday's things. We humans have a natural remedy for mending the pains of the past; we call it time. All we have to do is let time, like medicine, heal."

"It was the anguish and desolation of my people that threw me back to a time in my life when I experienced similar feelings. It was a bad time...one that I..."

Thomas looked away aware that Abban was watching him. He was certain his companion was wondering why he had stopped, but he had to stop for he was reliving emotions of the past and the emotions of the days and nights that followed.

He sat up and swallowing hard continued in a soft, slow voice. "Do you remember when I told you of the night we had supper with Jesus and we were sure He was going to reveal Himself to the world?" Without looking, he knew his friend remembered. "Well that very night, Jesus was betrayed and arrested and the celebration stopped quickly and the dream of being powerful died even faster."

"Who would have betrayed so great a Man?" Abban asked with a degree of shock in his voice.

"One of the Twelve who believed that he was doing the right thing. Do you remember I told you that we all had different ideas of Jesus? Well the one who betrayed our Lord had a very different idea. Now when I think of that poor Apostle I am sure he never stopped listening to himself. Had he done this he would have heard Jesus speaking to him. Now when I think of bygone times, I remember, after we went out to the countryside healing and teaching the people, how he never spoke or debated with us again. He knew the answer. He was so sure of himself. He did not need the Spirit of the Lord; he had his own spirit. Of course

I can only speculate what was in the Betrayer's mind, but I know that he stopped talking to us at great lengths. Somewhere in his journey, he left us on the road and went away, seeking different truths and different ways. Some of my brother Apostles believed he betrayed our Master in hopes of forcing His hand to act more quickly. Some even think the Betrayer wanted to get a higher position in the Kingdom to come. Oddly, for his sin, he will be remembered always and perhaps his need to be known will be fulfilled." Thomas took in a deep breath, "But the Betrayer was not alone that night, for none of us remained to help Jesus." He turned to look at Abban for he could sense the immediate feeling of disappointment coming from him.

"I know you think badly of us, and I know if you knew the Others you would find many of them disappointed and remorseful about their failure, but we now accept that it was not the will of God for us or anyone to have been brave that night. You see I—we—had to become like lost sheep, the sheep Jesus said we were, because He always seeks out the lost."

"Do you think that I am lost?"

"We are all lost until we accept that Jesus is the Way, the Truth and the Life."

The two men looked out over the river and to a town passing on the riverside. They could see the torches and the fires from the street and homes. They were like beacons in the night—earthly stars—blinking and flickering in the stillness of the night.

"And I was as lost as the Betrayer," Thomas stated softly.

Abban turned to look at him and Thomas returned the look.

"After Jesus was arrested, I ran the fastest and hid. After the Sabbath, I returned to the place of our Passover knowing that the Others would also be there. We were so predictable. Soon after my arrival, I felt the suffocating heaviness of the Room. It was filled with sadness and self pity. I regretted returning and I wanted to break out of that place and run far from all their stupidities, but how far could I run knowing that I shared in their stupidity? We all had been duped and we had no powers to rally the people or any powers to fight the Romans. Worse, we found ourselves hunted and condemned by our own people. We had lost our families, friends, our homes and even our religion because of Jesus. He left us with nothing. My despair was that deep and that cutting. I quickly decided that I would not stay long with the Others, but for reasons I could not explain, I stayed because of some unknown need. During the night when the Others were sleeping, I crept away. I went off under cover of the night cloaked once again with cowardice and weakness, yet with a degree of freedom. I do not know how long I wandered. I do know that several times I was nearly caught by the sentries of the solemn, midnight watch and the cock-crow watch, but I had learned how to hide well and was not discovered. Early the next morning when the City Gates opened, I made my way away out of the City. I wandered for several hours, grew tired and finally sat. When I looked I found myself sitting on a mount looking in the direction of Golgotha which was where they had hung and killed Jesus. I saw the distant and barren cross. It was stripped of life and dead just as I was. I cried to the Almighty asking for forgiveness for I felt I had taken my eyes off of Him and followed a false prophet. I begged The Almighty to forgive me for insulting the intellect He gave me. I promised I would not be so easily misled again. I was at that time, the lowest of low, for all that time I never once thought of Jesus, whom I had loved, or of His pain; I thought only of myself and what happened to me. I never thought I was that selfish, but I became that selfish. After a few hours of inner searching, I decided to leave the Others. I would go back to the Room, bid them goodbye and retreat from anything that would remind me of Jesus and them. I hurried back. Strong with certainty, my mind was free of all of my failings. When I arrived I became surprised. All their faces were glowing. They all looked so happy...so jubilant. They came running to me.

"'Thomas, we have seen the Master,' Jude Thaddeus said as he grabbed and embraced me.

"'Peter and John went to the tomb and it was empty,' Andrew shouted.

"'He is alive,' Simon Peter exclaimed.

"They were shouting and speaking together and this confusion was as hard to understand as what they were saying. As they rattled on and on, I began thinking that they had all gone mad. Their excited voices were thrown into mumbles as my mind distanced itself from them. I examined their excited faces and reasoned that they needed to believe such an impossible thing. Out of guilt, I expected that Simon Peter only wished Jesus was alive so that he could beg forgiveness. I could see John's grief being replaced by the possibilities of this event. I could understand Simon the Zealot's desire for this to be true for he needed to have a hero in his life. I could also imagine the Others having needs and desires for such a happening. They too did not want to be known as fools. I quickly ignored them and looked to James the Little with whom I had a bond. I knew him to be the most unbelieving of us all. He looked at me with a face no longer wearing its usual, annoyed disapproval. His eyes glowing with wonder, he remarked, 'It is true Thomas. He appeared to me and He made me believe.' I pulled away from them as if I just discovered they had leprosy and would contaminate me. I truly believed they were mad and I knew their insanity had desecrated the very death of Jesus. How could they say such things? How could they dare think such madness?

"'Have you all gone mad? How could you say such an unholy thing? Jesus is dead. John, you say you saw him die. You buried Him.'

"'And the tomb was empty when I looked in. He came to us today while we sat in this locked room. Thomas, we truly saw the Master,' John said with great conviction.

"'He appeared to us and stood in that place,' Philip added with equal conviction as he pointed to the middle of the Room.

"'Before we saw Him, He appeared to Simon Peter, James and even Lady Mary,' Andrew continued with a joyful look on his face.

"'And to the women and to Cleophas,' chimed Matthew.

"No! I thought. *I was not going to be fooled a second time.*

"'NO!' I shouted to them. 'You are all wishing this. You all need this to be true. Do you expect me to believe such a shameful idea? No. I will not believe it until I see the Master with my own eyes and feel His Flesh. I shall never believe until I see his wounds and place my finger where He had been pierced. No. I shall never believe what you say until I am that certain.'

"They all pressed around me, each wanting to assure me that what they said was true until Simon Peter called them away. The room became heavy with silence as Simon Peter walked to me. He stopped before me and with sadness said in a grave voice, 'Be careful of what you say, Thomas, for such disbelief will hurt the Master greatly. It would be like a denial.' His face twisted and twitched in pain. 'Let me remind you of the power we witnessed when Jesus was with us. He clasped the hand of the daughter of Jarius, and touched the brier of the son of the widow of Naim and called to His good friend, Lazarus. He showed power over sickness, sin, storms and even death. Remember these things, I ask you: If Jesus could do this for others, is it not possible that He could do it for Himself? What would stop Him from doing this one more miracle?'

"It seemed as though much time passed before Simon Peter broke his stare and walked quietly away. As I watched him walk, I wondered what had given him such insight. Had I missed what he had received because I was more concerned about what Jesus had done to me rather than what I had done to Him? Could it be that Jesus had given the Others insight and had forgotten me? Had He performed a miracle on all except me? I stood alone in the center of the Room—an outcast in their eyes. I watched as the Others mumbled and spoke softly to each other, possibly criticizing my disbelief.

"For three or four days thereafter, I kept to myself, in spite of the fact that my brother Apostles came to me and tried to comfort me and soothe my disbelief. Two major forces waged a war within me: Simon Peter's wise words and my decision to leave the Group. The longer I thought the more sure I became that I truly did not belong with them. I was not like them. They each had turned away, came back, and found sure hope in togetherness; I on the other hand did not come back with hope. I had no hope. I came back to leave. They all seemed to find some relief and forgiveness; I had no need for forgiveness. I had not hurt Jesus as much as He had hurt me. I had all the right reasons for leaving but I could not leave for something was holding me in place.

"On the fifth day something happened that completely changed my life. I was seated alone on the floor against the wall of the Room while the Others were seated in small groups around the room. Some had grouped themselves at tables eating—for it was midday—and others were standing in groups of two or three. Suddenly there was the scent of flowers, ever so sweet and poignant. From nowhere came a slight, mild, calm breeze that passed through the room, but not to cool us but to warm. There was a soft rumble, then a glow and when I looked up, there in the midst of us was Jesus. Many of the Others fell to their knees and soft reverent mumbles came from their mouths:

"'Peace be with you.' I heard Jesus say. He turned to me. His Face was drawn and offended, almost in severe pain.

"'Thomas. Come.'

"I could not rise to walk. My legs became like water. I felt the Master's eyes on me. I wanted to go to Him but I could not. I needed to go to Him, but I could not. I had to be near Him, but I could not move; so, like a child I slowly crawled to Him. My eyes were unable to look above the hem of his cloak for I could not bear to look at the hurt on His Face. His Feet—clean and immaculate—came into view and I saw the nail marks.

"'Come Thomas, seek the proof for your disbelief.'

"Inches from his robe I looked up and saw His Hands waiting for my touch. I saw His Side open welcoming my finger. I looked at His Face and saw three puncture wounds on His brow from the thorns.

"'Put in thy finger hither, and see My hands; and bring hither thy hand and put it into My side; and be not faithless, but believing.'

"All the emotions of life erupted inside me and rushed to explode. I cried as a child out of love, out of glee, out of fear, hope and faith.

"'My Lord and My God.'

"I fell on my face; my tears began wetting the floor. I heard the small sighs and sounds of pity, and I felt the love come from the Others.

"But Jesus said: 'Because thou hast seen Me, thou hast believed. Blessed are they who have not seen and yet have believed.'"

"You saw with your own eyes this dead Man alive?" Abban asked with great amazement.

"I saw that Dead Man living again."

"Tell me more of Your Master so I can see Him living again."

*

John traveled north to the City of Smyrna—the city of Homer— with Trophimus and Tychicus, disciples of Timotheus, to preach to his fellow Christians who were suffering under strong opposition from the local authorities. He found the city deeply entrenched in the worship of the Emperors and immediately came in opposition with the Roman and local authorities. His attack caused the arm of Rome to seek him out as a traitor and he was declared an enemy of the Emperor and his arrest was ordered. The local Christians saved John by giving the authorities a different name, but he was a marked man in Smyrna and he remained a fugitive of Rome. After spending several harrowing weeks in that city, mostly under heavy secrecy, he was persuaded to leave, so he and Tychicus traveled to Sardis, the one-time capital of the Lydian Empire, while Trophimus returned to Ephesus.

Sardis was a city that laid claim to the largest temples to the Roman goddess Diana, the goddess of fertility, whose cult following encouraged loose living. John approached the cult and their Temple priest with great zeal, but little success. He was offering the citizens of Sardis discipline, purity, and respect and it was not in line with their carefree life. He stayed in Sardis for several disturbing weeks. Unable to deal any longer with the debauchery that he witnessed, he returned to Ephesus promising himself he would someday return. Once in Ephesus he quickly became comfortable. He discovered that he enjoyed the serenity and the comforts that living in Ephesus gave him, yet he felt he had failed. For on his return he could not do anything but think constantly of the cities he had visited. He went into deep prayer, spending many days fasting and performing acts of self-denial for the people of these cities. Continually he asked God to afford him one more chance to return to Smyrna and Sardis to preach Jesus.

After being home for two weeks, he returned to his desk and unrolled one of Thomas' *papyruses,* still feeling the weight of his failure. Getting back to the scrolls was something he knew he needed to do, for he was strongly interested in Thomas' mission. The words Thomas wrote made him feel close to his brother in Christ, and he had the need to vicariously live the excitement and the adventure of foreign places. Thomas revived many forgotten events in the time Jesus had traveled with them, and what Thomas had experienced filled many scrolls. Instantaneously after unrolling a scroll, he fell into the rhythm of Thomas's narrative and read of the continued river journey down the Tigris and Euphrates and out of their delta and into the open seas. Thomas called the sea he sailed the *Mare Arabiae et Indiae* the Sea of Arabia and India. John never heard of this sea and suddenly felt ignorant and naïve and once again he wished he had not been so limited in his travels.

He read on.

Abban hired a larger vessel for our travel and we sailed close to the Parthian shoreline, needing to feel the security of the sight of land. This sea was sapphire blue and its swells were rhythmically timed to almost cause me to day-dream. The small swells lifted the boat ever so gently and carefully dropped it to meet the oncoming waves. The hiss of the boat cutting through the oncoming waves was like a lullaby and the soft spray of the salty water refreshed my warm face.

Thomas' description of the color and swell of the sea was so vivid that for one, quick, sudden moment John could almost smell the salty sea air.

Finally we arrived at the mouth of the great Sindus River where Abban hired another small, reed boat to carry us up river. On the very first day of our sailing, I saw dolphins, about fifteen of them, swimming and jumping in the brown-gray waters of the river. They playfully challenged us by coming ever so closely to our boat. It was a delight and a blessing to see them enjoying in simple play the world God had created for them.

John stopped reading, looked away, and out the small window of his room again felt the longing of such an adventure. After a few frustrating moments, he slowly returned to the scroll hoping Thomas would not re-awake his dissatisfaction.

Then they came to a place called the Sinh Plain. Thomas described the plain as silty land because it was often flooded by the river. They disembarked and continued by mules, and then changed to horses.

It was the first time, dear Brother, that I rode a horse. I tried not to look fearful or intimidated to my companions. With the help of the Master, I mounted the beast with confidence until he began to move, and then coaxed on by the evil one he galloped away. Unable to control him, I simply ordered the stallion in the Name of Jesus to stop and he obeyed immediately. From that time on, the beast was as gentle as a small lamb found in the fields of Galilee.

Abruptly, John stopped reading and walked away from the scrolls. For several precious moments, he imagined the feel of a horse beneath him and the superior, high feeling one had to have from riding such a beast. When he was satisfied with his imagination, he slowly went to the small table in the corner of his room, poured a cup of water from the jug and slowly sipped the cool water. He walked back to the scrolls and began reading again. He prayed not to have his frustration awaken.

Our small, reed boat continued north until we came to a small river port. We disembarked and began the rest of our journey on camels. These beasts had two humps and they were heavy, with thick coats like those we saw many times as children. The one difference that these beasts were far meaner and definitely more ill-tempered than those seen in Palestine. These animals bite and kick a great deal if they are provoked. The experience was exciting yet uncomfortable, but as we traveled I grew fond of my beast. The camel I had was a female and at night the guides milked her and this made her an instrument of kindness for she helped us. I did not remember that camels produced milk so this was very strange and unusual to me.

John lifted his eyes from the scroll and again looked out the small window of his room.

How would it feel to ride a camel? He questioned himself and closed his eyes to seek out his answer. An image of a camel—with two humps— came into his imagination. It was sitting on the earth with its legs beneath itself waiting for him to mount. He imagined himself mounting the animal and felt himself being thrown forward as the hind legs of the camel rose and then back as the front legs straightened out. Slowly he rocked to the rhythm of the camel's walk. What he envisioned satisfied his curiosity even though he was certain he had not captured the full experience of riding a camel. Feeling inadequate again, he heard himself say unexpectedly, *Most likely God knows what is best. I do not know if I could endure the many discomforts, unknowns, fears and great dangers that my brother Disciples had to bear in the Name of Christ, so I guess the Master knew what was best for me.*

He quickly returned to the scroll and vowed never again to regret his mission.

At long last we arrived at a small outpost that Abban said was at the border of the kingdom of his King. I was grateful for the rest because I was tired of traveling by sea, land, mule, horse and camel. It was sheer glee to return to walking with the feet God gave me. I was given heavy clothes and covers for my feet due to the cold. This country has many barren hills that rise and go flat. The mountains rise like giant eruptions of a land that screamed and needed to be noticed. Most mountain ranges have ice or snow on them just like the Armenian mountains. The mountains give off many waterfalls that cascade onto pools that move into the valleys. We passed many rivers and found the people selling their wares from their boats. Not only did they sell fish but also agricultural products. This was somewhat unusual to see for I never saw such a market. I could see the poverty of the people and the suffering that accompanied such want. At dawn some of the rivers looked burnished and had a mysterious heavy mist that resembled steam rising from it. I could not help but think that the steam was the exhaled breath of the earth in the chill of the morning air. The valleys that we traveled were plush with many small streams and large, blue rivers passing through them along with many peaceful lakes.

After two days of travel by foot, we again hired mules and continued up long, narrow roads until we came to a green valley that was edged with many, purple flowers. Abban told me that those flowers were used by the people as a spice. In the middle of this valley was large, open grassland and on this grassland were many, small tents. Milling around these tents were horses, a few camels, and some mules. Many men and soldiers were walking around; some seemingly playing games; others tending their horses or military equipment. These small tents circled a large tent; one of the largest tents I ever saw. The material of the tent was bright yellow with wide, orange strips. Long, thick poles anchored into the ground at equal angles held the tent tight. From these poles, streams of yellow and orange material flapped and waved in the wind. Sitting on the top of the tent was a round ornament that looked like a crown.

"That tent is the tent of King Gondophares. He has come to meet you," Abban stated with awe and glee on his face. The glee and the sheer look of admiration for this human King caused my heart to sink for I knew then that I would never save my friend Abban for Jesus. In my travels I had spoken to many sailors and camel drivers, horse tenders and muleteers which the Lord came to meet. I washed them in the many rivers and lakes on my way, but never had Abban come to that point. Oh, he was interested and attentive but never to accept Jesus as his Lord and Master. I felt a failure.

John fell back in his chair amazed. He read again and again the words, "I felt a failure." Instantly he felt a stronger attachment with Thomas. He could not help but smile with satisfaction at the revelation that he could share his feeling of failure, but quickly he corrected his moment of delight and knew he would have to seek forgiveness.

Perhaps all that we do is not enough. Oh Master, we love You that much! John thought.

Leaning forward, he continued to read after thanking God for Thomas.

We arrived at the entrance of the big tent and instantly an atmosphere of insecurity came over me. Abban was greeted warmly by several of the guards who were neatly dressed in sky-blue uniforms that appeared heavy and that covered them well below their knees. The uniforms were trimmed in black fur. Their legs were covered with white cloth held in place by leather stripping that wrapped around their legs. Their feet also had coverings. Before we were permitted to enter the big tent, we were taken to a small tent nearby and ordered to bathe, change our clothing and wait to be summoned. The tent we bathed in was warmed by an open fire. After bathing and putting on clothes, we waited. I prayed into the night and early morning. For the first time in a long time I longed for Galilee. Finally after many hours of prayer, I fell over with exhaustion. The next afternoon, Abban was summoned before the King. I was told to wait. Again I returned to prayers asking Jesus to show me what was to be my mission. Much time passed when I finally was escorted to the big tent. The interior of the tent was draped over and over with fine material of different shades of yellow and orange. Even the poles that supported the tent were wrapped with cloth. It was an amazing sight. The floors of the tent were covered with red rugs that were so soft I could feel its material through my sandals. Around the tent in a circle sat many richly dressed men all sitting on pillows. They were eating, drinking or puffing on a long tube that was attached to an ornate container. Standing in the center of the tent was King Gondophanes. He was a tall, thin man with black eyes that were set deep in his face. His eyes were barely visible because of his thick, heavy, black brows. His nose was long and pointed. A thick, heavy, black beard wrapped around his tan face and barely visible in his beard due to his red lips was a small mouth. On his head was a white turban that was jeweled with pearls and red, blue, green gems. His robe was golden and his sleeveless cloak was snow white. He was impressive, overpowering, but when he spoke I detected sadness and a worry in his voice. Besides, the King was a rigid soldier, holding an arched sword by his side. He was clothed in a black robe that matched his black beard and hair, and from his side hung a silver sword that captured my attention. It was a strange instrument of defense and I wondered if it was as good a weapon as it was beautiful. The soldier stood with his eyes lowered, and after Abban introduced me to the King, the soldier looked at me and I immediately felt a cold chill pass over my being. His eyes were full of distrust. I later learned that this man was Omende and he was the general of the King's palace guards. I looked for Abban but he had disappeared and I missed him immediately. I later learned that Abban had been dispatched on another mission and was soon to return. I turned my attention to the King who, when I entered the tent, had immediately raised his head and took in a deep breath. With a quick wave of his hand he ordered me to come closer to him. "You do not impress us as so great a man, Thomas, yet we are told you are. Tell us what makes people think you so?"

"My Master works through me, Sire."

"Do you firmly believe that a master would give a slave such greatness?"

"Yes, because He loves me and wants to save me."

I could tell the King was trying to hold back laughter, but the others in the tent began to chuckle and smirk. He looked around the tent and immediately there was silence. "Well perhaps He did save you, for He sold you to us and we are a benevolent Kingdom." The others in the tent began to mumble and I could hear small phrases of agreement and praises in their words, yet I could detect their fear of him. The King raised his hand and again everyone grew silent. I was impressed by his power and authority but still was intrigued by the sadness in his voice.

"Your Master sold you to us as a carpenter. Tell us, did you build something for Him?"

"Sire, I am still building for Him," I said as I silently thanked Jesus for the honor to be in Felix India to do His Will.

"And how long have you been a carpenter?"

"Sire, I am a fisherman by trade and a carpenter part-time but know only a little about carpentry."

"But your Master said you knew carpentry!" His voice was loud and tinted more with surprise then anger.

"I do in His eyes, so rest assured that if Jesus wants me to be a carpenter, then I will become a carpenter and you will not be cheated."

One of the guards spoke. "For your sake we hope you quickly become a good carpenter for he can be a very difficult King if he does not get his way."

"Then, you are like my Master," I replied simply.

The next morning I was taken before the King and given my instructions. I was to build a castle for him and his family on the very spot we stood. All the supplies and help I needed would be given to me but first I needed to draw him a building plan. I was discharged. When I returned to my tent, I found parchment, rulers, stylus and servants to help me. I spent the night talking to the servants about Jesus. Much to my surprise, I found Jews among them. I soon found that these servants were local people pressed into slavery to build the King's castle in lieu of taxes past due or future taxes to be paid. The stories they told me were sad. They spoke of their illnesses, diseases, hunger, cold, and homelessness. You have no idea how I ached and suffered for these people. Their poverty was far greater than the poverty I saw in Armenia, Osrene, and even Galilee. It seems Rome is not the only place of suffering, for India has misery also. Suffering and poverty are everywhere and the only hope we have is Jesus. During the night, I woke and by the light of a small oil lamp, miraculously began to draw plans for the King's castle. I knew that the knowledge to make a plan came from God, and by morning the plans were completed even to the ceiling decorations, portraits, furniture and sculptures. I asked for an audience with the King who seemed very annoyed by my presence, but when he saw the plans his disposition changed to sheer elation. He clapped his hands and immediately five men from nowhere appeared and rushed to the King. He whispered an order and immediately they produced bags of gold coins which the King had placed before me. "We have urgent news that requires we go back to my palace. This money is for you to purchase materials for our castle," he stated. "It should be enough to get what you need. Soon we shall return to see what progress you have made and we will supply you with more gold." By afternoon he and his entourage were gone except for several hundred slaves and the local people. The next day I gathered the laborers and began building the King's castle...

The King and his entourage were gone only a few weeks when word was received that his beloved brother, Prince Gad, was grievously ill. The news spread quickly among the people for the Prince was well loved. The news also was that the King was distressed by his brother's illness. It was rumored that the King's immediate advisor was deeply concerned, for they never saw the king so troubled. It seemed as if all life left him, for he sat and cried most of the day, and every night he would go with his family to keep vigil at his brother's bedside. After a week of watching his brother suffer, the King issued a decree for all to pray to any god or gods for the quick recovery of Prince Gad. The people gathered in prayer as ordered, and Thomas watched in wonder as the many different religions came to the surface. He later questioned the villagers and they assured him that the King was very tolerant of all religions though he was leaning towards the teachings of Zoroaster.

The Zoroastrians were virtually unknown to Thomas, but he soon learned they worshipped Ahura Mazda, the sovereign knowledge, and the belief of the never-ending battle between the forces of light and darkness. Their priests were Magi who had no great love for foreigners and were extremely power hungry. He knew he had to learn more about them. Within days he also was confronted by the Brahmins, the priests of the Hindu Religion. Their zeal was strong; their followers great. This faith was deep and entrenched in the daily life of the people. Again he knew he had to learn more about this religion so that he could properly debate them. More familiar to him were the remnants of the polytheistic Hellenistic religions brought by Alexander the Great of Macedonia. He also saw many varieties of nature religions with their worship of the sun, moon, fire and water along with the many, animal worshippers. He had seen these before and he knew their weaknesses and vulnerabilities. Finally, a small group of Jews came to his attention. He found they assembled for prayer in a small shed, and joining them, he quickly began to preach about Jesus. His success with the Jews was immediate and soon several of them joined him as he went among the other worshipers to preach Jesus but his success here was minimal.

Several nights later, in the silence of the late night, a group of men came to see him. They were not ordinary men for their robes and cloaks showed they were men of importance and wealth. One of the men, the oldest of them all, was respectfully led to Thomas. He was so fragile that Thomas reached for him and helped guide the elder to a seat nearby. Laboriously, the old man sat on a small stool near the Apostle, and after becoming comfortable, he leaned forward to within an inch of Thomas's ear and said in a fragile, low voice, "I am told you have come from a place called Judea."

Thomas nodded his head.

The old man sat erect, and slowly wetting his lips he said again in a fragile, low voice, "Good. Many years ago one of our kind traveled to your land in search of a King. He returned and told us that he had seen a King who was to become the King above all kings and one who was to lead many to their freedom. Do you know of this King?"

Thomas smiled and responded in a soft voice, "I do, Sir, for I am one of His Apostles. He has sent me here."

The other men in the group began to mumble with excitement.

The older man raised his hand and they fell silent.

"Did this King lead many to freedom? Out of Roman hands?"

"He led them to freedom beyond the hands and grips of Rome. He led them to freedom from death and to the freedom of eternal life."

Slightly perplexed, the old man, in an unbroken, long stare, searched Thomas' face.

Finally Thomas spoke, "He gave all a new kingdom: One above the rest, one that promises eternal happiness with the Creator of all life. The

King came to live and redeem us. He gave us the tools to build a life hereafter and to give us the keys to His Father's Kingdom."

"Where is this Man now?"

"He was crucified; rose from the dead and ascended to heaven where He sits at the right hand of His Father to rule and judge all people."

A small gasp and stir moved through the group and Thomas knew they were disappointed as well as shocked in what he told them.

"Does it disturb you?" he asked those around him. "His coming was told over thousands of years and all that was said of Him was perfected. He was the Messiah, the Savior of all mankind."

"Did you see this Man again after He was known to be dead?" one of the men in the crowd asked.

"Yes, and I doubted as you do, but I touched His Flesh and felt the warmth of the blood in His wounds and I believed, but if you believe in Him your salvation, your glory, will be greater than mine for you will see Him with eyes of faith."

The old man leaned forward and in a whispered voice, said, "Tell me more, kind Sir, so that I may see as you saw and believe as you believed, but Sir, be quick for my time is less than most men, and my need for a promise of a hereafter even greater."

So Thomas preached Jesus to these Magi for three straight days and many left believing. He returned to the locals with a newly found zeal. Though the *populous* were strongly entrenched in their ancestral religions, they soon became interested after he laid hands on the blind and sick in the Name of Jesus. His popularity grew and many more came out to hear him, but few accepted Jesus as the Christ. Nevertheless, he still preached Jesus and how faith saved many people in His time.

One day while preaching to the villagers, he saw soldiers in the crowd and within moments he was surrounded and ordered to follow them, which he did obediently. The small detail of soldiers escorted Thomas to the open plain that was the site of the King's castle. As he was led to this place, he saw Omende, the general of the King's guards, standing in the distance. His legs planted firmly in the earth were wide apart and his clutched fists were resting on his sides. He remained with his back to the detail of the soldiers and Thomas. He was dressed in black and this stark color served as a sharp contrast to the beauty of the landscape and the sky. A fast passing wind caught Omende's black cloak, it flowed and flapped behind him, then the cloak fell and hung lifelessly from his back. The land was quiet and still except for the sound of small birds.

"I was told by my spies that you had not yet started constructing the King's castle," he said. "So I came to see for myself." He turned to

Thomas. His face was grim and black but held a tint of enjoyment and satisfaction.

Thomas sensed he was facing the devil himself.

"I am so glad you have not disappointed me. I knew you were a charlatan."

"But you are wrong, good sir," Thomas spoke with mildness. "I have built the King's castle but not at this place."

Omende looked at him quizzically.

"I have begun building his castle in a better place. In heaven."

The general laughed and the sound of his laughter was heavy and sinister.

"You Jewish fool! Do you think the King gives a damn about your heaven? He has no need of a castle in your heaven. He has all the castles he wants here."

"So why if he had all his castles here did he ask me to make him another castle on this plain?"

"Insolent swine," a guard shouted and struck Thomas on the side of his face. Thomas reacted quickly and turned his other cheek, but Omende raised his hand and stopped the second slap from finding its mark.

Omende walked slowly to Thomas. His height overshadowed the Apostle. He leaned forward; their faces were inches apart, and Thomas felt his hot and unpleasant breath.

"Our priests say you have a sharp tongue and a clever mind with answers to all things, but that will do you no good, little man, for you shall never have the chance to speak to anyone again," his words did not need to be spoken, for the glee in his eyes and on his face were great.

"Guard, take this Jewish peasant away. Take him to the King's palace!" With these words he turned away and once again the breeze caught his cloak and fluttered it in the air.

The guards forcefully grabbed Thomas and began leading him away. "Wait!"

The guards stopped and spun Thomas around.

Omende turning his head asked, "Tell me Thomas, what have you done with the King's gold?"

"I gave it to the poor and needy."

"Then they shall suffer for taking it from you."

Thomas was tied in the back of a cart and led away. Though he could not see Omende, he knew the man was in sheer happiness and he thought: *Servant of the evil one, I shall have a greater day in the Name of Jesus.* For two days and nights he traveled until he arrived at the capitol of King Gondophares. Once in the city, he was tied to the back of the cart and dragged through the streets and into the castle. By the time he reached the castle gates, the flesh on his legs, arms and back was scraped and torn. Inside the castle he was stripped of his clothing and beaten with sticks and whips. The guards did not observe the Roman rule of inflicting thirty-nine lashes, for they beat him until he collapsed and was revived by the cold, salted water thrown on his wound. He was dragged down to the lower bowels of the castle and thrown into a dungeon. The stench of human excrement, waste and decay was so great that he was forced to take small, quick breaths in order to prevent getting instantly sick. Damp hay covered the rough, stone floor of the cell. Rats the size of cats raced around the cell squalling as they bothered each other. For some unknown reason, Thomas concluded they were feasting on the remains of a forgotten body and he uttered a quick prayer for the dead being. With determination, for he believed this was to be his fate, he crawled to the corner of the darkened cell and leaned his beaten back slowly and gently against the wall away from the cell door. The coolness of the stones chilled him. From this position, he could see the night sky through the small, cell window above him. The dark, blue sky and the stars reminded him of the many nights he sat with Jesus and the Others in the open Galilean countryside.

He was quickly distracted by the orange, waving light on the rough, stone wall opposite him. This light was a reflection of an open fire far below his cell window. He closed his eyes and for a moment could feel the light and the heat on his flesh. He slowly slipped away. His dreams were scattered with tableaus and cameos. He saw his parents and his twin brother who had died young. He saw his father, the carpenter, showing him the way to repair chairs, tables and damaged boats. These images of his youth came with quick statue-like images. Distant and echoed voices came to him and he recognized whose tone of voice they were. He saw himself walking to the Temple Gate on a High Holy Day, the feeling of the dry dust on his skin as he walked the roads of Galilee and the cool, soothing water upon wadding in the Jordan. He heard the penetrating voice of John bar Zachary. He saw Simon Peter, Andrew, John and James walking a dirty road following a tall muscular Man whose very stature demanded attention. He waved to John Zebedee, his friend, and saw John's young face smiling with pride and great joy. As the tall and well-built Man passed him, Thomas felt His shadow pass over him which immediately gave him a sense of peace.

The shadow seemed to linger on Thomas and when it passed something was extracted from him and without hesitation he followed the Man. He felt the outer chill of the night and the inner warmth of Jesus as they sat on the hillsides of Judea. The storms, the masses, the sounds, the faces and the places all came to him. He felt the presence of Jesus but then confusion entered his mind when thinking about the doubts of the Others. He felt fear and uncertainty. He remembered the parables and the turmoil they created within his mind. He saw the healings and the risings, reliving the astonishment of what he witnessed. The voices he heard were echoed and distant. The words he heard were so slow that they stretched and lingered in his ear leaving him perplexed as to their meaning. In his dream he heard himself say he was suffering from his wounds and this was causing him to fever and be confused. Abruptly all went blank and in the dark waters of his dreams he felt something tug at his sleeve. He turned and there he saw Jesus standing in the orange light of a large, charcoal fire on the shores of the Sea of Tiberius. Thomas knew where he was and what was going to be repeated and instantly he felt his heart race and his eyes water. He saw Simon Peter and John bar Zebedee coming to the fire carrying the fish they had just caught after Jesus had directed them to throw their nets on the right side of the boat. Simon Peter's clothes were wet for he jumped into the Sea and swam ashore. The fish were placed on the fire and the instant smell of cooking fish filled the air around them. Jesus offered them bread. Suddenly, as if pulled away from the Others, Thomas felt that only Jesus and he were living. Then Jesus looking into the fire, said to him: "Be calm, Judah Thomas Didymus, I will not rebuke you, but have one question: have you found what you wanted in Me?"

"Master, please do not be angry with me. John told us how he saw You dead. He told us You were marked and bloody and that water came from Your side. What else was I to think?"

"I understand Thomas, you believed Me to be dead, and to hear the Others say I was alive was indeed a vexing thing to understand and an even more difficult thing for you to believe." Jesus turned and looked at Thomas. "But did I not tell you I would be with you always? Did you not believe Me when I spoke these words? Yes you did. Did you know that I never die to those who believe in Me? That is what you denied, Thomas; you did not deny My Resurrection, but My never leaving you."

Thomas lowered his head. The heat from the fire and the warmth of Jesus' intense stare made him flushed and sweaty. He felt a heavy weight on his chest and he gasped for air. When he opened his eyes from his dream, he saw a large rat sitting on his chest and all around him were the others gnawing at the rags he wore and nipping at his open wounds. His first thought was to push his tormenters away, but soon he accepted that their licks and gnaws were tending to him. He slowly moved his head and surveying them and in a low voice said, "My dear brethren, have you been sent to do me kindness? See how good our God is to a lowly servant."

By morning the rats were away from him, gathered in the corner, timidly doing nothing. They became startled and their moods changed when they heard the latch of the cell door slide open. The sound of the door opening and the light from the torches jolted Thomas back to reality and he quickly protected his eyes from the brightness. Then he heard Abban's familiar voice. He was relieved. His guards looked at him in amazement, and it was then that Thomas realized his wounds had vanished. He smiled for once again he was blessed with a miracle from Jesus.

The guards cautiously led him to a large vat of water where he was washed. He was given clean, bright colored clothes and escorted to a small tent where he was greeted warmly by Abban.

"Thomas, I was so disturbed by what happened to you, but you infuriated the King and Omende so much that I am surprised you were not killed immediately."

"Where have you been?" Thomas asked.

"In the South, on another mission for the King. Looking for the clothes for the palace you did not build."

"But I did build him a palace. One in heaven. All the money he gave me I gave to his poor people and they ate, clothed themselves, and praised the King for his kindness. I am sure this made my Master very happy and that He will prepare a palace for the King in heaven."

"Thomas…Thomas, King Gondophares does not believe in your Master. He has no gods but himself."

"But he will believe in Jesus, of this I am certain."

"This is true, but it is up to your Master to prove Himself to the King." Abban smiled slightly as he walked around examining Thomas.

"The color of the yolk of an egg becomes you Thomas." He stopped before him and placed his hand on Thomas' broad shoulder. "You know the King's brother has been ill. In fact he is near death. I told the King of your Jesus healing the sick and returning those who had died, and the King was immediately interested. You must go to his brother and cure him as your Jesus did. If you do this all will be forgiven you and the King will return you to Judea." He smiled broadly. "You will be free, Thomas!"

Thomas lowered his eyes and moved away. "Abban, those things happened because Jesus wanted them to happen; if He does not will Prince Gad to be healed it will not happen. All is in the Hands of Jesus. I am only an instrument of His Will." Thomas turned and looked at Abban. "Just as you are His friend."

"Me? but I do not believe in Jesus!"

"True, but you have become His instrument and messenger."

"You can believe what you wish, Thomas, I have no control of that, but we must move fast, for the Prince is dying and the King grows anxious. Now tell me what potions, what herbs, what roots you need to cure the Prince."

Thomas smiled and said softly, "I need none of these things. I only need the Will of God and time to pray."

"But…the King will expect you to have these things."

"If this is what the King expects he may not receive the miracle he seeks. He must believe in the power of Jesus. Maybe healing his brother will be the way Jesus wants the King to come to Him." Thomas said as he walked to the opening of the tent. "Come let us do the Will of the Lord. Take me to the Prince but the King must allow me time to pray."

The King ordered everyone to leave his brother's room except Thomas and Abban. The air was filled with the wonderful scent of African frankincense which pleased Thomas. Those who remained were the queen mother, Prince Gad's wife, and his two young sons. They sat around the bed in silence and all that was heard was an occasional soft sob. Nothing moved in the room but the stream of tears from the eyes of the royal family. Thomas stood silently looking at the shallow breathing of Prince Gad.

The King cried silently. Suddenly, he was beside Thomas. Leaning close to Thomas he said in a low but definitive voice, "Make your God heal him or I will feed you to the wildest beasts in my kingdom."

Thomas looked at the King and with equal assertiveness said, "My God is never put to a test, Your Majesty, that is for humans. My God will show mercy."

"Then get Him to give the Prince mercy, Jew."

Thomas turned from the King and walked closer to the body of Prince Gad. Outside the room wailing could be heard from the professional temple mourners; Thomas instantly shuddered. He closed his eyes and for a long time remained still. His prayers were silent. After much time he raised his arms. He remained in this position for a longer time. Everyone in the room watching Thomas was mesmerized by his endurance. Thomas was not in this world; his mind and his being were transported back in time.

In his memory he was relocated to southern Galilee and was approaching the two mounts call Harmon. Jesus and the Twelve were walking along a dusty road that led to the main gate of the small town of

Naim. The sun was hidden behind a heavy cloud that covered all of the sky giving a gray hue to the day. James the Little, Judas, Simon Zealot and Jude were walking several steps in front of Jesus. They were in deep conversation. Jesus walked slowly and silently behind them with the other Apostles walking beside Him. Suddenly the air was full of wails and screams. Everyone knew that a funeral procession was nearby. Several of the Apostles hoped the funeral would be some distance away because rabbinic law demanded that all who came upon a funeral procession were to stand silently as the procession passed where they then were compelled to follow the body to the grave site. As the procession left the gate of Naim, the wailing grew louder. Thomas looked at Jesus and saw His face tighten with anguish. The closer the cortege came to Jesus the louder the laments were. As they passed, Jesus walked up to the mourners and said to them: "Do not weep." He walked to the bier and softly placed His Hand on it. The bearers stopped walking. Jesus walked to the body and removed the white cloth that covered the face. It was a young man. He closed his eyes and looking at the corpse said in a soft voice, "Arise, young man, I say to thee, arise."

With these words the man sat up and began to speak to all around him.

Thomas heard the mumblings of the past.

"Did you see what He did?"

"That was not magic!"

"He has great powers from The Great One."

Other sayings were a distant memory.

The fragrance of African incense burned his nostrils and when he finally stopped remembering he realized that he had his hand on the Prince's shoulder. Then in a loud voice he began to chant a psalm.

"I said: I will guard my ways, lest I sin with my tongue...' He felt a deep sadness come over him and he felt weak, but he continued; *"Lord, let me know my end..."*

He heard the sound of deep laborious breathing.

"Behold, Thou hast made my days but a short span...every man is but a breath. Man passes away like a mere shadow..."

The sound of the breathing pressed against his ears and he winced.

"Deliver me from all my sins..."

"Look, the Prince has opened his eyes!" someone shouted in amazement. Thomas did not hear them for he was far away.

"Remove thy scourge from me: I am perishing under the blows of Thy hand..."

"Look the Prince has moved his head in the direction of this healer and he smiles," another person said.

"Hear my prayer, O Lord…for I am thy guest, a pilgrim like all…turn thy angry eyes from me that I might be refreshed, before I depart and be no more."

Thomas felt a small breeze pass. It was like a slow exhale. He pulled his hand back and looked into the face of the Prince who was smiling at him. Slowly a glow came over the Prince's face and it traveled over his body. As he watched, he saw a mist slowly lift from the Prince. It had no form; it just flowed and lifted which Thomas watched as it ascended.

A scream loud and long pierced his vision and he felt chaos and confusion around him. He was roughly grabbed and he saw the face of the angry King inches from his face shouting at him. He was slapped and thrown to the floor. Just before he was hit again, he heard a loud moan from Abban and then all was dark.

When he woke he knew he had been badly beaten. His mouth was flooded with the warm sweet taste of blood. One eye was closed and he was unable to see from it. His knees and arms were scrapped clean of skin most likely from being dragged. In the cell with him was Abban and from what he could make out the poor man was as bad as he was. He tried to go to him but found he had been chained and was immobile.

"Abban. Abban."

"Thomas, I thought you were dead. The king showed no mercy; he continued beating long after you were thrown to the floor."

Thomas did not answer him. He was relieved that Abban was alive.

"Your God failed us. I was beginning to believe in your Jesus, but I cannot now. He proved as false and as worthless as the gods I have known."

"Abban. Hold your tongue before you damn yourself. We had seen a great thing. Prince Gad went to the Lord. I saw it."

"You are blind and foolish and I more than you, for I believed your story of the Man at the Gate coming back from the dead and having powers to heal the sick."

"But I tell you…"

"You will tell me no more! You are a charlatan and a thief. You robbed from the King and say you gave the money to the poor but they deny ever having received any money from you…."

They are too fearful to say otherwise.

"…and you killed the Prince with your mumbling and bad magic. I will hear no more from you, Thomas. The King has declared a national mourning and today Prince Gad shall be buried. After that you shall be beaten and killed in the most brutal way the King could find and I shall follow you to my death. No, Thomas, enough! I will not be told any more."

Thomas felt the weight of his friend's fears and knew there was nothing he could say or do, for all that had happened was the Will of the Lord, the Giver of Life. He quickly said a prayer asking Jesus not to hear Abban's doubts and to forgive him as He did that thief on Golgotha.

Suddenly, the cell door swung open and torches illuminated the blackness of the cell.

"Hurry, get him and also that other one and take them to the yard. The King wants them before him immediately."

"Have courage, Abban. I assure you I shall see you before Jesus," Thomas shouted as they rushed him from the cell and up the stairs to the courtyard where they stripped him and began wetting him with cool water.

He was dried, perfumed and given new clothes and led to the King.

The throne room was full of people standing in small chatty groups. Thomas knew them as advisors to the King. Among those present was Omende, who stood off to the side of the King with rage and hatred on his face. Thomas quickly rejected the advisor and placed his attention on the King who was pacing before his throne impatiently. When Thomas arrived, Gondophares stopped pacing, turned and froze in place. Once the guards departed the room, the King walked to his throne and sat heavily on it. In all this time he did not take his eyes off of Thomas. The silence of the room was thick and all eyes were on King Gondophares who did nothing but stare at Thomas.

"Leave us," he ordered, still not taking his eyes off of Thomas.

Omende and some of those present began to mumble and he shouted, "We said, 'Leave us!'"

The room emptied instantly of people and then it was swallowed by heavy silence.

The King rose from his throne and walked cautiously to the Apostle. When he was a body's length away from Thomas, he stopped and after several long, intense, unbroken stares, he started to walk examining him with his eyes. In spite of his wounds Thomas still looked strong and unbothered. After circling him, the King stopped before Thomas. Their eyes met.

The king said in a low voice, "What manner of man are you, Galilean?"

Thomas did not answer him.

"This is the second time you have come close to death, and the second time you are spared. Why is this so?"

Thomas did not believe the King wanted an answer so he did not answer him.

"You are destined to torment my tranquility. Even when you are not in my thoughts you have the power to send others to speak for you." The king stopped talking and Thomas wondered why.

"Last night in my dreams which were heavy with grief..." his voice trembled, "Prince Gad came to me. Glowing. Peaceful. There was a radiant light surrounding him. He told me he saw the house you built for me in that place your God calls heaven. My brother said to me, 'This palace is unmatched by anything seen by man. It is a magnificent palace greater then any seen in all of Rome.'" The King walked around Thomas. The Apostle watched him as long as he could. He once again became aware of how tall the King was for he was towering over him.

"What manner of man are you? What powers do you have that calls the dead to dreams that appear so real that one could catch the scent of a brother's flesh?"

"It is not my doing, King Gondophares, it is the doings of my Master, Jesus."

"But why did your God of such great powers not heal the Prince?"

"Because the Prince was ready to let go; I knew that the moment I entered the room. I could sense God was calling him. I had been summoned to help him answer the call of my Lord; to prepare him for his journey. The Prince had a mission: he had to be used by my Master to make your eyes see what was done in your name through love of the poor."

"Prince Gad was so happy. He never smiled as often and as wide as he did in my dream. Will this palace you built in my name be mine always?"

"Yes, but it will be better if you know of Jesus."

"I cannot..." The King returned to this throne and quickly sat in it. He was upright and majestic. "You know many hate you and have demanded your death, yet I do not know what to do with you. If I spare you, I shall be regarded as weak and afraid of the Power you know; if I kill you, I shall never learn of your God or His Power; if I ignore you others will kill you. What am I to do with you?"

"Listen to me."

"What?"

"Listen to what I have to say to you about my God. Allow me to speak of my God who is a God of love and of mercy to all."

Again the room was swallowed by silence.

"I will listen to your words, Thomas, with hopes that I will learn what to do with you. Teach me of your God."

*

For several moments John sat motionless and he felt a great void come over him. He was stunned by the news Tychicus had just given him.

"Are we sure of this report, Tychicus?"

"Yes, John. It has been confirmed by those in Alexandria and even by those traveling to Ephesus."

"What was his manner of death?" John asked because he needed to have closure.

"It seems he had been very successful with the pagans in Alexandria, especially the followers of the god Serapis. While the Christians were at the Meal, a mob charged the assembly and arrested him. They put a rope around his neck and dragged him through the streets of Alexandria. The rough, rocky surface of the streets cut his flesh. He was taken to the temple of the god Serapis. The conspirators gathered, beat and tortured him. The next day, they again tied a rope around his neck and repeated the street scene. By the time they reached the middle of the city, Mark was dead. They burned his body. Anianus, Mark's successor and three priests, Milius, Sabinus, and Sardenus risked their lives to bury Mark. It was their report that confirmed Mark's death." Tychicus cleared his throat trying to get John's attention for he knew that once John's mind wandered there was no way to become part of his world. I am sorry to bring you this news, John, but Timotheus insisted you know."

He looked at the Apostle and saw that far away look in his eyes.

"John. John. John, did you hear me?"

There was no response—John was away.

John saw young Mark before him. It was the very first time he noticed the boy. It was at the wedding of his sister Naomi to Joses. Mark and his family were guests. After that night, the young man trailed behind Jesus and the Twelve, and the boy was always eager to run an errand or to get something for them. His wealthy father, Aristarchus, was cousin to Simon Peter's wife and was at one time a procurer of food for the Roman Army of North Africa. It was on his father's side that he was cousin to Barnabas and a distant cousin to Thomas Didymus. It was to Thomas that Aristarchus complained that young Mark was never at home and always with Jesus. Thomas invited Aristarchus to stay and hear Jesus speak, and after that day Mark's parents became followers and supporters of Jesus. It was Artistarchus that Peter and John met that day carrying the water pitcher and whose upper room they procured for the Passover Feast. John had an attachment to Mark, most likely because they were both young. Suddenly, the likeness of Mark being at the Passover Feast came to John's mind. He saw the young man push aside the servant who was holding the bowl containing water and grabbed the towel that Jesus used to wash the feet of the Twelve.

This sight made John smile.

He stayed with us all that night and followed us as we journeyed to Bethany through the Garden, hiding in the bushes watching Jesus. He was there when Jesus was arrested and in fear, like so many of us, he ran but not before he lost his garments.

John stopped thinking and remembered the tears streaming down Mark's face as he later mentioned what he witnessed during those lonely hours of Jesus.

If it were not for Mark, if he had not been secretly there, we never would have learned of the agony of soul Jesus endured. When we told Mark of how valuable his witness was, his entire posture changed.

John stopped and lowered his head.

Mark is like you, John, he had something unknown to tell just as you have some unknowns to tell the world.

He closed his eyes and his mind was filled with thoughts.

I am lazy! I still have not gotten a beginning. Oh Lord, help me to do what You want me to do so that I can feel worthy to be Your servant.

Again a smile crossed John's lips as he envisioned Mark's excitement when he announced to his mother and all that he had been asked by Barnabas to join Paul on this journey. This image was a good way to remember Mark, so John opened his eyes and looked around the room. Tychicus was not there and again he knew he had neglected his friend. Somehow he knew that Tychicus understood him well enough to forgive him. He glanced at his "desk."

"When I finish this scroll I shall write Thomas and tell him of his cousin Mark's death." He said aloud. He slowly walked to the "desk" and carefully unrolled the last scroll from Thomas.

My dear brother Apostle,

It has been a long time since last I wrote and I have promised myself that after this scroll I shall have these all delivered to you where I am sure it will be several months before you receive them. I now have left the realm of King Gondophares which I had to leave because I was a virtual prisoner of the

King in his palace. I was under guard day and night not
because I found displeasure in the King's eyes but because
he feared for my life. His court, and in particular General
Omende, are not too pleased with the privileged treatment
that I am receiving. When it was discovered that the King gave
me more gold for the poor, they went into a rage and desired
to take my life. All my food and drink were tested by someone
to make sure I would not be poisoned. I abhorred this test-
ing for it endangered my Indian tester who was a father of
five children and indebted to the King. I spoke to this Indian
about Jesus and he believed and was baptized. His name is
Zenophus, a very humble and simple man, who now is a very
holy and devoted follower of our Master. He stopped tasting
food for me despite his insistence. We had to put all our trust
in the Lord. Zenophus was a great asset to my work and knew
his way around the palace. With his help I disguised myself
and left the pristine luxury of young King Gondophares' palace and went into the nearby villages to preach to the Indians.
Abban discovered me and reminded me that the King was
very selfish and wanted me all to himself, but the King had not
embraced Jesus no matter what I said to him. I told Abban
that I was not there for the King's pleasure but to do the will
of God. Abban is too careful of his temporal life. He told me
that if we were caught Zenophus would be the one punished.
This caused me to become fearful for Zenophus' life so we no
longer remained away from the palace, thus causing me to be a
prisoner of the King.

As you know dear Brother, God always has His way so soon
I was able to escape. My escape from King Gondophares'
kingdom can only be explained as an act of God. My rescuer
was a man named Siphor. He was a captain in the army of
King Mazdai in the south of Felix India. He came on a good
will visit with trade of arms as his main objective. His king was
waging war with a neighboring King and was in need of the

superior lances of Gondophares' army. In the course of his bargaining, Siphor mentioned to King Gondophares that his wife and daughter were tormented for years by an evil spirit. The King proudly announced he knew a man who could help, and Siphor begged to meet this man. I was summoned and Siphor begged me to leave with him. King Gondophares objected, but Abban, who I believe wanted to be rid of me for I was endangering his life, reminded the King that my life was in danger and suggested I leave with Siphor and return when things were safer. The King relented only after I promised that I would return as soon as possible. I blessed Zenophus and left him to care for all those we had taken to the Master. I was released along with Abban, my reluctant companion, and began my travels into Southern Felix India.

✻

The trip to the southern part of Felix India was quick and peaceful. Thomas delighted in knowing that the favorable weather and the hurry were proof that his mission was pleasing to Jesus. Within five days journey they seemed to have arrived in a completely different India. The large clouded mountains, with their chilled rivers and lakes and the open plains gave way to a flat land full of foliage that defied the seas. The trees and foliage came to the very edge of the land and stood brazenly against the sea. The air was consistently hot and humid. Looking onto the beaches and into the plush, thick and impenetrable vegetation was a new and different sight for Thomas. A new world was being given him.

At sunset on the sixth day of sailing, the boat came to a clearing on the edge of the jungle and the captain suggested they go ashore and camp on the open beach. Thomas welcomed the rest for his curiosity to walk on this new land became a daily distraction to his thoughts and prayers. The boat was too confining and he was restless and needed to meet new people and to feel again that overwhelming feeling of converting. The day was very hot and the features of the jungle with its many shadows and shades looked cool and relieving. The immediate feel of land under him gave him great joy, but much to his surprise the jungle was not at all cooling.

The very first night Thomas spent in the jungle, he was sure he found the center of silence in the universe, for wrapping itself about him was peace and stillness. The bushes and trees were motionless and reflected the silver tones of the moon. Basking deeply in this phenomenon, he felt the love of God. He stayed in this peace until midnight when softly an infant breeze casually passed through the bushes and trees. The breeze stealthily moved from vegetation to vegetation disturbing little; it was the jungle's night breath.

Abban, who had known and lived in the jungle for many years and who was sitting with Thomas, remarked how unusual the silence was but Thomas dismissed his remarks enjoying the blessing in that moment.

Finally, he spoke to Abban, "My friend, I think the jungle is sending us a message. The silence is in anticipation of Jesus' coming. The jungle is showing respect to us, his servants, for Jesus' arrival here in their world." He stopped and listened once again to the silence and then said in a soft reverent tone, "Yes, the jungle is sending us a message."

Thomas sat the whole night wrapped in the silence of the jungle and marveled at the gentle dignity of God. Being rapt in the presence of God, he began to pray.

The next day, tired and weary from hours of prayer, Thomas and the others boarded the ship to continue their journey down the coast of India. After two days of travel, they came to the shores of the Kingdom of King Mazdai. The crew quickly began to unload cargo, and just as quickly, the dock filled with people carrying and moving containers. Thomas surveyed the dock and the villagers with surprise. In northern India the people were light skin and fair of hair and light of eyes, but the people of this place were dark of skin with black hair and eyes. The northerners dressed modestly and with finery, but these southerners dressed scantly and more basic. He noticed quickly how these people shied away from the small party, ignoring them completely and thereby showing a great lack of hospitality.

Siphor hurriedly led Thomas, Abban and two Indian crew members who had come to Jesus and wanted to stay with Thomas as his disciples, through the village. Ultimately, they came to the outskirts of the village and found an old, weather-beaten hut with no roof surrounded by the jungle. Siphor insisted that Thomas and the others stay in the small village until he reported to King Mazdai that he returned with the arms agreement. He excused himself and was gone. Quickly the four men began making their living quarters more acceptable, and as night approached, they settled in with what they made. They made a fire and after purchasing some fish, cooked and ate them. As night came, they prayed together, and as always, Thomas spoke of Jesus, of His miracles and of His mission. Eventually, Abban and the others slept. Thomas sat listening to the jungle and after much time elapsed the darkness of night became dense and the shining tones of the moonlight began to fade.

Suddenly from deep inside the belly of the dark jungle came the piercing calls and cries of animals. Some cries were giving alarms; some were calls of need, others were loud pleas to be remembered in the darkness. The roars of tigers, the trumpets of elephants, the snorts of water buffaloes, the chirps of birds and shrills of monkeys sounded and resounded in jungle competition. He grew sad for he envisioned that behind the veil of the darkened forest, death existed unchecked, and innocence, gentleness and smallness were being victimized. He had the sense that there behind the forest veil was the very embodiment of the tormented soul of the world. The animal's calls were cries of the lost ones in the darkness of the world, in the belly of the world, who did not know Jesus. The sounds he heard were pleas to be saved from the unknown. When he considered this he knew he had an entire nation to save for Jesus, and he knew that he would have to work harder in this land than in any previous land he preached of Jesus. It was on that night that he felt a chill in the jungle air which never left him in all the time he was in this new India.

The next morning Thomas awakened early and began his day in prayer. As he was nearing the end of his long praises to God for loving the world, a small group of men came walking timidly to him. They were the villagers and they came to welcome him, and immediately Thomas began telling them of Jesus. By midday a large crowd had gathered to listen to this little man from far away talk of the great Lover. By mid-afternoon Siphor arrived with his sick wife and daughter. The two women were tied to each other and struggled with the servants who were leading them to Thomas. When finally they were before Thomas, their faces grew dark and sinister. They began cursing him with deep, muddy voices. In unison they accused him in a loud-tarred tongue of being a fake. Turning to the crowd nearby, their voices mellowed and they told the crowds that Thomas did not always believe in Jesus and that he was a doubter. Thomas ignored the women and the mumbles of the crowd as they began to show disbelief in his teachings.

He looked at Siphor and said, "I cannot cure your wife or daughter unless you answer me one question."

"Please ask your question, Sir," Siphor replied disquietly.

"Do you believe that Jesus will heal them?"

"Yes," Siphor shouted firmly. His voice was far from being in a military tone; his assertion far greater than any reply to an order from his king or general.

Thomas turned to the women. He closed his eyes and with a humble and gentle voice he asked Jesus to become present. Then with a loud voice he shouted, "Be still, Evil One!" His voice raced over the land through the jungle, across the sea and into the very ground on which he was standing. A small gentle breeze passed over them.

"Dark spirit, I made my doubts and denials become my strength, but your disobedience made you able to possess only the weak." He leaned forward and narrowed his look at the two women who threw themselves on the ground, rolling about fiendishly. He raised his hands to the sky and with a commanding voice said, "In the Name above all Names, leave these souls and return to your dark abode."

The two women in unison gave out a loud piercing shrill, so painfully long and hurtful that one thought the very marrow of the bones, the very will of the body, had been ripped from them.

Everyone in the crowd turned away or covered their ears in pain and protection.

Abruptly the day grew grey and a chilling breeze passed over the crowd.

Black and disfigured clouded forms spewed from the women's gaping mouths and swirled high above the crowd in search of refuge.

Thomas' face turned to rage and he threw a point finger at the forms and shouted with an almighty command: "Out of this place, Demon! Return to your hell in the name of Jesus who still has command over you."

The disfigured beings flew into the air and then plunged into the ground.

The screams stopped.

The sun beamed, the breeze stilled and the crowd let out a sigh of awe.

The two women slowly stood, looking unaware of what had happened. They walked to Thomas, their faces clean and aglow.

That day Thomas converted many. Among them was a noble woman named Migdonia, who had followed Siphor from the king's palace for she knew Siphor's wife and daughter for many years. Siphor, his family and Migdonia stayed with Thomas for days, and when they returned to the palace of King Mazdai they were questioned as to what had happened. Karish, Migdonia's husband, who was next in line to be king, forbade his wife to visit Thomas, but she disobeyed him daily, so he went to the King declaring a powerful sorcerer who possessed women had entered the kingdom.

Three days later the king learned that his wife, Queen Tertianana and daughter Azan, had been to see Thomas. He questioned them and they began to preach to him about Jesus and demanded the King change his sinful ways. The King angrily ordered Thomas and his companions arrested and jailed with a sentence of death. Thomas, Abban and many others were arrested immediately and thrown in prison. They were to be beaten and killed the next day, but during the night they were miraculously freed and were led unnoticed out of the palace to a boat manned by Arab seamen. Their angelic liberator told them to go further south. Obediently, Thomas boarded the small vessel but his two Indian companions, Ahalya and Dayaram, decided to stay behind and care for those who had become Christians.

It was then that he and Abban came to the place sometimes called the Land of Pepper on the southwestern part of India. They landed in a seaport called Muchiri at the mouth of a three-branched river called the Periyar River. The Arabs call this land Malabar. It was a large trading area. Thomas soon learned that traders from Phoenicia, Egypt, Parthia, Greece and Rome had conducted large-scale commerce here, primarily because of the hot spices, especially pepper, and cinnamon, ginger and other spices that grew there. The pepper from Malabar was so much in demand by the Romans that this part of India was jokingly called *Yavana Priya* the beloved of the Romans.

Thomas, with renewed zeal that equaled his fervor at Pentecost, paced the deck of the small vessel anxious to disembark, but for reasons unknown to him, he and Abban were told to wait. While they waited, Abban informed Thomas that he had heard of this place and that many valuable gems and pearls of all sizes and shapes were bartered here.

"I have heard there are many Roman coins here and even a Roman temple dedicated to Augustus with a garrison protecting the interest of the Empire. Surprisingly also, dear brother, you will find some of your countrymen here. Let me warn you that there are many rich and powerful people in this part of India that are set in their customs and ways. They lived by stations here. This may seem strange to us but to them it works so they keep the system in place. Be patient Thomas, and learn before you act," Abban advised softly.

Thomas looked at Abban with disappointment. He was sure Abban knew that he was here to do the will of his God and no system, riches, or contentment would deter him.

They were held aboard the ship until dark and were then allowed to go ashore. There they quickly found another empty and abandoned hut to sleep the night.

The next day, armed with a medium-sized wooden cross in his hands, Thomas walked in front of his hut and planted the cross firmly in the ground. As he drove the cross in the ground, he could feel the earth of India willingly take the wood. He had arrived at his destination.

Later that day, he and Abban went into the center of the town to buy some provisions. As they walked about, a young merchant seeing Thomas came to them and asked, "Are you Israelites?" Thomas answered that he was and the merchant immediately invited them to join the small community of Jews at the Sabbath that day at sunset. He quickly accepted, asked directions and went back to his hut and prepared himself for that evening by staying in deep prayer.

Just before sunset he joined them in their small, out of the way synagogue. They were hungry to hear the good news of Jesus. All through the night he spoke of the Christ, retelling the many parables, miracles and words of Jesus, and before dawn he had purified the small group of nine men. In their enthusiasm to become part of this ministry, they told Thomas of the large Jewish community that existed in the city of Cochin. Immediately Thomas had the urge to go to this other place but he felt he had to stay with this small band of Jews to make sure they were more established. He and Abban stayed with this community for several months. During this time, he visited several nearby villages and began preaching to the Indians and began having some success among the poor. However, Abban was anxious to be among more affluent people and suggested going to Cochin where he told Thomas there would be more success. Thomas agreed and they traveled to the city of Cochin.

As soon as they arrived in Cochin, Thomas began a strenuous campaign of preaching but he was not widely received. Every Sabbath, just before sunset, Thomas would walk slowly to the synagogue and debate and argue with the Rabbis and the congregation. He would return to his hut weary, disappointed and still without any conversions.

The Jews of India are so unlike other Jews. They have a far greater freedom than other Jews I have known. Though they follow the Laws of Moses with great vigor, they remain a bit indifferent to the rituals and Pharisaic Laws under which we lived in Jerusalem. A great deal of Greek influence has entered their way of life, so they observe the Laws in a casual way yet, seem to enjoy the fruits of the Law. They are very cautious of anything that may be radical; therefore, my coming with the idea of Jesus being the Messiah and Son of God has left them on guard. I am having a difficult time with these Cochin Jews, because Jesus and His charitable ways are seen as a threat to their status and wealth and also a threat to their security. In retrospect, they are not that free, for they are ruled by their successes and temporal values. They are very fearful of their delicate position among the people of this land. You have to understand, my dear Brother, that India is unlike any other world. Here the people are born to certain stations in life and they stay in that station until death. Unlike our world where a poor man can become rich, here in India if you are born to a low station you stay there. Each of the stations tolerates the other out of need, and this toleration is of the lowest degree. Therefore, any threat to this system is viewed as a grave menace to the whole of society. Preaching love, mercy and respect for all life is a very strange and dangerous concept to the Indians. The highest station includes the priest and scholars of the country — sounds somewhat like Judea? The priests are called Brahmin and they are very powerful. The people follow a religion of many levels of gods. It seems they have more gods than the Romans or Greeks, and though I find their Temple buildings wondrous and unique, I sometimes must look away for they have multitudes of profanities therein. Their religion is deeply entrenched in their daily lives, again this should sound familiar. So like Jesus I found much success among the poor and oppressed, which is the lowest station. The rich came to me with their sick and never want more than miracles. So our brother Jews are tolerated as foreigners in manners and customs, and are endured but not totally accepted. They walk a fragile path.

The script stopped.

John closed his burning eyes and rested. The quality of parchment had changed and it was somewhat difficult to read. Perhaps the parchments were old and the ink was faded, he was not sure what the problem was, except it was difficult to read. He made a mental note to forward these letters to Linus in Rome of Thomas' mission.

Slowly he stroked his beard, something he enjoyed doing for he felt great pleasure in the feel of the soft hair on his face.

He slowly laid his head on the parchment paper and his mind traveled back in time and he saw the Twelve together again. He heard the bickering, the laughter, and the small annoyances. They all came to life. Just before he slipped into sleep, he wondered how they all were capable of doing what they did and his last thought was: *Because the Master is still with us.*

✳

Abban was very concerned about Thomas. Seeing Thomas so distressed and defeated by his lack of success among the Cochin Jews made Abban regret his suggestion to go to Cochin. He was certain Thomas was beginning to doubt himself and Abban knew this was a dangerous thing. He could not bear to see Thomas so unhappy for he loved him. After many weeks of watching Thomas suffer, he suggested they leave and move on to another part of India, but this suggestion only enflamed Thomas with greater fervor, and still no one came to Jesus. In desperation, Thomas withdrew to prayer and fasting. Abban watched him become weak and sickly, but there was no chance of changing his mind.

Just when it seemed that Thomas had failed, a miracle occurred. A ship from ancient Persia arrived in Cochin, and aboard this ship were several Judeans. They told all the Jews of the fall of Jerusalem and the burning of the Temple. One man named Noam aben Aharon sought out the synagogue on the Sabbath. When he heard Thomas speak at the synagogue, Noam aben Aharon came forward and said that the Christians were the new Jews and then he told every one of the brave men and women who preached Jesus throughout the Empire. He told how the followers of Jesus were imprisoned, tortured and put to death. When Noam aben Aharon reported the deaths of several of the Apostles, Thomas felt silent and closed his eyes in pain. The thought of each death pained Thomas, but when hearing of Bartholomew's death he felt the most anguish for he heard Bartholomew was in India.

I should have gone to him, he thought as the pain spread over him.

On hearing this report, Rabbi Shamon rose to his feet and said with careful words, "Tell me Son of Judah, did these men die loving and still believing in this man Jesus?"

"Yes," Noam aben Aharon quickly replied.

The Rabbi turned to his fellow Jews, "For centuries our people have died believing in The Almighty and His promises. For centuries we have been beaten and tortured because we believed in Him. We suffered much for our belief. No other religion in our time can claim people dying for their beliefs." He turned to Thomas, "Thomas, I am willing to believe in Jesus for men do not give up life easily, unless they are certain their beliefs are true."

That night many came to Jesus. For the first time in a long time, Thomas felt the closeness of the Twelve, for he was certain they had all traveled far to come to his aid to convert these Jews. Soon after, the families of those in the synagogue became followers.

Thomas stayed many years on the Malabar Coast, traveling up and down, baptizing all the Jews he met. He soon converted those in service to the Jewish families, but these servants, caretakers, cooks and others were extremely careful in making their conversion know for fear of reprisals. Soon word spread and more Indians came to hear Thomas teach and many were baptized. For the longest time these conversions did not bother the locals, but then a few of Thomas' converts included several Brahmins, teachers and Pundits and when this happened the leaders of the Brahmins grew concerned. The Jewish community heard the complaints and expectedly the threats came thereafter. The Brahmins were not too pleased with Thomas or the Jews. The Jewish leaders in the region began to worry about these complaints and tried in many subtle ways to quench Thomas' desire to convert everyone, but it was not heeded. Soon the fragile peace and tolerance that existed between the Hindus and Jews were in danger of being fractured and as a consequence the life of the entire Jewish Christian community was in peril. When the Hindu Brahmin leaders started showing signs of hostilities to some of the Jewish merchants, the Jewish elders decided to approach Abban.

"The Brahmins are a very powerful group," Rabbi Shimon avin Alacar, the elder among the Jews told Abban in a slow, carefully worded tone, "and they have the power to destroy all that we have built here. Recently they have made it know to us that they do not like their people being converted. They have tolerated us because we never tried to change anyone to our ways. We never evangelized, but Christians need to evangelize. The Brahmins can cause Thomas and us much pain and trouble. What Thomas has built here could be destroyed with one quick sweep of their mighty hand. We need Thomas to see this but he never sees what is near; only what is far. Perhaps if you talk to him, you can persuade him to move to another part of India until all is made smooth in Malabar. Assuredly, what Thomas has done here will remain good, but he must be convinced that it is time to go. On the other side of India on the Mylapore Coast, there are some Jewish communities who will welcome him. We will send messages ahead telling of your arrival."

When John awoke he quickly adjusted his eyes and looked down at the empty parchment before him and remembered the break in Thomas' letter. He grew curious and wondered why there was no more writing. He unrolled the scroll until the large gap in the parchment ended. Slightly satisfied, he ignored his curiosity of the wasted parchment and began to read on eagerly. Refreshed, he could conquer whatever Thomas had to say.

I picked up my stylus again after many months, no, years since I started to write to you about India Felix. I had no idea where all the time went, but I promise you will receive these letters after I update you of all my work in the Name of the Lord. Forgive me dear Brother, but writing to you of what I do is unimportant. Many communities of Gentiles were started in seven different places on the Malabar Coast. Naming them would be tedious for you to read so I will simply tell you that they spread up and down the coast in prosperous cities, important towns and in small insignificant villages. What is amazing is the depth of faith these Christians have. They believe with complete childlike faith in the Words of Jesus and in the message He offered them. I believe Cochin is the crowning point of my Indian mission. The city is most unusual because of the many ships and nationalities that arrive there. I have been in India almost five years traveling to many places and during that time had only the Jews and very few Indians come to Jesus, but when I came to Cochin things changed greatly. There is a large Jewish community there, and at first those who came to the Lord were only our brethren who came very cautiously. I had a difficult time with these Cochin Jews, but eventually successes grew and this by a miracle but that is for another letter. After the Jews came to me, I was led and blessed by the Master. One day, as I was preaching to the poor Indians, a group of Brahmins appeared. They stood listening for the longest time. The leader of this group was called Maliyakal. He was a tall, thin man with black, piercing eyes, and a great questioning mind. The idea of One all-encompassing God intrigued him and soon he and I entered into a full discussion of the love from this One God. This group visited me for seven days and only Maliyakal debated with me or even challenged me. On the seventh day, I walked into the river and called all who wanted to be baptized and saved to come forward, and seventy-five Brahmins and their families came into the river. This was the first time I had suc-ceeded so well with the upper class. Besides, the Brahmin priests there were warriors of the princely and military classes, the martial nobilities, and the traders and merchants. Soon after, over three thousand came to Jesus, so I began looking for leaders among the new Christians. With God's grace and help, we continued to grow. The community is self-sufficient with its own leaders and elders. Being noticed, I was being elevated to a position of a demigod. I had to leave before things got out of control. Knowing Abban, who had remained faithful to me but who still was not a Christian, was home sick, I decided to return to King Gondophares. However, before I made my intentions known to Abban, we learned that the King had been killed in a war with the Parthian Empire. His kingdom on earth was no more and the community which we had set up was now in hiding for the Parthians were cruel rul-ers and did not tolerate any thing foreign, especially a foreign religion. I suffered with Abban but received comfort in know-ing that the King had finally arrived at the palace built for him among the Lord's mansions. Then my faithful friend, Abban, suggested going to the other side of India to a new ocean so we packed and began our trip across India. We traveled by land and rivers until we came to a place called Mylapore. It is

from this place that I now write you after many months delay. I
have decided to stay here for some time for I am doing the Will
of the Lord and baptizing all people in His Holy Name.

Again there is a gap in the writing and John presumed that what he
was about to read was written some time later.

I am writing many months later and I promise that this will be
sent off to you as soon as I make this last entry. How good is
our God! When I first arrived here, I was met with accepting
Jews. They warmly embraced me and within months they were
followers of Jesus. I saw for the first time in my life a yellow-
skinned man from a faraway place. When I first saw him I could
not stop looking at him. He was a short man with long, thin
eyes and richly dressed with brightly colored robes trimmed
with animal fur. He must have seen me staring at him for he
came to me and began speaking in Aramaic, which shocked
me and I replied to him which was equally shocking. You, of
course, know what happened yet each time this happens I
become so excited and humbled. The miracle of tongues takes
me back to that Pentecost feast and I remember the rush of
knowledge and understanding that we were gifted with on that
day. The Paraclete is still living in us. He is constantly in our
actions as well as in our thoughts.
After meeting this man, I decided that I wanted to journey to
this man's land to preach to his people especially after I baptized him and his many man servants and traveling companions.
But alas, my brother, after many months, things changed and
we were met with great hostilities and I was imprisoned for a
long time. I have lost much of my body weight and have grown
hairless. You will truly not recognize me. Abban was spared
imprisonment because he was not a Christian and he attended
to me while I was imprisoned. Those who professed belief in
Jesus were jailed, beaten or killed. Apparently my success
on the other side of India with the Brahmins followed me here

and my enemies waited in silence. The people here are led by a fanatical Brahman priest called Varuna the Ramban. This priest is a man who distrusts everything that is not Hindu. As I wrote before, I once understood that the followers of this religion believed in many gods, but now I learned that they believe in many celestial deities who are part of one god. You may think it is a religion much like the Greeks' and Romans' but it is not, for they believe in one god with many faces. They believe a god with no beginning and no end. An infinite god like ours. He is here, there and everywhere. They do not evangelize and dislike those who do. They tolerate others only if they leave them alone, but how can we when you and I are under a command to teach all nations. I hope you realize that eventually Varuna Ramban and I are destined to clash.

The scroll ended here.

John was disappointed knowing that this was the last scroll for he wanted to know more. This religion Thomas spoke of intrigued him. He made a promise that he would try to learn more about it. There was so much of the world he did not know and the feeling of being ignorant and so inadequate sickened him again. He always longed to know all things. He knew this was an attribute of God, but he seemed to have learned nothing in comparison to the Others. He moved away from his desk and walked across the room and through the heavy, wool curtain into the next room where Naomi was cooking. Since the news of her husband Joses' death, Naomi had grown quiet and pensive and no matter what John tried to do, he could not get her to respond to life. The only time she left the house was to do some shopping or to attend the Meal. Even her duties of charity such as visiting the sick and poor had changed. She had become a prisoner of the kitchen. She would cook for the sick and poor but not visit them and bring to them the joy of Christ. Now others delivered her wares and visited the sick and poor in her name.

"I will have some fish and grapes for you soon. Timotheus and the others send their regrets that they will not be joining us later."

"That is fine, for I am tired."

"Have you finished reading the scrolls from Thomas?"

"Yes. They just stopped abruptly. At the end of his writings he seemed to have grown tired of writing. He appeared to be very busy."

"Knowing Thomas, I am sure he will write again." She stopped kneading the dough, and wiped her forehead with the back of her wrist and looked at him. "Did you need something?"

"No, I just wanted to see you and ask how you were."

"I am well and thanking the Almighty for this blessing."

"So then we praise God," John replied and turned to walk back into his room. He walked to a small, wooden table by one of the chairs in the room and picked up the clay burning lamp by the handle and walked out into the small garden behind the house. He always enjoyed this time when day was ending and night was beginning its slow capture of the world. He would sit in the small garden and pray or most often think of his account of the Life of Jesus. Thomas' letter created many memories of Jesus. He had to clear these thoughts in his mind. He placed the clay lamp on the ground by the small stool he was to sit on, and slowly lowered his body onto the stool. Immediately, he went into prayer, and before he knew it his mind was back reliving those times with Jesus and the Others. Every physical characteristic on their faces came back to his mind. He heard their laughter and the change in their voices as they whispered concerns and precautions. He envisioned the cocky swagger in some of their walks, the pride and air of arrogance that some had at being chosen. He heard the cutting edge to some of their voices as they became impatient with each other, the small mockery of each other over a remark or observation voiced.

It is amazing that we made it work for You, Lord. He thought. *You knew us all well. You knew us better then we knew ourselves. We often wondered what we were to do; what You expected of us. We had so many doubts. During Your time with us, did You ever question, or regret Your choice of us?*

"We all had our darkness and doubts, but Your Spirit gave us light," he said aloud.

Then he heard the sound of wings flapping. He quickly lost yesterday's world and opened his eyes. Startled and confused he looked frantically around the garden but saw nothing. He rose quickly and walked back into the house. Naomi had burned the other lamps in the room knowing that he would soon begin to try once again to write his account. On the small table was his dinner consisting of fish, bread and grapes. He ignored it and slowly walked to this desk, being drawn to it by some unknown power. He rested his hand on the cloth bag that had contained Thomas' scrolls and with great surprise felt a small scroll under his hand. He opened the bag and quickly removed the scroll and just as hurriedly unrolled it. Immediately he could see that the lettering was different.

John Sahib. Teomaa Ramban told us that you were called the Sanam — one who was loved. We are honored to write you and ask you to please excuse our poor Aramaic. I am writing you at the command of Teomaa also known as Thomas. This letter will go with all those Thomas has written. I am Abban, a companion of Thomas. I am the bearer of sad news for Thomas has died. He made many enemies on the Mylapore Coast. Happily more friends came to your God willingly. In this place there are many merchants of Greek, Roman, Jewish, and Arab backgrounds. Thomas worked among them for many months and the Word of God spread to places Thomas could never go. One day a small group of Indians came to Thomas and they were followed by others and Thomas baptized them in the nearby river. He first was very successful with the poor Indians but then the rich and even the Raja Vizan of Muchiri and his family traveled to him to be received as a follower of Jesus. When the Brahmin, Varuna Ramban, heard of this, he sent several of his priests to the Maharaja Sahan pleading for help. He informed the Maharaja that Thomas was a danger to the government by converting many people to the Christian religion. He called it "a foreign infestation" that was filled with "equality to all" which, in Varuna's words, was speaking revolt against the government. Several weeks later, the Sahan arrived with a troop of soldiers to a place where Thomas was preaching. I was also there. When several rich and influential people came forward to be baptized, the Maharaja's soldiers grabbed Thomas and several of the others. I hid among the people and made myself safe. A cowardly thing to do, but now as I remember, it was the best thing for me to do. I followed the soldiers and Thomas until they came to the Raja's palace and was later told that Thomas was beaten badly and thrown into prison. The three Indian men who were taken with Thomas were immediately killed and their heads impaled on stakes outside the city walls. Their bodies were thrown in the jungle for the beast to devour. A week later, Thomas was taken before the Maharaja where he was questioned before the entire court and many of the people. When I saw Thomas my heart ached. His face was swollen and black from the beatings. His clothes were in shreds and his cut flesh could be seen. He was dirty, with dry blood and extremely weak. The Brahmin Varuna asked Thomas to worship the goddess Kali who represents all that is unpleasant in life; she is the eater and destroyer of time. Thomas remained silent. Again he was told to worship Kali and Thomas announced in a loud voice, "As my Lord and Master told the Evil one, 'The Lord thy God shall thou worship and Him only shall thou serve.' Therefore, I shall not worship an idol." With these words he raised his open hands to heaven. His hands shook and so did his body. Then he made a fist and with a might that only could have come from an Almighty Power, he thrust his fist at the image of Kali and the temple began to burn in great flames. Panic broke out and Thomas could have easily walked away from his guards but he stood there with his eyes closed, his lips moving slowly in prayer. He always amazed me with his ability to do such things so innocently.

A guard walked over to Thomas and raised his hand to strike him but Sahan the Maharaja stopped him and announced that Thomas was free to go. The Brahmins were furious and began protesting but Thomas was led away. After he was out of the palace, he walked alone into the city and then to the outskirts of the city to a small hill called locally Bachcha Pahadi. He ascended

this place. I stayed a great distance because I was so
ashamed of my desertion and of my cowardly retreat. I
had not yet realized that what I had done was the Will
of God. After some time, I finally walked up the hill.
In the distance I saw Thomas deep in prayer. When he
was in prayer it was impossible to interrupt him. I heard
him giving thanks to Jesus and asking for guidance
and help to continue his work among the Indians when
suddenly, like a swift bird in flight, a swishing sound
filled my ears. I knew what was going to happen. I called
to Thomas but he did not move. He jerked and swayed
only when the spear hit him in the back. Another came
flying by, and then another and another until Thomas
was pierced by four spears. Each of them still stuck in
his body. His clothing quickly wet with blood. I looked
up and at the edge of the forest stood Brahmin Varuna
and five soldiers. Varuna raised his hand and the fifth
soldier raised his spear and with all his might threw the
final spear that pierced through Thomas and out of his
chest. Thomas finally fell forward. I watched as Varuna
and the murderers backed into the forest.
I ran to Thomas. His eyes were open and he was smiling
but was dead. Moments later, many Christians came
to help me with his body. We took him to the bank
of the river and removed his clothes. When he was
stripped of his clothes, we found no marks on his body
from the spears except a spear mark on his right side.
I remembered his story of the day he doubted Jesus
and began to cry. I was not a Christian and though I
had witnessed many miracles I myself did not have
a miracle in my life to make me believe in Jesus, yet I
loved Thomas and served and believed in him. I heard
a voice say: 'Bring here thy finger...and put it in my
side; and be not unbelieving but believing.' I felt my

hand move on its own to the wound in his side and when my finger touched it the wound disappeared. Thomas was made whole and I had my miracle. I kissed Thomas' hand asking him to pray for me and then I asked those nearby to baptize me. I shall remain in India and continue the work of your brother and my brother. There are many here. We will be here for all time until God wishes for us to be made known.

I am your servant in Christ through Thomas Ishwar aik hais [God is one]

Abban. A Thomas Christian.

John fell into the chair nearby. His eyes fell on the scrolls he read in a basket by his desk.

How long ago did this happen? He questioned. *Oh, Thomas!* It most likely happened long ago, and he did not mourn his brother Apostle all this time. John settled his mind and began to mourn Thomas. Moments passed. From the garden he heard the flutter of wings and he quickly moved to the garden door. Just as he arrived, a swishing sound filled his ears and a breeze passed his face. It was a dove. It circled above John again and again. John watched with delight and had tears in his eyes for he now understood why the dove was there and who the dove was.

"Oh, Thomas, you have come to see me. Be not so uncertain. Go do what you said you would do many years ago—go follow Jesus. Be assured that soon I will be with you. Go. Go, my friend, and pray often for us."

The dove fluttered its wings and landed momentarily on an olive tree nearby. It turned to John and made a small cooing sound and flew off into the sky. John stood on his toes almost hoping and believing that this would make him closer to the dove as it climbed high into the sky. It was gone from his sight.

John felt alone. He sighed and softly lowered his head. He stood there for a long time and then with a mixture of joy and sadness he walked into the next room to tell Naomi of the good news.

CHAPTER EIGHT:

SIMON OF CANA, QUN'ANAYA ZEALOT

PROLOGUE

It seemed she had been gone a long time. John remembered daily every feature of her face. In his comforting moments, he envisioned the gentle motion of her hand. In his weary moments, her voice echoed in his ears, and he was soothed by her soft, controlled tone. Her small smile was his consolation when he was discouraged. The small nod of her head with closed eyes, which was her way of giving agreement, was his companion when he doubted that he was worthy to write the story of Jesus. When he spoke of her, it was always in peaceful tones and with love and respect; this was the way everyone spoke of her. The Twelve and the early followers called her Lady Mary to place her above all others. She was protected, and her privacy was defended with absoluteness; this was at her insistence, and in their wisdom the Twelve concurred. She was so well guarded that many of the early converts did not know who she was. Those who needed to know were only told that she lived. This again was the way she wanted it, for she firmly believed her part in God's plan had been completed. Her motherhood was achieved through God's Will and her humble consent. She regarded herself as merely a vessel that carried the Son of the Most High. In the eyes of many, He was born as the son of Joseph and Mary and stayed hidden in their parentage. This was the way the Almighty wanted it to be and this was the way they lived it. The memories of Jesus' youth were God's reward to them for having taken care of His Son, and this was all they claimed. Mary always believed that if God wanted the world to know of His Son's humble beginnings, He would have made this known; but He had not done this, and she again did the Will of God by keeping these times hidden. She remained the holder of the miracles and dreams and early occurrences; she told Luke only a few things because he came to her asking if Jesus was the Son of God at the time of His birth. She told him just enough to satisfy his needs and enough to let the world know that Joseph and she were the smaller part of God's plan.

Those early years were set apart from Jesus' mission. The universal meaning of Christ's mission was manifested during His public life. Still, Mary's wishes for anonymity did not always satisfy everyone. Some saw her simple part in the birth of God, and others saw a greater part than she was willing to admit. The early Jewish followers, who had always considered lineage to be so important, insisted on an account of Jesus' ancestors, and Mary knew this was why Matthew and later Luke provided genealogies of Jesus in their writings. Luke, needing assurances, came to her for confirmation of Matthew's genealogy. As uncertain as the early Jewish converts were, they quickly accepted her womanhood and allowed her to willingly and dutifully remain in the background, according to the Judaic customs regarding women. As the Gentiles came to Jesus, Mary's place in the community became more prominent. The Gentiles looked for more information about Jesus, and she represented Him in many ways. She conveyed His human nature. He was bone of her bone, flesh of her flesh; His face and hers were one. After all, she was His mother and the only human He could look like. It was conceivable that the Gentiles would go to her for advice. They easily could have perceived her as a high priestess or even a goddess. Coming from a polytheistic culture, this would have been a natural reaction. Gentiles would have felt comfortable going to a religion that reminded them of their old religion. But those who knew Mary realized that she was a very humble woman who, like her Son, suffered daily human pains. She suffered pains of cold, heat, and the chill of fever. She suffered the pains of loss. She had cloudy moments, and again like her Son she was tempted with fears and uncertainty. These were her private troubles.

Yet anonymity was not always hers, for there were occasions when the Twelve would ask for her prayers or seek her counsel, and she, after time in prayer, would tell them that she was speaking for Jesus. No one ever asked her to explain what she meant by this, for they understood these words. When she was asked, and only when she asked, she would contribute to a discussion. She often said, "What is happening now is the work of the Spirit of the Living God, for all this is His Will and I could never make things different."

Her silent presence was important to the Twelve, for she was a great source of encouragement and zeal. When the Twelve were arrested and beaten or when word was received of the death of one of the Twelve, she remained strong and steadfast and showed the same faith that she showed on Golgotha.

Above all, she was a woman of understanding; even when some believed she had been slighted, she remained understanding, John thought as he remembered the time a woman cried out, "Blessed is the womb that bore You," and Jesus responded with a blessing of His own. John recalled seeing Mary, who was not too far from her Son, with a glow of approval emanating from her face. He remembered how confused this look made him feel. Then there was the time that James the Little and some other relatives came to persuade Jesus to return home and tend to His widowed mother. Some listeners told the Master that His mother was outside, and Jesus responded in an unexpected way. His response did not hurt her and again John saw her face as she smiled with great approval. Later, he had watched as Mary mildly pulled her nephew James the Little aside and advised him to wait and see what was to happen before seeking to deter Jesus from His mission.

Some of the followers thought that Jesus had been disrespectful to His mother. At one time, even John was disappointed in Jesus over the treatment of Mary, but this perception changed one night not too long after Peter, Andrew, James, and he had been begun following Jesus.

✳

A cool breeze pushed its way through the open window of the room, spreading the chill of the early night. It passed over John, and with it came memories of a similar chill from a bygone night. Quickly the chill faded and was replaced by the warmth of family and friends. John heard the sound of the flutes, the harp, and the soft tempo of the drumbeat, and he closed his eyes and let earlier times return to him. A mental picture came into his mind and grew to full life. He heard the sound of mumbling voices, then loud laughter, and finally came the aroma of food and the scent of burning olive oil from the lamps. It was the wedding of his sister Naomi to Justus, also known as Joses bar Binyomin.

Zebedee and Binyomin, Justus' father, had been business associates, and their families were close.

Justus had often worked as a fisher for Zebedee; John had to reciprocate by working as a clerk for Binyomin in his open-air market. Soon it became apparent that Justus was interested in Naomi, Zebedee's daughter. When the interest became very obvious, a *shiddukhin* match was contracted, and after the normal engagement time had passed, the nuptials were set.

Justus' family was from Cana, and according to tradition, the wedding feast was to take place in the groom's father's house, and so Justus "kidnapped" Naomi and took her to his father's house; Zebedee, his extended family, and invited guests followed Naomi to Cana.

After the seven blessings were recited by the parents and the Rabbi gave his scriptural blessing, the large meal was eaten. In keeping with Judaic traditions and Temple dictates, the women and men sat in different sections of the room during the meal. The bride was seated under a *chuppaha* canopy with her ten white-dressed bridesmaids standing around her. Each of the bridesmaids daintily held an oil lamp. The groom was taken away from the bride for some manly discussions, and when he returned, the gifts were given to the newlyweds, who later would discretely slip away for some privacy. The celebration continued for days.

John was forcing himself to enjoy the celebration. Weddings had a way of tiring him. He understood the customs of his people and that the wedding feast should last for several days, but after the ceremony and one night of celebrating, the following days were forced revelry with continual food, music, and conversation. During the third day's meal, John momentarily relinquished his seat next to Jesus to get some fresh air. As he returned, he walked along the side of the room. He saw Jesus at the table picking a small piece of meat from a plate and putting it into His mouth. Near Jesus were Peter and Andrew and James. As he continued to walk along the perimeter of the room, he looked into the section of the room where the women sat, and he noticed Mary. She was sitting between her sister and John's mother, Salome, and her sister-in-law Mary Cleophas, wife of Alphaeus. The three were having a lively discussion and were laughing freely. Mary's face when she smiled blossomed into a picture of perfected joy. Her skin glowed and her eyes moistened with glee, and her small delicate mouth widened to reveal her splendid teeth. Her long, brown hair matched the color of her eyes. It was a pleasure to watch her laugh.

John's steps slowed as he gazed at Mary, and for the first time he noted that she possessed a singular beauty, and he wondered why he had not observed this before. The beauty he saw was more than a simple peasant beauty. It was a beauty that was deep and that radiated with pleasantness and—he hesitated until he realized the word—bliss. He found himself frozen in place and unable to move as he basked in this newfound beauty. He was distracted when he saw one of the wine stewards walk to his mother and lean over to whisper something in her ear. His mother's expression changed to deep concern as she quickly rose from her lounge and excused herself, but not until Mary had discovered the reason for sister's distress. Mary's disposition changed just as quickly as her sister's.

Salome somehow got her husband Zebedee's attention, and the two of them rushed out of the room and into the garden. John, now concerned by his parents' distress, followed them.

At that moment Jesus rose from His lounge and walked into the garden. Outside in the garden the wine steward was talking to Zebedee and Salome. Jesus walked by them but was abruptly stopped by His mother, who seemed to appear out of nowhere. She stood before Him.

"They have no wine," she said softly as her eyes moved over His face in search of something that only she knew.

"Woman, what is that to Me and to thee? My hour is not yet come."

Son and mother looked at each other for a long time. John, who was watching this, could tell that many unspoken words and many understandings were passing between them.

Mary's facial expression held a small delight, and Jesus' face was questioning. Suddenly, as if all had been decided, Mary walked away from Jesus; turning to the wine stewards, she said in a soft voice while indicating at Jesus, "Whatsoever He shall say to you, do ye." Then she walked away from the confused steward to Zebedee and Salome and whispered something to them, and they reluctantly left the garden with her. As she passed Jesus, she reached for His hand and touched it softly. Jesus looked down at her hand, and when He raised His eyes, Jesus saw a small smile on Mary's face. John knew he was witnessing something very intimate. Suddenly he became uncomfortable, for he felt like an intruder, but he could not look away. John watched as Jesus looked around the garden. Jesus saw several water pots of stone used according to law for purification. He frowned slightly. Jesus knew the purifications were not of Moses but of the Pharisees, so He attributed no validity to this law.

The wine steward walked to Jesus.

Jesus said in a low but commanding voice, "Fill the water pots with water." The wine steward ordered the servants to fill the pots to the brim, and when they were full, the wine steward looked at Jesus for further instructions.

"Draw out now and carry to the chief steward of the feast," Jesus said casually.

The attendant followed the orders.

Jesus stood in the garden alone; the silence was heavy. His face was illuminated by the shine of the full moon, and His garment shone brightly.

Soon Simon Peter, Andrew, and James came out to Him. He spoke softly to them, and the group walked out of the garden and away from the celebrations. John, bewildered by what he had seen and yet certain he had witnessed something of great importance, quickly followed the group, eager to relate the story to his brother. As he neared the edge of the garden, he was distracted by something moving in the bush near him. He stopped, squinted, and looked into the shadows of the bushes and trees. To John's astonishment, there hidden in the shadows, with a look of shock and bewilderment on his face, was the Zealot from Cana called Simon.

SIMON OF CANA, QUN'ANAYA ZEALOT

Clavos jolted from his sleep and lost his dream. His pulsating heart pounded in his ears. He grabbed his chest in defense and took a deep breath, hoping to control his heart, which seemed on the verge of breaking through his muscular chest. He struggled to breathe again. This method had worked before, but this night it was not working. With his free hand he wiped the perspiration from his forehead.

"Are you all right, Clavos?" Simon asked him.

Amidst a gasp, the ex-soldier mumbled, "Yes."

"Dreaming again?"

"Yes," he murmured in a soft, almost apologetic voice.

"Same dream?" Simon questioned sleepily.

"Of course."

"Jesus only wishes to help you understand what you dream"—Simon yawned, interrupting his sentence—"you still have not found peace in your soul. Search your heart and mind, Clavos, and give it to the Lord to help your lack of understanding." He yawned again. "It is something that all of the followers of Jesus had to do."

Clavos could not see Simon, for night claimed the room, but he knew that somewhere in the dark corner, Simon was there. He wanted to talk more, but he knew his companion was tired, so he softly said, "Return to your sleep, Simon, I have some praying to do." He stopped short of finishing his sentence with the word "again." He reached for a small cloth nearby and wiped his sweaty face and chest. Slowly he lowered his large body onto his sleeping mat. After a few still moments of staring into the night, he shut his eyes, not to sleep but to turn inside himself.

Again, Jesus, You have awakened me with my dream. I have relived that day so often that I need not dream it again, for it is etched deep in my existence. You allow this to happen, Lord, to remind me that I should be more charitable. I try, Lord, I try, but You know I am weak and need Your strength. Help me. Give me what I lack.

He remained silent, patiently expecting a sign—a light of understanding, a surge of strength—but nothing came, and in its stead he became completely at ease. He bathed in this tranquility for a long time until slowly he slipped smoothly to that place of night, where the mind lays numb and where unfinished thoughts and forgotten memories come to life.

The stage was set.

The preface was uttered, and so the dream came back again, back to that place, to that day.

It was a dream that was without people. Their forms were always gray and hazy, but their voices and noises echoed from that involuntary vision, so he relived in each dream the sounds people made.

✳

Clavos was preoccupied with preparations for the scourging when the Man was led into the dungeon. He had just finished scourging two rebels who also had been condemned that day. Those scourgings left him in an unusually heightened state. The overwhelming thrill of having power over these men was still exciting him. He was so frozen with this excitement that his normal lust for blood went unheeded. His back was to the Man as he reached for a cloth to wipe his brow. He heard the rough orders, the tearing of garments, and finally the sounds of chains ringing as they were threaded and dragged through the eye of the stone pillar.

The room went silent.

He took a sip of warm wine from a nearby wooden bowl, smiled, and reached for his favorite *flagrum*. This whip was of his own making. Several years ago, when he arrived in Judea, he braided the thongs into different lengths and carefully picked the most jagged stones, the sharpest animal bones, and the crudest pieces of metal and knotted them to the ends of each thong. He used this *flagrum* for Jews only because the bones knotted in the thongs were from swine. He never failed to mention this fact to the Jews before scourging them; it delighted him to know that he could add to their torment. He threw his *flagrum* behind him and with brute, hateful force, brought his body around and struck the Man on the back. Some of the thongs struck high and wrapped around the Man's face and throat. A roar of approval and the shout of the first count replaced the silence of the room.

(In his sleep, Clavos' head jerked, for the sounds in the dream startled him.)

Though he received instant gratification from the strike and from the loud approval of those in the dungeon, he was not satisfied. He wanted more. He wanted, needed, the cry—the scream of pain and surprise from this Man. It did not come. He looked at the back of the Man with anger. He quickly repeated his action, and again, there was no cry. He pulled the *flagrum* away and felt the tearing of flesh race up the handle to his hand. Again, with great force, he brought the *flagrum* around, and when it struck the Man, he again received silence. He heard the count from the soldiers, centurions, and tribunes and the sounds of enjoyment at the show.

(In his slumber, he started grinding his teeth.)

He felt the leather handle in his hand and heard the straps, with their knots of stone, metal, and bone, hit the floor by his feet. He rotated his hips and allowed the whip to stay behind him, and with one smooth but forceful twist, he threw his body around, pulling and dragging the whip through the air. The traveling whip sliced the stagnant air, and the swishing sound whistled loudly by his ear. The sound pierced his head and vibrated inside his ear, only to be replaced by the sound of flesh being struck. A cheer of approval rose from the soldiers in the room, but again, there was no cry, not a word, not a sound, from the Man. Clavos became openly angry. He had never been insulted in this way. His scourgings were painful, with many agonizing cries for mercy. He was certain that everyone in the dungeon would soon begin to laugh at him. He repeated the punishment again and again and again, each time becoming more and more enraged. He was breathing heavily, for he had not stopped his whip—he had allowed the Man no time to rest.

One of the Romans shouted, "Slow down, Clavos, and save something for the cross."

Everyone laughed loudly.

(Clavos took a breath of air in his sleep. It was so deep that his body quivered.)

He stopped abruptly and stared at the Man's back. It was black from the bruising and red with blood. Ribbons of bleeding flesh hung from the Man's back. His legs and buttocks were blackened from the contusions. He laid on another strike, but without force, for he had lost count and wanted to know how many more he could give before the Man would beg for mercy. Besides, he did not want to give more than forty, for he knew that the Jewish Pharisees had spies who stood watch to make certain that only thirty-nine lashes were given.

"*Viginti septem,*" he heard someone shout.

Only twelve more lashes to make this Man cry out, he thought.

Before he could start in again, something strange happened to him. He suddenly lost all interest in the Man. When he looked at the torn back, he felt an unfamiliar sense of regret, and he wanted to run to the Man and cover His nakedness.

(In his sleep, Clavos' eyebrows wrinkled with perplexity.)

"*Permanes,*" a Syrian mercenary shouted in poor Latin, but he could not "continue" because he was flooded with concern.

"*Verbera Virum,*" someone else shouted—"whip the Man."

He felt the urge to curse the Romans, but his anger was not at them, it was at the Man. In the past, when the scourged men were near death, he grew uncaring and fell into an aura of intense delight, but this scourging was stripping him of all joy. It made him feel weak, and he did not understand why he was feeling so peculiar. The Man's silence was an oddity. The Man seemed to welcome His scourging.

Again, he heard a shout in poor Latin: "*Permanes, Clavos, et ocius!*—Continue, Clavos, and swifter!"

He turned his body away from the Man, and with all the strength he had, he twisted his body. He heard the familiar swishing sound of the whip, and his face tightened as he waited for the hiss to die and be replaced by the sound of the thump. It happened, and he strained his hearing for the moan, the cry of pain, but it never came, and he simply let his *flagrum* fall to the stone floor. He slowly pulled the *flagrum* to him. He readied himself for another lash.

From the corner of the room came the command, "*Satis!*"

(A quick breath, almost a snort, came from Clavos' nostrils.)

The voice was that of Cornelius, the centurion in charge. "Enough!" he heard Cornelius repeat.

(Clavos exhaled a loud sigh of relief.)

He did not know if he had given the required thirty-nine lashes or not; he only knew that he was relieved it was over, and grateful that the spectators had not noticed the Man's silence.

Without looking at the scourged Man, he walked away. The whip in his hand became heavy and painful to carry, so he willingly allowed it to fall to the prison floor.

(In his slumber, Clavos' hands slowly opened wide as if they pained him, and once opened, they became stiff.)

He heard the chains being unlocked. Laughter, cursing, and mockery followed, but he could not look at what was happening; instead, his eyes were set on the dungeon floor, where blood washed the rough stones. He stood looking at the deep red fluid until nothing seemed to exist anymore.

He heard nothing, felt nothing. Nothing.

He felt the heavy pressure of silence press against him. It shut him out of existence and carried him away from all things. This strange feeling left him naked, numb. He did not know how long he stayed this way, in this place. Then he heard the sound of a fly buzzing and busying itself around the room. That small sound returned his senses to the moment. It was then that he felt the sting of the Man's blood on his body.

(Clavos flinched from this stinging feeling, and with the four fingers of his right hand he began rubbing the palm of the same hand.)

He quickly moved to a small clay basin nearby and scrubbed his face, arms, and hands free of the splattered blood. With a soiled cloth from a nearby stool, he slowly wiped himself dry. When he had finished, he reached for a cup of soldier's wine and in two large swallows consumed the warm liquid.

(Clavos wet his dry lips.)

As he lowered the cup, he wondered why he was so weary and weak.

(In his dormant state, he took a deep breath that expanded his muscular chest, and instantly he gagged and began to cough.)

His nostrils and lungs filled with the sweet scent of blood, and he felt queasy; he needed to leave the prison, needed the feel of air on his flesh. Suddenly, in the distance, he heard the sound of the mob.

(In his sleep he turned his head in the direction of the sounds.)

His ears filled with the shouts and cries. In a subtle way, he heard the undercurrent to the cries—the voices of delight. There always was a certain group of people who enjoyed the spectacle of a crucifixion, but the delight he heard was a different enjoyment. Above these sounds he heard the cracking whips, and he knew that the Syrian mercenaries were finishing the job he started. The sounds were above him, outside of where he was, and he quickly raced up the narrow dungeon steps with an urgency he never knew, and with a need to escape something.

(His breathing grew heavy.)

The closer he got to the street, the louder were the sounds of the whips. He wondered why these sounds bothered him and why they seemed so severe. Once out of the shadows, he felt the cool pleasure of outside air on his skin.

(He released a small sound of relief and squinted his eyes.)

After adjusting to the brightness of the sun, he saw that the crucifixion procession was moving through the narrow hilly streets of Jerusalem, some distance from him. He began walking to the mob and realized he would never get to see the Man because the crowd was so large. He quickly turned up a small side street and to his surprise, it was void of life. He hurried through the street, not realizing that he was in a full run, and when he thought he was about up to the beginning of the procession, he cut quickly down another street in the direction of the crowd. He was immediately greeted by the herald, the young German slave Namenlos, carrying the *titulus* and declaring in Latin the Man's crime: "*Iesus Nazarenus Rex Iudaeorum,*" Jesus of Nazareth, King of the Jews. Occasionally, he shouted in faulty Aramaic: "*Yeshu'a Natsaraya mulka Diyhudaye,*" Jesus of Nazareth, King of the Jews. Clavos promptly detected the lack of enthusiasm in the youngster's voice, and the scourger was curious why this was so.

He heard again his own thoughts: *By Hades, He is a revolutionary, a traitor, Who deserves to be beaten and crucified.*

He looked up at Cornelius as he rode by. The usual smug, superior look on his face was replaced by a look of pain, and Clavos wondered why. Next he saw Stephaton, whose eyes were searching the crowd. Clavos could not imagine what he was looking for until he recognized the military alertness on Stephaton's face; he was looking for an enemy. Lastly, he saw Abendadar the Syrian, whom he disliked, but he looked beyond him for the Man.

The Man stumbled by him. Clavos shifted his body and lowered his head, but still he could not see His face. He was close enough to Him to reach out and move the blood-soaked, tangled hair away from His face, but he couldn't because the procession passed too quickly. He looked at the other two condemned men with little care, for they had suffered under his scourging, and for one quick second he experienced the usual feeling of delight and pleasure. He pushed himself back through the crowd. Once free, he raced up the side street and again found it empty of life. He ran until he was sure he was ahead of the procession, then he raced up another street and came upon a tall, muscular African carrying the *patibulum* crossbeam. This surprised him, and he momentarily reeled back.

If the Man was strong enough to take my beating, why is He not strong enough to carry His own cross? He seems immune to pain. He never cried out!

The frustration and anger returned to him, and he wanted to shout to the Man now staggering behind the African: "Why did You not cry out in pain? Why did You not make a sound?"

(In his sleep, Clavos' face strained in anger.)

Then for one brief moment, he saw His face: it was covered with blood, spittle, bruises, and dirt. It was a non-face, for the nose was broken, the cheeks bruised and swollen, the lips cut, and the eyes sealed shut with blue, bloated flesh. He had no way of detecting or imagining the true features of the Man Who did not cry out. The procession passed on, and Clavos stood frozen. He felt the push and bump of other bodies against him, but he did not push back or react in his usual angry way.

The sounds of the people slowly grew distant and faded away. The sounds of the whips stopped.

All was blank. Emptied.

Again he felt the calm pushing against him. He actually felt it forcing its way through his skin, seeping inside him, moving inch by inch through him, soothing all the rage and hatred that had been living inside him all his life. *I must have contracted a malady*, he thought, hoping to understand this strange calmness. He had to be sick, for he knew no other explanation for the rare quietness he now felt. In defiance, he forced himself into anger for not hurting the Man. The lump in the pit of his stomach, the anger, the hate erupted and came back to life, and he felt safe again. He would not allow any illness to soften him, for these dark feelings were the only emotions he knew, and he could not live without them. Even the great kindness and unselfish love he had received from the Pulerius family could not calm his fury.

(He took a deep breath, inflating his lungs to full capacity, and this made his body tremble.)

In his dream he saw Tarcius in full Roman uniform.

(His face tightened, not for anger but for control.)

Tarcius Pulerius, a centurion, found him in the wilderness of Germania at the age of twelve. He was hovering over the body of his warrior father, who had been killed by the Roman Legions. Tarcius admired the boy's devotion to his dead father, and when it was discovered that all of the boy's family had been killed, Tarcius took him into his home and gave him to his son Talamius as a companion. Talamius treated Clavos as a brother. He was given an education and was able to speak and read Latin, but Clavos never lost his hatred of the Romans. Rome had taken the only love he ever knew, and nothing, no one, would ever be able to replace that love. All his love was left in Germania with his father's mutilated body. He encouraged feelings of hate to grow and fester deep inside him, and he hid them under a veneer of appreciation. Eventually, these feelings consumed everything he felt, and he became incapable of loving anyone or anything. When Talamius was of age, he became a centurion like his father, and Clavos went with him as an Auxiliary. Later, Talamius was killed on maneuvers, and Clavos was given his freedom, but he remained in the Legions. On account of his cruelty, he was made a *lictor* of prisoners. Here he could punish, kill, and maim others, and this elevated him to moments of emotional ecstasy.

His dreaming stopped here, as it always did, and his vision was filled with a black void.

(Clavos' breathing returned to normal.)

With small, shallow breaths, he rolled onto his right side and curled up, not to defend himself from the cold night air but to gather himself. In this catatonic state, he knew his dreaming was over, but this night his prayers were to be answered, for his dream continued.

(Clavos' breathing became heavy, and his eyes moved quickly, frantically, under his eyelids.)

He heard the sounds of treading feet. He saw them, moving one at a time over a dusty road. Then he heard the sound of labored, heavy breathing—it was his breathing, and the feet he saw were his feet.

A loud sound crashed into his dream. It was the sound of a hammer cracking against metal.

(He jumped in his sleep.)

Again came the sound of banging.

(Again he jumped in his sleep. A small whimper escaped his lips.)

He heard voices, laughter, and then groans and grunts, and when he looked from the dusty road, he saw Romans busily nailing the feet of the Man to the *stipes* upright. He looked at the soldiers around the cross. Among them was Dorimius, a *lictor* like him.

He slowly made his way up the side of a mount. He knew this place. It was called Golgotha. It was part of the city dump outside the city walls. It was infested with rats and other scavengers. Often the smell from this place passed through the city, but today that odor was stagnant, and the smell of decay settled on his clothing and stuck to the inside of his nostrils.

(His nose wrinkled at the offensive smell.)

He heard a voice—someone speaking—but did not hear the words. "What?" he heard himself say.

"Why were you not here? I had to do your job. Where were you?" He recognized the voice as that of Dorimius.

Ignoring Dorimius' questions and not looking at him, he asked, "Tell me, this Man on the center cross, did He cry out when you pierced His hands and feet?"

There was a long pause, and in his mind Clavos knew the answer, but still he waited.

"No," was the reply, and Clavos detected a surprised discovery in Dorimius' voice. "He never uttered a sound."

"Truly amazing, is it not?" Clavos said to Dorimius and himself.

He stood off and away from everyone on the mount. He was not with the soldiers; they were Romans, and he was not a Roman. He was not with the Pharisees; they were Judeans, and he was not. He stood away from the mother, who was stoically standing by the cross with a protective young man; Clavos was not of this family. He didn't seem to belong anywhere on that mount, yet somehow he fit there. He felt the warmth of the sun on his flesh. He sensed the stillness of the air. All sounds had died, except for the incessant buzzing of flies and other insects that swarmed around the body of the Man on the cross, adding to His suffering. He looked up at the Man. His face was draped with His blood-drenched, matted hair, and though he could not see much of His face, he stood mesmerized by the disfigured image he saw. The Man's naked body—whipped, cut, bruised, and marred—was the result of Clavos' cruelty. Again he became aware of the stillness around him: the motionless and muted world around him. Everything seemed to be on the verge of something. Not even the insects were heard. Everything seemed to be on the verge of something.

A small, insignificant whisper of air passed, and the Man's matted hair parted. Clavos saw one eye. It looked at him.

In a loud voice that seemed to resound from the highest heavens, the Man gave out a plea. His voice split the silence and stillness of the mount: *"Pater! Dimitte illis, non enim sciunt quid faciunt."*

His wording was perfect Latin; His voice, though loud, was tender. Clavos wondered how an ignorant Judean could speak Latin so well. How could a Man Who had suffered so much have the strength for so strong a voice? His wondering stopped when the words echoed again in his mind: "Father! forgive them, for they know not what they do." His hand twitched. The skin on which the Man's blood had splashed began to ache and burn.

(His face twisted in sudden pain, and he began rubbing his hands and arms.)

Again he heard it: "Father! forgive them, for they know not...."

Suddenly, his uniform became burdensome. He experienced a sudden demand to be rid of it—free of it.

A strong wind came from across the distance; it passed swiftly over the land and rushed on to the mount. There it twirled and whirled into a column of sand that rose into the darkening sky. As it passed Clavos, he gasped, for it took the breath from his being. As it continued away, it took something of him with it. Suddenly, he felt free, and without taking his eyes off the Man, he slowly began to remove his uniform.

Within his being, he heard echoing: "Father! forgive them...."

He stood looking up at the Man with wide open eyes, unaware of the heartless attack of the sand as it churned on the mount, whipping and stinging bare flesh.

Again the echo raced through his head: "Father! forgive...."

He was oblivious to all the changes in the day and to the chaos around him. He was unaware of the rain, the darkness, the wind, the moving earth, and the cold water blinding his eyes.

Finally, he heard one word—one scorching, stabbing word that echoed to the center of his being: "Father!"

The word became his cry, and instantly within half a heartbeat he felt covered, protected, and no longer fatherless, no longer without fatherly love. In an unnatural act, his knees buckled and he fell to them. When he felt the sand on his knees, he felt that all was natural. In a small, timid, childlike voice he sobbed, "Forgive me, I did not know what I was doing."

Someone came to him. He thought it was Namenlos, the young herald. He was pulled to his feet and led down the mount. He passed Dorimius, Stephaton, Abendadar, Longinus, and Cornelius; he looked at them in their stupor and found a bond with them, for he understood their frame of mind. He continued down the mount, feeling the rain wash over him and the earth move beneath him. As he walked, he felt a newness in his chest, a feeling of having left much of himself on the mount.

A short distance off, behind a large boulder and some nearby large rocks, he saw a man wet, shivering, and cringing in fear. He looked hard and long at this man, feeling that he knew him or should know him. He did not, but later he would come to know this man as the Apostle of the Lord, Simon of Cana, a Zealot.

✳

The first time Simon heard of Jesus, he was working for Zebedee on the shores of the Sea of Galilee. This was during the time that Simon called his "needing time"—a time when he needed *shekels* for a new cloak, robe, or sword. Usually, during this "needing time," he would hire himself out as a laborer in a field or vineyard, as a shepherd, or as a fisher. Being a fisher was his preference because he liked sailing, especially at night. Fishing at night left him in the middle of the open endless sky and the open restless sea. He preferred working for Zebedee, who over the years had become a father to his fatherless life. He enjoyed the company of the men in Zebedee's employ, and Zebedee paid in Judean *shekels*, not Roman *denarii* or Greek *drachmae*. Sometimes, he would help repair the fishing nets or help set nets for a catch. He would help clean and gut the fish and salt them for the markets.

One day, while cleaning and gutting the day's catch, Simon heard about Jesus. It was an unusually cool early morning as he expertly cut open one of the large fish. He overheard the sons of Zebedee and of Jonah discussing Jesus as they worked nearby mending their nets. They were speaking so excitedly that he thought they were talking about the man many called the Baptist, whom Simon had heard preaching many times in the desert. He appreciated the Baptist's criticisms of Herod, whom Simon regarded with great contempt, and the mild dissatisfaction John seemed to direct at the Romans, whom Simon hated more than death. He concurred with John's willingness to rebuke the Pharisees and Sadducees, whom Simon considered traitors because they appeased the Romans and Herod. John had called them "vipers" which was shocking to most, but to a Zealot, it only made sense.

After listening to the four men, he realized that the Baptist was not the topic of their conversation because their tone of voice was low and secretive. In those days, few spoke of the Baptist secretively. Simon's curiosity was piqued, so he strained to listen as he continued to gut the fish. He heard that the Man had a "clear-sounding voice"—a voice that "warmed the spirit." This Man had eyes "that read your soul" and that command "love and respect," and then he heard that the Baptist had called Him the "Lamb of God."

Talya! He smiled as he repeated the Aramaic word for lamb. He continued thinking. *How could someone be regarded so highly by these men when He is compared to a simple, helpless lamb?*

He looked at the four men nearby with complete pity and decided to ignore them. He would leave them to their ignorance and simple thinking. He finished gutting and cleaning the fish in his hand, and as he reached for another, his hand froze as he recalled another meaning for the world *talya*. There was a slang meaning to the word that meant "little male child," and as soon as he recalled this, his inner voice said, *God's child—the Son of God.* Instantly, Simon knew he needed to know more about this Man. He wanted to ask them to tell him more, but he did not want them to know that he had listened to their conversation.

Sometime later, by shear accident, Simon met Jesus at a wedding celebration in Cana. It was a wedding he was not supposed to be invited to. Even more accidental was his being seated by the Man as a result of mixed up table arrangements. Jesus began speaking to him, and within minutes Simon understood the conversations of Zebedee's and Jonah's sons. The gentleness of Jesus' voice soothed Simon's mind and inner being in a way that was utterly new to him. He soon discovered that he could not look at Jesus too long, for under His glaring eyes he felt naked. So every time Jesus spoke to him, Simon avoided looking into Jesus' eyes. He was certain that his avoidance was being noticed, for there were times when he could almost sense that Jesus was amused by this act.

Much to Simon's surprise, Jesus knew a great deal about him, and he was flattered yet curious as to how He knew him so well. More amazing was Simon's feeling that he knew Jesus all his life, and he felt a strong admiration and respect for Him. Baffled by this Man from Nazareth, Simon forced himself to break away from the celebration and seek solitude. He decided to take a stroll in the garden in front of the house. Sitting behind a bush on a small pedestal, he battled with himself about this Man. He was soon distracted by the sounds of other voices. Hiding farther into the bush, he watched all that happened between Jesus' mother, the wine steward, and Jesus. After Jesus and the sons of Jonah and Zebedee left the celebration, he remained, curious to taste the wine that had been declared "the best saved for the last." When he drank some and found it to be the best wine he had ever tasted, he acknowledged that he had witnessed a great magical trick, and he hurried to join Jesus and the others. He decided to stay with Jesus because he wanted to see more of what this Man could do, and because he needed a cause, for he always had to attach himself to some cause in order to maintain meaning in his life.

*

Simon's father and mother were killed by Roman chariot riders on a road in Galilee when he was very young. His father had been a laborer who never amounted to much. He was either fully employed or fully unemployed, and it seemed more of the latter. Soon after his parents' death, his father's brother took Simon to raise him. Simon never found himself at home in his uncle's house because his uncle ruled his household according to the old ways, demanding to be called *baal* lord or *adonai* master. His uncle was a convenient Jew. He observed the Law only to his own comfort. His uncle was also a laborer who worked in fields and vineyards and as a shepherd or fisher. His aunt resented having to care for another child. At a young age, Simon found himself belonging to a group of troublesome boys, and soon he acquired the reputation of being a disrespectful child. He enjoyed the idea of belonging to a group. Being in a group required little of him. He could hide in the masses yet still belong to something. Besides, the group made him feel good about himself, and he took some sort of devilish pleasure in being regarded as a rebel. His punishment for all his mischievous acts was severe. When his time arrived to begin studies of the Sacred Law and the traditions of his faith, the oldest and toughest Rabbi was assigned to him as his teacher, and this Rabbi did not hesitate to verbally abuse the young boy. At the age of thirteen, when he became a "man" and was required to recite the *Shema Israel* three times a day, he decided that he had no love for the establishment, be it Roman or Jewish. He joined several rebellious groups as soon as he could. When these dissolved or disbanded, or if he became dissatisfied with them, he would go looking for another. His only requirement when joining a group was that it was against authority. He did not have to believe in their rules or principles, just as long as he was accepted and could belong and they were against the establishment. When he was sixteen, he was sought out by the Zealots, for he was a perfect candidate, a "trouble maker." He quickly joined. It was the year of his uncle's death, and his aunt was glad to be rid of him. He was used as an informer and a spy. He enjoyed the secretiveness of his assignment and was often praised for the information he delivered.

As years passed, he became disillusioned with the Zealots, whom he found more inclined to crime and terrorism than to resisting authority. When he discovered that the Zealots were a silent military wing of the Pharisees, he wavered more. Then he discovered that the Zealots upheld the Jewish faith only to rally the common people, for without the common people they had no strength, but they had no sincere concern for the common people, whom they saw as potential subjects. Some of their tactics, especially those used against their fellow Jews, caused Simon to rethink his membership.

When he started following Jesus, he was at his lowest point of enthusiasm for the Zealots. So after many days of being with Jesus, he found Him radical enough to be interesting. He saw that Jesus' teachings threatened the establishment in a different way. His approach was not crime and rebellion, but rather silent resistance and preaching. It was a charitable yet forceful approach. Jesus' denunciations of the corrupt establishment caused many to follow Him. He was able to mesmerize the common people in a way that the Zealots could not. He offered true hope, not false political hope. He offered them not only labor and toil, but promises and rewards. He held their interest and their concerns, yet He was not afraid to identify evil when it was present. He was a Man for the crowds, for the poor and simple.

Simon approached the Zealots and told them he had gained Jesus' confidence and would report to them all the things Jesus did. He told them he was certain that Jesus would soon create a revolt against Rome and that His appeal to the impoverished masses—the most discontented Jews—would provide the Zealots with much-needed manpower. The leadership of the Zealots quickly agreed, for they knew Jesus' popularity was on the rise and they saw Him as a potential ally. Because Jesus was so openly against the Sanhedrin, they warned Simon to remain very discreet, for they did not want their silent allies, the Pharisees, to know of their interest in Jesus of Nazareth. Simon knew he didn't have to report to the Zealots, for they had spies who would report what Jesus was doing. The one thing that was true about his attachment to Jesus was his freedom from the Zealots and their strategies. Temporarily, and he truly believed it was to be temporary, he attached himself to another cause.

When Jesus called Simon from among the many to join the smaller group called the Apostles, he saw Barabbas, one of the leaders of the Zealots, in the crowd, and instantly he noticed the grin on Barabbas' lips. Simon knew that the Zealots were pleased, but he was fearful that his being with Jesus and His Apostles could endanger Jesus' mission. He was very reluctant to take his place with them, but he did because he needed to know more about Jesus. He was sincerely surprised at being chosen. It remained a mystery to him forevermore. He felt that he and Jesus had little in common from the three or four conversations they had shared. For reasons he could not explain, Jesus intimidated him. A strong sense of authority emanated from the Nazarene. Authority of any kind always made Simon feel uncomfortable, but Jesus' authority was somehow more intimidating. Simon could not find the source of the authority, but it was like no other authority he knew. For this reason and for fear of leading the Romans to perceive the Twelve as a group of Zealots, he remained in the background.

Several days after Jesus had called the Twelve, they were walking along a Judean road. As they walked, Simon fell behind them. He suddenly had become burdened with a very solemn mood. He felt a strange and strong need that demanded time. He slowed his pace, only slightly separating himself from the Others, and he kept his eyes on the back of Jesus' head. He could hear the mumbled questions from the Others as they questioned Jesus and debated among themselves, and he became annoyed at them. He slowed his pace more and fell a distance behind them, and in that instant he felt a stark, cold separation from life. This feeling was so powerful that it almost forced him into cries of anguish. Unfamiliar with such feelings, he hurried his pace and joined the Others. He pushed himself into their midst and instantly found comfort and companionship. From that day on, he knew he could not be separated from them; that day he found a group to belong to permanently. This experience surprised him, for his relationship with the Others was somewhat weak, yet he was included, perhaps as an afterthought, but still included. He had known James the Little and Judas before coming to Jesus. In the past, they had shown some interest in the Zealots, yet even they remained distant. There seemed to be a quiet distrust of him. Whether this was factual or imaginary he was not certain, but he understood the reason for the distrust: a Zealot in their midst would make the Romans suspicious. The Others knew that Simon and Matthew were philosophically opposed, and some worried that they would clash. Even the Zealots had once approached Simon with the idea of assassinating Matthew. Simon let the Zealots believe that he would consider their idea, but he thanked the Almighty that they never mentioned it to him again. He knew he could not kill Matthew, and even if he did, it would please the Pharisees more than the Zealots. Simon knew that he was drawing unneeded attention to Jesus' Twelve. This attention he did not want, for he felt it was detracting from the ideas and teachings of Jesus. He also didn't want the Others to become objects of surveillance, for he knew they were simple men of simple faith, and there was no malice in them. So taking the advice of the Zealots more seriously, he resolved to remain in the background. Consequently, whenever the group walked, Simon was always found in the back, and when they stood by Jesus, he was always in the back, stooped over and trying to go unnoticed. This was all a defense, for he had not yet reached a point of complete honesty in his life. If he had, he would have admitted that this backward attitude was typical for him for his life was filled with cautions and double cautions, with being a part of and not being a part of many temporary situations that were steps back and away.

As time passed, Simon started to find other things that separated him from the Others. Unlike them, he did not spend hours discussing what Jesus said or did. When they discussed Jesus, he found himself in silent disagreement with them, for he did not believe that Jesus was a great prophet or a messenger from the Almighty—and certainly not the Chosen One. A prophet would be more forceful, and a messenger more to the point, and the Chosen One would have appeared on a white stallion with weapons in his hands. He would not have been a poor carpenter from Nazareth with fishermen or part-time fishermen as His appointed ones. Even the normally cautious Judas saw Jesus as a Man of great importance, and he would often tell Simon that Jesus was "the greatest leader," "the greatest prophet." Simon disagreed with Judas but desired his convictions. The only ally he found in the group was James the Little, who said that Jesus was "misguided." James remained extremely skeptical of everything Jesus did, and rightly so, for James had known Jesus all his life. Simon saw Jesus as a clever Man with a strong, charismatic personality that inspired some people to listen to Him, some to believe in Him, and some even to follow Him. This charisma helped Simon to remain a follower, for he believed that the Israelites needed a compelling person to clear up their minds and show them the muddy mess they had allowed themselves to become. They had given much to the Romans and more to the Sanhedrin. They were so used to being conquered that they accepted it as their national trait. Jesus' tactics were unlike those of any other leader in Judea. He spoke of love, kindness, and compassion, and though Simon believed that these were not good tools for building a movement, he was confident that Jesus would put it all together.

Simon was amazed at the multitudes that came to hear Jesus preach, watch Him heal, and witness Him drive out evil spirits. The crowds made Simon feel lost in their midst. On one particular day, the multitude was larger than ever, and Jesus seemed pleased. Jesus was so pleased that He walked among the people. He passed through the crowd, touching and whispering to them. Finally, He ascended a small mount nearby. He walked to a rock and sat on it with His hands resting on His knees. He slowly looked over the countryside toward the horizon and the cloudless sky, and then He lowered His eyes. His look passed the many brown faces before Him. Simon and the Others were off to the side and slightly down the mount so that everyone was looking up to Jesus. He was at the center of them. Some of the Twelve sat on nearby rocks and boulders, but Simon stood back and away from them, yet near them.

Simon followed Jesus' gaze.

The crowd was settled down. Many sat on the ground or on their cloaks; others leaned heavily on their staffs. As Simon surveyed their faces, he knew that among them were the spies of the Sanhedrin, the Zealots, and the Romans, yet he could not tell who they were, for everyone looked serious. Simon smiled to himself in satisfaction, for it always delighted him that Jesus could so readily create these moments of eagerness and enthusiasm. He continued to survey the people. Hidden well under his cloak and hood was Joseph of Arimathea, and next to him was the Pharisee Nicodemus. Simon looked past them, and his eyes turned to a familiar face. His heart skipped a beat but then relaxed as he recognized the Roman Cornelius, a centurion. He was disguised as a commoner. Simon's eyes left Cornelius and moved around the crowd, and he saw the brazen, uncovered face of Barabbas. This man, though a Zealot, was also a criminal who delighted in living without scruples. In his early years with the Zealots, Simon had been a companion of Barabbas. Together they had attended several Zealot meetings, and they participated in raiding the Roman depot outside of Caesarea Philippi. It had been Simon's first revolutionary act as a Zealot, and he was exuberant. Later, he realized that his excitement was brought on by Barabbas, who had encouraged and praised Simon's courage. At that time, being young and foolish, he saw Barabbas as a great and dedicated leader. Barabbas had killed, and this made him even more intriguing. Simon knew he had no courage to kill, yet he considered anyone capable of this to be far superior to himself. Barabbas had a strong personality that drew men to him, but few men stayed with him, for soon they learned that he had no attachments to any cause but his own. He was a crude man with little regard for anything, and this included the Jewish faith and the Jewish people. Barabbas existed without faith, and to him life was cheap. He killed for the thrill and joy of it. He was called an insurrectionist, but Simon knew Barabbas was nothing but a criminal—a cruel man with hatred so strong that he gave off a foul scent. Simon looked away but could feel Barabbas' hard stare. In spite of being uncomfortable, Simon looked back, and for a moment he thought about walking to Barabbas. He refrained, for he knew that this would mark him as a sympathizer with the Zealots. With his attention away from Barabbas, his strong dislike for this wretched man returned. He kept his gaze away for a long time, and when he finally looked back to the place where Barabbas had been, he was gone. Simon sighed quietly and turned to look at Jesus, Who had remained speechless all this time.

The silence was heavy.

The anticipation was overwhelming.

Again, the feeling of being lost among so many came to him, and as it wrapped around him he recalled something from his past, something he had not remembered in many years. He once heard a Temple priest—the only one he ever trusted—tell him that there are "moments in life when *Adonai* unexpectedly comes to us, and these moments were created by the Almighty for the individual." After remembering this, he heard an inner voice say, "Listen, and find what you have lost."

Jesus spoke, and His voice carried across the plain, over the mountains, and into the distant valleys. Simon wondered how this Man of peaceful words with gentle, rhythmic tones could be heard so many paces away. Simon's wondering was never satisfied as he heard the words "Blessed are the poor in spirit" echo inside him. Simon immediately fell to the moment. This was his moment with *Adonai*. He wanted, needed to hold onto it.

Each blessing echoed inside him, and he questioned himself: "Do I merit such a blessing?"

In the middle of His teaching, Jesus turned slightly; He caught Simon's eye and said, "Blessed are the peacemakers, for they shall be called children of God."

From nowhere came a breeze—not the dry, warm breeze of Judea but a cool, refreshing breeze, the kind that soothes the human body and eases the human spirit, and with that breeze stillness instantly came into Simon. He knew this breeze was meant for him, that this calmness was for him, but he had to let this go amidst the sweet peacefulness that quickly followed. A question came to him: *Is this feeling from Adonai? Or is this feeling from Jesus?* He looked at Jesus with these questions in his mind, and suddenly he felt a new friendship with Jesus. He silently welcomed the peace and longed for more. That night, when they gathered around a warm fire, he wanted to talk to the Others about what had happened to him, but everyone was very somber and introspective, so he decided it would not be wise to start a discussion. He thought of going to Jesus and asking Him directly if what had happened was from *Adonai* or from Him, but he thought this to be too juvenile—and besides, Jesus had gone off to pray.

It was just a fluke, just a crazy, weak moment, he thought, but still he had the peace in him and it stayed with him, just as the need to belong with the Others had come to him and stayed with him. He remained restless all through the evening and then decided to go for a walk, and it was then that he came upon Jesus in prayer. Quickly and quietly he hid himself in the nearby bushes and watched.

Jesus was standing. The palms of His hands were opened to the deep blue night sky. His head was lowered and His face was hidden in the hood of His cloak. After a short time, Jesus raised His head; His hood slipped away and Simon could see that His eyes were closed. As He stood there motionless, His face gleamed in the moonlight. For the longest time He stood this way, and for the longest time He remained in silence. Then with graceful energy He seemed to wake up, and slowly a smile came to His face. Simon detected that it was a smile resulting from something agreed to or something understood. Simon thought that what he was witnessing was all very strange, and he hid deeper in the bushes.

Then Jesus spoke and prayed: "Give them faith, hope, and love, *Abba.* I do not want them to seek worldly greatness. Keep them as I found them in all things, but let them believe in You. Let them walk to You, each in his own fashion, each to the rhythm of his own steps. Keep them human, and with the spirit of trust, let them hear only what You wish them to hear." Again He fell to silence. "Abba, I ask that You give them a bond of companionship and souls of peace, serenity, and faithfulness. Give Your blessing to Simon, Simon, Judas, Matthew, James, Andrew, John, Jude, Thomas, Philip, Bartholomew, and James."

Jesus returned to silence, then clearing His throat with a slight cough, He turned and slowly walked away.

Simon slipped deeper into the bushes, and after many moments, he looked around. Seeing that Jesus was gone, he rose and began brushing himself clean. He looked in the distance and could see the campfire, and without hesitation he began walking toward the flames. As he walked, he vowed that from that night on, when Jesus went off to pray, he would follow Him.

I may learn more by observing Him, but more importantly, I will guard Him, for He has many enemies among the Temple authorities, the Herodians, the Sanhedrin, and the Romans.

He reached for his dagger as assurance. The feeling of bravery passed, and he heard Jesus' words in his mind. He remembered that Jesus called the Almighty "Abba." Simon was pleased.

How familiar Jesus must be with the Almighty. Could He be that intimate with Adonai? I like the feeling of referring to the Almighty as Abba. He thought perhaps he would adopt this practice of speaking to the Almighty in warm and familiar terms. It suited him better than being fearful of the Almighty.

He slowed his steps as fear captured his thinking.

Could I dare be that familiar with Him? Why not? Is He not my Daddy also? I will pray this way from now on, and I will pray more often.

He continued to walk, pleased because Jesus had taught him something new.

It is odd that Jesus would pray for us, He thought. *Why pray for us? And in that fashion?* After taking three more steps, he stopped. *He prayed "Simon, Simon, Judas…" He prayed for me before many of the Others! Why me before the Others?*

With great urgency he started back to the fire and the Others. He wanted to ask Jesus why He had done such a thing, but before he could get any closer to the fire, he stopped abruptly and said aloud, "Was I the first Simon or the second Simon?" His heart beat quickly as he grew anxious and fearful, wondering if he unwillingly had become important. In his heart he knew he would not have the courage to ask Jesus this question; it was too arrogant, but he knew he would have to spend more time watching Jesus in prayer.

Later, Simon observed Jesus in daily confrontation and debate with the Pharisees and Sadducees. This delighted Simon because of his dislike for authority, yet every confrontation started a debate among the Twelve. Some had a great fear of these leaders, so they were uncomfortable with Jesus' challenges. Others saw these officials as less threatening. Still others who disliked this group enjoyed it when Jesus rebuked and embarrassed them.

Simon was surprised to see that Jesus was so at ease with sinners. Jesus released people saying, "Go and sin no more" or "Your sins are forgiven." Of course, Simon wondered how Jesus could say this and it worried him, until he remembered Jesus' familiar way of speaking to *Abba*; this seemed to make him understand the authority Jesus had. The Pharisees often remembered the sin and not the contrition. Jesus always seemed to remember the open and humble people who came to Him, and He responded to the multitudes with simplicity and straightforwardness. "Poor in spirit" were the words Jesus used. The multitudes seemed to enjoy the parables, which were on their level. It was the Twelve who complicated the parables, and sometimes they reminded Simon of the Pharisees, always looking for profound meanings. Yet when Simon looked at his fellow Apostles, he found no hypocrisy among them—they also were poor and simple. Though they had sinned, some more than others, Jesus had accepted them, and not once had He mentioned their sins. Imperfect as they were, they were accepted by Jesus. This pleased Simon.

One cool day, as Jesus and the Twelve walked along one of the many dirt roads in Judea, they came upon a blind man stumbling along the road. Thomas, Jude Thaddeus, and Simon bar Jonah asked Jesus, "Rabbi, who hath sinned, this man or his parents, that he should be born blind?"

Jesus examined each of their faces carefully and answered softly, "Neither hath this man sinned, nor his parents; but that the work of God should be made manifest in him."

That night, when Jesus went off to pray, they debated. Simon went off by himself and began to ponder Jesus' words. He believed Jesus was saying that people and situations are placed before us and those situations are there for us to grow from. We are given our share of life, and what we have is to be used by us to glorify *Abba*. Others' deficiencies become opportunities for God's providence and goodness.

Simon waited then followed so as to watch Jesus. He found Jesus praying; He again was praying for the Twelve. This humbled Simon, and later that night, all curled up under his cloak in the cold night air, alone, he silently wept, for he had found someone Who cared for a sinful person like him.

Every time Jesus went off to pray, Simon would wait a little while then slip away and find Him. He was never missed by the Others. He continued watching Jesus in this way. Many times Jesus prayed for strength to do the Father's Will, and often for the Twelve. On one night, He asked that the Twelve be given understanding, for they were blind to what was taking place and were ignorant of the signs. These words made Simon sad, because he knew Jesus was correct. The Others endlessly debated and argued about Jesus. They argued as to whether He was a prophet or a new leader for a Davidic Kingdom. Though he did not know what signs Jesus spoke of, Simon vowed to become more alert and less cynical. That night, Simon prayed to *Abba* for understanding. He had the need to see Jesus as He was supposed to be seen. He then pleaded for the courage to be able to help Jesus make everything known to all the Others. In the many days that followed, Simon watched as Jesus calmed the sea, healed the blind and the crippled, cleansed the lepers, and even raised the dead daughter of Jarius. Simon soon understood the power and authority that Jesus possessed. He recognized that Jesus had received these things through a direct relationship with *Abba*. With certainty, Simon acknowledged that

Jesus was sent by *Abba*. He even began to understand the parables Jesus told. He did not know if what he understood was correct, but he was satisfied with whatever conclusions he reached.

One hot dry day as they walked on the shores of the Sea of Galilee, Jesus stopped to wade in the cool water. The Twelve stood watching with delight as Jesus splashed and kicked the water in many directions. It was obvious that He was thoroughly enjoying this simple part of God's creation.

Simon, who had been praying consistently for a long time and was now confident in his prayer life, turned to Simon bar Jonah and asked, "Simon, do you pray?"

"Why do you ask such a thing of me, Simon? Of course I do."

The Others, stunned at the Zealot's question, stopped and listened.

"Do you pray as Jesus prays?"

"Simon," Andrew interjected, "we all pray differently."

"But are you not curious to know how Jesus prays? After all, He prays far more than we do. Do you not wonder how He prays?"

"Do we really need to know this?" questioned James bar Alphaeus.

"Yes, I think so," Bartholomew answered for the Zealot. This support surprised Simon.

"Why do you think we should know this, Simon?" asked John.

"So we can know the Master better," answered the Zealot.

"To become more like Him," added Bartholomew, surprising Simon again.

"How can we learn to pray as Jesus does?" asked Jude Thaddeus in a small, timid voice.

"Simple," Matthew said. "We ask Him, as we ask Him so many other things."

Simon knew he had done a good thing, so good that even Matthew sided with him, so the Zealot took a few steps back, away from them, and let them decide who should ask Jesus how to pray.

And so it came to pass that Jesus was approached by Simon bar Jonah.

Simon said, "Lord, teach us to pray, as John also taught his disciples."

Jesus looked at Simon bar Jonah for a moment, then He said, "When you pray, say: Our Father who art in heaven, hallowed be Thy name. Thy kingdom come. Thy will be done on earth as it is in heaven. Give us this day our daily bread. And forgive us our debts as we also forgive our debtors. And lead us not into temptation, but deliver us from evil. Amen."

Having said this, He continued to speak as he walked among the Twelve, His eyes passing over each of their faces.

Finally, He stopped before Simon the Zealot and said, "And I say to you: Ask and it shall be given you; seek, and you shall find; knock and it shall be opened to you. For every one that asketh, receiveth, and he that seeketh findeth, and to him that knocketh, it shall be opened."

Having taught His Apostles to pray, Jesus wanted to be alone with them, so He told them to "come depart into a desert place and rest a while."

So they took a boat and crossed into a deserted place near Bethsaida on the northern side of the Sea of Galilee. When they arrived, they found a multitude waiting for them. Jesus began teaching them, and by evening the Apostles asked Jesus to tell the crowd to go so they could buy some food.

Jesus said to all, "Give you them to eat."

Turning to Philip, He continued, "Whence shall we buy bread, that these may eat?"

Judas Iscariot, who had been made holder of the purse, said, "Rabbi, we have not silver for so many."

"Not even two hundred *denarii* worth of bread would feed these," Philip remarked.

Andrew drew near to Jesus and in a low voice said, "There is a young boy who has five barley loaves and two dry fishes."

Jesus said, "Bring them here to Me."

Andrew led the young boy with his small basket to Him. Jesus placed His hand on the boy's head, smiled, and said, "You have done a great thing today, little one. You show no disrespect for sharing and giving. Years from now, people will hear of you."

Jesus turned to the Twelve. "Make them recline by fifties in a company."

The Twelve went among the people and ordered them to recline on the grass. As Simon walked among the crowd he saw Gestas, a ruthless and merciless robber, who befriended Barabbas. Gestas not only killed Romans in the cruelest of ways but also raided Roman supplies for his own profit and also robbed from Jews. He was a man who did more with a look than most men can do with their voices. Patience was not one of his virtues, nor was it ever part of his character. With his lack of forethought he was dangerous, especially to the Zealots, who liked to carefully plan their actions. Gestas stood in the crowd in full view of everyone. His face was hard and set firmly with indifference. He did not acknowledge Simon, which pleased Simon. Then Simon saw Dismas. He was a young man with light brown hair and a developing beard. He came into the Zealots shortly before Simon began to drift away, so Simon knew little about him. Simon did learn that he became a Zealot because he was seeking refuge. The closed society of the Zealots gave Dismas the anonymity and protection he needed. He robbed only Jews who were in the employ of the Romans. He had a great dislike for Samaritans, whom he beat and robbed, but he was unlike most Zealots in his willingness to listen and consider. As time passed, Simon found Dismas to be a man who was searching for something, and he appeared to have a truthfulness about him that made him a bit less cruel and a bit more intelligent than most Zealots. Seeing Dismas there did not bother Simon, for Simon could tell from the look of wonder on Dismas' face that he was enthralled by what was taking place. As their eyes met, Simon could detect a tinge of envy. He acknowledged the young Zealot with a nod of his head, but Dismas backed away and hid himself in his hood.

When all had reclined, Jesus took the five loaves, looked up to heaven, blessed and broke them, and gave the pieces to the Apostles to distribute. He did likewise with the fishes. When the people had their fill and they gathered the remains, they counted twelve baskets. The multitudes were not aware of what had been gathered, but when the Apostles saw the twelve baskets, they were amazed.

"Brother," Andrew said excitedly, "look, there are twelve baskets gathered."

"Andrew, Philip, have you counted them correctly?" James bar Alphaeus questioned.

"Yes," Philip replied curtly.

"How did this happen?" Bartholomew asked, looking quickly at the baskets near him.

Simon bar Jonah, aware that the multitudes were sensing that something miraculous had taken place, recognized that this could be dangerous for Jesus. He immediately quieted the Others with a few strong looks and a few grabs of their arms. He then turned to Jesus, and Jesus, sensing that the crowd was getting unruly, fled into the mountains alone.

The Twelve quietly took a few pieces of bread and fish and silently slipped away. Later, when they assembled, they boarded a boat anchored nearby and sailed to the opposite shore. Halfway across the lake, they burst into excited shouts and debated about what this all meant.

Simon looked back on the shore, regretting that he did not stay behind to follow Jesus and observe Him in secret. He was sure that more would be revealed in listening to Jesus than in listening to his companions. Simon knew that what happened was significant to Jesus' mission, maybe even a turning point, but he was confused as to how this was all done. It all seemed so unbelievable. Unlike the Others, who with great excitement rehashed the event, he was silent and filled with curiosity and completely unsettled. He heard the others state that it was a great thing; when Jesus came to power, he could feed the people forever. He heard the wise thought that all this came to be through *Adonai*. That was the wisest thought he heard from the Others. Unlike the wine at the wedding, which was done in private and for a few, this multiplication was done in public and for many. Suddenly, Simon realized that Jesus was sent by *Abba* to nourish the people as they had been nourished in the desert. He now clearly saw that Jesus was the New Manna for the Jews—Jesus was not merely a prophet, but a special herald and messenger from *Abba*. Quickly, Simon became fearful, for he knew that the Zealot leadership would hear of this and see Jesus as a provider for the people. They would try to use Him in their cause, and Jesus' mission would be jeopardized. A question then came to Simon's mind, and the question remained unanswered: *How many more can Jesus feed?*

Simon curled himself into a ball and tucked his cloak around him. The night's coolness had brushed against him and lingered with indifference in his body. He hated the chill of night, though he knew he should be used to it by now, for the chill of night had been his companion for many years. In spite of this, he shivered and settled deep in his cloak, hoping to claim some warmth and protection. He grew comfortable and longed to return to sleep, but he soon resolved that sleep was going to be elusive. For a few precious moments he was still, suspended between awareness and slumber. This time was broken by the heavy breathing and low moans coming from Clavos on the other side of the room.

He is back to his dream, Simon thought, and immediately he felt the pangs of sadness, for he knew that soon he would again need to wake his companion to interrupt the pain of the dream. He did not know what this recurring dream was. Clavos never told him and he never asked, but he was sure it had to do with the flogging that Clavos gave Jesus and with what had happened to him on that dark, turbulent day on Golgotha.

The mount…that day and all that was before it, he thought, and suddenly, in bits and pieces, people and places raced through his mind. Who these people were did not matter much to him because he only remembered his pounding heart, the sight of Jesus, and the pain he endured each time he looked upon Jesus.

After they had supped and celebrated the Passover meal, they began the walk to Bethany. It was a cold night with a different and added chill that seemed to come up from the dust and earth, and at the same time down from the sky and heavens. So they walked huddled together in one large group. As they approached the Garden of Gethsemane, they passed the many tombs and markings of the prophets and holy ones of old who were buried on the side of Mount Olivet. The white markers of the graves were like pale, silent sentries in the night. They gleamed under the silvery moonlight. The markers reminded Simon of candles waiting for a flame. Simon later learned that several of the Apostles ran to this place and hid behind the markers when Jesus was bound and arrested.

✳

His remembering stopped. The night's chill shivered him and broke into the present, and he smiled, recalling a similar chill that woke him from his intoxicated sleep that night in the garden. He remembered shivering and his teeth chattering as he became annoyed at the cold. In a daze, he looked quickly around the garden and saw Jesus off in the distance leaning against a large rock. At first he thought Jesus was sleeping, but then he heard Jesus speak. He strained his eyes and saw Peter, James, and John sleeping not too far from Jesus.

I thought they were going to keep watch with the Master. The Master should not be left alone. Perhaps I will go and hide near Him and listen to His prayers, he thought as his eyes grew heavy and shut; his desire to sleep returned to him. *But not tonight.*

Again he heard Jesus speak, and again he could not understand what He was saying. The demand for sleep grew too strong, so he wrapped his cloak firmly around himself.

Sorry, he thought. *Not tonight, Jesus. Tonight I will leave Your prayers to You.* Growing comfortable, he willed sleep to come, and then he thought, *This is the first time in a long time that Jesus has prayed alone.*

He was awakened again. He opened his eyes, and in the distance standing by a tree was the young boy Mark. It was the last thing he saw before he drifted off to sleep, and the last thing he thought was, *Then Jesus is not alone. Why would that boy be here?*

The arrest of Jesus perplexed Simon because he did not know why Jesus permitted it. So many times he had seen Jesus vanish when He was in any danger, but He did not that night. Bethany was not far—they could have made the journey in no time. Or He could have gone into the desert, for it too was within reach.

Why did He not escape?

After the arrest of Jesus in the garden, Simon followed the mob every place they took Jesus, but always from a great distance, always hidden in the darkness and in the shadows of the night. He followed not with courage or dedication, for at that time he lacked both these qualities; he followed out of curiosity, for deep inside he was waiting for choirs of angels, or *Abba*, or some powerful intervention from the Almighty.

He went to the house of the Chief Priests Annas and Caiphas, and in the darkness he heard Simon Peter deny Jesus. He remembered the prediction Jesus had made and wondered: *How did Jesus know that Simon Peter would deny Him?*

He followed the group through the night and morning, from Caiphas to Pilate to Herod and back to Pilate, always carefully hiding deep in his hood with his cloak wrapped tightly around him, as if he was still chilled by the departing night or the early morning dew. The only time he lost sight of Jesus was when He was jailed and scourged, and when Jesus emerged from this ordeal, Simon wept silent, tormented tears.

In the sun, in the crowd, in the darkness of his hood, he watched Pilate's offer of freedom for Jesus or Barabbas. Simon relaxed for he was certain of the outcome. Jesus had fed them, cured them, showed them mercy and understanding, and had recently been declared by the people their King. Barabbas was a criminal and a revolutionist. When the people shouted for Barabbas, Simon was dumbfounded. In complete disbelief, he watched Barabbas go into the crowd, soon to be swallowed up in their midst.

How could this happen?

He continued to watch the proceedings, paralyzed like a spectator at a Greek play, and as with a Greek play, it seemed that the characters were moving around at the whims of fate. He watched Pilate wash his hands, then, following the Roman custom of condemnation, he reached for a staff, broke it in two, and threw the pieces at Jesus' feet.

Solemn and seemingly regretful, Pilate then declared, "*Ibis ad crucem*"—Thou will go to the cross. Turning his head slightly, he said to the executioners, "*I, Lictor, expedi crucem*"—Go, prepare the cross.

When Simon heard Pilate speak these words, an odd feeling came over him. He first felt that Jesus deserved this, for He had permitted it, but soon his feelings changed to sadness, for he knew that Jesus was completely innocent. Simon wondered why this was happening—the beatings, the scourging, the crown of thorns, the carrying of the cross. How was all this related to the mission of Jesus? Then he began to feel foolish. He had allowed himself to waste three years of his life with a charlatan...

but still he could not break away from the proceedings. He was compelled to hide and watch.

Jesus was led away to His cross, and a lane was created by Cornelius and the Roman detachment for the walk to Golgotha, just outside the city walls. Suddenly, from nowhere, two others were led out to be crucified. Simon studied their faces and eventually recognized them as two Zealots. Like Barabbas, they were wanted criminals who under the cloak of the Zealots had profited from the terror they spread. As he watched these two men being led to their crosses, he thought, *If I had stayed with the Zealots and had become as these men, this could have been my crucifixion.*

He grew sad at this thought and found himself calling upon *Abba* for understanding.

He saw a young woman push her way to Jesus and wipe His bloodied face.

Where did a woman get such courage?

He watched an old, dark man push his way to Jesus and offer Him some water.

Why would a seemingly wise old man do such a foolish thing?

Finally, he observed the tall, muscular African pressed into service to help Jesus carry His cross.

That is what we should be doing.

Eventually, everything came to the mount called Golgotha. Many called this place "the place of the skull," but Simon never understood why they referred to this place by such a name. He did not see any similarity to a skull. Some people called it a mount, but he thought it just a hill. He had passed it many times and paid little attention to it, for it stood for death, a place in which Roman justice was delivered. That day, it seemed totally different to him. It looked pristine. The sand was bright gold, the bushes were green and full, and the rocks and boulders were clean in the bright, warm sunlight. Even the surrounding land was free of contamination. He cautiously approached the summit and quickly hid behind several bushes and a small boulder. This was some distance from the summit of the hill, but still he had a good view.

He arrived just as the Romans were nailing the charge above Jesus' naked body.

Simon read the charge in Hebrew: *Ha Yehudim u'melekh ha Natzari Yeshua.*

Turning his head away quickly, he said in a low, disappointed voice, "If only that sign were true!"

From his vantage point he saw Mary, the Master's mother, the woman from Magdala, Mary Cleophas, and even Salome Zebedee. And he was amazed to see John standing with them by the cross. The young Apostle was acting like the consoler and true follower of Jesus.

He seems so much taller. Where did he get such bravery?

When he heard the shouts of mockery and laughter from the members of the Sanhedrin, he cringed and hid deeper in his hood, crawling into the shadow of the boulder. He heard Jesus speak, but he was too far away to understand clearly what was said. The members of the Sanhedrin reacted with loud, abusive language.

Then Simon heard clearly: "If Thou art the Son of God, come down from the cross."

"Yes, Jesus, show them. Come down," Simon whispered.

"He saved others, Himself He cannot save."

"Yes, Jesus, save Yourself...save me. Help me now to believe in You," Simon whispered.

"If the Almighty loves Him, let Him deliver Him now."

"Oh *Abba*, where are You now?" Simon whispered.

Surprisingly, he heard Gestas, who had been crucified to the left of Jesus, begin to ridicule Jesus.

Simon for the first time showed some bravery as he stood and looked over the boulder. With great anger, he thought, *Gestas, you fool. You worthless fool. What have you ever done that could equal the good that Jesus has done?* He grew angry at his former companion and was on the verge of shouting something in defense of Jesus when he heard Dismas reprimand Gestas in a truthful and painful way. Gestas cursed Dismas for his stupidity and returned to his own agony.

Simon felt proud of Dismas and was pleased to see that he had been right about the man—he was indeed sensitive.

He watched Dismas turn his head to Jesus and in a loud voice, Dismas asked to be remembered when Jesus entered His Kingdom.

Simon froze.

For the third time in his life, the words of the Temple priest echoed in his mind. There are "moments in life when *Adonai* unexpectedly comes to us and these moments are created by the Almighty for the individual...."

His heart beat rapidly. His mouth grew dry. Simon's insides lurched as he envied Dismas for having the courage to come forward, and then he heard what Jesus said to the thief: "*Amen, Amen, amarna lachbam atte emmib Pardessa.*"

Simon crumbled to the ground. An instant flood of revelations came to him, and he saw things clearly. For the first time in his three years with

Jesus, he came to see that Jesus had power outside of this place and time and into eternity. He had power to take with Him another human soul. He had power into the beyond and into timeless life. He realized that Jesus had not come for the crowds but for the person. From the many around Him, He took but one, a robber and a sinner, with Him, and He granted this criminal a place in Paradise.

Warm tears washed Simon's face. They were not tears of sadness but of joy, for he now knew that Jesus could promise Paradise. He leaned against the boulder, ignoring the wind storm and the turmoil that was forming around him. He did not know how long he hid in this position, for when he awakened to time again it was dark and the world was foul. He walked away and into the darkness, regretting that he had not been zealous in his time with Jesus. For the remaining hours of that day and into the next, Simon walked in darkness. His mind was numb and blank. He saw no images, heard no words, felt no life. He walked and walked until he suddenly became aware of the smell of damp clothing and of dry mud on his feet, sandals, and cloak. When he looked up he recognized the Upper Room in the house of Mark's parents. With urgency he raced up the steps and knocked gently on the door. He was let in by Jude Thaddeus. The shadows of Simon's passing days entered with him, and these matched the shadows across the faces of the Others. He immediately became a part of their blindness.

Sometime later when Simon felt more open, he walked to Simon Peter, who was standing with John bar Zebedee. He waited until it seemed appropriate to interrupt the two, and as he stood there, he grew surprised at the size of Simon Peter. His body was thick and strong.

"Simon Peter, I do not know what is to become of us. Perhaps we will all return to our former ways, or perhaps the Lord has something in store for us. I only know that I must thank you for having been the one who always stepped forward...."

Simon Peter reached for Simon's arm. "Simon...."

"No please, let me finish. In the past, when it seemed I should have stepped forward, you did in my stead. I should have taken my sword to the High Priest's servant. I should have spoken to the Master about prayer, and I should have been more bold, for I had learned more than the rest of you."

He lowered his eyes in shame and to avoid Simon Peter's searching eyes. "For a long time, I watched the Master in secret. Every time He went off to pray, I followed Him and hid, listening to His spoken prayers. I heard His words and came to understand much of what He was doing and why. This was wrong, but even worse, I never told anyone what I learned."

"If the Master wanted us to know something, He would have told us Himself," Simon Peter stated. "I think He gave us what He wanted us to know. I believe He will tell us more when He wants us to know more."

"But I was a spy. I was deceitful. I was a coward."

"We all were spies. We all looked and inspected and re-inspected the Master. I was deceitful, for I was going to give my life for Him, and when the time came, I denied Him. I too am a coward." Simon Peter placed his rough hands on Simon's shoulder, encouraging Simon to raise his eyes and look at the big fisherman. "I believe you have done no wrong, Simon, and if you have, the Master will tend to it as He sees fit. It is not for me or any of us to be judges. Just remember, as I am now remembering, that He chose you, us, for a reason. Let us search our minds and souls for that reason, and let nothing else matter."

Simon walked away from Peter respecting him more.

Then came the holy women telling them they had seen Jesus, and they heard rumors of other people seeing Him.

Hidden behind the walls of that room, they were safe from the authorities and the people, and maybe even from Jesus, for they all feared that seeing Jesus would put them in a dilemma. They would have to acknowledge the contradiction of Jesus' life when they were assured of His death. The past days had filled them with enough confusion, and having to face the confusion of cold death and warm life was something they did not want. Even worse, they would have to face the Jesus Whom they had deserted. There was no doubt that confronting Jesus would be a profound struggle for them all.

In his thoughts, Simon believed that Jesus had risen. After witnessing Jesus and Dismas on Golgotha, he had come to believe that Jesus was all powerful, capable of all things. He had no doubts about this; what he doubted was Who Jesus was, and this he was sure would come to light when Jesus saw fit. Simon knew that somewhere, in all those many words of Jesus, He told them, but they were just too preoccupied with their own ideas.

When Jesus appeared, Simon was relieved and overjoyed. He wanted to reach out and touch Him, not for assurance but for comfort. He wanted to ask Jesus about death and the hereafter, about Paradise, about Dismas. But it became clear that Jesus was appearing to them for other reasons. He heard Jesus commission them to forgive sins—to forgive just as He had forgiven from His cross. Simon did not know how he was to do this. In his exuberance, he wanted to tell Jesus of his joy, but again he stayed away and in the back of the group, for he knew he was not "poor in spirit."

In the days that followed, Simon just let time and events flow over him as Jesus gave them His final teachings. When Jesus spoke to them, Simon listened carefully to Jesus' every word, committing all His teachings to careful memory. He acknowledged one gratifying conclusion: he was empty when Jesus was away and full when Jesus returned.

One night, when they believed it was safe to fish, they took Simon Peter's boat out on the Sea of Galilee. In the boat were Simon Peter, Thomas, Nathaniel, James, John, Jude Thaddeus, and himself. They fished for many hours and had no catch. In the early morning, they heard someone call out to them.

"Children, have you any meat?"

"No," they shouted back in unison.

"Cast the net on the right side, and you shall find."

"We did net on the right side," said Thomas, "and we had no luck."

"Have you not yet learned to obey, Thomas? What have we to lose by doing it again?" Simon Peter said as he led the others in hauling in the nets and casting them on the right side of the boat.

Instantly, the nets were filled with fish.

John grabbed Simon Peter's arm and said in an excited voice, "Simon Peter, it is the Lord!"

Simon Peter girted his cloak, for he was naked, and jumped into the sea while the Others in the boat rowed feverishly to the shore. When they arrived, they found Jesus sitting on a thick log with a burning fire, and over the fire were some fish and bread.

"Bring hither the fishes which thou hast now caught," Jesus ordered, and Simon Peter with the Apostles went and hauled in the morning's catch.

"Come and dine," Jesus said, and they sat and ate with Him.

After they had eaten, Simon and the Others went to tend to the rest of their catch, leaving Jesus, Simon Peter, and John behind to sit by the fire. Eventually everyone returned to the light of the fire and sat intimately around the flames and around Jesus—except for the Zealot, for he sat out of the circle. Even from this position he enjoyed the pleasure of being in the presence of Jesus.

Night came quickly and as night grew late, sleep soon came to the Apostles and Jesus once again was left alone in the night. Simon had remained positioned off and away. He rolled himself in his cloak and pretended to sleep. He was elated, for he knew he was being given the opportunity to make amends for sleeping that night in the garden. He knew this night he would keep watch with Jesus, and perhaps once more, maybe for the last time, he would listen to Jesus pray.

Suddenly, from the past he heard the advice of the Temple priest, and he knew and believed again that *Adonai* was to have His moment with him.

"Simon Qun'anaya bar Achyon."

He heard his name behind him, to the side of him, and above him.

Astonished, he froze in place. This was the first time he had been addressed by his full and proper name: Simon Zealot son of Achyon. Few knew his father's name, and therefore few people ever called him by his former name. He could not move. His heart crashed repeatedly against his chest, pounding and echoing in his ears and head.

"Simon Qun'anaya bar Achyon."

He heard it again, but this time the call came from the front of him—from Jesus.

"Come near, Simon. You do not have to pretend."

"Master," Simon said as he peeked out of his wrappings.

"Come!" Jesus said, and Simon slowly crawled to Jesus and into the light of the fire. "No need to hide any longer."

"Master, I did not mean to be disrespectful; I did not want to leave You alone. I just wanted to be with You."

"I know, just as I knew you were always hiding nearby, listening to My prayers. It would have been better if you had joined Me," Jesus said looking into the fire before Him.

"I am sorry, Lord, I did not know what to do." Simon lowered his head, not in fear but in contrition.

"And to guard Me?" Jesus turned to him and smiled. "Ah, but were you a watchman that was blind?"

Simon was unable to speak, for he had no answer to this question.

Jesus turned His face away and looked out over the sea. After a few moments He continued, "You were like the Others, you had many questions to ask and you did not come to Me in those private moments of watching. You had many thoughts about the multiplication of the loaves and fishes, and yet you asked no questions. Amen I say to you, soon you will not have to look far or wide for the meaning of that event. Know this: I will give the world bread to eat and I will give many baskets of fishermen."

Simon's mind was blank. He was in his moment; he felt the magnitude of this time, so he let the time flow and flood over him. He was like a large fish with a gaping mouth, wanting and needing to be fed.

"You have questions about your friend Dismas. He is with *Abba* and Me. He prays for you even now."

Simon drew near to Jesus. He sat on the sandy beach absorbed in his Master. From the crackling, yellow fire Simon felt heat on his face; and yet, he felt the chill and the aloneness of the dark night on the part of his face that was away from the fire.

Jesus continued to look off in the distance. "You are still puzzled about why I did not escape Gethsemane. You must understand that everyone who is to face the Almighty must have a Gethsemane. When everyone reaches their Gethsemane, they will conclude that they had been to all the places they had to be and had done all that they had to do. Like Me, they will know there is no other place for them to go. That night, My hour had come. Though you did not know it, My dear friend, there was the sound of trumpets that night."

The burning logs began to collapse into the fire and become consumed again and again. Simon became mentally aware of the fire but refused to be distracted from Jesus.

"We have much to say to each other, Simon. You have spent much time in silence, but soon I will come to you and we will talk of great things. This will happen when I come to you as a Watchman."

The fire snapped and popped loudly, and Simon, surrendering, turned to watch the fire. The flames leapt into the air with great vivacity. As he watched the fire self-consume, it began to take on a new life.

When he turned his attention back to Jesus, all he found was the large, thick log.

✳

With a deep, frustrated sigh, Simon sat up from his sleeping mat. He knew that sleep would not come to him now. He would remain awake all night long, and he had to find something to do, but this urge passed quickly when he again heard Clavos moaning in his sleep. He pressed his back against the wall of the hut and looked at the door. He could take a walk, but he was still too tired to do that, so he moved his eyes to the open window and looked up into the dark, starry sky. Within moments, his mind began to race to many places, seeing many people. It stopped for a moment then moved to another place, another person, until, exhausted, he stopped the racing and went into prayer. He recited the prayer taught to them by Jesus and then went on to one of the prayers of David.

I placed firm confidence in the Lord, and he bent down to me,
and heard my cry.

He drew me out of the pit of destruction, out of the filthy mire;
and he set my feet upon a rock, and strengthened my steps.
He put into my mouth a new song,
a song of praise to our God.

He recited from memory, like most Jews did, until he finished the psalm with a plea:

To do Thy Will, O my God, is my delight,
And Thy Law is in my very heart.

Now a little eased, he took a deep breath and waited, for it was time that the Lord spoke to him. Moments passed, and it did not happen. Instead, he saw the faces of the Others, and when the faces of James, Matthias, James, Bartholomew, Peter, and even Paul, Andrew, and Thomas came to him, he asked them to remember him before the Almighty, for their voyages and missions were complete.

Now his memory gave him faces and images of the many others who had touched his life in his mission. He again remembered a psalm of David and began to recite it.

I will bless the Lord at all times,
His praise shall be ever in my mouth.
Let my soul glory in the Lord;
let the humble hear and rejoice.
Glorify the Lord with me;
and let us together exalt His Holy Name.

Numerous faces of Judeans, Galileans, Samarians, Syrians, and Egyptians made their way across his mind, and finally he came to the Africans, and there his mental travels ended. These were the faces he knew best. This was the place where he was to be from the beginning. When the Apostles received their missions, this forgotten place was given to him; his lot was *Africa*. Upon learning this, he asked about this land and was told that it was a massive place, a strange land that sighed in delight and moaned in sorrow. Some said it was an important part of the Roman Empire because it was "the bread basket of Rome." As valuable as it was, it still was hidden in winds and openness, and it existed in the minds of many Emperors and Romans as an afterthought.

He learned of a synagogue in Jerusalem founded by North African Jews. He had seen a few of these Black Jews. They were rare, and because they were so few in numbers, they had to open their synagogue up to others, namely the Egyptians and the Libertines, who were the few Gentiles who had become Jews. He had intentions of going to this synagogue but was warned that Stephen, the deacon, had been there and was met with great hostility, so he cautiously waited until the "insults" of Stephen were forgotten.

He had seen a few Numidian slaves who traveled through Judea and other places. They were darker and taller than most Jews. They were muscular and always bare-chested. Their skin reminded him of a large black stone he found many years before on the shores of the Sea of Galilee. The stone was polished smooth with a sheen that made him feel there was a softness deep inside the hard exterior surface. The eyes of the Numidians were always deep black. In these black eyes, shadows existed that covered their dreams, thoughts, and feelings. Their entire being held a mystery that reached down deep inside the souls of their descendants.

Simon had been told that they were "good workers, stronger than any bull, and wild as the land that gave them life."

After drawing lots, he, like most of the Twelve, was ready to leave, but it was so difficult to say goodbye to home. All of the Twelve seemed to be similar to one another in their thoughts about leaving, except for James the Big and Matthias. They seemed to mill around Judea before departing on their mission "to teach all nations." During this time, they clung to one another and shared advice, courage, and affirmation.

Simon preached and spent much time in Palestine, then he crossed over the Jordan to Peraea and Ituraea before moving north to Syria and even as far as Osroene and Armenia. Eventually, he turned south and traveled to Antioch in Syria with the intention of boarding a ship for Africa, and there he was met by Clavos.

"I have been asked to join you and to be of help," the former scourger said.

"By whose orders?" Simon asked with great curiosity.

"Simon Peter, at the suggestion of John Zebedee and James Alphaeus," Clavos responded, assuring Simon that he had all the necessary credentials.

"Do you know where I am going?" Simon asked, looking off into the city.

"Yes. Wherever the Lord leads you."

Simon laughed. He liked this man, even if he saw the image of the beaten and bloody Jesus in his eyes.

"I am off to Africa."

"Good. I know the perfect person to help you. Do you know of Lucius of Cyrene?"

"No," Simon quickly replied, then he remembered. "Wait, I heard that name before, but I cannot put a face to it."

"Well, it matters not, for I know him and I will do my first service for you. Seemingly by the Will of the Master, he is in Antioch. He was supposed to leave for Cyrenaica with Symeon of Cyrene and Manaen, but he became ill. He will be a great guide and companion."

Simon looked blankly at Clavos, for he did not remember Symeon of Cyrene or Manaen.

"I will see him and ask him to lead us on our trip."

"Our trip?"

"Yes, I am going with you."

So Clavos led Simon to meet Lucius of Cyrene, and Africa.

*

Lucius was from one of the most privileged families in the city of Cyrene. His family for years had been merchants and traders. It was because of their wealth that Lucius and his family were frequent pilgrims to Jerusalem, and they were prominent members of the city's Cyrenian synagogue. His ancestors had converted to Judaism long before he was born. He had been told that their conversion was out of necessity because they were in the employ of Jews who came with the Phoenicians, the Greeks, and finally the Romans. As years passed, their faith in the One God became increasingly sincere and devout.

Lucius was in Jerusalem for the feast of the Passover during the time of the crucifixion of Jesus, and he had been forced to stay in Jerusalem for sixty more days on account of family business. He was among the many who heard Simon Peter speak from the landing of the Upper Room on the Jewish feast of *Shavu'ot* Pentecost. All the things that happened at that time made no difference to him; he ignored all that was taking place and continued on with his business.

Two days before his departure and a few days after he had finalized the purchase of a new *shofa*r horn and some other religious articles for the synagogue in Cyrene, he went to the Black synagogue in Jerusalem for the Sabbath. To his surprise, the usual docile services were in complete turmoil, and some of the people were debating with a young man named Stephen who openly declared that he was a member of "The Way." The hostility displayed against this young man was something Lucius had never seen before. The young man's courage captured Lucius' admiration, and soon even the words he spoke found a place in Lucius' heart. When Stephen was driven out of the synagogue, Lucius followed him to learn more of the Nazarene. It did not take him long to discover his faith in the Messiah and seek Baptism. A short time after Stephen was stoned to death, Lucius and many of the newly professed members of "The Way" left for Syria. The city of Jerusalem had become a death chamber with the Sanhedrin leading the hunt for members of the new sect. Within months they commissioned Saul of Tarsus, who left for Syria with death on his breath.

The next day Lucius, Clavos, and Simon boarded a ship. They spent the first day remembering bygone times. Simon knew that Lucius had been a part of some conversations among the Twelve, but Simon did not remember what was said.

"I am sure you remember that those times were fearful times, Simon," Lucius said with much sadness in his voice. Small shadows came across his face, and Simon knew that Lucius' memories of the past were painful. "When Stephen was killed, I and many others panicked and ran off to Damascus. We ran for safety. After we did this, we felt we had deserted the Twelve to certain death. We had much guilt."

"Yet we never thought you had deserted us. We knew that what you did was under the guidance of the Almighty." Seeing that Lucius still was not convinced, Simon continued: "It was the Lord's Will that you were to go to Damascus and that Paul should follow and thereby receive the Lord's message. We seemed to be milling around Jerusalem and Judea, and when we heard that you and others had laid hands on Paul, we knew that the Lord was indicating that we had to move on. You and your friends were following the dictates of the Almighty and received the first understanding of the universality of 'The Way.'"

Lucius rose from his chair and, looking down at Simon, asked, "Are you sure of what you say?" Seeing the look of certainty on Simon's face, he continued. "But we left out of fear. Truly, to have such a mission we should have had some courage and conviction."

"My brother, one never knows what the end of a mission is. We hear. We go. We pray and preach and leave the rest to the Almighty. As for courage, that also comes to us from the Almighty. I know several of the Twelve who went to lands far different from anything they had known. Were they afraid? Yes, but they knew that the Master was with them. As for fear, I had fears even before Jesus was arrested and crucified. I have found that fear can be a blessing that keeps us close to the Master."

"Do you ever think that what you do is wrong?"

Simon thought for a moment, then smiling, he replied, "When things go easy, I begin to have fears that I have made a mistake. When I am having difficulty, I believe that the problems I am having are obstacles put before me by the evil one, who is trying to stop me from fulfilling

God's Will. It is when things are difficult that I know I am doing the Will of the Almighty."

Lucius looked out to the distant harbor of Antioch, from which the merchant vessel *Mare Equus*, the Sea Horse, was sailing. He was glad to be going back to Cyrene and his family. Perhaps Simon's conclusion about difficulties was an indication that he was delayed so that the Will of the Master could be fulfilled.

Simon placed his hand on Lucius' shoulder.

"My brother, do you think it was by chance that you became ill in Antioch? That you were left behind by your companions? Do you not see the hand of the Master in this? You were detained so that you would lead Clavos and me to Africa. I would say that with so many of us going to Cyrene, we have much to do for the Lord."

Lucius smiled.

The ship moved swiftly through the Roman Sea and arrived at Apollonia, the seaport of Cyrene. Waiting far in the distance for the vessel's arrival was the unsettling Roman Province of *Africa*.

*

Africa first came to Rome as a result of three successful wars with Carthage, which was Rome's seafaring and trading rival in the Mediterranean. The Romans called these the Punic Wars because Carthaginians were known as *Poenici*, after the Phoenicians who founded the city. After these wars, Rome occupied the most fertile land around Carthage and called this new territory *Africa Vetus*, with its capital at the city of Utica. The rest of the Carthaginian lands were left to the Kingdom of Numidia under a client king named Massinissa. This situation pleased Rome, whose only desire was to prevent another seafaring power from challenging Rome. Even though Rome built cities and ports and gave the land a Roman look with amphitheaters, baths, and paved streets, the region was very loosely held in place.

When King Massinissa died, his kingdom was divided between his sons. The fragile bonds fell apart. One son, Jugurtha, who had been in the Roman Legions, tried to unify the divided kingdom. His enthusiasm led to the sacking of the city of Cirta, where many Roman merchants and settlers were killed, and this forced Rome into another war. Numidia's defeat added more territory to Rome, and to avoid Numidia's fate, some kings, such as King Bocchus of Mauritania, willingly became puppet kings, and this helped to stabilize the region and tighten Rome's grip. To gain better control, the Roman Senate rewarded veteran soldiers who fought in the Numidian wars with grants of land. These grants were for the most fertile lands along the coastline. The Roman colonists migrated in large numbers and joined the descendants of the Phoenicians, who were dispersed throughout the population of Africa. With these Romans came artisans, tradesmen, merchants, and their families.

Farther east along the northern coastline and close to Egypt, the Romans acquired more land. This area was called Cyrenaica. It had been a Greek colony known as *Pentapolis* because of the five cities of Cyrene, Apollonia, Barke, Tauicheira, and Euhesperides. This had been part of the empire of Alexander the Great, and after his death it became part of the Ptolemaic dynasty. When the Ptolemaic dynasty fell to Rome, Rome separated Cyrenaica from Egypt.

Rome did not take much interest in Africa because Rome did not hold this region in high regard. Its colonies were along the coast, extending inland about one hundred miles or less, and were held as military occupations. They failed to Romanize the native inhabitants of the region and remained distinct from these people. The native inhabitants, whom the Romans called *Barbarus* Berbers, were as hostile to the Romans as they were to the Phoenicians and Greeks. The Berbers, who called themselves *Amazighs*, free men, were desert tribesmen. They pretended to be obedient to the Romans, but they were actually elusive raiders who tormented the Romans. Hoping to resolve this situation, the Roman Senate created the provinces of *Mauretania Tingitana*, *Mauretania Caesariensis*, *Numidia*, and *Africa Nova* and *Africa Vetus*, but the entire region was referred to as *Africa* by the Romans. The Emperor Caesar Augustus then ordered the *Legio III Augusta* to guard the frontier of *Africa,* and they set up fortified stations in the interior called *castra*. This Legion stayed in Africa for four hundred years. The province remained the "granary of Rome," for it provided much needed foods such as grains, wine, fruits, olives, and livestock. It also supplied Rome with wild animals and dark-skinned southern Africans for the *Coliseum*.

✳

As the *Mare Equus* slid into Apollonia's harbor, Simon watched the excitement grow on Lucius' face. Lucius was so excited that his eyes moistened, and small pools of tears anxiously waited on the rim of his eyes for a blink to set them free. The ship was anchored, and as its ties were fastened to the docks, Lucius began waving his arms.

"Symeon! Symeon!" He shouted as he stood on his toes.

Simon followed his sight and saw a tall, muscular, dark man standing on the dock. When Lucius had gotten the man's attention, the black man began to wave back.

Simon looked away from the man and surveyed the harbor and the city. The dock was bustling. Everywhere people were carrying things. The full length of the dock was cluttered with warehouses, which were being filled by black men, most likely slaves. Many of the buildings were the back entrances to stores whose entrances were on the other side, the city side, of the dock, and this was where the newly arrived products were being sold. Away from the dock area, the seaport was peaceful and unruffled. On the surface, the city looked Greek, yet the feeling of Rome was everywhere. In the distance, Simon saw the white marble of the pagan temple shining brilliantly against the azure sky. For a moment he grew resentful, for he silently wished that God could have such a place of worship and that Christians could be that open with their faith. Farther in, he saw the theatre, and from the flags and noise coming from that direction Simon concluded that some gladiatorial event was taking place. He whispered a prayer for mercy if indeed this was the case. The palm trees swayed in a breeze, but the breeze did not cool the harbor or remove the odors associated with the dock. In the distance he saw green pastures and an occasional rocky hill that looked primitive and did not fit into the grandeur of the city.

"Come," Lucius ordered with excitement. "We still have a long journey before us."

"Are we not staying in Cyrene?"

"Of course, but this is Apollonia, the seaport. Cyrene is a day's journey inland."

"And our things?" Clavos asked.

"They will be taken ashore, Clavos." Then, seeing the concerned look on Simon's face, Lucius said with a small, joyous chuckle in his voice, "Relax, Simon, this is Africa. There is not much to worry about here."

They disembarked and were greeted by the tall black man. The moment Simon saw the man close up, he believed he knew him. He quickly raced through his mind trying to remember who this man was, but before he could make any identification, the man spoke.

"It is good to see you again, Simon," the man called Symeon said. Detecting Simon's confusion, he continued with a wide smile that flashed his ivory white teeth. "No need to feel uncomfortable, Simon, it is not necessary to remember me."

Simon felt embarrassed. He did not like the feeling of being known by someone he could not remember.

Symeon placed his big hand on Simon's shoulder and directed him through the crowd.

"Come, Simon, stop hiding in the Roman world and let me show you Africa," Symeon said, smiling.

They left the docks and traveled quickly through the city. They arrived at a *villa* in the western part of Apollonia. By afternoon, they were refreshed and had been invited into the *atrium* for some wine, bread, figs, and fruits.

"Later tonight, I have a surprise for you, dear brother Simon," the tall African said. "But for now, tell me, how are things in Judea? How are Simon Peter, James, John, and all the Others? And Lady Mary, how is she?"

He knows us all!

"They are all well. Many are in other lands spreading the knowledge of Jesus," Simon answered.

Who is this African? Why can I not remember him?

The African stopped chewing his food and looked at Simon long and hard, then as he resumed his chewing, he asked, "Simon, you look so uneasy. Is something wrong?"

Simon, with no hesitation, replied, "I am sorry, brother, but I cannot recall who you are and I am at a disadvantage. I must know who you are, or your hospitality will be wasted."

"Simon…." Clavos said, then stopped.

Simon looked at Clavos, who was now looking at their host, so Simon turned his attention to the African and found the man with his head lowered. After a few sensitive and warming moments, the African raised his head, and Simon saw tears at the edges of his eyes.

"That Passover in Jerusalem…."

A warm, large tear rolled down the African's face.

"…the day that Jesus died…."

The tears washed his face. They polished the African's dark skin, which now looked like a precious, highly polished black stone.

"…the arm of the Roman pulled me from the mob…."

The African had no need to continue, for Simon was on his feet. He rushed across the room and embraced the man whom history knew as Simon of Cyrene, father of Rufus and Alexander, the bearer of the cross of Jesus. The man's tears dampened the garment covering Simon's shoulder.

Oh Master, You have honored me in putting me this close to Your cross… help me to bear it…help my friend to bear it more easily, for he has been carrying it longer than anyone.

That night at dusk, they were taken by cart to a cave in the nearby hills. Assembled there was a large crowd of followers. When he entered the torch-brightened cave, the assembly stood in reverent awe. They were in the presences of someone who had walked, talked, eaten, and rested with Jesus. Being near Simon was like being near the Master. With great humility, Simon spoke of the love and the "blessings" Jesus gave on the mount. Simon was surprised by the gathering and was told that many were Gentiles. Simon immediately felt the universality of the words of Jesus and made a note that he would write to Simon Peter about the numbers of non-Jews who had come to know Jesus. He celebrated the Meal with them, and together they prayed. When it grew late, they silently began to slip away into the night. Simon agreed with the decision in Jerusalem to accept Gentiles with no restriction. The Gentiles had to be included in the salvation of Jesus. He would give thanks in prayer that night. On the trip back to their lodgings, Simon was told of the story of an old *magus* named Balthazar who told the Cyrenians of Jesus, and he heard that Symeon also had been spreading the Gospel among the Jews and Gentiles.

The next day they rose early and traveled by cart through the *Viridis Mons* Green Mountains. These verdant mountains seemed endless and were breathtaking, for they were heavily forested with lush valleys and fertile uplands. Later that day, when they arrived in Cyrene, they were met by a Judean whom Simon knew but could not remember. The Judean who met them was very alarmed, and he immediately announced that after they left Apollonia, the Romans began to arrest and detain known Christians.

"It seems that just hours before your arrival in Cyrene, a Roman *nuntius* messenger from Apollonia arrived and informed the *Urbs Consul* city magistrate that a conspirator of a revolt was coming to Cyrene. This *nuntius* messenger reported that one of the chief leaders of the Christians was coming to incite rebellion within the Jewish community. The gates of the city were immediately secured, and the Romans were stopping everyone who resembled a Judean. Many were arrested and held for interrogation. You got here just before the gates were secured. I am happy that the Lord heard our prayers and gave you safety," the Judean said as he embraced everyone, greeting them by their first name.

"It is unsafe here," Symeon announced. "We must leave immediately."

"But to leave now would be unwise," the Judean said. "Wait for dawn—guards are sleepy then, and we will have a better chance of escape. I obtained some old clothing in the street market and some henna and charcoal. One of our brothers gave us three camels that we can use for our journey. I also gathered provisions that should be sufficient." He turned to Simon the Zealot and, smiling warmly, continued, "This will not be luxurious, as in Judea, but good enough for Africa."

"The Lord bless you," Symeon said. "Come, let us hurry, for we have much to do before our departure."

The two men hurried about the room. Clavos was asked to help them, but Simon was ordered to relax and pray, which he could not do because he was wondering about the identity of this Judean.

Finally, the Judean came to him and began to paint his face and hands.

"We will make you look African," he said as he began applying a thick layer of dye to Simon's face.

"And you, brother, what is your name?"

The Judean applied several strokes of the dye to Simon's face and turned away to dampen the cloth with more dye. As he returned he said mildly, "In Antioch I was called by the Latin name Collactaneus. Much later, after I came to the Lord, I was called by the Greek name Syntrophos."

He stopped applying the dye and looked deep into Simon's eyes.

"You still do not know me, Simon?"

"I think I know you. I have seen you before in Judea, but not in Antioch."

"Those two names I gave you were names I used to cover up my true identity. Perhaps if I mention Joanna, the wife of Chuza, I might refresh your memory."

Simon thought hard. He remembered Joanna as a follower in the early days, and she had attended Lady Mary. Eventually, her husband became a Christian, and if memory served him right, Chuza had been the steward for Herod.

Again the Judean turned away to dampen the cloth with more dye.

"In Judea, I was named Manaen."

Simon grabbed Manaen's hand.

"You are the foster brother of Herod Antipas!" Simon exclaimed.

"Yes, I am." Manaen stood erect, expecting to be discharged, for perhaps the Zealot blood was not completely out of this Apostle.

"I saw you several times in Herod's presence. How did you come to be a Christian?"

"Through Joanna and her friend Suzanna. They often spoke of Jesus, so one day I went to see Him and heard Him speak the Blessings on the Mount. That day I ceased being anything insignificant and became someone great. Of course, I had to hide my beliefs, and when Jesus died, I waited with the others."

"The others?" Simon asked as he released his grip on Manaen's arm.

"Yes: Cornelius, Longinus, Stephaton, Abendadar, Dorimius, Nescius, and many others who were on the mount, Clavos and Symeon among them. We waited for the Twelve to come and instruct us. Finally, Simon Peter came to Cornelius' *villa*; we were all there, and we were all purified. We placed ourselves in the service of the Lord, and now we serve Him through you, the Apostles."

Manaen returned to applying dye to Simon's face.

"I was in Antioch when Paul and Barnabas came. We—Symeon, Lucius, and I—laid hands on Paul and ordered him in the name of Jesus to take his first journey. We did this with no authority from Simon Peter or any of the Twelve, but from the Holy Spirit, Who came to us and instructed us to do what we did. I know many thought us presumptuous and incorrect, but we did this not of our own accord."

"If Simon Peter said nothing to you, he must have known that what you did was from the Spirit of the Lord."

Simon suddenly remembered something, so he looked at Manaen carefully and said, "There is a large price on your head."

"It matters little, for Antipas has received an order of perpetual exile."

Thank God for His divine justice, Simon thought.

Early the next morning, while it was still dark, the five men dressed and prepared to secretly leave Cyrene. What they did not count on was Simon's lack of experience with camels. Never having ridden a camel, Simon looked awkward and frightened, so Symeon, disguised as a slave, led Simon's camel through the streets of Cyrene and out the city's southern gate. The group was not challenged, for the guards were too tired. Once outside the city, with the tension relieved, they traveled again through the *Viridis Mons* Green Mountains. After a day's travel, they arrived at the beginning of what the Romans called the *Crocus Mare* Saffron Sea.

Symeon slowly forced the camel carrying Simon to the sand, and Simon gladly jumped off. Together the small party of men silently stood looking into the Saffron Sea, the name the Romans gave to the great desert. They looked intently into the wide openness before them, each having his own ideas and trepidations. Simon was in awe of its enormity. The moment Simon's foot touched the sand, he felt a strong feeling of belonging come over him. It was unlike anything he had experienced before. This desert was not like the deserts of Judea; those deserts were crass and often hilly, with too many secret places, but this desert was empty—it was open and seemed to hold the fullness of the Almighty in it. He gazed into the desert, searching for his God, but like all journeymen, he knew he would have to venture out, away from security, to find his God. He would have to go into the desert. In that moment, the endless sky and the enormous desert made Simon know how finite he was. With tears in his eyes and with his hands opened in prayer, he began to chant a psalm, and soon the others joined him.

> *The earth is the Lord's and the fullness thereof,*
> *the world and they who dwell therein.*
> *For He has founded it upon the seas*
> *and has made it firm upon the floods...*

When they had finished the psalm, they fell to silence. Finally, Symeon said lightly, "A Roman once said this place was 'like a leopard's skin, spotted with inhabited places that are surrounded by waterless and desolate land.'"

"Are there such inhabited places?" Simon inquired without moving his eyes from the greatness before him.

"Yes. The Egyptians call them *oases*."

"Will we see such places? These *oases*?" Simon asked.

"Yes. Why?"

"When we reach one, I would like you and the others to stay there while I go into the desert. Alone."

Symeon looked at the Apostle and said, "If one is to go alone voluntarily into the desert, one must have a great feeling of God. This place is open and unprotected, without borders, and it leaves a soul that way."

The others encircled Simon, for his request was dangerous in their eyes.

"The desert is a place of death, Simon," Lucius added. His voice was heavy with concern. "It dies to itself under the plague of the sun. If you go, we will go with you."

"Yes, Simon, please reconsider your request," Manaen stated. "We know this place. It is not a homeland. It is only a home to emptiness. It is a place that constantly says to all who see it, 'Move on.'"

Simon remained silent, then he turned to look at Manaen, Symeon, and Lucius.

"My brothers, look out there. Do you see that petrified tree in the distance? See those stiff branches? They look like disfigured fingers reaching up into the endless blue sky, hoping to grasp a bit of heaven. That tree reminds me of myself, and I must grasp a bit of heaven." He returned his attention to the desert. "There is something out there that is calling me. I believe that I must learn something hidden in those grains of sand."

The men remained silently by him.

"Did not the Lord go into the desert?" Clavos asked, and all turned to him. "And did He not come out and preach to all? And are we not to imitate Him? I think Simon is being called to do the same."

The silence between the five men was only matched by the silence of the land around them. Then, suddenly, a dry wind slipped across the open space, and it made the sand swirl around them. As quick as it came, it was gone.

"Come, let us go," Symeon shouted above another wind. "Let us go together, and when the time is right, Simon will find his solitude."

So they hurriedly mounted the camels and began their journey into the silence of the desert. For two hot, dry days, they traveled. The more the desert swallowed them, the more Simon believed he was to find something in this barren place. Each hour the desert grew bigger, pulling Simon deeper inside its soul. He watched as the desert was carved and chiseled, changed and re-created by the relentless winds that whipped and shifted the sand. The sands moved and traveled at great speed. They grouped into mounds and then slipped into smaller mounds, until the massive heaps of sand formed again. Mountains and valleys of sand grew and died. Each minute, new worlds and images were made and re-made and un-made.

Simon knew this was a land where things went away, and it was a land that could sculpt a person into a new being.

Like God working in the transformation of a soul...never would it be the same...always would it change and become something according to the Will of God. The desert and the soul are always sculpted by the wind—the breath of God.

Finally they came to an *oasis*, and they kept their promise. They gave Simon a camel, water, instructions, and some provisions, and he went into the desert.

The first day, he suffered greatly from the oppressive sun, which attacked everyone who dared to invade this vast domain of death. The sun dried every fiber of his being. Soon, his very thoughts were dried up, and he was living without thought, unable to think. He lived on the sole desire to find some form of relief. The only thing he felt and knew was the silence of the desert and the low whisper of the shifting sands. They held him in place and time. The sound was almost capable of putting him to sleep. In the heat, he had the desire to remove some of his robes, but the first instruction the others gave him was to resist that urge. Occasionally, he saw a patch of weeds and pitied them, yet he admired their defiance.

The first night he found himself covered under a blanket of stars. The dark sky was as massive as the desert. It was a night of coldness, and this coldness matched the death of the land around him. He called out to *Elohim* in the night, when the death chill of the desert slipped under his clothing and into his flesh. In this chill, unlike the chill of any night, he sought warmth in the presence of *Adonai*. From the night he heard the voice of Jesus say to him, "Simon, this is the forgotten place of your being. You have no place to hide here, so you must find yourself and come to know Me as you knew Me but denied Me."

Simon began to weep.

In a loud voice that filled the vast emptiness of that cold night, he shouted, "Master, when did I deny You?"

All he heard was silence and the sounds of his own weeping. He ached for an answer, for a sound of another life, anything to replace the silence and chill of this place.

I had to be insane to come to this place, for the Almighty is alive. He would never dwell in a place as dead as this place.

This was his last thought of the day.

The next day, the sun burned down with blazing heat. When the sun reached its summit, his head ached from the heat and his eyes burned from the reflection of the sun off the sands. Looking ahead, he could see the warmth of the sand rising from the desert in waves and waves of heat. He felt he could not go on. His bare skin was tight and stinging. His back hurt from the constant to-and-fro motion of the camel. The silence was oppressive. It was crushing him, yet it invited him to stop and rest. It urged him to sleep and forget the journey. He hungered for the sound of another voice or any sound of humanity. He needed rest, shade, a bit of comfort. He needed water. He knew he had to ration his water, but his resolve was not as strong as it was the previous day. He continued his journey, longing for shade. Several times he saw a shadow fall over the top of a sand dune and he tried to reach the coolness, but the desert's breath moved it away, made it fade and shift away. He blinked his eyes several times in disbelief, and then with certainty he saw a group of rocks come up out of the sand before him. He urged his camel on, and the animal began a gallop across the flat sand. He was almost certain that what he was seeing was an illusion or some trick of the desert. Finally he arrived, and he tied his camel under the partial shade of one of the boulders. He hurriedly climbed the rocky island and faded into the shade amidst the great rocks. He fell to the ground and felt a cool piece of rock touch his face, and he exhaled a sigh of relief. He quickly relaxed.

He felt a wet cloth on his lips, then on his face, and he slowly opened his eyes. He jumped to his feet and, losing his balance, fell back against another rock, hurting his elbow.

"Do not be frightened, Simon, it is I," a man said to him in Aramaic.

Simon blinked his eyes rapidly and brushed his eyes with his hands. He recognized the man, and his reaction was to pull back and farther away. He could not believe that the man was who he thought he was.

"Simon," the man said again with a wide smile on his lips and a tenderness to his voice that made Simon feel utterly relaxed.

"It is I, Barabbas."

Simon looked hard. This is who he thought the man was, but this Barabbas had lost his look of defiance and had no dark shadows on his face. His eyes were gentle and kindly. This Barabbas had a white beard and hair. He still looked strong, but in a different way; his strength was not in his muscles but from deep inside his chest. This man smiled with care and joy. This Barabbas was not a criminal.

"I knew you were coming. I have been waiting for you."

"How did you know I was coming? Who told you?"

"It matters not," Barabbas said, extending his hand to Simon. "I just knew."

Simon firmly grasped the extended hand and was lifted to his feet.

"Come! Some water, food, rest, and talk," Barabbas said as he led him farther into the maze of the boulders and into a small, cool cave.

Soon Simon was eating and giving thanks to the Almighty for the gift named Barabbas.

"How did you get here?" Simon inquired as he eagerly chewed the meat set before him.

"That day, the day that Jesus took my place, I followed the march to Golgotha. When he promised my companion Dismas life everlasting, I knew that I had been freed by God. For two days I looked for someone who could tell me more about Jesus, but I found no one. I did get word that the Romans were looking for me, so I disguised myself and left Jerusalem. I went out into the desert, the wilderness of Judea, knowing I had to go there. I had to find something or come to know something. Somehow I knew that the wilderness would cleanse me and make my soul known to me. I do not know how much time I spent there, but when I left, my hair was white. I slipped away into Sinai and then into Egypt, and finally I came to Cyrene. By the Will of Jesus, I met Symeon and an old *magus* called Balthazar. Symeon told me of his experience of carrying the cross for Jesus and how that cross grew heavier with each step. Balthazar told me of how he journeyed to Nazareth to find a king and found a Child called Jesus. When Balthazar left Nazareth, he knew he had not only found a King but a Living God. He and Symeon instructed me and purified me. I preached with them for a while but then became a danger to them, for I was still a wanted man. So I came to live in the desert, seeking to be cleansed and then to die." Barabbas smiled widely. "Why do you look so surprised? Is there a better place to die? Is not this the place to go and leave all and then come back to life anew? Is not this the place to die to self and emerge as a new man?"

Simon did not answer him. He still was in that place where reality seemed too ridiculous to be real. Finding Barabbas in Africa in the desert was the work of the Lord. He knew there was more to what was taking place, but he did not care—he was too happy to be away from the sand and the sun.

"Simon, you have not yet reached your cleansing, but it will come, my friend, it will come. For now, let us eat and drink, then you must speak to me of Jesus, and then we will sleep."

They talked as the night became chilled, then cold, then icy, but they were safe in the warmth of Jesus.

The next morning, Simon saw the ashes of a fire near his sleeping place, and he heard the call of his camel. He rose slowly and looked around. No one was there—seemingly no one had been there at all. He felt hurried by a desire to find something waiting for him. He had no time to thank his host or to find the time to search for him. He had to leave quickly. He frantically gathered his things, carried them to the camel, loaded his belongings, and mounted the beast. The camel stood up, and they began their trek through the early desert. Simon decided not to look back, not to see if what he had experienced was a dream or something supernatural. It did not matter. He now was on a quest to cleanse himself.

That is why I came to this forsaken place: To find the Almighty and have Him change what was wrong in His eyes.

For many hot and dry hours, the camel sauntered with a repetitive and uninterested stride. The bobbing motion of the camel rocked Simon into a lethargic state. The heat from the sun was so heavy that Simon could feel an anger coming up from the sand in response to the heat. Simon began to pray. His mind and prayers began jumping from psalm to psalm, catching a sentence, a thought, here and there. From his parched lips he shouted aloud knowing that no one, no thing, would hear him but God.

Remember Thy word to Thy servant, by which Thou has given me hope…
O Lord, how many are my adversaries, many rise up against me…
Yahweh turned rivers into a desert,
and springs of water into parched ground…

On and on he recited one-line prayers, unable to concentrate on anything except the oppressive, hot, sandy day. Suddenly, in the distance he saw a column of sand twirling and swaying casually in the bareness of the desert. It moved over the sand toward him like a large, rolling, angry whirlpool. It was coming to him quickly and seemed to give a warning of destruction. He realized that this was a sand storm. He had been told that they came quick and furious. He stopped his camel and, remembering his instructions, quickly dismounted and forced the animal to sit on the sand. He firmly held the reins in his hands, and by the time he covered himself and lay next to the beast, the storm was all around him. The winds gathered the stinging sands. The very earth was pelting and attacking him. He felt the anger of the desert and its hatred for intruders. This was a place for no man, no one, just silence, heat, and death. The sand continued to pelt him, and he wondered if his camel was surviving. Just as his worries for his camel intensified, he became conscious of the sound of the wind that hissed around him, then he heard it: "Sssssssimon. Sssssssimon."

He ignored the sound, but it repeated again and again. Out of curiosity and against all that he had been told, he found a small opening in his hood and peeked through it. He saw a man standing by him. Simon looked hard, but he could not see who the man was because of the light that surrounded him. He became aware that the sand was swirling around the man and himself. They were in a funnel, and the wind, though moving, was not disturbing them. He wanted to stand but could not. The earth seemed to have embraced him, needing to keep him safe, far and away from all that was happening.

"Come out, Simon, it is time to come out."

He could not move—the need to remain in hiding was paralyzing.

"Lord, help…help me."

"I hear your plea. I would have heard your plea if you had asked it of Me. Come, Simon Qun'anaya bar Achyon. Come."

Simon stood up free of bindings, free of bounds.

"I forgive you for your denials of Me."

"Lord, I never denied you!" Simon stated with full certainty.

"Each time you heard something in My prayers and did not tell the Others, you denied Me. You had been blessed with those opportunities, blessed more than the rest, but you did nothing with this knowledge of Me. Your silence made you a mute among the Twelve. Your fears kept you far and away. As the Others debated among themselves, you debated with yourself. Even now you are afraid that association with the Others could bring down upon them the cold hand of Rome. I chose you, a Zealot, not for what you believed but for what you will become, and for what you held inside you. You were to be a Zealot for Me."

"I will be this for You, for You are my Lord and my Master."

The whirlpool continued around them, and a question bewildered him: *Why is not the sand pelting me or bothering me?*

As soon as he asked this question, the sound of the wind increased and filled the funnel, and Simon could feel the wind playing havoc with his hair, beard, and clothing. He staggered under the force of the wind.

"Tonight, Simon, find your place in the desert, and when you do, cherish your smallness. After this, you will be united with your companions and you will never hide again."

The sound of the wind stopped. The whirlpool was gone, and Simon found himself standing alone in the wide open, barren desert.

His camel bellowed, so he turned his attention to the beast and found it standing upright and free of any sand. Suddenly, he felt the first chill of the desert night, and he knew his traveling for that day was over. He quickly prepared for the long, cold, desert night. The azure sky slipped into dark blue, and the blue-gray world of the desert night came to life. The desert rolled endlessly before Simon. He sat leaning against his camel and began reciting psalms. As he prayed, he heard the sound of Jesus' voice intermingled with his, then he heard the voices of the Apostles, then many voices speaking in languages he could not understand. Mystified, he looked out over the sands and wondered where the desert ended, for it seemed to go on forever.

From nowhere came a thought: *This is like the Church! With many tiny bodies moving and going to different places, pushed by the wind, the breath of God, preaching and making a difference and changing the world. It will be endless. Eternal. Enormous.*

With a smile, he concluded that he was one grain of sand, one voice, only one of many.

He stood and raised his face to the sky and saw the millions of twinkling lights, acknowledging him and his finite life. Another thought came to him: *These are the many who have gone before the Master and who prepared the way for Him, for the Twelve, and all those who will follow the words of Jesus.*

From high above he heard, "When you walked with Me, you wanted to remain far and away—always an unknown. Is this still your wish?"

"Yes, Master. I want to be remembered and known only by You."

"So it will be. You will remain a mystery to all, the least-known among your brethren. I alone will know you, and when your time comes, I alone will remember you. You will not be a part of anything, but only a part of Me."

Simon fell to his knees, overwhelmed and in awe of all that he had heard and understood. Abruptly he began to chant in Aramaic the prayer of the Lord:

Aboon dabashmaya
nethkadash shamak
tetha malkoothak
newe tzevyanka
aykan dabashmaya

✻

"It has been three days since he left," Lucius said with worry shadowing his face.

"I know," Manaen concurred. "I hope he is well."

"The Master will protect him," Symeon added as he looked out into the desert. Standing far in front of Symeon was Clavos, who had begun to search the horizon every day for Simon.

Symeon returned to tending to his camel. Unlike the others, he feared for Simon not on account of the desert itself but because there were Roman patrols who roamed the area.

"Look!" Clavos shouted as he pointed out into the emptiness. "Look! There!"

The three men ran to Clavos.

"I see nothing," Manaen shouted.

"Look. There. I see something."

"I see it," Lucius said with excitement in his voice.

"I do not see anything," Manaen shouted again with frustration in his voice.

Symeon, shading his eyes with an open hand, stated, "Something is there, but is it Simon?"

The four men stood watching as the speck became a dot, then a blur, then a man on a camel, and finally Simon was before them.

His face was burned brown.

His lips were parched and split.

His hands were blistered and cut.

His hair and beard were white as the clouds.

✳

For many years Simon labored in Africa. He preached to Jews and Gentiles and "barbarians," enlightening many in the Way of Jesus. Over the years, he traveled many times from Alexandria in Egypt to Cyrene in Cyrenaica, Cirta in Numidia, Carthage in Africa, and the far western city of Tinges in Mauritania. He even converted many in southern Hispania.

He and his companions frequently warmed prison cells and bared their backs to the whip, and they were well acquainted with the torments of bodily pain, exhaustion, and frustration. Simon watched Symeon suffer crucifixion for preaching the Lord to a patrol of Roman soldiers in the desert, and he prayed as Manaen was beheaded by the "barbarians" for preaching against their god *Mastiman.*

After more than thirty years of preaching, Simon received a letter from Jude Thaddeus asking him to join him in Persia. Simon instantly began to pack his belongings. Clavos insisted on going with him. Simon blessed Lucius and made him the head of the followers in Africa, and he left for Persia to join Jude Thaddeus.

✳

Clavos awoke, refreshed and at peace for his dream finally reached completion. He found Simon sitting on his sleeping mat and staring out into the morning light. He knew that Simon had not slept, and he hoped this was not because of his recurring dream. Since Simon had not slept, their final day of travel would be short and they would camp earlier than normal.

They had traveled over deserts, mountains, plains, and grasslands. They had crossed shallow waters, wide streams, raging rivers, and stormy seas to arrive at the appointed place in Persia.

They were now one day away from meeting Jude Thaddeus and his companion Dorimius.

EPILOGUE

John wrote frantically, not wanting to forget any part of what he had dreamed in the night. What he was writing he had not witnessed, but it had been told to him by his brother Disciple Simon the Zealot many years before. He had forgotten about it and remembered it only after dreaming it. His *stylus* moved swiftly across the *papyrus* as he heard Simon's words in his mind. When he finished, he fell back in his chair, his hand warm from the strain of its ordeal.

Unexpectedly, a picture of the Zealot came into his mind, and he was bewildered as to why he seldom thought of this Disciple.

It is as if he has been erased from my mind intentionally, John thought as he moved away from his desk and walked across the room to get a cup of water.

The last I heard, he was in Africa, or was it Persia? Still, Simon is elusive to me.

He became more perplexed as to why he thought of Simon so infrequently. He walked out into the garden behind his house and took a deep breath. He closed his eyes to enjoy the fresh air, and there was Simon, telling him the story of the Samaritan woman at the well with Jesus. He watched Simon's face become animated with his retelling of the incident, and John smiled warmly. Finally, he opened his eyes, turned, and walked into the house, and as he walked he wondered how Simon had known of this event.

Chapter Nine

Judah Thaddeus Lebbaeus, Bar Cleophas

Prologue

John drank the cool water from the wooden bowl on the table near his desk. It was a hot day, and he was finding the heat more uncomfortable than usual. With the bowl of water still in his hand, he rose from his chair and walked to the door at the back of the house and out into the small garden. There was no relief, not even a small breeze. His need for relief disappeared as the silence embraced him in peacefulness. The silence pleased him, for it replaced the noise and clamor of the busy city of Ephesus. He found it difficult to think or pray because of all the activities and distractions of city life. Between the city noise and his preaching, his writing had suffered. The more he preached, the more he was sought. This was expected, for he was a disciple of Jesus and was fulfilling the Will of the Spirit. Now, because of his preaching, he was constantly being sought by the authorities, and this forced him to move from house to house to avoid arrest. After each move, he had to wait for his scrolls to arrive.

When a "dear lady" suggested that he move from Ephesus, he thought it a good idea. He settled in a *villa* owned by the "dear lady," a wealthy woman whom John had baptized along with her daughters and household; after his sister Naomi went to the Lord, the "dear lady" befriended him. Before dying, Naomi told the "dear lady" that John was writing an account of Jesus' time on earth. The "dear lady" continued to encourage John to write his account because she possessed a copy of Mark's writings and felt that much was lacking. John, still not completely committed to this undertaking, told the "dear lady" that Jesus had not commanded anyone to write of His life, but the woman would hear none of this: "What you say is true, John, but someone has already done this, and I hear that two others have written also, but yours will be the best of the four, for yours will be of love."

John silently disagreed because he did not think he was capable of writing anything worthwhile. He could not write a beginning, let alone tell all there was to tell about Jesus. Besides, he had read Mark's account and found it more worthy than had the "dear lady." John was so deeply moved by parts of Mark's writings that he had to control his tears. He had read Luke's writings and he knew of Matthew's account because he had read parts of it years ago. He could see that Luke had added more information to Mark's writings, as did Matthew. The last time he received a letter from Matthew, he was in the southern part of Egypt and was moving farther south. John was certain that he would never read the end of Matthew's writings.

The heat of the day returned to bother him, so he sat on a small stool in the shade under a fig tree near the house and took another sip of water. He heard the sounds of some birds in the distance and relaxed, enjoying the peacefulness around him. He closed his eyes to further his enjoyment. After a few empty moments, his mind was filled with the latest dilemma that had been troubling him. For the past few days, he had been contemplating more action between the Disciples. He was bothered by Luke's account, which made Paul seem to be the only Disciple. He should write of the Twelve, John concluded, and just as quickly he became uncomfortable. This would make the Twelve become important. *We are not. We followed the command of Jesus and gave our lives in following this command, and besides, there is still so much more to write of Jesus.* Again he decided that his doubt was a sign that he was to write only of Jesus. He was to write the story of Jesus and nothing else. Jesus alone was the example to be followed. He was certain that what Luke did was acceptable; it gave some history of the days that followed that great day of courage.

It is better to leave us to silence, he thought. *In fact, many of us rarely spoke. The silent ones.*

The faces of the silent ones raced through his mind.

If I were to write of the Twelve, what would I do with these silent ones? Would that not make them seem utterly unimportant?

Then, suddenly, he stopped thinking and his face wrinkled for a moment.

That quickly, he saw the young face of Jude before him, and he smiled.

Jude, a silent one, spoke up once. I remember.

"At our last supper," he said aloud. He was pleased that he remembered so quickly.

I suppose I am getting better at remembering things about Jesus.

He walked to his desk, searched for a *stylus*, and quickly began to write. After writing several lines, he stopped and looked out the window into the night sky.

He wondered: *Why, after all his silence, would Jude Thaddeus ask Jesus such a question?*

JUDAH THADDEUS LEBBAEUS, BAR CLEOPHAS

During Jude's mission in Parthia, he converted many Jews. These were the Jews from the Babylonian Exile who chose to remain in Babylon rather than return to Jerusalem after the repatriation. Their conversions to "The Way" were easy because, like so many in the Diaspora who were far from the strong hand of Jerusalem, they had become less rigid and prideful in their thinking. They still celebrated all the Jewish Holy Days and followed Jewish practices like monogamy, circumcision, and some dietary laws. Some practices had been adjusted according to local custom, and these concessions eventually led to the Jews being accepted by the locals. Once accepted, they prospered and led successful lives. Soon, these Jews traveled away from Babylon and into the surrounding territories and countries with the Parthian expansion. Consequently, Jude found Jews throughout the land of the Parthians. He initially directed his energies to the Parthians, but when he did he immediately became frustrated. In sheer desperation, he wrote to Simon for help, and Simon began the journey to Parthia.

Jude and his companion Dorimius, who had been with him for many years, waited for the arrival of Simon and his companion Clavos.

Jude sat mesmerized by the mountains through which he and his companion had journeyed. Yesterday, the mountains didn't seem so massive. They were just painstakingly endless. It had taken them many months to journey over them because they traveled at the base of the mountains where the land was wide, but also where the landscape was thick with trees and bushes. They never ventured higher. To go higher would have been a perilous invasion of the mountain's privacy.

Now that the mountains were part of yesterday and other yesterdays, he wondered how he had not noticed their massiveness. They seemed to fold into and onto each other; where one mountain ended the other picked up, leaving little space for anything but themselves. They were a jagged wall that cut off one world from another. The blend of gray, brown, and black shades left Jude longing for the sight of the beautiful green pastures on the other side of them. The sharp, crude, chiseled slopes made him long for the open, flat deserts of simple splendor that existed behind them.

Jude had once heard that mountains were the earth's prayers struggling to get the Almighty's attention. They had pushed their way up out of the belly of the earth and charged violently into the sky, believing they could reach heaven. The prayers were urgent, and that was why their eruption from the earth was so uneven and seemingly unprepared. Their jagged, hard form was a sign of their selfish desire to reach great heights and to be seen by the Almighty. He was sympathetic toward the mountains, for he knew and understood urgent prayer. Finding these thoughts pleasing, he accepted them. His eyes slowly scaled the side of the tallest mountain. Against the pure, immense, azure sky, the mountain fell to silence. Near the crest of the tallest mountain was a crown of thin, slow-moving clouds that glided along the side of the mountain. The clouds crept with reverence into the many caverns, caves, and gullies, seeping into the secrets of life in those dark places. Occasionally, in defiance, a slab of indifferent rock pierced the clouds. The crest of the mountain was capped with gleaming white snow; small slabs of rock rebelliously cut into the snow, declaring their independence. Eventually, the snow covered the stubbornness of the mountain and the crest was smothered by the pure-white snow that froze the mountain in place, stopping its growth and confining it to chilled repose. He was saddened that the mountain had not achieved its quest to go higher into the heavens. The mountain had pushed high, and *El Hashamayim*, God of the heavens, seeing it had neared close to heaven, met it and stopped it.

As a boy, while studying in the synagogue, he remembered wanting to know what the Almighty was like. He envisioned the massiveness of a mountain, and he felt humble and finite, the way one should feel in the presence of *Adonai*. He remembered his desire to climb a mountain—to draw near to heaven and, upon returning, to tell everyone that he had kissed the feet of *El Hashamayim*. But he knew that he was only a boy, and he had to wait for his time to be called to the mountain.

Without warning, he was inspired and thought: *This mountain is like Jesus. He is the answer to the prayers of mankind that charged and cried to heaven for a Messiah. He came and met our prayers. He lived as part of the earth, part of the heavens. He came so that no one had to climb the mountain. He is with us. He is Immanu-El.*

Immediately he went into prayer with psalms of thanksgiving. He closed his eyes and saw the face of Jesus. He was grateful for the gift of seeing and remembering Jesus, but he never spoke of this gift for fear of inspiring envy in those who were not so blessed. He was sure that others who had been with Jesus were as blessed as he, but still he was humbled. His eyes filled with tears of gratitude and happiness, for God had been good to him.

He was so deep in prayer that the Apostle did not hear Dorimius, his companion, come from his tent and greet the morning with a loud yawn. When Dorimius recognized that Jude was in prayer, he quickly withdrew and sat nearby, watching the Apostle in silence. He knew he should also be offering his morning prayers, but for him it was always difficult to pray in the morning. He was not a morning person; the Lord knew this, for He never placed a feeling of guilt within him. Eventually, Jude lowered his head and dropped his arms to his side, and Dorimius knew that the Apostle had completed his praying.

"Come, Jude Thaddeus. Let us eat breakfast. I have some wild berries, pistachios, almonds, and pears that I gathered yesterday from the trees and bushes at the bottom of the mountain."

Jude lingered a moment looking at the mountain, then he smiled with great satisfaction and turned to join his friend to break his fast.

"I should have joined you in prayer, but I knew you were in the presence of Jesus," Dorimius said as he opened the cloth bag that contained the treasure of gathered foods.

"I am sorry, I should have waited for you so that we could pray together, but I became so overwhelmed by the mountains and their majesty that I was moved into prayer."

"Do not trouble yourself. I will pray later, and if you wish, you can join me," Dorimius said quickly, knowing that he would not pray until nightfall.

"I will," Jude replied, appreciating his friend's thoughtfulness.

"It is natural for you to feel the presence of God in a mountain, for these mountains are mighty and strong. For years they have protected Rome from those Parthian barbarians." He divided the fruit and berries between them. "What is the word you Jews use to call God mighty?"

Jude raised his eyes in surprise. Dorimius never ceased to surprise him with his knowledge of the Jewish ways.

"*El Shaddai*. It means the Mighty and Powerful One. It is also understood to mean the Almighty."

"So it is natural for you to feel the presence of God in the mountains," Dorimius said as he continued to display the food he had gathered.

Jude sat down on the blanket and looked at the small bowl before him. He closed his eyes and offered a prayer of thanksgiving, and Dorimius uttered, "Amen."

Slowly the two began to eat.

"If my thinking is correct, we should be meeting Simon and Clavos within a day," Dorimius said between bites of food.

"God willing," Jude thought aloud as he casually reached for a wild berry. "It would be good to see them both again. It has been a long time."

They returned to their breakfast and silence.

"Do you miss seeing the others?" Dorimius asked with a mouthful of berries.

"No, not really, and that is because they are always in my heart. Sometimes I can close my eyes and see them as they were years ago."

"I know you were not of the same mind when first you were called. How did you develop such closeness?"

"With time, and Jesus. You see, when Jesus threw us together, we were all of different minds. Even those of us who were blood relatives were not of the same mind. After the excitement and pride of being called diminished, a great deal of discomfort and silence developed. We were like the crowds that followed Him. Let me give you an idea of what I mean. One day, I saw members of the Pharisees, Sadducees, Romans, Zealots, Publicans, Herodians, and Samaritans among the crowd. There were rich and poor, sick and healthy, young and old, fishermen, shepherds, traders, and beggars. There were the needy, the curious, the gossipers, those wanting to become great, the humble, and the undesirable. We were as different in our thoughts about Jesus as the people in the crowds were. We had our likes and dislikes among each other—just as Levi finds favor with you and the Zealot does not. What held us together was the Will of Jesus and our own ideas and desires of Who He was and what He was going to do for us. Of course, with the coming of the Paraclete, we were made to be of one mind, but still different—for even now we say the same things but differently."

"In all the time you were with Jesus, did you not confront Him and ask Him what He was about?"

"We tried so many times to get Jesus to tell us what His purpose was. We were so confused by what we saw, heard, wanted, and understood. I myself, on the night of His arrest, asked Him openly when He would 'manifest himself to the people.'"

"And what did the Master say to you?"

"He did not answer me directly, but instead He said, 'If anyone loves Me, he will keep My word, and My Father will love him, and We will come to him and will make Our abode with him.'"

"And did you understand this?"

"No. I think Bartholomew, Philip, and even Levi understood Him, but I did not. Now, of course, I know, thanks to the Paraclete."

Dorimius wiped his hands on the blanket he was sitting on and reached for another fruit. The fruit was sweet and helped to satiate his intense hunger.

"You must understand, Dorimius, that most of us thought that Jesus was establishing a new Jewish kingdom, and most of us believed that we would be in high places in that kingdom."

"Did you not know that He was speaking of a heavenly kingdom?"

"No. You see, it mattered little what Jesus wanted—we were fixated on what we wanted. We needed an earthly kingdom. We thought this had been promised by *El Shaddai*, and so it was the natural thing for us to envision. We never thought of any other kingdom. There were some Jews who believed we should have nothing more than Palestine. I believed differently; when Jesus spoke of sins forgiven, rewards for goodness, and love, I believed this was to be the way He would rule—with great justice and with freedom from everything Roman, everything Sanhedrin. I saw Him raise people from the dead. Watching Him raise the dead made me believe that the kingdom He was to establish would be free from death. I thought that with this power, Jesus would raise up David, Solomon, Joshua, and other great leaders who would lead Judea to greatness. But no matter what Jesus did, I always believed that He had chosen us to be the governors and lords in His new kingdom."

"Why do you Jews always desire to be free of Rome?"

Jude stopped chewing. This was a sensitive topic, for Dorimius was a true Roman and disliked hearing that other people and nations did not love Rome.

"We are a people needing our own, just as you need yours."

They returned to eating in silence.

"And you? What did you think?" Dorimius asked.

"About what?"

"About Jesus being a great warrior Who was sent to liberate the Jews?"

"This may surprise you, but I believed early on that Jesus was the Chosen One of God. I believed that He would put an end to death, so in my mind, He had to be the Messiah."

Dorimius did not seem surprised by this, and Jude was disappointed. Dorimius was like so many others who asked him the same question and were not surprised by his answer.

All the berries and fruit had been eaten.

Dorimius rose from his blanket and went to get some water for washing their hands. As he walked away, he thought, *It is amazing that anything was accomplished with these twelve selfish and confused men. Poor Jesus, He must have been very frustrated and disappointed in them, yet He knew that they would become great men. He is a loving God and always endures mankind's slow movement to Him.*

He got the skin containing their water off the back of one of the donkeys, grabbed a cloth, and returned to Jude, who again was looking at the mountains.

"Still entranced by the mountains? Surely you have seen mountains before."

"Yes, many times, but this range of mountains has come to mean something more. I am so captivated by them that I think I will write John bar Zebedee a letter about them. John and Simon are the only ones I have written. Poor John always felt incomplete because he did not travel like the rest of us."

"Did I not hear he was in Rome, and in Greece?"

"Yes, but he wanted to do more. He is the resigned Apostle."

"That is understandable when I consider the extensive travels of some of the Twelve."

"And that is why he must constantly deny his own will. John wanted to leave Jerusalem the most. He found so many bad things in that city, but it all matters little now, for Jerusalem is no more. You Romans have seen to that."

Jude's implication offended Dorimius. He refused to believe that Rome was somehow inherently bad.

If Rome were not in Africa, those Berbers would be attacking merchant ships, Dorimius thought. *If Rome were not in the north, those Germanic barbarians would destroy civilization and enslave us all. If it were not for Rome, the savage Parthians would be killing and maiming people throughout the empire. Did Jude Thaddeus really think that Rome would allow little Judea to lead a revolt and go unchallenged? It was the fault of the Zealots and their supporters. Maybe I should remind Jude Thaddeus that Jerusalem's fall was the fulfillment of Jesus' prophesy and thus should not be mourned.*

He quickly regretted his thoughts. He understood the need for freedom. He understood the heavy hand of Rome and the strangling grip it had on its citizens, for he had felt both the hand and the grip. Had he known Jesus before Golgotha, he might now be able to see Him in the same light as the Twelve did.

Had Clavos been on time at Golgotha, I would not have been required to nail Jesus to the cross. I would not have that guilt on my soul and mind forevermore.

Suddenly an image of a hand and wrist was before him. The hand was rough and calloused and clearly had worked at a hard trade, yet as he forcibly gripped the hand, he could sense gentleness from it.

This confused him for a moment.

His recollection continued and he saw himself pull the left hand and lay it flat against the rough wood; he held it in place by putting his knee on the Man's arm. Dorimius looked to his side for his hammer and nails. In complete shock he felt the Man's hand slowly wrap around his hand. His first reaction was to pull away, but the grip was friendly. He made his hand remain where it was because he was confused and because he felt a goodness and peacefulness in the gripping hand. The Man's hand grew warm, and Dorimius roughly pulled his hand out of the grip as if to defend it from the warmth. He looked at the face of the Man being nailed, but the face was turned way. He was accustomed to being cursed and spat upon while nailing a criminal to a cross—never had he been treated with calmness.

Frightened and bewildered, he shouted loudly, "Will someone come and help me!" He was suddenly annoyed with the world and everyone around him.

A mercenary came and grabbed the Man's hand and held it in place.

He placed the nail against the flesh then heard the swishing sound of the hammer as it passed through the air. The hammer smacked against the nail. For the first time in all his years as an executioner, he felt the nail pop through flesh, but the Man did not say a word.

Experiencing again the feeling of the nail breaking through the Man's flesh made Dorimius tremble. He closed his eyes tightly. In his vision he saw blood spurt from the broken flesh and splatter on his hands and arms. He quickly opened his eyes, escaping the sight. His hands were trembling as they always did when he remembered Golgotha. His insides quivered; he placed his hand over his stomach and pushed hard, hoping to stop the sickening feeling.

In the distance, echoing through the mountains, he heard the hyenas laugh.

The breeze of the hammer passed his ear and returned to the nail. The nail resisted him, for it had hit the crude wood of the cross. He looked at the Man. His face was stoic and distant.

The Man did not say a word.

Dorimius drew a deep breath, breaking for a moment the image in his mind. He felt his legs shiver—a typical reaction when he remembered these things. They were too weak to hold him upright, and he crumbled to the dirt.

Again the air passed his ear as the hammer searched for the nail. When it struck its mark, it slipped and slammed against the Man's wrist. A deep purple mark appeared, yet the Man did not say a word.

He heard someone say, "He is secured, Dorimius, get to the other hand. Let's hurry and get off this damned hill."

Someone roughly bound the Man's left arm to the cross with crude rope.

By the time he had gone to the other hand, someone had pulled the Man's arm taut. He placed the nail against the flesh and raised the hammer, then he stopped. He leaned close to the Man's face. "You have to cry for mercy, Jew. You have to do this!" he said in a low whisper into the Man's ear. When he raised his head, he saw on the blistered, swollen, split lips a smile.

Dorimius shook his head to clear it of this disturbance. He closed his eyes tightly. His breathing was in short quick gasps as he thought, *Please, Jesus, let me know. Was that smile a defiant sneer? Was it a smile of understanding? Were You laughing at the stupidity of a mere man? You have performed miracles for others, but You have given me nothing. You gave me nothing to help me understand what has been clouded by guilt.*

He envisioned those around the cross, but they returned in his mind like spirits. The only beings truly alive were he and the Man. His thoughts returned to the Man. He could not understand the silence or the sensation of the flesh breaking or the smile on the Man's face. He looked into the Man's eyes, searching for something, an explanation, but the Man's face was solemn and his eyes were filled with gratitude.

Suddenly he was distracted by the sound of a scream. He snapped his head in the direction of the cry and saw a young woman with long brown hair crumbled to the ground, and standing beside her was a stoic woman. Her face was tight with pain and sorrow. She was attended by a young man who appeared to be in complete disbelief. Dorimius later learned that this man was John. He then heard a voice say that the stoic woman was the mother of the Jew.

Ah, so You get Your strength from Your Immi mother, he thought, looking back at the Man. *Well, let me see if I can get You and her to cry out.*

With great force he pounded the hammer against the nails, ignoring the sensation of punctured flesh and life. Again, he struck, with no care, but with greater strength, yet the Man did not make a sound. Again he slammed the hammer. Many believed he did this to hasten the nailing, but actually it was his savage desire to hear the Man cry, moan, yell. The Man did not make a sound.

Again, with brute force, he continued the hammering, and he never heard a cry.

When he finished, he had blood on his arms, hand, breastplate, and face. He retreated from the cross, knowing he was defeated; he could not deliver the hammer to the feet of the Man. He sat on the sandy ground and turned his back to the cross, and to the Man.

Let someone else finish this Jew off, he thought.

Now people began to move around him; they were no longer spirits, and he wondered why they came to life now and not before, when he needed companionship.

He watched as the other soldiers raised the *patibulum* to the *stipes*. The Man's mutilated body lurched and dangled until they nailed His feet and tied Him securely to the cross.

Still, the Man made no sound.

He turned his attention to the other criminals who were to be crucified, and he heard their cries.

That is what You were supposed to do! Why did You not?

Quickly he glanced over at the mother as she stood by the cross.

Why does she not wail and lament?

Finally Clavos, the one who was to be the executioner, arrived. He quickly walked to Clavos with resentment in his mind. He wanted to reprimand the German for not being there to do his job, but he was taken aback by Clavos' question: "Tell me, this Man on the center cross, did He cry out when you pierced His hands and feet?"

From that moment on, Dorimius was a different man.

He took a deep breath, and his remembering was over. He opened his eyes, and the bright morning sun instantly attacked them. He instinctively shaded his eyes with his hand. Feeling the wet perspiration on his forehead, he longed for a bath. He could feel perspiration race down between his shoulders and continue farther down his back, then he realized that his entire body was wet from perspiration. He knew it was not the heat of day. It was because he had been soaked that day on Golgotha.

✴

Jude never thought of himself as a good Jew. He followed the Mosaic Law because his father and brothers expected him to, but it was all external, with no devotion. Why he was this way he did not know. He was not as intelligent as they were and did not feel he should question his religion. So he was an oddity; he sulked in dissatisfaction with himself and his arrogance. He envied his father and brothers for their devotion, and this envy soon caused him to question everyone around him. He felt guilty, but this guilt did not induce him to stop questioning. Secretly, he began a quest to find out why he was so irreverent, and he discovered things about himself that he disliked. His problem, he realized, was not with religion, for he believed in the Almighty and had great respect for all He had done for His people. His problem was with the Jews. He did not like the way his people interacted with *El Shaddai*—much performance with little substance. Why did the Jews keep the One True God to themselves? Why did they not bring His Truth to the world? Why were they scattered all over the world and not defending their Promised Land?

Then one day he thought, *If I, who am not that intelligent, ask these questions, surely those with greater intellect must also ask these questions.* He knew of others who were also superficial in their beliefs, and he concluded that not all Jews were true Jews. In all this he still had a gift of hope, and this gift gave him dreams for the future and for change. He hoped every day for something to change him back to being a good Jew, but instead he became numb to the devotion of those around him and learned to stop feeling guilty.

As time passed, he had no revelation, so he started a feeble venture to find answers. Having no direction, he simply went to the one source he knew: the Holy Scriptures. In his search, he came to the promises of a Chosen One. He had heard of the Chosen One but never considered Him to be relevant to everyday life. The Almighty had done much for His Chosen People—why should He promise more to His ungrateful people? Truly, the Almighty was more faithful than His creatures. The more he read, the more he became certain that things would be set right by the Anointed One. The Anointed One would be a corrector of all things: one to perfect that which was in place.

On the day he came to this conclusion, something strange happened. It was so strange that Jude grew weak in his legs. Having come to these conclusions regarding the Anointed One, he heard a voice, a strange voice; it disclosed to him that the Anointed One was then, now, in his midst. He knew he had to find Him. It was because of this voice that he followed after anyone who remotely resembled the Anointed One. He even investigated the Zealots, for he thought that one of their charismatic leaders might be the Chosen One. It was among the Zealots that he met the man known as Simon the Zealot.

Then one day, it happened.

He heard a voice that caught his breath. It was a voice so loud and so forceful that he felt a shiver deep in his soul. He walked to the voice and found a man standing in the river preaching repentance. He heard John raise his voice against King Herod and the Pharisees. Instantly, he believed that John was the One, but still he moved cautiously. He secretly went to see John, and from a distance he listened and observed. He waited for a sign that he was the Promised One, but nothing came. He began to spend more time with John. Several times, he was late for his duties, but the fact that he had not been reprimanded encouraged him to stay more often with John, and the secrecy of his actions made him feel like a rebel—a feeling he enjoyed. Somewhere in his thinking, he came to believe that what he was doing was pleasing to *El Shaddai.*

One day, he heard John speak of a kingdom to come. This announcement overwhelmed Jude; though he was not completely sure what John meant about "a kingdom to come," he was comfortable with the idea of something better in the future. To his own surprise, he began to pray the psalms, which he seldom did outside of home and temple. He even became more sincere in listening to his father and brothers and the rabbi.

Months later, the Baptizer was approached by some representatives of the Pharisees, and they questioned John regarding why he was baptizing. John's face grew solemn, and looking away from his questioners, he said in a clear voice, "I indeed baptize you in water unto penance, but He that shall come after me is mightier than I, Whose shoes I am not worthy to loose: He shall baptize you in the Holy Spirit and fire."

Jude was stunned.

He questioned himself: *One greater than the Baptizer? Who could be greater than John?* And in a moment he thought, *He would have to be the Promised One!*

From that day on, his visits to John were limited. He was soon put to work with his father Cleophas and was not able to slip away. He was given one thing after another to clear up, straighten out, or put together, and though he did what was expected of him, his mind was on the Baptizer and the last thing he had said.

Finally he was able to see John, and it was on that day that he was surprised to see his "forgotten" brother, Levi, in the crowd. Levi was "dead" to the family because he was in the employ of the Romans as a tax collector. The family was forbidden to utter his name or have any contact with him, but Jude would usually greet him with a smile or kind gesture. As time passed, Levi responded in like manner, and eventually the two would go off to a secluded place and talk. Levi would ask about the family and sometimes give Jude money to give his father, but Jude would not take it. Levi accused Jude of not forgiving him, but Jude had no way of explaining the money to his father. "I am not clever enough to make up reasons or to be convincing when challenged."

Levi understood and vowed to find a way to help the family; after all, he was a wealthy man.

The next day, when Jude saw Levi in the crowd listening to John, his first thought was to get his attention. But as he observed his brother, he discovered that Levi was going to great lengths to remain hidden under his hood and cloak; he was even crouching in the hope of hiding his tall, lean body. So Jude made no sign of acknowledgment.

Three days after seeing Levi, Jude got a second surprise: he saw his brothers James, Joses, and Simon walking into the river to be purified. Even he had not been so bold as to be baptized. Again he hid, for he was sure that his brothers would be angry because he was there. He hid behind a large tree trunk, cautiously watching his brothers as they came ashore dripping and talking to each other. They were concerned about something. He followed their sight, and to his surprise he saw Jesus bar Yosef walk into the river toward John.

"What is Jesus doing here?" he asked in a voice only he heard.

He watched in amazement as Jesus and John stood in the water speaking to each other. He wished he had positioned himself closer so he could hear what was being said. John led Jesus into the water, and when Jesus emerged, the water around the two men became sapphire blue. Jesus' garment was white as snow and dry. These things became secondary, though, as he caught a glimpse of John's smile and Jesus' look of joy.

John's voice boomed across the countryside: "Behold the Lamb of God! Behold He Who takes away the sins of the world."

The words traveled through Jude's head and to his chest, and his heart beat quickly as he thought, *This is the One! This is the One John said would be greater than he.*

He realized he was no longer behind the tree. He was out in the open. His mind told him to return to his hiding place, but his body froze as he thought, *But this is Jesus!*

He jumped behind the tree and pressed his back against it. He closed his eyes as he felt the deep stab of disappointment. His thoughts raced on and on.

How could this be? Truly John is mistaken. Jesus is just a Nazarene, a poor laborer! How could John see Jesus as being greater than he? And are they not cousins? Did John know when they were growing up that Jesus was the One? He closed his eyes, trying to ease the distress he was experiencing. His thoughts would not cease. *He's one of my brethren! How could any thing of importance come from my family? We are simple Jews that did nothing for El Shaddai or any of His prophets. No! John is wrong! I have been fooled!* He took a deep breath in an effort to settle his conclusion, but his thoughts were not to be ignored. *How could this be? I played with Jesus as a child. He did nothing extraordinary. He spoke and walked as I did. He played and ran and got hurt as I did. He answered to Yosef and Mary just as I answered to my parents.*

With little forethought, he came away from the tree and walked in the direction of the empty river bank. There he found John sitting alone, inches from the edge of the water. John looked old. Jude walked slowly to him.

Scarcely knowing what he was doing, Jude requested, "John, baptize me with your water."

John looked up into the young man's face, and recognizing something in Jude's eyes, he quickly rose to his feet. He stood looking over Jude's face, then a small smile came to his lips.

"You are Jude Thaddeus, sometimes called Lebbaeus, are you not?"

"Yes," Jude replied with little surprise; this was a day destined to be full of surprises.

"There is no need for that now, Jude Thaddeus."

"I know," Jude affirmed.

John was startled.

"You know?"

He looked at Jude closely, and resolved, "Yes, of course you know." John looked away for a moment, then back at Jude.

"You have been blessed above many. You have been called before many others will be called. For your sake, young Jude, do not make known what you know or what has been revealed to you until the Almighty has made it the right time. Know that you will suffer much because of this revelation. You will find torment in knowing what you know."

He turned and walked into the river.

"Come, Jude Thaddeus. You have been chosen and given knowledge. You are one of those destined to serve the Almighty. Come, let me give you my water, then go and find Him Who will give you His fire."

Jude walked into the warm river and emerged from his hiding.

Once on the shore, he looked to see where the crowd had gone. He left John alone in the Jordan. As he raced, wet with earthly water, confident and with a smile on his face, he thought, *I have found the Holy One!*

When he reached the crowd, he found Simon and Andrew bar Jonah, James and John bar Zebedee, and others he knew, but he was disappointed because Jesus was not with them. He had disappeared. For the next few days, he waited for Jesus to return. After weeks with no sign of Jesus, the crowd diminished. Jude's great enthusiasm waned, and he began to debate his belief that Jesus was the Chosen One. The things that John had said and the way John had instructed him eased his doubts, but still he did not know what to do.

Time passed, and so did his fervor.

On a day when all that had happened was far from his thoughts, he heard a rumor that "a new prophet" was preaching, and immediately he knew it was Jesus. He quickly did what his father wanted of him and slipped away. As he traveled, he heard those around him speak of Jesus doing unusual things. His excitement grew. As he neared Jesus, Jude thought of the Baptist's warning, so he resolved to be careful. He was under a tormenting mandate not to tell anyone that he knew Jesus was the Chosen One. His greatest fear was of his brother James and his parents; he would never lie to them. So he cautiously walked to where Jesus was and, upon hearing His words, willingly found a new and different peace.

As time passed, when he would speak to his brothers about Jesus, he would act innocent and say that he heard this or that about Jesus, and many times he would evade all their questions.

On the day that Jesus chose His Twelve, Jude was standing in the crowd. All were watching Jesus. Upon hearing each name, Jude nodded his head in agreement. When his brother Levi was called, he wanted to shout with joy, for he believed his brother was being forgiven.

At first, Jude thought Jesus would call only three or four to His side. As Jesus continued, Jude thought he would call seven, and when He passed seven, Jude began to yearn to be among those called. Jude counted ten men, and suddenly he heard his brother James called. Jude looked immediately at Matthew and was surprised to see no reaction from him. Putting aside James' dislike of what Jesus was doing and his feeling that Jesus was avoiding His duties as a widow's son, Jude knew his brother was a good choice, for James was an honorable man.

He knew he would not be called, for he had nothing to offer. He would not be good at protecting Jesus, as Judas or the Zealot would, nor did he know people in high places, as John and James, Levi, Bartholomew, Simon, and Andrew did.

Perhaps He will call one of my other brothers, Simon or Joses. I am certain Jesus considers me too young.

He looked up at Jesus longingly. He wanted to raise his hand to be noticed, but Jesus was looking the other way, away from him.

Jude lowered his head in shame.

Like a soft, whispering echo came one name: "Jude," followed by, "Jude Thaddeus Lebbaeus bar Cleophas." He looked up and felt Jesus' piercing eyes on him, and then he felt the eyes of all around him. Jude's legs instantly grew weak, and for an instant he could not move. Soon, a path was made for him, and he walked up the mount to Jesus. When he reached his place, he went to his brother James' side. He glanced over to Levi and smiled humbly. He looked below at the crowd and saw faces of surprise, indifference, and even envy.

As he calmed himself, he heard once again John's words: "You have been blessed above many. You have been called long before others will be called." It was then that his eyes filled with tears. He vowed to *Adonai* that he would keep these words close to him and remain quiet. As he traveled with Jesus and watched Him cure the blind, lame, and possessed, he became certain that his cousin was indeed the Chosen One. So again he remembered the other thing John had told him: "Do not make known what you know or what has been revealed to you until the Almighty has made it the right time."

There were times when he wanted to shout to the whole world what he believed, especially to the other Apostles, but his fear of betraying the command of John pressed him into continued silence. Meanwhile, the Others debated everything Jesus said, and without coming to any conclusions. All of the Twelve had been followers of John the Baptist, and with John's death, they needed to follow someone. At first, many of them believed that Jesus was simply an extension of John.

There were times he wanted to be a hero—to go to the Temple and tell the Sanhedrin what he knew. He knew they would welcome his knowledge, but as time went on, Jesus and the Temple Authorities grew apart, and he smothered his desire for heroism. Nonetheless, Jude was perplexed at the tension between Jesus and the Authorities.

Why would Jesus permit strife between Himself and the Authorities? If He is the Chosen One, should not the Temple Authorities agree with His plan? How can Jesus establish a new order if the current order opposes Him?

On other occasions, he thought, *Jesus is right in condemning the Pharisees and Sadducees—they are nothing but the toys of Rome. Jesus is only continuing the Baptizer's campaign. If Jesus is to find a new order, He has no need of those "vipers." We Twelve will be His new leaders.* Other times, he thought, *Jesus is making too many enemies. He is endangering us.*

The greatest temptation to reveal what he knew was when Jesus went off to pray and Jude listened to the Others. They complicated Jesus' actions with their personal opinions and doubts. The temptation was so great that there were times when he simply walked away. It all seemed simple to him: Jesus was healing the sick to get people to believe that He could do all things. Jesus fed them, and if they stayed with Him, He would be their provider. He spoke of shepherds and Samaritans, kings and emissaries, all to show that He knew their world and understood their struggles. When He calmed the seas and the wind, He showed that He had power over all creation and that He was a true messenger of the Almighty. So Jude remained silent and purposely hidden within the Twelve, hoping to be forgotten, and he watched as the Others continued to trouble themselves with debates and fears. It seemed the longer they stayed together, the longer and louder they disputed. As he looked around at the Twelve, he soon saw that Simon, the one called the Zealot, and Levi, whom everyone now called Matthew, were also quiet and without opinions. He wondered if they had been blessed as he had been.

Finally, he stopped worrying about the Others, knowing that Jesus, as John had said, would baptize them with fire, but he grew impatient with Jesus as he waited for Him to reveal Himself. Often, he found himself vacillating between patience and frustration. His urge to tell someone what he knew grew stronger. When there was a miracle, Jude expected them to rush to Jesus and acclaim Him, but instead he heard people questioning how this was done or by what power Jesus did such things.

At each miracle, Jude would think, *Now Jesus will tell them who He is*, but Jesus never did, and Jude would fight off the urge to declare his knowledge. Eventually, he became calm and accepted Jesus' timing, but he was struggling to see what Jesus was trying to establish, and he was uncertain of what he and the Others were to do. At times, his anxiety caused Jude to doubt his loyalty to *Adonai* and to Jesus.

One day, an official of the Temple came to Jesus. His name was Jarius. Many of the Twelve knew him and had seen him secretly listening to Jesus' preaching. Jarius told Jesus that his daughter was ill. He asked Jesus to come and "place" His hand on her, "so that she will get well and live." As they set out for Jarius' home, the Temple official received word that his daughter had died. Jarius began to weep and lament.

Jesus calmed Jarius, saying, "Fear not, only believe."

Jesus proceeded to Jarius' house.

The words Jesus spoke to Jarius had a strong effect on Jude, for he knew that he also had to obey the command given to Jairus. When they arrived at the house, Jairus let Jesus, Simon, James, and John inside while the Others stayed outside. After a few moments, Jesus and the three Apostles came from the house and walked away. Nothing was said, but Jude saw the expressions on the faces of the three Apostles and knew that something of great importance had taken place. He needed to find out what had happened, so he stayed back as Jesus and the Others left.

Some time passed before he walked along the side of the house and heard the sounds of joy and happiness, and when he looked in, he saw Jarius' twelve-year-old daughter eating and talking and laughing. Afraid that he would be discovered, he moved to the other side of the house. As he walked away, a servant of the household, whom Jude knew, came hurriedly out of the side door.

"Batar."

"Ah, Jude Thaddeus, how have you been?"

"Fine, fine. A small question: I heard that Jairus' daughter has been ill. How ill is she?"

Batar looked around quickly, then pulling Jude close to him, he whispered with restrained exuberance, "I tell you, she died. I know she died. She was beginning to turn cold and black, then Jesus came in and said, 'Why make you this ado, and weep? The child is not dead, but sleepeth.' Some of the mourners mocked Him, but nevertheless, He took her hand and said, '*Talitha koum.*'"

Batar pulled Jude to him. In a whisper filled with exhilaration he said, "And the girl got up and walked." Batar backed away from Jude and said in a less restrained voice, "Then Jesus told the household in a commanding way that no one was to tell what they had seen."

Jude broke Batar's hold, pulled away, and looked at him as if he had lost his mind.

"But was she sleeping?" Jude asked.

"No. She was dead. I know it. You take me for a fool. I tell you, she was dead."

Jude rushed away from Batar and did not look back. He knew Batar was no fool, but this seemed impossible.

Batar could be mistaken. He could have made a mistake, he thought. *Jesus said she was sleeping, but if she was dead, then Jesus can give life to the dead.* Overwhelmed by this conclusion, Jude began to tremble, and he reached for the wall of a nearby house to steady himself.

What am I to do with this new information? I must tell someone. Whom can I tell? James? No! He still sees Jesus as lacking respect for His mother.

Matthew? No. He would not be of any help, for he would remain silent also. There is no one! Oh Adonai, when am I to know the right time to speak? As he walked on, he grew more and more uncertain of his duty and what he was to do with his knowledge. *John was right, this is a heavy burden and one I fear I am not worthy to carry.* He stopped walking and thought, *And Jesus asked Simon, James, and John not to say anything, so I must also wait until He is ready. But when will Jesus announce Himself?*

As the second year passed, Jude grew more impatient with Jesus. He was becoming weary of all the parables and enigmatic teachings. Jesus would need to start talking in plain words in order for the Twelve to know what they were to do in His kingdom. Of course, Jude had no idea about what this kingdom would be. He didn't know whether Jesus was setting up a Jewish kingdom or another kingdom far greater than anyone could imagine—greater even than Rome.

There were times after miracles when the people wanted to take Jesus and declare Him king. The Twelve, who firmly believed that this was Jesus' destiny and who wanted Jesus to declare His kingdom, would rush to protect Jesus. Even Jude helped hold the people back, but later he wondered why he had done such a thing. It seemed to contradict his desire for Jesus to reveal Himself.

One day as they approached a town called Naim in Galilee, Jesus asked Judas Iscariot and Jude to go on ahead and buy provisions for the Others. Several of the Apostles were not with them because they were tending to family matters, so they planned to reassemble in Naim for dinner. Jude and Judas Iscariot promptly walked into Naim to do what they had been asked to do. Jesus and the Others followed.

As Jesus approached the town, a funeral procession passed by. Jesus, with compassion, stopped the procession. He touched the bier and said to the dead boy: "Young man, I say to thee, arise." The boy sat up.

The entire incident happened quickly, and it left many in amazement and disbelief.

When Judas and Jude and the other absent Apostles joined those who had witnessed this miracle, they were told what happened. Judas demanded to know what had happened after the man rose from his bier.

Simon bar Jonah said, "Most of those present were filled with fear; some became hysterical, and still others began running into the town shouting, 'A great prophet has appeared among us.'"

Jude's heart beat rapidly. *This is it!* he thought.

Then a group started shouting, "The Almighty has come to His people."

The Almighty has come! El Shaddai! They know!

"The people raced to Jesus and we had to hold them back, and when we turned to see if the Master was safe, He had disappeared."

Jude fell into disappointment, which later turned to frustration that lingered for several days. The Others, who normally paid him little mind, began to question him about his mood. He made feeble excuses, which they accepted, and they soon returned to paying him little mind.

In his private moments he wondered why Jesus did not seize the opportunity of Naim.

What better time? He would have had all of Galilee with Him in a day. What better moment? Why did Jesus not take that moment and make Himself known?

He began to wonder if Jesus wanted to be known at all—would He ever permit the truth to be known?

Within days, Jude became bitter and depressed, for he acknowledged that now others knew who Jesus was, and consequently he no longer felt special. He should have realized this sooner—he was too young, unintelligent, and meek to have been the only holder of so great a truth.

As Jude followed Jesus for the third year, a marked change took place in him. He withdrew deeper inside the Twelve and became the most silent of them all. In the winter of the third year, Jesus and the Twelve went up to Jerusalem for the festival of the Dedication of the Temple. While they were walking in Solomon's Porch, Jesus was unexpectedly surrounded by a crowd of Pharisees who continued to question Him as they did on Mount Olivet after Jesus had forgiven the adulteress. Their questioning was very confrontational and Jude was not close enough to hear the exchange of words, but every so often he would hear Jesus' response. Jude was certain that the responses he heard by Jesus were intended for him to hear.

Jude heard Jesus say, "...I am not alone, but I and the Father that sent Me. And in your law it is written, that the tesimony of two men is true. I am one who gives tesimony of Myself and the Father that sent Me giveth testimony of Me."

Jude fell against one of the columns of the Porch and sank into complete disbelief, not because he thought the time had arrived for Jesus to reveal Himself, but because he could never have dreamed of questioning Jesus so directly.

Then he heard Jesus say, "You are of this world, but I am not of this world."

Again they came after Jesus and Jude heard, "If God were your Father, you would indeed love Me. For from God I proceeded, and came; for I came not of Myself, but He sent Me. Why do you not know My speech?"

Jude heard no more, for he suddenly realized that the problem was not with Jesus but with everyone else. Jesus had revealed Himself in many ways, but no one heard Him. In one crushing moment, Jude realized that those around Jesus were still as stiff-necked as those who lived in the days of Moses.

His thoughts stopped and he heard Jesus continue, "If I glorify Myself, My glory is nothing. It is My Father that glorifieth Me, of whom you say that He is your God. And you have not known Him but I know Him…Abraham your father rejoiced that he might see My day; he saw it and was glad."

Jude heard the question: "Thou are not yet fifty years old and hast thou seen Abraham?"

Slowly, Jesus looked at the questioners around him, and with a voice that held the power of many ages, He said to them: "Amen, amen I say to you, before Abraham was made, I AM."

A roar went up from those gathered, and Jude heard the shout: "Blasphemy!"

The Twelve were in confusion. Jude found several of the Apostles going to Simon bar Jonah trying to force him to say something. Others pulled and poked at each other in disbelief, and then he saw his brother James standing with his eyes closed and his face raised to the heavens. He believed that James was asking the Almighty to forgive Jesus.

Jesus continued to talk, but the excitement was too loud for Jude to hear what He was saying. After He finished speaking, some men began to push against Jesus, and some raised their fists and open hands to Him. Some of the Twelve saw people gathering stones to cast at Jesus, and they reacted by moving to protect Jesus from the anger of the crowd, and again, Jesus escaped. When the Twelve noticed that Jesus was gone, they scattered in different directions to get away from the mob; this was a tactic they often employed to ensure that no one could be singled out for a mob attack. Eventually the Twelve reassembled, and they went beyond the Jordan into Perea for safety. They stayed in the largest town in Perea, called Bethany beyond the Jordan, so named to distinguish it from the town of Bethany near Jerusalem. They continued to travel through the Jordan Valley and came to the town of Salim, which was the place where John had been baptizing. While they were there, Jesus healed many of the sick, and people came to Him and said among themselves, "John did no signs such as those this Man is doing, but all things whatsoever John said of this Man are true." Many in Perea came to believe in Him.

It was during this time that Jesus received word from Martha and Mary of Bethany in Judea that Lazarus, their brother, was ill.

Jesus grew sad when he saw the concern the Twelve had for Lazarus, a close friend to them all, so He said to them, "This sickness is not unto death, but for the glory of God; that the Son of God may be glorified by it." His words did not comfort them; they simply ignored what He had said and continued to grieve. When He did not rush to Lazarus, they looked upon Him with disbelief.

Jesus turned and walked away. Slowly, they followed Him. When they had walked a short distance, Jesus turned His head and told Matthew and Jude to go to Bethany to the house of Lazarus and tell Martha and Mary that He would be coming. Matthew and Jude left immediately, but Jesus did not change direction to follow them. Instead, He stayed on in Perea.

When Matthew and Jude arrived in Bethany, they found Lazarus gravely ill and his sisters in distress. For two days they stayed with the family and Jesus did not come, so Matthew announced that he would take the road to Perea. When he met Jesus, he would apprise Him of Lazarus' grave condition and urge Him to make haste to Bethany. Within hours after Matthew's departure, Lazarus died.

Jude stayed with the family knowing that Jesus, Matthew, and the Others would arrive soon.

Servants were dispatched to inform all family and friends in Bethany, and even as far as Jerusalem and Galilee, that Lazarus was dead. Within hours the house was filled with mourners. As was the custom, professional mourners were hired with several flutists who played softly as the mourners waited for the corpse to be made ready for viewing.

Jude watched as the body was washed and anointed with nard—the same ointment that Mary, the sister of Lazarus, had used to anoint Jesus. He held the strips of linens that were to tie Lazarus' ankles. He held the shroud of linen that was used to cover the entire body. When this was done, Lazarus' face was covered. The covering of the face was usually of the best material that the family could afford. In Lazarus' case, it was a very expensive silk fabric. Lazarus' body was then carried to the upper chamber of the house, where family and friends came to pay their respects and grieve. It was by the door of this upper chamber that Jude stood watch for Jesus, Matthew, and the Others.

After eight hours of bereavement, the body of Lazarus was placed on a bier and carried from the house through the streets to his tomb. His sisters and all the female mourners walked at the front of the procession, lamenting and wailing. The male mourners followed the bier. The procession stopped several times so the mourners could throw dirt or dust on their heads. When they arrived at the tomb, Martha and Mary tore a piece of their clothing off the sleeves of their garments, and the wailing increased. The body was placed in the tomb, and as the servants rolled the large boulder over the entrance and sealed it, the mourners began the *Kaddish*—the prayer for the dead.

Jude joined the male mourners, and as he spoke each word, he felt his throat tighten and his eyes water, for certain words took on more meaning for him. Suddenly, this prayer became his cry to *El Shaddai*.

> *Yitgaddal v'yitqaddash sh'meh rabba...*
> "Exalted and sanctified is God's Great Name
> in the world which He has created according to His Will
> and may He establish His Kingdom,
> may His Salvation blossom and His Anointed be near
> in your lifetime and your days and in the lifetimes
> of all the House of Israel, speedily and soon..."

Jesus arrived four days later.

When news was received that Jesus and the Others were nearby, Martha left the mourners and went to meet Jesus.

Upon seeing Him, she cried, "Lord, if You had been here, my brother would not have died, but now that You are here I know that what You ask of God, God will give to You."

Jesus said softly, "Thy brother shall rise again."

"I know that he shall rise again in the resurrection of the last day."

Jesus said in a resonant, firm voice, "I am the Resurrection and the Life, he that believeth in Me, although he be dead, shall live. And every one that liveth, and believeth in me, shall not die for ever. Believest thou this?"

Martha, in tears, replied, "Yes, Lord, I have believed that you are Christ the Son of the living God, Who has come into this world."

Soon Mary came from the house followed by many mourners, including Jude, and seeing how she and those with her were crying, Jesus became troubled and made a small grunting sound of disapproval.

"Where have you laid him?" Jesus asked with a small edge in His voice.

"Lord, come and see," Mary said sobbing.

When they arrived at the site of the tomb, Jesus stood silently looking at the tomb, which had been hewed into a cave. A large boulder had been rolled over the entrance, sealed with thick rope, and anchored into the side of the hill. He began to weep and everyone looked on with growing sadness. Several of the Apostles wept with Jesus, for it was obvious that He truly loved Lazarus. As the moment lingered on, several mourners complained that Jesus had done so much for the poor, the blind, and the ailing but could do nothing for His beloved friend.

Overhearing what was being said, Jesus groaned. His frustration and impatience were apparent.

He took a long, deep breath and said, "Take away the stone."

An uproar went up from the mourners. Martha openly objected by reminding Jesus that Lazarus had been dead four days and the stench of death would be great.

Jesus looked at her intensely and said, "Did I not say to thee, that if thou believe, thou shalt see the glory of God?" He turned to the Apostles standing near Him and ordered, "Remove the rock."

Reluctantly, Simon, Andrew, James the Greater, Simon the Zealot, and Judas walked to the tomb. After breaking the seal, they strained to move the boulder from the entrance of the tomb. With great exertion, they finally managed to open the tomb. Everyone looked at the black open wound on the side of the hill. As soon as the Apostles moved the boulder, they hurriedly walked away and covered their mouths with their cloaks. Several people began to cough and gag violently.

Jesus raised his face to the sky, and in a loud voice He said, "Father, I give Thee thanks that Thou hast heard Me, and I know that Thou hearest Me always, but because of the people who stand about have I said it, that they may believe that Thou hast sent Me."

With His face still toward the sky and His eyes closed, He said softly, "Lazarus."

Abruptly everything went still. There was no breeze, no moving clouds, no sound of trees or bushes moving, no birds in flight.

The stillness was oppressive.

The stench of death was heavy in the stillness.

Jesus lowered His head and, looking at the black gaping hole, said in a louder voice, "Lazarus."

The name charged over all the land and penetrated the very earth; it passed through the mountains and hills and tumbled down the valleys.

In a deep voice that came from the moment of the beginning of time, Jesus called, "Lazarus, come forth!" The words entered and vibrated deep inside every living thing nearby and left every heart beating faster; every one, every thing, felt life in a heightened state. Everyone waited for the exhale of breath, of new breath. A sudden strong wind, which seemed to come from the very breath of Jesus' mouth, spread across the land, and everyone standing felt the strength of this wind as it passed and pressed against their bodies. Every tree and bush, even the blades of grass, swayed in the passing wind.

Just as suddenly, the winds stopped and the ruffled earth returned to calm. The stench of death passed, and in its stead was the sweet smell of flowers.

At the mouth of the cave appeared a being; he was bound with winding bands and his face was covered.

Confusion broke out everywhere. Many ran away yelling, some in fear and others wanting to tell the world of this prodigy. Some stumbled and fell, some dropped to their knees in prayer, and still others simply collapsed.

Jude's emotions shot to his head and he wanted to shout to everyone, finally, that what they had seen proved that Jesus was the Chosen One, but he froze. The only thing free in his body was his pounding heart.

Sometime later, he heard his brother James in a hushed but commanding voice say, "Jude, close your mouth and stop looking so foolish."

Many came to believe in Jesus after that day, and others went to the Sanhedrin. Later, the Sanhedrin questioned Lazarus, who told them he remembered nothing but the sound of Jesus' voice.

From that time on, Jesus was a Man marked for death.

✳

Dorimius walked along the lake looking out over the calm waters. A morning mist delicately rested on the lake. The thin gray clouds that crowned the lake gave it an air of mystery as they rose from the lake like steam. He was told that such sightings were signs that the Olympian gods had come to bathe. The mist was the gods in vapor form coming to watch Aurora, goddess of the dawn, give birth to her son Sol as a new day. He once believed these things, but now he knew only the true God. His new God made these things for man to admire and enjoy, and the longer he looked at the mist moving over the water, the more he became aware of God. A sense of creation came to him, and he felt humble. Immediately he stopped walking, feeling that there was something he should do to show appreciation for this sight. He whispered a short prayer of thanksgiving. After praying, he grew sad as he acknowledged that he was not a complete Christian. Though he had been baptized by Simon Peter and was instructed, he found himself forgetting to pray. He seemed to pray only when those with him prayed or invited him to pray. He never seemed to be motivated to pray on his own. He watched his Christian family pray constantly. He was always amazed that other Christians could instantly be moved to prayer. Another thing that amazed him was the constant presence of God in the minds and lives of other Christians.

They seemed to be more in tune with God than he was. He was sure that his lack of prayer was the reason.

I only think of Jesus when I remember Golgotha or when I remember hearing the news of Jesus' rising from the dead. How impossible that was—I saw Him dead. I know He died. Yet He lived.

What he thought of more often than God was his Roman life, with all its comforts and gratifications. His bygone days leaked into his daily thoughts and became demons in his mind, making room for few other things. Rome was a soft life that catered to the senses. No matter what he did, he could not dismiss the shadow of these delights. They seemed to remain near him at all times, always ready to slide back into his mind and make him regret his new life. Daily he battled these desires for comfort. In this new life he felt the cold, rain, and heat with intensity. He knew the hardness of a bed of earth, rather than the softness of a Roman couch. He had the meagerness of simple food instead of the meals of delight and variety. He could not understand why, after all these years, he still longed for that good life. He should be rid of it. He had recently been tempted to return to the Roman ways, but he could not, for the opposite of this shadowy side was the splendor of the light of Christ. In this divine light he lived with Jesus, Who hopelessly conquered him with the desire to be good, to do good. Unlike the other witnesses and miracles on Golgotha that day, he got no look, no nod. All he got was silence, and that silence had become a clanging cymbal that sharply sounded in his mind and left him only partially sure of the way he was to go. He had little doubt that Jesus was the Savior: He had come from God and was God, and His mission was to save mankind from endless death. In spite of this, he still longed for the good life, and this contradiction left him adrift in stormy waters. He sighed at his dilemma and slowly began to remove his clothing. It was morning and he had to bathe. He stood facing the lake, the mist, and the blazing orange sunrise. He remembered a morning like this in Rome. He walked into the water, and the chill of the lake greeted him.

He shivered and thought, *Oh for the comfort of a Roman bath!*

Bathed and refreshed, he dried himself as best he could and began walking the short distance from the lake to their camp. When he arrived, he found Jude deep in prayer. He slowly and quickly walked up behind Jude and took up his position in prayer, annoyed that once again he had forgotten his morning prayers.

"Let us do something unusual and a little exciting," Jude said with a childish grin on his face. "How about going fishing for tonight's dinner?"

Dorimius was not that excited at such a venture. He was not a fisherman, but he knew this would please Jude. Also, it would make Jude reminisce, and this would allow him to question the Apostle about Jesus. So they made two fishing spears from some nearby tree branches and waded into the lake, and with great patience they waited for a fish to greet their spears.

After they were blessed with three fish, they returned to the site, cleaned and cooked the fish, and sat down for another day of waiting for Simon and Clavos.

"Was there ever any jealousy among the Twelve?" Dorimius asked after Jude had explained how the Twelve began to grow into a tightly knit group.

"No! Never jealousy," Jude stated, then he rethought and added, "Well, resentment perhaps, but never jealousy."

Moments passed, and Dorimius knew that Jude was thinking back.

Jude was remembering his desire to follow Peter onto the water when the Lord told him to "come" to Him. He remembered watching Peter put his foot onto the unsettled waters of the Sea of Galilee, and could see Peter's toes wiggling. He remembered wanting to feel the water that way. When Peter began to walk carefully to Jesus, he longed to have the same experience, but the Lord had called only Peter, and Jude stifled his desires. But still to this day, he wished he had been the one who walked on the water with the Lord. He swallowed hard to dissolve his selfish desires and thought back, remembering one incident when there was some dissension.

"There was one time when some of us became angry at James and John bar Zebedee...no...we were angry at their mother, Salome, who asked Jesus if her sons could be given the highest places of honor. Many of us knew that she did this partly because she was Lady Mary's sister, and she thought that meant something. Jesus offered the brothers His chalice to drink from."

"But did they not understand what Jesus meant by the chalice?" Dorimius questioned, then after a short pause he asked, "What do you think Jesus meant?"

"That they would have to suffer death, just as He would. Some of the Twelve have done this already. There are only five of us left. When James the Greater, John's brother, died, many of us expected John to follow, but that did not happen and it will not happen until John has written his account of Jesus."

"Is it completed?"

"Not to my knowledge." A wide smile came to his small mouth. "And knowing John, I am sure his will be more profound than the accounts of Mark and Luke."

"But I heard that your brother Matthew has also written an account."

"Yes, he has," Jude confirmed with a bit of pride. "Well, I think he has by now. I only read a small part of it." He stopped and looked off into the distance, then turning his head back to Dorimius, he continued, "Yes, we can expect John's account to be far different from the others."

"Have you ever written anything of Jesus?"

"No."

"Why not? I would imagine that all of the Apostles would want to do such a thing."

"Perhaps so. We each saw Jesus in different ways, but I am sure that our accounts would largely duplicate one another. Besides, dear Dorimius, Jesus never instructed us to do such a thing, but He did instruct us to go and 'baptize all nations.' That command is what we must obey. Mark and Luke have made Jesus present in words; Simon Peter, Andrew, Thomas, and James have made Jesus present even where the words are not read."

Dorimius reached for a cool piece of cooked fish and pensively chewed on it as he pondered Jude's words.

"I am certain that the Others have written letters to the communities they founded, and I am sure they have written to each other. I know I have written to the Others and to my communities. In fact, I did pen a letter to the Church, and I understand it has been copied and read to the Greeks and Asians."

"What did you say in this letter?"

"Oh, a very simple message: I told the faithful to remember our common goal of salvation. I warned them of false teachers who speak against God's grace and love. I challenged them to be spiritually firm in order to fight for their faith. Finally, I gave them the blessings of mercy, peace, and love, which are the three things I believe Jesus offers to all of us unconditionally." He stopped and smiled delightfully, as if he was revealing a big secret. "Actually, my message was similar to Peter's in his letter to the Church."

"Do you really think that mercy, peace, and love are the three things Jesus offers to us?"

"Yes! He offered mercy to all who came to Him. His daily life was of mercy. Mercy is the essence of His promise. The first word He spoke to us when we first saw Him in the Upper Room after He rose from the dead was 'peace.' He always gives us peace. Of course, we have to understand what that peace means to each of us. As far as love is concerned, He gave

His life with love. Oh yes, Dorimius, those are the three things Jesus offers to us unconditionally."

Silently they continued their meal, but Jude knew that Dorimius would be asking questions again—he always did. He needed to ask questions. Jude suspected for a long time that Dorimius was experiencing spiritual dilemmas, but he never wanted to talk about them. Jude knew it was through his questions that Dorimius was getting answers to his problems, so Jude answered his inquiries. Though he strongly wanted to help his companion, he knew it would be in the Almighty's time, so he waited.

They continued their meal.

"I heard that you and the Others often tell of the times when Jesus spoke to you in private moments. Did He ever speak to you in private?"

Jude smiled, "Oh, yes. I had my private moments. After all, Jesus had to minister to us also; He had to save us first."

"Did anyone tell you of their private conversations with the Lord?"

"My brothers, James and Matthew, did."

"And you, how many times did you speak to Jesus in private?"

Jude reflected for a quick moment then said, "I guess I should remember them all, but I do not. I only remember one, and that was the most important one."

"And when was that?" Dorimius asked with childlike curiosity.

Jude sat back and became comfortable as he felt the excitement of that moment returning to him. For one fleeting moment, he held that remembrance to himself, wanting to bask in all the emotions.

"It was the night of our last supper. We left the Cenacle. As we walked the narrow streets of the Upper City, the place called Sion, we were conversing loudly. We were still experiencing the joy of the Holy Day. It seemed like the night would not end. As we passed through the Lower City and came to the southernmost part of Jerusalem, called Ophel, I suddenly became aware of being alone with Jesus. For some reason, we had fallen a great distance behind the Others. I do not know how this happened, but it did. I remember thinking that this was planned, that Jesus had wanted this to happen, that possibly He was displeased with how I questioned Him during the Paschal meal. I had asked when He would manifest Himself to the people. I was angry at myself for being so presumptuous. For a long time we walked in silence, and this made me more and more uncomfortable. Soon we neared the Water Gate, which led to the Valley of Cedron.

"I wished Him well, and He smiled. We walked a little farther, and then Jesus said in a very solemn voice, 'Jude Thaddeus, you have been a trustworthy friend. You, like Simon Peter, have been blessed with the knowledge of Who I am.'

"'Lord, I....'

"Jesus raised His hand, and that gesture demanded silence.

"'Even though you knew this, you remained silent, though I often heard you wondering why I would not make myself known to all.'

"Jesus turned His head and looked at me.

"'If I had manifested Myself to the people at the times you thought were the proper moments, I would have done their bidding and not the bidding of My Father, the One Who sent Me.'

"I could not say anything: I could not even look at Jesus. All I could think was that I had hurt Him, and I felt that somehow I had failed in my mission.

"Jesus sensed this, so He continued: 'Know now that My manifestation is soon at hand, and all will be made known, but not until I do the Will of My Father. When I do the Will of My Father, you and the Others will be lost, and you will soon find that all of you will have to manifest Me to the world.'

"We walked farther. Then, He spoke again: 'Your youth has left you anxious; you have tortured yourself these past years. I know that during these years you lost faith and hope, but *Abba* understood this and has forgiven you. Stop worrying about asking for My forgiveness, for it has been given you.'

"I felt so unworthy, so humbled, that tears of gratitude welled up in my eyes.

"'You have comforted Me by your constant silence, and that silence was a sign of your trust in Me and My Father. For being so comforting, Jude Thaddeus, I will one day return that comfort to you. For now, remain steadfast, for I know you are not completely sure of Who I am, nor do you understand what is to take place. You will not be spared doubts, for soon what has been revealed to you will be tested, and you will be lost in a maze of confusion. Remember what I said to you this night. Remember and believe in what has been given you and in what you know.'

"We had passed through the Water Gate. Jesus rested His right hand on my shoulder and looked at me with a grave, encouraging smile. Finally, He spoke to me: 'I entreat you, Jude Thaddeus, remain silent in your knowledge and surrender to the Will of the Spirit, Who will come to you. Someday the very heart that you nurtured with belief, yet which was filled with hopelessness, will be pierced.'

"I grew tense, for this last thing He said frightened me.

"Then Jesus continued, 'Continue to hope and all will be well. Someday your hope will make you known throughout the world, and you will be sought after by those filled with hopelessness.'

"We continued on to the garden. Then came Golgotha. Jesus' prediction came true. In the days that followed, my knowledge was tested, and though I assured the Others, this did not seem to satisfy my disbelief. My life had been thrown into turmoil, but I could not let go of three years of believing in what I came to know. He sent the Spirit to comfort me, and now I make Him known to the world."

Jude tilted his head to the right and looked at Dorimius. "You seem disappointed, Dorimius. Did you expect a greater story? What I have told you was important to me, and I am sure Jesus knew this, and that is why the moment was made to happen. Jesus gives to each person what He believes they need; if more is needed, the person should go into prayer and ask for more."

✳

Dorimius rose from his blanket and walked out of the partially roofed hut. It was a hot day, and he longed for a cup of cool water or better, a cup of cool wine. He shook his head, trying to forget his desires.

My longings are becoming more frequent. Stronger! he thought as his face tightened with disappointment. From the corner of his eye, he caught Jude watching him, and for one fleeting moment he felt that Jude knew his thoughts.

"When you were with Jesus and the Authorities were getting angrier with Jesus, were you or the Others afraid?" he asked, knowing that his question would end Jude's speculation.

Jude, accepting the trap, said, "At first we were terrified because these were the leaders of our people. They had control over us, even more than the Romans did, because they controlled our religion. As time passed and we saw the power Jesus had, we knew He would protect us from the leaders." He stopped and looked at Dorimius. "In recent years, I have thought often of Jesus' protection of us. I find it ironic that we expected Jesus to protect us, and yet Jesus did not expect us to protect Him. I am sure that He knew we were not strong, that we still had worldly desires and ambitions."

A shiver raced through Dorimius. He was certain that Jude knew his longing for Rome. He walked quickly from the hut and found the hot, dry, blazing sun strangely refreshing.

After a long absence, Dorimius returned to the hut. He had been with Jude for many years and had traveled with him through Syria,

Osroene, Armenia, Mesopotamia, and finally Persia and the Parthian Empire. He never told Jude of his desire to return to Roman life. This day, as he walked alone, he knew he had betrayed himself. He decided that he would talk to Jude about his desires and failures. He returned to the hut, eager to blurt out his dilemma, but he found Jude on the shady side of the room in prayer. Dorimius did not know what to do. He never prayed this much. Over the years, these times of impulsive prayer would occur after Jude had preached and baptized, and even then Dorimius did not know what to do. Jude's posture of praying, with his eyes closed as in a trance, puzzled Dorimius. With no immediate solution, Dorimius sat in the shade and waited, determined to speak honestly to Jude. His anxiety was so strong that he had to bite hard to keep his mouth shut, for he wanted to shout Jude out of prayer and talk about his problems.

Suddenly, Jude opened his eyes and, looking at Dorimius in surprise, said, "Oh, I did not know you were there."

"What were you doing?" Dorimius demanded.

Jude sensed an urgency in Dorimius' voice. He softly answered, "I was remembering yesterdays. You, I, and many others are blessed, for we saw Jesus and know His face."

Dorimius looked out of the hut and said coldly and with regret, "I only remember His hands."

"And that is more than many know and remember," Jude quickly replied, and then sensing the need for more he added, "but that does not satisfy you, does it Dorimius? You have need for more."

Dorimius turned and looked at Jude. "When I was on Golgotha, I received no miracles like Longinus or Abendadar. I received no revelations like Nescius, or Namenlos, or Cornelius. I got nothing, yet I cannot turn my back on Jesus. He captured me."

"And how did He accomplish this capture? What did He do to you?"

Dorimius knew this was the moment of truth, so he blurted out, "He did nothing. He said nothing. He only gave me silence."

Jude smiled and declared, "How blessed you are!"

The Roman reeled in shock. "Blessed? How can you say that?"

Jude smiled slightly at the thought that Dorimius still had a touch of Roman thinking in him.

"Do you not remember me saying that silence was one of the blessings that Jesus gives all of us?" Seeing no reaction on his companion's face, Jude, with great warmth in his voice, continued, "My friend, Jesus gave you the one gift He had left to give: He gave you His consent to your actions by His silence." Seeing that he had not convinced Dorimius, Jude went on, "I believe you have taken the Master's silence as something bad or meaningless—this would be a great mistake. Silence was always a great gift of Jesus, for it was in His silence that He spoke the loudest, like when He stood before the tomb of His friend Lazarus—that silence was deafening. Everyone around Jesus knew what He was feeling. Jesus was also silent before Herod; that silence was more powerful than words. We know Jesus' silence was innocence. Herod knew this and could not confront Jesus, for Herod feared innocence. Likewise, we know of His silent moments before Pilate, and that silence was like a mighty storm. So you see, Jesus' silence speaks loudly. To me, silence is ever associated with the Almighty. It is a blessing to receive and a greater blessing to have. Silence was the only thing God experienced. Before He created the world, there was silence, and it was out of silence that the words of creation were spoken. Because it is so closely related to God, we humans struggle to appreciate it. It is a foreign thing to us; we do not know how to become a companion to it, because we are the noisiest of creatures—noisier even than our nearby hyena friends. Humans associate silence with death and are fearful of it. But silence is not death, it is life—through silence, the Almighty speaks to mankind, and it is our responsibility to hear the voice of God in silence."

Jude stopped and looked at Dorimius, whose face was expressionless.

"I am not like you, Jude. I need things to happen to me; I need things to be shown to me. You speak of listening and being still, but that is not my life. My life was and is filled with here and now. I am one who hears orders and carries them out. I do not have the capacity to fight off the distraction of a hyena's laugh. I am weak and unable to turn away from material things, especially things of my former life. To me, silence is a barbarian's attempt to harm me. I cannot hold silence and hope for a soft breeze or a tiny breath of air to give me meanings and directions. I need things to be said to me."

He stopped, and Jude knew he was hesitating, maybe even debating with himself to go on; finally, he broke his hesitation and said in a clear voice, "I long for the Roman life because it is there and it speaks to me of good things. I long for it so much that sometimes I want to run away." He stopped speaking and lowered his head, seemingly in shame. "The silence I got from Jesus froze me in time; it caused me to want more, and for the past years I have waited for more—but I only relive Golgotha and hear silence. I pray for His help, but my prayers go unheard; my life seems confined to Golgotha."

It was out! Now the air from a deep breath filled his lungs and replaced the stale air that had choked him for many years.

Jude's heart ached with his companion's pain. He heard the cry and struggle in Dorimius' words. Ten years of companionship had made this man like a brother to him, but much to Jude's disappointment, Dorimius remained distant and not completely in the realm of Jesus. During this time, Jude surmised that Dorimius was punishing himself for having nailed Jesus. He tried on many occasions to help the Roman, but Dorimius would not permit conversations about his spirituality. Now, for the first time, Dorimius spoke openly of his life as a Christian, and Jude sensed it was too late.

"Jesus comes to us in His way, not ours. He meets us half way; we must travel the other half to Him. That is the way love is; you go so far to meet someone, and that someone must come the other distance. Love is when two halves become one. So it is with Jesus. He came to you, now you must go out to meet Him."

"That is the problem! That half way voyage is far off! You and others can talk with much certainty because you heard Jesus. All I know is His death, which I helped to bring about, and His silence." In exasperation, he rose and walked around the hut. "Maybe I do not love Jesus, or maybe He does not love me. He would certainly be justified in despising me."

"You are wrong! You did not kill Jesus, and He loves you. He did not condemn you from the cross—He saved you for something else. Dorimius, everyone who comes to Jesus feels guilty and unloved. It is part of the conversion. Jesus had to come to redeem us because we needed to see God's love and witness God's forgiveness. These are the messages of Jesus' mission."

Dorimius looked at Jude. His face was draped with sadness, and he said softly, "But I do not find either of these things in what I do. I am the embittered brother in that story Jesus told of the son who squandered all his inheritance and then returned—like him, I feel unloved and even unimportant. I feel forgotten, and now I feel like I want to squander my inheritance."

A long silence filled the space between the two men.

Jude lowered his head and closed his eyes, then with great pain, he said, "Then I will release you. You have to find Jesus. Our journeys have somehow allowed you to lose Jesus. You must find Him again. Let yourself go into silence. Wait, and you will hear our Lord's words, for you lost Him in the silence that torments you."

Dorimius searched Jude's face. He could not find a line or wrinkle that could hide a lie. After a short time, he said, "So you think I will hear the voice of Jesus by being still and silent? And you? Did you ever hear Jesus' voice in silence?"

"Yes. In my silent prayers, I hear His voice daily."

Dorimius looked at Jude then turned his head away so that Jude would not see the envy in his eyes.

✳

Later that night, as the chill from the mountains slipped down and settled into the valleys, they slept. Jude slept in the comfort and warmth of the memories of Jesus; Dorimius slept in the hard, damp silence of the night, and through the night he heard the sound of the hyena's laugh.

The next morning, Dorimius opened his eyes and found Jude deep in prayer. He slowly, quietly slipped out of the hut and walked hurriedly away. He did not feel like praying; he was hungry and was determined to find some fruits. As he walked, he looked up at the nearby grayish-purple, white-capped mountains. They seemed more ominous. He turned his head away, not because he was afraid of them but because he did not have the patience to be bothered by them. As he walked, he looked off into the distance and spotted two small specks. He stopped and looked harder. Soon, the specks became dots. He waited until he was certain—today he needed to be certain. When the forms began to look like images of men, he called out to Jude.

"Jude Thaddeus! I think they are coming!"

Within seconds Jude was beside Dorimius, straining his eyes.

"They are people to be sure, but I cannot tell if it is Simon and Clavos," Jude stated. "If they get closer, I will be able to tell by Simon's walk. His left foot always turns a bit more to the left."

The two men stood watching, and then a smile slid across Jude's face.

"It is them! They have arrived."

When the two Apostles were close enough to each other, they ran, and just before they collided into each other they stopped.

"Simon, your hair is all white!"

"Jude Thaddeus, your hair is gone!"

They laughed and embraced like two children.

Clavos and Dorimius stood by looking on with amusement.

✳

"You have been on the other side of these mountains too long, Jude Thaddeus; you have missed a lot of history," Simon said lightly. "The Judeans revolted, and Rome threw them out of Jerusalem and out of many other places in Judea and Galilee." Simon's voice was excited with pride. "Cestius Gallus, the Governor of Syria, sent the Twelfth Legion into Galilee, but they were routed by the Judeans and the Galileans."

Simon's voice softened. "Sadly, the Jews killed the rear guards of the Legion—about four hundred Romans."

"Who led this foolish revolt?" Dorimius questioned with a tone of mockery in his voice.

Simon looked at him in surprise, then remembered that this was a Roman like Clavos but apparently, unlike Clavos, still a Roman.

"The Zealots," Simon replied timidly.

"You once were one of them. Did you know these Zealots?" Dorimius asked again, only now his voice was caustic, especially when he sounded the name "Zealots."

Simon hesitated for a moment. He looked at Jude and Clavos and found them looking at Dorimius with caution. He was certain they had heard this same tone in Dorimius' voice.

"Yes," he replied softly. "I knew many of them. I am not proud of what they did. They made things worse for the Jews, and when Titus finally breached the outer wall, and then the second wall, he had no mercy in his heart. Many were killed and sold into slavery."

"And those leaders you knew? They are all dead?" Dorimius asked coldly.

"No, some are still holding out at a place called Masada. Titus still fights there. He has greater numbers, and the Jews will not be able to hold him and his mighty army off forever, though Masada is a difficult place to breach."

"You are wise to think this way, Zealot, for Rome is mightier than all things," Dorimius stated, and then he abruptly rose and walked out of the hut and into the night.

The three men sat silently for a moment, then Clavos remarked sadly, "He has not changed. He still is a Roman first."

"We should not judge him, or anyone; that is the duty of God," Simon interjected quickly.

"He must be excused," Jude remarked, apologetically. "For a long time, he has been in a spiritual dilemma. I pray that Jesus will speak to his heart, for I have not been of any help to him."

"Then we will join you in your prayers, Jude Thaddeus," Simon remarked softly and simply.

Early the next day, Jude and Simon stood outside the hut and watched as Dorimius walked away from them. His body grew smaller and soon formless, then it became a dot, then a speck, and finally it was no more. He was on his way back to his Rome, but he agreed to stop in Ephesus and inform John that Simon and Jude were among the Parthians.

"He never felt comfortable with the Parthians and was in constant turmoil with his guilt of the cross. I could tell he was in retreat. He never prayed on his own, but only when he found me in prayer, and he never found peace or the understanding of silence. He did not know it because he was afraid of silence. Silence would bring to him again the sounds of the hammer."

"We must leave him in the hands of the Master," Simon said looking into Jude's disappointed face. "Jesus did wonders with us, did He not? We will leave him to Jesus, and when the Master picks the right time— Dorimius' time—he will hear the call. Until then, we will pray to remind the Master of a lost sheep."

✳

For the next ten years, the two Apostles worked together in Parthia. They remained cut off from the Roman and Jewish worlds and knew of no other world but that in which they labored. The Parthians had a different lifestyle, and they readily adjusted to their new environment. Unlike in Rome, there was no heavy controlling hand from the Emperor, because the Parthian Empire was not centralized. It was composed of many small kingdoms and even some city-states. Each kingdom and city-state had its own kings or rulers, and these small realms functioned independently, with their own currency, armies, and in some instances, their own sets of laws. Yet like Rome, the Empire was composed of many different nationalities and languages.

The Emperor Vologases I, like the emperors before him, was in reality an overlord. The Emperors of Parthia for years had been called "the king of kings," for they were indeed kings over many other kings.

The smaller rulers were important to the survival of the Empire, and they were respected by the Emperor, who knew he could not rule without them. These rulers also had an important role in choosing a new Emperor of Parthia. Many of them sat and voted in the Royal Council, which appointed the Emperor. One of these sovereigns, and his descendants, even had the sole honor of crowning every newly appointed Emperor. The Emperor had two capitals, Susa and Ctesiphon, and he traveled between them constantly. His wealth came from tributes paid to him by the eighteen kingdoms. Because Parthia was central to the silk trade, a toll was placed on all silk passing through the empire. Tolls, which made up a large part of the Imperial Treasury, were also placed on all goods coming into and going out of the seaports, especially the seaport of Siraf.

The Parthians were a very difficult people, and Jude was appalled at the looseness of the government and of the various laws, customs, and morals of the local peoples. There were no laws governing marriage; consequently, marriages were quickly made and quickly dissolved. Marriage had no social value. Divorces were granted for the most frivolous and dubious reasons. Adultery was expected; fornication and illegitimate children were commonplace. The fathers of children born out of wedlock could take the child from the mother, and in some cases they would sell the child into slavery—the mother, and women in general, had no rights. Injustice was the norm. In cases of murder or robbery, the accused were put to death even before evidence was gathered. Life was cheap. It had no purpose other than to produce food and products to make life comfortable for the rich and powerful. The general populace survived in a loose form of slavery; they were subjected to abuse by the local royalty and authorities. They were taxed unjustly and received few benefits for their sacrifices. Even in death the human person was cheap, for the dead were not buried but taken out of the city limits and left to be devoured by wild animals.

The Parthians benefitted greatly from the influence of the Zoroastrians, who like the Jews and the followers of Jesus, believed in one Supreme and Loving God, Whom they called *Ahura Mazda* the Wise Lord. They also believed in the complete triumph of good over evil, individual judgment of life at the time of death, and life after death through a resurrection. They maintained a vague faith in a messiah who would come and save all living things from darkness. The followers of this religion believed in a strong moral code and were deeply concerned for their countrymen.

When Jude came to these believers and spoke of Jesus and the One God, of judgment, and of life after death, these people were not very receptive because he was not offering them anything new. The belief in *Ahura Mazda* was so similar to Jude's preaching that many walked away, though some did come to believe that Jesus was the promised Messiah. His successes remained few until he came upon the "fall-aways," a group of idol worshippers who followed some practices of the Zoroastrians and whose priests were known as *magi*. These *magi* were seekers of their own power, and those who followed them did so blindly and in fear. Often, Jude found himself in direct conflict with these *magi*, and eventually he decided to write Simon the Zealot and ask for his help.

SIMON AND JUDE

Two days after Dorimius left them, the three men journeyed north to the city of Ecbatana and on to Lake Matianus near the border of Armenia. They preached there for several years. Their efforts were fruitful, for they found many converts in the rural areas but sadly not among the Zoroastrians, who were strongest in the cities. At times, there were great debates with the Zoroastrian *magi*, who came out of the cities to listen to these men from Judea. Though the debates were heated, the Apostles were never arrested, imprisoned, or in danger of death. The *magi* were educated and mostly non-violent, and they enjoyed the mental stimulation of religious debate. This tolerance, however, was not shared by all of the Parthians. Many Parthians were uneducated and deeply set in their ways. Most of the uneducated lived outside the cities. They were controlled by self-ordained priests who led the people in different versions of Zoroastrianism. Most were pantheists or idol worshippers who were dominated by superstition and the powerful *magi*. The *magi* of these religions were not as tolerant as the Zoroastrian *magi*, but their attacks on Christianity and the Apostles were feeble and at times completely worthless. They were unable to match the Apostles' intellect and could not defend their beliefs, so many people sought the forgiveness and love of Christianity. Charity, compassion, and the pursuit of virtue were new concepts to these people.

As the years passed, the three began to travel farther south into the land where idol worship was more prominent, despite large pockets of Zoroastrianism. Simon and Jude had to adjust to each village because it was common to find different gods being worshipped in each place. Their pantheism led them to worship lions, tigers, birds, and serpents.

In the south, the *magi* were deeply entrenched in the government, and their grip on the people was absolute in some places. They controlled the rulers of the city-states and wielded powers to change the course of the government. To keep their believers deceived and controlled, they often staged spectacles.

When Simon and Jude came into the south, the *magi* found themselves at a loss, for the conversions to Christianity were rapid and numerous, so that even the Apostles trembled at their success. Fearful that the kings would hear of these successes and become curious, the *magi* prevented the Apostles from coming into the major cities. This was an easy thing for them to do because they controlled the law enforcement in the cities, but this worked to the benefit of the Apostles, for they concentrated more on the nomads, the poor, and the unwanted.

After a year of watching the Apostles' successes, the *magi* went out to the countryside and met the Apostles. They began an abusive verbal campaign against them. These attacks, though frequent, proved unsuccessful. It was obvious that they could not match the power that seemed to radiate from Simon and Jude. At a loss, the *magi* watched as rumors of the Apostles drew the city dwellers out to meet Simon and Jude. In desperation, the frightened *magi* sought help in plotting their revenge.

On a warm, dry day, from a large crowd that stood listening to Simon and Jude, there came a tall, thin man whose deep, black eyes created dark shadows over his face. The first thing noticeable on his tanned face was his long, thin, beak-like nose. He had a black, heavy beard that was curled and oiled. His hair was raven black and held in place by a gold band that wrapped around his high forehead and tied in the back of his head. His hands were large, with long, thin fingers that had many rings on them. His fingernails were long, just long enough to begin to turn down. Thick, heavy, black hair covered the back of his hand. He wore long sleeves that hid his thick, hairy arms. His body was delicate; it was obvious he had never worked a hard day in his life. His glare was full of hatred, and it was obvious that he was a man of little tolerance. His name was Zaroes. He was known as a High Magus, one of the Supreme Magi, and he was known for his violence and hatred. He stood above the crowd. The moment Jude saw him, Jude felt a surge of coldness race through his body, and from nowhere a thought came to Jude: he remembered his brother Matthew telling him of *magi* coming to see Jesus after His birth, and he wondered if they had looked like this *magus*.

Simon was speaking to the people and was seemingly unaware of Zaroes' presence. Instead, he was watching another *magus* who was standing directly before him and whose extravagance was distracting the Apostle.

The man was short, fat, and round. Everything about him was round. His face, nose, ears, shoulders, and waist were in rotund harmony. His fingers were short and chubby and well trimmed, and on each finger he was wearing large rings of every gem and color. Climbing up his arms and wrists were bracelets of various sizes, designs, and precious metals. His hair and beard were curled, perfumed, and glossy black. A thin gold band wrapped around his head, and it was tied at the back of his head in a neat bow. His heavy black eyebrows darkened his deeply set eyes. A finely embroidered cloak flowed over his body and partly covered the long, loose, white-and-gold robe that fell in front of his protruding stomach. He stood looking at Simon in an unbroken stare and with a petulant smile on his face. His name was Arfaxat, and he also was a High Magus, one of the Supreme Magi.

From the crowd came a rasping, cracking voice: "Tell me, Jew, where is the image of your God?"

Simon turned his attention to Zaroes.

"Jesus the Christ needs no image," Simon replied plainly.

"You want us to believe in a God Who has no being?" Arfaxat chimed in, drawing both Apostles' attention.

"Jesus is the living image of the One God. His love is given freely to all people," Simon stated with equal plainness.

"What a pity, for I know some ugly people," Zaroes said with a chuckle.

"And some diseased people," added Arfaxat with great amusement.

Many people snickered and laughed.

"He loves all these people," Jude said, taking a small step in Arfaxat's direction.

"But who needs a God that wastes His time with the weak and wretched?" Zaroes shouted.

Arfaxat turned to those around him and echoed, "Yes, what kind of God is that?"

"A God that loves unconditionally," everyone heard Simon shout above the laughter. Then silence returned, and he continued: "He is a God Who created us and stays with us always."

"Whose love is so great that He became one of us and suffered, heat and cold, pain and sorrow," Jude shouted looking at Zaroes.

"A God so full of love that He gave His Son as a sacrifice for our salvation," Simon stated as he walked slowly to Jude's side.

Everyone looked to the *magi* waiting for a reply, but before one came, they heard Simon question in a booming voice, "And where is your god, O High Magus? Stuck in a stone? In a beast? Away from the people, and seen only when visited?"

Jude cleared his throat, and with an equally loud voice he said, "Your god sits in an image made from the very ground you stand upon. How great does that make your god? Tell us of your god's love and care, and of his need to be among his people. Tell us, where is your god?"

There was no answer. The *magi* had disappeared and returned to their city fortress. That day, many were taken to the nearby river to be reborn in Jesus the Christ.

For the next year, these two *magi* confronted the Apostles. They challenged every teaching and insisted that the Apostles were impostors and charlatans. Several times they accused Simon of being a "murderer" and Jude a "betrayer." They often accused the Apostles, and all Christians, of being "cannibals" for eating the flesh of their God, while the Apostles showed that the Meal was the manifestation of God's love and presence among His people.

After it was reported that Simon and Jude had performed a miracle in the name of Jesus, the *magi* came; they were disguised, but the Apostles knew they were present because they could sense the hatred and evil.

One day, several Christians came to the Apostles begging them to be careful because the *magi* were plotting against them. So the Apostles and Clavos retreated slightly. Later, a larger group came to them and begged them to leave, for their arrest was imminent. They decided to go into the desert and refresh themselves in prayer and fasting. They traveled in the heat of day and enjoyed the cool desert nights. Though they did not rush their travel, they found they had traveled far, and soon they felt the loneliness of distance. They prayed asking for something from the Master to confirm their desire to return to their Christian family. At dusk on the third day, they saw two doves flying in the direction of their former mission. They believed that this was a sign, so they celebrated the Meal and went to sleep.

During the night, as they slept, they quietly were surrounded by Parthian soldiers. They were arrested, taken to an army camp, and imprisoned in a heavily guarded tent. They were told that they were being detained as spies and that they would be brought before the commander of the Parthian Army. At morning, they were shackled and led to the tent of Prince Baradach, who was preparing for a campaign against an army from India. The prince was seeking godly guidance from the *magi* Zaroes and Arfaxat. The two *magi* had just finished predicting his success in battle when the three Christians were escorted into the tent. Upon seeing the two Apostles, the *magi* immediately demanded that they be killed.

The prince, whose spies informed him of these men, was curious and said to them, "We hear much of your God. Tell us what your God is saying of this war against the Indians."

The Apostles instantly knelt, and after a few moments of prayer they rose.

Simon said, "At this hour tomorrow, your war will be over."

Zaroes walked to Simon and Jude and laughed at them.

"That is exactly what we told you, Your Highness," he snorted.

"I said the war would be over, not won," Simon said with a small smile of satisfaction on his face.

Jude quickly added, "There will be no war, Prince. The Indians will come with a peace offer and war will be avoided."

"That is nonsense. There will be a glorious victory for the prince, and he will receive great rewards from the Emperor of the Parthians," Arfaxat yelled.

"My Lord, truly you cannot believe the words of these allies of the Indians. They are both Romans and Jews, and we all know that the Romans and Jews are in league with the Indian barbarians. I beg you, most kind...."

The prince slowly raised his hand and stood up. Immediately everyone in the room, except the Apostles and Clavos, bowed.

"We will see. It is our intent to break camp tomorrow and advance on the Indians. We will see if these Jews are correct. If their prediction is true, we will trust in their God. In the meantime, all of you will remain as our guests." He turned and looked down at Zaroes and Arfaxat. "You *magi* can return to the comfort of your tents."

The prince turned and looked at Simon, Jude, and Clavos. "Guards, take these foreigners to their tent, feed them, and give them the comforts of honored guests. No one is to go near them until this time tomorrow."

Looking at the *magi* he said, "If these men are correct, we will have a lengthy talk with them about their God, and we will not need to see you *magi* again." He turned quickly and looked at the three men of Christ. "But if the *magi* are correct, you will be tortured and killed. We have spoken. We have made ourselves clear. Now go and leave us to our planning."

The *magi* quickly backed out of the tent. The guards came and directed the Apostles and Clavos to a new and larger tent with food, water, and sleeping mats.

The next morning, Simon and Jude rose and immediately began their morning prayers. A few moments into prayer, they became distracted at the sounds of clanging armor, galloping horses, and shouts of rough commands outside and around their tent.

Suddenly, guards appeared at the entrance of the tent and roughly ordered the Apostles to follow them to the prince's tent. Sensing danger, Simon turned to Clavos and in a low whisper ordered him to stay in the tent—"but if you see an opportunity to escape, take it."

Simon and Jude exited the tent and followed the guards to the prince. As they walked, Jude said in a low voice that held no regret, only joy, "My brother, I think the Master is calling us."

Simon smiled brightly.

When they arrived, they were immediately escorted into the presence of the prince, who was being dressed in his armor by a group of black slaves.

Without acknowledging their presence, the prince said, "Apparently your God was incorrect, Jews. Our spies tell us that the Indians are advancing toward our camp."

He acknowledged them with a quick glance.

"You lose." He spoke plainly and without emotion. Turning away from his prisoners, he ordered in a loud, commanding voice, "Guards, bind them in chains and take them away. We will send you instructions as to what to do with them."

The Apostles were roughly rushed away and brought back to their tent. They found all the luxuries, as well as Clavos, gone.

They immediately went into prayer, not out of fear, but to ask God to forgive their murderers. They prayed for a long time, and their sincerity drowned out the world around them. They did not hear the loud, long blare of the trumpets or the beat of the ceremonial drums, nor did they hear the sounds of marching feet.

Sometime later, the flap to their tent was thrown open. Prince Baradach walked in with an uneasy smile on his lips.

"Your God has proven to be a greater God," the prince said as his eyes searched the faces of the two men, hoping to find the secret to their power. "This morning, at the very hour you said, the Indians arrived and sought peace. After seeing their armies, I know that the battle would have been theirs—but still they came for peace."

He looked around the tent, and disapproval covered his face.

"We will see to it that you are made more comfortable. Please accept our hospitality with gratitude, for the peace agreement has given more than we expected. The Emperor will be pleased. We will tell him of the power of your God, and we will see to it that the Emperor rewards you with an audience. You are free to stay among us and enjoy our hospitality, with my blessing."

He nodded his head and turned, but as he walked out of the tent he said, "Your counterparts, Zaroes and Arfaxat, are not to be found. We will search for them, and when they are found, we will attend to them in the manner intended for you."

He left the Apostles, who simply continued with their prayers, only now they offered prayers of praise and thanksgiving. As they were finishing their prayers, slaves and servants came into the tent and began to place Persian rugs on the ground. They built a fire and carried in large amounts of food, wine, and water. The two became uncomfortable; slowly, yet politely, they left the tent and walked out of the prince's encampment and away.

Once away from all that opulence and luxury, they proceeded to a new place far from Prince Baradach.

For two days, they traveled without any direction other than the feeling that they were in pursuit of the two *magi*. Unknown to them, they had passed from the domain of Prince Baradach into another princely kingdom, whose inhabitants were deeply immersed in idol worship.

On the third day, as Simon and Jude came out of a great arid strip of land, they saw in the distance an unbroken stream of black smoke rising into the clear, azure sky. The smoke seemed to intrude upon the beauty of the endless sky. They did not know why this smoke bothered them, but they did know that it meant a pagan sacrifice was taking place. They walked in the direction of the black smoke; they did not speak to each other, for their eyes and minds were fixed on the smoke. Somehow they felt compelled to reach its origin. Less than an hour later, they were climbing the mountainside where the smoke originated. They soon came to a clearing and saw a large assembly of people with their arms raised to the sky. Occasionally those in the assembly would bow and chant response to the calls of the *magi* conducting the worship.

The Apostles immediately recognized the gray stone idols as the gods Lahar, who was the Mesopotamian god of cattle; Nisaba, the Babylonian goddess of grain; and Ama-Arhus, the Akkadian goddess of love. This place was known to the locals as the temple of the three gods, but to others it was a place called Suamar. The idols were carved in the mountainside, with grim, blank eyes and stern faces. Before each idol was a small altar crudely cut from the gray stone of the mountain. In the center of the three idols was a large elevated stone altar. The thin, unbroken black smoke was coming from this altar. On the altar, burning, were a calf, a bundle of wheat, and some flowers. Off to the right of the idols, sitting on a small, high balcony, was the royal family dressed in eloquent clothing, bejeweled and crowned. Standing before the altar with their silky robes were Norbcan and Ecotum, two *magi* who were calling on the gods to provide livestock, wheat, and love to all those in the kingdom. Their prayers were filled with pleas tinted with anguish. These were gods of earth, and the thin stream of smoke rising to the sky was a sign that their sacrifice was not pleasing to the gods. The Apostles descended the mountain and walked through the assembly of people, into the clearing, and up to the altar. As they neared the altar, they drew the attention of the *magi*, who cried out, "Sacrilege! Your Majesty, these men stand on the holy ground of our gods."

The Apostles ignored all the cries and continued to walk to the altar where the *magi* Norbcan and Ecotum were standing. Simon reached the height of the altar and, turning to the people, declared that he had been sent by the true and only God.

Norbcan with rage denounced Simon as a murderer and a follower of a God Who was merely a Jewish criminal.

"We are messengers of the God of Love, the God Who died for our sins and came back to life, as He promised, to give us eternal life," Jude shouted in response to the accusations.

"They teach a false God, one that has no body and that cannot be seen. A ghost!" screamed Ecotum. "What need do we have for such a God when our god is here and visible?"

Norbcan turned to the royal family. "Your Majesties, order these men away from here, for I fear that they desecrate our holy grounds."

"This is not holy ground," Simon said with a small sneer on his lips, "this is ground infested with your deceit."

"Some time ago," shouted Norbcan, "this man told the Supreme Magi Zaroes and Arfaxat that his God was everywhere, but they now say that this holy ground is infested. See the lies of these men. By their own words they condemn themselves."

Jude turned to the assembly and said, "You have come here to ask for livestock, wheat, and love. I promise you all these things in the name of my God, Who is the provider of all things; He is the life-giving bread and the unending giver of love. He is not a silent God made of stone but One Who speaks to His people with undying affection and patience."

To Jude's surprise, the people fell to the ground, and when he turned he saw that the ruler had risen from his throne.

"Strangers, you speak of great things from your God, and we are curious. You say He is here. Good. Let us see Him."

The queen, who was standing by the king's side, smiled.

Jude looked at the crowd before him. Slowly, he walked into the crowd and through it until he came to an old woman whose eyes looked empty.

"You are blind, are you not?" he asked her in a voice loud enough for all to hear. "Have you been blind all your life?"

"All my life, sir."

"If I tell you I can make you see, would you believe in Jesus Christ, the Son of the Living God?"

"I would, sir, and I would become His voice among all others who are blind."

Jude led the woman through the crowd. As they walked, the woman touched others in the crowd with her swaying, extended arms and searching hands. When they reached the clearing, Jude dropped his staff. It fell to the ground softly and without making a sound.

With both his hands, Jude grasped her head, and in a loud voice he said, "In the name of Jesus the Christ, Savior of all those who are blind, I command you to see and become His witness."

The woman trembled for a moment then slowly opened her eyes. She had no color in her eyes, but she shouted, "I can see! I can see!"

Those around her fell back. Those who knew the woman began to rush forward to confirm her sight. Jude reached for his staff and raising it to the sky demanded silence.

He said to the woman, "Tell me, what color of clothing does the king wear?"

The woman turned her head toward the king and with a wide smile declared, "The handsome king is wearing the color of the sky."

The people broke into sheer chaos. Many rushed the Apostles begging to be cured—men on crutches, women on litters, children and infants—all were pushed and pulled before the Apostles amidst cries for help and healing.

Simon joined Jude in his attempt to calm the people, and they settled down. The formerly blind woman walked to Jude and fell to the ground to kiss the hem of his garment.

"No!" Jude corrected her sternly. "Give thanks to Jesus Christ."

The woman stood up and declared, "I believe in Jesus Christ, for He has cured me."

The people began to proclaim Jesus in mumbles and in prayers, and many fell to their knees with tears in their eyes, announcing their belief.

Jude turned to the balcony, but the royal family had disappeared. When he turned to the altar, he found Simon standing alone. The *magi* were gone.

The long, thin stream of smoke from the sacrificial altar had stopped rising because the sacrifice had cooled.

For many months, the Apostles labored among these people. They won many converts, and the fruits of their mission were abundant. During this time, seven thousand were baptized. But the Apostles were growing concerned, for it had been a long time since they had heard from Clavos, and they were uncertain of his whereabouts. They feared that perhaps he had been killed.

One day, a young boy with few teeth came upon them and told them he knew where they could find their manservant. They eagerly asked him, and they were told that he was in the city of Suanir. This city was a stronghold of a group of *magi* who were deeply committed to idol worship, yet their concern for their friend was far greater than their concern for themselves. They decided to follow the boy under the cover of darkness. That night, they slipped into the city and separated in search of their friend. It had been arranged that at the end of each day's search, they would meet near one of the city gates and then find lodging for the night. For two days they were unsuccessful, but on their third day, they were approached by a beggar with one leg. He told them that Clavos had been in hiding for many days and that he could take them to him. They fed the man and gave him some clothing and asked him to lead them to Clavos. They were led to a small side street and found themselves surrounded by a large group of *magi*, who quickly laid hold of them. They were led to the temple.

The temple was a huge building influenced by the Greek style, with tall, thick, gleaming-white columns and a pyramid roof. The arched entrance and hall to the temple gave way to an open court. When the Apostles arrived in the courtyard, there were people sitting, standing, kneeling, and prostrating themselves in prayer. Along the sides of the interior of the building were numerous rooms used for the needs of the *magi* and the royal worshippers. The walls were plaster of lime and ash with decorations of various plants, flowers, and animals. The floor was gray and of a material unknown to the Apostles, but as they walked on it they felt the hardness of the material under their feet. At the center of the court was a large altar that was covered with flowers, food, fruit, and livestock, all of which were offerings given by the people. Beyond the courtyard and directly behind the altar was a large doorway that led to the sacred chamber of the temple.

The idols of the "divine triad gods" stood tall, grim, and stoic above the many *magi* present. In the center was the god Ba-al-Shamin. The pagans believed him to be the god of all gods—the lord of the heavens. His face was painted in flesh tones to make him look human. He wore a beard as a sign of authority. In his right hand was a spear with lightning rods charging from the point, and in his other hand he held rocks. These signified his power over the heavens and the earth. He was wearing Parthian-style trousers. To his left was Yarhibol, the sun god; he had a burst of sunrise behind his head and was wearing a tunic. He had no beard, and his hair was curled and fell onto his shoulders. To the right of Ba-al-Shamin was Aglibol, the moon god, who resembled the sun god but had a group of quarter moons behind his head.

The Apostles were taken into the sacred chamber. There were sixty-six *magi* all dressed in flowing cloaks of gold and white. They were around the sacrificial altar, and among them were Zaroes and Arfaxat. Zaroes immediately shouted attacks against Simon and Jude, accusing them of poisoning the minds of all Parthians with lies and magic. Arfaxat chimed in, calling them impostors and worshippers of a lawbreaker Who was crucified by the Romans. The accusations continued; throughout the barrage, the Apostles remained silent.

Finally, an elderly man, richly dressed, rose from his chair. Because of his age, he was assisted by another *magus*. This man was known as Somindoch.

Immediately all the shouts and accusations ceased.

"Tell me, Jews of Jesus, why do you not answer your accusers?"

The Apostles remained silent.

"Do you not know that these accusations are serious in the eyes of this assembly?"

Again they remained silent.

Other *magi* began to grow angry at what they saw as impudence. Somindoch slowly and gently raised his hand, and all fell silent.

"If you show us that you are not our enemies, we will let you go and permit you to continue preaching your God. To show you that we are willing to live in peace, as we do with the Zoroastrians, we will even offer you the honor of being called *magi*."

"But your Supremeness," pleaded Zaroes, "these men are violators of our gods."

"They even know of charms and magic that look believable to the ignorant," added Arfaxat.

Somindoch looked at them sharply, and the look drained the *magi* of any courage they thought they had.

Somindoch looked at the Apostles. "My friends, to gain favor with us you must do one thing in exchange for freedom and priesthood. You must adore our supreme gods."

Mumbles of approval echoed in the sanctuary; even Zaroes and Arfaxat were smiling.

Simon and Jude looked at each other, then Simon said, "We will not have strange gods before our God. Your gods are stone idols that stand for nothing but deception and fear. My God is alive and full of love."

"Blasphemer!" shouted Zaroes as he rushed to Simon intending to strike him.

"Stop!" Somindoch shouted.

Zaroes complied instantly.

"You think your God is so great, Roman Jew?"

"Far more powerful than your god," replied Jude.

Simon took a few steps toward the idols and in a loud voice shouted, "In the name of Jesus, come forth, Satan. Show your true image to these people, whom you have fooled for all these years. Let them see your true, hideous face."

From nowhere came a moan that echoed throughout the temple, and seemingly throughout the entire land. It startled the *magi*. It was so loud, so painful, that those in the courtyard rushed to the entrance of the sanctuary to see who it was that cried so painfully.

"In the name of Jesus Christ, you are commanded, evil one, to leave this place," Jude shouted.

The moan became deafening.

From one of the idols came a loud, torturous moan. A black, smoky image seeped out of the stone. It lingered for a short time, then with a louder scream it flew out of the sanctuary.

Everyone was in a panic, except the Apostles. They silently made the sign of the cross in the air.

A second scream was followed by a third, and again black deformed images seeped from the stones and flew away, screaming and crying as they vanished.

The idols trembled violently and finally crumbled into a mass of dust and clay.

Jude turned to Somindoch and, pointing at the destroyed images, shouted, "There are your gods! Now hear the words of my God: 'I am the Lord your God, you shall not have strange gods before Me.'"

But the *magi* had vanished; Simon and Jude alone remained amidst the destruction that God's justice had wrought.

"Jude Thaddeus."

He did not have to turn, for he recognized the voice, but when he did, he saw an image in the doorway, deep in the shadows cast by the setting sun.

Jude rushed to him and they embraced.

"Where have you been? We have searched for you for days."

"I was told that you would be here in Sunair," Clavos said, "and I came here looking for you and Simon. I was led all over the city by a boy and a beggar who claimed to know your whereabouts."

"And we came to this city in search of you."

"Where is Simon?"

"As I came in, he was hurrying out the door. He told me that a messenger came and said that the *magus* Zaroes waited for him by the river, for he now believes in Jesus and wants to be baptized."

"I hope this messenger was more reliable than the ones I have been dealing with."

Suddenly Jude's eyes widened.

"This boy who helped you, did he have few teeth?" he asked Clavos hurriedly. "And the old beggar, did he have one leg?"

"Why yes, how did you…" but before Clavos could finish, Jude was running from the room and down the dusty road.

"Follow me. I think Simon is in trouble."

Clavos followed. They raced through the city gates and around the east side of the city walls to a patch of trees.

Jude suddenly stopped and, breathing heavily, ordered Clavos to stay well behind him and hidden.

Clavos obeyed and fell behind. He watched Jude race through the closely spaced trees and disappear into the brush.

When Clavos finally arrived near the clearing, he fell to his knees in shock.

Jude stood about three hundred paces ahead of him. Clavos could hear his heavy breathing and then the utterance, "Jesus, forgive them."

In front of them was the torn body of Simon.

He was tied upside down and hung between two trees in the shape of the Greek letter *chi* X. His right wrist and leg were tied to one tree and his left arm and wrist were tied to another. His right leg had been sawn off at the hip. It dangled and hugged the tree. His left hand, wrist, and arm, which had been sawn off at the shoulder, rested on the grass still bound to the tree. His chest and face were covered with the blood that streamed down his ripped stomach. The saw that had been the tool of torment remained in his body at his stomach, where his murderers had stopped.

Clavos, who had seen much blood and death in his life, was sickened by the sight. The pain that Simon must have endured brought chills to his body. He had heard that the Parthians killed Roman prisoners this way, but upon seeing it, he could scarcely believe it. He closed his eyes to blot out the horror before him, and he could hear Jude praying that Jesus would welcome his faithful Apostle. Clavos, with his eyes closed, silently joined in this prayer.

Suddenly he heard the sounds of running feet, and when he looked up he saw three muscular men charging at Jude with a small tree trunk that had been cut to a point. Before he could shout a warning, they had reached their goal. He heard a loud thump and then a loud moan as the tree pierced Jude's back and partially exited the front of his body. The three men then planted the tree trunk into a prepared hole nearby and secured it in place. They left Jude's body impaled upon it. Blood began to flow down the sides of the trunk as Jude's life seeped away.

Clavos, horrified, remained on his knees—expecting, wanting, needing to be next. But all was quiet and all was still, except for the flies and insects that began to swarm the bodies of the two Apostles.

Clavos thought of Golgotha. He silently prayed to Jesus asking Him to accept the souls of the Apostles. Finally he uttered, "Father…." Soon he felt the same warmth he experienced on Golgotha. "My Father," he said with joy in his heart, "forgive them, for they know not what they do."

EPILOGUE

After his release from the Roman prison in the Asian city of Philadelphia, he sensed that something extraordinary had happened to him. He did not know what it was, but something had changed in his mind and in his body. He first noticed this change when he tried to return to his writing. He found that he could not concentrate on anything for long periods of time. His mind simply would not function in a disciplined realm; it seemed to wander and would not stay on one thought long enough for him to write what he was thinking. Every sound, even a passing fly, was a distraction, and once distracted, he could not return to his writing. He would look for excuses to keep him away from the parchments. After many days of difficulty, he finally returned to his writing, but his thoughts came slowly and they had to be drawn forcibly out of his head. His writing became an onerous task. In addition, he noticed that he was always physically tired. His nights were filled with dreams and of times forgotten or overlooked in his writing. He would wake from these dreams and make mental notes, but inevitably when morning came, his mental notes were forgotten. He felt new bodily pains, and though he was one who could endure pain, these persistent pains were nagging, and he could not overcome the depth of the discomfort they created. They, too, were distractions from his writing. All these things puzzled John. He was certain that they all were caused by his imprisonment, but he could not see how this imprisonment was any different. He had already seen many prison cells, and he could not understand why he was experiencing such a great effect this time. Instead of writing, preaching, or teaching, he spent hours and days trying to determine the reason for this different experience. His arrest brought him much contentment, for it made him closer to Jesus. He had joyfully defied the authorities in a theater where a performance ridiculing Christian Baptism was taking place. The outdoor theatre used for gladiatorial events was crowded with spectators. It was a perfect forum for John to declare Jesus the Christ. Though he was not able to stop the performance, he was able to alert the crowd to Christ's message of love and forgiveness. He was dragged away from the theatre, kicked, beaten with sticks, and punched by soldiers, who as usual found sadistic pleasure in this abuse.

He remained defiant before the Roman Magistrate Aplius Mairius Gaudius, and after hours of interrogation, he was finally sentenced to death. With joy in his heart he accepted his fate, welcoming his chains and his time in the cold cell. During the night, he had a dream about his work being found and destroyed by the Romans. This saddened him, and he began to sob in his sleep. He saw thousands of strange people in strange clothing crying and wailing, because they did not know the story of Jesus. In his dream he begged Jesus and Lady Mary to forgive him for failing in his duty, and when he woke he was outside the city walls, sleeping with beggars. This miraculous release was a direct sign to him that he was to finish his writing. So he returned to his home determined to continue his writing. Then things grew dangerous for him, for he had been declared an escaped prisoner and was wanted by the authorities of the Roman Province of Asia. He notified the "dear lady" of his dilemma, and she provided him with a small hut outside of Ephesus, away from roads and commerce and everything else. Alone in this hut he faced his troubles, and though he was bothered by his lack of writing, he knew that this was Jesus' way of preparing him for something important, so he impatiently waited.

Jesus will make it happen, for He now knows that I miss writing about Him. I know now that this is what I must do. I must do this, not for me or for now, but for all those strange people who need to know about Jesus. I will wait until Jesus makes it happen. I will not go to Jesus or be with my brother Disciples until I write this account of my Master.

For years John remained away from the world, yet not completely without the world. He was in constant contact with the many Christians in the area through two families, who gave him news of the fall and sack of Jerusalem, of the persecutions against Christians, of the volcanic destruction of the city of Pompeii, and of the growth of the Church. These two prosperous Christian families, who lived a short distance from his hut, were his only connection to the outside world. Both families had sons who, because of their youth, were used as messengers. Their visits were so frequent that they became John's companions. The two youngsters, Papias and Polycarp, filled John's life with questions and youthful curiosities. Their innocence brought him amusement, and their enthusiasm for knowing gave him hope.

Papias was the son of Stabius Alpinius and Luvena, both Roman Greeks who had been baptized by the Apostle Philip. During a local Greek persecution, Stabius and his daughter were arrested. His wife and son were away when this happened. Stabius was beaten and released, but his daughter Muriella was held. She, like so many others, was given the opportunity to worship the Roman gods, but she refused and was beaten, raped, and beheaded. Worried that his fearless young son Papias would declare his belief in Jesus, Stabius left Greece and moved farther east.

The other family was that of Nestor Diliponius, a Roman Christian from Armenia who had been in the company of Jude and Simon when they had preached in his country. Nestor had been a civilian employee of the Armenian-Roman government and had served at that job for several years, but when he became a Christian, he left and bought property in the Asian countryside to raise sheep and goats. His son, Polycarp, was fifteen and a student of Greek philosophy. He was a true follower of Jesus and openly told his family and John that he wanted to be a presbyter.

It was with the coming of these two boys, Papias and Polycarp, that John began to write again and not as slowly as he had in the past, but with a new energy. The two youngsters, who did not know each other until they met in John's hut, became friends. Together, they would visit John and spend hours questioning him about Jesus. Their visits were blessings to John because they helped him to remember details that he had forgotten. They would supply him with parchment, *papyrus*, and *stylus* and would then listen to him read what he had written. Their questions about his writings helped him to refine his wording. Soon, they began copying his scrolls. John daily thanked God for the companionship of these fervent young Christians.

John, still cognizant of his dream, entrusted the boys with storing the scrolls. They hid them in their parents' homes and in a mountain grotto that served as a crypt for their families and for the celebration of the Meal.

Then one cold day, Papias came running to the hut, followed closely by Polycarp. It was the tenth month in the Roman calendar and the month of *Kislev* in the Jewish calendar. The weather had grown cool, sometimes cold, and some of the beauties of nature had been stilled and browned by the chilling winds.

"John, you have been betrayed, you must leave! We have come to help you prepare for your escape. Hurry!"

John's first thoughts were of his manuscript. He quickly gathered his scrolls and ordered Papias to take them to a safe place. Papias quickly grabbed the scrolls from John's arms, threw them in a cloth satchel, and raced out of the door.

Polycarp had found another satchel and began throwing into it clothing and some provisions, and he roughly grabbed John's arm and pulled him from the hut. They ran for a short distance then slowed to a quick walk. Feeling there was enough distance between them and the soldiers, they slowed down and rested. As they ate, Papias appeared. He assured them that all had been taken care of: the scrolls were safe and he had been sent by his father to stay with John.

Papias opened the small cloth package he was given by his father and revealed fruits, nuts, and a small piece of fish with some barley loaves. They sat, said a prayer of thanksgiving, and ate.

Suddenly, Papias stood erect.

"What is it, Papias?" Polycarp asked with alarm. "Oh, how strange."

John's curiosity grew, so he stood, but before he could find what the two youngsters were looking at, they ran to a large tree that stood in full bloom.

He followed the two gleeful youngsters with his eyes, but they were lost in the thick bushes.

"What is it?" he shouted with vicarious excitement.

"Look at them. Up there in the tree!"

John looked and saw two doves jumping from branch to branch in an effort to be noticed.

This sight startled John, and he felt his heart beat loudly.

The boys began to jump up and down like two children in an effort to shoo the doves.

"No, No! Do not let them fly away," John shouted. "Please, let them be!"

His words went unheard and the two doves flew out of the tree and up into the sky. They seemed to be playing with each other as they swirled, turned, soared, and swooped. Suddenly, they stopped their acrobatics and flew directly to John.

His mind went to the only two Apostles who were together. The moment he had this thought, the doves flew away side by side into the blue, cloudy sky.

It was then that he felt two heavy hands on his shoulders.

"John bar Zebedee of Judea, Christian, you are under arrest in the name of Imperial Rome."

He looked into the bushes, knowing the two boys were hiding and safe. He smiled.

He turned to meet the Roman soldiers who had found him.

CHAPTER TEN:

JOHN BAR ZEBEDEE OF BETHSAIDA, APOSTLE

PROLOGUE

John woke and found himself sitting on the cold, rough stone floor of a Roman cell and instantly felt the pain in his backside. He did not want to move, for he knew that this would cause greater pain. Even though he could not see his face, he knew he had many open wounds there, and he then gently touched his swollen face with his equally swollen hands. He shivered each time he touched his chin, cheeks, and lips. He knew he had lost several teeth for he tasted the warmth of blood. He knew his eyes were swollen for he could not see well, and he was certain his nose was broken. With great care while in pain, he moved his legs with hopes of getting to his knees to pray. He needed to thank Jesus for having survived the worst beating he had ever received. He could not move his legs; they were tightly chained to the cell floor. Disappointed in not being able to kneel, he slowly concluded that his legs were in worse shape than he thought, for he felt the open flesh, the bruises and tenderness of his legs. Carefully, he wiggled his toes and moved his legs ever so slightly to see if they were broken; they moved and he thanked God. He took a deep breath and the pain in his chest caught him. He froze needing to avoid the distress, but the pain lingered. He threw back his head in agony but with determination smothered the cry of pain, and instead got relief in a soft moan.

Broken chest? He questioned himself. *Most likely.*

He looked up at the narrow, small window high above him. Through the window he could see the dark, starry sky. The world seemed so distant to him at that moment. It was out there but he was in a place far from it and far from its reach. He wondered if this was the feeling all prisoners shared.

Is this not what all the followers of Christ must feel? Being a part and yet apart from the world? Are we not to separate ourselves from the world? He allowed this question to seep into his mind and did not bother to answer for the answer was clear to him, yet not wanting to leave things undone he replied, *Of course! And for some it is the hardest thing to do.*

His thoughts turned to the many Christians who were unable to endure suffering and who instead denied their God and worshipped the Roman gods or the Emperor himself.

He took a slow, shallow breath and rested his head against the damp, stone wall.

The cell was cold—they always were—and it reeked with the odor of human excretions—they always did. In all these odors John detected a different aroma and for a moment this scent left him guessing as to what it could be. It was a sweet smell yet it was stagnant in the air, and slowly he deduced that what he smelled was blood. He wondered how many other Christians had been there before him, under the same sentence, and suddenly he felt their courage *in absentia.*

A deep chill attacked his body and he shivered.

Jesus had a night such as this. He was beaten and was left in a Roman cell like this one, and He shivered from chills and felt the pains of broken flesh. His thoughts momentarily stopped, then continued. *I share Your agony, Master, and I offer it to You in forgiveness of those who are about to kill me.*

He felt a heavy sorrow in his heart for those who harmed him and hoped that in His mercy Jesus would forgive these men as He had forgiven the many on Golgotha. He became quiet and the stillness of these thoughts gave him comfort. For the first time in a long time, John felt sure he was being Christ-like and he became joyous and took great pleasure in the moment.

My last night on earth and with this thought he felt the run of excitement in his stomach and grew pleasantly happy and smiled a painful smile.

He rethought the earlier part of the day and most of it was filled with pain and hurt. He felt blessed and grateful that he did not remember all of the beating, but he remembered enough to make him re-feel the cut of the whip, the punches and kicks, the slam of the iron and wooden rods against his back, head and chest. Apparently he became unconscious during the torture, and he was certain that the Roman Auxiliaries still did not stop their punishment. He did remember his cries to Jesus to forgive his tormentors and his refusal to worship the Roman gods.

Thank you for helping me remember those times with certainty Master, and may my suffering be offered for the sins of those who do not yet know You, he thought.

He went into prayer, remembering the many times Jesus prayed alone and he again felt close to Jesus.

Suddenly he thought: *Why did I permit Jesus to pray alone so often? Why had I not joined Him when He went off to pray? What made me so indifferent to prayer at that time and why did not the Twelve join Jesus? Instead we allowed Jesus to go off...alone. We just sat and talked, ate some more, or slept.* Unexpectedly a small degree of satisfaction came over him and again he tried to smile with his bruised lips. *We gave into human weakness! Whatever He found in us to be called His Disciples is a mystery to me.*

Again he felt a small degree of satisfaction for standing by Jesus, but the fact of being at the Cross and with Lady Mary had never fully satisfied him for he did not defend Jesus. He should have died with Jesus. He quickly dismissed his wandering thoughts and returned to prayer. Mentally, he began to recite a Psalm—his favorite Psalm. As the Psalm unfolded in his mind, he became calm. When he came to a part of the Psalm that held a special meaning for him, he spoke the words aloud.

"...The eyes of the Lord are upon the just; His ears open to their cry..." he returned to silence as the Psalm rolled through his mind.

"...The just cried and the Lord answered them, and delivered them from all their troubles..." he said as his voice grew louder and then faded back into silence.

"...Many are the trials of the just man; but the Lord delivers him from all..." A moment passed, then he said aloud, "...The Lord delivers the souls of His servants..." and he finished the Psalm in his mind.

Bathed in complete peace, he tried to smile in spite of his sore and tender lips and cheeks. As the pain subsided, he welcomed the gift of stillness and he closed his eyes in peace.

He was under the sentence of death. He did not fear death but he feared dying. Death was a gift and dying was the payment for this gift. He silently prayed for his dying to be bearable, and if this was not possible he then prayed for the strength to endure the sufferings that would be inflicted on him. He became joyful when he knew he would see Jesus and Lady Mary again, and his parents and fellow Disciples. His thoughts froze and he remembered Simon and Jude and again saw their doves flying up and away. He longed to be that high—that far—and that close to the Almighty.

All the Others had suffered and so shall I, he thought with naked certainty.

At peace and in total calm, he slipped into sleep.

He dreamed.

He was walking into a large room that was filled with old men wearing their *talliths* shawls. They were hovering over two large tables and were immersed in reading the many scrolls piled and opened on the tables before them. Occasionally they murmured or grew excited and loud at some of their discoveries. He sensed they were making comparisons of two documents. Over the shoulders of one group, he saw they were reading copies of the prophet Isaiah, Micah and Jeremiah.

He heard one man say, "That is what is written. He did fulfill this prophesy!"

They are discovering that Jesus fulfilled many prophesies of the Books, he concluded.

A breath of air was frozen in his throat.

My work!

Startled, he opened his eyes and the darkness of the cell enveloped him giving him a deep chill to his bones.

"It is not complete," he said aloud.

How could I leave this place with my account not being completed?

He wondered if Papias and Polycarp would finish it.

But how could they? They never knew Jesus!

There were so many other things he had to write. He covered the vital parts: the Death and Resurrection of Jesus. He told many of the stories but not as many as he should have recorded. He wrote of many miracles but not nearly as many as he should have, and above all else, he still did not have a beginning to his account.

If I die tomorrow my work will be incomplete. Oh Master, I have failed You. Or is it, Lord, that it was not meant for me to accomplish? Perhaps someone else was to undertake this mission, one who was far more qualified than I? You know I always believed this, for You knew I never was certain. Everyone was so sure of my duty, but not I. Even You, dear Master, when I prayed to You for assurance You remained silent. You never even helped me find my beginning!

A deep sadness settled over him as he felt the heaviness of his own failure. Even if Mary, Peter and others were wrong he still had not done his part. He grew sad and as his failures intensified he forgot his anguish and felt empty.

"O Master, I come to You not completing what You have set before me."

A tear came to his swollen eye and he felt the burn as the tear slipped from his swollen and tender eye down his cut face.

JOHN BAR ZEBEDEE
OF BETHSAIDA, APOSTLE

In spite of the pain from his swollen ankles and his difficulty in breathing, John stood shackled and unwavering before the magistrate, Corlidius Albus Tranacus.

Corlidius was a young Roman magistrate who had recently been assigned to the Roman province of Asia. From the quality of his robes, the refinement of his hair and care to his body, it was apparent that he was a wealthy Roman Patrician. His uniform was of the finest quality and in perfect military condition, undoubtedly due to the hard work of a slave. He sat in his chair erect and with great majesty. It was obvious from his appearance that he was not a man of the military. Around him were many men who had been carefully picked to advise and guide him to success in his quest for greater things.

Corlidius looked at John for the longest time with amazement. He wondered why he had paid great sums of money to traitors and informers among the Christians to have them deliver John to him. Obviously this thin, beaten, bloody man was not a threat to the mighty hand of Rome or the Emperor. Yet to have captured one of "the originals" would sit well with the Emperor in Rome.

Before the young magistrate would say anything he would tilt his head to the side to be advised by a man whom John suspected was either a chief advisor, or a teacher of the young Corlidius. One thing was certain; the advisor knew much about the Christians.

"Tell me Jew; is it true that your Jesus died on the Roman cross?"

John looked directly at the advisor and then Corlidius, "Yes."

Corlidius tilted his head to the side and then questioned, "He was truly dead?"

"Yes. I saw Him die with my own eyes."

"They broke his legs?" Corlidius said with great satisfaction.

"No, they pierced His Side and blood and water came forth."

"A trick. You Jews are always good at tricks."

"He was not pierced by a Jew but by a Roman, who also saw what I saw and came to believe as I believe."

"Liar!" Corlidius protested, as he leaned forward from his chair. Getting no reaction from John, the Roman smiled and leaned back to his side and again the "advisor" whispered something to him.

"Just what do you believe?"

"That Jesus of Nazareth is the Promised Messiah; that He came into this world to save all from eternal death; that He died for our sins and will judge us all when we die. If we repent in this life, He promised us Paradise."

"And do all Christians believe such nonsense?"

"Yes."

He titled his head to the side and asked, "And tell me, John of Galilee, where is this Paradise?"

"With Jesus. Wherever He may be."

Corlidius laughed.

"Now come, John, you seem intelligent enough to know better."

"I do know better, that is why I believe what I have spoken."

The advisor leaned close to Corlidius' ear to whisper something but the magistrate brushed him away angrily and quickly rose from his chair, racing down the steps to John. He stood inches from John's face.

"You try me, Jew, and your arrogance angers me." He turned and hurried back to his chair. After he sat he reached for his scepter and declared, "Scriptor, let us make all this legal, write that the Jew, John bar Zebedee of Galilee, a Christian and a traitor, refused to worship the Emperor Titus or the Roman gods and for these insults and because I wanted to maintain the devotion to my Emperor, I have condemned him to death."

He leaned forward in his chair, narrowed his eyes, and between clutched teeth said, "It will give me great pleasure to have you crucified like that criminal Jesus of Nazareth."

John's sense immediately grew sharp and he quickly said, "Mighty Sir, that would please me greatly."

The Magistrate threw back his head and laughed; his laughter pierced the noonday stillness. You could almost feel the mockery in the tone of his enjoyment.

"You Christians are a crazy lot," Corlidius continued with a wide smile of delight on his lips. "To me it matters little how you die, but because you want so to die the death of your God, I will think of a more unique and unpleasant death that suits a stupid Christian pig such as you."

He suddenly stopped smiling and fell back in his chair and with revulsion on his face shouted, "Guards, take this filth away from me. He disgusts me."

Two guards rushed to John and violently pulled him away.

"Watch him with your lives, guards. I shall have to consult my gods for an appropriate death for this Christian unbeliever and Jewish traitor."

As they roughly pushed and pulled John away from Corlidius, John looked over his shoulder at the Magistrate and prayed a prayer of forgiveness for having been the cause of the Magistrate's hate. The guards pushed John into the nearby dense forest. They walked along a small, narrow, dirt road, and as they led him along, they cursed and abused him. After walking some distance, they came to a clearing and forced John to sit. They tied him tightly to the trunk of the tree and went off a short distance and began to gamble and drink cheap, soldier wine.

John immediately began to pray, thanking Jesus for allowing him to become an instrument of His Will. He then prayed to Lady Mary petitioning her to be with Jesus when his death arrived and begged that he be greeted kindly.

Moments passed and the once cloudy afternoon became clear and sunny. John basked in the glory of the day. He softly rested his head against the tree trunk to which he was tied and soaked in anticipation of his new life. Now he will be with the Disciples and many others who gave their lives for Jesus. The list of names passed through his mind and with the names came images of the past. They were all young, vibrant and filled with the love to serve and do the will of God. Then came the image of Jesus and John's nostrils were filled with the sweet scent that always accompanied this Image. He smiled as he felt himself lean forward and once again rested his head on the shoulder and chest of Jesus and heard the soft heartbeat of life within His Master. Contented with this image, the smells and the sounds, he felt himself slip into a euphoria that he once experienced a year ago.

This will be my tomorrow, he thought, *for all time and eternity.*

The images of the other people who had walked with Jesus continued through his mind. They all raced hurriedly through his memory and finally they stopped and John felt a cool, soft breeze and the heat of sunlight on his face. He was once again on Golgotha. Immediately, he felt the need to cover Jesus' nakedness, a need that remained with him all during the nailing to the Cross. He sensed his arm wrapped casually around Lady Mary's shoulder. She stood sternly and bravely by the Cross. The only signs of pain were the silent streams of tears that channeled their way down her face. He wondered at her courage and silence. He believed she knew more of that moment than he did.

The sun ceased being warm and John felt the breeze slip away to become a passing wind, fresh and chilling. He watched the gamblers, the mockers, the haters, and the uncaring and indifference of others as they walked by the Cross. He saw Magdalene's body shake with sorrow as she clung to the base of the Cross at Jesus' feet. He looked to Salome, his mother, and then to Mary of Cleophas and finally to Joanne, Susanna and the other Holy Women.

He remembered thinking: *Where are the Others?*

After that he grew numb and colder.

He heard the man on the right of the Cross plea for mercy and Jesus' promise and John felt a yearning for such a promise and even envied the man he knew as Dismas.

A shiver scurried up his back and as it reached his head, his teeth chattered. He looked around and found night had come to day, and then he felt the rage of the wind as it charged the mount and attacked everyone which even made the crosses sway.

Jesus cried out "It is consummated."

He saw the flash of the lance.

He heard the sound of flesh being pierced, a sound which caused him to wrench and gasp.

He saw the pallid blood gush from the cut. The fluid ran ever so slowly down the side of Jesus' chest.

He heard the cries of conversion and witnessed the faces of the Roman soldiers. He saw the changes from anger, hate, and iciness to peace, love, and warmth.

He remembered thinking: *They are Gentiles. What has Jesus given to them that He did not give to us? How could these strangers declare their belief in Jesus and not us who were with Him all this time?*

It was then that John felt the depth of being abandoned. A feeling he was sure Jesus felt and lived through during his arrest, beatings, and death.

Where are the Others?

His thoughts and revelry were disturbed by the laughs and sounds of the soldiers near him. He opened his eyes and saw a man walk out of the forest and into the clear. The man was an older soldier but he walked passed the guards with an air of authority. As he approached John he became timid. He stood silently in front of him; his tall muscular body towering over the Apostle.

John looked up. The man was haggard and looked very troubled. For a quick moment John believed he knew this man.

With a mild tone the man inquired, "Do you know who I am?"

John examined the man more closely. Again the face was familiar but John was not too eager to search his mind.

"No. Should I?"

"No. It is just as well that you do not."

The man turned quickly almost as if he needed to escape John, but before he had gotten too far, John remembered the face.

"I remember you," he shouted after the man.

The man stopped and for several minutes stood motionless; he did not even show signs of breathing. He turned slightly and over his shoulder looked back at John. It was obvious he was debating whether to return to John or to ignore him. Finally, he slowly turned and walked back to John and once again stood over the Apostle.

"I had hoped you would not. In the world in which I am now living, no one knows who I was."

"The Lord knows who you are; you cannot hide from Him."

"One thing is for certain, you Christians are full of rhetoric."

"We do not have rhetoric, for we are filled with the Spirit of the Lord," John replied simply.

John examined the man's face more closely. The face was taut, almost frozen. In the man's eyes he saw a well-repressed agony; it was a familiar sight to John. He could see the pain coming from the man's soul.

"Why do you torment yourself so much?" John asked with great pity and compassion in his voice.

"I do not torment myself!" the man exclaimed, then, as an afterthought murmured, "Only since I met you has the torment returned."

"You know you have been forgiven."

The man stood frozen by John's words and as a defense closed his eyes.

John cleared his throat and murmured to the Roman, "Tell me, do you deny what I have said about the Lord having forgiven you?"

The man thought for a long while and then responded in a low voice, "I do not know. I never knew."

"Because you never wanted to forget what happened. That should not be your worry. What is important is that the Lord has forgiven you."

The man looked long and hard at John. This time he was searching John's face and as he did this for a moment John saw that the Roman was wavering.

"Why did this have to happen?" The man asked. "Why did you allow yourself to be captured?"

"Because you are to be my Dismas."

"What?"

John smiled slightly. "Nothing." He grew serious and continued, "I believe this was to happen so that you would be given another chance. The Lord really wants you and He is chasing after you."

"Do you not know that I have orders to have you killed?"

"And like Jesus, I am willing to die, so do not let my death or His death be the reason for you to deny Him. I remember Peter telling me of your Baptism, Dorimius, and I remember him saying your face was aglow. You and the others at Cornelius' villa were the first non-Jews to join us. All of you wanted to help us; that is why Peter assigned each of you to one of the Twelve and because you knew your world better than we did. All of you did well; some have even died for Jesus."

"I was the least ready to help. I could not forget my sin. Jude Thaddeus tried to help me but I could not forgive myself."

"So you left him and all that you knew of Jesus?"

"Yes. I could not pretend any longer."

"Was it all pretend? It seems something was there, I can tell."

"Yes, there was something there but it was not enough."

"In faith, the smallest 'something' can be enough for salvation."

"Rhetoric, again! We go around in circles; there is nothing more to be said," Dorimius said as he walked away briskly.

"You still remain incomplete, Dorimius." John said in a raised voice but the soldier continued to walk away. In desperation John said, "Did you know that Jude Thaddeus was dead?"

Dorimius stopped. He felt a strong tuck in his stomach that caused him to swallow hard.

"When? How?" He asked over his shoulder.

"I do not know. But I know he is dead, as is Simon." John replied, finding Dorimius' concern a sure sign he was not completely away from Jesus.

"Clavos?"

"Still in Parthia, I believe."

A young *legatus* messenger came running to Dorimius. The poor boy was out of breath and his face was flushed and full of perspiration. He immediately captured John's sympathy, for the youngster looked so hurried and uncomfortable. The young messenger gave John a quick, curious look. The look was tinged with sympathy. He hurried to Dorimius, whispered something to him, and the news drew a loud sigh from the former missionary. Dorimius nodded, and the boy ran away. Dorimius walked to the guards and spoke to them in a very low voice.

The guards struggled to their feet and together walked to John and untied him. As they did this, one of the guards said to him, "The *consul* magistrate has prepared a new and different death for you. He will not allow you to be crucified like your Precious God, but he shall have you boiled in oil."

John smiled.

In complete disbelief the guard looked into John's eyes.

"You Christians are confusing," the guard remarked as he roughly pulled him to his feet. With the point of his finger the soldier directed John to walk through the forest.

"I do not understand you Christians. If you live you will have more time to poison the people." one guard said.

"Is it not better to live than to die?" asked the other guard.

"We believe there is life after this, and that afterlife is better than what is here."

"Pleasure is the only life," the first guard said with a wide smile on his lips while the others smirked in agreement.

"That is not true, for pleasure is fleeting. What I am speaking of is eternity," John replied softly.

Shaking his head vigorously, the second guard said to his companion, "I told you they were confusing."

"And better off dead," added the other guard.

They came to a large clearing in the forest. In the center of the clearing was a large *lebes* cauldron sitting on a huge fire. Steam could be seen coming from the cauldron and occasionally the boiling oil would splatter over the side and instantly be consumed with a loud sizzle. Sitting around the clearing were soldiers. Some were eating, some were drinking cheap wine, and others were napping. Several were merely sitting around enjoying the shade of the nearby trees. Three other soldiers were chopping down a small tree and stripping off the branches.

As Dorimius and the young *legatus* entered the clearing, all the soldiers came to some form of attention by standing or fixing their uniforms and helmets.

Several other guards with a *Scriptor* scribe appeared in the clearing.

The *Scriptor* shouted, "Christian, you have one last chance; renounce this Jesus of Nazareth and give sacrifice to the Emperor Domitian of Rome."

John shouted, "There is only one God and He is Jesus, the Christ."

"I will make note of the Jew's refusal," the *Scriptor* said with authority as he glanced over at Dorimius, who nodded his head slightly.

"Proceed with the execution," The *Scriptor* casually ordered and quickly turned and left the area followed by the guards who escorted him.

Two soldiers ran to John and roughly pushed him to the ground. The dry earth clung to his perspiring, bruised face and some dirt hit his eyes and filled his mouth. Two other soldiers pulled at the ropes that were tied around his chest and upper arms. When they were satisfied they were secure, they bound his feet.

Additional soldiers came to John carrying the tree trunk they had stripped of branches. They slipped the trunk between John and the ropes that bound his arms, chest and feet. Six soldiers lifted the trunk and carried John to the *lebes*. They dropped the tree trunk on the lip of the *lebes*. As soon as the tree trunk touched the lip of the hot cauldron, it smoked and burned.

"Renounce your Jesus of Nazareth and you will be saved, John bar Zebedee," John heard Dorimius shout to him.

"Never! I will worship only He who is the Son of God and the Savior of the world."

"Then die, Christian," he heard a strange voice shout.

The steam from the boiling oil wet John's face and warmed him and to his surprise the moisture on his face from the steam grew cool and soothing. The dirt that had clogged his wounds and eyes were cleaned. He saw and felt no pain.

He looked down at the bubbling oil just inches away from him and cried loudly: "Lord Jesus, Thy will be done. Forgive these men who wish to harm me and give them Your Love; let them come to know You as I do."

The tree trunk began to sag and John felt the heat of the oil touch his skin as his clothing became wet with oil. He waited for the pain, but none came. He closed his eyes wanting to have no sight of earth. He wanted to clear his mind to prepare for the sight of Jesus.

Suddenly the trunk snapped and John was plunged into the boiling oil.

John expected an instant burn, but instead he felt nothing. He felt the rope around his chest, upper arms, hands and feet peel away; he even felt the disintegration of the tree. He was floating. He saw a bright light. He knew the brightness was from the Almighty. The light moved to John, pressed against him, passed through him and took with it part of his humanity. He felt completely free and drifted above everything. Suddenly he was surrounded by a multitude of people. All their faces were somber. There were people of his time for he could see their clothing was similar to his, but he also saw people who were strangely dressed: Men with no beards to cover their faces and women with no veils to cover their heads. At first glance they were aimlessly milling around, then abruptly they stopped. All looked up and unexpectedly they began to walk in the same direction. Their walk was not easy. Some stumbled and some fell but they rose again. John looked ahead and saw people walking through deserts, across turbulent rivers, and over hills and from deep valleys towards a huge mountain. It was a mountain whose summit was crowned with pure, white, glistening snow and hanging thickly around the summit were large, billowing clouds in which he could hear the sounds of singing. He could not understand the words of the song but he knew it was a holy prayer of praise. All of a sudden he realized they were not singing a song but repeating one word over and over again. He deciphered the word and wanted to know it so that he could join in the voices. He quickly felt as an outsider and was certain he was not supposed to be witnessing these events.

Suddenly he heard a loud voice say: "And who will see your dove?"

He knew the meaning of the words but wished to ignore them. Meantime the singing grew louder. He opened his mouth to sing, to say something but all he heard was a loud, screeching sound. It was the call of an eagle in flight; it was in the oil around him and when he opened his eyes he found himself standing waist high in the boiling, bubbling, steaming oil and looking into the frozen, shocked faces of the soldiers.

He heard a screeching call and he turned his head to the sky and saw an eagle circling above him. The sun blinded him. The last thing he heard was Dorimius shout, "Remove him from the *lebes!*"

*

The news traveled throughout the Christian and Roman worlds that John, one of the Twelve was dead. It traveled so swiftly that within days Philip, and within weeks Matthew, the two remaining Apostles, knew of it. The Christian world mourned; the Roman world rejoiced. All this did not surprise John. He attributed the rapidity of the traveling news to the clever mind of Dorimius who had managed to calm the soldiers who had witnessed John's survival by persuading them to swear to the Magistrate that John was dead. He reminded them that if it was discovered that the execution was bungled the Emperor would be extremely angry and they would face their own demise. Some soldiers and Dorimius hurried John away and hid him in an abandoned hut. When darkness came, Dorimius arrived with a cart of hay that became John's hiding place.

They journeyed back to Ephesus only at night, the one place John would not be sought. The journey was long and made covertly. On the journey, Dorimius extracted from John a promise of complete silence, for if it was discovered that John was not dead, Dorimius and the detachment of soldiers would truly face death. John agreed but insisted on notifying the "dear Lady" for he knew she would be the only one able to hide him. As they traveled, John spent most of his time in prayer for God to protect those men who endangered themselves for him. This trip reminded him of his trip back from Rome. Like that trip he had to rely on the cleverness of a Roman soldier, but unlike that trip where he felt he had done the will of God, this trip he felt he had not. The other half of his trip was trying to recapture Dorimius' soul, which he failed to do.

As they traveled along, John became ill with fever and the aches and pains from his beatings returned. When they arrived at Ephesus, he was immediately pushed into hiding and was attended by the "dear Lady" who once again provided him with living quarters. She arranged for him to hide at her widowed sister's secluded *villa* in the mountains above Ephesus.

For the next several weeks John laid sick and helpless.

The "dear Lady," her sister-in-law Alivia, and the Christian servants tended him, believing he would die. All the wounds and beatings he ever received were reopened. Carefully they applied ointments and herbs to his body but he never reacted or showed any signs of life. For days they watched over him until one day he woke and asked for food. At the "dear Lady's" insistence he remained in bed and was gently cared for by the household servants who were sworn to secrecy.

His illness took a heavy toll on him. He was a different man. He was a frail, aged man. His small-framed body was stooped over and void of muscles and tautness. His beard and hair had thinned and grayed.

When he began to gather his senses, he started to remember some of his visions. They came to him in bits and pieces but he knew he had to remember them. As he grew stronger, those who attended him noticed that he had lost more than his physical appearance. He was frail and a man defeated. All day they talked to him, even questioned him about Jesus, gave him only good news and kept the household light and happy. John slowly responded but still was not the man they once knew.

Weighing on his mind was the episode in the clearing of the forest which depressed him each time he remembered that time. Why wasn't he honored to become a complete witness of Christ? He began to feel he was unworthy of so great and so noble a death. Perhaps he had not done as much as the Others had done? Perhaps he did not have as many converts as the Others?

These questions led him to despair which became a disease that festered and scarred his spiritual life. When he felt hopeless, he immediately went into prayer asking for forgiveness. He begged for a slither of understanding, but nothing ever came to clear up his confusion.

Soon he discovered that he lost the desire to write and his pain grew greater as it became more obvious that he had lost everything that day in the clearing. If he was to simply write an account of Jesus but lost his ability to write, what was his purpose in life now? He started a journey to find this purpose but soon learned that sometimes finding the source of pain is greater than the pain.

After months of prayer, he came face-to-face with his problem. He concluded that ever since the Death of Jesus he had lived the warm sense of comfort, but since that day in the clearing that comfort was gone. In its place he felt an abandonment that had plunged him into a deep, dark place away from all feelings of being or of belonging to anyone, or anything, including God. He could not understand why he had this feeling of being unloved. It was so alien to him. It made him feel barren and nude and his every thought echoed in this emptiness.

It was at night, and every night, that he felt his heaviest emptiness. The seriousness of nighttime, the slumber of life, came to be God turning His back to him and leaving him parentless. Every night he heard his own sobs reverberating inside his empty being. Every night he felt the wetness of tears dampen his friendless soul. He was kept awake for hours in a dark room or behind his covered eyes cringed and enclosed within himself, suffering the sole wounds of an unwanted solitude. It was more painful than all the physical tortures he had endured. In the somber night he would hear an inner wail, his own wail, and the sound slashed deep into his soul.

Even in the daylight when life was all around him in nature, he knew somewhere in a corner, in a shadow his emptiness, his oneness, was lurking and ready to pounce back upon him. His only escape was through his prayers, but soon the blackness began to seep into them and he was left with no refuge. He suffered continuously, begging for Jesus to come back to him, to allow him the memories of life with Him.

How did Christ expect him to live after being loved with a love that was greater than all love?

How did God expect him to live in emptiness? Or survive living a lifeless life?

His questions remained unanswered as he struggled day and night with the feeling of being unloved.

He begged for help; none came.

A full calendar of days passed when in his sleep he began to re-dream the vision he had in the cauldron. He again saw people of different ages walking to the mountain and once again he heard the singing of the angels. Each night the dream developed new, haunting images, numbers, colors, symbols and other allusions. On different nights he saw sealed scrolls, four horsemen, twelve city gates, a Lady childbearing, demons, dragons and angels. Always, every night, the angels sang their one word song over and over. Some nights he felt the phrase was in Latin, and then other nights the word was sung in Greek and other nights Hebrew, but it mattered little because he could not decipher what was being sung. Because he could not understand his dreams, his loneliness intensified.

When it seemed safe, the "dear Lady" came to see him and when she saw how he had dwindled down to skin and bones she immediately demanded to know what was bothering him.

"You have not completed your task, and that is the reason you are still here. Christ wants you to finish what is yours to do. Each of the Twelve had a different task; yours is to write an account as no other can. When you have completed what Christ has set for you, then you will join Him in Heaven."

"John," she continued, "you did not deny Christ. You still showed your willingness to die for Him and to remain faithful to His Church. Is that not a martyr's death?"

John looked at her in complete silence and slowly began to feel the stupidity of his ways. After all, God is the Controller of time; our call is not for us to decide. Tears slowly welled up in his eyes and found their way down his pale, thin face and wet his gray beard.

I have died a martyr's death without dying, he thought. *The "dear Lady" is right. How stupid and foolish I have been. How self-centered I allowed myself to become. Lord, forgive my challenge to Your Holy Will.*

The "dear Lady" stoically sat nearby as she watched John sob and wash clean all the waste he had experienced in months passed.

Slowly he returned to his work, and it was then that he began to write letters to several churches and to the "dear Lady."

When he learned that a cargo ship was leaving Ephesus and going to Egypt to travel down the Nile, he composed a quick letter to Matthew who was in Egypt to tell him that his brother, Jude Thaddeus, had died. This letter was very compelling and he found himself giving Matthew other information. He told of his work on an account of Jesus and that he had read parts of what Matthew had composed, and then mentioned Luke's and Mark's writings. He wrote this being sure that Matthew knew of these things. When he finished, he gave the letter to Papias who delivered the letter to the Christian captain of the ship who assured John that the letter would be delivered.

John returned to his account of Jesus' life and soon noticed his writing style had changed and he began to write more deeply and more vivid; he felt his words flow more easily. With the knowledge that his account was to be his life long mission and for all Christians, he tried to find a beginning to his account, but nothing he wrote was satisfying to him or seemed to fit into what he was writing.

On and on he wrote his stories without a beginning.

CHAPTER ELEVEN:

PHILIP OF BETHSAIDA

PROLOGUE

S oon after returning to his writing, John became well enough to begin
celebrating the Meal, now being called the Breaking of the Bread,
with the household. The joy of speaking about Jesus filled him with
new zeal, and to celebrate the Breaking of the Bread was an even greater
joy, for he knew he was following the Master's instruction to "do this in
remembrance of" Him.

Alivia, the mistress of the house and the sister of the "dear Lady,"
had a young son named Tinius who became John's companion. The boy
moved in and out of John's mind with his constant inquiring about Jesus.
The questions he asked were questions few people asked about Jesus, and
they caused John to reminisce.

"Did Jesus have an earthly father? What was His mother like?"

"Did your mother like Jesus? Did your father ever meet Jesus?"

"When you played with Jesus, what games did He like the most? Was
He good at hiding when He played 'find me'?"

"Was He a good swimmer? I bet the fish helped Him swim because
they knew Who He was."

"Did you know any of the other Apostles as children? Which Apostle
did you like the most?"

"Did Jesus like to eat figs? Or bitter grapes? Did He really have to
learn how to be a carpenter? After all, He was the Son of God, and He
knew all that stuff."

The boy's questions continued, and John answered them with the
same simplicity in which they were asked. Sometimes he listened to the

boy's questions with a great deal of self-control, and sometimes they were so innocent that they made John smile. These questions reminded John that many of the things Jesus did would remain unknown. To know all things about God is unnatural. God should remain a mystery. To know all makes God natural, but to leave things unknown adds to the magnificence of the Almighty.

John knew that his account of Jesus would be far different from those of the others. His account would not be simply history—it would show clearly that Jesus was the *Khristos*, the Anointed One, Who offers the world eternal life. He was certain the others had been inspired by the Spirit of the Lord, and he was also certain that his message of God's love in giving His only Son was fundamental to his writings. John believed that the Almighty wanted him to be the presenter of His love. His message could not be written as the other writers; his writing was to stand alone.

The "dear Lady," in order to keep John away from Ephesus and therefore from danger of discovery, had Papias and Polycarp, two friends of Tinius, come to stay at the *villa*, and John's life became full. Now John had three inquirers, and it didn't take John long to conclude that the emptiness that God had given him was really a preparation for the fullness he now had. Again, the memories of long ago came anew to him. The three forced him to remember days, times, phrases, small details that were forgotten. Some would find their way into his account, but most simply made him melancholy, and some helped him to realize new things about his relationship with Jesus. He saw that over the years his relationship was different from those of the Others. He had a closer bond with the Master, so close that he was permitted to rest his head on the Master's shoulder. As he recalled this, he grew pensive, wishing to rest this way again. He longed to hear the beat of his Master's heart—the beat that echoed and vibrated until it reached his very soul. A heartbeat that reached out into eternity and held everlasting time. It was not a loud echo but a soft, even sound that calmed John into semi-existence. Each time this happened, he was certain that being with the Almighty would be a similar experience. It was when he had rested his head on Jesus' chest that John was certain he understood what Jesus was trying to say to the world.

As he retold stories and incidents about Jesus, John recognized that the way the Twelve questioned Jesus about His mission was no better than the badgering of the Sanhedrin or the Romans. Worse, the Disciples had judged him, just as the Sanhedrin and Romans had. He could remember times in which the Twelve doubted Jesus' ability to forgive sins. They also doubted Jesus' right to condemn the unworthy, asking by what authority He did these things.

None of us were worthy to know Him; none of us were worthy to be called by Him; none of us were worthy....

One day, while walking slowly along one of the many dirt roads that led to the *villa*, Polycarp, Papias, and Tinius began questioning him about the Crucifixion.

"So you were there when Jesus died? Were you not afraid?" Tinius asked.

"Yes, I was there." His memory flashed images that sent chills through him, and for a moment he was not with them—he was back there, on Golgotha. He retreated willingly from the images and shook his head so as to free his mind completely. "I do not know why I was not afraid. I just knew I had to be there, so fear was not present in my mind."

"That's odd."

"No, not really, for when it comes to defending what you believe in, you forget all that can harm you."

"If that is true, then why did not the Others stand with you?" Papias asked simply.

John was stunned and unable to think; when he finally gathered his thoughts, he said in a soft voice, "It was what I was expected to do."

"It was your first mission," Polycarp said in an ordinary tone.

A flash of reality shone in John's mind, and he stopped walking. Not wanting to look shocked, he distracted his companions by pointing to two rabbits running across the field, and the youngsters gleefully ran after the animals.

Alone, John felt a tightness in his chest, and he began to breathe in quick, shallow breaths.

Oh Lord, forgive me. How vain and undeserving I have been. Yes, it was my first mission. A mission I would not have given to any of the Others. When all were away, I was there. You gave me my mission then. How unforgiving I have been, thinking I had done nothing for You.

His eyes began to fill with tears. He quickly found the sleeve of his cloak and used it to wipe his eyes. He glanced up and saw his companions walking to him, looking dejected and defeated.

"What happened?"

They exploded with excitement and began telling John their ordeal. They laughed and joked about each other. For one quick instant, John felt that he could join in their excitement, but then he became filled with his own excitement, for the young men reminded him of the Twelve after they witnessed Jesus perform something extraordinary.

How childlike we also were, he thought.

He remained silent, smiled, and heard nothing of what they related, for his mind was away and filled with faraway thoughts.

When finally the three had finished their jovial tale, they saw that John had grown silent, and they too became silent, knowing that he had wandered off again. This happened often when they were with John. It did not slight them, for they knew he was off to visit a time or place that belonged to Jesus, Lady Mary, or the Twelve. They waited until he returned.

A little later, along the dirt road, they began to question him again.

"Did you know from the beginning that Jesus was the Messiah?"

"No, but I did know He was my friend and my relative, and I loved Him."

"Did you know Jesus as a child?"

"Yes."

"Tell me, what was He like?" inquired Tinius.

John smiled. "He seemed to be an ordinary boy." Seeing the disappointment on Tinius' face, John continued, "Sorry, Tinius, but He did not reveal Himself until much later. He was very quiet and pensive, and perhaps unusually somber. He played games and played with toys. I remember overhearing my mother tell my father of how quickly Jesus learned things, and when she spoke to Him, she felt that she was being guided. I remember her saying that Jesus was to be a great person and that His Father—and she stressed the word Father—would be pleased with Him."

"That does not surprise me," Polycarp interjected with a smile on his face.

"Indeed, no surprise."

"What made you realize that Jesus was the Messiah?"

"Oh, there were many occurrences that gradually formed my faith. Also, I witnessed many things that the Others did not see."

"Did any of the Others know that Jesus was the Messiah before His death and resurrection?"

John thought for a while and carefully made each of the Twelve pass through his mind, then he said, "Perhaps. I am sure my brother James knew. I know Peter knew because he had openly declared it with the help of the Almighty, and maybe there were two or three more."

"Tell me, what is the one thing about Jesus that you remember most?"

John sighed aloud, not from anger or frustration, but from the difficulty he was having in being honest with them.

"I remember all things about Him."

"Come now, John, you must have one thing about Jesus that you always recall with delight."

John looked at the three young men walking with him. He could see their desire to become, even in a small way, a part of the past, and of Jesus. He smiled, understanding their curiosity and cherishing the opportunity to speak to them of Jesus.

"I remember His voice. It was soft and mellow, yet it traveled far. I was told by many that no matter what distance people were from Him, they could hear His every word." John wet his lips and added quickly, "I remember His eyes. They looked into you. They never searched, for that was not His way, but they looked and directly found whatever He wanted or needed in you."

The three were baffled by John's remarks. "Jesus had a way of reading your soul, your silent, hidden, and forgotten thoughts. You would know He was doing this, and unless you had some things to hide, you welcomed it. It made you feel close to Him and, in some mysterious way, close to the Almighty. If He ever found something that He needed or wanted, He would bring it to the surface."

"In other words, Jesus never looked for greatness, only what little we could give Him," Polycarp said.

"And He used what we alone could offer Him," Papias added. "Just look at the way He worked through each of the Twelve."

"Yes," Polycarp answered quickly. "Just look at your brother James. He loved to travel, and sure enough he traveled the farthest."

"And look at Philip. He was sent to Greece because he was the most Greek of you all."

"All went where they were supposed to go."

"And even you, John. You were given exactly what Jesus wanted you to do. You were to tend to His mother and stay close to home where each of the Twelve could write you. You became their anchor amidst the rough waters of deprivation and persecution."

John merely continued to walk.

Even the young and innocent knew…were certain…only I, John, did not see or know.

That night, when the *villa* was still and even the soft shuffle of servants' slippers was silenced, John forced himself to remember what he could of Jesus as a child; to his surprise, there actually was very little he could recall.

Nazareth was quite a distance from Bethsaida. His contact with Jesus was usually during a holiday, a funeral, or a wedding. He was much younger than Jesus, and this also contributed to his lack of contact. He was certain that Jesus had gone to the synagogue at the age of five to study and had continued until he was fourteen, at which age He was expected to know the Torah and the Law of Moses.

His brother, James, who was near Jesus' age, once told him that at the age of five Jesus knew the Torah and challenged the *rebbe* teachers. Jesus' questions were so challenging that He was given private instruction. James laughed and then said that few teachers would take this job because they could not answer all of Jesus' challenges.

John recalled one time when Jesus and he were alone; Jesus said that John had a great challenge before him and that He believed that John could help Him. John childishly asked how he could help Him, for Jesus was so smart, and Jesus said, "Watch and see. Be patient. Wait and watch."

John remembered finding Jesus writing on a large piece of pottery, and he asked Him what He was doing. Jesus replied, "I am writing a prayer to My Father." John thought that excellent and decided to write a prayer to his father, Zebedee.

Still another time, John found Jesus in prayer. John stood quietly off to the side and watched. He found Jesus smiling occasionally, and then He lowered His head, and each time He raised His head His face was glowing. After finishing, Jesus looked over at John and asked if he knew a young man named Philip.

"Yes," John replied, bewildered by such an odd question. Jesus smiled and said, "Soon you will find him to be one of the best friends you could ever know."

John's night of remembering continue for many hours.

The next day, news came to John that the nearby churches of several cities were having internal problems. People were teaching false doctrine, asserting that Jesus was not the Redeemer or the Son of God. Though John knew of the good faith of these communities, he also knew that the greatest dangers to Christianity would come from within. Unable to do much about this situation, John wrote to his old friend Philip for help. Philip was in Greece, not far from Ephesus. He was certain that Philip would come to help the troubled churches. He was equally certain that Philip's daughters and his sister, his constant companions, would arrive with him. It would only be for a short time—until John was well enough to return to his duty as shepherd of the region.

So he wrote to Philip, the Apostle.

PHILIP OF BETHSAIDA

Hermione walked quickly to the door, opened it, and roughly pulled her youngest sister through the doorway, and then she shut the heavy wooden door behind her.

"What took you so long? Father is ill. He has a fever, yet he still wants to follow John bar Zebedee's request to go to the Province of Asia. I told him he should wait. Even Chariline has spoken to him, but he will not listen. You are his favorite; speak to him before he does something he will regret."

"Sister, why are you so troubled? You and I know that Father will do what he wants to do."

"But this is folly. Please do not take this lightly. Father is ill and has been for some time."

Hermione brought her hand to her mouth to stop herself from saying anything that would be displeasing to others. She was the oldest of Philip's four daughters, and the worrier in the family. She was determined to protect her father from anything she felt would harm him, but her protection was sometimes carried to extremes. She often had to be reminded that he was an Apostle of the Lord and, consequently, he was at the call of the Lord.

"I think it very thoughtless of John bar Zebedee to ask Father to come to assist him. He knows Father's age."

"But if the Church needs Father someplace, then he must go. Besides, how would John know Father is ill? And you forget that the authorities think that John is dead; if he exposes himself to the public, he will surely be arrested."

"I can see you are going to be of no help."

Chariline walked quietly into the room. Seeing her two sisters standing far apart alerted her to the fact that there was a disagreement, so as quickly as she entered the room she tried to leave, but Hermione immediately drew her into the debate.

"Irais wants Father to go to Ephesus in the Province of Asia," Hermione blurted out.

"I did not say that I wanted Father to go; I said that if he is needed, he will go, for he is an Apostle of the Lord," Irais retorted, impatient with her sister's distortion of the truth.

"Well, Chariline, tell Irais what you think," Hermione ordered.

"I...I think it is...a bit unwise," Chariline stated weakly. "After all... there is his age to consider...."

"See, Sister, she agrees with me."

"I do not care who sides with you, Hermione, I believe it is entirely up to Father and the Will of the Lord."

The three sisters stood silently, and after several moments passed, Chariline, with her head bowed, announced timidly, "Mariamne is coming. I told her of John's request, and she said she was coming to talk to Father."

The three sisters continued to remain silent.

"Mariamne seemed less disturbed about the request than we are," Chariline continued. "She thinks that it would be very good for Father to get away and to visit our sister Eutychiane."

"Eutychiane is not able to tend to Father properly. She is not well, and besides, her dear husband has not time for family," Hermione chided.

"Well, maybe it is time her dear husband comes to know the meaning of family. I think the idea is splendid," Irais remarked as she began walking into the next room.

"Where are you going?"

"To see Father."

"No, let us wait for Mariamne to arrive, and then we will speak to Father together."

Not far from the room in which the sisters were talking, in a smaller room, sat Philip. He had finished writing John of his intention to leave Attica and go to the troubled cities of Philadelphia, Laodicea, and Sardis. In the letter he joked that he had sailed the Aegean Sea more times than Paul of Tarsus.

Immediately after completing the letter, he heard the voices of debate and knew that the topic was his intention to travel from Greece to the Province of Asia.

There always is a debate, he thought with feelings of both annoyance and acceptance. *It seems that my daughters, and before them my wife, always feel that I need more assistance than that given by the Almighty.*

He accepted the fact that his wife and daughters felt that they had to be a part of his decisions, for he believed that one of the tasks of females was to mother the males in their lives. Unlike many Greeks, who believed that women were slaves, inferior to men, Philip believed that women were the caretakers of men.

Yet with all the faith and all the holiness of my daughters, they still forget that I am an Apostle of the Savior first. They, like their mother, my dear Esther, still have much to learn.

His thoughts conjured up the image of his small, fleshy wife with her long black hair and true Semitic features. She had been his wife for many years, for they married very young. After their marriage, he moved to Greece to help her father in his small fishing business. A few years after, Esther's father died, and Philip managed the business. Eventually Esther brought forth their first child, and they then began having children in quick succession. After delivering her fourth daughter, Irais, his wife suddenly died. A widower, considered by many to be advanced in years, and with no one in Greece to raise his daughters, Philip sold his business, bade his many Gentile associates farewell, and returned to Bethsaida, his birthplace in Galilee where his sister Mariamne lived. She took charge of the four girls, and Philip worked for Zebedee, an old friend of his father. Becoming a fisherman was not Philip's choice, but he was not young and he had few other skills. He had learned fishing from his wife's family and from the Greeks. It was a job that Philip did not like because it held few excitements. He enjoyed the challenges of management; fishing was much more dull. Fishing forced the human person to become a slave to the whims of nature and the stupidity of the fish. He was a Greek Jew, educated in Greek philosophy, logic, and mathematics; he had little need for the boredom of fishing. He became a fisherman to feed his family. His lack of enthusiasm often caused Zebedee to criticize Philip's lackadaisical attitude or his lack of forethought in completing a task. Philip knew that this made him appear stupid, but he cared little, for he knew that he was more intelligent than most men.

It soon became obvious to everyone that Philip was not hired for his fishing skills but for his ability to deal with the Greeks from the Decapolis cities that surrounded the Sea of Galilee, with whom Zebedee did much business.

The Decapolis consisted of ten cities colonized by Greeks in the era of Alexander the Great. Nine of these cities were on the east side of the Jordan, with only one on the west side. They maintained a blend of Greek and Jewish cultures in an uneasy understanding. Both sides frowned on the practices of the other. Though most of the Twelve lived and worked in the area around the Sea of Galilee and knew some of the local language, it was Philip who felt the most comfortable in the Decapolis. Often, when dealing with the Greeks, Philip found friends from Greece who were visiting someone in one of the cities of the Decapolis. Early in his fishing career he met another unwilling fisher named Nathaniel bar Tolomai, called Bartholomew, and because they were a bit above the others in station they became good friends. Bartholomew was a man who enjoyed the higher and better things of life; he possessed a degree of refinement that equaled Philip's.

One ordinary day, while cleaning that early morning's catch, Philip heard Simon and Andrew speaking of a prophet named John. For reasons Philip could not explain, he found interest in their conversation, and he wanted to see this John and hear him. A few days later he went to the Jordan and was instantly captivated by the man, and he felt compelled to return again and again. Philip was confused by this. He was not easily impressed by other men, but John had certainly impressed him. His voice was full of great authority, and Philip wondered where John had acquired this authority.

The man wears animal skins! He looks like a beggar! He is a radical—a man of great zeal and enthusiasm in his calling…but why? Is he a reformer? He endangers himself in order to make a difference. A true prophet!

Still, with all his uncertainties, Philip began spending many hours listening to this man. One day Philip stepped into the Jordan to be purified, though he later questioned this decision. As he walked to John, the Baptizer's facial expression changed and a smile broke John's stoic face. Just as quickly as the smile appeared, it disappeared, and John looked long and hard at Philip. Then in a low, personal voice he said, "He Whom you search for, He Who is greater than I, will call you, and to Him you will owe much."

At that moment Philip had a change of heart. He wanted to push away from John and run, for he thought that John was a sham, but he ignored this reaction and permitted himself to be purified. As he emerged from the river, he felt a tinge of relief, which he disregarded as he walked to the river banks. On shore, he never once took his eyes off John, wanting to find more in the prophet's words. John's words had left him feeling helpless and in the hands of a destiny that frightened him, for he was not searching for anyone, nor was he listening for a call. John's prophecy was thoroughly illogical.

He returned home and told his sister what had happened; she, believing that all men had a purpose, encouraged Philip to return to John and learn more of what he meant, but the next day Philip suppressed his curiosity and returned to fishing. He would not become a follower of a misfit who made absurd predictions. He slowly began to tear down any extraordinary ideas he had about the Baptizer. He concluded that John was a man who was willing to destroy something that Philip considered the foundation of Judaism, and yet John offered no replacement for the foundation he was undermining. Even if he agreed with John's condemnation of the Herodians and the Sanhedrin, he could not imagine a better system for protecting the holiness of *haShem* The Name, or the Jewish people.

A nation cannot become great or strong if it does not believe in Theos God, he thought, remembering what some Greek philosopher had once said.

Many days passed, and on each day Mariamne asked him if he had seen John. He evaded the questions. To his surprise, the feeling of helplessness that he experienced at the Jordan returned to him. This feeling then became a daily occurrence, and as time passed the feeling became a torment.

Days later, Philip heard Simon and Andrew say that the Baptizer had pointed out a new prophet. The two brothers were so excited by this new prophet that they could hardly contain themselves.

A day later, Philip overheard Zebedee angrily complaining that he was short of help because Simon, Andrew, and his sons had gone off to follow a new prophet. Philip, having experienced the "thunder" of Zebedee, did his work with great care. The day was heavy with duties and soon took its toll on Philip. Finally, he had a lull in his labors. Philip walked away from everyone, especially Zebedee, who would find more for him to do, and sat by one of the boats that had been beached on the shore of the Sea of Galilee. The boat was on its side and rested on two large rocks, creating a safe, shady haven. Philip glanced around quickly to make certain that no one could observe what he was about to do. Seeing no one, he quickly went under the boat and enjoyed the shade. From a small satchel he was carrying he removed some fruit, a few nuts, and a small piece of unleavened bread. He said his prayers of thanksgiving and slowly began to eat his midday meal. During the meal he uttered a small prayer of thanksgiving for the peacefulness around him.

Several still moments passed.

Unexpectedly, a gentle, caressing breeze passed under the boat. It was soft and so soothing that Philip instantly experienced a moment of comfort and relief. Suddenly, on the sands of the beach, he saw a shadow. It was a large shadow that spread over the sand and equaled the length of the boat. He never looked to see who cast the shadow, for it surely was cast by the tallest man in Creation. He heard a voice softer than the breeze—more caring, more caressing, yet with a power so intense that Philip almost lost his breath.

The voice said, "Come. Follow me."

The shadow moved away from Philip, and without a thought Philip rose, leaving his meal, and followed the shadow, the voice, and the Man Who spoke to him.

The next day, Philip found Nathaniel bar Tolomai and brought him to Jesus by saying to Nathaniel, "Come and see. We have found Him of Whom Moses and the Prophets did write...." To Philip's surprise, he believed his own words.

In the following days, Philip joined the followers of Jesus, and when he was chosen as one of the Twelve, he continued to hold some rank among them. It seemed that his being the oldest had something to do with his being regarded so highly, but he liked to believe that it was because he was better educated. He wasted little time in using his position of authority to guide the Others.

When the Sanhedrin began their campaign against Jesus, Philip reminded the Twelve of the many philosophers and prophets who had been regarded as renegades and troublemakers. He was certain that many of the Twelve wanted no part in a confrontation with the Sanhedrin, but being of a Greek mind, Philip enjoyed a degree of independence more readily than they did. Besides, as Philip saw it, Jesus was offering His followers an alternative: another "kingdom."

When Jesus began teaching with parables, Philip pointed out to the Twelve that Jesus was doing more than merely telling interesting stories—they were stories with subtle yet profound meaning. He told them of Plato using parables to teach others. From that time on, the Twelve debated the parables of Jesus. Even after Jesus explained the *mashal* parable, they would debate its meaning. And when Jesus began performing miracles and cures, Philip explained to the Twelve that miracles were a suspension of natural laws: a *phenomena* that they were witnessing and therefore had to believe. He added that if Jesus was able to suspend natural laws, then He must have some authority from the Almighty. From that time on, the Twelve accepted Jesus' miracles as part of His mission.

Philip became the theorist among the Twelve, but this position was not acceptable to all. Some thought him to be nothing but a pretentious old man with bits and pieces of knowledge; others believed he had a normal measure of common sense and nothing more. Whatever the reason, Philip enjoyed authority among the Apostles and often offered his opinions regarding the teachings and actions of Jesus.

One cloudy day, as the small group of thirteen walked the road from Capernaum to Bethsaida, Jesus and Philip were walking side by side. Jesus softly said to Philip, "Stay back with Me and let us talk."

Philip was elated, for this would be their first opportunity to be alone; Philip immediately concluded that Jesus was about to ask him for advice.

"Do you know the story of Adam and Eve?"

"Of course, Master," replied Philip, slightly insulted at such a rudimentary question.

"Do you really know the story, Philip?"

Philip became offended and replied quickly, "Master, I have told You I know the story. Why do You ask me again?"

Jesus, looking away, said softly, "Tell Me, what great sin did Eve and then Adam commit?"

"Disobedience," Philip answered without hesitation, and he looked to Jesus to find approval.

"And what greater sin than this did they commit?"

"Is there a greater sin than disobedience, Master?"

"Yes. One more dangerous than all sins," Jesus replied with simplicity as He looked ahead.

Frantically Philip ran *Bereishit* Genesis through his mind, for his need to be correct was overpowering.

"Envy," he responded with confidence, and then to confirm his answer he added, "They wanted to become like *haShem* so they were guilty of envy."

Receiving no reaction from Jesus, he quickly added, "Selfishness."

Again, he received no reaction from Jesus.

Philip felt his confidence shaken as he searched for the correct answer.

"This sin that I speak of is the master of all sins, Philip."

A few uncomfortable moments passed between the two. Finally, Philip said in a low voice that showed his disappointment in himself, "The sin of pride, Master. It was the sin of pride."

"Yes. It was pride: the sin that puts self above My Father and all others." Jesus turned and looked at Philip then gently placed His hand on Philip's arm. "Heed me, Philip, pride is stalking you. Be no companion to this sin, for it destroys your relationship with My Father. This sin will find a place in one of the chosen, and the Son of Man will suffer on its account."

Philip quickly pulled his arm away from Jesus' touch. He did not know why he did such a thing. Was he insulted by the implication that he was a great sinner, like Adam? Did he pull away because he was shocked to find out that his pride was so obvious? Or did he move away out of surprise upon realizing that Jesus knew him so well? Soon, the reason mattered not. He regretted pulling his arm away, and for the rest of his life, when he remembered that moment, his regret intensified. From that day on, Philip withdrew and was not so willing to be of help to the Others. Soon after this, the Others began to think of him as the shy, somber-minded Philip. Nonetheless, they retained a certain respect for him, for he had a greater sense of the Gentile world. When they neared Bethsaida, Philip went to his sister's home and told her of Jesus. Seeing the joy on Philip's face instantly persuaded Mariamne to go to Jesus. Within days, she and Philip's four daughters—Hermione, Eutychiane, Chariline, and Irais—joined the other women and children traveling with the Master through Galilee.

One day, Philip's daughters approached their father with other children and asked if they could see Jesus. Philip, being concerned for Jesus' rest, told the children to go away. The children pressed on and began to get close to Jesus, but Philip stood in their way. He pulled his daughters aside and began to scold them for their disobedience and persistence.

Suddenly he heard Jesus say, "Suffer the little children and forbid them not to come to Me: for the kingdom of heaven is for such." When Philip turned, he found Jesus' stern, disapproving eyes upon him, so he gladly allowed his daughters to go to Him. From that day on, Philip knew that his daughters would be servants of Jesus.

Later that day, when the Others were occupied, Philip found Jesus standing next to him.

"Tell me, Philip, would you wish to deprive your children of the love that the Father has given the world?"

"No, Master."

"Learn from children, Philip. We must all be like children when we go to the Father; in their simplicity, they find the Father more readily than can the greatest of minds."

Jesus walked away leaving Philip humbled.

The Jewish Feast of *Sukkoth* was approaching, and Jesus told the Apostles that He wanted to go off and pray. They got into a boat and crossed the Sea of Galilee, for several of the Apostles knew of a deserted place just outside of the town of Bethsaida: Julias, in the Tetrarchy of Philip. As they came ashore, they found a large crowd waiting for them, and Jesus immediately became filled with compassion for these people, for He knew they had traveled long and far to see Him. He spoke to them and healed many of the sick. Later in the afternoon, the Apostles, who had grown hungry, began to press Jesus into dismissing the crowd.

"Tell them to go back to their homes for their meal," one of the Twelve said.

Upon hearing this, Jesus turned to Philip, who was the nearest to Him, and remarked that the Twelve should feed the multitude. Philip was confused but somehow knew that this was a test; unable to find a solution, he replied timidly that they did not have the money for such an undertaking. Jesus' attention was drawn away from Philip as He was approached by Andrew accompanied by a boy with five barley loaves and two fish. They followed Jesus' instruction to feed the people, and when they were all fed and the Twelve had gathered up the remains, they became excited. Philip, off to the side, watched as the reality of the miracle began to spread over the crowd. He felt someone standing behind him, and before he could turn to see who it was, he heard Jesus say, "You see, Philip, the Father always provides for the humble."

The crowd, now realizing what had taken place, suddenly surged toward Jesus, but He was gone.

That night Philip became depressed, for it seemed that he was being reprimanded by Jesus. Though they were gentle reprimands, they bothered Philip, and seemingly it was happening to him alone.

Over the next few months, he discussed this thought with Bartholomew and with John Zebedee, and they both dismissed it, insisting that Philip was being over-sensitive. Believing that perhaps they were correct, he forced his feelings to pass, but occasionally the thought returned, causing him to withdraw further.

As the years progressed, Philip began to see that he was a great deal unlike the Others. They were less adventurous and less aggressive than he was. He differed from the others in that he did not believe that Jesus was a secular leader; Jesus had never given any indications of this. What Philip did see was Jesus' power in forgiving sins and asking for repentance; Philip was sure that the kingdom Jesus spoke of was not a material kingdom. At least this is what he thought. Unlike the Others, he didn't know or care what part was to be his.

They traveled through Galilee, Judea, and Samaria, and several times they crossed the Jordan River into the Decapolis. They watched as Jesus grew in the favor of the people and the disfavor of the Sanhedrin and the Pharisees. As time passed, the Twelve grew close because they had the bond of Jesus, Whom they all loved and wanted to serve.

✳

It was a hot, humid day.

The blistering sun beat down on the winding, dusty road along which the thirteen men were walking. The scorched earth heated their sandals, making their footsteps uncomfortable. They were perspiring and often wiped their foreheads with the sleeves of their robes or hands. All of them walked the road wishing for relief—be it water, shade, or a breeze. They were approaching a small village just outside of the Decapolis city of Scythopolis, the only Decapolis city on the west side of the Jordan. Passing them on the same road was a caravan of merchants who were heading west to one of the Mediterranean seaports. As the group passed, some of the Apostles stopped by the road to allow the caravan to pass, while Jesus and the remaining Apostles continued to walk to Scythopolis. Philip watched as the caravan passed. He could tell they were Greeks from their clothing. He thought back to some of his friends in Greece, many of whom had family, friends, or business associates in these cities.

From nowhere, he heard a voice. It was a familiar voice that caught his breath. He quickly turned his head. At the end of the caravan were three Greeks whose faces were so familiar that he had to grab a nearby tree to steady himself. Suddenly his face brightened as one of the three men glanced at him. The man stopped walking and yelled out in surprise, "Philippos!"

Philip and the man ran to each other and embraced. Soon the other two Greeks joined the embrace.

"What a strange thing," shouted Alastor, the oldest of the three Greeks. "Yesterday we wondered if we would find you in Galilee, and here you are among the Greeks."

"My dear, dear old friends, what a blessing to see you again," Philip responded gleefully.

"Philippos, you look younger," Thales, the next oldest, said as he slapped Philip on the back.

"And you, Thales, are still a liar, in spite of your desire to speak and know the truth," Philip said in jest.

"Good friend," Usiris, the youngest and quietest of the three, said as he gave Philip a hardy embrace.

"Usiris, I see you still are putting up with these old foxes."

"They are like bad habits, so hard to get rid of," Usiris replied with a wide, warm smile.

"And what, besides the usual mischief, brings you three to Galilee?" Philip asked, still smiling and still flooded with joy.

"Money," Alastor replied quickly.

"We were here on business, visiting some of our associates and relatives," Thales added.

"And you completed your business and were hoping to find me?"

"Yes, but we could not find you, so we were returning to Greece," Thales answered.

"And you, my friend, what are you doing here?" Alastor asked Philip.

"Missing the Greeks, no doubt," Thales added.

"I am traveling with friends, and we were just passing through on our way to the Jordan," Philip replied, but then he became disappointed with himself for not speaking the whole truth.

"And where are your friends?" Thales asked, looking around and finding no one near them.

Philip looked around and said plainly, "They must have gone ahead."

"You look well, Philip. How are your daughters?" Usiris asked timidly.

"They grow quickly and are with my sister, Mariamne, in Galilee."

"You travel just with friends and no family? A single man again?" Alastor remarked with a small smile on his lips.

"I…I travel with a prophet."

The three men glanced quickly at each other and then returned their eyes to Philip, and he could immediately see that they thought he had lost his senses.

"You mean like one of the prophets of old?"

"A Jewish Prophet?"

"Interesting."

"Yes, but this Man is a new prophet; He is different."

"And what makes this Man different?" Alastor asked suspiciously.

"I believe this Man is the Chosen One," Philip said, certain they thought him a fool.

"The Chosen One?" asked Thales.

"Your Messiah?" questioned Alastor.

"Yes, the One promised by *haShem*," Philip replied, feeling a renewed confidence in his answer.

"What drew you to this conclusion?" Alastor asked with a show of interest.

Philip began to walk behind the caravan, leading the Greeks farther away from the town and from Jesus. As he walked, he began telling them of his new life. They walked some distance, listening silently and intently to Philip as he spoke feverishly about Jesus. Philip soon recognized that the three Greeks were silent because they were not as enthralled with Jesus as he was. He knew these men and expected them to ask many questions and to debate with him, but they remained silent; soon Philip assumed that they were merely being polite. He continued on with his stories of Jesus' miracles, and finally he told them of the teaching Jesus gave from the Mount, and suddenly the three men became vocal.

"I find what you say very interesting, for each thing Jesus said begins with a *makarios* blessing and ends with a reward—a dispenser of goodness for something done," Alastor stated with a quizzical look on his face.

"Yes, that is unusual, but more unusual is that the rewards are not here on earth but in *ouranos* heaven," Thales remarked blankly.

"*Ouranous?* Thales?" Philip uttered with a small smile on his face. "Many years ago you told me that you did not believe in such a place."

"Old age, my friend, often brings hope of immorality. Besides, you have made me knowledgeable of your ways and have converted me in some of them. *Ouranous* is now a real place to me, a home that I hope to share with you and others," Thales declared with sincerity.

"But first you must be blessed," Usiris declared pensively.

"Ah, yes, that first," Alastor corrected himself.

"But, my dear companions, let us not forget that these *makarios* blessings must be known here on earth if we are to get to heaven," Alastor added, pleased that he had made so important a statement.

"You do not mean we must know them, Alastor, you mean we must do these things in order to be blessed with heaven," Usiris corrected.

Philip and the two Greeks looked at the young man with astonishment.

"You are correct, my young friend," Alastor said.

They continued to look at the young man who was gazing off into the distance.

"These words of Jesus are shocking. They rearrange many ethics of our world," Alastor said, wanting to continue the conversation.

"Yes, and His words speak of kindness and compassion, and such things are not common in our world," added Thales.

"They speak of how we are to get to *Theos* God," Usiris muttered.

The three men again looked at the young man who was still gazing off into the distance.

"Yes, Usiris, I believe you are correct," Alastor murmured flatly.

The four men fell silent.

"Yet there is a paradox in these sayings. How can you be blessed and happy with mourning, or poverty, or persecution?" Alastor asked.

"Because the joys of heaven will be greater than these hardships," Philip answered. "Jesus, I believe, by these blessings has given joy to hardship and reward to endurance and patience."

"Philip, for a Jew, you are sometimes very perceptive," Thales said with a smile. "Perhaps being friends with us has given you an intellect after all."

"Well, I still am not completely in agreement. I still cannot see why this prophet expects humans to do such things," Alastor said.

"Because no one can live without joy, and Jesus brings us true joy. This Jesus also speaks of love. Love of self, of friends, of neighbors, and of God. These blessings are of God and to God, and…." Thales paused, trying to find the correct word.

"From God," Usiris said. He turned to look at his three friends, from whom he had learned many things and through whom he had been richly blessed. Slowly, his eyes passed over their faces. "So perhaps we should be asking Philippos something: By what authority does Jesus speak?"

"Yes, Usiris is correct again. Is Jesus of God?" Alastor asked.

"Or is He from God?" Thales asked

"Or…is He God?" Usiris asked. They all looked at the young man and then slowly turned to look at Philip, who simply smiled and said, "Come and see."

Philip began walking back to the city where he would meet Jesus, knowing that his friends were curious enough to follow.

The three Greeks stayed with Jesus and the Twelve for three days, then they returned to Greece. Three months later, they wrote Philip saying that they were returning to Galilee. Philip had privately predicted they would do this, for he knew the three had not experienced enough of Jesus to satisfy their curiosities or their understanding. Philip was certain that they had retreated to Greece to familiarize themselves with the Jewish scriptures and to stabilize their thoughts.

While home in Greece, the three did just as Philip suspected. They studied everything they could about the Jewish prophets and the various writings concerning the Anointed One. They had lengthy discussions with Greek Jews and relayed to these Jews what they had witnessed and heard while in Palestine. The three appreciated how Jesus used *parabole* parables, for the parable was an old and respected Greek form of educating.

Usiris reminded his companions that Jesus was unique among Jewish prophets in using this form of teaching. Jesus, he remarked, was fulfilling prophesies set down by King David: "I will open my mouth in parables; I will utter things hidden since the foundation of the world."

"I am certain," Usiris said in a deliberate tone, "that Jesus will fulfill many other prophecies. What I do find amazing is how frequently and thoughtfully Jesus tells these parables, as though He has been pondering them since He was a young man, and maybe even as a child, or…" he stopped and looked at the others, then added with some delight, "before He was born."

The two older men disagreed: Usiris was being too idealistic.

One thing the three agreed upon was that this form of teaching was wasted on the crowds and Jesus' close followers, with the exception of Philip, for the true meanings of the parables could only be understood by trained minds, Greek minds. A Greek would examine and dissect such parables for the hidden meanings. The three agreed that the parables Jesus taught were profoundly spiritual, but in a cruel and secular world they would go unnoticed. Jesus had to be naïve and idealistic to think that His message of love, compassion, peace, self-denial, and sacrifice would be accepted. They concluded that Jesus was a great teacher but a poor philosopher, for only Greeks were good philosophers. What had amazed them was His personal history: He was but a Jewish carpenter's Son, and yet He was so wise, so reflective, that He gave the impression of a well-educated person with an all-knowing mind. They all admired Jesus' power of speech. His words flowed smoothly and distinctly. His responses to those who challenged Him were swift and poignant; indeed, Jesus seemed to know the questions before they were asked. At one time, through their observations, they suspected that the Jewish leaders were allies of Jesus and were only attempting to elicit His eloquence, but soon they dismissed this theory, for they could not explain the frustration that Jesus created among the leaders.

The first time they saw Jesus perform a miracle, they concluded that He was a clever charlatan, a great magician, but they found no conspirators among the crowds. What they did uncover frightened them. They found that the leaders of the people were setting traps for Jesus by hiring poor and lowly individuals to act as though they were sick. These hirelings were told to call out to Jesus and ask His help for a cure. If Jesus had cured the impostors, the leaders would have been able to reveal Jesus as a fraud, but when these fakes called out to Jesus they received a disapproving look and no assistance. The Greeks were bewildered at how Jesus could tell the difference between the fakes and the people in need. The three had to conclude that the miracles were real, and then they wondered and debated: How did this Man get such a gift? How does He have such power over nature?

The miracles baffled the Greeks; they could not find any solid explanations for them until Usiris softly uttered, "Perhaps we cannot explain these miracles because they are not on our level. Obviously, they are from a higher power, maybe a divine power." Seeing the shocked look on the faces of the others, he continued with equal softness, "Let us not forget that Jesus is not of our culture, but of the Jewish culture; think of the prophet who said, 'God himself will come and will save you. Then shall the eyes of the blind be opened, and the ears of the deaf shall be unstopped. Then shall the lame man leap as a hart, and the tongue of the dumb shall be free'—perhaps he was speaking of Jesus."

They then debated Jesus as a prophet. They knew that if Jesus was a prophet the Jews would not accept Him, for they rarely honored prophets during the prophet's life. This historical fact saddened them and made them concerned for Jesus' safety. They finally had to face the fact that a prophet must make prophesies, and they had heard none from Jesus. Over and over they relived their time with Jesus, and they could recall no prophesies. So they did not feel comfortable in declaring Him a prophet; besides, they could not understand why a prophet would choose the poor, ignorant men of the Twelve as His *apostolos* Apostles.

Next, they scrutinized the idea of Jesus being the Anointed One.

Alastor remarked, "If Jesus is the *Khristos*, He should make Himself known. To fulfill the expectations of the Anointed One, Jesus would have to give signs of leadership that would release His people from the domination of Rome and the corruption of the leaders of Judea. I do not see this happening."

Thales stated, "I agree with what you say, for all Jesus offers His followers is sympathy, guidance, and love, and these qualities do not make rulers or generals. I doubt that He is the *Khristos*, for I do not see what His anointing would represent. What is He anointed to do?"

Usiris did not agree with his friends. He believed that Jesus was an extraordinary Man on an extraordinary mission: a mission unlike any man had undertaken since the beginning of time. These were his feelings, but still he searched for proof. He declared once, "If Jesus is the Anointed One, we must remember that He is here for the Jews, and it will be for their benefit. We are Gentiles and will not be blessed by Him."

The two older men agreed.

✳

The three men arrived in the Phoenician city known as Tyre. They intended to stay a few days in Tyre visiting with Photios, an old friend, and then they would travel south into Galilee to find Jesus and Philip. While resting at Photios' home, they him asked if he had heard of Jesus.

"Of course I have! One could not help but hear of Him. Every Jew and non-Jew in Syria and Judea has heard of Him. The Judeans and Galileans travel much, and they are not men who keep secrets."

Photios looked at the three men and knew from their faces that they wanted to know more, so with the desire to create envy in them, he announced, "I even went to see for myself if Jesus was worthy of all the rumors I had heard."

"And what did you find out?" Alastor asked as the other two Greeks leaned forward to hear what he had to report.

"What I heard of Him I found to be true, but sadly I also learned that He is in grave danger. Many plot against Him."

Photios began to tell them of the great hatred that the leaders of the people had for Jesus and of the numerous plots to capture or discredit Him. He was certain that the leaders staged confrontations and debates with Jesus in the hope of using His own words against Him. Photios was certain that Jesus' enemies were looking for a weakness in His followers so as to catch Jesus at a disadvantage.

"I truly believe they will succeed, for men will do anything for money and fame. Yet Jesus seemed fearless and continued to speak to the people and perform miracles. He even eats and converses with tax collectors and sinners, and this makes me admire Him greatly."

The three Greeks were surprised by Photios, for as he spoke his voice was above his normal flat tone; they could see that he truly liked Jesus. Finally, Photios told them that Jesus had fed large numbers of people.

"Are you sure that is what He did?" asked Alastor.

"As sure as I am of your name," Photios asserted.

"How can you be that certain?" Thales inquired.

"I was there," Photios replied.

The Greeks fell to silence.

Finally, Alastor said in a low voice, "We must speak to Philippos."

"Yes, and soon," added Thales.

"Well, you will not have to go very far, because I hear rumors that Jesus and His friends are in Tyre."

The next day they went searching for Jesus and the Twelve, and by midday they had found the place where they were staying; much to their surprise, there was only a small crowd. As they approached the Twelve, they realized that Jesus was not among them. Philip, upon seeing them, walked lightly to them; they warmly embraced and moved off to the side away from the Twelve.

The Greeks immediately realized that Philip had changed. His pride and arrogance were gone; he was a man of timidity and self-control.

They asked for Jesus.

"Jesus needs rest," Philip said to the Greeks. "He is at the house of a friend. He sought refuge here before and found He could maintain some anonymity among these people. When He came here previously, He spent hours talking to us, explaining many of the things He did and said. Now He needs to be away from the huge crowds of people who hound Him. He needs a respite from the demands for miracles, and further-more He needs to be away from the scrutiny of the Sanhedrin and the Herodians. Among the Gentiles, He can have some peace and obscurity."

Alastor, who knew Philip better than the others, immediately asked, "Philippos, you are worried. Why?"

"Things grow dangerous for my Master. His enemies grow bolder and confront Him more often, but instead of hiding Himself, He grows bolder and does things that further anger the leaders."

"What are your fears?" Thales inquired.

"They may harm Him," Philip replied as he turned to look away.

"The people will not allow such a thing. They love Him," Thales said.

"The people are afraid of the Temple leaders. They will do nothing."

"Perhaps they will do more than you Twelve will," Usiris said.

Philip looked at the young man and for an instant wanted to lash out at his veiled insult, but instead he looked away, discovering a new fear in his thoughts.

"Tell us about the feeding of the people," inquired Usiris.

Alastor and Thales looked quickly at the young man and Alastor coughed as a sign of annoyance, but the young man decided to ignore him. Alastor realized that Usiris was oblivious of Philip's fragile condition.

Usiris ignored Alastor further by repeating his question.

Philip's expression changed quickly. He took a small step closer to them and began to tell them the story of the feeding. He told them of how they divided up the people so that it was easy to count five thousand men, and how they fed them and gathered the remnants.

"I have told you exactly how it happened."

Alastor pressed Philip: "How do you think Jesus did this?"

"I do not know. The Others sincerely believe it was a miracle and that He will feed all of Judea when He reveals Himself."

"But you do not think it a miracle?"

"I know it happened; I know it was real and I know it was spectacu-lar...." he stopped and shifted his eyes to each of their faces. They were waiting for him to make a denial of Jesus, or of himself, but he could not. He stood erect and said, "Yes, I suppose it was a miracle....Yes, it was a miracle. Jesus seems to be able to perform miracles at will."

"You have made a bold claim, Philip, one that is against logic and nature."

"Jesus is not a normal Being, I told you that." He looked at them and could sense their doubts. "I believe He is the Promised One. I make this statement not from the logic you wish me to have or from the intelligence that you seem to worship, but I say this…in faith."

"The same faith you have in your God?" Usiris asked timidly.

"Yes," asserted Philip, and he felt pleased with his affirmation.

Instantly he saw Alastor's and Thales' brows arch with dissatisfaction, but when he looked at Usiris he saw a glimpse of understanding on the young man's face.

Thales, whose face was twisted with uncertainty, asked, "And the people, what did they do when they saw what Jesus had done?"

"They wanted to make Him king."

"The perfect time for Jesus to declare Himself their *Khristos*," Alastor stated with excitement in his voice.

"But Jesus disappeared."

"What?"

"When we turned to find Jesus, He was gone. We later found Him on the other side of the Sea of Galilee."

"He just disappeared?"

"Yes, He simply was gone."

"At a time when the people would have declared Him king?"

"Yes, I know. We all believed it was the perfect time for Jesus to claim His kingdom, but He was gone."

"The time was not right," they heard Usiris say, and they looked at him.

"And why do you think that, dear Usiris?" The annoyance in Alastor's voice was obvious.

"Because if Jesus is teacher, prophet, or Messiah, He will not allow Himself to be made king through a riot, for this would be contrary to His teaching."

"I believe you might be correct, Usiris. He would have been king by their wishes and not by His," Philip said as he inched closer to the young Greek.

"I disagree," blurted Alastor as he turned and walked a few steps away.

"So do I. If anything, it proves Jesus a fake," Thales roughly remarked. "I believe it proves that Jesus does not want to be a king."

"Perhaps not of this world," Usiris simply said.

"What did you say?" Alastor shouted.

"Perhaps Jesus' kingdom is not of this world."

With astonishment Philip said, "Jesus used those very words!"

The Greeks retreated into silence as they tried to imagine what other kingdom there was.

Knowing that the Greeks were perplexed, Philip decided to give them more to think about. As he was set to speak, he looked only at Usiris for support, for he felt he had a believer among the three.

"If you think that feeding the multitude was a great thing, let me tell you of how Jesus brought a boy and a girl back from death."

Instantly he felt the older men grow skeptical, but from Usiris he saw a smile, a look of clarity, and a nod.

*

Later, the three Greeks retreated for the night, and during their meal the two older Greeks discussed the news that Philip had given them. They talked late into the night. Usiris listened and never spoke. He heard the others speak of Jesus as being the *Khristos* and of the possibility that He came to save the "Chosen People." Because they had heard Jesus speak of sin and repentance, they believed that Jesus was also a holy Man, most likely a prophet.

Usiris listened and never spoke.

They debated and debated, around and around, back and forth, until they came up with a conclusion that left them exhausted and confused. They concluded that Jesus might be God.

Usiris listened and never spoke.

They thought of this for a while then concluded that if Jesus was God, then He was working against the laws of nature and the principles of Aristotle. For Aristotle had said that God co-exists with all the working natural causes, but this God of Philip's was working against nature by feeding many with little and giving life to the dead.

Usiris listened and never spoke.

They finally resolved that whoever Jesus was, He was here for the Jews and not the rest of the world, and therefore He would do things only for the Jews and the rest of the world would never know of Him.

Usiris listened and never spoke.

Tired, they decided to ready themselves for sleep, and in the morning they would go to see Philip and bid him goodbye—they had decided to return to Greece and their Olympian gods and to leave their Jewish companion in his own foolishness. They talked a bit more of unimportant things. They were finished talking about Jesus, for they had found their conclusion and needed to search no more. They had satisfied their own minds. The fire they had made was glowing and dying. They blew out the candles, and each went to their beds and fell quickly into silence.

In the dark, they heard: "I always believed in one God. I always thought that if Zeus was the king of all gods and the god among gods, then he should have been able to do what all the other Olympian gods did."

Alastor and Thales turned their heads in the direction of Usiris' voice, and in the dark they could picture the young man's face.

"So I believe, like Philip and the Jews."

In the dark they waited for Usiris, the less significant, to say more.

"Plato said that God was a force, just a force, and therefore could not give hope or love. He said that God is not an almighty caregiver, nor is He able to help the needy or the suffering."

Alastor slowly sat up, and Thales rolled on his side in the direction of the voice.

"Plato also said that if God can do all these things, if He can give hope and help the needy, then He is a living God. I think what Philippos and his friends are blindly following is a living God—a God Who is not selfish—a God Who gives love and Who wants not only the body and mind of men, but more."

There was silence in the room, and then came the sound of Usiris moving on his bed trying to find comfort for sleep.

"The questions I ask are these: If this God of Philippos can receive love and give love, can He be a God of all people? Is the God Philippos is walking with satisfied with a few or with many? And who am I to say I am not wanted?"

*

There had been a bad windstorm that day, so Jesus and the Twelve stayed in the house of one of the Jews who was a follower. Jesus enjoyed this time alone with His Twelve, for it gave Him time to see if they understood what He had said to them. By midday the storm had passed, and Jesus readied Himself for a trip to another part of Tyre because He had been found out and a crowd was beginning to form around the house. Among these people were the three Greeks. Jesus and the Apostles came from the house and walked quickly down the narrow dirt street in the direction of their next destination. A small crowd followed, and from the crowd came a well-dressed elderly woman. From her appearance it was clear that she was a woman of wealth, and in spite of her age she was well attended to. It was also obvious that she was Greek; she was not a follower of the Olympian gods but of the god Baal.

The woman approached Jesus quickly and fell before Him. At His feet the woman cried, "Have mercy on me, O Lord, Thou Son of David: my daughter is grievously troubled by a devil."

"The woman is Greek, and yet look how she grovels," Thales murmured in shock and disapproval.

"She is in need," Usiris replied.

Jesus did not reply to her pleas or acknowledge her; He just continued to walk away from her in haste.

Alastor leaned forward and whispered in Usiris' ear, "Well, my dear wise friend, there goes your all-encompassing God."

The woman quickly stood up, her beautiful dress dusty from the dirt and her face smudged with grains of sand.

Again she called out to Jesus.

"Send her away, Lord, for she crieth after us," one of the Twelve said.

"Yes, Lord, she draws attention to us," another of the Twelve added.

Jesus called back to the woman: "I was not sent but to the sheep that are lost of the house of Israel."

"By Zeus, He has rebuked her because she is not Jewish! You are wrong, Usiris, the Man is not for all people," Alastor affirmed.

She raced before Jesus and His Apostles and said again, "Lord, help me." Her eyes were wet with tears that wanted to fall but with stubbornness stayed around the edges of her eyes.

Jesus looked at her and said, "Suffer first the children to be filled; for it is not good to take the bread of the children, and cast it to the dogs."

"I will not hear more—He called that Greek a dog!" Alastor said angrily. He threw his cloak over his shoulder and turned, ready to walk away.

But the woman persisted and touched His arm; for a moment she looked into His face, and then she said, "Yea, Lord, for the whelps also eat under the table of the crumbs of the children."

Thales and Alastor smiled proudly at the wise response the woman gave Jesus.

"She speaks with the logic and intellect of a Greek," Thales whispered.

Jesus looked at the woman and said with warmth and compassion, "O woman, great is thy faith; be it done to thee as thou say. Go thy way. The devil is gone out of thy daughter."

He walked away.

The woman stood allowing the tears to flow down her soiled face, and finally she wiped her tears and rushed away.

Usiris turned from Thales and Alastor and hurried away. The two Greeks raced after him, and when they were next to him, Alastor said in a gasp, "So you were right, my friend, Jesus is for all, so why are you walking away?"

"To follow the woman and see. I need to see if what Jesus said comes true."

As they neared the woman's house, they heard screams and cries of joy. It was as Jesus had said—the daughter was free of the devil.

The woman invited all her neighbors to celebrate with her, and she invited her three countrymen to join in the celebration, which they did.

Later the next day, Alastor said, "We must go find Philippos and talk to Jesus for there is much more for us to learn."

So they traveled back to the place where they had last seen Jesus, but they could not find Him. The next day, they heard that Jesus and the Apostles were returning to Jerusalem. They immediately set out after Jesus. As soon as they crossed into Galilee, they began hearing rumors of the danger Jesus was in and of the plots to stop Him. These rumors intensified as they moved closer to Jerusalem, and the threats to Jesus became more real. When they finally found Jesus, He was in Jerusalem. As they mingled in the crowd, they heard talk of Jesus having raised another person from the dead, and they heard of His triumphal entry into that Holy City. The men were elated with the news of Jesus' triumphant entry into Jerusalem and were certain that Jesus had declared Himself. Expecting to hear of further triumphs, they rushed in search of Him, but instead they heard of a plot to kill the man raised from the dead and a conspiracy to capture Jesus and place Him on trial.

This troubled the Greeks greatly, so they sought out Philip and said to him, "Philippos, we must speak to Jesus. Please arrange it."

Philip saw the look of urgency in their eyes, and he could tell from their gravity that this request was important. Not wanting to appear proud in Jesus' view, Philip decided to go to Andrew, who was also sympathetic to the Greeks. While Andrew listened to Philip, he never took his eyes off the three Greeks. Finally, the two Apostles went to Jesus and told Him of the Greeks' request.

As they spoke to Jesus, He had His face turned away from the Greeks.

Softly, Jesus said to Andrew and Philip, "Tell them to come to Me."

Philip and Andrew withdrew, and the three Greeks walked to Jesus. When they arrived, they bowed to Him.

"*Didaskalos* Teacher," Alastor whispered, "we seek to help You."

Jesus looked at them for a moment with a puzzled expression on His face, then His face cleared and assumed a look of understanding.

"There are many here who plot against You. They intend to do You grave harm," Thales whispered.

"Come with us to Greece where You and Your ways will be understood and appreciated, and You will be safe," Alastor pleaded.

Jesus lowered His head and seemed to be deep in thought. Finally, He raised His head and said, "Come, stay with Me."

"We cannot do that, Teacher, for we see a great sorrow for You, and we do not want to witness the death of so great a Teacher as You. We Greeks lost Socrates out of jealousy and have lamented his death for centuries. We do not want to lose You as well."

Jesus turned abruptly and walked away.

"The hour is come, that the Son of Man should be glorified," Jesus said. "Amen, amen, I say to you, unless the grain of wheat falling into the ground die, itself remaineth alone. But if it dies, it bringeth forth much fruit. He that loveth his life shall lose it, and he that hateth his life in this world, keepeth it unto life eternal. If any man minister to Me, let him follow Me. And where I am, there also shall My minister be. If any man minister to Me, him will My Father honor."

The Greeks heard what Jesus said.

"He rebuked us."

"No," replied Usiris, "He found us to be a confirmation of what He knows is to come. I believe that we are messengers to Him. He has not rebuked us, we have rebuked Him. I think, brothers, we were instruments in His plan by confirming what He was supposed to do. I think He is supposed to die."

Jesus continued, "Now is My soul troubled. And what shall I say? Father, save Me from this hour. But for this cause I came unto this hour."

"My goodness, Usiris, you are correct."

Jesus went on: "Father, glorify Thy name."

A voice came from heaven, a voice that all heard.

"I have glorified it and will glorify it again."

Jesus looked over His shoulder and then said, "This voice came not because of Me, but for your sakes."

The Greeks stood along the street as Jesus went on, and when they looked up they saw only Philip standing in the street. His eyes pleaded for them to join him.

"What are we to do?" Usiris asked.

"I will not be a part of this—not even a witness to so great a loss. I for one am returning home," Thales said.

"Yes, I think we should be away from this place, for I have a sense of great sorrow, and even death, surrounding this Holy City of the Jews," Alastor added.

Usiris looked at them for a long time, then at Philip. He silently promised to return, but for now he, too, needed to go to Greece to think and learn more of himself.

"Let us return to Greece," he whispered, and he turned to begin his voyage. Alastor and Thales followed him.

They learned that Jesus was all that people said He was, but they could not do what He asked of them, for they could not follow a teacher to His death. They wanted only to remember the great things He had done. They knew that eventually Jesus would come to them in a different form, and they were certain that He would come to find them.

As Philip watched his friends leave, he felt something being torn from him, and a void replaced the missing thing. He knew they had done what they had set out to do, but this did not ease his pain. He watched as they continued to walk, and suddenly his heart leapt with joy as he saw the three of them wrap their arms around each other's shoulders.

I never saw them do that before, he thought. He smiled, for he knew that Jesus had done what He was supposed to do.

✳

Philip threw himself behind the rock and hid. He wanted to seize the moment and grasp his senses, but he was too scared to do even this. He pressed his cold, sweaty body against the rock. His heart was beating rapidly. His body was trembling. His mouth was dry from panting. His emotions and thoughts were twirling around inside him, and he could not control the disorder.

Get a hold of yourself, Philip! Think! he shouted in his thoughts.

He closed his eyes, and in his mind pictures began to flash quickly; voices raced and rushed together to become distorted babblings. Occasionally a word, or several words, became clear.

"Awake, the hour has come...."

Jesus stood in the moonlight, His face silver and His white robe tinted light blue.

Soldiers were all around them. Some of their faces were blank and lifeless, and others had faces of anger and hate.

"Hail, Rabbi...." Judas looked so strange. His eyes were hidden in the shade of his brow, and his face was white and black.

"Whom do you seek?"

The tender, even sound of Jesus' voice cut the chilly night air.

"Jesus of Nazareth…." came the feeble reply.

A knife flashed. An ear fell. A miracle was performed.

"Let these others go…." Jesus spoke not as a request but as a command.

The soldiers rushed and grabbed Him. They had found their lost courage, and now secure in their numbers they were rough, mean, and hateful.

The Twelve ran.

Peter, who was the one who had vowed to stay with Jesus, ran. John, who had sought and begged for His love, ran. The Zealot, who had defended other causes, ran. The young Jude and the old James ran. Bartholomew and Matthew, who had money to pay for their freedom, ran. James and Andrew, who had the strength to haul loads of fish onto boats, ran. Thomas, who bravely had volunteered to follow Jesus and die with Him, ran. Even Judas, the betrayer, ran. Some ran faster than they thought they could, and Philip ran the fastest of them all.

He never could remember how long he sat behind the rock hiding, but by the time he decided to leave he was vested in the cloth of desertion. He knew he had betrayed Jesus as much as Judas; he had hurt Jesus as much as Judas. He knew he was lost, in an empty world without any hope; his three years of great hope were drained from him. He knew he had to find the Others; perhaps they could rally the people and save Jesus.

How would we do that? Who would follow men with no courage?

He had to think.

He knew he had lived a night of great hate. It was "a night unlike any other night," and he wanted to be washed clean of it, for he smelled the stench of hate and cowardice. Over and over he called himself *pseudadelphos*, false-brother, and each time the word cut deeper and deeper into his being. He discovered a new Philip, and he disliked him. He slowly rose away from the rock, and as he walked in search of the Others, he wept. The wet tears burned his face, for they came from wounds far from the human eye. They were tears from a slashed soul. As he walked away from the safe rock, he grew numb, knowing his tears and his sorrows were for himself, not for Jesus.

✳

His hands were wet and trembling slightly as he reached into the cup for his lot.

Please let it be Greece, Jesus. Please let it be Greece.

He returned to his place and slowly opened the small parchment. His heart stopped beating for a moment as he read, *Go North.* With great pain he shut his eyes and allowed the sting of disappointment to penetrate his being. He took a deep breath with the understanding that the Master truly needed him where he was assigned. He opened his eyes and looked down at the parchment and continued to unfold it; when the words *Then go to Greece* were revealed, he again closed his eyes and allowed the surge of happiness to flow through his body. With a wide smile on his face, he thanked Jesus for this blessing.

Like so many of the Twelve, Philip stayed in Judea, Galilee, Perea, and Samaria for a long time. He and the Others were reluctant to leave their beloved homeland, in spite of their profound apostolic zeal. Some did leave, immediately or a short time after drawing their lots, and some stayed long after all the Others had left.

✳

When Philip finally did leave Galilee, he traveled north into Syria, Cilicia, Laodicea, Asia, and Phrygia, and then into Thrace and Moesia. He labored in these Roman provinces for more years than he had intended, but his successes were so astounding that he continued to stay and build up what the Paraclete had done through him. Finally, after thirty years of labor, he arrived in Macedonia and Greece. In Greece, he was joined by his sister and his four daughters, who came from Galilee. They came to stay with him and give witness to Jesus.

After preaching in the cities of Thermum, famous for its temple to Apollo; Actium, the city that every four years celebrated Roman games of archery, wrestling, and writing; and Megalopolis, believed by the Greeks to be the place where Zeus defeated the Titans, he went to Demetrias and later Sparta. Finally, he arrived in Athens, the place of his earlier life, and in Athens he continued what Paul of Tarsus had started during his short but intense visit. Paul never returned after his successes, so Philip claimed Athens and the surrounding area as his mission, and after Paul's death Philip labored through all of Greece and converted many to the way of Christ.

Also in Athens at the time of his arrival was his Greek friend Usiris. Alastor and Thales had died several years before his arrival. Usiris had abandoned the gods of Olympia and their Roman substitutes and had begun a life of prayer and goodness in imitation of the Master. He had heard the news of Jesus' death and resurrection through Paul, and upon Philip's arrival in Athens he was eager to receive Baptism. Usiris was baptized, and soon his wife, family, and household followed.

Usiris instantly left his business to his family and began following Philip, and he even gave him a house to live in just inside the walls of the city of Athens, near the main street called the Panathenaic Way.

*

Athens was a large city. It was a city held in great respect and affection and was regarded as the seat of the wisdom of the Greek mind, though it had lost much of its power to the Roman system of government. Many roads led to Athens. They came from many directions and from many different worlds. In the center of this metropolis was an open area called the *agora*. Surrounding the *agora* were official government buildings, social buildings, temples, baths, and many shops, workshops, and stalls for the selling of various commodities. Goods and merchandise from all over the Roman Empire and beyond were sold in the *agora*. Here in this open place, women, young ladies, and their female slaves gathered in the early morning hours to purchase goods and hear the news. It was also in this place that many ideas, theories, philosophies, and religions were discussed. One of the important buildings that surrounded the *agora* was a long open-sided structure with a terra cotta roof called the *stoas*. In the *stoas*, men gathered in the mid-afternoon to share news, debate, discuss philosophy, and listen to new thoughts. It was here that Paul and now Philip came daily to tell the Athenians of the salvation that was coming to them from humble Galilee. In the *stoas*, long debates took place between Philip and the noble and learned men of Athens. These people of status were known as *agathos*, and they challenged Philip and Usiris every day. They even invited Athenian Jews to debate Philip, and finally they sent for members of the Sanhedrin in Jerusalem. The results were astonishing: Philip proved to be a noble and well-informed preacher, and soon many decided to follow Christ, even some of those from Jerusalem.

As the Faith grew, Philip found the Greeks to be a tough breed of Christians who strengthened their belief in Jesus with logic and philosophy. When the Roman persecution came, they stood ready to die for their beliefs.

*

Philip sat in the *andron* of the house Usiris had given to him. He was certain that his daughters and their discussion would soon come into the dining room. He was not listening to the mumbled conversation from the other room, but instead, for some unknown reason, he was listening to the past. He was hearing a debate among the Twelve. They debated whether to allow Jesus to go to Jerusalem. They knew that it would be unsafe. The debate was at the time of Lazarus' illness and eventual death. Though Lazarus was quite old, he was very active and young in appearances, and his illness surprised them all.

Jesus received word of His friend's illness and showed little concern. The Apostles were perplexed by this lack of concern, but at the same time were relieved for they believed a trip to the Jerusalem area would be dangerous.

A few days later, Jesus turned away from the crowds and said to the Apostles, "Lazarus, our friend, sleepeth, but I go that I may awake him out of sleep."

Andrew said to Jesus, "Lord, if he sleeps, he shall do well."

"Yes, Lord, this is a good sign," Philip added.

Jesus glared at the two men and with slight frustration explained, "Lazarus is dead. And I am glad, for your sakes, that I was not there, that you may believe." He turned and began walking away, and over His shoulder He said softly, "But let us go to him."

None of the Apostles followed Him.

"It is unwise for Jesus to go. His enemies wait for Him," Simon Peter stated.

"I agree. It is unwise," Andrew said.

"Truly, He knows it will be dangerous to go near Jerusalem. Just days ago the people wanted to cast stones at Him," Bartholomew stated with great concern as he looked past the Apostle to Jesus, Who was walking alone a short distance from them.

"And what of us? If we go with Him, would we also put ourselves in danger?" inquired James bar Alphaeus.

"If we go, we will be suspected of any crime they say Jesus committed," James bar Zebedee said, seeing the same fear on the faces of those around him.

"We should stay here and let Him go," Judas Iscariot stated carelessly.

"It seems that Jesus is willing to challenge the authorities, and I know we all agree that this is very risky," the Zealot remarked.

"We must do something, for Jesus is going alone. We cannot make Him go alone," John whispered, and they all looked at him.

"But what should we do?" Philip asked.

They continued to debate until suddenly Thomas broke out of the circle, and passing through the Apostles he declared, "Come, let us go, that we may die with Him."

Slowly, the Others began to walk after Jesus until they were together again.

Jesus knew what awaited Him. He knew all that was to happen to Him, and He was following the Will of His Father, Philip thought, then suddenly he became sad. *Oh, how lonely that short walk was for Jesus. He was walking alone with none of us with Him. He truly must have been the loneliest Being in the world. How cruel we were to Him. How unwilling we were to die for Him when He so wanted to die for us.*

Without warning he heard silence, and he knew that the debaters would be coming to see him. He smiled warmly, for their concern pleased him, but their efforts to persuade him would all be in vain, for John's request had been answered in a letter that was already on its way. He glanced away from the food before him on the small table by his couch and saw his three daughters, his sister, and Usiris entering the *andron.*

"Father, I want you to know that I am completely against your journey to the Province of Asia. I am concerned about your health and your age. You have labored far and wide for the Lord, and you should now consider letting others do His work," Hermione said without hesitation.

She walked to the far side of the dining room and sat on one of the couches.

"I think you will find that Chariline agrees with me, and that your good friend Usiris is also against it," she continued as her sister Chariline walked to her and sat by her side.

Philip was not surprised. His daughter Hermione always disagreed with everything he did, and Chariline followed Hermione, for she feared her older sister.

Philip looked at his two daughters and understood their concern, for he had been ill and he was tired. He was sure that soon he would hear again: "Come, follow Me."

Philip looked at Mariamne and noticed a small smile. She had known for many months that he was ready and willing to set out again. He looked at his daughter Irais and captured her quick wink. She was always the childish one, and the one who never wavered in understanding his commitment to the Lord.

"Well, I take it that dear Mariamne and daughter Irais raise no objection to my going. And I am certain that Eutychiane would enjoy seeing her father closer to Ephesus, so let us count her vote as yes. So if my calculations are correct, that leaves it at three in favor and two against."

He turned his head to Usiris.

"And you, dear friend, make it three against three. This leaves me with no other choice but to say that I love you all and know that you mean well, but we must all remember that we are called to obey the Will of our Lord Jesus Christ. For some reason, it is important for Jesus to have me in Asia and near Ephesus. I will go knowing that you are deeply concerned. I wrote John some hours ago and told him that I would be leaving in two or three days."

"Father, I have a bad feeling about this trip," Chariline said softly, and everyone in the room looked at her in surprise, especially Philip. He smiled warmly at her and felt his eyes water.

"Come here, Chariline," her father ordered, and she timidly walked to him. He slowly and painfully rose from his couch and kissed her softly on her forehead; then, opening his arms wide, he invited his other daughters to him and kissed them softly on their heads.

Slowly and silently, the daughters left the room.

Mariamne walked to her brother and embraced him. "Brother, you had no other choice, and you understand the ways of Jesus far better than we do."

He kissed his sister on the forehead, and she silently left the room.

"I will go with you, my friend," Usiris remarked.

"I expected you to do that."

"I want you to know that I also have a bad feeling about this trip, Philip."

Philip lumbered to the couch with hopes of completing his small meal before going into prayer. As he walked, he said, "I have always believed that Jesus had a bad feeling when He went to Jerusalem for the last time, and still He went. If Jesus the Son of God had to die, what makes you think that I will live forever?"

"So you also have a bad feeling?"

"Doing the Will of God is never a bad feeling, Usiris. It may be unpleasant, but it is not a bad feeling."

"It is not so much your death—think of the pain you will endure."

"My pain could never compare to that endured by our Lord."

Reaching the couch, Philip slowly sat in it and enjoyed the comfort. He looked up at his friend, who still held youth on his face and in his mind.

"Tell me, Usiris, how do you like being a Christian?"

"I feel honored and blessed...even unworthy."

"I have always felt that way as an Apostle. You and I have known Jesus by sight and by sound, and even by spirit, so indeed we are honored, blessed, and unworthy. I long for Jesus, my friend. It has been too long since I last gazed upon His glorious face."

Usiris left the room in silence and in tears, for he knew his friend was going to his death.

✳

The Roman Province of Asia encompassed the regions of Lydia, Caria, Mysia, and Phrygia. It was often referred to as Phrygia, but in Roman eyes it was a proconsulship province created with the blessing of Emperor Caesar Augustus. Soon after this status was given to this region, many new cities and towns came into being. In each city, new temples were erected to the Emperor, and the province became a great center of Emperor worship. Some of the province's "venerations"—holidays honoring the reigning Emperor with processions, sacrifices, and prayers— were greater than any other in the Empire. At times, these services were better attended than any celebration of the old established Roman gods.

The fervent worship of the Emperor caused many problems for the Christians, as their refusal to participate in celebrations and worship instantly made them traitors to the Empire. Christians moved and worshipped in secrecy, and they even devised a system of recognition that only they knew and understood. If a person was a Christian and wanted to know whether another was a Christian, he would draw an image of a fish in the sand or chalk an image of a fish on a doorpost. The Greek word for fish was *icthus*. This word formed an acronym for a Greek phrase meaning "Jesus Christ, Son of God, Savior." In this coded way, the Christians knew each other and maintained a degree of safety, but nonetheless many were arrested, beaten, and martyred.

For two years, Philip, his sister, his daughters, and Usiris missioned in Asia, laboring tirelessly in the cities of Philadelphia, Laodicea, Smyrna, and Sardis. Philip addressed the various disorders and conflicts in these communities and established charity banks and schools. When he departed from a city, he would leave faithful and strong presbyters to continue on. Philip traveled to the southern area of Lycia and north to the city of Pergamum in the Province of Asia to preach and teach. Philip was preaching on the banks of the Caicus River when the proconsul and his entourage arrived in that city. Pergamum was used by the Romans as the administrative center of the Province. Mariamne was standing on the road, inviting all to come and hear her brother preach. Among the travelers was the wife of the proconsul, Lady Nicanora. At Mariamne's insistence, Lady Nicanora, who was sympathetic to Christianity, stopped to listen to Philip speak. Before day's end she was baptized.

Leaving Pergamum, Philip, his family, and his friend traveled south to Ephesus with hopes of visiting his other daughter Eutychiane, her husband, and hopefully John the Apostle. After a few days of rest, the group was to return to Philadelphia, Smyrna, Sardis, or Laconia, but just as they neared the city, they were warned by a group of Christians that an arrest had been issued for Philip by the proconsul. The proconsul was angry over the conversion of his wife and had her confined to her *villa* after publicly denouncing and beating her before the people of Pergamum.

So the group took a detour and headed for the city of Hierapolis.

✳

Hierapolis, located southwest of Ephesus in the Roman Province of Asia, was called "The Sacred City" because it was naturally blessed with many hot mineral springs. These springs were believed to have miraculous and medicinal powers, and people from all over the Empire came to them to strengthen or restore their health. The minerals were so bountiful that many of them cascaded down the hillsides and over rocks like white rivers. The springs inspired the people to build many temples to the many gods. There were several cults to the Roman gods, and these cults set up sanctuaries in and around the city. There was a temple to Apollo, the god of healing and medicine, light and sun, arts and music. There also was a temple to Aphrodite, the goddess of love, lust, and beauty. The largest cult was to Poseidon, the Greek god of the underworld. Poseidon was also responsible for earthquakes, which were common in this area. This cult, with its priests and high priest, called the land around Hierapolis *Plutoriaum*, after the Roman god Pluto. This was the one cult that inspired fear in many people.

Like Laodicea and Colossae, Hierapolis had a large Jewish population as a result of the relocation movement of Antiochus the Great of the Seleucid Empire, who conquered this area and Judea. These relocated Jews were later joined by other migrant Jews. By the time Rome conquered this territory, the Jewish population was large and well settled in Hierapolis and the surrounding towns. These sons and daughters of Jacob became very independent and accomplished what Antiochus intended: they invigorated the economy through their hard work, peaceful ways, and unselfish lifestyle.

During the reign of Emperor Tiberius, Hierapolis suffered an earthquake, followed by a larger and more destructive quake about forty years later during the rule of Nero. This quake nearly destroyed the entire city. So Nero had the city rebuilt in the Roman style. He commanded that all streets be arranged in a rectangular fashion. All the streets were to be parallel to the main street that ran through the middle of the city.

While Paul of Tarsus was in Ephesus, he preached to many neighboring cities, Hierapolis among them, and he left large Christian communities in the area. Though Hierapolis benefited to some extent from his missionary work, it remained a pagan city. When Philip arrived, he found himself entangled in a nest of fear, hatred, distrust, and rivalry among all the different religions. Within his first week, he found himself in conflict with the high priest of Plutoriaum. For a long time, the priests of Poseidon had held the people in complete control. They were able to extort large sums of money from them and demand illicit favors—all because of a simple trick they performed that left the people in awe. Many of the caves around the city emitted poisonous gases into the air, and anyone who entered these caves was killed instantly. Birds, rabbits, and calves were used to demonstrate this fact. Every week, one of the priests would walk into a cave and stay inside for a number of minutes, eventually emerging with no sign of harm. This "miracle," of course, was nothing more than a hoax. The priests had learned that by holding their breath as they walked into the cave and, once out of sight of the people, rushing to one of the high rocks and standing upon it, they could be safe from the poisonous fumes.

When Philip witnessed the control the priests had over the people and the injustice that the people endured, he immediately went to Plutoriaum and confronted the High Priest, Calpherites. Calpherites ordered that several chickens and three lambs be chased into the cave, and as soon as they neared the cave, they fell dead.

The High Priest, smiling and confident, then challenged Philip to enter the cave and live.

Philip, with greater confidence, walked toward the cave and stopped.

"See, he is afraid, for the underworld is waiting for him," Calpherites said with a wide smile on his lips.

At the opening of the cave, Philip called aloud to Jesus, asking Him to show the people the true God, then slowly he walked farther inside. As he neared the entrance to the cave, he momentarily looked back at all who were there, and then facing the darkened cave he fell to his knees.

Calpherites, bellowing with a loud laugh, turned to the hundreds present and shouted, "See, the Christian is about to die, for his God does not have the power of our god."

The people looked beyond Calpherites, and some gasped.

The High Priest turned, and to his amazement he saw Philip rise and walk into the black cave.

"Fear not, my people, he will surely die. This man, Philip, is of a false God that is not powerful like our god. He will be called to the underworld by Poseidon. Watch and you will see, he will not come forth alive. He will die!"

Philip was consumed by the open black cave.

All was silent. Not a tree branch wavered. Not a cloud in the sky moved.

Death's calm had gripped and stilled the earth.

Moments passed.

"He surely is dead," one of the priests stated.

Calpherites turned and ordered, "Lepides and Manchetes, go and bring out his body. Show all that only we are true servants of Poseidon."

The two quickly obeyed. Just as they came near the opening of the cave, a strong wind passed over everything. The people shielded themselves from the sands and the debris that was stirred by the wind.

Just as quickly as it came, the wind stopped.

"Look!" someone in the crowd shouted.

The two priests near the cave stood motionless.

Calpherites turned and reeled back in shock.

Philip was standing at the mouth of the cave. His face was as white as the chalky deposits that flowed over the nearby rocks and filled the hot spring waters. As he walked into the daylight, he looked down at the dead lambs and chickens. He slowly moved his hands over their bodies, and as his shadowed hand passed over the animals, they sprang to their feet and stood silently by the Apostle.

"The Lord Jesus Christ is the Lord of life, death, and life again. Heed my voice for I give you words of forgiveness, love, and mercy. Jesus is the Son of the Living God. He moves among you, not like Poseidon who hides in dark places and kills out of loneliness and hate, but as the passing wind and the breath of your lives."

Philip walked over to Calpherites and stood next to him. Addressing the people, he continued, "Let what you see here today be a revelation to you that Jesus the Christ is not subject to the folly of false priests or of the false gods of Rome, Greece, or any other nation. Know that I am His servant and have come in His name to free you from tyranny and show you the way to Him."

He began to walk away and was quickly joined by his family, Usiris, and the animals.

"If you wish to know of this greater God, come and see."

In the following months, Philip missioned throughout the Province of Asia. Somehow he was always a step ahead of his enemies, who were growing more numerous. The Romans were still seeking his arrest, but they were not as persistent as the leaders of the pagan religions. On several occasions he was beaten and left for dead by these pagans, but each time he survived and returned to his attack on them and their gods. The leaders of the pagan religions were beginning to believe that Philip was invincible.

After each arrest, Philip would momentarily retreat to a more conservative way of preaching, for he always feared for his daughters, his sister, and Usiris.

It was after one of his worst beatings that Philip went into hiding in the city of Hierapolis. One day, during his recuperation, his family and Usiris were out buying provisions and meeting secretly with the local Christians. Philip was visited by Lapadines, a fellow Christian whom he knew and trusted. Lapadines told Philip that the High Priest of one of the pagan cults had been ridiculing Jesus and attacking Christians in the northern part of the city. Several Christians had been killed, and many were beaten or discouraged. This priest, Mendites, was the High Priest of a cult that worshipped Asklepios, a serpent-like god known for his healing powers. The temple was about one hour's walk, just northeast of the city.

Philip, though sore and weary from his latest encounter with the pagans, thanked the Christian. Fetching his staff, he went out to meet Mendites. It took him less than an hour to get to the temple, and he marveled at God's mysterious way of hastening his steps.

Standing on a small hill overlooking the temple of Asklepios, Philip could sense the presence of evil—its stench was so strong that it disturbed his stomach.

The temple was nestled in a small canyon. The area of the open air temple was lined with large white columns that stood at the base of the canyon walls. Small wooden seats were used for the large congregation. The congregation sat facing the altar, which was a large, roughly cut slab of rock resting on several tree stumps. Standing behind the altar with his back to Philip and the congregation was Mendites. He stood before an image of Asklepios with a large green tree behind it. The tree trunk was split, and two heavy, large branches, one on each side of the image, appeared to be embracing the stone image of Asklepios. The High Priest's black-and-gray, finely woven cloak billowed at the command of the passing wind. He was deep in idolatrous prayer, and his voice carried through the canyon and spilled out into the surrounding land.

Philip looked up at the rocky image that was the center of everyone's attention. It had not been carved by man, but by nature. Its shape was truly that of a snake. It soared from the earth into the sky, penetrating the beauty of the blue heavens. Its presence in this lofty place was an act of defiance to the Almighty. Philip whispered a quick prayer to Jesus for strength. He walked down the side of the hill. Halfway down the hill he was met by Lapadines, who greeted him with a smile. Before Philip could realize he had been betrayed, the temple guards were upon him, and he was roughly taken away.

EPILOGUE

It was late; it was a warm night.

John, with Polycarp, waited for Philip's daughters, Eutychiane and Irais, to arrive. He was concerned about a visit at this late hour.

When they arrived, the daughters quickly revealed the reason for their visit.

"My father had intentions of coming to see you," Eutychiane said. "But we sent word to him to stay away because the Romans and some Greeks were waiting to arrest him. We sent Lapadines to warn him."

"You remember Lapadines?" Polycarp asked.

"Yes, I do. He was one of Paul's converts. He came to Paul through an encounter with one of the priests of Asklepios; he is a good man."

"Mariamne sends her warmest regards," Irais said, changing the conversation.

"Please return my regards. You and Mariamne have helped my dear brother Philip greatly, and I am sure our blessed Savior will reward you."

"How have you been, John?" Irais asked.

"Well, and still working on my account of Jesus. I have completed most of my writing and am nearing the crucifixion; there is much sadness in reliving that day." He paused, then added with a sigh, "And still I have no beginning. No, that is not true, I have several beginnings, but not one that pleases me."

"I am sure the good Lord will confirm what beginning you are to use with a sign," Irais said with great confidence.

The room filled with a sudden silence. John realized that they had other things on their minds.

"Tell me, how is our brother Philip?" John asked, sensing this was the reason for their visit.

The two looked at each other and then at John. Their faces changed from casual to serious.

"He has done what you have asked him to do," Irais stated quickly. "He has strengthened the cities you were concerned about. Now, he is traveling to other cities around Ephesus, preaching and baptizing."

"We worry," Eutychiane said softly.

"Over these few years, he has aged quickly. He has endured many punishments for Jesus, and he is now frail; we come asking for his release from any further obligations here."

John was speechless. In all these years, none of the Twelve had asked to be relieved of a mission. He had asked to be allowed to go on foreign missions after Lady Mary left them, but Peter said it was not in his power to do that, for the calling came from Jesus. He looked blankly at the two women and closed his eyes. He knew this request was not for him to grant. With his eyes still closed, he asked, "Has your father asked for this?"

"No."

"He does not know of our being here."

"Then do you not think it is for him to ask?"

The room was silent, and John could not avoid opening his eyes to see what his question had created. The two sisters sat on the verge of tears. They were torn between two loves: Jesus and Philip.

John recognized their dilemma and immediately remembered something Jesus said. "Remember the words of our Lord: 'They are not of the world, as I also am not of the world.... As Thou hast sent Me into the world, I also have sent them into the world. And for them do I sanctify Myself that they also may be sanctified in truth.'"

John cleared his throat, and with the tenderness of a father he said softly, "I cannot do what you ask. Let us put our trust in Jesus, Who will make what is wrong in your eyes right. Or let us trust that He will find a way to make His servant Philip well again."

They left.

The next day, John was finishing a letter to a Christian named Gaius regarding a troublesome fellow Christian name Diotrephes who had grown in error. John knew he had to be careful in what he wrote, for he did not want to create ill will between Gaius and the dominating presbyter, Diotrephes.

Just as he was nearing the end of his letter, Papias stormed into the room to announce that the proconsul Corlidius Albus Tranacus had been called back to Rome. John immediately praised God, for finally he would be free to travel and preach among the Ephesians. Suddenly, he thought of Philip. He asked Papias to wait, and rushing to his desk he found a piece of parchment and his *stylus*. He wrote a quick letter telling Philip he should return to Greece and thanking him for all his help.

This is the work of the Master, John thought as he sealed the letter with wax and gave it to Papias with the directive to go to the house of Eutychiane.

After Papias departed, John offered a prayer of thanksgiving from the writings of David:

Thou hast given him his heart's desire, and denied him not the request of his lips…he asked love of Thee; Thou gavest to him length of days forever and ever.

When he had finished, it was near sunset, and he hurried back to his desk to continue his letter to Gaius. He cut the letter short, writing that he would soon be seeing Gaius.

John returned to the front of the house. Picking up a small piece of unleavened bread and a chilled cup of wine, he sat. The day seemed to be perfect. Philip would be returning to the safety of his beloved Greece, and John would be free to go where he wished. He took the bread in his hand and broke off a small piece of it. Instantly he remembered the Last Supper. He smiled, for whenever the faithful thought of bread and wine together, they remembered that glorious Passover meal.

From the past, he heard Jesus' voice: "I am the Way, and the Truth, and the Life. No man cometh to the Father but by Me."

From the corner of the room he heard Philip ask, "Lord, show us the Father, and it is enough for us."

Jesus said to Philip with a tinge of disappointment, "Have I been so long a time with ye: and have ye not known Me?"

Then Jesus' tone changed to that of a teacher. "Philip, he that seeth Me seeth the Father also. How sayest thou show us the Father?"

John stayed motionless, as he always did when he remembered the past, and this state became a cherished resting place for him.

"John? John, where are you?" Papias called from the garden in the back of the house.

"In here, Papias. What is so alarming?"

"You must see this," the young man said with delight in his voice.

"What is it?" John questioned with vicarious joy.

"Look!"

John walked out into the garden and saw a dove sitting on a wooden stool. Its open wings were spread and resting on the stool; its legs were hidden under its white body.

"Oh no!" John exclaimed as his mind went to Matthew.

"What is wrong? It is unusual to be sure. It followed me all the way home from Eutychiane's house. It just flew before me—like a guide. When I arrived here, it flew to that stool and would not be shooed away."

John leaned on Papias for support.

"John, are you unwell?"

John gazed into the heavens as he sat opposite the dove.

As always, he was filled with joy and sadness.

"John, where are you? There is a man here to see you. He has been at the door."

Polycarp appeared in the doorway with a short, black-haired man. On seeing the man, John knew the dove was not Matthew.

"Come, sit, and tell me what happened," John said with his eyes set on the dove.

The Greek looked surprised. He slowly walked to a nearby stool and sat.

"I really do not know what to tell you. I was sent by Mariamne and the daughters to tell you, but it seems you already know."

John looked away from the dove and at his Greek guest.

"My name is Usiris."

John recognized the name from Philip's letters.

The Greek continued, "Yesterday we left Philip alone under the pretense of getting provisions for the household, but we all were on a different and secret mission. I went to the faithful in Hierapolis and told them that Philip was too weak to preach; a presbyter had to be named. Mariamne went to see the women of charity, telling them that they would have to do more because she needed to spend more time with Philip. Irais and Eutychiane came to see you.

"When Mariamne and I returned home, Philip was gone. It did not take us long to conclude that he was preaching, and we became concerned, for he had received a bad beating two days before and had not regained his strength. We hurried to the *agora* but did not find him, then we heard that an important Christian had been killed. We questioned the man who made the statement. He told us to go to the temple of Asklepios. We ran, and when we arrived we found Philip dead." Usiris cleared his throat and swallowed hard in an effort to control his grief. "He had been nailed to a large tree that stood behind the pagan altar. The tree looked like the Greek letter *gamma* Y. His hands were nailed and tied to the two large branches, and his feet to the main trunk. He had been dead for a number of hours."

John slumped in his chair, so the Greek stopped talking.

Polycarp left the room and quickly returned with a cup of cool water, which seemed to refresh the Apostle momentarily, so Usiris continued.

"There was a man there who said he came upon the crucifixion and found Philip near death; he was calling out to Jesus. The man said he heard Philip say, 'Lord, I heard Your call; I came to see. Lead me as You did before—I will follow.'"

John looked back at the stool and the dove. It looked so at peace—confident and unafraid.

"Thank you, Usiris. Please tell Mariamne and the daughters that I mourn with them, but I mourn with great joy, for Philip is with the Master. The peace of the Lord be with them and you."

Usiris rose and was escorted back into the house by Polycarp and Papias.

John returned his attention to the dove, and after a few moments he said softly, "Go, my good friend, and join the Others."

The dove flew to John's shoulder and stayed there, cooing. Suddenly, summoned by an unheard command, it flew away. John watched the dove as it soared. He longed to join it.

As the white speck vanished, John closed his eyes and instantly saw Jesus walking on the shores of the Sea of Galilee. Philip was running to Him. As Philip was walking beside Jesus, John heard Jesus say, "You have pleased Me, Philip, to the end. Come, follow Me and I will show you to the Father."

CHAPTER TWELVE:

LEVI MATTHEW BAR ALPHAEUS

PROLOGUE

———————

After preaching, John walked away from his listeners knowing that he accomplished much and that a wave of joy would wash over him. It had nothing to do with his pride, for he knew this joy was Jesus' way of agreeing with what was done in His Name.

On one particular day this wave of joy seized him. He was on his way to the city of Laodicea at the request of the city elders and as he walked the road to the city, he was becoming aware of how long it was taking him to arrive at his destination. Suddenly, John sensed something unusual; he was to satisfy the Will of God and once again become an instrument in God's Hands. He continued to walk, waiting for God's moment to mature. As he looked ahead, he saw a group of field workers sitting on the side of the road. They had stopped working for their mid-day meal. He asked to join them and quickly offered them his provisions. Without delay a friendship grew between them, and John began speaking of Jesus. He told them of the time Jesus multiplied a meal for the thousands. The men listened politely. He told them of Jesus' Death and Resurrection and gave himself as witness to these things. Some of the men looked intrigued but most were politely disinterested.

Suddenly a shout came from the road and everyone turned to see who called out to them. They watched as a spry, elderly man walked from the road to them. His face was beaming with a wide smile.

"*Salvete mei amici*. Good day, my friends. Can a weary traveler join you for an old fashioned conversation?"

The traveler was invited to join them. He walked quickly to their place of rest and meal. He was a short man with a large chest and thick, bulging arms. The scars and marks on his arms, face and neck made everyone conclude he had been a soldier or a gladiator. He sat with the men and asked what their conversation was.

Some men told him that John was sun-struck, for he was telling them tales about a Man named Jesus who did unbelievable things; some concluded that Jesus most likely was a great magician.

The traveler asked them why they thought Jesus was a magician.

"He fed many from scraps," one worker said sarcastically.

Some men shook their heads in disbelief.

"He died and came back to life again," added another worker.

Some of the other men snickered.

"Well I know not about the feeding of many, but I do know of this Man Jesus dying and coming back to life again."

Suddenly the men grew interested.

"I saw this Man die. In fact, I helped put Him to death and entombed Him, and I later saw Him come from that same tomb."

John sat wondering who this man was. Truly the traveler came to help him bolster his story of Jesus, but he needed to know who he was.

The men began to ask the traveler questions, and the man smiled and told the workers that he made a crown of thorns for Jesus and fashioned it like the crowns of the East. He placed the crown on Jesus' entire head and pressed it deep and hard into his skull.

"Making that crown was not an easy task," the traveler said. "In fact, I cut and pricked myself many times. Even now my fingers still show scars and some of them have never healed."

He showed the men his fingers and they could see marks and cuts, and yes indeed, some of the marks seemed on the verge of bleeding.

"Later I was told by the Legionnaire who pierced Jesus' side that He was truly dead. Then I was placed on duty to watch the dead Man's tomb to assure that no one would steal His Body. People believed that this would happen so they persuaded Pilate, the Roman Procurator, to post guards. We stayed our post all night and the next day began rotating the duty. I was given the early morning, sunrise duty. So for two mornings I watched the tomb. On the second morning of my watch as I walked in front of the tomb a strange feeling took hold of me. I realized that there were no birds chirping, or the buzz of flies, or the sound of any animal, not even the smallest breeze slipped through the trees or the bushes. The early morning frost had suddenly warmed. I never experienced anything like this in all my days as a Roman soldier or anytime.

"Suddenly the earth shifted and clashed into itself, and a strong gust of wind came rushing. It did not come from across the land; it came down on me, from above me and it rushed beyond me to the tomb. There was nothing but this wind around the tomb and the stillness around me. As I fell to the earth, I could see that the huge stone that covered the tomb split and rolled away. There was a sudden flash of light. It was blinding. I shaded my eyes and this made me able to see a Man—the Man I crowned—the Man who died—standing at the entrance of the tomb. His Body was still marked by the nails, by the piercing and even by the marks of the thorns. When the wind died, and the earth stopped moving and the light was gone there was no trace of the Man.

"There was only an empty tomb.

"There was the morning chill; the sound of birds and insects and life.

"All the men on my detail were in shock. Some remained blind for hours thereafter and others became speechless for hours and still others, like me, needed to talk to someone and tell them what they witnessed. Afterwards, a group of women mourning, came, and when they saw the empty tomb they left yelling, 'He has risen!'"

"Later, a young man," he pointed at John, "this man and an older man came running. They went in and came out of the open wound on the side of that mount with great joy, yet with confused looks."

"This man…" again he pointed to John, "asked me, 'What happened here?'

"And I could not answer him, except to say, 'I saw Him. He lives again.'"

The laborers stared at the traveler as though in a trance. They were completely taken by his story. They were not alone for even John who was sitting nearby was in shock reliving that dramatic moment. He was stunned by the power of this man's witness for he had never heard that day explained in such a manner.

"This is the same story this man told us. Can this all be true?" a worker said.

"Our gods have never died and returned to life," another added.

"True all they do is eat, fight and become angry."

"And toy with each other! Let us not forget that!"

John saw the opening and softly said, "But Jesus is not like your gods; He is the Son of the God of mercy and love. It was by Jesus' love and death that we can follow Him into Paradise."

"Tell us more," one of the workers uttered and John began telling of the undeniable humanity of Jesus and of the greater part of His Nature: His Unquestionable Divinity. He spoke of the signs Jesus gave through miracles and the fulfillment of prophecies; next he told them of the glories of Jesus and of His many parables and discourses.

Suddenly John realized that he was reciting his written account of Jesus and he became elated. He turned to thank the traveler but discovered he was gone. Looking onto the road, he saw the stranger walking toward Laodicea. He jumped to his feet, quickly gave the men a blessing, and promised to return in a few days, but, now he had to find the traveler and talk to him. When he traveled some distance from the workers, John realized he had lost the man so he continued on alone.

It was not until John was some distance from the workers that the workers realized they had eaten most of John's provisions and that much still remained.

Two days later, as John traveled the same road back to Ephesus, he came upon the same workers. Again, the men were enjoying their midday meal and walking to them again offered to share his provisions.

He sat down and without delay began speaking of Jesus. After a short period of time, they heard someone shouting to them.

"*Salvete mei amici*, hail, my friends! May I join you?"

Everyone's attention turned in the direction of the voice and they saw the traveler from days before walking to them.

The men greeted him warmly and John looked at the man, wanting to know more than life who this man was. The man quickly sat among them, crossed his legs and began eating some grapes. He listened as John continued his teaching. As the workers asked questions the traveler simply smiled or nodded his head to John's answers. Before returning to work, the men asked to be baptized and John took them to a small brook nearby and purified them.

After the last one of the workers had become a Christian, the stranger looked at them and said in a very simple tone, "My dear brothers, in this act you have been given the life-giving waters of Jesus Christ by the hands of one of the Twelve men who knew Him, walked with Him, ate with Him and followed Him. Eleven of these men have earned their crown of thorns and soon this one will be called."

The men turned and found John's face glowing with joy.

When they returned to ask questions of the traveler on how he came to this knowledge, he was gone.

The men returned to work and John continued on his journey home. He was walking very slowly, enjoying the sound of his lonely steps on the Roman road when suddenly a name jumped into his head.

He stopped walking and he said aloud, "Coronius! His name is Coronius." Pleased with himself and happy that the stranger now had a name, John continued to walk praising God and then thanked Jesus for His care, when suddenly he heard the stranger's words: "...eleven have earned their crown of thorns..."

Eleven were not dead. Only ten, he thought quickly, then he stopped and began looking up to the sky and in the trees and everywhere searching for the dove, who was to be Matthew.

LEVI MATTHEW BAR ALPHAEUS

Matthew's mind jolted from slumber and for a few confused moments he could not remember where he was, but when he remembered he instantly felt the pain. A surge of disappointment raced through him. Slowly he accepted the reality that he was still living. He had hoped it would be over; that he would have simply slipped through the gate.

In that weak moment he felt the bending of his humanity and he murmured, "I am so tired. Tired of moving; tired of suffering; tired of doing; tired of living."

The words were no sooner out of his mouth when he grew shameful for having spoken them.

Aloud he prayed, "Lord forgive me! I am sure You also had these tired feelings for I can remember the weary look on Your Face. I remember the times You raced away needing to be alone. You were hounded and pursued by many and You longed for peace, rest and the return home."

Matthew grew quiet and felt like sleeping again. He needed to sleep; he was weary.

With a painful smile he thought, *But Lord, You did not stop; You went on to do as You were commanded. I must be like You and will experience my Gethsemane and my Golgotha.*

He had an itch on his face and though he often ignored such small annoyances he felt he needed to pamper himself just a little, so he slowly and painstakingly raised his hands to his beard. He surmised his itch was from lice or fleas and that he most likely was full of them. Inspecting his surroundings, he concluded his prison had been a hut. It was a round, roofless hut with a wooden door of holes, broken and splintered wood held together loosely with many other pieces of wood. It reeked of the smell of animals so he concluded it was, before his prison, used as an animal shelter.

He was thirsty, but he knew that asking for water was futile. He remembered being told he would not be given any.

Outside he heard the loud and rough laughter of his captures. The flickering flames blazed through the cracks in the door and reflected off of his cut, bruised, and dirty face. He could feel the heat, then the chill which made him sleepy. He felt himself slipping into darkness and in an effort to delay the blackness of sleep, he tried to remember the many times he had been a prisoner and how his captures had built a large fire.

I have been in jail fifteen or more times. I can count them all, but I can only recall one other time when there was a large fire. He thought.

He remembered and said aloud, "It was in Dura. In Mesopotamia."

The instant satisfaction from remembering this first fire quickly slipped away as his consciousness slid into a dark place; he stayed empty for a moment. Finally, darkness came to him and he began to dream of his yesterdays.

*

Fifteen years after the Twelve pulled lots for their missions, Matthew left Judea and Galilee. His reason for this delay was a selfish one. He wanted to enjoy the reunion with his family who for years had rejected him and considered him dead. For a short time he helped his brother James the Little in Jerusalem, but he became a liability to James' mission, because his past was known, so he slipped away into silence. For the next several years he lived apart from everyone and preached little. He knew he had a mission like the Others for the parchment paper with his assignment was carried always. It hung in the small, leather purse that dangled from his cincture. He knew he had to leave but he was constantly tormented by a gnawing knowledge that when he left he would never return. He remained in this self-imposed seclusion and prayed. One day, his aunt, Lady Mary, took him aside and softly said to him, "You are one of the educated of the Twelve. It is up to you to write what you witnessed. You must let our people know that Jesus is the Messiah. Show them that He was the new Moses and above Moses."

So Matthew began to gather material especially "...the book of the generations of Jesus Christ..." He sat with his dying father and got the genealogy of the family to establish that Jesus was of the House of David as prophesied by the Prophets. He remembered his uncle Yosef and recalled the whispers his parents had when they thought they were alone. He remembered the strange tale he overheard Yosef telling his father about the three foreign men who followed a star. He remembered how sad and tearful his parents became when they got word that Yosef and Mary had to flee to Egypt to avoid Herod's wrath. At that time he wondered why his uncle had to do such a thing. Why would Herod want to harm a gentle and 'just man' like Yosef?" He went to Lady Mary and she told him the circumstances and reasons for the actions of those bygone days. With part of Mark's narrative and several small scrolls of the sayings of Jesus that the Twelve had jointly composed before they left Jerusalem, and his own remembrances, Matthew began to write. He remembered Lady Mary's words and made a great comparison between Jesus and Moses. He wrote in Aramaic for his common countrymen because he believed that they being the Chosen Ones had the right to know that Jesus was Divine, the Son of God and their long awaited Messiah. His writing came quickly and within a year his work was completed.

After completing his account and leaving it with his brother James the Little, whom he later discovered had copies made, Matthew left for Syria where he spent time trying to convert the Jews. Among these Jews many knew him as a publican and they berated him with insults and calls of being a traitor. His life in Syria grew hard, as hard as it had been in Judea and Galilee. He seemed destined to be tormented by his past as a "sinner." His reputation was a hindrance to his teaching among the Jews, so he turned to the Gentiles and it was there that he found success and it was at this time that a young man arrived to be his companion.

"Who sent you?" Matthew asked surprised and slightly pleased that someone remembered to give him a companion.

The young man hesitated for a moment, then smiled and answered, "The Holy Spirit of the Lord."

Matthew smiled.

"And by what name am I to call you?"

"I am known as Namenlos."

Matthew knew the name, so he quickly walked to Namenlos and embraced him saying, "Welcome, friend of the Holy Spirit of the Lord."

Namenlos was a young man who "that day" was on Golgotha. In his young mind Namenlos knew what he was witnessing was wrong. He heard of Jesus, and what he heard was nice and caring things. He heard Jesus showed great kindness for the poor and downtrodden; that He fed the poor and cured the sick. To young Namenlos, Jesus' only crime was He was nice to people.

The injustice he witnessed that day made him sad. He pitied those involved for they were captured by the moments of an awakened nightmare.

"Jesus of Nazareth, King of the Jews."

Each proclamation he shouted, as he carried the *titulus vitium* title of crime, caused a stir inside him. Each word pained him for it scraped and tore at his throat. He felt foolish for mutilating himself; his words acting like daggers that wounded him and like a fool he was the cause of these wounds. Unsure of why this was happening, he resolved that he had to know more about this Man and what was happening that day. As he moved through the procession and to the hill, he registered in his mind the faces and names of all the Centurions, Legionaries, and Mercenaries who were on the hill and carefully watched their every action. After the Man died, he continued for days to watch and follow those who had been on the hill. He believed and knew they would lead him to the understanding he needed.

Days later, while passing Abendadar, Calvos and Dorimius, he overheard their whispers and their reliving all that happened to them on the Mount.

He was nearby when Cornelius, Nescius, Longinus, and Stephaton met in secret and talked about the strange things they experienced.

On that day Cornelius secretly invited all those who had been inflicted with an interior wound to meet some of the "friends of Jesus." Namenlos clandestinely followed them to Cornelius' *villa* and stole his way inside. He waited in the shadows for the arrival of those who would help him understand the wounds that boiled and scarred deep inside him. At the moment of Peter's arrival, Namenlos felt a warmth and a desire so strong that his thoughts, bones, and insides wanted to scream out. He felt a great enlightening come over him and to this young boy came knowledge so great that it was hard to contain. He felt sorrow, grief, joy, love, and understanding all at once. It became difficult for him to contain the tears of excitement that welded up in his eyes as he walked out from the shadows and into the bright light of the fiery torches of the room.

Years later when he told John the Apostle what had happened, the Apostle walked to him and embraced him, saying, "My son, what you experienced that night, we Twelve had experienced on Pentecost. What happened that night in Cornelius' house was the second Pentecost."

He was not allowed the joy of manifesting his Pentecost because Peter, Cornelius and others said he was too young to preach and too young to join one of the Twelve as a companion. He kept his beliefs to himself as he continued his life with the Roman Army as a slave. When some of the wealthy, Jewish Christians learned of his conversion they purchased his freedom. The young boy immediately asked to go with one of the Apostles but was again told to wait until he got older. Meantime, he served as messenger between Christians or as a guard when the Christians assembled secretly for the Meal. He was eventually given the noble task of taking the Meal to the sick, dying and those in prison.

Namenlos remained in Palestine, helping wherever he could and eventually began going among the slaves in the Roman Army, speaking to them of Jesus. Many were baptized secretly and they in turn preached and taught other slaves and camp followers.

What many failed to see was Namenlos having received the gift of belonging: A feeling he never had before in his life. Part of the gift he received in Cornelius' house made him feel he was at home! He was never with his parents. His mother was a slave from *Germania* and was sold and taken to Syria and Palestine. She found favor with a Roman Officer, a Centurion, in Palestine. She became pregnant and at childbirth died. Namenlos was given by his unknown, Centurion father to another woman to be raised. This woman was a cold woman and kept him in servitude. When he was nine, she returned him to the Romans who put him into service as an occasional messenger or occasional companion to Roman children, but his primary duty was belonging to the corp of *praeconor* herald.

He was given a uniform, a small replica of a soldier's uniform, and the job of walking behind the Centurion who led the procession of those to be crucified and proclaimed the crime of the one condemned to death.

So it was on that day he became the herald of "Jesus of Nazareth, King of the Jews."

✳

After years of preaching in Sidon, Palmyra, Antioch, and other cities in Syria, Matthew and Namenlos headed northeast to the Euphrates River that served as the border for the Provinces of Syria and Osroene. They arrived in the city of Nicephernium which was a major, river port to the upper part of the river and a city just inside the province of Osroene. They traveled down the Euphrates into Mesopotamia, which was not part of the Roman Empire and where many Jews from the Babylonian Captivity still lived. Matthew hoped that here, away from any knowledge of his past he would find peace and do the bidding of the Master to "teach all nations."

They traveled down the ancient river and stopped at Dura for provisions. Dura was a large city but not as expansive as other river ports on the river. It had a small, Jewish community of merchants and businessmen. Matthew and Namenlos quickly found where these Jews met for the Sabbath and then joined them. As a gesture of kindness, Matthew was asked to read from the Holy Writings. He stood in the synagogue and in a loud, clear voice read:

"I will raise up a prophet out of the midst of their brethren like to thee; and I will put My words in His mouth and He shall speak to them all that I shall command Him. And he that will not hear His words, which He shall speak in My name, I will be the revenger."

He looked over the congregation and continued, "I bring you tidings of this Promised One, Who is the new Moses. He, who came to do His Father's will, to die on a Cross for you and yours. I bring you the truth that Jesus, the Divine One, is your Messiah. Jesus is the one whom you have longed for; He is the one whom you have expected; He is what you have yearned for all those centuries." He closed his eyes and slowly opened them to see a mass of shocked faces around him. "I come to you today with the words *El Shaddai,* The Almighty One, spoke from the mouth of He Who was His Only Son and I shall repeat His words for your salvation."

Having captured their attention, he proceeded to speak of Jesus, and they all listened and soon many came to be purified. From that day on, Matthew and Namenlos were welcomed in Mesopotamia and remained there for many years.

After the council meeting in Jerusalem and the decision on circumcision, Matthew returned to Dura. He and Namenlos wasted no time in going among the Mesopotamian Gentiles to preach Jesus but they quickly discovered that this was no easy task. They learned that in one city there were fifty different gods. Some districts duplicated others but on the whole each had a different god which caused the two men to face many gods. The temples to the deity became the focal point of city activities, for it was near the temple where merchants sold, citizens purchased, sorcerers worked, and government functioned. In most cities, the priests or priestesses had complete control of the people. They dictated to the populous every second of their existence and ruled with fear and by magic, or well-staged theatrics. The citizens believed that every facet of life, seasons, and success was due to the gods and the appeasement of these gods was their only function.

One day Matthew went to the temple of Dura to preach to the multitudes. Namenlos had taken ill and was resting at the home of a Jewish Christian. While Matthew preached, he was confronted by an unknown, veiled woman. Those around him knew who she was for they began to shirk and scatter as she walked slowly to Matthew. As she approached, Matthew heard someone whisper she was Qulara, the priestess of Enki, the god of water, of wisdom and protector of the city.

The priestess was wearing a multi-colored garment of blue and green that flowed loosely around her. Her garment was one, complete piece of cloth. It streamed over her and was a toy in the breath of the warm, afternoon breeze. Her face was covered by a green veil that was thick enough to obscure her facial features.

Matthew immediately acknowledged he was facing a woman of great strength and dominance. He never faced a woman adversary, so this rarity spiked his curiosity.

In a loud voice, the priestess denounced Jesus and Matthew and those of Dura who succumbed to the spell of Jesus. She called Jesus and Matthew weaklings and messengers of falsehoods.

It was not until she stood before him did Matthew realize the height of this woman for she overshadowed him by six *zereth*—hand spans. He was sure many men cowed before her but he knew he would not, so he stood upright knowing this effort was only a show of courage. For an instant he closed his eyes and waited for Jesus to take control.

"Well, little Jew, what is this I hear of you speaking of a God of love and forgiveness?"

"I speak of the only God. The God of love who offers all people forgiveness for their sins and transgressions."

She laughed and her laughter vibrated the interior of Matthew's body.

"And what, pray tell, will such things do for these people who need food to eat and water to drink and loins to be satisfied?"

"Jesus is Living Water and He gives Himself to eat and He nourishes the soul as well as the body."

"And where is this Man you speak of?" She waved her arms in a grand gesture as she turned her veiled head, looking around the area. It was a well staged mockery. She stopped abruptly and turned to Matthew.

"Does He hide behind a little man like you?"

"He is a God that is unseen but always with us."

She laughed and the sound of her laugh again vibrated Matthew's insides.

"You speak in riddles, like all Jews who live among us." Turning to those around her who had been listening to the Apostle, she continued, "Why are you people so ignorant and stupid? You know that Enki is ever present to your sight and he provides food and leisure for you. Listening to this little man only angers our god, and if floods come to us it will be the fault of you stupid people. Go about your work and business and bring your goods to the temple as offerings of forgiveness, and I will pray to Enki for your safety."

She began to walk away and many followed after her. Matthew spoke to her in a loud voice.

"I was told that you believe your gods sit in a council of fifty and that they allow many spirits to roam the world. Am I correct?"

She turned.

"Yes, we hold that as faith."

"Can you see these spirits?"

She did not answer, but he could feel her eyes on him and instantly felt her hatred and anger press against him.

"Jesus lived with us, died, and rose again and is now unseen like a spirit. He cannot be seen, but we know He is here. We know this and feel His presence, for He projects love, mercy, and understanding which are also unseen. He punishes only the sinners and not the innocent or the ignorant."

"Your Jesus could not be a spirit for He never came here."

"Do you think you have the only god? What of the Romans? And what of the Greeks who conquered you? And before them, what of the Babylonians and the Assyrians and the Parthians and all the others who have passed through this land? Did they not take their gods with them and to you? Did not the Jews among you take their God with them? As you have a council of fifty gods to help rule these people, should you not also admit that there is one god greater than all gods? Of course you do! That One Greater God is the God I speak of; the God above all other gods. The God who loves us so much, He gave His Beloved Son as a sacrifice for our sins and for our freedom to enter eternal life. Tell me, High Priestess, are any of your gods equal to this or caring enough to perform such an act of love?"

Before any answer could be given he was surrounded, bound, and taken away. That night he was tied to a tree in the orange glow of a large fire. His capturers chattered in loud voices. They sang soldier songs and their revelry continued into the chill of the dark night. In the distance he could hear the sound of water, of men playfully splashing in water, and he surmised his capturers were bathing. His body throbbed with need to become clean again. As the night turned to dark morning, some of the men settled down and Matthew, bruised, tired, hungry, and thirsty, slipped into sleep. Just as sleep was slowly gripping his world, he heard some of the men gambling and the jingle of their coins alerted Matthew. He froze as the sound of the coins echoed in his ears and pounded in his aching head. With much regret he followed his mind as it raced back many years to another place and time; it settled on a hot, sunny day in Galilee.

Levi was sitting in the customs-house collecting levies and customs tolls from those coming or going through the town of Capernaum. With him that day was one of the chief publicans, Zacchaeus, and Zacchaeus' Roman friend, Isidorus. They had just returned from some nearby farms and large land-owner's *villa* where they had collected property and produce duties. Unlike Levi, Zacchaeus and Isidorus were of the group of Publicans known as the *Gabbai*. These Publicans collected taxes for the Romans and their revenue came from real estate, income, livestock, and produce. Levi was a collector of tolls for King Herod. He belonged to the group of tax collectors or publicans known as *Mokhes*. Their duty was to collect taxes on imports, exports, shipping and river crossings, as well as taxes on articles purchased, harbor taxes, market taxes, as well as bridge and road tolls.

Until the two Roman Publicans arrived, the day was an ordinary day with plenty of jingling coins exchanging hands. After they arrived, the bartering between several of the citizens and Levi became heated and the groans of resentment became edged with deep anger, resentment, and hatred. Oddly he was even certain he could hear the unspoken curses of those passing his custom post. Sometimes, Levi found these silent words were far more poignant than the sounded ones. He tolerated these offenses and continued his occupation of collecting taxes—someone had to do it. He came upon this job after having collected the Temple tax, which was the Temple offering levied on the faithful Jews by the Temple authorities. There were about twenty-four assessments that were to be paid to the Temple and anyone over the age of thirteen was expected to pay half a *shekel*. There were no exceptions and no matter what a person's financial status or what hardships they might have to endure, they had to pay this tax or face expulsion from the Temple. In addition, one-tenth of all the produce or income one made was taxed, but Levi did not collect this tax as it was done by others.

This position as a Temple collector made his family proud for as they so often told him, "You are doing the work of *El Shaddai*."

Despite his family's pride, Levi was dissatisfied with his job. It bothered him to collect money for the Temple when the demands were so severe. The authorities appeared heartless and lacked any compassion for the poor as they lived comfortably in the Name and in the Shadow of the Almighty. They condemned and shunned all that was being done wrong by the people, but did nothing to help the people who were in need of a bit of compassion. They put the Law and their interpretation of the Law above *El Shaddai's* compassion. Once Levi began to realize all the monies that the Temple collected and how much was used to create comfortable lives for the Chief Priest, he stopped respecting the authorities and grew disenchanted with his job. The Temple priest's quotes from Scripture that Abraham had "given the tithes of all he had wont to the Almighty" did not appease Levi.

Then one day, Zacchaeus came to him and asked if he would be willing to work as a Publican for Herod. The money was better, much better, and with this employment came a household for him to keep as long as he remained in the employment of Herod. In a moment of avarice he agreed in spite of his knowledge that this would alienate him from his family and countrymen. The moment he agreed he felt independent; a personal trait he always had and nurtured with selfishness. He knew he could be more compassionate and reduce a tax here and there. Besides, lowering a tax because someone looked in dire need would be a loss to his revenue and not Herod's. Of course, this benevolence towards those being taxed was not completely accepted by the other Publicans, who extorted all they could from the people by adding more to the taxes for their own benefit. The more the other Publicans complained to Levi about his charity the more he ignored their reprimands.

He took the position and immediately started a life of comfort. He wore expensive clothing and enjoyed the best food and wine. He had servants, slaves and others in his employ. He made new, influential friends and was wealthy enough to give parties and entertain, yet in it all, he was still unhappy because he had a void in his life. Though he felt lost without his religion he believed it was his family's rejection that was causing this void, especially the rejection by his brothers whom he greatly missed. To reduce his guilt, he began to find ways to help his family, and he clandestinely began providing them with funds and benefits. When his father sold his catch or did carpentry work he would give the merchant *shekels* to give his father as a token of appreciation for a job well done. When his family bid for jobs he would provide funds for the bid to be accepted. He enjoyed the anonymity of giving. Still it hurt to see his family walk by him with their eyes of indifference. It caused him physical pain when they walked away from him, refusing to make any eye contact. Only his youngest brother, Jude Thaddeus, would sneak away and seek him out. They talked but only in shaded places and this kept Levi abreast of his family.

When Jewish High Holidays came, alone at home, Levi mourned his lost family and truly missed his religion. This void in his life soon became a festered sore. Then he came to realize that what he despised in the authorities of the Temple he had now become.

It was after one of these Holidays that he went to hear John the Baptist preach. He followed John for several months, magnetized to the man in spite of the condemnation of John for his present and former employers. Eventually he stopped going to John when John made him feel worse about being a Publican and made him truly feel like a sinner.

Suddenly, his mother's brother approached his custom's booth. He paid his tax and walked hurriedly away without a glance in Levi's direction. Levi wanted to call out to him but knew better and in that fleeting moment he felt the pain of alienation.

Zacchaeus immediately noticed Levi's pain. "It still bothers you, that you are ignored by these small minded people?"

"Those small-minded people were part of my life for many years, Zacchaeus. Unlike you, I have a family that I still love."

"You will always be a Jew, Levi, regardless of all the good things money has done for you," chimed Isidorus.

"Yes, I suppose I will always be a Jew even if I do not go to the Temple or observe the many dietary laws."

"But they hate you, just as they hate me and Isidorus."

"Yes, but I do not hate them."

"Well I pity you, and more them for they do not really appreciate what you do for them. I know you do not like to hear this, but they are borderline barbarians," Isidorus said with an air of Roman superiority.

With a smile on his lips, Levi replied, "I will forgive you because your Roman ancestors never knew the value of traditions." Looking at Zacchaeus, Levi said mildly, "And you Zacchaeus, I sympathize with you for like me you have lost the glory of being a Jew and together we have forgotten our ancestors' obedience to *El Shaddai.*"

Another Jew came to the custom's booth and Levi quickly calculated his tax. He extended his hand to receive the *shekels* and as they fell from the Jew's hand and landed in his palm he heard the jingle of the coins. The sound was deafening and Levi jerked his head in an attempt to clear the sound from his senses.

Above the din he heard Zacchaeus say, "Look who comes now."

Levi saw a small group of men coming towards his booth. He knew most of the men. They had been friends and associates of his former life. The sight of these men did not bother him, but what instantly bothered him was that among them were his brothers James and Jude Thaddeus. The moment he saw them his heart beat fast.

Levi heard the jingle of coins off to his side.

Suddenly from out of the group of men came a different face, yet a familiar face, and for one sudden moment Levi lost his breath. The

Man walked away from Levi and stood opposite the custom's booth. The man Levi knew as Judas paid the passage for the group. Judas held out the coins, not wanting to touch Levi, and the coins fell through the air and landed heavily in Levi's palm. The coins clashing together sounded like loud gongs. Quickly he twisted his head in an effort to be free of the sounds. His efforts were curtailed as the coins suddenly grew warm in his palm. They nearly seared his skin and just as he was about to let the *shekels* fall, he heard the Man opposite the custom's booth say, "Come. Follow me."

The Man walked away and the others silently followed Him.

Levi cupped the warm coins in his hand and extended his arms to Zaccheaus who reached for Levi's hand.

"Zaccheaus, mind my post for me. I shall be back."

His hands opened wide and the coins fell to Zaccheaus who immediately felt their warmness.

Levi walked after the group.

In the distance, Levi heard the sound of more clanging coins.

＊

The shouted orders woke Matthew from his slumber and after his eyes and mind wiped the dying end of slumber away, he could see soldiers and people running about in complete turmoil.

For a moment he had to recollect where he was, *Oh yes, Dura. I am in Dura, Mesopotamia.* His thoughts and dreams of his yesterdays were again only memories. He watched as his guards hurried around adjusting their uniforms and equipment as they formed into some remnants of a guard patrol on duty.

A large crowd of civilians had gathered on the river bank and milled about in expectation of someone's arrival.

A loud horn blared and Matthew looked around for the trumpeters but could not find them. The sound of drum beats pounded in a slow precise beat; its timing was the cadence of someone walking. Then, he heard the sound of flutes. Their melody slowly curled, twisted and unfolded from the instruments reminding him of an awakened serpent in search of prey. Matthew instantly became uncomfortable as he felt their timbre slither and worm around him. A procession of men appeared; quickly identified as eunuchs. Their faces were stoic. Matthew could see they were captives in mind and body. Finally, an image appeared that he quickly identified as Qulara. Her tall body covered from head to toe with a long, green-gray garment of sheer material. Everything was covered except for her big hands, which were clutched tightly. Occasionally the tip of her feet would peek out from under her long, flowing clothes. Even with all this covering, Matthew felt her eyes full of hate for him.

Qulara walked to the edge of the river with her robe and dress flowing and fluttering in the wind that was coming off the river. On the river, people were fishing and boats were sailing up and down in commerce and recreation. The sails of the ships billowed in the constant breath of the river. Some fishermen were pulling their morning nets into their boats. The green-gray river flowed in a normal drift. Several eunuchs rushed to Qulara and slowly removed her garments. Her naked form held no femininity. Her body was big, distorted in a strange and disturbing way. Her face was masculine, square with big features.

Matthew realized she was the first non-Jewish woman he ever saw naked.

The blasting horns, pounding drums, and wining flute became still.

Qulara walked into the river and everyone present fell to their knees and began to chant praises to Enki, the river god. In prayer they asked Enki to give them a sign that would help them know what to do with the unbelieving Jew. She continued into the green-gray water until her naked body was submerged completely. Everything became silent except for the infantile sound of the passing breeze. All was still except for the boats and ships slipping across their aquatic roads.

A long time passed. Then suddenly one of the eunuchs stood up and pointing to the river shouted, "Look at the water!"

Everyone looked toward what the eunuch had pointed out and they all saw the green-gray water turn brown.

The people screamed and shouted exclamations of fear and soon complete chaos broke out on the riverbank.

Out of the river emerged Qulara with her skin stained brown. As she solemnly walked to the riverside, several eunuchs ran quickly to her and covered her stained body with garments. After she was covered, she raised her arms above her head and declared, "Enki has spoken, and the Jew must be given to him. The infidel's body will satisfy our god and our river will be purified."

A mob turned to Matthew. They dragged him to the river bank and left him on the wet sands. The guards grabbed his hands, tied them tightly behind him, and then tied his feet. They put him in a sack bag and began filling the bag with rock and stones and then secured the opening of the sack around his neck. From nowhere a wooden raft appeared and the guards boarded the raft and dragged Matthew on it. They pushed off the shore and moved half way across the river and then stopped.

The drums and flutes played and Qulara standing with raised arms suddenly dropped them to her side. The guards rolled Matthew off the raft and into the river. He quickly disappeared from the surface of the river and all that could be seen were bubbles erupting on the surface. The people cheered and shouted praises to their god Enki.

Moments passed.

Some of the people started to walk away confident that their god was the greatest god. Qulara and her entourage began to walk away to sounds of flutes and drums.

Suddenly someone shouted, "Look!"

Everyone looked. Screams of amazement filled the air drowning out the sounds of Qulara's instruments.

Standing on the river water, free of the sack bag, ropes, and rocks and in dry, clean clothing was Matthew.

"Lord Jesus, show the innocent Your power," he shouted as he raised his arms from his sides to his shoulder making a cross of his body.

Instantly the river ceased to flow.

Fishermen on boats rowed frantically but they could not move. The sails went flat. Everything froze in place.

People began screaming and ran about in panic demanding that Matthew return their river to them, but he remained in the form of a cross as the sun brightened and cast a long, large shadow of his form over the river. Many of the people covered their eyes because the sun was so bright.

Suddenly the light faded and they found a clean, dry, un-marred Matthew standing on the shore.

The people rushed to him demanding to know more about Jesus and on that day he purified many in his Master's name.

✳

Matthew immediately lost the past and all its memories and returned to his prison and his pains. The fire from his captives was no longer bright and the reflections through the cracks in the door were flickers. Thunder rumbled across the sky and when he looked up he saw the night sky enraged. Again thunder pounded and echoed all around him. Lightening zigzagged across the thick blackness. These two prefaces to rain crashed and grumbled several more times and then together they threw the rain from the skies. His parched lips and feverish body felt the downpour and immediately Matthew smiled to himself and instantaneously became thankful.

"You are so good to me, Lord. You hear my every request and grant it," he said aloud. He quickly lifted his face to the emptying sky and opened his mouth wide to enjoy the water as it filled his mouth and extinguished his fiery thirst. His warm and feverish body was simultaneously refreshed and in his suffering he found contentment. Grateful, he again thanked the Almighty, for the rain had also rid him of the insects that had tormented him all night; even the rodents scurried in search of better shelter. The rains continued and soon small streams of water funneled their way to him, carrying the filth and mud of the hut to his open wounds. Some of his wounds burned and stung, but he found no discomfort in these things; instead he started to rejoice for once again he was being Christ-like and this was the challenge he and all humanity had to face. He believed that in pain, suffering and in dying humans were most close to Jesus.

Rethinking this belief returned his mind back to that day on Golgotha and the sight of Jesus looking just as wounded, just as dirty, just as wet as he was. Matthew acknowledged that Jesus on Golgotha was washed clean by the rain as a sign he had completed his work on earth, and was rinsed clean of human life. He, on the other hand, was being made dirty by the rain for he still had to live and still had work to be done on earth. The rains were cooling, but the rains on that Golgotha day were not. The rain singed his skin as he hid behind a thick bush a great distance from the Cross.

Unexpectedly, the day became dark as night and in that darkness of Golgotha, for the first time in hours, Matthew found rest. He believed the darkness was from the Cross; it was the shadow of the cross. It shocked him to see that he found respite in the distant shadow of the Cross.

Suddenly, he realized all was dark.

How could I be in the shadow of the Cross when night and darkness are all around me?

Then Matthew found his answer: The darkness was indeed the shadow of the Cross, for the shadow had covered the world; it would never fade away, never to go away even in the darkness of night. Even in the blackest moment in time, the shadow of the Cross would be there, scarred into the earth and the memories of human beings.

His journey to distance himself from the shadow of the Cross began the night before, in Gethsemane, when he was the first and the fastest to run. Even before Judas blistered the Master's cheek, he ran. He had the right to run for he knew that the Temple guards would have delighted in bringing a publican to the Chief Priest of the Council.

How far he ran, he did not know, but he eventually found himself crumbled behind a bush struggling to breathe. The moment he stopped he felt guilt so he struggled to his feet and ran some more. He again stopped, and struggled to breathe and again felt guilt. So again he ran, until he finally had to stop or die. On the ground and wet from perspiration he struggled for air. Suddenly he believed he would not live. The air he labored for was too heavy to take. The guilt of deserting Jesus was severe. He was unworthy of the air that *El Shaddai* provided.

How could I enjoy a gift from the Almighty after I have forsaken Jesus who was of the Almighty?

The question burned into his mind and he cursed with shame and his lost manliness. Finally he collapsed into sleep and when he awoke he was greeted with the mid-day sun. He quickly raced back into the center of Jerusalem and there heard that Jesus had been crucified.

How could this be? Why would this be?

He hastened to Golgotha to witness, in hiding, the death of his Lord, Jesus.

For the first time in his life he cried. The rain masked his tears so he cried as a hidden sinner.

✳

The rain continued to fall and small puddles of water were forming inside his prison. It was a hard, continuous downpour that reminded him of the storms he had witnessed in Galilee. Some of them were so violent that the thought of them returned fear to him.

Why is everything reminding me of things in my past? It seems this is my night to think about my yesterdays. Why is this night forcing me to remember bygone days and places? Am I to review my life?

Suddenly an exciting thought came to him and it elevated him above the deplorable conditions of his present life.

Perhaps, Matthew, he thought, *the Good Lord is preparing you for your death.*

With a peacefulness he had not felt in many years, he rested his head on the post that he was loosely tied to and smiled with naked joy.

✳

Matthew remained and labored in Mesopotamia for many years, going from city to city and attacking the different gods in every city. In many cities he and Namenlos were arrested and beaten, but never did they seem to be in complete harm's way.

In their closing years in Mesopotamia they met a group of Jews from Parthia and Persia who asked them to return with them to a small Jewish community just over the border that would be receptive to their message. So the two missionaries and the small caravan of Jews departed for Parthia. All the way to the border, Matthew taught his fellow travelers of Jesus. When they arrived in Parthia, at the first stream they came to, they left the road and the group was purified. Soon a crowd of curious people formed and Matthew began to speak to them of Jesus and the longer he spoke the more people gathered. Suddenly from the back of the crowd came whispered news that a royal escort was coming. Most of the people scattered in different directions but several people stood with Matthew and Namenlos. Abruptly on the road came a contingent of royal guards riding their sheen, black stallions. The guards charged into the crowd hitting many with their galloping horses and others with sticks and clubs. Screams of pain from broken bodies were heard everywhere and when they had finally cleared a path to Matthew, Namenlos and the Jews, the soldiers dismounted and stood at attention.

With equal suddenness three figures appeared on the road. Their long, flowing garments flapped and waved in the wind. Their faces were decorated with black ink in swirling and curling designs. Their ears, lips, and noses were pierced with gems and gold. In spite of the heat of the day, they defiantly appeared cool and refreshed.

"That is Queen Fulvana, and the Crown Prince, Rumec and his royal wife, Butivare," one of the Jews whispered. "One is as cruel as the other and they are greatly feared by all."

Everyone fell to their knees and bowed except Matthew and Namenlos.

"Kneel, Matthew, or you will be killed," one of the Jews said to him.

"I bow to no man," Matthew replied plainly.

"You!" the Queen shouted and pointed with long, bent fingers at Matthew.

Her voice was harsh and grainy. It was not a human voice but a voice from the distant hollows.

"You!" The one word was likened to a shrill and sent shivers through everyone's body. When she continued, each word was pronounced with a drawl with tints of hissing sounds.

Her voice caused Namenlos to say, "Matthew is that…." But before he could continue he was silenced by a hand over his mouth.

"Shh, never ask! That will put you at a disadvantage. Know! And always be ready," Matthew advised in a whisper that was sharp with experience.

"You Galilean! You do not belong here! This place is not for you to walk on for this is the holy ground of the great god of the mountains, Janpai. Go or you and those who are with you will be tortured and placed on the mountain for the protectors of Janpai to devour."

Matthew bent and with his right hand picked up his wooden staff, and with his other hand reached for a fairly large rock which he held tightly in his hand.

"I am here in the Name of Jesus, who is the Anointed One, the Christ. He teaches peace and tortures no one. He instead offers love, forgiveness and the promise of eternal life with Him and His Father."

"Bah!" shouted the Crown Prince. "Your Jesus was nothing but a criminal who was crucified by the Roman pigs."

"He could not be that great a God, for you deserted Him when He needed you the most. Have you forgotten your disloyalty, Roman tax collector?" added the Royal Wife of the Prince.

"Go!" added Prince Rumec.

"And never return," shouted the Queen. Her words were strong with authority.

"We will not allow imperfection to desecrate our holy land," screamed the Royal wife of the Prince.

"No!" Matthew shouted back as his word reverberated throughout the mountains.

A guard moved quickly to Matthew with his drawn sword. He raised his sword with the intent to strike him but his hand froze and trembled in mid-air.

Matthew's face was soft and loving. His eyes unblinkingly searched the man's face until the man dropped his sword and fell to the ground sobbing.

"Go!" the Royals shouted in unison.

"No! For you do not speak from your own hearts but from the heart of another."

"Go!" the Queen shouted and she raised her fist to Matthew.

Matthew immediately reacted to the Queen's gesture and raised his staff to her. Soon her hand began to tremble out of control.

"No! You who are within these souls; you Legion and Evil One, identify yourself. Give me your name!"

A long howl came from the Royals followed by a harsh growling voice, "Kill him!"

No one moved.

"Give me your name! Now!"

"My name…" said Butivare in a deep, manly voice.

"My name is…" Rumec said in a strangled and harsh voice.

"…Asmodaeus," shouted the Queen Mother.

Suddenly a gust of strong, cold wind raced across the land. Many covered their faces to protect their eyes and others tumbled and fell to the earth, unable to hold their posture.

"Stop! In the Holy Name of Jesus, I order you to stop!" Matthew shouted and with all the strength of his right arm he planted his staff into the ground and the wind was gone. "You demon of the hollows; you destroyer of man's will and soul, in the Name of Jesus, the *Messiah* of the world, be gone! I cast you out of these souls and send you to the pits of your domain. GO!"

Matthew threw the large rock in his hand to the earth with great force and as soon as it hit, the ground erupted in heaves and shivers. The innocent ones who were standing nearby in awe of this battle of good and evil crumbled to the ground, screaming and crying for mercy.

From the three Royals came unintelligible screeches. Their three bodies jerked and quivered and eventually collapsed to the road in a mass of rich rags. In their stead, standing in their place, were three dark clouds with no form. From the forms came loud and long wailings that increased to a deafening pitch; then the forms began to fade until there was nothing there. The earth weakened to stillness.

Matthew uttered quick words of thanksgiving and then called the Royals to him.

As they timidly walked to Matthew their faces were cleaned of ink and their piercings healed. On that day they gave themselves to Jesus and all their entourage followed.

When the King heard of this and saw the change in his family, he ordered Matthew and Namenlos to be arrested. Several days later they and several of the Jews that had received Jesus were captured, beaten, and thrown in prison.

The King gathered all his priests and ordered them to ask the god Janpai to return the royal family to their former selves. The priests went to the mountain but none returned, so when guards went to seek them, they found all the priests dead. Next, the King demanded that his queen, son, and daughter-in-law abandon their new God and return to Janpai, but they refused even after the King had them beaten. Defeated, the King decided to leave his family to their own insanity and let Matthew and Namenlos go free, but during the night he had a dream. The demon that had lived within his family appeared to him and told him he had to kill Matthew by fire for this was the Apostle's greatest fear.

So the next day the King had the Apostle and Namenlos tied to a withered tree and stacked huge amounts of wood and kindling at their feet and set a fire, but the dry wood would not burn because it suddenly had been made damp and wet. The King attempted three times to have a fire started and each time the same thing took place. Frustrated, the King called on the demon in his dream and suddenly his head was thrown back against his throne. His crown flipped from his head and fell to the ground, rolling around and around the foot of the throne. He shook and shivered and finally slipped onto the ground before his throne, next to his fallen crown. Slowly he rose from his vulnerable position and looked grimly at Matthew and Namenlos. His mouth was foaming and his body wet with perspiration. His royal garb was no longer pristine gold but now stained brown and black. He appeared more muscular and taller then he was. The black ink and dye on his face had gotten darker. Again, he ordered the fire to be set. His voice sounded like the growl of a wild beast.

A wide smile crossed his lips as the fire began to catch, but suddenly the smoke from the fire changed directions and began to blow into the face of the King who immediately began to cough and choke. When finally the smoke cleared he found Matthew free of bondage and standing with his arms extended in the sign of the cross.

The King screamed and ran from the room and onto the balcony. He flung himself over the railing to his death.

When everyone looked, Matthew and Namenlos had disappeared and the tree to which they had been tied was charred.

It was soon after this encounter that Matthew received word from John bar Zebedee and Luke that Lady Mary was near death. They requested him to return to Ephesus immediately due to Mary's request to see all of the Twelve for the last time.

"We will never be able to get back in time," Namenlos announced. His face was sad for he had been in Lady Mary's presence often and had grown fond of her.

"Fear not, my young friend, for the Lord Who makes all things possible will allow this if it be His Will," Matthew said softly and he immediately went off to pray.

He prayed for many hours and though he grew tired, he could not stop his prayers; he knew this was what he had to do. Late into the night, he felt himself being moved to another place; he relaxed and made himself go.

✳

"Matthew, are you well?" and he heard the urgency in Namenlos' voice.

"What?"

"Are you well? You have been in prayer for three days and though you spoke to me and others you never seemed to be totally here. Shall I seek a physician for you?"

"No, my young friend, all is well," Matthew replied.

It has happened again, he thought and again gave thanks to Jesus for the gift of being in two places at the same time. Remembering where he had been, he became joyful for he saw the Twelve together once again. He slowly rose from his mat and looking down at Namenlos said, "Mary has died and her last wish was granted."

✳

Matthew and Namenlos stayed in Parthia and Persia for many years when they finally returned to Syria. In Syria, Matthew met a group of Egyptian Jews who told him they were baptized many years before in Jerusalem. They told him of the many Jews in Egypt who were there from the days of Jewish slavery and of others who had returned to Egypt in frustration for being in the desert for forty years. Matthew quickly volunteered to join them, for he could see the need to convert these Jews and to continue the work of Mark, who was killed.

Matthew and Namenlos boarded the merchant ship *Profundum Turba* Restless Sea and left Antioch, Syria for Egypt. His first night on the *Mare Nostrum*, Matthew prayed. He felt he was in one great temple; the temple of the first days of creation and felt united with God. He wondered at the darkness and the feeling of being lost in the massive depths of the sea and sky; and appreciated the stealth, almost fearless glide of the ship through the darkened waters and the dark, blue sky, yet he still had the feelings of hope and guidance within the moon and the stars.

The soft sound of the sea captivated him and he surrendered to its whispers. The whispers spoke of the many hushed secrets of the sea; they tantalized him with their undetermined mysteries. The sea became a huge, open book of nameless things and these confidentialities would only be known when the sea wished them to be known. These privacies were there to be discovered if one could understand the hissing whispers of the sea's words.

In daylight, the blue sapphire water was a reflection of the sky and the smell of the salt reminded him of Galilee, of fishing, and of Jesus and the Others.

For three days and three nights Matthew stood on the deck of the ship. The Sea reminded him of God. It was mighty and endless with mighty powers over life and death. The sea, like God, brought humans memories of home and of being away from one's final home. The whispers of God, like the hissing of the sea, were mysteries. All that is God can never be known, in spite of God being an open book, in spite of God sending prophets, for man had too narrow and human an intellect. This was the reason for Jesus' coming: God became Man and because of this men now could know something of God, which was impossible of them before His coming. They could "hear" the whispers of God and understand their meaning.

These thoughts brought tears to Matthew's eyes and he fell to his knees in open prayer.

"O Lord, once again You have taken me into Your trust to show me Your ways, and once again I am Your humble servant. Let me do Your will without fear and let me always see You as I see You tonight."

Sometime during that night he was joined on the deck by Namenlos and the three Egyptian Jews: Yaniv, Nisim, and Oshri. When they found him in prayer they stood nearby listening and watching.

"Father, Lord of heaven and earth, to You I offer praise; for what You have hidden from the learned and the clever You have revealed to the merest children."

"What form of prayer is this?" Yaniv whispered to the others.

"I know not," replied Oshri while Namenlos shook his head in agreement.

Matthew fell silent and when he began to pray again, they joined him for they recognized the prayer from Isaiah, the prophet.

"The heavens are My throne,
and the earth is My footstool.
What kind of house can you build for Me;
what is to be My resting place?
My Hand made all these things when all of them came to be.
This is the one whom I approved,
the lowly and affected and who trembles at My work."

Aware of the presence of others, Matthew relaxed for a moment, then opened his eyes and greeted the four men with brotherly love. The five men stayed on deck all night talking and asking Matthew one question after another about Jesus. Their questions were endless; their need to know insatiable.

The hours passed on and into the early morning darkness.

Finally, Nisim asked, "When did you really know that Jesus was the Messiah, the Son of God?"

The moon reflected off of Nisim's face. Matthew looked at his companion's moonlight face for a long time because the face looked unreal, macabre.

Matthew answered him softly, "There were three times really. The first was when Jesus sent us out two by two. He commanded us to do this by saying, 'Go ye not into the way of the Gentiles, and into the city of the Samaritans enter ye not. But go ye rather to the lost sheep of the House of Israel. And going, preach, saying: the Kingdom of heaven is at hand. Heal the sick, raise the dead, cleanse the lepers, cast out devils; freely have you received.'"

"And did you do all that was commissioned of you?" asked Oshri with anticipation.

"Yes."

"You healed the sick, raised the dead, cleansed the lepers, cast out devils?" inquired Nisim.

"Together we did these things but we did not do all of them individually. For example, I did not cast out a devil but I did heal, raise and cleanse. My brother James healed the sick and cleansed a leper; and Jude healed the sick only, but the Twelve did what Jesus asked of us."

"How did you feel knowing you could have such powers?" asked Namenlos.

"I immediately knew it all came from Jesus. He had let His powers go just long enough for us to see what He could give us and what we could do in His Name. It seems Jesus wanted us to know that we could be blessed. Some of the Others were a bit more uplifted and felt they would inherit these powers. I understood that this power, given for a few moments, was from *El Shaddai* and therefore I concluded Jesus was of and from God. He was the *Messiah*."

"Do you think Jesus knew what you were thinking?" Namenlos asked

"Yes. I am sure the Master knew what each of us were about. I am sure He knew that without Him we were not going to work. We enjoyed each other somewhat, but lacked thinking as one. I am often saddened by the fact that we did not fully live according to Jesus' teachings. I know we frustrated Him, for many times I could see His exasperation. We sensed the love He had for us individually, but we failed to transform His love for us into a love for each other. My brother James remained cold to me for a long time in spite of my trying to warm things up between us. One day he came to me and said our father had asked to be remembered to me. Days passed without a word between us. Finally Jude came to me and begged to go to James and ask him to tell our father, Cleopus, that I wanted to speak to him. I did this and things slowly warmed with James. Still, I believed James had a bitter taste in his mouth for me, that is, until Jesus rose from the dead. After that event James was a true brother to me. He made me proud of him for he preached Jesus with great strength and conviction. He died telling the Jews of Jesus' love and sacrifice for them."

"Did not any of the Others think as you did about Jesus being the Messiah?"

"I do not know. Perhaps Peter, James and John did for I knew they witnessed happenings that the rest of us did not. Many times when we debated they were the ones who were most forceful in saying that Jesus was an Anointed One. Others may have had a small feeling."

"It is amazing how twelve of you could have done what you did. Look, most of the Roman Empire knows of Jesus," observed Yaniv.

"I agree with Yaniv and our amazement should be doubled when you realize that after Jesus was arrested and crucified we thought Him a fake. We gathered together not out of need for each other for suddenly we were strangers once again, but out of fear. My brother James was the leader of the idea to disband and return to our homes and former selves and go into hiding. That seemed an impossible thing for me to do, for how does one leave being a tax collector and then return to being a tax collector, and remain hidden? It was totally unacceptable, so I remained strongly in favor of staying together as a tribute to Jesus if not for any-thing else."

"Do you think you changed any of their minds?"

"I do not know, but I know we stayed together and were together when Jesus appeared to us on that first day of the week."

"You said there were three times you knew that Jesus was the Messiah, what was the second and third time?" Namenlos asked.

"The second was the miracle of Jesus going back to His Father and the third was private."

"Tell us about Jesus going back to His Father," Oshri pleaded.

"None of us expected such a happening. It was just an ordinary day and we were happy for having Jesus with us. We knew Jesus had died and came back to life, but none of us knew what was supposed to happen next. We were content having things just the way they were. Jesus had eaten with us, rested with us, and talked to us. His death was something that just happened. We had no idea why He had suffered or why He lived again. We were just relieved to have Him with us again because we were now secure and felt His strong protection. After all, He had done what no other being had ever done—He died and lived again. He had beaten death. One day, we walked to Mount Olivet which is a mount on the east side of Jerusalem just beyond the Valley of Kidron. This mount has a long history among the Jewish people, but that was far from our minds that day for we walked listening to Jesus.

"He said: 'Thus it is written and thus it behooved Christ to suffer and to rise again from the dead on the third day; that penance and the remission of sins should be preached in His name, unto all nations, beginning at Jerusalem. You are witnesses of these things. And I send the promise of My Father upon you; but stay you in the city till you be endued with the power from on high.'

"'And these signs shall follow them that believe: In my Name they shall cast out devils; they shall speak with new tongues. They shall take up serpents; and if they shall drink any deadly thing, it shall not hurt them; they shall lay their hands upon the sick and they shall recover.'

"He stopped walking. I remember there was a great, soft stillness around us and I grew curious as to why this calm came over us. Jesus walked a bit up the mount and turning to us, smiled. His face shone as bright as the sun. He raised his right hand over us as to give us a blessing, then his feet rose from the ground. His eyes were fixed on us as he continued to ascend. We were stunned but none of us became too excited, though I did hear a few gasps and a few low, murmured prayers. Jesus kept His eyes on us for the longest time and finally He looked up into the heaven. He was enclosed by clouds and simply vanished. Just then a small, gentle breeze passed and we were standing dumbfounded and alone again. So we gathered our thoughts, followed our instructions, and returned silently to Jerusalem.

"Some time later we were joined by many others who believed in Jesus. Lady Mary and my mother and Salome, the mother of James and John, and Lazarus' sisters, the lady called Madeleine, Suzann and Joann also came to be with us. We told everyone what we had witnessed and they accepted what we said in spite of it being extraordinary. By this time most of us would believe anything seen because so many extraordinary and amazing things had taken place. The extraordinary was now part of our lives.

"This ascension was a great revelation to us. You see, none of us saw Jesus actually rise from the dead, but to see Him ascend before us transformed many of us. We all seemed to enter a place of euphoria for we believed that a new phase in our relationship with Jesus had begun."

"I have read your account of Jesus' life, and you did not mention His going up to heaven. Why did you not mention it?"

"I knew Mark had written of it and Luke also, so I did not desire to retell what they said. In writing what I did, I felt I had to be somewhat independent from the others for if we all wrote the same thing nothing new would have been known of Jesus. I hear that John is writing an account also and that his account is written on a different level which soars above the rest. With his words, John entered into the profound depths of the mystery of Jesus."

The moment was disturbed by a sailor who came on deck and set several torches afire. The torches gave the faces of the five men an amber and orange glow.

"Thank you, Matthew," Yaniv said as he suppressed a yawn.

"Yes, thank you, I need to know more, but sleep comes to me quickly, perhaps tomorrow and in the days and nights to follow we shall hear more of Jesus," Namenlos said.

"I am here as the servant of the Lord," Matthew replied.

The men quickly bid their good-nights and covered themselves with their cloaks. They moved and tossed into comfortable places and soon the world fell back to silence.

Matthew took a deep breath and let the dark, morning air fill his chest.

They did not ask me about the other time I learned that Jesus was the Son of God, he thought and for a quick moment he was relieved that they had not asked him. He never revealed to anyone that other moment.

He rested his head on the side of the ship's cabin and his eyes looked at one of the torches. The flames from the torch were flicking and fluttering while the other torches were at a steady, even burn. The flames to this torch reminded Matthew of the flames of the many, large fires the Twelve built for Jesus and themselves when they were not sleeping in a house provided by a friend and outside along the shoreline of the Sea of Galilee or on a hillside.

With no surprise, his mind moved back to his first night after being called when he sat by a large fire on the shores of Galilee just outside of Capernaum.

The fire was big and it snapped and spit sparks into the air. Levi sat mesmerized by the small embers shooting into the air. Slowly he began to relive the strange events of that simple day. After hearing "Come follow Me," he lost sight of his life and his focus was on Jesus only. He could only hear the words, "Come follow me."

Alone by the fire, he forced himself to exit whatever trance he was in, but to his surprise leaving this unfamiliar place left him hungry to return. Also, to his surprise the place he was in was a warm, comfortable place—

like home—and he felt a joy that had long been devoid from his life. He wondered what he was to do with this new-found feeling and for some inexplicable reason he found he wanted to tell the world of his discovery.

Again he examined the events of the day. Things came back to him like a lazy dream. He had invited Jesus and His followers to his house to dine. He was so pleased that Jesus accepted; he did not care if Jesus' followers came. Matthew's brother James, Simon the Zealot, Judas Iscariot, and Jude Thaddeus reluctantly stayed outside in the courtyard and refused to sit at the table.

Zacchaeus and his friend Isidorus attended as did several other Publicans. Levi knew these Publicans dined in a defiant pleasure to the Pharisees and not for interest in hearing Jesus.

During the night Zacchaeus spoke caringly to Levi and said, "I believe I know what you are thinking of doing, Levi, and I warn you not to be taken by this Man, Jesus, who is but a prophet and who like all Jewish prophets will be disregarded by the people. You can see you are not welcome among His followers. Just look at your own family and those radicals who refused to enter your home to dine with you. This is unhealthy. Stay away!"

"I know what you say is true, but I need time to test this Man. I know Him from youth. He is my father's relative, and I never thought He would be so compelling. I must spend time with Him to see for myself. Give me this one request, dear friend."

Now while they were eating in the house of Levi, the Pharisees came and said to those eating in the courtyard, "Why does your Master eat with Publicans and sinners?"

Jesus hearing this turned his attention to them and said: "They that are in health need not a physician, but they that are ill do. Go then and learn what this meaneth: I will have mercy and not sacrifice. For I am not come to call the just but the sinner."

On hearing this Zacchaeus said to Levi, "Spend time with this Man, and tell me of Him later."

After dinner, Jesus and His followers walked out of the city to the shores of the Sea of Galilee. Levi followed them by walking a short distance behind them. He heard their raucous laughter and muffled conversations and found himself longing to be with them.

The group stopped and from the group came Jude running back to Levi with a wide smile on his face.

He invited his brother to join them with the words: "The Master wishes you to be with us."

Levi timidly walked to the group and was greeted by none and ignored by all. With Levi in their midst they continued on to the sea in silence.

On the shore, they built a large fire and sat talking, joking and singing songs. With each passing moment Levi's feeling of unwelcome began to cloud his need to stay and follow Jesus.

The night passed on and soon all the men were settling down to sleep. Levi sat alone on a large petrified tree trunk watching the fire burn. He felt more than disappointment; he felt foolish.

How could you have been foolish to think you belonged here? You have a brother who has not looked at you all night, and two others who despise you and in another time would have killed you. All of them look at you with distrust and disdain.

He resolved when all were sound asleep that he would creep away and never return.

How can I have allowed myself to do such a foolish thing?

Anger and self-pity intoxicated him like a heavily drugged wine. He waddled in it and was more determined that he had to leave, but still he could not do so.

I heard rumors that He cured a leper and the servant of a Centurion and even spoke blessings on a mount that caused many to follow Him. I heard He fought the devil, and even cured Simon's mother-in-law. I have to see if all these things are true. I cannot leave unless I learn the truth. Perhaps a few more days or at least one more day. Yes, I shall give Him one more day.

Suddenly he realized that he had not spoken to Jesus all night.

Quickly he looked at the human forms wrapped in their cloaks and only counted eleven. Jesus was not there! He jumped to his feet and looked around the shoreline and even the side of the hills and mountains, and he could not find Jesus. Within an instant he felt completely abandoned.

"Why do you look so far, Levi for something that is ever near?"

Levi looked down and to his side. There sitting on the petrified tree that once he alone occupied was Jesus.

"Come, sit with Me. I always enjoy this quiet time of night. Come and enjoy it with Me."

He wanted to know how Jesus could have appeared and seem to have been sitting with him all along, but he simply could not think. Levi fell on to the tree drained of all reason and explanation. He was caught once again by the Voice and the Face of Jesus and immediately he was placid. He had the strange feeling he was surrounded by ancient, new, and future ages. The beach was suddenly crowded.

He looked at Jesus' face and watched the blazing light become consumed and softened on His face.

"Levi is a good name. Levi was the third son of Jacob from whom the Levites descended. I am sure you know that the tribe of Levi was the only tribe that refused to worship the idol of the Golden Calf because of their strong belief of *Abba*. Truly you have a noble name, but, sadly, a name that is not without sins. Levi was quick to anger and destroyed an entire town out of revenge and, of course, did help sell his brother Joseph into slavery, but you know all that."

"Why did You call me to You? Did You not know I would not become a part of these others?"

"Yes. But you are the third son of Alphaeus, and you are priestly yet you grew in anger and you have sold people and yourself into slavery."

Jesus pushed his hood back and turned to face Levi. "I needed a Levi," He continued. A small smile crossed Jesus' lips as He said, "Why did you follow Me?"

"I felt a need to be with You and a desire to find You out and because…"

"You needed to be found and you needed to find yourself."

"Yes. I was growing tired. I felt You would give me rest."

"This I knew and these were the other reasons why I asked you to 'follow Me.' I read your soul and knew your hurt and your need. Do you believe this, Levi?

"How did you know this?"

"I know all things."

Jesus turned his face away and looked into the fire that seemed brighter and stronger.

"Are you not the Son of Yosef and his wife Mariam, relatives to my father?"

"Yes, for the here and now, yes, but I am the Son of Another."

"Do not be cryptic with me, cousin, for I knew You as a child. We played together. We enjoyed childhood together."

"I knew you saw Me as being different."

Jesus turned His Face to Levi.

"Deny it not, Levi, for you thought I was 'extraordinary and too kind to survive in the world we played.' Am I not correct?"

Levi was speechless, for he remembered thinking this when playing games with Jesus; in fact, he remembered using those exact words. He knew he never told anyone what he felt or thought; so he wondered how Jesus knew.

"You will not leave Me, Levi, for you have a strong need to know and because you know that something important is about to happen. There are many who do not and will not trust you. You will be pointed at and reminded of what you were, and the Others who have been chosen will look at you and always remember what you were. If ever they question you remind them that I, Jesus of Nazareth, the Son of Man, chose you and nothing more is needed to be said."

Jesus paused and then continued. "Some day people will come to love you, and I promise you will be remembered by many ages and your name will be known more greatly than some of the Others who have been called."

Jesus stopped. His eyes were soft and warm and His Face, now partially shadowed by the flickering fire, was heartfelt and gripping.

"I shall give you a new name, just as My Father gave Jacob a new name after he wrestled with My Father's angel. This new name will partially separate you from the man called 'Levi.' Because you will be a gift from Me, I shall make you known as *Mattiyuahu.*"

Matthew knew that the name meant "Gift of the Lord" but still, he needed to know so he asked calmly, "Lord, by what right have You to give me a new name, when You said that my name, Levi, was so great a name?"

"Matthew, I will tell you and though this will be made known to you, you will not believe it until My Father and the Comforter come to you, but I am *Bar'El*, the Son of God. I am the promised one, the *Messiah*. I am of God, born of woman, Who came into this world to open the gates of Heaven to all who were faithful; I came to keep open the gates for all who will believe in Me and know My mercy, love and forgiveness. You are one of the first I give redemption to, if you so wish it, for none of your own will forgive you your sins, save Me."

Out of emptiness and openness came a surge so great and so intense that Matthew was forced to clutch his chest for his breathing had stopped and he ached for air. He seized hold of the dead tree beneath him for fear of falling over. He was so overwhelmed with surety and wisdom that he suffered in controlling his desire to yell and proclaim to all the sleeping and silent world, that finally, he had been vindicated, and finally he had arrived back home among his ancestors, with his people, in a family.

When morning came, the Others found Jesus and Matthew sitting on the log, refreshed. From that day on he was known to all as Matthew, the gift of the Lord.

✳

The ship traveled to the Egyptian port of Alexandria, which was one of the great cities of the Empire. It was founded by Alexander the Great, who wanted a great city named in his honor. Because of Alexander the city grew in prestige and flourished as a great metropolitan, commercial, and educational center. The city was the home to the *Bibliotheca Alexandrina*, the Library of Alexandria, which was the largest known library of scrolls in the world. It was the home of the *Mouseion,* the House of Muse, which made Alexandria the center for literature and science. It boasted a large population, for it was home to Greeks, Africans, Romans, Syrians, Numidians, Arabs, and Jews. Its Jewish population was surpassed only by Judea. It served as the home for many different religions; the most famous being the Sarapis. This religious group was responsible for the death of Mark who was the writer of the first account of the life of Jesus.

Immediately after disembarking, the three Egyptians led Matthew and Namenlos to the northeastern part of Alexandria which was the area that housed most of the Jews in the City. It was from this section of Alexandria that Matthew labored for many years. He preached among the Jews and then among the Gentiles who traveled through Alexandria. Matthew and his companions also traveled the Nile and visited Jews and Gentiles in the cities of Memphis, Oxythynchus, Antinopolis, Ptolemais, and numerous towns and villages. As the numbers of Christians grew, Matthew left Yanif and Nisim in charge of several communities with the understanding that they were to spread the teachings of Jesus. Oshri continued to travel with Matthew and Namenlos.

In the year 66, the Emperor Nero named General and Equestrian Tiberius Julius Alexander *Praefectus Aegypti*, Governor of Aegyptus. Tiberius Julius Alexander was well known to the Alexandrian Jews, for his wealthy family was from Alexandria; he was a Jew who had abandoned his religion for Roman glory and wealth. He was also known to Matthew for he had been procurator of Judea under Emperor Claudius and had permitted the persecution of many Christians in Judea. His arrival made many Jews fearful and within months their fears were justified. Egyptian Jews were suddenly targeted and their activities were curtailed in a number of cities. Julius Alexander deployed several legions against the Jews of Alexandria. The attacks spread. Then the governor was told Christians were among the Jews. He ordered attacks against the Christians because he remembered his unpleasant experiences with them while procurator of Judea. The Christians and Jews in fear scattered throughout Egypt.

Yanif and Nisim were imprisoned, tortured, and martyred along with hundreds of other Christians.

After many near-arrests, Oshri, Matthew, and Namenlos finally went into the desert for safety taking with them many Jews and Christians.

Unexpectedly Julius Alexander was summoned to Jerusalem by General Titus to serve as second in command to end the Jewish revolt.

Many years after the governor's departure from Egypt things still did not return to what it was. The Jewish and Christian population sat very precariously in an Egypt that never again seemed safe for them.

While in the desert, the three Christian leaders found a different kind of mission. The nomadic desert people listened to Matthew just long enough to get a small idea of Jesus; then, would move on to their next destination. Soon another caravan would pass and they would ask Matthew to tell them about Jesus. When Matthew asked how they heard of Jesus, they replied they had heard of Him from other passing nomads. So the mission to the desert people was partly done by the desert people themselves, for it was spread by mouth from caravan to passing caravan. Though this was a great and new form of evangelizing, Matthew was very slow and cautious to baptize these nomads. His concern was their lack of community, which was the basic element of Christian life. He worried that there would be a lack of sharing and more specifically the sharing of the *Agape,* the Meal. The *Agape* had become a great part of the belief in Jesus and was at the center of their worship.

As expected, Matthew found himself having disputes with many local religions which had beliefs based on animal and nature worship, but his success against these religions was usually quick. It was in the large cities of Upper Egypt that Matthew faced his strongest resistance, for in these cities the cult of *Serapis* was deeply entrenched. It found a stronger following among the rich and influential. It was fashionable even with Vespasian, a future emperor, who became interested in the religion while living in Alexandria.

During Matthew's stay in Egypt he saw the Church persecuted by the Emperor Nero and later in smaller measure during the reigns of Vespasian and Titus. When the Emperor Domitian came to power Matthew began to hear rumblings that alerted him of greater dangers. Domitian had been told Christians were cannibals because of the Meal and that Christians practiced incest because they were all "brothers and sisters."

Then came the decree from Rome that *Imperator Caesar Domitianus Augustus Pontifex Maximus Pater Patriae* was given the title of "lord and god" and Matthew knew that the Christian world was in peril, for now all subjects of Rome had to acknowledge Domitian's divinity. Not to do so would be anti-Roman or anti-state.

Following this decree was the announcement that Jews had lost their right to practice their religion and were now subjected to the religion of Rome.

Domitian's Persecution began in complete madness and continued until Christians and Jews were reduced to hiding among the dead, in mountains, deserts, or in lands outside of Roman's reach. They had to do this or face the decision between death or denial of their faith. These persecutions forced Matthew to remain in the desert and enter metropolitans under disguise. His visits to the suffering Body of Christ was quick and quiet. He did this at the insistence of his fellow travelers and those Christians around him who hid their identities. They found ways to avoid open celebrations of the Emperor's birthday and festivities of his military conquest, for it was at these celebrations that adoration of the Emperor was demanded and "a pinch of incense" was required before his image. To the Christians this small act was succumbing to idol worshiping and a denial of their God.

Oppressed, but not dissolved, the Christian communities lived on, surviving on the wits and ingenuity of the faithful. Jesus was discussed behind closed doors or in places that were far from appropriate for God. Though distrust and suspicion were always in their minds, the Christians still continued to love and perform works of charity and it was these very acts of charity and their willingness to die for their beliefs that caught the minds and souls of others. Soon the act of persecution became an asset for the Christians because it became a symbol of their convictions.

For seven years the persecution savagely continued and many were jailed, tortured, and killed. In all this time, Matthew and his companions were able to remain free, though at times they narrowly escaped the authorities. Finally Matthew got word that the governor of Egypt had issued an order for his arrest or murder. Soon after this he heard that similar orders were issued for Philip and John. Immediately Namenlos and Oshri prepared for a quick retreat into the southern Egyptian desert.

Under the cover of a dark, blue starlight and moonlight sky, the three traveled down the Nile to the city of Thebes. They did not enter Thebes for they learned that the Roman detachment in the town was on full alert and in search of Christians, so they traveled around the city by route of the desert. While in the desert they fasted, prayed, and did penance. Often they were visited by caravans and nomads and when this happened they preached of Jesus.

The conversions of only these few did not sit well with Matthew, who believed he had to do more for the suffering Church. He grew restless. He longed for an open assembly of people or the open, green countryside where rivers flowed as living water. He noticed that Namenlos and Oshri were very content with this minimal living and he was happy for them, but his life was a life of greater obedience; he had to follow the commands of Christ if he were to live a fulfilled life. In his past he had always been happy with his life of exile, which is what Jesus had given him, but this exile was too severe, so he prayed for help out of his dilemma.

Several weeks later, the three men camped at a seldom-used oasis that was sometimes used by desert caravans. The oasis was surrounded by several small, jagged hills that had hidden caves which helped make it a perfect place to be protected from the desert storms and sun.

Soon after their arrival a caravan passed where they had camped. It was a diminutive caravan with a small contingent of soldiers on camels. The soldiers were dressed in bright orange and white garments. Several soldiers had their swords drawn and the others carried bows by their sides. Walking beside the soldiers were about ten armed men who wore white robes with hoods. Their robes were held close to their bodies by a gold strap from which hung a sword.

In spite of the heat the travelers look refreshed as they made their way slowly towards Matthew and his companions. Even the camels looked invigorated as they moved with soft exactness, their heads high in an air of arrogance. Three camels were burdened with splendidly decorated, tasseled canopies. The canopies swayed in a slow, lazy rhythm with each step taken by the camels. Two canopy riders were visible and robed in fine garments that waved in the desert breeze twisting, dancing and flowing behind them creating grand images of unknown royalty. The third canopy had a sheer drape around it which obscured the rider. All three camels were guided by attendants who were robed in white and gold garments with glimmering, jeweled swords hanging by their sides. Matthew, Namenlos, and Oshri watched the caravan's slow approach and the closer it got to them, the more they concluded this was no ordinary convoy.

"Are they royalty?" Oshri whispered as he looked at the approaching visitors with great interest.

"They could be very successful merchants," Namenlos remarked, mesmerized by the parade before him.

With a broad smile on his face, Matthew thought, *I think these strangers are the answer to my prayer.*

The caravan stopped some distance from the small, rocky refuge and after a few still moments, one of the camel attendants slowly began walking to Matthew and his companions. The attendant was a tall, thin, black man who was dressed in a white robe that covered every part of his body except his dark hands and a small part of his black face. He wore a white turban that came across his face revealing only his eyes. Across his waist was a gold strap that held his sword by his side. He had his hand on the sword as he walked cautiously to the three men.

"Do you think they are hostile?" Namenlos asked.

"No. If they were they would have attacked by now and had us prisoners," Matthew replied as he walked slowly to meet the man.

Matthew and the man stopped about arms length and stood silently examining each other.

"My master would like to know if you are friendly," the man said.

"We are men of peace and of God. You are welcome to share our small provisions."

The man removed the cloth that covered his mouth and Matthew saw a wide smile on his black face. He thanked Matthew and quickly returned to the caravan. After a few moments the caravan continued its slow, swaying approach to the small, rocky island of hills. When they were close the camels stopped and the three men in the canopies dismounted. They were instantly surrounded by soldiers as they walked to Matthew. The soldiers stopped several steps away from Matthew and stepped aside. From their midst walked a tall, well-dressed man. As he walked to Matthew a large, warm smile crossed his lips.

He stood before Matthew and said in a joyful voice, "*Pax vobiscum.*" Peace be with you.

Matthew smiled and replied, "*Quod vobiscum*" And with you.

The "master" quickly drew a sword from the side of one of the guards nearby.

"Matthew!!!" Namenlos yelled as a warning.

Matthew, without looking away from the African, raised his hand to his companions.

The African pointed the sword to the sand and drew a fish.

Matthew looked at the sign curiously. He surmised it was a symbol of Christ or something Christian but he was not sure. If it was either of these things he was ignorant of it as its use was made known and practiced after he left the center of Roman rule.

So Matthew bent over and with his finger traced a cross.

"*Per sanctam crucem suam*" by His Holy Cross. The "master" proclaimed.

"*Sumus unum*" we are one, Matthew quickly replied.

The African exhaled with relief as he looked around at his guards who returned his smile.

Matthew walked to him and embraced his fellow Christian.

*

That night in the chill of the desert's darkness and around a fire, the African told the three Christians an amazing story.

"My name is Calashas. I am the chief eunuch in the royal house of the Kingdom of *Askum,* often called the Kingdom *Axum*. The Hebrews call us the country *Cush;* the Greeks called my land *Aethiopes* and the Romans call us *Aethiopia.*

"There are many believers of *HaKodosh* The Holy One in the Kingdom of *Aethiopia*. Our first king, Menelik, was descended from King Solomon and Queen Makeda. The people of Jerusalem called her the Queen of Sheba. She was a young queen with little experience in ruling but when she heard of Solomon's wisdom she went to him seeking some of his wisdom to rule her people better. She and Solomon became enchanted with each other and begot Menelik. In addition, the Queen came to believe in the One God *El Echad* of Jerusalem. Since the time of her return many of us have believed in *HaKadosh* and we now call ourselves *Bet Isra'el* House of Israel. We do not speak much of the language of Jerusalem and because of our distance we do not follow many of the rules and regulations of the Judean people. Our teachers are priests called *Kohanim* and they teach us only the *Torah*. We knew little of the other Writings.

"Several years ago I and my entourage traveled to Jerusalem as an ambassador from *Bet Isra'el* and our then Queen, Candace, with hopes of getting more information about our beliefs for my fellow Aethiopians. On my way to Jerusalem I passed through the city of Gaza and there I met a *Reb*, teacher of the Law, who showed me the many writings of the Holy Scriptures that we Aethiopians did not have. I was amazed at all the scrolls there were. The scrolls that most intrigued me were the ones written by the Prophets. I purchased a copy of these scrolls and I started reading them as I continued on my way to Jerusalem. We were traveling on a road that was seldom used and I was so confused by the book of the prophets, especially by the Prophet named Isaiah, who wrote:

'He was led as a sheep to the slaughter; and like a lamb without voice before His shearer, so He openeth not His mouth. In humility, His judgment was taken away. His generation who shall declare for His life shall be taken from the earth.'

Suddenly I saw a man, a Galilean, walking by my litter and the man asked me 'Do you understand what you are reading?'

"He was an elderly man with age and experience engraved on his face.

"So I said to him, 'How can I understand, unless someone explains it to me?'

"A smile came to the man's face and I knew immediately that he was the one who would explain all things to me.

"I asked him, 'Tell me of whom is the prophet saying this? Of himself? Or of some other man?'

"I invited this man, who called himself Philip, on to my litter and he instantly began to speak to me of Jesus."

Calashas stopped speaking and looked up at the dark, night sky and after a moment of silence he lowered his head to speak, "So as a follower of Jesus the Christ, I returned to my country and began to speak to *Bet Isra'el* of the Prophets and that the long awaited *Messiah* had come. I told them what I learned from Philip but there were many things I did not know. There were so many things I could not teach them, so we suffer for more."

The eunuch looked at Matthew and with deep sincerity said, "You sir, are the one who is to come to my people and tell us of the Master."

Matthew looked at the man and felt his spirit being pulled away from him; he knew he had to follow this dark, tall, lean man to the forgotten land of the forgotten.

Early the next day the caravan with its new members began to travel south. They traveled along the banks of the *Nilus Fluvius* Nile River. Their destination was the Egyptian city of Syene.

Immediately the two groups of men bonded. Matthew soon learned that they were all believers in Jesus, so the next night he instructed them and celebrated the Meal, now called the *Agape*, with them. It was the first time the Aethiopians had partaken of the *Agape* and they became completely jubilant and stayed in this euphoria for the rest of the trip. When the Aethiopians learned that Matthew was one of the Apostles they became confident that God in His goodness had truly blessed them and wanted them to be directed by one who lived and knew the Christ first-hand.

In prayer one night, Matthew was reminded of the day he pulled his lot and he remembered it read: *Go to the Lost Tribes* and so he finally understood that his mission had been to go to Aethiopia for they were the lost tribe.

In a few days they neared Syene. The city of Syene was the southernmost outpost of the Roman Empire. Stationed at this outpost were three Roman cohorts who guarded the border with Meroe and the other independent kingdoms of lower Nile, which included Aethiopia. The city was a large trading center for Rome and these African kingdoms. The city was also famous for the red granite called syenite that was found in the nearby desert hills. This red granite was used by the Egyptian Pharaohs and Roman Emperors for public buildings and especially for their temples. The city was unique for it was composed of two islands in the Nile River and the port city itself which was on the east bank of the Nile River. On the larger island of Elephantine was a pit which the Greek mathematician, Eratosthenes of Cyrene, declared was the starting point for all measurement of the earth's surface. Because of this theory, Elephantine and Syene were famous.

As they passed through the main gate, Calashas, as a precaution, reminded everyone that the Romans were looking for Christians. He asked them to be silent and not to draw any attention to themselves.

"We Aethiopians have no fears for we are not of their domain, and they know that nearby, just across the border, is the Meroe army who do not like the Romans and who would love to find an excuse to confront their archenemies. We are safe but you three must remain unnoticed and be extremely careful, for if they suspect you are Christians they will ask you and you will be killed."

They passed through the city with little problems, but near the border the military was more noticeable.

"Perhaps we should have taken a boat down the river," said Namenlos.

"Just as guarded," replied Calashas.

They were stopped by several Romans soldiers.

"Do you have any merchandise to declare before we begin our search of your camels?" a Legionary asked roughly.

Calashas bowed to the Legionary and kept his head low as a true, servant eunuch would. His obsequious posture was routine to him but embarrassing to Matthew and the others.

"Kind sir," he said, "we are about the Aethiopian Queen's business and we have nothing of worth that needs to be declared."

The Legionary ignored Calashas and with the help of several soldiers began looking through the camel packs. After several anxious moments the search was over and the Legionary waved the group on to continue its voyage.

The camels and men continued on their way and when they were well past the post and near the border, they heard a shout, *"Sistete!"* Stop.

The caravan halted instantly and Calashas whispered, "This is trouble."

A Centurion walked to the group. His footsteps were heavy and each step dug deep into the sand. From the look on his face everyone could tell he was not too happy being where he was and was going to make the most of any opportunity that came his way.

"You are Aethiopians but these others do not look Aethiopian. Where are you from?"

The group remained silent.

"You do not have to tell me. You look German," he said as he looked at Namenlos.

"And you look Egyptian," he said pointing to Oshri.

Then turning to Matthew he said with a grin on his face, "You are a Jew. I would know your features anywhere for I was in Judea for many years and fought the rebels at Jerusalem until reassigned to this place."

He walked around Matthew, Oshri, and Namenlos, looking at them very closely.

"I would bet one or all of you are Christian. Am I right?"

He stood in front of the trio and waited.

The moment of truth was upon them.

"So are you Christians?"

Matthew knew the others would not deny this question any more than he would and as he was about to admit Christ, he heard Oshri shout, "*Jesu vivit in aeternum!*" Jesus forever lives, forever! When Matthew turned he saw Oshri running with great speed away from the caravan, the Romans, and the border.

"Get that Christian pig!" ordered the Centurion as he ran after Oshri, and soon many guards, and then all of them, began to run after him.

"Hurry! Go!" Calashas shouted to the members of the caravan. They began to move at top speed to the border.

Namenlos grabbed Matthew's arm and pulled him along.

"Come Matthew, Oshri has given us our freedom and other chances to serve the Lord. Come!"

Matthew looked back as he was pulled over the border. In the distance he saw the soldiers continue their chase.

The desert wind moved across the sands and gathered some of the sands around the caravan. For some unknown reason and only for an instant there was the sound of music in the air around the caravan. There came a scream of pain, and then silence and death.

Matthew lowered his head and begged Jesus to wait for his noble servant with open arms.

By the time the Roman soldiers returned to their post the caravan was over the border and moving quickly under the protection of the gleeful Meroe border guards.

The land was flat and spread before them like an endless calm sea of sand, but in the distance the land erupted into gray, misty, curtained mountains that defiantly dared any potential conqueror. The sight of the land and the mountains instantly made Matthew feel weary. The death of Oshri had left him numb and Oshri's final proclamation: "Jesus forever lives" moved the Apostle to appreciate the Egyptian more. The man had sacrificed his life for them and the only thing that seemed proper was to steal the moment given to them and run to safety.

After several days of mental torment and anxiety, Matthew had a dream that cleared his thinking. He dreamed that Jesus once again was seated in his house in Capernaum dining with the many Publicans. He heard Jesus say, "I came not to call the just, but sinners." The rest of the dream, though he lived it, was lost to the haze of memory. All that he remembered were Jesus' words.

The dream put Matthew at ease and he released the last part of himself to the will of God; Matthew had nothing more to do with his life except to guide "…all the sinners…"

They traveled for several days and came to a river port town.

"We will travel down a tributary of the Nile. It will take us south and east into Aethiopia where things are more civilized. Rest yourself, Matthew, for when you arrive you will be put to many hours of work for the Lord Jesus," remarked Calashas with a small grin and delight in his voice.

They boarded a small boat and sailed the Nile. For two days they sailed and finally came to a place, in the middle of nowhere, where they disembarked, for beyond that point the river had rapids and waterfalls.

"We are not far from the border of Aethiopia," Calashas announced with controlled excitement.

As they disembarked, Matthew was aware of a faint, continuous sounding roar that seemed near but yet far. He pushed this sound away until the next day when again he became conscious of the faint roar. As they traveled the sound became more noticeable. Out of curiosity Matthew asked Calashas what it was he heard.

"That is the sound of the great waterfall. Some people call it the smoke of fire and worship it as a god."

"A waterfall? That can be heard so far from its source?"

"It is not just any waterfall, Matthew; it is a great waterfall. In a day or more you shall see it, and then you will understand."

The next day they continued their journey. This time they traveled by horses which was a new experience for Matthew and though he learned to rein a horse quickly, he still moved along slowly and carefully, never wanting to provoke his animal.

As they traveled, the dull, thunderous sound grew more present. Midway through the first day, Matthew was aware that his clothing was moist and by the time he stopped for the night the roar was loud and angry and his clothing was still damp.

Calashas woke Matthew and said, "Sir, before we say our morning prayers, come with me and see the smoke of fire."

They walked a distance and came to a cliff that faced an enormous waterfall that cascaded and threw itself onto the land below. The water came from many places but lived and acted as one. The roar was deafening. The air was wet. It moistened everything near it. Crowning the falls from one end to the other, above the roar, arched over the wet air, was a rainbow, wide, delicate and promising.

Matthew was in awe of the sight and fell to his knees to thank God for giving him this picture of God's almighty Beauty and Power. That day they rested but Matthew could not find rest, for he was perpetually excited by the sound of the falls and the thought of God and His power.

Late that night in the orange glow of the night fire, while others slept, Matthew had a visitor. The man appeared to him from nowhere. Because the fire was his only lighting, Matthew presumed that his visitor's long robe was red. His face was painted red and his black hair shimmered in the moonlight and fire. The man stood before the large fire.

In a deep graveling voice he said, "I am Samac, high priest of the Fire God. We know who you are. We know why you are here and we have been told that you hope to harm us. Our god will not allow this! You are warned to go and leave this place for we are men who will do harm to you and your friends. Be wise. Leave this place."

Matthew stood and faced his visitor; his defiance inflated him and he felt taller than he knew he was.

"You are a being of the night, Samac, and you have no place here for I do what is demanded of me. You and your god will not stop me. So be gone and bother me no more. The next time we meet you shall be vanquished into eternal darkness."

Then quickly Matthew found himself alone. All was still and silent around him except for the small snapping and crackling sounds from the fire and the distant roar of the falls.

Early the next morning the sounds of the falls were replaced by the sounds of blaring trumpets, muffled drums and wailing.

Matthew ran from his tent to Calashas and the other Aethiopians. "What is wrong?"

"It is a funeral procession. Muxa Answada, the son of King Muska Answadi, has died and the Royal family is taking the young prince to his grave. This is a sad thing. In spite of the high priest Samac's power and need to control the king, the king remained a kindly king and his son promised to be of the same character. He is a young boy of about twelve cycles. This king is of a small kingdom that is subservient to my Queen. It is a sad day."

Matthew looked at the procession as it slowly and solemnly passed by a nearby road. Large poles with long, flowing, orange, silk cloths were waving in the breeze. Behind these banners were the muffled drums and drummers followed closely by trumpeters. They were followed by a litter carrying the body of a young boy who was richly dressed. His body was partially covered with a blanket of red, yellow and white flowers. The bearers of the litter were black Africans wearing long, orange, hooded robes. Their heads were bowed in silent respect and their faces hidden under the hoods. Behind the bier rode an elderly man more richly dressed than anyone. He rode a blinding, white horse. On his head was a crown. His face was grim and glistened with tears. He was surrounded by six guards dressed in white and black.

This must be King Muska Answadi, Matthew thought.

Behind him walking with her head held high and with great grace and dignity was a young woman, also richly dressed, greatly bejeweled, and wearing a much smaller crown on her head.

"Who is that young lady behind the king?" Matthew asked.

"That is the King's daughter, Princess Ephigenia," whispered Calashas.

"A noble lady," Matthew observed, and this observation was not for Calashas or any of the others, but for himself.

"Odd thing about this procession," Calashas observed, his face wrinkled with perplexity, "There is no high priest or any priest present."

"Who do these people worship?"

"They worship the fire god, and Samac, the high priest and his many magician priests tend the Royal Family constantly. Besides, it is normal for the priest to be present for such an occasion," Calashas said as he began walking towards the procession. "Come, we must go and present ourselves in sorrow for this is the custom."

Everyone followed Calashas to the roadside. The Aethiopians stood side-by-side and all bowed from the waist.

Just as the procession neared, the trumpets blared and everyone stopped. The only sound that was heard was the soft breeze slipping through the trees and nearby bushes; even the roar of the waterfall was soft.

From the corner of his eye Calashas saw Matthew walk onto the road.

Calashas became concerned. He immediately stood erect and walked after Matthew, hoping to intercept him and explain to the King that there was no disrespect, but only that Matthew, a foreigner, was ignorant of local customs.

The guards quickly rushed to stop Matthew but they never neared him. He looked at them and they froze in place. Continuing, Matthew walked to the bier, placed his hand on it. He closed his eyes and lowered his head and from his mouth came the thunderous command: "Muxa Answada! In the Name of Jesus the Son of God, breathe!"

A strong wind came charging across the land. Its force attacked all that was standing. It pushed and unbalanced some. In the wind came the sound of a long, choking gasp; a throaty, rattling sound of air struggling to fill the body and give life.

And the first word from the prince's new breath was "Jesus!"

The Royal Family was baptized soon after and the King asked all his people to embrace Jesus as their Savior. Many did convert but some remained in the grips of the Fire God.

Matthew stayed in this kingdom preaching and teaching for many days.

Calashas, Namenlos, and the rest of the caravan moved on to Aethiopia with the idea to prepare for Matthew's arrival. They promised to return in six months.

During their absence, Princess Ephigenia, filled with the Spirit of the Lord, dedicated her life to Jesus and sought to be secluded from the royal life. She decided to commit herself to prayer and penance. She approached Matthew with this idea and he immediately took her vow to prayer, penance, and solitude.

Soon after, King Muska suddenly died.

At the death of her father, Ephigenia was given a large island located on a lake near the great "smoke of fire" waterfalls. She approached Matthew and asked permission to set up a colony for women who also wanted to dedicate their lives to Jesus through prayer, penance, and solitude. Matthew gave her this permission and the princess, along with about two hundred women of her court and among her people, settled on the island and had a large building constructed to house them.

After King Muska Answadi's death, his brother, Hirtacus, became regent of the small kingdom because the King's son, Muxa Answada, was still too young to rule.

Hirtacus was an ambitious man with an equally ambitious ego, so he began to consolidate his power with hopes of taking control of the kingdom. One of the first things he desired was to marry and as he looked around he felt that his niece, Princess Ephigenia, would be the perfect wife for him. She was beautiful and truly worthy of him. A marriage to her would seal his claim to the throne, so he asked Matthew to help him win the hand of Ephigenia.

Matthew rebuked him quickly by saying, "Do you suppose to take the hand of one who has been given to God? By what authority do you suppose to have more love and meaning to her life than God? Neither you nor I have the power to take a soul or person from the Almighty. Marriage to the princess would never be allowed."

Hirtacus was enraged and so he secretly ordered that Matthew be killed.

Two days later, as Matthew knelt in prayer, two servants of the fire god and hirelings of Samac threw a blanket over Matthew's head and clubbed him.

When Matthew woke, he found himself stripped. His hands were pinned to an old, dead tree. They were held tightly in place with rope and two small spears that pierced each hand. His feet were also tied and were fastened to the sides of the tree with large nails driven though his ankles.

One of the men smiling said to him, "We did not want to give you full satisfaction of being crucified like your Master so this is the best we would do."

Another said, "We shall make you go to your Master on the wings of our god."

With that they began to gather kindling and when it seemed enough, they poured tar over the wood and over Matthew and set it afire.

Through this entire ordeal, Matthew was awake and in prayer. He called for Jesus to forgive his murderers.

Suddenly the sound of the roaring falls stopped and the land was still.

As the fire grew Matthew smiled for before him was Jesus; His Face aglow from orange and yellow flames, just as He was that night long ago on the shores of Galilee.

EPILOGUE

John for days searched the skies for a dove but none was seen. His mind was clogged with questions. He wondered how Coronius could have knowledge of Matthew's death, for Matthew was in Aethiopia and that was a great distance from Ephesus. How could Coronius know of news from that far-away place? And if Coronius' knowledge was correct, where was the dove?

After a few days of wondering, he discharged Coronius as being mistaken and happily abandoned his search.

He returned to his account of Jesus. For reasons he could not explain his writing was suddenly not an unwanted chore. He experienced great joy and peace in writing. Some of the things he wrote of had been forgotten with age and time. As he remembered, his thoughts rushed through his body and broke into letters that seemed to fall onto the *papyrus*. He could not control his hand as time, places and people came to life on the *papyrus* beneath his *stylus*.

After finishing one scroll, he moved quickly to the next, fearing that if he stopped to rest or even to pause he would lose the moment. As he frantically wrote, he mentally acknowledged that he had seen and experienced more than the other Disciples. What he knew and saw made him the most eligible Disciple to record Jesus' life and that from the very beginning nothing more had been asked or expected of him. With this thought he became thankful to Peter, Lady Mary, and others who had pushed and encouraged him on with this task, and finally he conceded that they knew more about John than he did. More importantly, he was sure that they had been directed by the Master to persuade him on to fulfill this mission. As he continued to write his account, tears of joy and happiness blinded his eyes. On and on he wrote tirelessly into the night and into early morning and with the new day his hand ached as did his back and shoulders.

He was exhausted.

He unhurriedly struggled to his feet and had to quickly grab the back of his chair to steady himself until his legs found their strength.

Ah, John, you are not as young or as flexible as you were three years ago. I think age is catching up to you.

Unsteadily he walked to his small bed. His eyes and body spoke of rest and sleep. When he arrived near the bed he fell face forward onto the cool covering. Before his head touched the pillow his eyes were closed and as he lost the morning light, he thought: *Still I have no beginning to my story.*

Chapter Thirteen:

JOHN THE EVANGELIST

The persecution of Christians initiated by Emperor Domitian was the worst that John had witnessed in his long life. He had watched many local persecutions, but none compared to what he was now experiencing. The persecutions of Nero, though violent and extensive, were not nearly as organized and as widespread as those of Domitian. While Nero concentrated on the large cities, especially Rome, Alexandria, and Ephesus, Domitian had extended his suppression to all the provinces and even into towns and villages. Fear and suspicion were everywhere. Husbands, wives, fathers, mothers, sons, daughters, friends, associates—all were betraying each other.

When Domitian assumed the title of "lord and god," John knew that being a Christian would become life-threatening—many would die for their belief in Jesus. This new title was widely accepted, and soon in ordinary Roman conversations "lord and god" was the way to refer to the Emperor. Domitian had been declared equal to the Roman gods and goddesses. Silver and gold statues of the Emperor were erected throughout the Empire, and everyone was expected to venerate and worship the Emperor as a god. Most polytheistic and pantheistic religions complied quickly, but Christians and Jews resisted.

There was no doubt that Christians were anti-Roman, for they believed in another King, a Savior, Who was to save them from all evil. The Christians also believed in another kingdom, a kingdom far superior to that of the Roman Empire. To Christians, the worship of any god other than the one true God was a denial of their religion and the damnation of their immortal souls. So a confrontation was inevitable, and soon thousands were imprisoned, beaten, tortured, and killed for their beliefs. Some had simply disappeared, through their own volition or by the arm of Rome. The carnage continued, and each day John heard of more tortuous forms of execution. Beheading, crucifixion, stoning, and spearing had become too commonplace for the new persecutors, so these forms of murder were replaced by flaying, burning, and feeding the faithful to wild animals.

John waited.

He had prepared himself. His writings, now almost complete, were hidden in several safe places. His legacy to the Church was under the protection of God.

The latest reports told him that Domitian's killers had taken the lives of Philip and Luke. Now only Matthew and John remained.

He felt it was only a matter of time before he was arrested, so he blessed those who had remained his friends and companions over the years and discharged them into the care of the Lord. He spent days in prayer, resigned to the idea that there was no place to go, no other place to hide. He had been hiding too long. It was time to stop hiding and leave his fate to God.

Many days passed, but he remained free.

Could it be that I am so well hidden that they do not know where I am?

One day John received a message that a Christian in a *villa* outside Ephesus was dying and had asked for him. He walked to the *villa* and visited the dying man, blessing him and preparing him for his journey into eternity. He stayed with the family and comforted them. After the man died, John began his journey back to his home.

It was a beautiful, warm day. John found it particularly enjoyable, for the countryside seemed unusually peaceful. He came upon a small hill that had on its crest a large tree. He walked to the shade of the tree, sat, and rested against its trunk. Gazing into the countryside and all its beauty inspired in him prayers of thanksgiving. At peace, comfortable and in the presence of God, he nodded off to sleep.

He was awakened by the sounds of shouts and curses. He instantly jumped to his feet and rushed in the direction of the sounds, only to find a Christian being murdered.

A small group of men and young boys had found the Christian as he was trying to speak to workers in the nearby fields. John instantly recognized this man, despite his bloody, disfigured face. The killers were beating him with their farming tools.

Coronius! John thought as he watched the man's body crumble to the earth.

John ran to the man and shielded him with his body.

"The man is dead! Leave him!"

The killers looked at John, and with blood still on their hands and tools, they quietly returned to whatever they were doing before the killing began. John cradled Coronius in his arms. When he looked down at his face, he found a wide smile on his lips. John envied his dead friend.

Later that day as John rested at home, he accepted that his actions made him a marked man. Roman spies were everywhere and their accusations often led to executions.

When John realized what he had done—that he had marked himself as a Christian and forfeited his hidden identity—he knew that his arrest was imminent.

I am tired. I am willing to go to the Lord, he thought. His desire to spread the Faith was becoming less intense than his longing for heaven. *Please, Lord, understand that I have been waiting for You to call my name and have longed to join You for many years.* He felt the humility of contrition swell in his chest, and he closed his eyes to let the feeling become complete.

Suddenly, a face screened the sunlight from his eyelids, and his heart began to beat quickly. Confusion settled in as he gradually sensed the identity of the face—it was Judas Iscariot, the betrayer.

Why should I think of Judas? Perhaps in longing for death I have failed in my commitment to the Lord. Then quickly he thought, *Lord, I am Your servant. I have loved You more than most. You know I would not be willing to go against Your will. If You wish that I stay longer, I will accept what is to be…but please do not make me wait too long, for I am weary.*

The face of Judas lingered. He quickly opened his eyes to rid himself of the image, but as he did this, he noted that Judas' face appeared deeply shadowed.

Judas was a forgotten man. For years after the betrayal, John and the Others only mentioned Judas in disdain. His name was hard to pronounce, and his image was perceived as a temptation. His voice was recalled with difficulty because it had been lost in the silence of his final sin. As the years progressed, John became less severe. His anger toward Judas mixed with compassion, and now he mostly pitied the poor traitor. John prayed for mercy upon Judas' soul, but he knew that the words of the Master left little room for hope: "Woe to that man by whom the Son of man shall be betrayed. It were better for him, if that man had not been born."

John felt the weight of Jesus' words. They were heavy and fixed. Still John knew that Jesus was a Man of mercy. He had witnessed Jesus' mercy so often.

John stopped thinking, needing to be careful that he was not about to think anything against God's will.

So many came to Jesus for mercy and left with his forgiveness.

He heard Jesus' voice: "Go, your sins are forgiven."

Jesus and forgiveness; Jesus and mercy are synonymous. In his final moments, Judas could have asked for forgiveness, could have screamed the Name of Jesus aloud or in his mind. Would not his plea be heard? Would not the God of love for all forgive him? Did not Jesus in a loud voice at the last moments of His life forgive all: everyone who hit, punched, whipped, and nailed Him? Did He not forgive the denials and desertions of the Twelve? God is love, and if this love is abused and then replayed with pleas of regret and contrition, can love and mercy be forsaken?

It disturbed John that one of the Twelve would betray Jesus, and for years it frightened him. In hindsight, John believed that any one of the Twelve could have done what Judas did. Several of the Disciples had their own agendas. All were free and all were trusted as much as Judas, but Judas became the weakest link. It fell to him.

John wondered if somehow Judas could be excused from guilt.

Was he perhaps fulfilling a mysterious mission from God? Did he not bring about the death that gave life to all the world? He stopped thinking for an instant; then quickly continued. *No, the Father would never will evil. Judas had free will. It was his choice and his responsibility. Jesus knew what Judas would do, and He did not stop him.*

As John walked to a small basin on a nearby table to refresh his face he thought, *I am certain Judas' name will be remembered more than some of the other Twelve.*

He refreshed his face with the cool water from the basin and as he washed his face, the image of Judas returned to his mind.

Perhaps we were wrong in acting with such bitterness. We judged Judas but judgment is reserved for God.

John reached for a small cloth nearby and dabbed his face dry, spending a great deal of time wiping his salt and pepper beard.

Jesus called Judas...the son of perdition...oh...the unspeakable consequences of sin. Jesus, have mercy on us all.

John stopped wiping his face and slowly took the cloth away.

Jesus would have forgiven him; yet, we Twelve struggled for so long to let go of our anger. We felt that he had also betrayed us by destroying our trust in him. No! that is not it! He showed us that we could have sinned also.

He made us come to see ourselves. We resented being reminded of our own betrayal of Jesus, of our own cowardliness. Judas showed us that we could have sinned also. That we, for money, power, self-regard, could have betrayed Jesus. Judas frightened us for he, his thoughts, his demons were so close to us and often with us.

Just then John heard the sounds of horses and the commands of one in authority, followed by the rattle of swords and the sounds of regimented footsteps.

He slowly turned and faced the heavy wooden door.

Finally, the time has come!

Suddenly all was quiet.

Then he heard the sounds of fluttering wings, and he did not want to turn around. There was no need. He took a slow, shallow breath and closed his eyes. He knew it was a dove. A face instantly flashed through his mind. It was Matthew.

The door to the house was thrown open; it slammed against the wall, and with the gust of wind that forced its way into the room came the cold feeling of aloneness, for now John knew that he alone remained.

Suddenly, the world was a bigger place.

John was taken to a jail and thrown to the stone floor of a dark cell.

For many days he saw no one. He heard no one. He lost time.

The flow of day to night and night to day moved together into one dark emptiness. He cried not from pain, of which he had his fill, but from joy—for he would soon be with Jesus.

In his slumber John dreamed of conversing pleasantly with the Other Apostles as they walked down a peaceful Judean road. It was one of those rare strolls when they were relaxed and not struggling to understand one of Jesus' stories or miracles. They were, instead, joking about Philip's baritone voice, Jude Thaddeus' tinny, high pitched voice, and finally about Thomas' complete inability to carry a note.

"We should thank the Almighty that the rest of us have good voices to compensate for our friend's inadequacies," James the Little remarked.

Soon their teasing moved on to Bartholomew's and Matthew's helplessness when they passed a food stand.

"They always have to stop and look," John heard himself say.

"You can see their mouths salivate," James the Big said with laughter in his voice.

"That is because they always want of a good meal," Peter contributed.

Finally they laughed about Judas' tight control of the purse and of Andrew's willingness to spend money for everything of less importance.

"Andrew has rich man's blood and a poor man's purse," Simon the Zealot declared, and they all laughed.

"And I have a poor man's blood," Judas stated.

"And a poorer man's purse," joked Jude Thaddeus.

In his dream, John felt the feeling of closeness that had become part of their small group. He loved these times, for they showed how much had changed among them. They now understood that they were all imperfect, and they knew that they could rely on one another to compensate for their weaknesses.

Then John thought, *Where is Jesus?*

The dream ended.

Later, in another dream, he was running with Peter. They had been told by Mary Magdalene and the other women that they had gone to the tomb to anoint the body of Jesus, but when they arrived the tomb was empty! It was still early morning, so under the security of darkness, Peter and John raced out of the Upper Room, down the stairs, and onto the streets of Jerusalem. Running would draw attention to them, so they stopped their racing and simply walked as fast as they could. They walked quickly through the city, carefully passed the house of Caiaphas, and then traveled along the city wall to the Gate of Yaffa.

After passing through the Gate, they began to run as fast as they could to Golgotha and to the tomb which was only a short distance from the Mount.

John wanted the women to be wrong. If His body was somehow desecrated, it would be more pain and sorrow for Lady Mary. He could not bear to see this final insult to his Master, or to Mary.

Peter did not believe the women, but he knew something had happened and he needed to see for himself what that something was.

"John…are you…sure that the tomb…was secure?"

"Yes, Peter…. Joseph of Arimathea, Nicodemus, and I made certain. In fact, three Roman soldiers helped us, and I assure you, they checked."

They ran.

"Who would have done…such a thing? Who would have…taken Jesus?" John asked, breathing heavily.

Peter's heavy breathing and gasps for air were all that John heard.

They ran farther.

"Simon…this frightens me."

"And…me."

They ran more.

"Do you think the…women are right?"

"I …do not, ah…know, ah…but something has happened."

When they arrived, dawn was just beginning to break. John took the lead and arrived at the tomb before Peter. The sight of the gaping, dark wound in the side of the mount greeted him, and he froze at the entrance of the tomb and peered inside. The morning light spread through the entrance and onto the stony floor, leaving the interior appearing dull, gray, and dreamlike. Peter arrived, rushed passed him, and went into the tomb. He saw the cloth folded on the *loculus* burial niches. John followed Peter in; when he saw the cloths, he said to Peter, "This is the shroud that covered the Master. Look, you can still see the stains on the shroud. And look at that *soudarion* small cloth! It is the cloth Lady Mary put over the Master's face. Look how neatly these cloths are folded. Who would have done this?"

"I know not," Peter replied. "Come, we must go to the Others and tell them what we have seen."

They left the tomb and hurried back to the city. The morning light had arrived, so when they reached the city walls, they walked quickly through the gate and rushed to the Upper Room. As they neared the Upper Room, Peter grabbed John's arm and said, "I know not what has happened: I do not know if Jesus' body has been stolen…what I do know is that I feel we are about to be surprised by a great event…. For the first time in days, I have hope springing inside me."

Again he dreamed.

Jesus and he were walking down a road. John did not recognize the road, for it was unlike any Roman road or dirt road he had ever seen. This road was paved smoothly and had no gullies or holes. It looked like it was newly made. As he walked, the surface under his foot cushioned and welcomed his steps.

Jesus was smiling as they walked, and John felt left out of Jesus' moment of joy.

"Why do You smile, Master? Have I again said something naïve?"

"John, I smile because I am pleased and happy."

"In what are You pleased and happy?"

"My Twelve have served me well." Jesus' smile grew wider. "And you, John, must not fret. What you have done I willed for you to do. Amen, I say to you, of all the Twelve, you will be read the most and quoted the most. Some will call you the greatest of writers. Your writings will be admired for their distinctive eloquence. Men will debate what you have written, yet you will bring comfort and assurance to many."

"Lord…."

"Oh John, learn to accept what is given you."

"Yes, Master."

They continued to walk, and then suddenly Jesus stopped. He folded His arms across His chest and slowly began to stroke His thick beard.

For an instant, John thought that Jesus was being pensive, but John caught a mysterious gleam in His eye.

"John, there is one more task you must perform."

John felt himself grow weary; he had hoped that this visit was Jesus' way of calling him home.

"But Master, I am alone...."

"And so was I—many times."

The two looked at each other, and John felt his heart grow warm. He knew that he would do whatever was asked of him.

"What I ask of you is most important. I shall send a messenger to you, when you least expect it, and the message will tell you what to do and then you will be free."

Jesus placed His arm around John's shoulders and embraced him.

"Lord, do not make me wait too long...let me come to You soon."

"If I wish you to remain until I come, what is it to you?"

John remembered these words from long ago, when Peter asked what was to happen to John; remembering these words calmed him.

He pressed his head to Jesus' chest and heard the soft thump of Jesus' Heart.

The dream ended.

The door to his cell opened. He was ordered out. He walked slowly to the door, covering his eyes from the painful radiance of the flaming torches. Once outside the cell door, he was prodded by the wooden end of a lance and taken outside into daylight. His eyes hurt again. Out in the open, he took a deep breath of clean air, and coughed.

"What's the matter, Christian? Fresh Roman air too good for your stinking body?"

Before the soldier's remarks even cleared John's mind, he was splashed with cold water again and again until the stench of the cell was rinsed from him and his clothing. He was marched down to a nearby brook and told to strip and bathe in the frigid water. He did as ordered willingly, for he needed to be rid of his cell and his time in the darkness. He believed that this washing was somehow preparing him for the new thing Jesus had asked him to do.

When finished bathing, he was given a white robe to wear. He was bound and roughly marched away; as he walked, he prayed silently.

Have mercy on me, O God, for men do trample upon me, they oppress and attack me…my foes are forever treading on me, for many fight against me…in the day when fear comes upon me, I will trust in Thee…in God I put my trust, I will not fear; what can man do to me?…for Thou hast delivered my life from death, my feet from stumbling, so that I may walk before God in the light of the living.

A smile came over his face, and he remembered the smile on the face of Coronius the day he held the dying man in his arms. He knew he was again to face death, but he was sure that he would not die. Still, he was happy to show that he was ready to die for Jesus. The anticipation of his trial was an overpowering joy. He wondered if all the Disciples had experienced such joy—if they also loved the idea of dying unto perfect life. John was outside of the moment and in a state of separation from his body. His steps glided upon the earth; his body moved with light gracefulness, and his mind filled with soft, comfortable things.

Suddenly, he was hit in the back with the wooden end of a lance, and he fell to the ground. The solid fall jolted him back to reality. He slowly looked up from the dirt and saw a young Roman seated on a polished bronze chair. He wore a Roman uniform unlike any John had ever seen, and this led John to believe that this was no ordinary magistrate. This was a man of higher rank. The young Roman's hair was as dark as a moonless night, and his face was tanned and free of any imperfection. Black hair covered his muscular arms and legs. His breast plate was white and gold.

He raised his hand ever so slightly, and immediately two soldiers grabbed John and forced him to stand.

The Roman leaned forward, and after a few examining moments, he smiled.

"It amazes me how these Christians look so ordinary, and yet they claim to be different because they believe that the criminal Jesus is a God. Do you not agree, Dorimius?"

John suddenly looked at the man standing by the Roman, and he recognized Jude Thaddeus' former companion. His first instinct was to greet Dorimius, but he stopped. He examined Dorimius and saw a man lost, estranged from himself. He was standing motionless and at full attention. His face was lined; his skin was loose. His hair was completely white. Old age had claimed him.

"Christian, I am under direct orders from Emperor Domitian, our lord and god, to dispose of you as I see fit. He has waited a long time to have you in his grip, for by your death we will end this Christian stupidity."

Dorimius unrolled a scroll and began to read in Latin:

"*Ego, Imperator Romae, tribuo...* I, the Emperor of Rome, give to Proconsul Antonius Primius Topius the authority to destroy the Christian leader John of Galilee and Ephesus, a traitor and false teacher of the criminal Jesus of Nazareth. For the crimes against the Senate and the people of Rome, and for the sacrileges against me, a living god, this death is justified. Signed and sealed by *Imperator Caesar Domitianus Augustus, Pontifex Maximus, Pater Patriae.*"

Dorimius slowly lowered the scroll.

The proconsul stood and was given his scepter. He announced, "John of Galilee, Christian, you shall be put to death by the drinking of hemlock from your own hand...."

John heard no other words. His mind was filled with Judas, and he shouted in terror, "No! I will never drink it thus. I will go to my Lord and God at your murderous hands, and never by my own."

Someone struck his head; John staggered and lost his bearings for a moment. He felt the blood from his head crawl down his neck and back.

"Take this slime away from me and give him three hours to drink his due, and if he refuses, force it upon him."

John was roughly led away to a large tent. The interior was empty, except for a stool and a small table. The tent suddenly became filled with guards. He was forced to sit. Dorimius entered carrying a plain wooden cup.

John watched the cup as it was placed on the table before him. To his surprise, as the cup was placed on the table, it made the sound of a heavy door being slammed shut. The sound startled him.

From the past he heard, "Say that these my two sons may sit, the one on Thy right hand and the other on Thy left, in Thy Kingdom...."

"You know not what you ask."

Jesus looked at James and him, the sons of Zebedee.

"Can you drink the cup that I shall drink?"

And the two said, "We can."

Jesus said, "My cup indeed you shall drink...."

John looked at the cup of hemlock and smelled its musty odor.

He thought, *Master, was it Your plan that James, my brother, should be the first to die for You and I, John, the last to die? Was this the cup You spoke of? One at the beginning, and one at the end?*

Dorimius stood nearby, and when John looked up at him he realized they were alone in the tent.

"John, please, do what has been asked of you."

"Dorimius, I cannot, for it will make me like Judas, who ended his life by his own hand. How am I to face my Lord and Master with hands stained of my own blood?"

"John, if you refuse, I will be forced to administer the cup, and I will spend the rest of my life in torment for having killed the last of the Twelve. Please, spare me that anguish, for I have been tormented enough by my own denials."

John looked at the cup, and suddenly he saw two hands embrace it. He heard, "Drink ye, all of this. For This is My Blood...."

✳

Suddenly, the island was there, looming in the distance. Its gray, misty appearance seemed to convey its purpose. It was an island set apart for unwanted things. It was an island with the sole purpose of punishing. It was an island people never went to, but were sent to.

Its very existence was an obstacle.

To a fisher returning from an expedition or coming out of a storm, the island would have been a happy sight, but to the passenger aboard the Roman ship *Neptunus Altissimus*, Neptune Most High, it was a heartbreaking sight. The exiled John bar Zebedee was arriving at his new home, the island of Patmos. By his side was his guard Dorimius, who had secretly provided John with all the things he would need to be comfortable.

Dorimius had been ordered to escort John to Patmos because Proconsul Antonius did not know what else to do. The hemlock did not kill John, and Dorimius explained to the Roman that this was the second time that John had defied an attempt at execution.

"Perhaps," Dorimius volunteered, "John has a great power over death. Perhaps, Sir, it would be wise to exile him and let him die his own death as his powers grow weak. Look at him, Sir, he grows weak with age. How much more time has he?"

Antonius, seeing no other option, in the name of the Emperor ordered John to be exiled for life to Patmos, a remote and sparsely inhabited island off the coast of the Province of Asia.

Patmos at one time was an important island to the Greeks. They believed it was the refuge of their goddess Artemis, so they built a temple on the island. When the Romans arrived, they used the island, because of its isolation, as a penal colony. Most of those who were exiled to the island never received a trial or even formal charges. The island was used mostly by Roman Emperors eager to rid themselves of troublesome family members, associates, and, in later years, Christians. The island was dotted with many bays and coves, which were beautiful and sometimes even breathtaking. Its coastline was jagged and erratic. The island's surface was mostly flat, except for some low mountains that were farther inland. These mountains blended into a small, barren plateau. Most of the inhabitants were Greek, but owing to the influx of exiles, people of many nationalities lived there.

Immediately upon his arrival, John was whisked away by Dorimius and taken to a cave that was not too far from the shoreline. The cave, which became John's home, was, thanks to Dorimius, very livable. The cool cave would make the long, hot days more bearable. Several chairs, stools, a table, and a small bed were provided for him.

Just before Dorimius returned to the Province of Asia, he presented John with a gift of parchments, ink, and a *stylus*—these were the only things John had requested. He truly wanted and needed these things. He had a new mission, and these articles would help him to complete that mission.

During his seemingly lifeless moments after taking the hemlock, John re-dreamed an old dream. It was the dream from the cauldron— the dream with horsemen and scrolls, gates, and dragons. He traveled through the dream, going farther than he had gone before, and then he heard behind him a great voice: "What thou seest, write in a book...."

He awoke.

His mind raced. His mind was excited with a new knowledge—a command. A command and affirmation he always needed to hear: "What thou seest, write in a book..." Finally, he knew. He was to write! He was always to write! That very day, John passionately began writing the *Apokalpsis* Apocalypse.

He wrote so feverishly that he knew there was none of his humanity in the words he was writing. What he was writing was being dictated to him, and he was the scribe. He spent many days occupying himself with his writing. When he was not writing he was in prayer, and when he slept he was in dreams.

Again he had the dream of thousands of people walking up a mountain, and from the mountain could be heard voices singing. Years ago, when first he heard this singing, he believed the voices were singing a psalm. Later, he realized that they were singing one word over and over again, but on different intonations.

For many months, John remained in the cave to complete his writing. When he had finished the last thing that his Master had asked of him, he went into the village below and began to preach and teach the good news of Jesus Christ. Many listened, but few came to the Lord.

John lost track of time as he preached daily to the inhabitants of Patmos. The believers in Jesus slowly increased. Those who believed demanded a structure in which to worship. They found an ancient, partially ruined pagan temple and used this as their place of worship. The few authorities on the island allowed the inhabitants to practice their new religion, knowing that they were far from the hands of Rome and that it was best to keep the peace by letting them do what they wanted.

One rainy day, as John busied himself in his cave, a warm comforting feeling came over him. He stopped what he was doing and looked around the cave, but he found nothing out of the ordinary.

A short time passed.

"John."

He knew the voice and turned. Standing at the mouth of the cave was Dorimius. He was not in uniform. His hair had waned, and what was left was unruly. His face was warm yet deeply creased. His shoulders, though still wide, slumped.

Gazing at Dorimius, John discerned that the old Roman had returned home—he had come back to the Faith and was humbled and worthy of serving the Lord.

Dorimius reeled back in shock at the John he saw before him. John had aged a great deal. He had lost much weight and looked withered. Before coming to Patmos, Dorimius had decided to stay on Patmos and let John travel home alone, but he knew he would have to take John back to Ephesus.

Dorimius, hoping to hide his shock by conveying his important news, blurted out, "Domitian is dead. The persecution is over. The new Emperor, Nerva, has pardoned you and all who have been exiled. You are free to return to Ephesus. I am here to take you back; Polycarp and Papias await you."

✳

Ephesus seemed strange to John. He had lost his excitement for the city and immediately longed for the privacy of island life. On their arrival, Dorimius informed John that he was returning to Patmos with the intent to continue John's work among the inhabitants, a small duty that he felt was meant for him. John was elated, blessed him, and sent him on his way.

Polycarp and Papias greeted John with concern, and they quickly loaded him on a litter and carried him to a small *villa* outside the city. His presence, it had been decided, would temporarily remain a secret for the sake of his health.

With these two young disciples, John felt protected and at ease. The two young men assured him that his account of Jesus was safe. Polycarp added, "And John, in your absence, I read what you have written. It is indeed very profound, and you have done a great service to Jesus. You make known that God is love and make clear that Jesus is equal to the Father in His self-sacrificing love. You give to all the followers the idea of discipleship in the name of Jesus Christ. When I went to teach in Philadelphia, Thyatira, and Pergamum, I used some of your writings to explain the love of God."

"Polycarp was very successful," Papias added, gleefully. "Many were eager to know more about Jesus."

John smiled and felt fulfilled.

"I was surprised by your beginning. It sounded so unlike the rest of your writing. It seemed you had copied from the writer Mark, by beginning with the ministry of John the Baptizer."

"I still have not found my beginning," John said softly and weakly. He took a deep, weary breath and slowly exhaled. "It seems I am writing an account without a beginning. I have waited for the good Lord to enlighten me, but it seems I am unworthy to understand what He speaks."

The two disciples looked at each other with sadness. From the tone of John's voice, they could sense that he was deeply troubled by this lack of a beginning.

"I need to rest," John said, as he walked into another room. "It seems my age is the predominant part of my life these days."

He disappeared behind the curtain.

In the days, weeks, and months that followed, John spoke frequently to the Christians in Ephesus. Many saw that his health was failing and grew fearful, for he was the last of the Twelve. What were they to do without the Apostles?

John recognized their fears, so he decided to release his account of Jesus, in spite of the fact that it still lacked a proper beginning. He gave his two disciples permission to find scribes to copy what he had written, but before the scribes started, John called Polycarp and Papias and said, "Take a *stylus* in your hand and copy what I say." He dictated to them the story of Jesus and Peter on the beach.

"Why would you wish to add this to your story?" Papias asked.

"To show that Peter was above us all—to him was given charge of the Church. I need to recount the remedy of Peter's denial of our Lord." Seeing that his two disciples did not fully understand, John continued. "After the Twelve are gone, others, such as both of you, are to carry on for Jesus' Church. Just as Peter was followed by Linus and he followed by Cletus, Clement, and Evaristus, so it must go on. The Church will never die. I desire to put this in my account to show that the Church will go on long after the Apostles are dead. The grace of our Lord Jesus Christ will endure."

Smiling, the two disciples began to write as John continued to add to the end of his account. Finally, he dictated, "There are also many other things which Jesus did; which, if they were written every one, the world itself, I think, would not be able to contain the books that should be written."

He watched as the two men wrote what he had said.

"I already wrote something like this, but I want to state it again— there are many other things that happened, but through time and human weakness, I have forgotten them. On this account, I beg the mercy and forgiveness of my Lord."

He sighed aloud, and in a very low voice he said, "It is finished."

He closed his eyes and thought, *I need a beginning.*

Two days later, John became ill.

In his delirium he asked his two disciples, "Where are the letters I received from the others?" The two men looked at each other and sadly realized that the letters had been lost. Constant travel was the cause of their disappearance. John's account was certainly the most important thing to preserve and protect. Other things seemed unimportant. With regret, they wished they had cared for those letters as much as they had cared for John's account of Jesus. They did not answer him, for they did not want to distress him, so John never learned that they had been lost, as had so many of the other events in the lives of Jesus and the Twelve.

For the next few days, John remained sick. To everyone's surprise in the days that followed, he improved, but he looked more aged and fragile. His appearance concerned the two disciples, and they called together the elders of Ephesus. It was decided that John should be watched very closely.

A week later, John became ill again. This time, his body burned with high fevers, and many were called to his bedside.

John dreamed.

Again, he saw the multitude of people climbing up the side of that high mountain. Again they were strangely dressed and without beards. They wore no cloaks, but clothes that covered their legs. The women walked with the men as equal partners, showing their ankles and hair. Again, he heard the singing coming from the mountain, and again he could not understand what was being sung. He knew it was one word repeated over and over, such that it sounded like a phrase.

Suddenly, John heard the word! It was a word that resounded from the earliest days of Creation, and John found himself lost in timelessness.

He heard, in Hebrew, the word—*Bereishit.*

He heard it clearly, over and over again: *Bereishit, Bereishit, Bereishit....*

There was silence, and John froze; he forgot to breathe.

Then in Latin came, "*In principio erat verbum....*"

Then finally in Greek, "*En archê ên o logos....*"

GENESIS! John yelled in his thoughts.

John jolted from his meditative state and, with a spring to his body that he had not felt for many years, he was out of his bed. He hurried to his desk, grabbed a *stylus*, and began to write:

"*En archê ên o logos kai o logos ên pros ton theon kai theos ên o logos...*In the beginning was the Word and the Word was with God, and the Word was God.... All things were made by Him, and without Him was made nothing... In Him was life, and the light of men. And the light shineth in darkness and the darkness did not comprehend it...."

The two disciples and the others in the room stood by, amazed at John's energy.

Rapidly John wrote, "He was in the world, and the world was made by Him, and the world knew Him not. He came unto His own, and His own received Him not...."

He wrote on, and the words seemed to pour out from his soul, and from the souls of many others who had died believing.

He came to the words, "And the Word was made flesh and dwelt among us, and we saw His Glory, the glory as it were of the only begotten of the Father, full of grace and truth...."

Then he stopped. Looking longingly into the heavens, he collapsed.

They carried him to his bed, and he said to his disciples in a weak voice, "Write, for I have found my beginning." He continued his account until he had tied the narrative together.

Finished, he closed his eyes and fell into a coma. The room was filled with awe at his determination to complete his work.

Again he dreamed.

He was sitting beside Jesus, and slowly, with great confidence—for he knew that what he wanted to do would be accepted—he placed his head on Jesus' chest. Again he heard the soft heartbeat. The beat had always comforted him and made him at peace. But this time the heartbeat sounded different. It sounded muffled, like muffled drums, then suddenly he realized it was not Jesus' heartbeat he was hearing—it was the beat of his own heart.

He opened his eyes and saw that it was night.

My dove will not come at night, he thought. He closed his eyes and heard the sound of muffled drums.

The next morning he woke. The air had been touched by the morning chill. He looked and found many Christians around him. He looked at the open window and waited. He knew this was the day.

When the others woke, they found him awake and staring at the window.

He was washed and dressed in clean clothing, and he was even given some food and wine; all through this, he looked at the window.

At the ninth hour, he heard the sounds of wings fluttering. He struggled to sit up, and his companions rushed to help him.

His face glowed with anticipation and excitement.

It is time, he thought.

Suddenly a young eagle appeared on the windowsill.

John's face froze in shock.

"No!" he shouted. "Where is my dove? Lord, do not make me wait longer...."

Polycarp jumped to his side.

"John, what is wrong?"

"My dove. Where is my dove?"

He closed his eyes and slipped away into sleep.

Again he dreamed.

He heard loud, manly laughter, and the sounds of heavy feet on a dirt road. The rising dust from the road concealed the makers of the laughter. He tried to make a clearing in the dust by waving his hands, but to no avail. The laughter was louder; suddenly the dust cleared, and ahead he saw the Others. They were smiling and waving to him. They all looked young and vibrant.

"Come, John, what is taking you so long?"

He ran to them and they embraced him warmly, and together the Twelve continued to walk.

The sound of muffled drums grew dull.

He opened his eyes, and there on the sill sat a white dove. It suddenly became very impatient as it flapped its wings and seemed to jump up and down on the sill.

"My dove," John said, and the sound of the muffled drums was no more.

*

All in the room sang praises to God. Some of the women cried. Papias closed John's staring eyes and covered his face with a *soudarion* small cloth.

Polycarp looked to the windowsill and saw the dove as it lifted away. He quickly ran to the window to watch the dove fly into the heavens.

"Why was John so worried about a dove?" the disciple said aloud.

The other disciple joined him.

"Did the dove fly away?"

"Yes."

"I wonder why John was so interested in seeing a dove."

"I do not know, but look there." The disciple pointed to the sky. "There are other doves in flight also. See them flying?"

The two disciples watched as the last dove caught up to the others.

Suddenly, there was a distant rumble of thunder.

"How unusual, that on a clear day there should be thunder," the disciple said surveying the blue sky.

"How odd."

"Yes, I know. Why should it thunder on such a sunny day?"

"No, not the thunder. Look at the doves. Count them," the disciple said.

"I count twelve doves!"

"Could it be?"

"What else could it be? Twelve doves! Twelve of them!"

The Disciple's eyes watered with joy.

"Yes, the doves of Galilee."

Principium…the beginning…

ABOUT THE AUTHOR

Vincent M. Iezzi is a long-time resident of Philadelphia, educated in Catholic schools for sixteen years. He attended King of Peace grade school, Southeast Catholic High School, and La Salle College. After service in the military, he was employed at the *Philadelphia Inquirer* and *Daily News* for thirty-five years.

Upon his retirement, Iezzi began writing books. *Coffee with Nonna* (Servant Publications) has been successfully received, and the sequel *More Coffee with Nonna* (Servant Publications) is equally successful. Iezzi wrote a child's novel, *The Garden and Forest Behind Grandpop's House* (AuthorHouse) and a book of short stories, *Small Drops of Ink* (Trafford Publications).

Iezzi has been a Eucharistic Minister for many years at Jefferson Hospital in Pennsylvania. He also spent the past thirty years as a CCD teacher. He belonged to the Holy Name Society, the Saint Vincent de Paul Society, and Father and Sons. Iezzi is a fourth-degree member of the Knight of Columbus, a member of the Sons of Italy, and the National Italian American Foundation.

Iezzi is a professed member of the Order of Franciscan Seculars (Secular Franciscans), a membership he held for the past twenty-five years, and has served as Minister Prefect of his Fraternity for more than fifteen years.

He is married to his wife, Mary Ann. Together they have been married more than fifty years and have two married sons: Robert (married to Tina) and David (married to Danielle). The author and his wife have eight grandchildren: Kristine, Michael, Robert, David, Jessica, Giavonna, Eric, and Dominic; and one great-granddaughter, Gianina.

About Leonine Publishers

Leonine Publishers LLC makes fine Catholic literature available to Catholics throughout the English-speaking world. Leonine Publishers offers an innovative "hybrid" approach to book publication that helps authors as well as readers. Please visit our website at www.leoninepublishers.com to learn more about us. Browse our online bookstore to find more solid Catholic titles to uplift, challenge, and inspire.

Our patron and namesake is Pope Leo XIII, a prudent, yet uncompromising pope during the stormy years at the close of the 19th century. Please join us as we ask his intercession for our family of readers and authors.

Do you have a book inside you? Visit our web site today. Leonine Publishers accepts manuscripts from Catholic authors like you. If your book is selected for publication, you will have an active part in the production process. This epic book is an example of our growing selection of literature for the busy Catholic reader of the 21st century.

www.leoninepublishers.com

CPSIA information can be obtained
at www.ICGtesting.com
Printed in the USA
BVHW032212040122
625508BV00014B/50